RUNAWAYS
AND THE
LAST OF THE GUALE

by Jack Anderson

Cover Art: Islands and Marsh painting by Joseph Byrne
Chapter Intro Photos: Bill Anderson, Billy Harrell, Buddy Maetens and
Michael Stone

Paperback ISBN: 978-1-959563-25-9
Hardback ISBN: 978-1-959563-26-6
eBook ISBN: 978-1-959563-27-3

Published by:
Maudlin Pond Press
P.O. Box 53
Tybee Island, GA 31328
www.maudlinpond.com

For my mother,
Adela DeSoto Anderson

INTRODUCTION

Oye tu! Esta bien? (Hey you! Are you okay?) My Hispanic mother yelled this to me while pointing to the poor job I had done cleaning the Tybee Island Museum display glass.

She had the job of cleaning the museum every morning, and I helped her before school. She mopped, while I sprayed cleaner on the display case glass and wiped off the finger, and sometimes nose, prints from the previous day. When she yelled, I was cleaning my favorite display case and somewhat lost in my imagination about the two characters on the other side of the glass and what they were doing. It was six thirty, and I had been asleep just twenty minutes before at our home about a block away, and I was still somewhat sleepy-headed and easy to drift into an imaginary or fantasy game I usually played to offset the boredom of the task.

The two characters were about eight inches high and were classic-looking pirate types. One was pointing a flintlock pistol at the other, who was standing in a hole with a shovel and had dug about knee deep so far. There was a treasure chest sitting there, waiting to be placed once the hole was deep enough. The setting was on the northwest side of Tybee Island, Georgia, behind some small sand dunes with the mouth of the Savannah River in the background, and across that, the distant profile of Daufuskie Island, South Carolina. My imaginary fantasy game was to fast forward the scene ahead with different options, kind of like an extrapolated fantasy based on fact. Would the pirate with the gun let the man finish digging the hole, then shoot him so no one would know where the treasure was hidden? Would the man digging, quickly heave a shovel of sand in the other's face and wrestle the gun away and shoot him? After my mother yelled at me, I moved on and cleaned the next few cases without being distracted because they only contained objects and writing. Then I got to another display case and began cleaning and drifted somewhat dreamlike into the scene and waited for what conjured. My mother didn't yell this time but tapped me on my shoulder and caused me to jump, as that part of me that was away reeled back with a jolt. She must have been next to me for a few seconds before tapping me, because when I saw her face, she had a quizzical look like she must have been thinking something might not be right with me.

This work with my mother was my introduction to history, and Tybee Island had a lot of history, particularly the north end of the island, with the Tybee Lighthouse, and the Martello Tower, and the Civil War bombardment of Fort Pulaski from the beach. The museum itself was a historic structure, being built into part of Fort Screven, an Army fort built as a coastal defense in the late eighteen hundreds. Our home, near the fort, had been a mess hall, and most of the buildings on the north end of the island were for the soldiers and officers and things like a bakery, movie theater, parade ground, and all. When the fort closed in 1947, the buildings became available, mostly for low-income housing, and our post office address remained Fort Screven, not Savannah Beach, like the rest of the island. Unlike today, in my youth, the north end of the island was where shrimpers, crabbers, and fishermen and workers lived and was the somewhat poor end of the island but the more colorful and fun end. We had the quarter-mile-long abandoned fort to play in, the Tybee Lighthouse which also, at the time, was a U.S. Coast Guard Station, and various, still abandoned, Army buildings to play in. The north beach wrapped around to the mouth of the Savannah River and was where ships were always coming and going and were fun to watch. I remember lying in bed on a still morning and listening to the prop wash of the ships and on a windy morning hearing the bell buoys. The Tybee shrimp boats came by the north beach, from the docks at Lazaretto Creek, on their way out to the ocean, and I knew who the captains were and went to Tybee school with their sons and daughters. We also had on the north end of Tybee beach, a huge pipe that went out past the breakers and dumped out the island's sanitary waste. It was fun (and somewhat treacherous) to walk out to the end and see the thousands of mullet fish thriving on the effluence. There was also a city sign near that part of the beach that said, "Black Beach." Many of us on that end of Tybee were poor but rich.

Back to the fort and museum. Mr. Snell, almost singlehandedly, built out the concrete interior of a portion of the fort into a museum, and all the show cases and did a masterful job. One of the fun things to do for me and a friend, Richard Campbell, was to look for artifacts left from colonial times, the Civil War times, and the more recent Fort Screven era. We would bring those items to Mr. Snell to identify, and he would tell us what they were and give an explanation about them. Colonial era pipes, bottles, civil war cannon balls and rifled cannon projectiles and thousands of bullet shell casings and bullets form Fort Screven. Being a historian, he liked to tell us stories about those things. He liked that we were interested in his stories and encouraged us to keep looking.

One subject that he liked to tell us about that there were no evidence or relics of, was about the indigenous people of the area. He said the Guale were a mix of tribes that inhabited the sea islands of Georgia. What I remember most fascinating, in his story, was that they had an annual inland migration to and from the Piedmont area of the state, about a hundred miles away, to trade the salt that they had learned to gather from the salt ponds near Tybee, and that the word "tybee" meant salt in the indigenous language. He said they planned their migration during the summer and early fall when it was miserably hot and the bugs were bad and when the hurricanes came.

Mr. Snell liked to talk about the Tybee Lighthouse and how in olden times it was the most important thing on Tybee because it marked the entrance from the Atlantic into the Savannah River and how it was the most popular place for deadly duels. He told of how many times it had to be rebuilt because of hurricanes and how they finally moved it back behind the tall dunes where it sits today, although those tall dunes are no longer there. As kids, we would climb to the top of Fort Screven, which is about forty feet high, and from there have to climb another fifteen feet in some places to the top of the dunes. The fort was built into those dunes for protection from incoming fire. About 1959 or so, big dump trucks began rumbling by our house, loaded with dune sand to some road project somewhere, till the back of the fort was bare and the ground was leveled to a few feet above sea level and is now a parking lot and restaurant location.

The Tybee Lighthouse is right by the Tybee Museum. It was fun to watch the operations of the U.S. Coast Guard Station and what all they did. They had a boat at a government dock at Lazaretto Creek, and I saw it daily patrolling the local coastline plus they had another boat on a trailer, pulled by a giant four wheel drive vehicle, that they launched daily for the more inland waters. From my backyard I could watch them up on the lighthouse cleaning the glass, scraping and painting, and other maintenance work. Occasionally I would yell at them, and they would yell back. The Tybee Lighthouse is a big part of my story, and there is one detail pertaining to it that I should mention how I was inspired to include it. My uncle, William DeSoto, a career Army man, knew how much I liked to mess about in boats. He gave me a small one-man survival raft complete with Army rations. The rations contained various canned and dried foods and other things. One was a couple packs of Lucky Strike cigarettes, which I secretly smoked, and the other was a distress signaling mirror device with an aiming feature so you could reflect sunlight to a place you wanted to send a signal. I reflected it to the Coastguardsmen up on the lighthouse and was reprimanded indirectly through my mother, and I didn't play that anymore, but this method of communication is used, in my story, from the lighthouse to surrounding islands and Savannah.

Most of the story takes place between Savannah and Tybee and the group of small Islands south of Tybee called "Little Tybee," and further south to the town of Darien, Georgia. There are four islands in South Carolina in the story. Just two or three miles across the mouth of the Savannah River from Tybee are Turtle Island (closest to Tybee) then a half mile east of there is Daufuskie Island and a mile east of there is Hilton Head Island. The fourth South Carolina sea island is Saint Helena Island. It is about twenty-five miles north of Tybee and is much bigger than the other three islands combined and is the most of the South Carolina islands involved in the story.

My visits to Saint Helena Island, in recent years, were to see an old friend, Sidney Snellgrove. He lived in the island community called Frogmore. Sidney (now deceased for three years) was somewhat famous and a luminary personality and among other things, one of the most well-known barkeeps in modern history. I first met him at Myrtle Beach in 1966 where we were lifeguards. Then we crossed paths again a few years later, hanging out in Key West, when the place was poor and a hippy haven. You could buy a house on Duval Street for $1500. Anyhow, Sid was a bartender there on Duval Street and ended up buying a place for very little money. That place was Sloppy Joes. Anyhow, I didn't see Sid again for twenty-five years and during that time, Sid did very well financially, and bought a beautiful and historical plantation house and place called Tombee, in Frogmore, and I heard he was in the area and visited often. There is a book called "Tombee, Portrait of a Cotton Planter" by Theodore Rosengarten. It is the actual journal of the plantation owner and master, Thomas Chaplin, written between 1845 and 1858. No frills or glamour, just plain facts of life in that era and occupation.

I should try to explain just how remote and isolated the coastal islands of Georgia and South Carolina were during colonial times. Now you hop in a car and cross many rivers over long bridges and huge areas of marshland on expansive causeways and get to the coast in thirty minutes to an hour. It is near impossible to imagine what it was like to traverse those distances across marsh and rivers back in olden times. Before power boats, wind, oar, and tidal power were the way a boat was moved, and sails and oars were little match for the strong tidal currents, particularly in Georgia where the difference between high and low water is seven to ten feet and the surge in and out is a powerful force and can be three miles an hour. Winds are variable and blow from all directions and at different speeds, but the tides are like clockwork; six hours in and six hours out, they ebb and flow twenty-five miles inland, flushing out the low country and activating myriads of life.

Savannah is about twelve miles from the Atlantic Ocean, as the seagull might fly, if it flew straight, but the river snakes its way, and it is further as a fish would swim. A sailing ship with a deep draft coming in from the Atlantic, guided by a local pilot, would first have to get by and over the treacherous shoals deposited by the mighty Savannah River for miles out into the ocean. Once over the shoals, and into the river, sails could sometimes be useful, but unlike the ocean, the river is constrained by its banks and sand and mud bars, and a hard grounding could mean hours or even months to get off. So, once in the river, drifting was the safest and the surest way to get to port, but terribly slow. A ship would drift for the six hours of incoming tide at a mile an hour or so, and when the tide shifted, it would drop an anchor and sit for six hours for the tide to go the other way, then when the tide started back, lift the anchor and drift toward port again. A ship would have sometimes a dozen pulling boats that were used to keep it in the channel and away from shallow areas. Anyhow, drifting to get a ship in a tidal river was slow but dependable and was how it worked in olden times before engines.

The areas along the Savannah River from its mouth at Tybee Island and the port of Savannah, particularly on the South Carolina side of the river, was often referred to as "No Man's Land." It was a rare and mostly uninhabitable area with some dangerous aspects. I first heard of it from an old time Tybee patriarch named "Pop" Solomon, around a campfire when I was about twelve. He said we should never go there because if the big rattlesnakes the size of a man's thigh didn't bight you, the huge wild hogs and alligators would eat you, and if that didn't happen, the moonshiners would shoot you. He said the moonshiners liked it because people, including the law, were afraid of the rattlers and hogs and alligators and stayed away. This prompted me to go there as soon as I could, however, I knew to go on a very cold day when the snakes couldn't move good, and I went often over the years and never saw another person but did see a lot of big rattlers and hogs and alligators and the remains of busted up whiskey stills. Now, almost sixty five years after I first went, the land along the river has been built up by soil dredged out of the river and about to become a thoroughfare to a new container port. Miles and miles along the river and a mile or so back, the land is forty feet above sea level now. This is the sand that was destined to wash out of the river and continually build up on the beaches of Daufuskie, Hilton Head, and Tybee. This dredging is to deepen the river to enable bigger and bigger ships to enter the port of Savannah. Some believe another consequence of this deepening of the river channel may be affecting the aquifers and threatening the fresh water source of the area.

More than fifty-five years or so after leaving Tybee, traveling a few years, then raising a family in Marietta, Georgia, and a career in carpentry and custom home building, I went back to Daufuskie to restore/remodel a historic Gullah house and residence of a longtime friend, Bo Bryan, and my sense of place and history rekindled. I had visited Daufuskie often starting in 1959 when the Gullah community was thriving and intact and like a third-world country with moss draped two-rut sandy roads and oxen carts, and brightly colored house trim to keep the "Haints" out. Daufuskie is now about 60% developed, but the Gullah community is gone with only a few remnants remaining. However, there has been a renewed interest in preserving the Gullah homes and way of life. Anyhow, Bo's house had been the home of Sarah Grant, the matriarch and midwife of the Gullah community, years before when the culture and community was intact. Her husband was the island undertaker in the house, and it was said, "They had them coming and going."

I ended up doing several other historic projects there for the Daufuskie Historical Foundation. I restored the Maryfield schoolhouse where Pat Conroy taught the Gullah children and wrote about his experiences in his book, "The River is Wide." Also, I restored the Jane Hamilton School, which was a school for the island Gullah children. The restoration and conversion was into a museum and now is the Gullah Learning Center. The structure itself had a dual historic significance in that it was also a "Rosenwald" building. Another historic building, next door, that I worked some on was the Mount Carmel Baptist Church in its conversion to the Billy Burn Museum. This was something of a circle back to my historical museum and lighthouse beginnings on Tybee, easily visible from the south end of Daufuskie, a couple miles across the mouth of the Savannah River.

Anyhow, Bo Bryan is a writer from Myrtle Beach, South Carolina. He wrote a historical fiction book called, "Shag," about the African origins of a popular southern dance and is the current "Poet Laureate" of Myrtle Beach. While I was working on his house, he had many interesting guests. One was a man named Wilton Earle, an accomplished writer from Anderson, South Carolina. Wilton had spent the last six years living in Savannah, researching material for his next book. The book was to be about a runaway slave community in a remote area near Savannah. He told some general information about his research like how the multi-generation group of runaways remained hidden for seventy-five years and even how it was six months after the Civil War ended before they knew that they could come out of hiding. Unfortunately, Wilton died six months later from cancer.

For some reason, I was smitten with the idea of runaways in the areas of my youth and it would not be gone from me. I ordered books about runaway and maroon communities in the southeastern United States and books about the testimonies of runaway slaves, and the more I read, the more I got hooked. I learned that most runaways did not get far or stay gone long. Some made it to western states, and some made it up north, but there were laws that allowed slave catchers to go there and bring them back. If a runaway made it to Canada, they were free, but that was no easy task. However, there were some hidden places in the southeast where groups of runaways sustained themselves free over multiple generations. Most notable and most remote was in the Great Dismal Swamp in eastern North Carolina where cabins were built and multiple generations lived and died. Another area was in the Congaree Swamp east of Columbia, South Carolina. In Georgia, there was an area between Savannah and Augusta that was home to several communities that would get raided and gather again further into the swamp. The Okefenokee swamp in southeast Georgia was probably the best place to hide in Georgia. Black Seminoles who were run out of Florida took refuge there because it was so impenetrable and had all the hazards that kept people out, and it became known as a refuge for runaway slaves.

I began thinking of the vast marshlands near Tybee. I learned about the Savannah Newspaper archives going back to the early 1800s and began searching for all things concerning Little Tybee, and almost all references were reward offerings for runaway slaves having last been seen in boats headed for the islands southeast of Savannah. Having grown up semi-feral, I had traipsed over most areas and began thinking of what places were the most difficult to get to that could support a group of runaways. Where would I go if my life depended on not being found? Where could I be safe from slave hunters? One of the islands in the group of islands called "Little Tybee" would be my choice. Seafood is plentiful in the area and easy to get. Oysters don't need catching, just picking up at low tide, and all the river banks are covered over with them, and fish, clams and crabs are plentiful. Water can be had on any of the islands just a few feet down, but the higher above sea level a coastal island, the better the quality of the water is. The islands of Little Tybee are low lying islands compared to the other barrier islands of the Georgia coast. The one island of the Little Tybee islands, I would pick is far out in the marsh and about seven to ten feet above sea level, higher than the other nearby islands. Getting there is difficult. There is a myriad of creeks that are only navigable at high tide, and you can't walk across the marsh without sinking up to your waist or further. Other difficulties are storms, heat, bugs and snakes and alligators. Anyone familiar with the area would choose a hurricane, sweltering heat, and snakes and alligators, all at once, over a cloud of flesh eating gnats. The more difficulties, the better the refuge. After deciding where I would go, a story began to form in my head about runaways on Little Tybee. The Guale Indians that Mr. Snell from the Tybee Museum, all those many years ago, also got involved.

Then, in my research, I found something in Tybee history that had been obscured for two hundred and fifty years. I learned that Tybee was one of two places, during and shortly after the Revolutionary War, that was a destination for runaways slaves to go, because it became known that British ships would take them on. The other place was Sullivans Island, near Charleston, South Carolina. The slave population in South Carolina was greater than the population of white colonials, and after a few slave rebellions, the colonials lived in fear of a major slave rebellion. Many militia groups formed to watch for and capture runaways. One overzealous militia group came across the river to Tybee, dressed as Indians and massacred hundreds of runaways and shortly afterwards, the same thing happened on Sullivans Island.

While this is a historical fiction story, some things in it are true and one is the slave massacre, according to several historians. There is an excellent article by Jim Piecuch "Preventing slave insurrection in South Carolina and Georgia" in the Journal of the American Revolution.

The exact location of the event was not given, but my best guess is that it probably happened on the south end where the Back River comes in from the Atlantic, and what I call the back door to Tybee. It has a shallow inlet, not deep enough for ships, but deep enough for a ship's boat and small craft. The north end had the lighthouse and Lazaretto Landing with the Quarantine Station and much more activity. The south end at the Back River would be a better area to hide.

I really wished for a book to be written about all this and that I had the ability to do it but was plagued with learning disabilities my whole life and barely made it through high school and flunked out of college. I pleaded with my longtime friend, Bo, to write it but he had a manuscript going. Next I tried to interest another writer friend on Daufuskie, Roger Pinckney (recently deceased), but he was not inclined. I was just an amateur historian with ideas, but those ideas stayed fresh, and I began to visualize a story with runaways and Guale Indians helping them in a sea-island environment something like the fantasies while cleaning the Tybee

Museum display glass all those years ago. It became like an inner silent video that only needed words to be a real movie. Had my mother seen me during these inner distractions, she would again wonder if something was wrong with me.

Something unexpected happened that ignited those ideas into possibilities. My wife, Mavis, and I liked museums, both art and history themed. We visited one of the best folk-art museums in the country in Augusta, Georgia. It is called the Morris Museum. It is filled with the really good folk art, room after room full. Folk artists had no formal art education or training. They simply painted from what they felt inside. From that moment on, I saw no reason I could not write my own story, and that is what I did. Some were facts, and some was fantasy that I tried to make believable. The biggest enjoyment came in periods when I felt like I was being told the story to.

The stories I listened in on, as a child, from people like the old timer Pop Solomon and the Tybee Museum curator, Mr. Snell, inspired me to hunt for artifacts and treasure on and around Tybee. I found bits and pieces of both. However, the real treasure and artifacts I found was the story that had been hidden within myself.

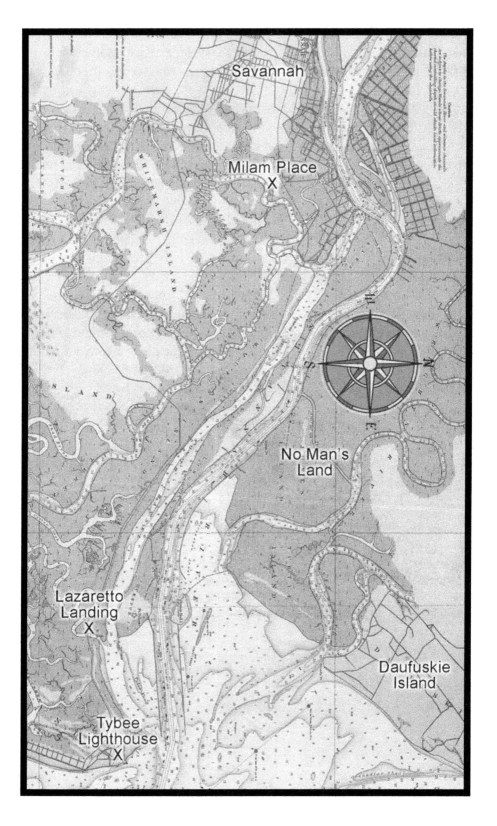

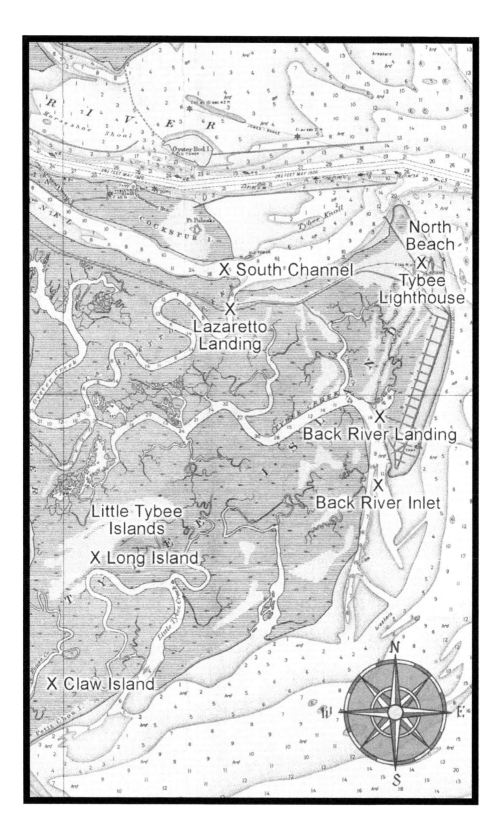

TABLE OF CONTENTS

1.

Martin and Mary

After Captain Martin Milam had given the order to shut down and heard the running gear stop on the Southern Ice and Works steamboat, he looked out the pilot house window at their surroundings and then looked at the chart, spread out on the table, at where they were stopped at. They were on the southwestern side of a large island on the Georgia coast called Saint Simons, in the Mackay River. They were on their way back to Savannah, after having delivered eighty tons of ice to various sea islands and coastal towns between Savannah, Georgia, and Jacksonville, Florida.

The Captain was at his desk, with his log book open and his first mate, Thomas, came in and told him that the anchors were set firm and the mooring lanterns were filled and hung and how many cords of wood they had burned this day as well as how many were left. Mary, the Captain's wife, came into the pilothouse and asked Thomas if he wanted supper with them and he said he would. She told Martin that they were having the same supper as everyone else tonight. It was crab stew from crabs that were trapped the previous night and Martin said that was his favorite. She told him it had already been sent up from the galley and to come on while it was still hot and there was plenty of it if Edward wanted to join them too. Martin stepped out and down to the engineer's quarters where Edward was finishing his daily report when he heard the Captain knock. Captain Martin asked him if he would like to join him and Mary and Thomas for fresh crab stew. Edward said he would like that very much.

Mary greeted Edward and asked if he would like his usual drink and he nodded and she poured four cups of iced sweetened yaupon tea, adding a little rum to each. Edward proposed a toast to Captain Walter Milam, Martin's father, and they raised their mugs and sipped some while the stew cooled.

Martin said he thought the weather would be fine for them to take the outside route in the morning to Tybee and come in at the Savannah River and anchor for the night at the Lazaretto landing, instead of following the inland rivers to Savannah. Mary always liked going that way because she would see her brother Daniel, the Tybee lighthouse keeper, and his family and visit the place where she was raised. Her mother and father, Charles and Margo Dyer, had been the lighthouse keepers before her brother, Daniel took over. Martin said that Lazaretto Landing was his favorite place to stay for the night. He always liked seeing Daniel and had many fond memories and adventures there and on the Indian Islands, just across the Back River from Tybee. He added that going outside would get Edward and Thomas home with their families sooner and they both liked that.

In good weather, travelling along the coast, a few miles offshore was quicker than the inland waterway. They could leave Saint Simons early and be at Lazaretto in the not too late afternoon. The inland waters were better in foul weather but could be slow. There were a lot of shallow areas, especially at low tide. Running slightly aground was routine and usually meant waiting for the tide to rise a bit to move forward. If they grounded out with the tide going down, they would have to wait hours for the tide to finish going out and to come back in and that could be seven or eight hours. Bumping the bottom was a regular thing, but the Captains boat was built to bump without damage. She was built with sixty foot planks of Southern Yellow Pine heartwood from nearby Darien. Her thick planking was fastened to steel hull framing.
There were two wide steel skegs, one under each prop and running gear, for protection when bumping the bottom or grounding out.

When they finished the crab stew and biscuits, Captain Martin got up to walk around the boat and visit with his crew. Edward and Thomas excused themselves, saying they had some more work to do. Martin walked out and down the stairs to the main deck and found the crew gathered as usual, watching the sunset and telling stories and carrying on with each other. They liked seeing Captain Martin every day and sometimes he would stay and listen to a story or two. They all particularly liked it when he would tell a story but his story telling lately had been with Mary every night, after supper, for the last nine months.

When Captain Martin returned, Mary was removing some old notebooks from a big earthen croc. She sat with one notebook ready to read its contents to Martin. This had been their routine for almost a year. They were nearing the end of about thirty notebooks that had been stored in several earthen crocs, the lids sealed with beeswax, and buried for more than ten years. The notes were written by Mary, documenting the history of Captain Walter Milam, Martin's father, the Milam place and Mary's family history, and many adventures and news worthy items over the years beginning with Mary's grandparents and parents. It was also all about the Milam place and family, from its beginnings and even of Captain Walter Milam's life in England before his coming to Savannah. About a third of the notes were about a runaway slave community on a remote island and the last eighteen of the hundred thousand Guale Indians that had once thrived on the Georgia coast, who helped the runaways survive. Little Tybee is what those islands are called now.

It also included a big event that happened when Mary was very young. During and just after the Revolutionary War, a large group of runaway slaves had gathered on Tybee where it was known that British ships would often, anchor a mile or two out in the Atlantic, and send a ships boat in and carry a few away. An overzealous South Carolina militia group came over to Tybee, dressed as Indians and massacred a few hundred runaways. One eight year old girl survived and was raised and treated as a family member by the Milam family. Alice, with the Milam's help, in secret, was educated but her biggest gift was a somewhat enlightened way or presence that could be felt by those around her.

There was another group that Mary spent a good amount of time documenting. They were pilots and their crews out on the north beach of Tybee, in front of the lighthouse. They were there every day, with their swift pilot gigs, to race out to incoming ships to gain the job of guiding them through the changing and hazardous shoals of Tybee Roads, to the Savannah River entrance. There was one particular pilot that everyone loved, including all the people in Savannah, named Captain Jones. His eyesight failed and he no longer could go out and he lived in a driftwood shanty on the beach and Mary and her lighthouse keeping family sent him his meals. Captain Sandy was what he became known as. The less Captain Sandy could see, the more his uncanny knowledge of predicting the weather increased. People had little jingles or chanties to sing about him and his telling of the weather and tide information. He said he got it from his pet seagull and a pet clam in Davy Jones Locker. His daily reports became a major interest in the Savannah newspaper and a common conversation around the town. Not only was his weather predictions famous, but his sea stories and wisdom was a big part of Mary and Daniel Dyer and young Martin Milam' lives.

As one of two children of light keepers on Tybee, Mary had the solitude and aptitude to read much more literature than most. She had an ample supply of books that she could get brought to her from Savannah's best library on the weekly supply boat to the lighthouse. She had decided that all the adventure and intrigue that had happened around Tybee and Savannah was more than any of the books she had read and that she should write her own story. Almost obsessively, she began a daily journal of happenings, and there were many. She sat and wrote her conversations with her parents, Martin's parents, members of the Milam place, pilots and their crews on Tybee beach, the leader of the last of the Guale Indians on the islands south of Tybee, the people of a runaway slave community on those same islands, and Alice, the survivor of the massacre. Because of the nature of much of what she documented, she could not share her work, so, she kept her notes buried in clay pots till a time would come when she could write it all into a nonfiction book and publish without fear for her family, the Milam's, the runaway slave island, the few remaining Guale Indians that aided the runaways, and Captain Sandy and others. In the early 1800's, had these stories been told, it would have brought very serious trouble to those involved.

Years passed and Mary became the wife of Captain Martin Milam, living on the big steamboat, delivering ice along the southeastern coast. After a few years, she decided it was time to string all her notes into a story and had Martin dig up the crocs and bring them aboard the ice boat. Mary wasn't so much interested in a finished work right then, but most interested in stringing her notes together while the stories were still somewhat fresh in their minds and she would wait for the appropriate time to write a complete and proper book of it all. As she began to write the story, from her notes, she needed Martin to help her reconstitute the content and context of the events since he was involved in many of the stories or very close to people that were. She would read the notes, and they would discuss the details, till the story was refreshed. Then he would tell it, and she would write it, dressing things up somewhat in between his telling, which was more a documentary than a novel.

As a child, Martin had been plagued with learning disabilities and missed a formal education. He had failed, miserably, at the school in Savannah and defied all efforts by the school master to teach him to read and was made fun of by the other school children and eventually became sickened by the experience till his parents withdrew him from school and was homeschooled by Alice, the massacre survivor and adopted sister of Martin and daughter of the Milam's. Alice realized that Martin was reading the words backwards and drew a large compass rose on the blackboard and taught Martin to see a page in terms of North and South and begin his reading from East to West because she knew Martin loved all things about boats, ships, and water.

During the sessions at the end of every day of rehashing the events in Mary's notes, Mary recognized that Martin's retelling of the events in her notes was simpler and more fundamental and had a childlike and guiles clarity that anyone could understand and appreciate, regardless of their level of education. He would tell and she would write and she was pleased with this process. It was not proper literature, and the grammar was minimally correct and sometimes awful, but the content and feeling of the events was real, and that was what Mary wanted more than anything. As things progressed, they looked forward to working on it together at the end of every day. They both cried and laughed often. The reconstitution of the events brought an even greater level of meaningfulness than they were able to understand at the time it happened.

Here is what Martin told and what Mary wrote, having dressed up the words some.

2.
CAPTAIN WALTER MILAM

Captain Walter Milam was a young captain in the British Navy assigned to a top secret research project on the east coast of England. He had risen in ranks quickly not from battle experience but from his intelligence and amiability. This plus the fact that he was a son of the light keeper at the eastern most lighthouse in England where research work had been going on for a few years, experimenting with a new lighting technology, specifically for lighthouses. Captain Milam never could have guessed that after six years in the Royal Navy he would find himself full circle back at home with a dozen helpers assigned to the most urgent Naval project of the time, that of trying to concentrate a light source to create a beam of light that could be seen from afar.

For more than a thousand years, men had wood, then coal fires on towers to help guide ships. Later candles and oil lamps were used. However, no one had been able to focus that glow into a "light beam" or "shaft" of light. Now in the 1760's making a light beam was an intense and secretive endeavor in England. The immediate need and purpose of the research was for a lighthouse, but the implication for other uses was vast.

England was an island nation and boating was a practical way to obtain food from the sea as well as traveling from one part of the island to another and to the mainland of Europe and beyond. English boat building advanced out of necessity and ahead of most of the rest of the world. Its seafaring capabilities enabled it to become a world empire with more merchant and military ships than any other nation.

The new "light beam" could enhance England's coastal navigation safety and security and could be used all over the world where British ships regularly traded. Up until now, a ship sailing close to land at night was a perilous adventure, especially in stormy or onshore winds or both. Thousands of lives and uncountable fortunes were lost every year. Far out in the sea a ship, even in a storm, was many times safer than a ship near shore at night, oblivious to where the edge of land was. A lighthouse, visible from fifteen miles out could be the biggest thing ever to happen to Lloyd's of London, the maritime underwriter insurance company and to the fortunes of the British maritime trade.

The sources of light for lighthouses started out as wood fires, then coal was used and more recently fish oils and candles, but were all sooty, high maintenance, or not bright enough. Then an Englishman in about 1765 began experimenting with something called a catoptric parabolic reflector. It was a large bowled out object lined with hundreds of silver-plated small pieces of metal with a light source in the middle to achieve a beam of light. An English clockmaker was also involved to create a way for this parabolic apparatus to revolve.

Advancing these systems became the work for Captain Milam and crew, working from the lighthouse he grew up in. Experimentation went on seven days a week with Captain Milam positioning himself at different distances out in the sea, with a crew in one of the local fishing boats adapted to the purpose, so that multiple settings could be recorded. Not only different distances of visibility were checked but also varied weather conditions and degrees of darkness were part of experiments and recorded information.

Much time was spent altering the light source and fuels. Some quickly sooted up the reflectors, and some were too dim. But gradually improvements were made but none of the things being used sounded as good as rumors of a new lighting device being secretly developed in France. A Swiss scientist/engineer, with his laboratory in France, had been working on a lantern with a light source set in a column of glass with a wick that burned oil and made minimal soot. The column of glass was cleverly designed so that air was drafted to the point of a flaming wick, causing an oxygen rich combustion that created a brilliant light fifty times brighter than the biggest candle. It burned continuously for hours with a minimum of soot.

This was what the English needed, an efficient and powerful light source to accompany their catoptric reflector to concentrate light into a beam. Secret agents were sent across to France to learn about this new lantern. Meantime, work continued on the catoptric reflector, and a major advance came when, instead of metal plate reflectors, silver plated glass was used and a big increase was attained in capturing more light and focusing it into a more concentrated light beam. Prototypes were built and installed and tested and visibility went from three miles to six miles.

Then the break came when a young woman spy was covertly inserted as a house servant to the French inventor of the new lantern. She was able to see the apparatus multiple times while cleaning the workshop every day when the inventor and his helper left. After making detailed drawings she was soon on a boat returning to England with the stolen technology.

Within a month after her return, a prototype was built. The new lantern placed in front of the new reflector lined with mirrors worked much better than expected. The result was the first ever powerful and concentrated light beam the world had ever seen.

Captain Milam had to go sixteen miles out before the light beam could not be seen. Work continued feverishly for another year before the new apparatus was ready to be in operation. This work not only involved the light beam but also a code of communications by intermittingly blocking the stationary beam to create flashes at various time lapses that would enable accurate communication for miles at night, in clear weather by coded flashes. Communication during the day, in clear weather, was enabled by a device called a "Heliotrope," invented in Germany. It reflected the sun's light into the same coded flashes to a desired location, using a hand operated shutter.

This new lighting for efficient and safe navigation was needed on the entire coast of England, but the most urgent need was in the American colonies where the profits from the vast American resources had begun to exceed anything ever imagined. Huge riches were only limited by the security of England's colonies from the French and Spanish and safe access and egress of the thousands of ships being invested in by banks all over the world to trade with the new world. Vast American natural resources were an unprecedented wealth potential for England, even compared to their successes in other parts of the world.

There was much planning to do in how to bring this new technology to America and how to apply it. This is where Captain Walter Milam was designated for an even greater role by appointment of King George III himself. There was a new bigger and much improved lighthouse being built east of Savannah on an island called Tybee to be completed by 1773. This was to serve as a day and night marker to the entrance into Tybee Roads which led into the port of Savannah, which was in a boom of commerce from all over the world from its slave-based production of cotton, rice, indigo, and more. Trade was unlimited by the large volume of raw materials but limited by safe access and egress of ships into the city of Savannah.

Ship Captains needed a safe and sure way to find the city along the coast and a guiding light to safely get in close enough for local pilots to come aboard and take over. Equally or possibly even more important than a navigational aid, was security of the city. The English rightfully felt threatened because of French settlements to the north of Savannah and a large presence of Spain on the South Georgia coast and all of Florida. From the river entrance it was about fifteen miles to the port of Savannah.

Many rivers and vast stretches of marsh separated Tybee from Savannah so land travel to and from was impossible. Ships of war could come up the river and not be identified until they were near the city, and this made Savannah and its residents vulnerable. The day and night ability to communicate by flashes of light provided the city to know, in real time, what was happening at the rivers entrance from the Atlantic.

All these factors were why Captain Milam was assigned the job of going to Savannah with the new light beam and signaling technology and having it installed in the new lighthouse. Ships could be guided in from the ocean by the powerful light and the lighthouse keeper could communicate daily with the leaders in Savannah about new ship arrivals and any change of conditions along the coast that might affect the security of the city. The other equally important thing that was his mission was to set up a support facility, between Savannah and Tybee, that could thoroughly support the lighthouse operation, including all lighthouse supplies of oil, hardware and maintenance facilities and food and supplies for the lighthouse keepers and guards and draft animals. Preparations were made and officials in Savannah were informed. A ship was prepared and loaded and careful plans were followed.

Several sites for the support operation were tentative, but final selection was to be left for Captain Milam when he arrived. The light beam and signaling device was kept top secret because it would be a couple years after Captain Milam's arrival before the lighthouse would be completed. Only Captain Milam, the Royal governor of Savannah, and a few of the Captain's officers knew anything about it.

Original plans had been to arrive before the new lighthouse completion, select a site and build a support system, then select a keeper and train people in Savannah in the new code messaging operations. An extended delay happened because of unrest between England and the colonies, so the Captain and his ship with the new light beam apparatus and provisions did not arrive until a few months after the lighthouse was completed.

The selection of the new keepers had been pretty much settled on to be the same family that had been at the previous operation before it was destroyed by a hurricane. The proposed property for the support plantation was adjacent to a large plantation owned by the Englishman who had been building the new lighthouse. It was about four miles east of Savannah and ten or so miles from the Lazaretto landing on the west side of Tybee.

It had all the necessary requirements including a high elevation bluff facing east with a direct line of sight to the new lighthouse on Tybee and to the west to the high bluff of Savannah. A house for Captain Milam was planned to have a covered deck on the third floor with a view toward Tybee and Savannah making communication possible, weather permitting, by day with sun reflecting mirrors and at night by shuttered light beam signals from the lighthouse.

This was to be the most highly technical lighting and communication system in the world. There were plans to do similar set ups in Charleston and other cities of the American coast. Navigational aid, coastal security and, weather permitting, real time communication was an advanced plan by the British. The particular location selected for the Milam place was because a supply boat with multiple oarsmen could, with the tide, row to the Lazaretto landing in four hours, or go the other way and row to Savannah, with the tide, in about an hour. Also, the site was on a deep-water river that branched off the Savannah River less than a mile. From this site, there were also other river passages to the south end of Tybee that could be used during times when the Savannah River was too rough. In addition to the multiple river passages and just as important, the land was fertile for growing crops. Also, the man in charge of building the new Tybee lighthouse had a huge plantation near where he staged his construction of the lighthouse from. He was a devoted loyalist to the crown and was favorable to facilitating any and all development of the new Milam site.

With unlimited funds and urgency by King George III himself, Captain Milam arrived in Savannah ceremoniously with much fanfare set up by Governor Wright. These were times of much tumult in the colonies. The positive news of greater security and prosperity provided by a new lighthouse on Tybee was good to promote loyalty to the Crown because rebellion was in the air in all the colonies.

The British had recently won the French and Indian War and had added to their holdings in Canada and indirectly in Florida. However, in the seven years it took, the war expended a lot of their wealth.

They believed that the colonies should bear the cost since they were the beneficiaries of the war so the British initiated several laws called "Acts" that were basically levies or taxes on goods. There was the Stamp Act, the Sugar Act, the Townshend Act and the Tea Act. The colonials reacted harshly to all these and talk of a rebellion was everywhere. There were hopes that the arrival of Captain Milam would diminish some of the hostilities. However, a few months after his arrival, colonials dressed as Native Americans boarded a ship in Boston and dumped the whole load of imported tea overboard. Things went downhill from there. The British proclaimed "The Intolerable Acts" whereas Boston Harbor was closed and Colonial Councils that governed each colony were replaced by a British Governor and British troops were sent to every colony. It was law that colonials had to provide housing for them and the troops and officers were pardoned for any hostile actions toward the colonials, which only further incited the Patriots toward rebellion.

All this was an unexpected happening and environment for Captain Milam but his mission was top priority. With the current events put aside and his late arrival, he and the Governor wasted no time in setting out to accomplish their work. Captain Milam quickly met with and approved the new lighthouse keeper and assigned him a list of things to begin. He went over how things were going to work once they got the support plantation squared away. Next he met with the lighthouse builder to discuss the plans for installing the new light beam apparatus. He looked at the site for the plantation and was pleased and approved it. His plan was to moor this ship by the 200-acre site, in the Wilmington River, and he and his officers would live on it while they supervised work there and on Tybee. He let Governor Wright know what he needed and within weeks, there were 150 workers; carpenters, masons and slave laborers and a makeshift tent camp with cooks, servants and a few nurses to begin the work.

Land was cleared, surplus ballast stones from ships coming into Savannah and oyster shells for tabby were hauled in for foundations and barges full of lumber were floated up. Plans were drawn up and work commenced, proceeding at a fast pace. The first buildings were six slave cabins, then the main house, then agricultural outbuildings, a wood shop, blacksmith shop, and last, a boathouse set at the edge of the river. Several wells were dug, and sanitary waste systems were installed, and fields were cleared then made ready for planting.

Captain Milam met regularly with the Governor to discuss progress and needed labor and building materials and to stay apprised of current events in the colonies, which had continued downhill. The patriots had formed a Continental Congress late in 1774 to declare rights and increasing grievances. More British troops were coming in from England to every colony. Polarization between loyalists and patriots became more and more defined and hostile.

Governor Wright gave orders to Captain Milam to hold off installing the new light beam apparatus in the lighthouse and to install the first and less powerful parabolic reflector with candles which they had brought as a backup instead. The latest, more advanced catoptric reflector with mirrors and the new lantern was to remain hidden on his ship due to the insecurity of the times and concern that in a revolt the secret technology could be stolen. This was a disappointment to Captain Milam, but his orders were to continue as planned because his mission was much more than just installing the lighting, so he continued with all the other aspects of it.

The lighthouse at Tybee was set up with the parabolic reflector with tin plates and large candles. No one knew of what the real plan had been, except the Governor, Captain Milam, and two of his officers, and more recently, the new lighthouse builder living nearby.

The candles with the reflector were a huge improvement over what had been in place, with a light beam that could be seen five miles out in darkness. All were impressed and suspected nothing of what the original plan was. Hiring pilot boats and crews provided temporary provisioning of the lighthouse and keepers. This way of provisioning continued until the Milam place could build its own supply boats, train its own crew and begin producing food and supplies regularly, which wouldn't happen till later.

With the lighthouse set up, Captain Milam was able to spend most of his time closely supervising the work on the farm, which was rapidly progressing. More to his liking, he was also able to spend time getting to know the people of Savannah. In those last few months of 1773 and during 1774, something happened that he did not expect. This new American spirit infected him. There was a lot of angry political talk going on but that was minor compared to hustle and bustle and growth of the city. New opportunities were everywhere. Ships were coming and going to and from everywhere in the world with new products and technology and ideas.

Many languages could be heard at the wharfs and excitement filled the air and there was never a lull in activity. It was vastly different from the Captain's home in England where things seldom changed or not at all, and old routines were followed and there was a vast separation of wealth. Here there were small and large businesses. Most were new businesses and they all meshed in a cacophony of clamoring busyness that was harsh and unstructured but harmonious and productive.

Happy and hospitable prosperity was the mood. Same was true at the work going on at the Milam site. The workers were industrious, self-motivated and happy. They expressed themselves openly without the somewhat subdued or glum working attitudes of Captain Milam's homeland, where people worked hard all their life without a glimmer of hope for betterment because the wealth and opportunity did not trickle down. In America, betterment and opportunity could hardly be avoided. England was great to him, but he felt an excitement here that he hadn't felt there.

His gift of getting along with everyone and all the good work and generosity of wealth and spirit made him one of Savannahs favorite characters at all levels of society in a short time. He got along quite well with the patriots and the loyalists and somehow managed to escape the quarrel, even though he was still a captain in the Royal Navy. His work was uninterrupted and focused on the plantation and he had no time to take sides.

Captain Milam had removed the more advanced light beam apparatus from the ship and hidden it on land, sharing the location only with his two officers. They eventually followed the Captain's lead in swearing allegiance to America as the war ended.

After the war the advanced and intended light beam was installed in the Tybee lighthouse. Ships could then see the Tybee lighthouse from fifteen miles out at sea and nighttime signals could be sent to the Milam place and relayed to Savannah. Daytime signals by sun reflecting mirrors, when weather permitted, was carried on every day.

Savannah now had all the safety and security systems that were originally intended and soon other seaports in America acquired similar systems. When conflicts arose again with England early in the next century, this served America greatly. All of these great deeds of the Captain became known and served him and his family well in later years. The friends he had made during the most troubling times did not forget his good deeds and he was credited for saving Savannah and creating the vast wealth and security that came about because of his public service.

Because of this, he was able to operate his place in ways that were outside of social norms that would have meant severe punishment to anyone else. He treated the slaves on his place as servants and respected them as fellow human beings, instead of subhuman. He operated his place like he had his ship.

3.
THE MILAM PLACE

The Milam Farm was not like a typical southern plantation. There were slaves that were treated as servants. There were no crops of cotton or rice or indigo that had to be grown and marketed. For security, it was located not far from the original fortification guarding the city called Mud Fort, which later became Fort Jackson in 1808. For convenience, it was four miles down the river from Savannah and about ten miles to the Lazaretto Landing on the west side of Tybee.

The ten miles between there and Tybee was "no man's land" of floodwaters, very large snakes, alligators, wild hogs, and outlaws. For these reasons most people stayed away. The story was that if the snakes, alligators, and hogs didn't eat you, the outlaws would.

The light house was first built on orders of James Oglethorpe in the early 1700's. It had been rebuilt several times because of storms. Originally, it was not actually a lighthouse, but a day marker without any lighting that marked the entrance into what was called "Tybee Roads" which was the passages into Savannah from the Atlantic.

The lighthouse was critically important for ships to regularly and safely come from England to supply the new colony before it was able to sustain itself. The newest tower at Tybee was much bigger and more visible, especially when the new light beam apparatus was installed.

The lighthouse operation consisted of a keeper and his family, plus two armed guards, and draft horses. Lighthouse maintenance supplies and lamp oil, food and water for people and horses, guard rotation, medical attention, and incidentals had to be regularly attended to. Plus, daily communications to and from the lighthouse to the Milam place and from the Milam plantation to and from Savannah. There were four guards who worked in rotation. Two stayed at the lighthouse for a month and were taken back to Savannah for a month while the other two were brought to Tybee.

Tybee was very remote. Other than the lighthouse operation, it was without law and order. The lighthouse was planned to be a fenced and guarded compound strictly regulated and supplied and coordinated by the

Milam place with regular and uninterrupted support. Captain Milam had a way of being completely thorough in all he did. He saw that the Milam place was complete in all ways to more than adequately sustain itself and the Tybee lighthouse operation. Just sustaining itself was ninety percent of the work.

There was a blacksmith's shop, a woodworking shop; vegetable gardens; a horse barn; fields for grains like corn and oats; a poultry house for chickens and eggs; beef and dairy cows, twenty slaves with living quarters, a boathouse and boats, a lamp oil storage facility, and a three-level home for Captain Milam and his family.

Captain Milam did not like the idea of slaves because his family in England had always been against it, but it was part of his naval directives. The current Governor Wright, who owned hundreds of slaves, selected them. Walter Milam treated his slaves as servants, which was against the current conventions. His place was isolated from Savannah and self-sustaining. What and how things happened there were different and by Walter's orders. Any news of his unconventional ways was overlooked because of his good favor and popularity, and the security and stability he provided the city. Treating slaves as human beings was perceived as a threat to the economic and social system. Those that did could be systematically cut off socially and financially, tarred and feathered, or intimidated by threats to family members and even lynched.

Milam maintained two supply boats, a boat house and boat shop as well as highly trained slaves to row the six oared twenty-eight foot sleek, easily driven, narrow vessels similar to a Captain's gig. Three men rowed hard for an hour, and then rested while the other three took a turn. One helmsman guided the boat, skillfully avoiding any unfavorable river eddies and taking advantage of the swift river current. Weekly trips to Tybee were timed with the tidal flow, which was six hours in and six hours out, gaining about an hour each day in timing.

A typical load would have eggs, meat, potatoes, oil and any lamp maintenance supplies, relief guards, and various sundry items that were requested on the trip the previous week or requested by sun reflected signals. The supply boat would return to Savannah the next day with the incoming tide and occasionally the same day, time and tides permitting. Every week a loaded boat could leave the Milam place, as the tide started out and in the six hours of its outgoing, reach the landing, at the west side of Tybee at Lazaretto creek in about four to six hours, depending on wind and weather.

On a typical supply boat day, the two lighthouse guards, in horse and wagon, would travel the one and a half miles from the lighthouse on the northeastern point of Tybee to the Lazaretto landing to pick up the supplies and haul them back to the lighthouse. A narrow road, connecting the few marsh hammocks between Tybee and the Lazaretto landing was maintained with mountains of oyster shells left near the landing by native Americans over thousands of years. Two bridges were built and maintained over the two creeks. The six oarsmen and one helmsman, operating the supply boat stayed at the Lazaretto landing in a well maintained shanty overnight and would return to the Milam place the next day with the incoming tide.

They also maintained a railway at the Lazaretto landing to slide the boat up above the high-water line while not in use. It consisted of a pair of eighty-foot-long pine timbers, hewn flat on top and set parallel about three feet apart and anchored into the bank with cedar pilings. A winch at the top, similar to a ships windless, turned by two to four men was used to drag the boat up the long, low sloping railway above the seven to ten foot tidal surge. Barnacles had to be regularly scraped off the rails to keep them clean and smooth. Two times a year, two or more boats were brought down with extra workers for maintenance on the small roadway that connected the low lying hammocks and the two bridges. More oyster shell were hauled and spread and repairs and maintenance on the bridges was done.

All this to keep a lighthouse operating every day seemed like a lot, but the commerce provided by ships being able to come and go safely from all over the world sustained and enriched the city and the lighthouse was the sentinel that guarded the city from foreign invasion and provided safe entrance to the river. As word spread worldwide of the modern Tybee lighthouse with the light beam and highly desirable goods available in the city, Savannah flourished in prosperity previously unknown.

In clear weather there was a communication network between the lighthouse keeper and the Milam's and then from the Milam's to Savannah. A log was kept of ships coming in from the ocean into the river and their origin and those exiting the river into the ocean and the number of ships moored, waiting to come in. Coded flashes did this from a mirrored reflector box with a shudder, at the top of the lighthouse to the third floor of the Milam place and from the Milam place to the bluff of Savannah. Also tide and weather information was shared and requests for any additional items or personnel needed to come on the next weekly supply boat. These codes that had been developed by the Captain during the light beam experiments in England were learned by his assistants and taught to appointees in Savannah. They passed the info to the city leaders, and it became the daily news to all the residents of the city. The lighthouse became federally operated in 1790. the Milam set up stayed the same except that the yearly contract was with the United States government, instead of with the state.

4.
WALTER WANTS TO GIVE UP ON AMERICA

Although there were many changes and difficulties, Walter Milam completed his mission and the lighthouse was operating with the new light beam system. The Milam place was operating smoothly, sustaining itself and making weekly supply trips to supply the Tybee lighthouse. Walter had become an American and married a woman from Wilmington Island, just a few miles down the river from the Milam place. They were expecting their first child, and then a disaster happened on Tybee.

The war had been over for a few years. But everything had not yet returned to normal. During their occupation of Savannah, the British had liberated many plantations nearby. Thousands of slaves were set free, some returned and some were aided by the British who took some to Canada and a few back to England. Many escaped to Florida where they were helped by the Spanish and Native Americans. There were two locations where the British ships would take on runaways and they continued to do it, even years after the war. Those two places were Sullivan's Island, near Charleston and the south end of Tybee. Both places became known and large numbers of runaways gathered there.

During this time in South Carolina and Georgia, the slave population outnumbered the colonials. There was always fear of a slave rebellion. Militias were formed to patrol the roads for runaways. Some zealous South Carolina militias instigated a raid, guised as local Indians, and slaughtered more than 200 fugitive slaves on Tybee Island in the grizzliest attack ever witnessed. To most at the time, these runaways were subhuman chattel, like farm animals getting out of their enclosure. The purpose of the massacre was to instill fear in the slave population so they would not run away and news of it spread all through the slave population.

There were some survivors of the event who were helped by the Guale Indians. The Guale inhabited the dozen or so low lying islands scattered across the vast marshes just south of Tybee. This group of islands was called "The Indian Islands" then, but now is called "Little Tybee." These small, low lying islands were the last of a much larger area given to the Indians by a treaty in about 1740 by James Oglethorpe. In about 1790, the time of the slave massacre, less than a hundred of the Guale Indians remained of the one hundred thousand of them on the sea islands of Georgia from the Savannah River to the Altamaha River. At the moment of the attack by the militia group, there were several dugout canoes and Indians that had brought fish and crabs and conchs across the river to the group of runaways and unloading them onto the river bank. When the shooting started they hurried away with as many runaways that could fit in the dugouts. However, it was falsely told that the few survivors were taken away and eaten by savages.*

In the morning, on the day of the massacre, having heard the commotion, the Tybee lighthouse keeper, Charles Dyer, went with his two guards to the other end of the island to investigate and saw with horror a scattered heap of bloodied dismembered bodies strode over the riverbank and along the edge of the woods.

A hundred feet or so from the main carnage, where the sandy beach ended and marsh began, and in some pluff mud that was about to be flooded by the incoming tide, he found a young girl almost completely submerged in the semi liquid pluff mud and she still had signs of life.

He gathered her up and as he started walking back with her mud coated limp body he noticed a curious sight. There was a white man with his face painted Indian style, with his pants pulled down and a large part of his forehead blown out by a bullet exit. He paused for only a moment at the grotesque body and continued, thinking he needed to get the girl back to the lighthouse compound where she might be able to be saved.

He was so distressed at the situation with pieces of chopped up bodies heaped up in a bloody mess that he signaled Captain Milam that afternoon with a brief description and to come on the supply boat the next day and to bring both boats with extra men and supplies.

On the next days early morning outgoing tide, both boats were launched from the Milam place, one with supplies as normal and the Captain, and the spare boat with ten men and their provisions. They arrived at the Lazaretto landing by noon and were met by Charles Dyer, the lighthouse keeper with his guards and two wagons. Charles described the scene to the Captain and crew, and they set out.

*   *While this is a historical fiction story. The fugitive slave massacre did happen on Tybee. Where on Tybee is not known, but is my best guess to be the south end of the island where comings were less than on the north end where the lighthouse was and where the Savannah River flowed to and from.*
    The internet has multiple references to the slave massacre on Tybee about 1790. This is one: JOURNAL OF THE AMERICAN REVOLUTION: "Preventing slave insurrection in South Carolina and Georgia" by Jim Piecuch

After crossing the last bridge to Tybee, the two wagons and men separated, one continuing to the lighthouse with the weekly supplies and the other headed to the southwest end of Tybee, with the men walking behind. When they got close to the place, Charles Dyer gave everyone a rag to tie around their nose and mouth and warned them of what they were about to see. Nothing he said prepared them enough for the scene. Bodies of men, women, and children, scattered in the edge of the woods and all over the riverbank and narrow beach.

All were horrified and some fainted. Some bodies had been carried out on the previous high tide and the rest were washed up to the top of the beach. The ones slaughtered in the woods remained in place, and it was obvious that many were killed before being able to rise. All the dead were black except for one light skinned mulatto and the white man with his pants down with part of his head blown away. Charles had the Captain come see the white man's body and when he did, they looked at each other with a grim mutual understanding of the guise of the attackers and the gross motive of the one with his pants down and the young girl found alive nearby.

The Captain, being the leader he was, was first to begin moving the bodies to a central spot on the bank for a funeral pier. He was then helped by the others and the solemn task was completed as the sun lowered to the west across the marsh. All the bodies were piled up and the whole group began gathering fat lighter roots and logs and, in an hour or so, they piled them entirely over the body pile and as the sun was setting, Charles Dyer poured ten gallons of lamp oil on and put a flame to it. Unbeknownst to this group of men, there was another group of people across the river watching what was going on in awe and sorrow and they stayed and watched the entire night as the huge flames released the spirits into the sky. Captain Walter Milam and the group waded into the fresh incoming tide and washed themselves clean and returned to the lighthouse where they collapsed.

The next day, the regular supply boat with most of the extra men went back to Savannah and the others stayed until the following day and returned with the Captain and the little girl, who, when was washed of the mud was found to be uninjured, physically, but was in a zombie type shock.

When the first boat returned to Savannah, the story was told and within a few days it spread to all the neighboring plantations and beyond. Most slave owners were glad because in their crude mind, this would instill great fear in the slaves to keep them from running away. There was always a fear of a slave rebellion and a hostile and bloody takeover. As intended, the news of the grizzly massacre struck fear in the hearts and minds of the slave population in Georgia and South Carolina. Militia lead slave patrols continued to increase and it was a common sight to see them leading beaten and bloodied captured runaways in chains.

Once back at the Milam place, Martha (Walter's wife) took over the care of the young girl. She attended to her every day continuously with warm food and talked to her lovingly as if she were her own. Martha was about six months pregnant, and her nurturing spirit was at full bloom. After a month she had given the girl a name and called her Alice, as she spoke to her often. About a week before Martha gave birth, Alice seemed to somewhat come out of her trance and shock. Martha had hugged her often every day and on this first day of coming out of her trance, she hugged Martha. When Martha gave birth to her son, he seemed like her second child, with an older sister named Alice.

Walter had closely watched Martha nurturing the little girl. His respect for her grew as he saw her steadily nurse and comfort her. He too became attached as if she were his own daughter. He vowed that if she did not recover, he would pull up anchor from Savannah and disown his allegiance to America and see if they would take him back in his homeland and if they wouldn't, his next move would be to the new English province in Canada. He had come to learn of the South Carolina militia responsible for the massacre and could not rest knowing they were just across the river and bold enough to come again to Georgia. This and the fact that many plantation owners reveled in the attack and took advantage of it to maintain fear in their slaves was hard for him to live with.

His mind became full of doubt and for the first time, questioned his existence and purpose in America. He had ideas of offering to take all his slaves to Canada with him and they could be free to do what they wanted. The colonials in the area knew the story of the massacre and some blamed the Brits for having run off many Patriot plantation owners, jailing some, and setting the slaves free during the war.

Many blamed the slaves themselves for leaving their protective confines and slave life and made sure that their own slaves were aware of the massacre to keep them in fear and less likely to run off. The bare facts of the event were horrid enough but by the time the story had been spread by telling and retelling, the horrors of it grew even worse. Slaves that were planning to run away changed their minds and even ones that were on the run returned. Everyone knew about the massacre, but only a few of Walter's closest friends and allies knew that Walter and Martha had taken the little girl that survived in as their own. Walter was of a mind to leave but was finally convinced by his friends to stay.

Alice did get well and so did Walter, but he never forgot his feelings about it all. Her recovery and Martha's care and the new son gave Walter hope and inspiration. He shed the dark cloud over himself when his inner light got relit by the little black angel that they had taken in.

Alice became a daughter, and a facilitator for Walter in the health and well-being of his whole operation. Martha taught her to read and basic math and showed her their library where she became a hungry reader and self-learner. Her dialect changed from being in the Milam's company, but she never forgot her first Gullah-Geechee dialect.

Alice became a subdued legend. Subdued because the slaves knew that if she were raised too much, a reaction by the colonials would happen that would not be good for her or the Milam place. Her story and glory was repeated and told often, but only in the secret meetings of the slaves all over the south. She became a heroin of the enslaved underground meetings that helped keep the hidden light of freedom alive. Because of her preferred treatment and education by the Milam's, she could have been envied and thought ill of, but she had a way of not causing any negative reaction from any of her slave relations. From her extensive reading in the library, she had the ability to be able to communicate both in her own strong Gullah/Geechee dialect and in the Queen's English and as she grew, she had a way of understanding both cultures.

The Gullah/Geechee dialect was more than a combination of African and English but was also slang, used to understand each other without the white man knowing what was said. It was continually crafted and was affected by not only words but by very timed glances and tones and volume of voice. A white overseer could be in the presence of a slave group and think he knew what was being said and be completely wrong.

On the other hand, the white population tried to maintain the Queen's English out of tradition and to differentiate themselves as elite. Although Alice could not join the elite, she understood the nuances and the necessary postures of her position. She used her bi-cultural knowledge to enhance the life of the whole Milam place in her acquired ability to communicate both ways.

Life for the people on the Milam place was very different than most of the south where the miserable plight of the enslaved people was beyond description and people were inheritable property, subject to cruel treatment without a right to testify against their owners. Slaves were so brutally beaten that sometimes ended in death and this was usually done openly to strike fear in the other slaves. They had no more rights than a dog. Some ran away but usually didn't get far. If they made it to a free state up north, there were laws that required them to be returned.

Some made it to Canada where these laws did not apply. Marriage was allowed sometimes because a married man was less likely to run away, but there was a fundamental conflict to slave marriages. How could a man and women pledge their life to each other when they did not own themselves but were owned by their master? By a whim or desire to profit or a financial need, the owner could decide to sell off a family member or sell the whole family to different buyers, or as often happened, use their power to separate as a threat to keep them obedient. Often their food was like animal food and living conditions were terrible. Somehow the spirit of these people was never snuffed out. In many instances they were a happier lot than their owners. It should be very clear, that this is not, in any way, to say that there was anything good about slavery, but simply a testament to the strong spirit of the enslaved and absconded Africans.

The Milam place, being four miles downriver from Savannah was somewhat isolated and unto itself. It was self-sufficient and independent from the normal commerce and activity of the area. They produced everything they needed to sustain themselves along with what was needed to supply the lighthouse operation. Most of what was produced was needed for the Milam plantation itself, with only a small portion needed to supply the lighthouse, but that is how it had to work. The Milam income came from the federal government contract that was renewed every year, for maintaining the lighthouse.

Again, Walter's popularity and importance to the community and his strong allies he had established early on, allowed him to operate outside the norms on his place which became like his ship where all the crew were considered valuable to their success and survival. It evolved from the understanding of equity of all people having been taught to him by his Quaker family in England. The ownership of the slaves was dumped on him through unusual circumstances, but Walter never considered them slaves and never treated them that way. He never had the fear that his success depended on his domination of another race of people or the fear of what his fellow compatriots may do to thwart his nonconventional ways. There were those that talked against him but none powerful enough to do it openly.

Time passed and Walter and Martha's son, Henry, grew up with a passion for learning and education and began attending the small school in Savannah, starting at an age much younger than normal. When he was fifteen and about to be sent to The College of Charleston in South Carolina, something very unexpected happened to Martha and Walter in that she became pregnant. Although Martha was much younger than Walter, this was a time when she was without the stamina of her first pregnancy.

Alice became her attendant and they spent most of their time together and became even closer.

Alice was an intimate listener and Martha confided many things about her early family life and the sisters she was very close to and remained in contact with and her mother and father and relatives. These topics prompted Alice, for the first time, to let herself very slowly begin to remember her life before the massacre and rescue. Up until now, it was like she had been born at eight years old to Walter and Martha, and her earlier life did not exist. The memories were there but it was too horrid to recall. Yet now she slowly allowed her consciousness to venture into those first eight years and dwell there instead of avoiding it. She remembered her parents, her brother and even her mother's mother who had died when she was five. Her mother's father and her father's parents had never been known. She was terribly sad in these memories but also grateful to at least have warm thoughts of her past. There was a big question that lingered about the ending of her first life, and she needed some help with that.

When Martha was within a week or so of giving birth, Alice asked if they could talk, and Martha knew it must be important because Alice had few requests pertaining to her own self. Alice began by saying that in order to ask her question, she had to tell the story of her earlier life and that it might take a while. Martha said that was not a problem because the doctor had told her to do nothing much more than sit and rest. Martha was surprised because Alice's conversations were never about her past, as if it did not exist. Alice explained and thanked Martha for the particularly intimate times they had been having for the last few months and how listening to her talk about her life and family had prompted her to recollect her own early life.

She said that she could clearly recall her life now, back to about age three but that she particularly remembered the last four months before the tragic event. Martha encouraged her to take as long as she needed and that they had plenty of yaupon tea to keep them stimulated and she would tell Walter that she was fine and to leave them be for a while even into the night.

Alice began by saying she was the second born to a slave mother and father on a plantation near the coast of South Carolina. They had a typical rough life of slaves but had a lot of relatively happy times early on because they had a somewhat kind master. Her brother was a few years older, and at an early age, they both were forced to toil with their parents, but she said she had many fond memories and feelings. They managed to find play even in their bondage.

Their master died and his son became the new master and things went from being bad, but tolerable, to terrible. He was mean-spirited and thought that the way to succeed with slaves was ill treatment and severe punishment to get the most work possible done. Beatings became regular and all were required to watch the beatings and they lived in fear every day. In one instance, Maliki, a beloved older slave with a lifelong leg injury, was ordered to go fill up two croaker sacks of oysters for the supper of the owner's family, so at low water he headed out across the marsh to the creek. Walking through marsh mud and especially the pluff mud at the creek edge is difficult for someone with two good legs and near impossible for an old man with one bad leg. After a long time, he managed to get the two bags filled but could only make slow progress back with one bag so hours later and past time for supper preparation, he struggled back with one bag of oysters.

By then the master had been drinking and he was in a rage because of how long Maliki had taken and he ordered everyone out of their cabins to see him beat the old man. He beat him until he lay as though dead and ordered a couple slaves to carry him to an open shed and chain him to a corner post. The night was very cold and the next morning, Maliki was dead. They were all horrified more than ever before. His beating was such a horrible spectacle to see him get whipped until he was covered with blood and his flesh was exposed and some of them were glad that he was dead and possibly out of his misery.

A few weeks later, word was out that the master was planning to sell off some of the slaves and that Alice's brother and father were to go to an upstate plantation and that her mother was to go to a plantation where the sole purpose of the slaves was to make babies to be for sale. Alice's family was terrified and her father made plans for them to run away. His job had been as wagon and buggy driver for the old master and he was familiar with all the plantations between there and Savannah and it was common knowledge for runaways that if you could make it to a remote island called Tybee, near Savannah, there were often British ships that would take on runaways and take them away.

After a few days of secretly packing some food and supplies, Alice's family plus a few other slaves made their escape in the night. It was the scariest time of their lives but the idea of being separated was more frightful. Plantation slaves often harbored runaways for a night or two and gave them food to go and Alice's father's familiarity with the area really helped the band of runaways make their way toward Savannah without being caught. The back door was always open in the slave houses of every plantation. It was standard operating procedure to take in, hide, and resupply a pipeline of runaways. It would have been easier if it had been fewer in the group, but they managed, and their courage and fortitude was restored by the good people at each stop.

The group was helped down roads and over rivers and their last stop was on an island within sight of Tybee called Daufuskie, but still three miles across the water from Tybee. The owners of this plantation were only there part of the year, and the slaves were left with tasks to be done while they were gone and a slave overseer to watch over them. The overseer was lazy and didn't oversee much so Alice's group had a few weeks to rest from their stressful plight and were glad. They thought maybe it wouldn't be so bad if they could just stay there and be slaves but were told that others before them had tried that but once the owner found out, he had them returned to where they had run from. They waited for a time when two boats were available, the weather was good and the tide was right and then loaded up and were rowed across the water to what they hoped was the last stop before their final escape on a ship. When they landed on Tybee, it was the middle of the night and near the lighthouse, so they headed for the other end of the island where they had been told that there was a group of runaways waiting for their time to catch a ship. The instructions from the slaves on Daufuskie was to follow the beach south to a river, then go west for less than a mile until the sandy river bank ended at a creek and to wait, and that is what they did. The night was almost over, and they hid behind a small patch of myrtle trees in some small dunes.

Shortly, as morning broke, they saw about a dozen log boats with little, small dark red skin Indians in them pulling up to the river's edge. Then out of the edge of the woods came at least a hundred blacks running down to the boats and in a few minutes, unloaded about twenty or so baskets of fish, conchs, crabs, and clams. Some had a big fire going with a big pot and some began cleaning the fish on the edge of the river.

After a couple hours, half of the crowd went back up to the edge of the woods and Alice's father ventured out and approached a small group of people doing something to a large pile of marsh grass. They were using large old oyster shells to cut off the bottom six inches or so and put it in a big cooking pot with water on a fire.

Alice's father approached slowly in a humble way and was cautiously received as the group viewed from the hidden spot behind the dune. After a few minutes, the situation relaxed and he motioned to the rest to come and said they told him to go up in the woods and ask for Gabriel.

One of the group he had been talking too went with them. As they entered the edge of the woods, they were amazed at how many people there were. Most were resting or sleeping or talking quietly. They were led to a thin light skinned mulatto man, sitting with a few others, weaving palm frond leaves into large baskets like the ones used to hold the fish they had seen being unloaded from the log boats. When he saw them approaching, he got up to meet them and smiled graciously and they were greatly relieved. The group were all given a warm drink of yaupon in a large clamshell and sat with the man.

He began by saying his name was Gabriel and he had come here about six years ago during the war. He was the son of a slave mother, and his father was the plantation owner's son. Gabriel told the story of how his plantation, near Beaufort, South Carolina, had been liberated during the war and he and fifty other slaves were brought here to await a ship out. Some were taken on a ship then and the rest were told to wait to be picked up when another ship was leaving, and sailors would come in a longboat and pick some more of them up. More sailors did come and take some and leave a few supplies, but word had gotten out about the place and more freed and runaway people came who were told to go to Tybee and to go to the sunset end of the island. People came and people went but the numbers grew and, even though they had plenty of seafood to eat, a lot became sick from the poor water and close quarters, and they were without adequate shelter from the rain, cold, heat, and worst of all the bugs. As the group became famished and sick, most were ready to walk to the lighthouse, on the other end of the island, and give themselves up and become slaves again.

About that time, some native people from across the river came with one of them that appeared to be their leader. She came every few days and began to show a few of them how to fend for themselves with things they could do like how to get fresh water and plants they could gather to eat. She could speak English and showed them things that helped them feed their selves and how to dispose of their waste in a way that did not poison the small area that they were on, making most sick. She showed them how and where to dig a few wells and how to maintain them to keep the water clean. The clean drinking water had the most immediate positive effect because they had been drinking water with a high salt content and polluted by their waste. She showed them how to find plants that when rubbed on the skin deterred mosquitos and gnats somewhat and how to make baskets and low shelters out of palm fronds.

She left them two log canoes that were used to gather oysters and shellfish and how they should drag them up under the cover of trees when not in use. Every week her people brought fish and other seafoods for them because even though she taught them how to fish, they were better at it and shared. She cautioned them to not go back toward the end of the island where the lighthouse was and not to go onto the islands across the river where her people were. She preserved and bettered their lives and made it possible for them to stay and wait for a ship out.

Gabriel then explained that if they waited, in a month or so, their time would come to be taken off and that while waiting, to do what they could to help in any way possible. He said that there was always at least a dozen of the group on watch for any person or boat coming into the area so everyone could retreat and hide at the edge of the woods. Alice's father asked him why he had not gone himself with the British sailors to a ship to freedom and he said that he liked helping others find their way and that his family had been sold off separate from him and he knew that the chances were slim but they could end up here and he missed them terribly. The brother he missed the most was fathered by a different man but they had the same mother. So, he waited and prayed that he might see his brother or any of his family again.

After a week or so, they became more comfortable, although there was lingering fear that they would all be discovered and captured. However, even here in fear, it was better than what could have happened had they stayed. Alice liked hearing from Gabriel about the Indian lady and hoped that she might get to see her, but Gabriel said that after about a dozen visits, she had not come back. He said he wished he could see her again too. Her people still came about once a week at just before daylight but left very quickly after the seafood was unloaded. They seemed shy or afraid and wanted to leave quickly.

Every month or so a ships boat with British sailors would show up after dark and six to twelve runaways would load up and go. There was never any fuss about who went next. It was generally known who had been there the longest and they were designated to stay in a spot on the edge of the woods closest to the riverbank. The sailors only came in good weather and waved a lantern a few hundred yards out before landing. Sometimes there was a small amount of discussion after they would tell how many they had room for on the ship and if it was six and there was a family of more than six or a close group from the same plantation that wanted to stay together, they would bow out and the next who wanted and had waited could go. Alice never heard a cross word the few weeks they were there. Everyone was so thankful to be where they were and there was no real authority other than Gabriel's simple guidance, and everyone was humbled and cooperative.

One morning Alice's family was up early with about half of the community waiting for the Indians in the log boats. The sun had peeked up just a little on the other side of Tybee, enough to shed light on the islands and marsh beyond us yet leaving our area in a thin shadow of darkness. In that edge of night, the log boats silently nudged the riverbank, all side by side.

In less than a minute, a half dozen of us were wading beside every boat and quickly setting the baskets on the edge of the water so the Indians could leave quickly as usual. They didn't turn the boats around but simply turned themselves around in the boats and faced the other way and one from each boat was out pushing what had been the bow of the boat off the bottom and a couple had already jumped back in and began to paddle out when a thunderous roar of explosions went off.

There was immediate panic and consternation as a thick swarm of a hundred Indian men with guns and long knives came from behind the sand dunes, sweeping the beach with a blaze of bullets. At the same time another roar of gun fire came from the edge of the woods where the rest of the community were still sleeping or just rising.

Alice's family and a few others were on the edge of the water about to begin the task of hauling the fish baskets up the bank. In the chaos, they had no direction to go except in the water and Alice's father grabbed the tail end of the nearest boat for a moment just long enough for them to jump in and she saw the last two boats leaving with a few extra passengers in them.

As they were leaving the bank, Alice looked back and a monster of a man came running full speed into the water after them and just as the depth of the water slowed his progress, he reached out and plucked her from the boat and tucked her under his arm and as she looked back toward the boat she saw her father, mother and brother, wide eyed in horror at the sight of her being hauled away.

When they reached land, Alice saw, still within the grasp of the man, the slaughter taking place. She heard the continuous gun shots, the hideous screams of the attackers and cries of the victims. The river bank was darkened by bodies, some in heaps where they must have piled on to try and bury themselves in each other to escape the slaughter. The man carried Alice like a sack of potatoes, down the edge of the river, hacking at wounded people with a broad sword.

He could have dropped her and hacked Alice up like the rest but she felt she was being saved for him to have later. As they got to where the sandy riverbank stopped and mud began, he dropped Alice down and ripped her clothes off and she could see his face for the first time. His white face was splotched with paint like an Indian and he had buckskin garments, but he was a white man and he was breathing heavily and his breath stunk as he bent down over her with his pants pulled down and then suddenly, his head jerked back and he fell, half naked in the muddy edge of the river.

Alice got up on my hands and knees and saw his hideous face again, this time colored with gushing red blood with part of his forehead missing from a stray bullet from all the gunfire. She continued her crawl along the river to where the mud became pluff and then laid down flat on her stomach and sunk in the pudding like mud almost completely.

Alice lay still in the mud and her attention changed to the commotion still happening a few hundred feet away. Gunshots and screams continued but diminished with only an occasional scream and a gunshot and then she blacked out.

When Alice came to again, she was in a bed at the light keeper's house being looked down on by several people. She thought she had been having a nightmare and was glad it was over but didn't know where she was and who these people were. They were smiling and although Alice was confused, she was not afraid.

She hadn't understood what had happened, yet she had one recollection that was troubling and it was of the horrified faces of her family. Then she blacked out again. Alice didn't wake up again until the next day. When she did, there was a man looking down at her, smiling and assuring her that everything was going to be ok. That was the Captain, and she said she would never forget the feeling of relief and comfort she experienced from him at that moment. That was like day one of her life and everything before that was closed off or bottled up and put away in a locked cupboard of her mind.

"You and Walter were my saviors and every day I am thankful for what y'all have done and now you have been listening for so long. The question I have that prompted this need in me to recollect those past unpleasant events is, could my family still be alive?" They were very much alive when I last saw them and the brief experience I had of the Indians was of their kindness, so, I have reason to believe that there is hope.

Martha had been listening intently to Alice's story and the intimacy she felt for Alice was even more than she had ever felt with any of her family, including her sisters, who she was very close to. While she listened the whole time, there was someone else, right there with them both, feeling that same intimacy and only the stretched thin skin and flesh separated him in Martha's swollen stomach. Martha could feel a glow from him in her stomach that emanated out and covered the three of them. She remembered a similar feeling when her other son, Henry was in her stomach when Alice was first brought from Tybee.

After a few minutes of silence, Martha said that she would speak to the Captain about the possibility of a search for her parents even though the Indian Islands were generally considered off-limits. Alice said how good it made her feel that she might have hope for seeing her family again or confirming that they were gone forever.

A few days after Martha and Alice's talk, Martha gave birth to her second son, Martin. It was an easy birth at home with the midwife from town and the very close attendance of Alice. The whole place had looked forward to the birth. It was a celebratory time and every member of the Milam place came by the big house to pay respect to Martha and Walter. Walter had Alice make a big pile of sweet treats and Walter passed them out to everyone.

Martha's breasts were dry but somehow Alice's became full, and she nursed Martin for six months until his cheeks were fat and rosy. Although Martha was not neglectful, she became less and less involved in the direct everyday care of little Martin. She began spending most of her time with her sisters and her parents who were getting up in age. Since Martha was the youngest, it was customary for her to care for them. In the meantime, Martin was with Alice all day, every day and soon became the darling of the Milam place.

Alice liked to spend a time every day at the cabin of the family that she was fond of because it reminded her of her family. Jacob and Ellie had a daughter, Maggie. Jacob was the helmsman of the supply boat and Ellie worked in the poultry house. As Martin grew he and Maggie became inseparable. Maggie was a couple years older, and Martin learned much from her and her family, including how to talk in the deep Geechee dialect. His mother was with her family a lot and Walter was off in Savannah every day and Henry was off at college. So Little Martin was almost always with Alice, usually at Jacob and Ellie's house. When Martin was eight, Ellie had her second child, Thomas, and from early on, Martin was like his older brother.

By then, Henry had graduated from College of Charleston. Henry had immediately started to take control of the place and implement all the things he learned in school and doing a fine job of it. Walter spent most of his time in Savannah all day visiting his old friends and enjoying his self after so many years of hard work and adventure. He was a welcome sight in the Savannah taverns and was never at a loss for a story. Some original, many times repeated, and all exaggerated.

When Walter did see Martin, he became concerned about the way Martin talked. Walter could barely understand the strong Geechee dialect his own son was speaking. He remembered that Henry, at five, was perfectly understandable to listen to, however, all his early learning was in and around the big house and not among the workers. He and Martha had talked a few times about how it didn't look like Martin was going to be ready for school even if he was late to start. It wasn't that he wasn't smart or bright but seemed a bit slow. He seemed to live in his own world or slightly absent from the present one. They had no less love for Martin than Henry. Their habits had changed and they were greatly confident in having Alice take full time care of him. While Alice spoke in a proper dialect around the Milam's, as soon as she left the big house, her dialect changed back to her roots.

5.
THE BOATHOUSE

Jacob spent every day except Sunday at the boathouse. He was on call even when he was at home for any emergency on the river. The boatmen alternated Sunday duty, half one Sunday and the other half the next. Two days a week were spent on the weekly supply trip to Tybee. The other days were spent in preparation for the next trip and maintenance.

The boathouse was a well planned and executed operation in all seriousness. It was the all-important link to always keep the lighthouse operational. The boatmen were trained in boat operation and swim and rescue skills. Besides the supply trip to Tybee, they were on call around the clock, seven days a week for any accidents on the river. The boathouse was a long building with a large door on one end facing the river. There were two eighty-foot-long parallel wooden rails made from pitch pine trees, flattened on top, leading from the low water mark going straight up to the door opening in the boathouse which was a few feet above the high water mark. The tidal swing was about seven to nine feet from low to high but could be as much as ten or eleven feet. The two rails extended to the boathouse and abutted two more that were level and extended, down the middle, almost the full length of the interior to within about twelve feet from the end. On a platform built across the end of the rails was a simple log winch with four sprockets where a man could walk behind each sprocket, pushing it in a circle and turning the vertical log in the middle and winding or winching a long rope attached to the boat at the river's edge. Within five minutes the boat could be winched up into the boathouse. Once pulled toward the back of the boathouse, the second boat that had been put side on two short rails could be moved over for the next trip.

Launching was letting the boat slide back over the oiled rails until it got to the top of the ramp, then with the rope still attached, holding back the pressure on the winch until the boat slowly lowered down near the river's edge where it was then chocked with a flat sided log and loaded with the supplies before slipping into the water.

The boats were alternated every week. The boat that was used got a thorough cleaning, was inspected and had any necessary maintenance performed. After a couple days drying time after being washed clean with fresh water, every square inch got a fresh thin film of whale oil wiped on and it was ready for service the following week. There was an oiled canvas that stretched over the bow and covered the first eight feet of the boat. This kept perishable supplies dry. It was kept up by removable battens and lashed on each side. In the back of the boathouse was a small area with a wood stove and some wooden chairs for the boatmen to relax. The boatmen spent adequate time resting, so they would be ready for the all-important supply trip to Tybee. The trip to Tybee was like an Olympic event of highly coordinated muscle power and boating skills at full tilt in a loaded boat. Three men rowed hard for an hour and then the other three would take a turn and this rotation would continue until they got to Lazaretto Creek and landing. The boats were long and narrow and easily driven.

The helmsman's job was to steer the boat, taking advantage of the current and winds while avoiding mud bars and eddies, choosing and maintaining the most direct course. On a calm day it was an easy task, and the trip could be made in four hours or even a little less if there was no wind against them. Without any current, the boat could make two to three miles per hour. The current on the outgoing tide was about two miles per hour so the combined speed was four to five miles per hour depending on wind speed and direction. A direct line from the boathouse to the Lazaretto landing was nine miles but the curves and cutbacks in the river made it further.

The weather was good only part of the time. The worst weather was when it was cold, with a strong wind coming out of the east or northeast. The current going out against the wind would create a steep chop of four feet or more in places. Rowing in those conditions could make the trip difficult and take as much as eight hours. The trip back could be equally difficult but less stressful because the boat was not loaded and there was no urgency of supply delivery and if the elements were very bad, they could stop along the way for the night. Sometimes in the worst weather they would take the longer but calmer route to the south and put in at the landing on the Back River on the southern end of Tybee.

A job as a boatman was an elite status because of its importance and skill. The helmsman was usually a little older and had been an oarsman previously and was somewhat the boss. The boats and boathouse operation was something that Captain Milam had copied from England where it was a common thing at the many coastal settlements there, mainly for rescue and recovery purposes of fishermen on their rugged coastline, and also for taking pilots to and from ships.

The boathouse was Martin's favorite place to go to. The men were usually busy but purposely took leisure time to be at maximum strength for the supply run, so there was idle time of laughter and joking. Martin was somewhat of a mascot of the boatmen, and they all loved him. Alice could leave him there with confidence. They taught him how to swim in the river by age three. By five he could swim like a fish. He helped with the boats and came to know about their maintenance and operation at a very young age.

6.
THE DUGOUT

One day when Alice went to the boathouse to retrieve Martin, she found him down by the edge of the river with Johnny, one of the boatmen. They were scraping thick mud off a small derelict dugout Indian canoe that had drifted up on the bank nearby. It was split on both ends, waterlogged and it barely floated. It had a layer of rot and decay about an inch thick on the entire surface, in and out.

It was waterlogged and heavy, but Johnny and a few of the boatmen had dragged it above the high water line, where the seven-year-old Martin enthusiastically began scraping the mud and the layer of rotted wood on the surface that had decayed while being neglected for a long time. With large oyster shells, the size of a man's hand, they scraped until they got to the firm and intact solid wood. Johnny noticed Alice come up, but Martin was so intent that he didn't even look up or appear to hear Alice say it was time to go home. She admired his intense scraping and left him at it for a few minutes. Alice was struck by the way Johnny was looking at her. She felt a connection and slight attraction and a moment of a feeling she had never experienced.

Johnny could feel her slight recognition of that moment but in an instant it was over and Alice moved to take Martin's idle hand to head home. He continued scraping with the other hand until she was able to pull him away. Johnny assured him that they could continue their work tomorrow so that he would go easier with Alice, and she ever so slightly, acknowledged his help and smiled at him, leaving him in a mesmerized stupor.

For the next few days, Martin was off early and headed to the boathouse, scraping his new salvaged find, with Johnny's help. After it was scraped clean and smooth down to the new wood, Johnny told Martin as they dragged it into the corner of the boathouse that before they could repair the cracks and seal the whole thing with oil, it had to dry out thoroughly for a month or so and they slid it back near the wood heater.

Johnny was pleased to help Martin on his boat but was particularly pleased every day when Alice came to take Martin home. He thought all day about what pleasant things he might say to her but was choked up and almost speechless when she came. Alice also looked forward to seeing Johnny but kept her thoughts to herself. Gradually they exchanged some pleasantries and something began to open in Alice that she had never anticipated.

Every day Martin came to the boathouse and went straight to the corner where his boat was. Johnny had told him that as it dried it would gradually get less heavy. Martin should turn it each day so that it would dry evenly because one side faced the wood heater. Johnny suggested that while they waited they could make a small sail rig for his boat and that suited Martin just fine. Johnny said that the sail shop in Savannah had lots of scrap sail cloth and that the Captain knew everybody and that he could ask him to get a piece. Martin was quick to go with Alice that day so he could ask his father about some sailcloth.

That night Martin waited for his father to come home from Savannah. Walter's nose was red and he had a slight odor of rum and was surprised to see Martin meet him outside as he left his horse to be taken care of. He could see that Martin had something important on his mind. Before they could get into the house and in his best English possible, Martin asked his father if he would get him a piece of sailcloth about the size of their dining table from the sail loft in Savannah. Walter had been having some social drinks with his friends in Savannah but not so much that he was without his usual quick wits and before he answered Martin he had an idea. He had been having a hard time bringing up the subject of school to Martin because he knew that it wasn't something he wanted to hear and something inside Walter sympathized with Martin, but he believed that it was his duty to have him educated. So, his answer was yes he would get Martin some sailcloth but when he brought it home, they were going to talk about school. Martin was both pleased and dismayed but mostly pleased so he agreed.

In a few days, Walter came home, and Martin saw he had a bundle with him and he went out to meet his father, quite excited. Walter said he had what he wanted plus extra material and some leather to reinforce the tie downs and a needle and thread for binding the sail edges and some small rope that he would need. He then said that according to their agreement, they needed to talk about school. Of course, this was not what Martin wanted to hear but he was a good boy and loved and respected his father and so they sat down on the porch. The Captain explained that he knew how much Martin enjoyed his life with Alice outside every day with everybody on the place but that he needed to begin school before too much longer. He said that he knew that he and Henry were different and that he loved them both. He told Martin that Henry hadn't liked being outside and playing with everyone like he did and had preferred being in the house and particularly in the library where his reading skills were beyond his age. They noticed this and suggested to Henry that he could start school early if he wanted to and he liked the idea and even though Henry was a few years younger than the other students, he soon excelled and in a few years became one of the youngest ever to enter The College of Charleston in South Carolina and graduated at eighteen years old. Henry had been fifteen when Martin was born and went off to college shortly after. When Martin was about three, Henry finished college and came back and was very busy attending to the place and a few other business ventures. He was soon married and had a child on the way. Henry and Martin loved each other but had not much in common, other than family.

Walter went on to explain that he and Martha had discussed Martin's schooling in light of his situation and that he would start school at ten instead of six when Henry started. Martin listened to all this as best he could but it was difficult to maintain his attention as usual. The bundle of sail-cloth was on the table next to them and every time his mind would drift, he glanced at the bundle and painfully increased his efforts to listen to his father. He liked hearing about starting school at ten because that meant later, and he had a lot of living to do before then. Martin agreed to what his father had said and was given the bundle. He was so excited that he slept less than usual and was off early the next morning to the boathouse.

Johnny helped him lay the sail out on the floor and they found a dead, dried out sapling pine tree for a mast. Then, with the help of Jacob to draw out a shape for a simple sail, they cut it out. After some practice and Jacobs help again, Martin began hemming the edge of the sail all around, sewing in leather pieces at the corners where ropes could attach and hold tight without tearing out. By the time they finished the sail work, Johnny inspected the boat hull and announced that it was dry enough to begin the next step.

Johnny liked how long this took because Alice came by every after-noon to retrieve Martin. He was slowly beginning to have just a little control over himself when he was near her. He had always been able to talk well without stuttering and stammering, but when he was within a few feet of her, he felt like he could hardly talk or think clearly. His heart raced and he had nervous tremors. Today he did better because Martin was so intent on sewing a few inches more hem line, that she couldn't pull him away although she didn't try that hard because she was pleasantly surprised at how focused and concentrated he was. Although Martin was happy he had a hard time concentrating on any one thing and completing a task. Often, he seemed in a fog or in dreamy way. When Martin resisted going with Alice, Johnny told him that while he was gone on the supply boat for two days, he could finish hemming the sail and seal the mast with oil. The idea of a mast grabbed Martin's attention and he quit his sewing for a moment and Alice was able to pull him away toward home and she smiled real big at Johnny and left. The smile made Johnny feel a kind of good he had never felt and was mesmerized for a few minutes until he heard Jacob yell that he still had work to do to get ready for their supply run the next day.

That night, the wind began blowing hard out of the northeast and as Jacob lay in his bed, he knew what that might mean. Northeasters usually blew for five or six days and made the supply trip to Tybee difficult. It was Jacob's job to decide things about the important supply trip to Tybee every week so he was up early the next morning to look at the weather and the wind and decide what to do. Traveling on the river was always dictated by the tides and wind. Since the land would often shield the wind in most directions, tides were usually most important but for the trip to Tybee from Savannah, a hard northeast wind was a big factor because it blew in from across the ocean and blasted up the river with a lot of force.

With the wind blowing hard up the river toward Savannah and the mighty tide flowing out toward the ocean, steep waves formed and battered the bow of the boat, and the violent rocking motion made it difficult for the oars to dip and pull effectively and the wind against the bow as it lifted each time made it very difficult to make progress.

With his knowledge and experience, in light of the increasing wind, Jacob decided to take the longer route to Tybee, through a maze of smaller rivers and creeks that circled around to the south end of the island to what they called the "Back River landing."

It was farther and took longer, but during a strong northeaster, easier and safer. Some northeasters were not so strong, and they could manage but the wind was howling on this day so Jacob knew they would need to go the back way to Tybee. It took longer than the six hours of the outgoing tide so the last few miles had to be rowed against the incoming tide and their trip would take all day. He would tell Henry Milam to signal the Dyers that they would be coming in at the Back River instead of the usual Lazaretto landing, but they would suspect it already, knowing the conditions.

There was a regular routine on supply run day. The boat would be let down near the water and held in place with a log. Different people would bring the different items that they were responsible for. Lamp oil and supplies, eggs and vegetables, meat packed in salt, and every month two new guards would go to relieve the two who had been at Tybee for a month. Jacob watched to see that everything was stowed securely. When it was, he and the men climbed on the boat, the log pulled out and the boat would slip the few feet into the river.

As the boatmen started rowing, Jacob would sing a chantey verse and the boatmen would sing a chorus in rhythm with the rowing and the people on the bank sang with them. Their soulful singing would separate as the boat went away and when the group on the bank couldn't hear the verse from Jacob, they stopped.

Between the Milam place and the Savannah River, a small river turned south. It was the first of many rivers and creeks that led down and around to the backside of Tybee. There were many curves and cutbacks and a much longer route, but during a strong northeaster, it was a better way to go. It was not only more difficult for the oarsmen but was also more work for Jacob at the helm. He had to constantly search the water surface and marsh grass to steer the easiest route. The oarsmen paced themselves for the extra hours of work and there was less of the talk and carrying on with each other to conserve their energy. They wanted to get as far as possible before the tide would start in and be against them.

As Jacob and crew got within about three miles of Tybee, the tide had shifted and started in. Progress slowed and the men had to pull harder on the oars. This longer way went by the Indian Islands to the south of Tybee. As they rowed they noticed a group of Indians on the southern bank of the river shucking a big pile of oysters that had been brought in by log canoes and piled up on the edge. This activity had been going on in this spot for so long that a long high pile of shells had accumulated along the edge of the river. They were busting the end of the oysters with a rock, then with a flat piece of fire hardened oak, prying them apart and dumping the meat into dried gourd containers leaving the heavy shells on the bank. This made the trip back to their camp easier.

The Indians saw them from a long way off and recognized the boat and watched carefully as they came closer. Normally, they would have fled to the interior of the island but over the years they had become familiar with the lighthouse supply boat full of blacks. Blacks did not frighten them like the colonials. Generally, the colonials left the Indians alone and stayed away from their islands. Most considered the Indians as "subhuman" and believed that they were cannibals that could sneak up on a man without him ever knowing it and kill him and have a feast. There were always stories of colonials going into their islands and never coming back.

When people went missing because of a boating accident it was assumed the Indians had killed and eaten them, but this was far from the truth. Often they rescued accident victims that would have otherwise died and took them across the river where they were able to walk to the lighthouse for help. However, the cannibal fears kept most colonials away and that was a good thing. The Indians had become increasingly shy over the years for various reasons. Some whites, when drinking, would sometimes take pot shots at them for sport without any regard of them being any more than animals, then brag about their bravery in fighting off the Indians.

Bucking the current, the supply boat slowly made its way past the group at a close distance and the boatmen and the Indians eyed each other closely. Jacob noticed something that seemed odd to him. The Indians were all dark but with a reddish tint but what caught Jacob's eye was one of several children playing in the edge of the river was black. This sight was curious to Jacob, but his attention switched back to constantly scanning the surface of the water to read and detect any eddies in the current to steer for that might increase their speed.

There were another two miles to go and only about two hours of daylight. This would be slowest progress of the trip because the current got stronger as the tide came in more. They could hear the strong northeast winds blowing above them and stayed on the lee side of the islands and marsh.

The oarsman was aware of the optimum speed over the surface of the water before the bow would try to lift and the stern would lower where a little extra speed cost a whole lot more effort. They stayed just a hair below that speed and were gaining only about one mile an hour toward Tybee after taking away the speed of the current. As they rowed east on the Back River and faced west, they could see the sun setting as they pulled onto the landing. The two lighthouse guards were waiting with a wagon. They hitched the boat up to the horse drawn wagon and laid green palm fronds that the guards had cut and had ready, down on the bank, then hauled the boat up above the high-water mark and began loading the supplies from the boat onto the wagon.

After the boatmen had rested a few minutes, they helped finish up and the guards and wagon headed back to the lighthouse. As usual, when the supply boat was coming to this landing, the guards had brought a tent down with bedding and set it up for them. They brought a prepared meal of giant clunk biscuits and bacon and a dozen baked potatoes, all wrapped in a big piece of sailcloth to keep it warm. Margo Dyer, the wife of lighthouse keeper Charles Dyer, was famous for her big biscuits and the boatmen always looked forward to them.

While the supplies were being unloaded into the wagon, Jacob had strolled up over the small dunes to the edge of the woods. They only used this landing two or three times a year. He always had a special feeling when he came. He had come with Walter the day after the massacre and stayed and went back in the boat with Walter and the little girl survivor. Each time Jacob came there he would begin to feel a strong presence of life, not so much around him but more so inside himself. He had become accustomed to and cherished that feeling within himself. He felt warmness in his chest as each breath came and went and a strong feeling of gratitude and richness of life and at the same time a reverence for the people that had died there. All the boatmen knew the place was special, but Jacob felt it most because of his family's close tie with Alice, beginning just after she was rescued. Martha had known about Jacob's wife Ellie having a gift for healing and she sent Alice there a few days a week when she had first arrived and it had helped Alice. Jacob and Ellie became like her second set of parents in her new life.

Jacob saw the wagon leaving with the last of the sunlight and walked back over to the group who were opening the big sailcloth on the sand with the still hot food carefully wrapped inside and they had set aside a portion for Jacob and waited until he returned to eat. They knew and felt some of what he was feeling and joined in the reverence for a few moments before eating.

This side of the island was normally the most pleasant side because the wind most often came out of the southeast and kept it comfortable enough during the hot days and a little warmer in the winter, but the most important benefit was that the onshore breeze blew the bugs to the other side of the island. This was the end of the island preferred by people for thousands of years for these same reasons. People never liked bugs and preferred moderated temperatures.

The next morning came with Jacob boiling a big pot of grits. There was two hours after sunrise before the incoming tide began. One man was throwing a net early, catching a few shrimp and baitfish and several others were using his catch for bait with hand lines to catch some whiting fish to go with the grits. They were cleaned and fried in a pot of grease and eaten with the grits. As they ate, they could hear the wind blowing above them and could see across the river where the wind was t blowing waves up on the oyster covered banks of the Indian Islands.

After they finished breakfast, they took the tent down and folded it with the sailcloth ground cover for the guards to pick up later then used the palm fronds again to slide the boat down to the river and with the tide just starting in, headed back home. They kept a short mast and a simple sail rig stowed and today was a good time to put it to use. They set the sail and most of the way was with the wind on their beam and a little on their stern, and shifting their bodies to ballast the boat, they were mostly blown the whole way, and by midafternoon, they were winching the boat up the rails back at the boathouse. The weekly supply trip was the rhythm of the Milam place. Although most of the work of the operation was to sustain everybody there, supplying the lighthouse with its needs was the primary purpose.

Martin had finished his sail sewing and was ready for Johnny to help him rig the sail and do the repairs to the boat hull and getting it sealed and ready to go. He waited and stared at the last bend in the river that the boat came around before it got to the boathouse. Finally, he saw the tip of the mast and sail before it rounded the bend and he got excited. With the wind fully behind them, Jacob steered the boat right up onto the riverbank in front of the boathouse.

A few people that had finished their tasks were on the bank waiting with Martin and all helped guide the boat onto the rails and the three oarsmen who had not been rowing, went inside the boathouse and pulled down the rope from the winch and attached it and then went up to the winch platform and began walking around and winding the rope in. One took a bucket of grease and coated the rails and the boat slowly slid up and into the boathouse. Martin wanted Johnny to help him immediately, but Johnny's work was not done and by the time it was, it was almost time for Alice to be coming for him, so the men did their usual ritual and sat a spell talking about their trip by the woodstove to each other and a few others that joined them.

Martin was disappointed that work on his boat would have to wait until tomorrow but sat entranced listening to them talk about the trip, particularly the part about seeing the Indians. His attention was never held by anything more than hearing about them and the Indian Islands. He vowed that when his boat was finished he would go there. All the boatmen, except Jacob, laughed. Just then Alice came, and Johnny slipped into his usual dumbfounded way but managed to walk with her and Martin a little way toward the big house.

The next morning Martin was at the boathouse early. Johnny was busy but Jacob and the others were partial to Martin. Jacob told Johnny to go help him and they would do his share of few tasks for the day, which was only cleaning the boat from the day before with fresh water and a few other small things.

Henry in the wisdom of his father was aware that what these men did was of utmost importance and the two day trip they did was intense and physically exhausting and if they were not allowed proper rest, the vital supply trip could be compromised, so the day after and the day before a trip were light days as far as work and they were encouraged to rest, almost as if resting was a task. Some slept and some fished on the edge of the river.

Johnny hung out with Martin and helped him restore his boat. First, they got some pine pitch and heated it slightly enough to fold in some dried moss and pressed it into the two split ends of the hull. As it cooled it caked up hard and filled and sealed the cracks, and then they dragged the boat outside and built a big fire, then they laid one side of the boat near the fire, not close enough to burn but close enough to heat up the wood and they slathered on whale oil and the warm dry wood sucked the hot oil deep into the fibers and sealed the wood from moisture and stabilized it. After doing both sides, they tipped it up on its side with the hollow inside facing the fire. After it was scorching hot, they laid it flat and upright and poured about a half-gallon of oil onto the bottom of the boat and swirled it up onto the sides until it had all penetrated in. They turned it upside down and slathered on one more coat to the bottom and sides. With the hull now dried, and waterproofed, it was light and would stay that way even after a few years in the water.

Johnny told Martin that after the boat was done to always leave it above the high water line so that it wouldn't get carried away with the tide. Before the next weeks supply run, Johnny finished rigging the little dugout but when he was done, it was the day before the weekly supply run and he told Martin that when he got back, they could try the boat out.

While Johnny was on the boat trip, Martin practiced on dry land with his new boat. He got some help dragging it to a level spot high up on the bank, then cut about fifty saw palmetto frons and spread them out about three levels thick then dragged the boat on top of them so he could with ease turn the boat hull at different angles to the wind and get a feel for it. It turned easily on the wax like surface of the frons. He practiced by turning the boat from one side to the other and moving the tag line from the sail to the other side of the boat to come about.

Another thing he did was practice taking the stick holding up the upper corner of the sail out and wrapping the sail quickly around the mast and lifting the mast out of its hole. Martin was paying all of his attention to his dry land sailing, and he did not see a man quietly walking up to the rear of his boat. The man stood there a few minutes, unnoticed because Martin was facing forward and in a deep fantasy of being on the river somewhere near the Indian Islands, seeing Indians as he swiftly sailed by. The Captain was amazed at what this young man had accomplished and how he was handling the boat, even if it was on a sea of palmettos. When he spoke, Martin jumped as his attention recoiled back into himself and was delighted to see his father smiling at him. What a surprise because his father rarely was home much except at night and was rarely out around the place anymore. He spent most of his time in Savannah while Henry handled everything. This was a good surprise and the Captain spent the rest of the afternoon with Martin teaching him what he could on dry land.

He warned Martin several times that doing what he had been doing on land was going to be a lot easier than doing it in the water and he tried to explain what the force of the wind would do to the boat and how the strong river current would play into things. Alice came and was very surprised to see the Captain there and Martin in a boat on top of a bed of palm fronds. Martin showed his father and Alice how fast he could untie the sail and wrap it around the mast and lift the mast up and lay it in the boat. Then the three walked together back home. On the way, Martin asked his father when he could go along on the trip to Tybee with the supply boat. The Captain was surprised at the question. He trusted Jacob and all the boatmen's skill and their attention to safety but the Savannah River could be a dangerous place and everything was wild and uncivilized beginning just a few miles out of Savannah and wild on Tybee, except for the Lighthouse compound. He told Martin that his longtime friend Charles Dyer, the lighthouse keeper, and his family would certainly take care of him for the night but he may be uncertain about the trip there and back. Martin pleaded to his father to let him do it once before he started school in the six months and his father said he would see.

The supply boat got back the next day, arriving at the boathouse just as the tide was about to turn and go back out. There was no time for Johnny to help Martin on his boat but Martin and Alice, along with half a dozen others, were waiting at the edge of the river for the boat to come in and all pitched in to get it up into the boathouse and listen to anything that may have happened on the trip.

Other than seeing a ship grounded at low tide, the day before, near the entrance of the river, it was a routine trip. As the sun set, Johnny walked with Alice and Martin all the way back to the big house and Martin asked Johnny if he would help him try his boat out the next day, Johnny said he would and Alice smiled at Johnny and it set his head spinning.

Martin could hardly fall asleep that night because he was so excited about his boat finally going in the water and was up before dawn and out of the house and at the boathouse as the sun was just coming up in the east where Tybee was. As just a sliver of the sun was above the edge of the marsh, Martin could see three masts, silhouetted, of the ship that had been stuck on the sand bar that the boatmen had talked about. As the tide had risen it had floated off and drifted in the current, of two tide cycles, toward Savannah, then anchored at where Martin was seeing it.

The boathouse crew arrived, and Johnny told Martin they needed to wait an hour or so until the morning chill burned off. Jacob excused Johnny from his work and the whole crew was looking forward to seeing the boat and Martin go after watching them work on it for the last few months. While it was warming up, Johnny helped Martin get the boat down to the edge of the river and was talking to Martin about what to do. He was pleased and surprised that Martin had practiced so much on dry land while he had been gone and also amazed that his father had come and taught him a few things. Johnny reminded him of the strong river current and that it was as important as the wind in operating the boat. He also said that the Captain had left something at the boathouse the day before with instructions that Martin was to have it at all times on his boat and he better go get it before they left. Johnny left and returned with two things, one he said was from the Captain and one he had forgotten about previously and showed Martin a small cake of grease in his hand and reached down and smeared it in the hole that the mast went in through the thwart, and Martin was pleased and knew exactly what it was for. He knew it would make the mast easier to slip in and out and spin when rolling out the sail, but he was puzzled about what the other item was that was about as long and round as a man's leg. Johnny said his father had seen them on the deck of a ship at the docks in Savannah and inquired about them.

The Captain said it was something made up north for fisherman that fished in small dory boats launched from a schooner out at sea. It was a long canvas sock stretched over something round and hard inside but was not very heavy. Inside was a type of tree bark from Portugal called cork. Several long pieces were fastened together with pine pitch and then rounded over on the edges and slipped in the canvas tube like a leg in a stocking. The ends were connected by a small rope to grab on to. Walter had said these had saved many fishermen and crewmen from drowning in boating mishaps and Johnny laid it in the water and it floated and was difficult to push down under the water.

Martin didn't really like the idea much because his boat was small and barely big enough for two people and this thing might be in the way. Johnny said that his father said that he was not to go without it and that was all there was to it. They got the boat in the river and Johnny was amazed at how Martin sailed the little dugout so easily. He had seen the palmetto fronds and Martin had told him what he did to practice. His father had shown him some things and he just looked like he was born to sail a boat. He remembered what he was told about the current and how the wind could be unpredictable on the river because one bank of the river was high with trees on top of that and the wind would sometimes be blocked and sometimes the wind would swirl over and swoop down and blow in sudden burst and to let out the sail quickly if the wind got too forceful.

Just as they were crossing over the middle of the river, Johnny leaned over quickly and tipped the boat over so far that the mast and sail laid down on the water, and Martin was a little shocked, but Johnny was doing something that the Captain had asked him to do. Walter wanted Martin to know about how to get the boat back upright in case it ever happened, and with a narrow boat like that it was certain to happen often. Johnny shoved the cork float to Martin, and they saw that it easily held them both up in the water and then tied it to the boat so it couldn't drift off. Next, Johnny showed him how to first slip the mast out and make sure that the tag line from the sail was fastened to one of the metal cleats they had made then swim around to what was the bottom and grab the edge sticking up and use his weight to right the hull and use the paddle to swoosh out most of the water in the hull before crawling back in. The other thing Johnny saw that was good is how buoyant the dugout was now that it was dried and sealed. They practiced sailing in all directions for a couple hours until Johnny was confident that Martin was able to handle things on his own and then it was time to go in.

For the next few months, Martin was obsessed with his new boat. He went back and forth from the Milam place to the wharfs in Savannah, sometimes sailing there and paddling back or paddling there and sailing back, depending on wind and tide direction. He loved the excitement down by the wharfs. There were boats and ships of all sizes and loading and unloading and different languages and a constant stir of activity and a unique smell that was a combination of the marsh mud, the smell of Savannah, hemp rope, horse poop, pitch pine ship caulking, exotic cargo of all kinds, and horses and wagons bringing in goods and loading up goods and the clip clop of their hoofs on the ballast stone pavement between the wharves and the river. It was a very colorful place and was almost like a different world from the city of Savannah, which was just up on the hill a few hundred yards away and it quickened Martin's blood every time he was near. He sometimes tied off his boat and walked around looking and listening to things. Martin always brought a smile to the men on the boats and docks, and some knew who his father was and some didn't, and many had seen him sailing out in the waterfront every day.

There were some men he saw, and he didn't have a very good feeling about them. There was something about the look on their faces and how they carried themselves. Martin had always been a little slow in thinking and understanding what people said and had compensated by being sensitive to other more subtle ways. He had learned to look at their faces, particularly their eyes and also the way they carried themselves to understand a little about them.

Walter and Martha had noticed how he had to have things repeated and he seemed slower than Henry had been in communicating. Martin may have lacked the kind of knowledge Henry had, but he had a sensitivity about people that Henry didn't have and he was a natural born sailor. His father always looked, from the Savannah bluff, for his little white sail amongst the many boats and ships in the river. After a few months, Martin knew every detail of both sides of the river from his home to Savannah, but his father had forbidden him to go any further, either way, but that did not stop him from thinking about places beyond.

Martin asked his father again if he could go on a supply trip with Jacob and the crew. His father said he would send word on this week's trip, asking Charles Dyer if he could spend the night at the lighthouse the following week and if he agreed, then he could go. Martin could hardly contain his excitement as word was sent, approval granted, and the trip was planned. Alice was not really happy about it but had total confidence in Jacob and the rest of the boatmen and the Captain's judgment. Martha trusted in what Alice thought about it and the Captain had already given his consent. He remembered his early experience on boats in England at about Martin's age and was proud that Martin was like he was. He knew that Martin started school soon and he wasn't sure how Martin would handle that enclosed environment after what he had been accustomed to.

7.
TYBEE

The afternoon before Martin's trip, Alice came down to the boathouse to get Martin. She wanted to be assured by Jacob that Martin would be watched closely. Of course he would, Jacob told her because Martin was precious to him and the crew. He said Martin would have seven pairs of watchful eyes on him during the boat ride and that he would be with the two guards going to the lighthouse from the landing and Charles Dyer would go with him back the next day. Alice felt better about it.

While Alice was there, Jacob wanted to talk to her about something he had seen on their trip two weeks ago when they had gone the back way to Tybee. He told her about seeing the Indian children playing in the water and their dark red skin and then seeing one with black skin. He said he wasn't sure what to make of it but couldn't forget it and thought he should tell her. Alice was like a young matriarch, not only of the Milam place but of the neighboring plantations and her opinion and wisdom was always sought after, particularly in the secret slave meetings. She didn't have an answer to Jacobs's information, but it was curious to her. She always listened carefully to any news about the Indian Islands because of the unknown fate of her family. She thanked Jacob and asked him to always watch closely of anything unusual when he was in the area. Like everyone on the Milam place, Jacob had heard the story of Alice many times and the uncertainty of the fate of her family, and this was why he had brought this news to Alice.

The outgoing tide began early the next morning. After the supply boat was loaded they slipped it down the rails where it splashed into the murky sediment filled water of the Savannah River with an excited Martin seated near the stern by Jacob. Johnny had put the cork float by him and this greatly pleased Alice. Alice and the workers who had just loaded the supply boat joined in the usual chantey as the boat pulled away. The three pair of oars made sound as they dipped in the water and was followed by a grunt of the oarsmen as they pulled hard on the oars in unison and that set the rhythm for the chantey for those on the boat and those on the edge of the river. Martin was wide eyed and in awe. It was a calm day and the trip down the river was uneventful, but for Martin, every mile was exciting. He had been on an overland trip to Charleston with his mother and father to visit Henry but had never been to Tybee and the lighthouse but had heard so many stories about it. On the Charleston trip, they had only seen Charleston harbor but not gone to see the ocean.

They pulled into Lazaretto creek about noon and the wagon was there waiting. A line was hitched to the boat and winched up and the supplies were loaded off. Charles Dyer had come, instead of sending the guards, to personally escort Martin to the lighthouse. Martin could see the lighthouse a mile or so away to the east. After all was unloaded, the boatmen were given their covered dishes of food prepared by Margo Dyer and they made themselves comfortable and started eating outside of their little shanty because there were no bugs out today. Martin could see some old dock pilings, barely standing and thickly covered with oysters and asked Charles Dyer what that had been and was told that it had been kind of a hospital and quarantine station years before but had been relocated onto the far end of Cockspur Island a few miles away and Martin had remembered seeing something there on the way down.

The trip from the landing to the lighthouse was more excitement for Martin. It was not much more than a wide path built up in the marsh with white oyster shells, connecting a string of small low hammocks, barely above the high-water mark. There was a small rickety bridge over a very small creek that was, at low tide, only a few feet wide and a few inches of water with very soft, muddy banks. The bridge was more of a walkway over the soft mud for fifty feet or so. It was the kind of mud that a man would sink in past his waist if he tried to walk in it. At high tide the creek would be seven to eight feet or more deep and twenty feet wide. A half mile or so further, they came to a larger creek with another rickety bridge and the horses were hesitant to cross. And after that, they came onto the island of Tybee where the path changed from oyster shells to sand and they were on the northwest end of the island a few hundred yards from the ocean. They were between the sand dunes and the tree line up on higher ground and the lighthouse was in clear view ahead.

Martin could hear the sound of the ocean waves and in between the dunes see across the wide mouth of the river to some islands a few miles away. Charles Dyer steered the wagon to an opening in the dunes so Martin could look out toward the ocean. He was in awe. They arrived at the lighthouse compound and entered through a stockade type fence that enclosed about two acres and there was a house for the Dyer family and a horse barn and a guard shack and a couple storage buildings, one being solid brick and Martin knew that was where they kept the lamp oil.

They first went to the big house where the two guards off loaded things into the house and left Charles and Martin before going to the oil house and then the barn to unload the rest. Charles Dyer took Martin into the big house to meet his family who had been out on the large front porch waiting. The Dyer's had a son and a daughter. The son, named Daniel, was thirteen and his daughter, Mary, was ten. Visitors were rare and they all studied Martin closely. Charles' wife, Margaret (Margo) had a table full of food inside and they had delayed their mid-day meal until Charles and Martin arrived and then went in and filled their plates and came back out to the porch to eat. After the big meal, Charles suggested that he and Daniel and Mary show Martin around and said he could best show Martin the area if they went to the top of the lighthouse. Martin was both excited and a bit afraid. It helped that Daniel and Mary were along because they smiled and joked a little and made Martin feel comfortable.

They entered a small gabled structure abutting the base of the light-house and then through a doorway through the thick brick base and Martin looked up and was a bit dizzy as he saw the upward spiral of stairs. First went Mary and then Martin and then Daniel. Martin was more afraid than he wanted to let on, but the casualness of Daniel and Mary eased his fears somewhat. He had never seen anything this big. As they climbed multiple flights, they passed a few small, glass window openings and Martin could see the ground getting further away. He was both afraid and excited. They finally made it to the top where Daniel first showed Martin the giant glass reflector with the strange glass lamp and the odd gears under the revolving platform that rotated and the crank that was wound each day and automatically rotated the light slowly all night so that ships north, south and east and the people in Savannah, to the west, could see the light beam intermittently about every thirty seconds on each rotation. Then they went outside on a walkway that went around the top with a guardrail.

Daniel first showed Martin the view back toward Savannah where they had come from. He could see the sand dunes they had come behind and the beach going back toward Lazaretto and where the beach sand ended, and the mud and marsh continued to where Lazaretto creek branched off to the south from the South Channel. He saw the big and small creek they had come across and the oyster shell path strung along the hammocks out to the landing at Lazaretto creek where the boatmen were spending the night.

Then Daniel, looking north, pointed out three islands, Hilton Head, Daufuskie, and Turtle Island. He mentioned that Turtle Island was a dangerous place where the worst kind of men hid out. Slave smugglers, thieves and murderers and worse than them were the large number of huge rattlesnakes that would kill a man in twenty minutes by its bite and if neither of those got you, the huge wild boars would, and that Martin should never go near there. Facing east Daniel told Martin that his father's Irish homeland was on the other side of the ocean there and that was where the strong northeasters came from.

Next he walked around a bit more and told Martin to look down the beach southward to where the Back River flowed out the south end of Tybee into the ocean and to follow that beach line around the south end of Tybee to where the beach ended, and the marsh began, and a small creek went back through Tybee to a small group of huge old Longleaf pines. He said that this was the landing spot that the supply boats used when the weather was too bad to come down the Savannah River.

He also said that this was where the slave massacre had been, and Alice had been found in the pluff mud and that directly across the Back River, from there, were the Indian Islands. Martin's attention perked as he mentioned this and he did not know why but whenever anything about the Indian Islands was talked about, he became keenly attentive to know every detail. Daniel pointed out the dozen or so of those islands scattered out in the marsh over to the next big inlet several miles away. Martin asked if the Indians were friendly toward the colonials and Daniel said that he had never known of an incident of them being aggressive, but everyone thought that they were cannibals and ate people if they came into their area. He said that they actually were very shy and reclusive and seldom were whites able to see them except occasionally at a distance. Contrary to the popular belief about their savage reputation, he knew of several occasions where colonials, stranded in their area by a boating mishap, were taken across the Back River and dropped off on Tybee by the Indians and those rescued made their way here to the lighthouse seeking help and were fed and sheltered and sent back to Savannah on the return trip of the next supply boat.

Daniel pointed northwest and warned Martin a second time. He said that here on Tybee was mostly safe but across the Savannah River around Turtle Island was not a place to be. Desperate outlaws came here from all over this country and the world, seeking escape from whatever laws they had broken and were dangerous and went there along with slave smugglers and every other kind of lawless activity. He said they went there because everybody was afraid of the snakes and wild boars, and outlaws and stayed away.

He said that Tybee lighthouse was mostly a beacon for law-abiding ships seeking legitimate trade, but there were also ships smuggling slaves and goods, using out islands as cover and most of their comings and goings were at night and they used the lighthouse to find their way too. Also, even after the massacre, there was an occasional runaway slave hiding on the south end of Tybee and he knew that boats came in the night from Daufuskie with a few more sometimes, but not as many as in the past but the word was still out that this is where British sailors would come and take them out to a ship, having just loaded up in Savannah and heading back to England.

They next walked around the walkway to the back side of the lighthouse looking west and pointed out a distant tree line of a long island, silhouetted just slightly above the marsh and told Martin that the Milam place was toward the north end of that tree line that was higher ground. Just as he pointed it out, a light from the Milam place flickered. Daniel said it was three o'clock and Martin knew what that meant.

It was the time every day, weather permitting, that communication could happen because the sun had passed far enough overhead to be able to reflect its light with a mirror westward. Daniel went to get the mirror box and returned with a wooden box, open on one end with a mirror inside against the back wall of the box. He set the apparatus down on a flat square shelf permanently attached to the top of the guardrail. The shelf had a mechanism underneath that allowed it to be turned or adjusted to any angle and tilt needed. Daniel began to adjust the box by turning it in the direction he wanted and then tilting it up so that it was pointed between the sun and the Milam place. Then, by sliding a thin flat piece of wood in grooves in the sides of the box in front of the mirror creating a shutter that he could lift up and down to expose the mirror in a series of flashes visible to the operators on the third floor of the Milam place. First, five quick flashes to acknowledge the signals they first saw and then a set of flashes saying all was well (meaning the supply boat had arrived successfully with Martin), then a series of flashes messaging the current weather and tide conditions and some ship information that was on a piece of paper Charles had prepared and gave him.

Daniel's hands deftly and quickly operated the shutter and the slide and tap of the wood was mesmerizing as he altered multiple timing and pauses to communicate in code to the other side. Martin had seen this happen from that other side and on this day, the Captain had made it a point to be at the signaling station to affirm the safety of Martin.

Daniel Dyer next talked about the night signaling using the lighthouse beam. He said night signaling was rarely done and only when there was something very important, on a day that was cloudy when the sun reflecting mirror would not work. Unlike the mirrored day signals, it could be seen from the bluff in Savannah and every night from nine to ten o'clock a security guard was stationed on the Savanah bluff to watch for a message that hardly ever came but it was simply a safety routine for any emergency that may happen. Daniel said it was done as a practice twice a year, once on the second Sunday in December and once on the second Sunday in June. Martin was impressed with Daniel's professional way and his skill and knowledge. Mary hadn't said much but was attentive at watching Martin listen to Daniel. The lighthouse operation had fallen on Daniel, and it was expected that he would be the next light keeper.

When they went down, Mary suggested that they go down on the beach and show Martin their favorite things to look for that the tide may have left like crabs and fish left in the tidal pools. They walked up and over the big dune between the lighthouse and the beach. Captain Jones was sitting in a weathered chair and his face brightened up when he heard them walk up. He was there alone because both crews had taken their pilots out to ships and returned to Savannah for a night.

They introduced Martin to the Captain and when he heard who his father was, he was surprised and delighted because he was a longtime friend of Captain Milam and greatly respected him. Although Captain Jones was here every day, his age and poor eyesight prevented him from actually doing any piloting and his wife had died and his children were grown and gone but this was the life he had always known, and this was where he intended to spend his last days. He stayed in a small one room shanty patched together from driftwood that was a landmark of the north point beach of Tybee. The pilot crews brought him a few necessities and some food and Margo Dyer sent him food every day.

There was a routine that he went through when Daniel came to visit, and as usual he reached into his pocket and pulled out a small white clay pipe and loaded it with tobacco, then the Captain would tell a story of some sort. Afterwards, Martin told about the boat that Johnny had helped him fix up and said he wanted to bring it here one day and take it over to the Indian Islands. Mary said he would be eaten by the Indians and Martin said he didn't believe that. Daniel told Martin that Mary was just making that up. Captain Jones pointed across the water and said that if she had been talking about Turtle Island, she would have been correct, but not by Indians, but by hogs, snakes or slave smugglers.

It was getting late, and Daniel said he had other things to show Martin, so they said goodbye and they headed back up over the high dune to the lighthouse. They then took Martin to the barn and the guardhouse. Martin had seen guards being brought from Savannah to ride the supply boat to Tybee. He had heard his father say that there was a time when guards were needed at the lighthouse but didn't think they were needed now. Then they went to the barn and fed handfuls of corn from the feed ben to the two small, big footed "Tacky" horses that were greatly appreciative of the snacks. Mary said she loved the tackies and told Martin if he came back again for a longer stay, she would take him riding on the beach and he said he would like that.

The sun was setting, and it was time to clean up for supper. There were two metal tubs on the front porch for the boys to bathe in and one on the back porch for Mary. Daniel showed Martin how to haul well water from the kitchen pump to the tubs and then to add a little hot water from a pot kept hot on the wood stove, to knock off a little of the chill. Mary had a tub on the back porch, and they hauled water for her before they bathed themselves.

Afterwards, while waiting for the call to supper, Mary showed Martin her one doll and her desk where she did her studies every day, taught by her mother, and her cat that was one of many living outside but was the only one allowed in the house. Mary had her own small room about the size of a large closet and Daniel had a space in the loft where an extra pad of stuffed quilts was made up for Martin on the floor.

After supper, they sat up by candlelight in the loft for a while and Daniel told Martin stories of storms and shipwrecks and all sorts of happenings. Martin was envious of the adventurous life of Daniel here on the edge of the mighty Atlantic, as he drifted off to sleep.

The next thing Martin was aware of was tapping noises of a broomstick on the floor below his bed from downstairs by Margo Dyer. Martin stood up a minute before going down the ladder. He went down and woke up Mary and they asked if they could go to the Lazaretto landing with Martin and were told they could.

Margo Dyer had been up an hour earlier and had eggs and grits and biscuits made for everybody, including plates of food for the two guards in the guardhouse and asked Daniel to take them out to them. Charles told Mary that they needed to leave to take Martin back at about noon because the supply boat would be leaving on the incoming tide, which started about an hour after noon. Margo said Martin could have an early lunch there or she could send an extra big biscuit with the ones she was sending the boatmen for lunch. Before Martin could answer, Mary said she wished he would eat there with them and he said that was just fine.

Daniel came in and asked Martin if there was anything he would like to do or see today, and Martin said he wouldn't mind going back up in the lighthouse again and maybe another trip to the beach. Daniel said if there was time, they could ride in the wagon to the Back River landing and Margo said that might have to wait until Martin's next visit. Martin said he would like that when he came back.

After breakfast, the three of them went up on the lighthouse again and Martin was not afraid like he had been the day before. He went very slowly around the balcony and spent most of his time looking south at the rivers and creeks around the Indian Islands. He told them about having to go to school soon and how he didn't like it but had promised his father that he would try it and said he would rather skip school and just go around on his boat until he got old enough to learn how to be a ship captain.

Mary said he needed to at least learn how to read because a ship captain had to read things. She said she loved to read because it was like going somewhere without leaving her room. Daniel said he didn't care to much for reading but was glad he knew how because he liked to read the old daily logs his father had kept from when he first came to Tybee to be the light keeper, even back when it was just a day marker without a light. He knew he would have to learn to read and write to be a light keeper when his father quit but it had been difficult but Mary had learned easily and could now read faster than him. Mary saw that talking about school and reading and all had made Martin uncomfortable and said they should go down and feed the horses and then go back down to the beach.

There were two pilots and crews down on the beach today. Captain Jones was sitting out in his spot and Daniel handed him the sack of food and the Captain asked him to set it in his shanty and he asked if they had brought Captain Milam's son back and Martin answered they had and went over and put his hand on the Captains shoulder. Captain Jones asked Martin to tell his father that he wished he would come to Tybee one of these days so they could see who could tell the best lie that sounded the most like the truth and laughed. Martin said his father was good at telling a big story, but he hadn't been around long enough to know if they were all true. Daniel said the Captain was an awful good storyteller and so were the pilots and their crews. The Captain said the vastness of the sea brought out the depths of a man's imagination. He said it was not morally wrong to entertain with a good sea story that was mostly a lie, but it was very important that it be based on a small amount of truth.

Martin told the Captain about his boat again, and how he wanted to bring it to Tybee and go over to the Indian islands. The Captain told him that he had lived with the Indians on one of their islands for a while and got Martin's complete attention. Martin asked him if that was a sea story that was mostly a lie with a little truth and the Captain smiled at Martin and said it was the truth and although the Captain could not see very good, he could feel how he had Martin's complete attention. Mary told the Captain that Martin was leaving on today's tide, and they should be going back to the house. The Captain told Martin that it would be better to wait so he could tell him the full story. Martin was disappointed and wished he could sit and listen for a few hours but knew how important it was to leave on the tide and told the Captain he would be back as soon as he could.

They walked back up and over the big dune to the house where Margo had them an early lunch ready. During lunch, Margo told Martin that she wished he would come back and stay for a while next time and Martin said he would like that. Charles asked Daniel to go hitch the horses and bring the wagon around to the back. While they sat, Martin said how much he had liked Captain Jones and Charles said everybody liked the old man around and it was uncanny how he was almost blind but could predict so well what the weather would be for a few days or a week ahead. Martin said he hadn't heard that about him and Charles said it was so. Mary told of how the Captain said telling a tall tale was morally fine as long as it contained a little truth. Margo looked at Charles to say something about that and Charles said he guessed it was up to the listener to find the small bit of truth and went on to say that a tall tale could have a lot of richness and value and as long as it didn't cause anybody harm, it was fine with him. He said that in Savannah, they had a theater building where actors and actresses were paid to act out stories that were made up by people that were paid for making them up and they were no more the truth than the tall tales of the Captain and pilot crews. He said people paid good money to go to the theaters and be told those tall tales with a lot of fanfare. He said it was entertainment and there was no moral wrong in it and neither was there any in a sea story because it could be rich in entertainment for people that didn't have the money to go to a theater. Mary said it was like that with some of the books she read and she really enjoyed some of them, but she liked history a lot and preferred stories of things that really happened. Daniel came in and Margo said they should be going and told Daniel to get the sack of biscuits for the boatmen and she went and hugged Martin and told him that it was a whole truth that she liked him coming and wanted him to come back again soon.

Martin liked seeing the ocean, but he really liked seeing the vastness of the marsh grass and the narrow oyster shell roadway connecting the low hammocks from Tybee out to the Lazaretto landing. From the roadway to the south and southwest, the marsh grass looked endless like the ocean but he knew the grass had a far edge that just couldn't be seen and that the ocean had an even farther edge but just couldn't be seen and he knew he wanted to someday travel on the edges of both.

Martin's attention was reeled in by the wagon slowing and Charles saying that it was time to bring in more oyster shells on parts of the road as the wagon wheels bogged down a bit. Martin noticed how the big wide hooves of the tacky horses spread even wider as they plodded in the marsh mud and were still able to pull the wagon through the soft spots. He remembered how odd the tackies had first looked to him because they were small horses but seemed to have feet the size of larger horses and now he understood now they were perfectly suited for not sinking so easily in the marsh mud and he understood why they were called marsh tackies.

Jacob and crew were ready and waiting for Martin and when they got off the wagon, Charles hugged Martin and told him to come back soon. Daniel awkwardly hugged him and said he hoped to see him and his new boat he had talked about, and Mary hugged him and surprised him with a kiss on his cheek that made his blood flush and was surprised and unfamiliar with the feeling of it. Charles shook Jacob's hand and Jacob knew what Charles wanted to hear and said for him not to worry because they would watch over Martin and motioned for Martin to come on and get in the boat.

The tide was low, and it was a long way down the two rails to the boat and Martin easily walked down one, holding onto the rope that came down from the winch and when he got in, they let it down the rest of the way into the water and they cranked in the line and within less than a minute all were aboard and Jacob started a chantey with a verse and the crew sang the chorus and they departed in a rhythm of the oars and gospel blues.

Charles, Daniel and Mary watched and could hear their singing until they turned out of Lazaretto Creek up into the south channel toward Savannah. Charles could see in his kids' faces that they had liked Martin's visit. Mary asked her father when he might come back, and Charles said it might be a while because Martin was finally starting school. Daniel said he didn't think Martin would last long in school and Charles said that his brother excelled in school and Mary said that Martin was smart enough but was slow to catch on and had a way of being distant and seemed to have difficulty keeping his attention on anything other than boats or the Indian Islands, and she agreed with Daniel that he may not be right for school and Charles said it was very unusual for the two of them to agree on something.

Martin watched carefully at the building on Cockspur Island since he had learned that it was the quarantine station that had been at Lazaretto landing. He was sitting back by Jacob and Jacob saw him staring at the place and told him it was a place of death and they had to move from Lazaretto because Lazaretto was no more than a marsh hammock and low and not big enough for all the bodies to be buried on, but Cockspur was higher ground and big enough for a lot of bodies. Martin asked why so many people died there and Jacob said sickness killed half and sadness killed the other half. He said he had seen the ships unloading people at Lazaretto before they moved to Cockspur, and he had not felt the same since. Martin asked what he meant. Jacob said the first thing that hit him was the smell and stench of it then seeing the poor souls leaving the boat was hard to look at because they could hardly walk from being cooped up and laying down in their own waste all the way from Africa. They say that half always died on the way but there was still more than a hundred got off the boat the day he saw it and he reckoned half of them died there at Lazaretto.

Martin asked Jacob why things were like that, and Jacob said that was a much bigger question than he had a mind to answer. He told Martin that his father's place was different than any place he had ever heard of, and he was lucky to be there and his father had always wanted to free them all and was ready to close his place down and move to Canada when the massacre happened and Alice came. Walter's friends in Savannah couldn't talk him out of it but it was your mother that had the right words for him to listen to. She told him what might happen to us if he shut things down and it was what made him stay but he would set every man or women free that wanted to go and he had me tell them all that. Also, it was little Alice that warmed their hearts and was a big reason his father decided to stay.

Jacob said that at the time, his father made it clear that if there was anyone that wanted to walk away from the Milam place, he would give them money and pay for a lawyer to manumit them. Martin asked him why he and his wife didn't go. Jacob said they knew how terrible things could be on the outside and they knew that if they couldn't make it on their own, the state could repossess them and sell them back into slavery. He told Martin that nobody would stop anyone from walking away from the Milam place and the only reason they might come looking for them would be because they would be concerned about how they were doing, but not to bring them back. He added something that Martin never forgot. He said that they all knew that they were free to go at any time and would be helped to go if they did and knowing that made them feel free where they were at because they had a choice.

On the way up the river, Martin saw two bateaus pulled up on the bank on the South Carolina side of the river and he wondered what they might be up to since all he had been told was that it was no man's land and not a place to be. He was thrilled when they overtook two ships that were drifting with eight pulling boats on each, keeping them in the channel. They passed close by, and the Captains waved over the side. One was a

Dutch ship and the other was from France and he wondered how long it took them to cross over the ocean and what it would be like to be in the middle of the ocean and having an empty horizon in every direction. He didn't know if he would like that. He wasn't afraid of it at all but simply thought he liked the edge where ocean and land met.

Alice was waiting with a few others as they eased up on the riverbank at the boathouse and she lit up when she saw Martin. Her next look went to Johnny and her beautiful smile made him melt and feel good all over. Martin got out of the boat and Alice hugged him as a mother would hug her child. She said it had only been two days, but the Milam place was not the same without him there and Jacob laughed and said how Tybee was not the same now that he had been there because he had seen the look on Charles and Margo and Daniel and especially Mary's face when he left.

All Martin could think about was going back to Tybee with his boat and sailing all the way around the island. He had a perfect memory of the ocean and rivers surrounding Tybee from his view from atop the lighthouse. He could start at the landing and go east toward the lighthouse and follow the beach around passing the pilot shack and then follow the long stretch of beach to the Back River and follow that to the west to Lazaretto Creek that circled back to the landing.

The image of the circular route around Tybee was etched in full color in his mind's eye. His mind went back to the Back River landing and then over to the Indian Islands to the south. He wanted to visit every one of the dozen or so Indian Islands scattered throughout the marsh that Daniel pointed out. He told Alice that the Dyers wanted him to come back for a week after he had completed some school and Alice didn't say it but had some doubts about Martin going to school. She, more than even his mother or father or brother knew he was special in a way that may not fit with a classroom.

8.
SCHOOL

Martin turned ten and it was time for him to start school. His father took him in his carriage the first day and went in with him to meet the teacher. It was one room with an iron wood stove in the middle. Walter had imported the stove from England earlier when Henry first attended.

Mr. Peeler, the school master, had also been brought from England and he greeted Walter and Martin when they came in. He asked about Henry and went on and on about what an excellent student he had been and looked at Martin and said that he looked forward to seeing him excel like his brother. He asked why he had not started earlier like his brother and Walter said it was his and Martha's thinking that Martin liked the outdoors so much that they would let him delay school a few years.

Mr. Peeler couldn't understand this reasoning but said nothing about it but would later understand. Martin had not said anything yet, but when Mr. Peeler asked what he liked best about the outdoors, Martin answered back about his friends at home and his boat and going to the boathouse everyday but better than anything he liked his trip to Tybee and seeing the Indian Islands. Mr. Peeler only understood parts of his answer because of Martin's strong Geechee dialect and he tried unsuccessfully to hide his shock at Martin's speech, out of respect for his father, and asked how he came to speak like this. Walter said that it was because he and Martha were so busy that Martin was mostly raised by their black house servant and spent most of his time with the workers children on the place. He was careful not to let on about Alice being a family member. Mr. Peeler said that they would work on that, and Walter said he wanted Martin to speak as good as Henry. Walter told Martin that since this was his first day, he would be back to pick him up and take him home.

There were only nineteen students in the school ranging in age from seven to seventeen. Mr. Peeler was a very dedicated teacher and took each student as his full responsibility to educate and refine. He would soon find out that Martin would be his biggest challenge ever.

The students were divided into three groups based on age. This way, Mr. Peeler could teach each group at the level of instruction suited for them. The students not being instructed were given assignments to work on while they waited for their session. Martin was the odd student out because his age and background did not match any of the others. He didn't mind because being alone allowed him to daydream about being on the river. There were just a few windows and that is where most of Martin's attention was. Out the window, there was a small space between two buildings that blocked the view of the river, and Martin spent most of his time trying to get a glimpse of any ship or boat passing by that space.

When it was Martin's turn for instruction, Mr. Peeler began by telling Martin they needed to work on his language skills before they could attempt any other subjects. Martin did not have a problem with his speech, but he was willing to try, mainly to please his father.

Mr. Peeler began by saying basic words slowly and having Martin repeat them. This exercise was difficult for the other students in the class to not hear and they could not always control their snickers or laughter especially when Mr. Peeler accidentally repeated Martin's slang.

This practice was all Mr. Peeler knew to do with Martin. He should have started with the basics of learning how to read, which he did after seeing that he wasn't getting far with word repetition. He brought Martin the basic reader book. Henry had taught himself to read in the library at home and had advanced quickly. Martin, on the other hand, opened the book and just stared at the letters and words in bewilderment. Mr. Peeler pointed to the large letters of the alphabet that were painted across the upper wall behind his desk and explained to Martin that these were the building blocks of the English language and that each had a different sound and when combined created a word and when words were combined it made a sentence and when sentences were combined it could make a story and there was a certain way to say the words which is what he intended to teach Martin.

Most of this went over Martin's head but he tried his best to listen and comprehend. Mr. Peeler got Martin a pen and ink well and some paper and showed him how to dip the pen and scratch out the shape of a letter. This captured Martin's attention because it was a little like sewing or coating his boat with oil. He was told to copy the three simple words on each of the first five pages while Mr. Peeler worked with other students. When Mr. Peeler came back to him he was pleasantly surprised at what a good job he had done even though they were in reverse order. Martin was happy to see him pleased and said that it was a little like making the sails for his boat but had to repeat himself several times before Mr. Peeler could understand what he was saying.

This seemed like progress to Mr. Peeler, and he then had Martin copy a few short sentences. Mr. Peeler watched as Martin began and he was surprised that Martin started at the right hand side of the sentence and was slowly "drawing" each letter of the word until he completed the last letter, which normally would have been the first letter. This confused Mr. Peeler but Martin was a little proud of his drawing. On the next sentence Mr. Peeler instructed Martin to begin on the other side of the sentence first. Martin didn't understand why it made any difference but agreed. The other thing that Mr. Peeler noticed odd besides how Martin seemed to draw each letter was how he kept his non drawing index finger on the letter of the sentence he was drawing. Mr. Peeler asked him to hold his hand in his lap while he worked, and this stunted Martin's already slow progress. He couldn't successfully find the letter that was next, so he was allowed to use his finger again.

Mr. Peeler had never had a student as difficult or like Martin. He didn't see how he could begin to teach Martin to read so he simply went through a routine of saying words and having Martin repeat them and then assigning him pages in the book to copy. This went on for the first few weeks and one day Walter came to pick up Martin instead of Willy, who took care of the horses and mules and was the carriage driver at the Milam place.

Walter was curious about Martin's progress. Mr. Peeler was apologetic about the slow progress but that he was trying his best. Walter said that he was told that Martin seemed ill every afternoon but after he was home a while he seemed to get better. Mr. Peeler said that Martin continued to try but that toward the end of each day his attention became quite dull. He also said that Martin had not had any success making friends with the other students. They couldn't understand his speech and his impaired skills were made fun of and Martin didn't fit in very well. This last part of the report disturbed Walter more so than his slow learning. He said he might get Martin some help at home.

Martin was silent on the ride home and had a blank stare at the surroundings and Walter noticed his unusual behavior. Martin was normally actively seeing everything and excited about what he saw. When they got home, Walter suggested he walk down to the boathouse because he knew this was his favorite place, but Martin said he would skip it today and would rather go to his room. This was a big surprise to Walter. Alice had come out to meet them and Walter asked if they could talk about Martin. Martha was there so Alice made some yaupon tea and they went into the study, and it was unusual for the three of them to be together. Martha was always with her relatives and Walter was off with his friends in Savannah. Alice was always the one in charge of Martin but since he started school she only was with him in the afternoons and some of that time he was at the boathouse, but she had noticed his dull character lately and commented that today he didn't even care to go to the boathouse and that was very unlike him.

Walter began by telling about Martin's slow progress at school and him being kind of a loner with no friends and how he didn't have his usual excitement on the ride home. Martha was surprised and said how easy it was for Henry even though he had started at a much younger age. Walter said Mr. Peeler said Martin was even writing his sentences backwards, starting from the end of the word instead of the beginning and he didn't think it was arrogance, but he may just be seeing things differently than normal. He also said that Martin had a difficult time paying attention and was most interested in looking out the window. Alice said that Martin had difficulty keeping his attention on one thing unless it was something about boats or Tybee or helping at the boathouse. Walter said that at least he could function at something even if he couldn't do well in school. He said that Mr. Peeler had been having him repeat proper pronunciation of words, three sessions a day for twenty minutes each time but that the only difference was that Mr. Peelers pronunciation had suffered and that the rest of the students could hardly understand his slang and that was partly why he hadn't made friends. This pained them all because they knew what a good boy Martin was, and he was obviously having a problem and not feeling well about it.

After a few minutes of silence, Martha said that maybe Martin should be taught at home the way that she had taught Alice and they still had the books they had used but she didn't think she would have the time to do it. Alice said she would teach him the basics. Walter said that there were already suspicions about them in light of Alice's obvious literacy and refinement. Martha said that they could say that he was being homeschooled by her, not Alice, since seldom was anyone else ever there to leak the truth. Walter said he was still concerned about Martin's slang Geechee way of talking and that if Martin was not around people speaking the Queen's English, how could they expect him to change. Alice, who was the first to notice what a bad experience Martin was having at school, said that she could try to help in that matter while she taught him to read and write.

Walter said that homeschool may be best and that it was not at all necessary for Martin to be like Henry and that he himself was a late bloomer as far as schoolwork because he had liked nothing much but boats and the ocean and he had now reached the age of sixty-seven years and it all worked out fine. He suggested that they give Mr. Peeler one more week and watch to see if Martin adjusted any better and if it didn't, Martin should leave school.

Alice was pleased with the plan for Martin. She had known from early on that Martin had certain disabilities that affected his ability to learn and pay close attention to instructions. She knew that he would be fine doing something that more suited the things he was good at and liked. His gifts were a very likable personality, similar to his father, and an enthusiasm for all things in the natural world. She never liked the idea of school for Martin, but even though she had become more like his parent than either Walter or Martha, she deeply respected and loved them both and would never do anything to disappoint them and she accepted always their wishes over her own.

Martin stayed in his room after school the next week and this was highly unusual. Martin had a strong desire to please, and especially to please his parents, so he got up and ready for Willy to take him to school in the mornings. This he did for four more days and then on the fifth day, when he came home and went to his room, he did not come out. Martha went in to see what was wrong and she could not wake him up. She was near panicking and called Walter and when he saw how Martin couldn't get up he sent Willy, first to get Alice, who had gone to take some leftovers from last night's supper to Jacob and his family, and then to get the doctor in Savannah.

Alice was there shortly but it would be a couple hours before Willy could get back with the doctor. Alice sat on the bed by Martin and held his head up and he tried to open his eyes, but they just rolled back into his head. Walter and Martha were upset but did not know what to do. Alice kept one hand under his head and with the other hand caressed his face gently. Every sound coming from outside they thought might be Willy with the doctor. Finally, they heard a single horse, and it was the doctor. He had told Willy he could get there faster on his horse than in the carriage. He came in and quickly said hello and went straight to Martin's side and began to check his vitals and ask Martha if anything unusual had gone on. She said nothing that they knew of but that he had recently started school and his health had gradually gone down since he began. She said that Willy said that Martin was fine in the mornings going to school but that he was ill every afternoon after school. The doctor said there was no fever, and his lungs were clear, but he was a little concerned about his grey pallor that in adults could indicate melancholia. He said it would be unusual for a child to have melancholia, but it sounded like he was having a hard time adjusting to school and rest was all he knew to recommend and that he would come every day to check on him and that he should have plenty of fresh water and juices and soups and food when he wanted. He also said that if his condition worsened to come for him.

The doctor left and Alice sat on the bed beside him again. Martha brought a pitcher of fresh water and a damp cloth to freshen his face. Walter and Martha left but Alice stayed the rest of the night and was there when the doctor came back the next day. By the time he had gotten there, word had gone out to everybody on the place and a dozen or so had gathered outside the front door in prayerful hopes for Martin. Jacobs's wife, Ellie had brought a broth she had made and sent it in with Martha when she had come out to meet the doctor. Henry had come and was in the room with Alice when the doctor came in and asked immediately if he had shown any improvement. Alice said he had hardly moved, not even to go to the toilet but had used a bedpan she had brought him. The doctor again checked his vitals and examined him all over for any signs of discoloration or rashes. He found nothing unusual, except the same grey pallor.

Alice stayed by Martin and every hour or so tilted his head up and put a spoon of the broth that Ellie had made up to his lips. After several attempts, he swallowed a spoonful and by afternoon he was swallowing several spoons full. She sent word for Ellie to make some more and requested to know what it was. In a bit, Ellie came back with it herself and told Alice that it was simply egg white and water cooked together. While it was still warm, Martin swallowed half a cup and Alice went to tell Walter, Martha, and Henry and from them word spread to others that Martin had improved.

The next morning, Martin drank a full cup of the broth and asked for some bread and soon after, sat up in his bed for the first time in days. He didn't know that days had passed and asked about missing school. Alice explained that he didn't have to go to school anymore and that she was to teach him how to read at home and help him speak to where he could be better understood by his father. She added that this was his father's idea to dispel Martin's idea that he had to attend school, and that his education from now on, aside from the basic home schooling, was to learn how everything on the place worked.

After hearing this, Alice noticed that Martin's face lit up for the first time in a while and the grey pallor changed to a rosier look. In a few days he was better and was close to his normal health. Walter went by to see Mr. Peeler and explain what had happened and that Martha was going to homeschool Martin and that he was pleased at how hard he had tried to teach Martin and it was not his fault and that Martin needed special educating. This made Mr. Peeler feel better because he had tried in earnest but had seemed to have failed. Walter later talked to Martin and told him how happy he was that he had tried so hard at school even though it had not worked out. He said that he wanted Martin to learn everything he could about the farm operation so he could be of help to his brother who knew how to balance everything but sometimes lacked the practical knowledge of how things worked.

Walter also told Martin some things about his own childhood in England. By the time he was thirteen, he could manage a crew of eight sailors on a small sailing ship and by seventeen he became an officer in the British Navy and a captain by nineteen, the youngest ever. So, he said that Martin, at ten, was ahead of even him in his sailing skills and that being a captain was about the most dangerous occupation there was but it seemed what Martin might be best at one day.

And then one more thing his father added and that was for Martin to not feel any burden of responsibility right now and to enjoy his youth and all things would come naturally. The next thing he said caught Martin by surprise and that was he hoped that Martin could, after learning the different operations of the Milam place, could spend at least a month at the lighthouse on Tybee to get an overview and all.

Visiting the lighthouse, the sickness, and school, all in the last few months was more than enough for a ten-year-old, but in some ways, Martin's learning had been stunted but in others he would learn things in advance of his age. Within a few days Alice gathered the books that she had been taught from and set a schedule for Martin to begin his basic education. There were no other students for Martin to compare himself to or hear snickers at his slow learning and Alice was a good teacher. She didn't bother trying to have him repeat pronunciation after her but was simply careful in how she talked around him and used the Queens English to try and affect a slow change in his speech. After a few months of being with her in the big house every day for about three hours, there was slow but solid progress in his reading and a little in his speech.

Early on, in his first reading lesson, she realized that Martin was not seeing things normally, sometimes progressing from the right side of a sentence and moving to the left or even starting at the bottom of the page and moving up. She stumbled on a helpful process one afternoon when Walter came in with something to show Martin. They were just finishing up with lessons and Alice noticed how excited Walter was to show Martin what he had. It was a rolled-up scroll, and he laid it down on the table and carefully unrolled it, placing a book on each side to hold it open. It was a nautical chart of the Savannah River from slightly west of the city and continuing east to Tybee and including a few island's north and south. Walter said this had been in the works for the last year or two by the best map-making outfit in the country.

Martin was totally fascinated and for the next hour sat spellbound as his father went over every river and island and navigational hazard. Martin recognized some of the drawings from having looked out from the Tybee lighthouse a few months back, and especially looked closely at the area south at the Indian Islands and to the big islands to the north of Tybee. Walter indicated the compass rose at the side of the chart and explained to Martin that this was true to a compass reading. Martin knew what a compass was but had never understood how it could apply to a chart in navigation. It was enlightening to Martin but also to Alice who had stayed and watched over Martin's shoulder as the Captain traced every detail with his finger over the whole chart. Alice smiled to herself as a creative idea occurred to her.

The next day when Martin came into the library for his schooling, Alice had written several simple paragraphs on the big chalk board and in the corner of the board, she had drawn a large compass rose with the four directions indicating North, South, East, and West and told Martin to begin starting at the Northwest corner and read across to the east. Martin smiled a big smile of humor, gratitude, and understanding. From that day on, Martin saw everything in terms of a compass rose. Not just on a book page or a lesson on the chalk board but which way the front of the house faced and what direction he looked out his bedroom window, and which way the river went, and which way was Savannah and which way the boathouse was, and which direction was Tybee. Everywhere he went he gained a natural habit of which direction he was going.

Home schooling didn't go faster but was easier now that he could orient his attention properly. He was painfully slow, but he learned to read. His speech got only a little better around the house but reverted immediately when he went to see Maggie. He had been so busy lately and hadn't been to play with her much and told her about being in school and how terrible it was. She said that she hadn't told him because she knew how hard a time he was having with school and how he had gotten so sick, but Alice had taught her to read and was bringing her books from their library every week. She went and got a book and opened it and read a half page and showed it to Martin and asked him to read some.

He looked at it and said it was a much harder book than he had been learning on and he couldn't read it. Maggie said that it was supposed to be a secret that she was being taught but thought it would be fine for Martin to know she was. Martin said that he didn't know why but it was hard for him to learn to read, and he was slow at it.

Besides Martin and Maggie's schooling, there was something else going on with Alice that was causing her to experience feelings she had never had. She and Johnny began to regularly see each other, and Johnny gained some ability to better overcome his strong feelings for her and compose his thoughts slightly enough to have an extended conversation. This came more natural for Alice than it did for Johnny, but Alice was patient waiting for him to clearly commit his liking for her before she let her own feelings be known to him. For obvious reasons, it was not easy for Alice to let herself be vulnerable, however it did happen, and they both gained a noticeable glow when together that was easy to see by the others on the place. Johnny was bright and so was Alice, but Alice had the advantage of literacy, and her position of privilege allowed her to see a bigger picture of how life and society was.

Although her situation was very different than just about any slave in America, she had perfect clarity of how things were for most all enslaved blacks. She attended the secret slave meetings and heard about the atrocities that happened to slaves on nearby plantations and even now, an hour did not go by without her grieving for her family and the memory of the look of horror and panic on their faces when they saw her snatched up and out of the canoe, however, Alice maintained a normalcy of life and her and Johnny were in love.

Alice had learned that Johnny had been handpicked, as a child, by Governor Wright and given, along with all the rest to Walter in the beginning of this all. She knew that Walter agreed with his previous countrymen who banned slavery in England recently but was now an American and outside of his homeland, was compelled by the laws and institutions of the land. She knew that had it not been for the important role that the Milam place played in the safety and security of the people and institutions of Savannah, Walter and his family would have been charged with treason or terrorized or both for their way of doing things.

Although the Milam place was like an island to itself, it helped that they were close to Savannah. Places further out were more subject to local intimidation and lynching of whites that did not conform to conventional treatment of blacks. Many of their devout church member friends always exchanged pleasantries on Sundays but maintained a social distance during the week but the social snubs did not bother the Milam's.

Particularly, Alice knew that the church did not sanction the marriage of slaves. This didn't bother her as much as it hurt her. Although her life was unique and full in many ways, she was not without the need to be accepted openly by her fellow human beings. This didn't matter to Johnny because he did not understand life much beyond his job, the farm, and his weekly trips to Tybee. Johnny never spoke to Alice about his family.

Alice and Johnny's love blossomed and it affected the whole place in a spring like way. Johnny had gotten over most of his nervousness when around Alice and they had discussions about marriage. Alice took the lead on these talks and in doing so Johnny was brought up to a bigger understanding than he had ever had in his life. Alice questioned things he had not ever given any thought to. She explained how that, similar to his weekly supply trips to Tybee, white people, for a long time had been sailing to Africa, a place across the ocean, capturing people, chaining them, then hauling them in the bowels of a ship and selling them here in America. And, how slaves were raised, just like pigs or chickens or cows so they would have children and those children were sold for profit and Johnny said that was what his beginnings were. He had almost completely repressed his feelings and memory of those events but in the lucid moments with Alice, visions and feelings awakened in him from his early life and he sobbed in Alice's arms. She regretted, in a way, to be causing him this sorrow but knew she was doing the right thing. She went on to explain that in most instances, slave marriage was only temporary and the vows of giving yourself to another didn't make much sense when you didn't own yourself to be able to give yourself away.

This particular subject struck Johnny to a depth he had never known. It sounds impossible, but because of his circumstances and in the confines of a slave society, he had never known or been aware of having a "self." His life had not been his own and he had never considered that possibility. He had always just been a possession of someone else and this concept of "self" had never, until now, dawned on him.

This was a very powerful experience between Alice and Johnny, and it went beyond the matter of their marriage. It was about the most intimate of all human experiences and what the essence of the very religion that would not sanction their marriage was supposed to be about. This clarity of talk and understanding was the experience of one person with a lit candle lighting the candle in another by simply revealing what they already had within themselves. Johnny had always been a human but now he was aware of it, and he was becoming whole. After some time, Alice told Johnny that she would talk to the Captain about performing the ceremony.

9.
MARRIAGE

When Walter heard Alice's request for him to perform the marriage ceremony for her and Johnny, he was as pleased and proud as he had been when Henry had gotten married, and maybe more. When word got out, the whole place was happy and excited. Everyone there knew Johnny, but everyone there and the surrounding plantations in Georgia and South Carolina were familiar with Alice from her attendance and stories at underground slave meetings and word reached out far and wide.

Alice's story and fame was known by only a few of the white people in Savannah and surrounding areas, mostly old and close friends of Walter. Walter was a wise man. He knew he had many allies in Savannah and he knew he had some enemies as well. He also knew that many who were friendly were simply being pleasant for social reasons and he had learned to sense their false friendliness.

Within two weeks, the wedding took place. Work on the Milam place was stopped except for the most important things and for a week there was a holiday feeling of celebration. Work that could be put off was left undone. The ceremony took place in the Milam's yard and house with everyone, including a few of Walter's close friends from Savannah, who knew the story about Alice.

From Savannah to Charleston, in the secret slave meetings, the legend of Alice and her marriage was a topic and her fame continued to inspire and kindle the flame of freedom. Henry had a small cabin built for Alice and Johnny halfway between the big house and Jacob and Ellie's house. This suited Alice perfectly because of the love and attachment she had for both families.

During this time, Alice continued educating Maggie and Maggie's hunger for learning grew greater every day and she and Alice became very close. Alice also imparted the knowledge of self to Maggie as she had to Johnny. It was easier with Maggie because she was never denied her own self, but she had not ever understood the importance of self-knowledge in all people's lives and how slaves were deprived of it.

Maggie, at a young age became another lit candle by Alice, and she grew in understanding, and continued her learning from the Milam library and books that Henry would get from the Savannah library. Maggie came to want to see the world beyond the Milam place.

10.
PRACTICAL EDUCATION FOR MARTIN

As Walter had requested, Henry had Martin begin a hands on education of every aspect of the Milam farm. He began by assigning him to Ellie and the poultry operation which was very important because eggs were nutritious and could keep for weeks. Martin was shocked to learn that it took between 600 eggs a week for all the people on the Milam place plus the Dyers at Tybee and guards and the boatmen when they stayed over at Lazaretto and some for Captain Jones and some occasionally for the pilots and crews on the beach.

After a few months with Ellie, there came a few months at all the other working operations. There was the animal and food crops and all that went into that including vegetables, grain, and lots of corn, and sugar cane making sugar, and winter and summer vegetables. There was farm animals to work, shelter and care for including pigs, beef and dairy cows, and a few goats. Martin spent some time in the woodshop and metal shop and helped in the building and maintenance of the houses and farm buildings and water and sanitary waste systems.

After a few years, Martin had finished helping in all the aspects of the farm and gained an understanding of how much work it took for the place to sustain itself and what a small part of it all to provide for the lighthouse. He asked Henry why they just didn't buy things from local farmers. Henry explained that from the beginning, their father had thought about relying on outside suppliers of the different needs but had come around to the way they were doing things because his original orders were to, with his best understanding and at any and all expense necessary, to provide quality provisions and supplies for the lighthouse operation. He added that as a result of them being so self-sufficient and independent, they were able to operate more as they wanted. He said he didn't know if their father had planned that part but it was a good thing.

Martin's next assignment was more to his liking. With his practical knowledge of how things got produced and maintained, Henry had him start to see that the provisions and supplies were included, in proper quantities, and carefully accounted for, securely stowed on the supply on time

82

boat every week for the all-important supply run. Organization record keeping was the hardest part for Martin, and he was slow at it, but he persevered and was a success. He had not forgotten the dreadful experience at his attempt in school or how inadequate he felt from the snickers and ridicule he had gotten from his class mates when he struggled to learn and how each day was a miserable experience and how sick he felt, nor had he forgotten how relieved and appreciative he felt when Walter said he didn't have to go back to school and that he was just as smart as Henry but in his own way. Gratitude and a chance to prove his value motivated him to triumph over his disabilities and learn the workings of the Milam place.

Martin had been fourteen for a while and Henry told him that he was, in a month or so, going to be floating a barge loaded with building materials down the river to Tybee. Both the bridges needed rebuilding and the roadway across the marsh connecting the hammocks to Tybee needed a lot of work, plus there was repair work on the bricks on the lower part of the lighthouse that was in need of repair. He had spoken to their father and they thought he should go to complete the last part of his learning process. He wanted Martin to watch the bridge maintenance and have the full experience of what a working lighthouse was about.

Henry went on to say that there was one other thing that he wanted Martin to be a part of and it didn't have anything to do with the Milam place directly but could in the future. He said he had made a good friend in college named John Wilcox and Martin said he had heard Henry mention his name and Henry added that he and John had stayed in touch regularly by letters. Henry knew how Martin's attention was sometimes hard to keep and he told him to sit tight and try to listen. John had gone to work for a company in Darien that operating a huge sawmill. Henry went on to explain how the mighty Altamaha River dumps out there into the Atlantic and about how the vast source of inland timber is floated down the river to the sawmill in Darien and Darien had become the biggest timber export location of the entire east coast. He said the mill has a process to mechanically saw logs by damming up every high tide in a big holding area, then releasing it through a shoot and turning paddle wheels which drive a circular saw blade to cut the timber. Some of the logs are sawn into lumber and many are left sixty to eighty feet long, squared off, and slipped through a big square hole in the bow of the ships and hauled up north and all over the world. The logs serve as the ships ballast and before they are loaded, the ships ballast stones are taken out and left on the riverbank. Martin said their father had told him about the paving on River Street was from used ballast stones.

Anyhow, Henry continued, the timber freighting ships, sailing from far up north got their ballast stones from creeks but sometimes when the creeks were frozen they couldn't get them so they began sawing big pieces from frozen lakes and slipping it through the big doorway in the ships bow. When they got to Darien, only about a fourth of it had melted and the remaining ice was shoved out to make room for the timbers and left on the bank to melt. A camp of sawmill workers was near there and in the hot summer days they began leaving their beer and drinks in this discarded ice during the day so that when they got off from work, all hot and tired, their drinks were cold and frosty.

They built a wooden box and put chunks of the ice in it and began leaving vegetables and meat in the box to preserve them. Soon, people from town were coming down to haul the ice to their homes to keep food and beverages cold and some people were even making a frozen desert with cream and sweetened with sugar and fruit.

John thought this might be something that we could use here and at the lighthouse to preserve meats and produce and he thinks it might grow into a lucrative business one day. So, John wanted him to come down and see things for himself and they could talk about the possibilities because he thought there could be a huge future in it. Henry said he had told all this to their father and he had suggested that Martin go along because they often looked at things differently and that could be beneficial.

Anyhow, Henry said he knew Martin would like what he had to say next and said they were to leave for Darien on a coastal trading boat the next week if the winds were favorable. The plan was to leave on the outgoing tide from Savannah, spend the night at Lazaretto, and leave very early from Tybee and be at the Altamaha Sound by afternoon, if there was favorable winds, and from there make their way into the port of Darien by wind and tides the next day. They would have a few days in Darien before the same boat would be ready to return to Savannah, if wind and weather permitted. The trip was agreed on and just like that, Martin was set for his first coastal sailing adventure.

When Alice heard that Martin was going on the trip, then going off to Tybee for a month or two, she asked him to come see her before he left, and Sunday afternoon would be a good time if he could. Martin agreed thinking he could see Maggie too before his trip because he had been so busy that he hadn't seen her in a while. After Sunday midday dinner, Martin walked over to Alice and Johnny's house. The boatmen alternated Sundays to be on duty, and this was Johnny's day on, so it was just Alice and Martin. Alice started by telling Martin that she was having a baby in about seven months and Martin burst out laughing so hard that Alice did not know what to think even though she joined in the laughter. Martin saw her consternation and said that he didn't know if that would make him a brother or an uncle. They both laughed again.

Alice had some yaupon tea made and she served them both a large cup with more in the pot. Martin took this to mean there was something important to talk about. He was right, because it was two hours later and two more cups of tea until Alice was finished talking. It was a rare thing for Martin to sit and listen that long again after his recent talk from Henry.

Alice talked about a lot of stuff he had never heard about her life before becoming a Milam family member, and how awful it was and how close she came to dying on the Back River at Tybee during the massacre. She told him that there was never a waking hour that passed that she did not see, in her mind's eye the images of her family and their horrified expressions as they were carried away in the log boat as she was hauled away under the arm of the brut.

She said her daily prayer was that they were still alive and that she might see them again. She said how thankful she was for his mother and father who had nursed her back to health and taken her as their own and teaching her to read and the library where she was able to educate herself and especially them giving her good understanding about the world around them and the wrongness and evil of slavery. Either the caffeine in the yaupon or the intimacy of Alice's story held Martin rapt.

Alice's clarity and sincerity, combined, set Martin up for the importance of what Alice had wanted to talk to him about. She told him that he had not been off the Milam place much except his month away at school and he had not even been prepared for what happened there and he was about to go to another city and then Tybee for a month or more and possibly much further places than that if he became a captain as most thought he would.

She began by saying that the place that he had been raised in was vastly different than the places he would probably go. She said that, as the kids at his school laughed at him for being different, others in a different and more grown-up world could react in more serious ways about peoples differences. She went on to tell him about the poor crippled man that was murdered on the plantation her family had ran away from and where her mother was to be sent and where her father and brother were to go. She also related local punishments of slaves and how awful some of the plantation owners were to their slaves. Martin told her that Jacob told him about seeing the pitiful people being put off from the ship at the quarantine station when it was at Lazaretto and all about it and how many dies coming over in the boat and how bad it was and all.

She took a long time to explain to Martin how the Milam place came about but that his father didn't believe in slavery and all and he said Jacob had told him that everyone there could leave and they would be supported in leaving and could come back if they wanted and Jacob told him that being able to go if he wanted to, made him feel free where he was at. Alice said his father considered his place like his ship and all hands were given equal respect as human beings and that the only reason he got away with this was because he had done so many great things for the city and was highly respected by many and by the most important people in the town.

There were those however, that if they thought they could get away with it, would do harm to Walter or his family or his properties. She said she wanted to make Martin as aware as she could about all these things so he would not venture out clueless into a world much different and harsh than the world he knew. Also, there was one other subject she wished to talk about and that was her family. She knew that most thought that the Indian Islands were a dangerous place, and most would advise him not to go there, but she knew by his way, that he would surely be going there at his first opportunity. She added that from her experience of the Indians, while she was on Tybee, they were peaceful and compassionate because they saw that her people were starving, and they brought food and helped.

Also, she was told that when they all became sick eaten up by bugs and were about to surrender themselves back to their owners, she was told about an Indian lady that came every day for a while and showed them how to get fresh, clean water to drink and how to dispose of their waste properly and how to cook the tender part of the marsh grass and several other plants and how to harvest the plentiful seafoods. She said that Martin would probably not be in any danger there and she had a request of him.

Before Alice could say another word, Martin said that he knew what she wanted and from the first time he heard his parents talk about her ordeal, he vowed to himself to go and look for her family. This made Alice very happy, and she hugged him. She remembered the special time when she had her long and intimate talk with Martha while Martin was still in her womb and how she felt as if there were three of them there together. She felt the same intimacy again now.

Alice was very happy and satisfied that they had been able to talk before he went away and how good Martin understood what she was saying. Martin was feeling the same way and her talk had filled him with the most clear and good understanding of himself and the world around him and felt a sensation of gratitude from within inside of himself. Again, she had used her lit candle to light the candle in Martin. This was the gift that Alice gave everyone she was around.

Martin left Alice and Johnny's house and headed to Maggie's house, and he could see that they were all out in the yard. They saw Martin and were happy to see him and Ellie went inside to get him a drink of water and a few sweet treats. News flowed quickly and they knew he was going away for a week or so and then going away again to Tybee for a good long while.

Jacob and Ellie hugged Martin and Jacob said that Martin was already as big as him. Maggie smiled at seeing them embrace, then they all sat down and laughed and carried on in an excited Geechee clatter and jabber conversation. Maggie's little brother Thomas loved Martin and followed him everywhere. After a while Jacob and Ellie went for a stroll around back to look at and talk about the different chickens that ran loose in the yard leaving Martin and Maggie and Thomas alone.

Martin told Maggie about where he was going with Henry and that he wasn't particularly excited about going to Darien but was more so about sailing in the large cargo boat to and from. He said he was excited about the trip coming up, but more excited about the long Tybee trip afterwards.

Maggie told Martin that she was reading the best book she had ever read. She said that Walter had brought it from England long ago when he first came and had kept it hidden for all these years and had only gotten it out once for Alice to read years ago, then put it back behind a loose ballast stone in the house foundation. Martin asked what kind of book would have to be kept hidden like that? Alice said that, here in the south it was considered treasonous material if anyone was caught with it and severe punishment could be dealt out. It is a book by an American slave from Africa that was educated by her masters and was very bright and wrote about things that promoted equality for all and interpreted Christianity in a way that included all people including Africans. Maggie said her name was Phyllis Wheatly and she wrote a lot of poems and Martin asked her what a poem was and she said it was some sentences strung together in a beautiful way that sometimes caused you to think about things and sometimes the words rhymed and she saw he didn't know what that was either and she said boat rhymes with float and cat rhymes with rat. Maggie said she was memorizing as many of her poems as she could because she loved them and, unlike having to hide the book, what was in her MIND was in a place no one could FIND, and they laughed.

Martin was in awe at Maggie and all that she knew and he thought that she was smart like Alice. He didn't understand all of what she was saying but he got the gist of it and felt her passion for what she was saying. Maggie said she wanted to read him one verse from a poem she wrote that he would like.

Ode to Neptune (first verse) by Phyllis Wheatley:

While raging tempests shake the shore,
While Aelus' thunders round us roar,
And sweep impetuous o'er the plain
Be still, O tyrant of the main,
Nor let thy brow contracted frowns betray,
While my Susanna skims the wat'ry way.

Martin didn't understand some of the words but knew it was a storm at sea and the boats name was Susanna and he imagined the boat in a furious storm. He smiled at Maggie in appreciation of her effort to memorize and recite this to him.

She said next was just a sentence or two taken from a piece of her writing that she could not forget.

"For in every human breast God has implanted a principle, which we call love of freedom. It is impatient of Oppression, and pants for deliverance."

Martin didn't fully understand it all but got the gist of it and was entranced and mesmerized by Maggie's brief recitation. Martin found himself peering into the depths of the beautiful twinkle in Maggie's eyes. Maggie saw his stare and broke the silence by asking what he thought, and Martin stammered and said that he had to be going.

They chatted small talk a bit more and Martin said that she obviously had been a better student of Alice than he was, and Maggie said that it was only that she was older but Martin knew better. They hugged and Martin headed back to the big house. He was feeling much different on the walk back than when he had set out three hours earlier.

On Monday, Henry brought word to Martin that they were to leave on Tuesday at about noon on the beginning of the outgoing tide. The cool northwest wind that was expected had started today and the Captain wanted to be moored off Tybee Tuesday night so they could leave early Wednesday morning and he hoped they could sail the entire length of the Georgia coast and moor outside Darien that afternoon ready to catch the early incoming tide into the port of Darien the next day.

Henry said that Walter was going to take them by carriage to the dock in Savannah, where they would board the boat they were going on. Henry was not as excited about the sailing trip as Martin was. He had wanted to take overland transportation, but Walter wanted Martin to get the boat ride. He knew the Captain and the boat and was confident of their safe passage. Henry told Martin that he was going to have Johnny do his job of checking that everything was loaded onto the supply boat since it was the same day they were leaving. He said they were both leaving when the tide started out, but the supply boat would be a few miles ahead because his and Martin's boat was leaving from Savannah.

He said that because Johnny could not read to go through the checklist Martin had made, Alice could help him, and they could continue filling in for him while he was at Tybee next month. Martin said he had gotten accustomed to that job every week and would miss it. This comment caused Henry to pause a moment to himself. He was slightly taken aback at the maturity that had come over Martin and that he had grown to his same height. He smiled, inwardly, at the wisdom of their father for having them do this trip together.

On their ride to town the next day, Martin was thinking about the things Alice had talked to him about on Sunday. He wondered again about the people he would meet in Darien. He also thought how different this carriage trip was than the daily trips he had with Willy taking him to school a few years back. He would never forget that awful time, especially the trips home in the afternoons. Henry had his head down in an account journal of some kind, but Martin was eyes wide open at every sight along the way.

Walter told Martin to learn all he could from his sailing trip. He said the boat they were going on was much bigger and had bigger sails but used the wind just like his small boat. He explained that this boat was a design from up north that worked very good for these waters. He said that it was called a "sharpie." It had something in the middle that dropped down called a centerboard when they were in deep water and could be hoisted back up when they were over shoals and shallow water and that the centerboard helped stop the boat from slipping sideways when under sail and move forward into the wind better. With the board up, it could pass over shoals that deeper boats could not. It wasn't a boat for going across the ocean but was perfect for coastal cruising or inter island cruising like to Cuba or the Caribbean. Martin knew about those places from his hours running his finger over all the islands on the globe in their library, especially those areas along the east coast of America and down to Cuba and around.

They were soon clip-clopping along the ballast stone paving of River Street. Just about everyone knew the Captain and waved. The smell and bustle of activity always excited Martin. He was even more excited today because they were part of the activity. They pulled along a sleek vessel about sixty feet long with two tall, raked masts and a long bowsprit and it had the look of going forward even while sitting at the dock.

Captain Ben Graham saw them coming and yelled out to Captain Milam. He laughed heartily and called Walter a landlubber and said how awful that boat with wheels he was in looked. Walter laughed and told him that he was so ugly that he did people a favor by being at sea. Their banter was their way of greeting and how they expressed their appreciation of each other. Captain Ben Graham knew he had special passengers coming and had all his cargo loaded and was ready to go when they got there.

Walter introduced Henry as the smartest and kindest farm master in Georgia or South Carolina. He introduced Martin as the soon to be best captain of those two states as well and added that it would only happen after Captain Ben retired. Captain Ben said he knew nothing of any type of management on land but that he had a wealth of knowledge of boats and the sea for any aspiring young lad that wanted to learn while looking at Martin. Henry and Martin were led to a small cabin next to the Captain's cabin. Captain Ben told Walter that he should come back another time and they could see who could tell the biggest and most interesting lie, but the tide was slack now, and soon to start out and it was time to go.

Farewells were exchanged, lines were freed and three pulling boats with lines attached to the sharpie watched the Captain and when he nodded his head, they heaved on the oars and the boat inched away from the dock. The Captain had ordered the centerboard to be dropped and a small jib sail set shortly after leaving the dock and the northwest wind filled it and the Captain steered down the middle of the channel.

At a safe distance from the dock, the pulling boats were let loose. Away from the Savannah bluff, and the slack tide beginning to gently move outward and with the wind having room to fetch up a bit, Captain Ben asked that the small jib be replaced with the larger jib and the boats speed picked up a bit. In about an hour, they were passing the Wilmington River that led to the Milam place.

It was a particularly high tide, and the river was full and wide and the wind had picked up more and the Captain shouted in a robust way to fly the wings, and the crew set about at making the huge gaff on top of the mainsail free to raise. The Captain came into the wind and the two crewmen used the windless to hoist the huge mainsail.

Martin and even Henry were in awe and even more so when Captain

Ben steered the boat back before the wind and once the big jib was set out to the opposite side of the mainsail, it was like two large wings filled with wind and the boat surged forward powerfully, even without a sail up on the foremast. Now, with the sails set and a high tide with a deep and wide river with plenty of room to navigate, Captain Ben left the operation to the two mates, and turned his attention to Martin, seeing that Henry was occupied with some papers below.

"So young man, how were you plagued with the idea of a life at sea, especially when you have one of the nicest home places in the state? You need to know that for every ten that attempt your choice, nine go back to the hill and for every ten that remain, only half survive. Now what say you?" Martin was slow to answer because Captain Ben was larger than life and an intimidating character but not because he didn't have a good answer and finally when he did, it was a question.

"What else is worth doing?"

Captain Ben laughed so loud that any animals or people that may have been on the far bank of the river could have heard and he bowed to Martin and said that he still had that question sometimes. Then he said that his mates were well in control and that he would begin to do what his father had requested of him and that was to show Martin the ropes.

He directed Martin to come over to the tall lanky mate at the wheel and formally introduced Martin to Ashley, who exuded likability, in his guffaw way, as the Captain brought attention to him. Martin felt he had known Ashley for much longer than having just met him. Then he called Ken over and had Martin meet him. Ken was also likable in an instant and had a disheveled way and comfortable demeanor.

The Captain looked at Martin squarely and with one of his thick weathered hands on his shoulder, he told Martin that the first thing he would teach Martin was that the most important thing to remember was that your mates were the most important parts of any ship and Ashley and Ken were the best he had ever had. Then he showed Martin the centerboard trunk with a gear-actuated crank on both sides to raise the huge centerboard up into its shallow position within the trunk. He pointed to the four huge cargo hatches on deck and told him that they were cargo holds and lifted one and pointed to the crates of metal sawmill equipment stacked inside. He told Martin to look at how each crate was fastened so it couldn't shift and said that shifting cargo had sunk many ships. He said that he specialized in hauling sawmill hardware that was brought into Savannah from Europe and he delivered it to different places along the coast from Virginia to Florida and that hardware was the best kind of cargo because it was heavy and not too bulky and could be stowed low where it provided excellent ballast. Martin acknowledged that he had to think about that in loading the lighthouse supply boat every week.

The main cabin house was very basic with almost closet sized rooms, one with two bunks and one with a single bunk for the Captain and a small locker and a simple shelf for a desk for him to write in his log book. The access area to the separate quarters served as a narrow galley and room for four or five at a narrow shelf for a table in the middle. One third of the galley was for a small iron wood burning cook stove and there were a few cubbyholes for utensils and a few pots hung up on hooks. It was very basic.

Captain Ben said that their trips were seldom longer than five to seven days and most were one or two days going, a day or two in port to off load and sometimes on load and a day or two to return, and he most always allowed for a few nights on the hill in between trips so the sparse accommodations only had to be tolerated two and rarely three days at a time. Most of the volume of the boat was for cargo.

As Captain Ben was showing Martin the last area of the boat, the lazarette, where they stowed sails and ropes, and it contained the toilet, Ashley called out that they were approaching a ship in the channel, which the Captain always wanted to know about. This was a large ship, heavily laden by the looks of its low free board, that had dropped the anchor an hour or so earlier when the tide started out and would wait for the tide to turn back toward Savannah to raise the anchor and continue on its way to port.

Without needing an order, Ken dropped the jib to slow the boat down and Ashley steered to within talking distance of the ship as was usually done so that the Captain could hail the other captain. This was done out of courtesy and caution for any news or warnings from whence each vessel had come. When Captain Ben saw the ship captain come on deck he yelled a greeting and that all was clear to port and the other yelled all was clear to sea. Before they had completely passed, the Captain asked if Martin would like to help Ken raise the jib back and Martin jumped to it.

After Martin was done, the Captain went below again and motioned for Martin to follow. He sat on the edge of his bed at his small desk and pulled his logbook and a quill and small inkbottle out of a cubby. He opened the log to a page with today's date that had a list of the cargo he had taken on in the morning and recorded the sighting of the ship, its position, its origin, type and size, and the fact that it was loaded. Captain Ben told Martin to always record things in the log as soon as possible after they happened so information would not be forgotten.

Martin knew that the supply boat probably left the boathouse shortly before they had departed Savannah and that put them about five miles ahead, but that they were, with the strong northwest wind in their sails, moving faster than the supply boat and as they came around every bend in the river Martin strained to look for it.

When he finally did see it, he showed the Captain and crew and Henry. For the next hour, they watched as the smaller boat came closer into view as they gained on it. So far, this was the biggest thrill of the trip for Martin and Henry even put down his work to watch. It was a beautiful sight to see the perfect rhythm of the oarsmen as the six oars waved ahead to catch a bite in the water to propel the boat swiftly forward. The boat itself was a beauty with a sweet shear line that swooped down from the bow to the stern gracefully. The Captain and his crew had passed the supply boat on the river before but without the special connection they had on board today and they shared Martin's thrill. Captain Ben nodded for Ashley to come by with the jib side to them so they could give Martin the biggest thrill by passing very close.

With the wind behind them, Ashley was able to come so close that the loose foot of the jib was over the supply boat. Martin loved all seven of the boatmen and they him and they were a beautiful sight as they all smiled big and their white teeth showed so pretty against their dark faces. Jacob was a regal sight, stoic and steady at the helm.

As the big sharpie moved by, not a word was said but much was exchanged in love, admiration, and respect and Martin never looked ahead again and watched the supply boat till it was a mile behind them. When he did look ahead again, he was amazed at how far they had gone.

Two hours later they were coming about at the mouth of Lazaretto Creek and with the mainsail struck, easing into the creek with the jib and dropping the stern anchor and sails, and the outgoing tide swung the bow around facing out of the creek so they could more easily leave in the morning. Then they let out a lot of the stern anchor line and set the bow anchor and hauled in the stern line so both hooks held fast, and they were directly across from the boatmen's shanty at the landing. Martin watched and learned and was amazed at the grace and ease that this maneuvering was done, all by Ashley and Ken with the Captain pleasantly relaxing.

This was always Captain Ben's regular mooring when he came the day before to set out from Tybee into the Atlantic and going either north or south. It was a routine they had gone through more than a hundred times.

Not long after they got settled the two guards with the mules and wagon showed up and right after that, the supply boat came in and the supplies were quickly loaded up but they didn't haul the boat up the ramp as usual. Martin saw that several baskets from the wagon were loaded in the boat, then with Johnny at the oars and Jacob at the tiller, they rowed out to the sharpie and handed over the baskets before returning to the bank where they were quickly winched up the ramp.

To everyone's surprise except the Captain, a fantastic meal was in the baskets, sent by Mrs. Dyer that included her giant three egg and bacon biscuits, potatoes kept warm wrapped in a cloth bundle and fresh plum preserves from the plum tree thickets around the lighthouse. As they had been leaving the wharf that morning, Walter, with only a wink and a nod to Ben and a quick hand to mouth gesture, had let Ben know what to expect that afternoon. It was a real treat, especially being unexpected by the rest, and all enjoyed. Even Henry was beginning to loosen up a bit and relax. The smooth trip and the big meal and the comical bantering of Captain Ben and Ashley and Ken combined to make Henry glad that they had not gone over land to Darien.

After watching the sun set, Captain Ben said that they needed an early start in the morning to clear the channel before the tide started moving back in. Henry and Martin found their bunks very cozy and comfortable. They slept solid and the next thing they knew was a bustling about in the galley by Ashley frying some dough in lard to go with the leftover plum preserves for breakfast. Martha had sent a large tin of dried yaupon leaves, enough to last the Captain and crew for months and Ashley had a pot, briskly boiling with a generous amount of leaves in it. They all sat in the little galley and had tea and crispy fried dough and preserves. It was a simple but good breakfast, and everyone ate with little talk.

Afterward, the Captain went in his cabin to pen the new date in his log book and record the mooring location and approximate time, tide and weather conditions of their departure. Henry retreated to the cabin and Martin and crew went on deck.

11.
DARIEN

At the landing across the river, the boatmen were up and getting ready to leave on the incoming tide. They had a little more time before departing before the tide began in, whereas Captain Ben wanted to catch the last of the outgoing or at least the slack period so he could shoot out onto the east side of Tybee without bucking a current. Once offshore, there would not be much of a tidal current to worry about.

Ashley and Ken, with a slight nod from the Captain, began the routine of departing Lazaretto Creek. Knowing that the tide would be flowing out this morning, they had anchored with the bow out the afternoon before. They first, using the windless, brought the bigger bow anchor up to beneath the bowsprit and secured it and the line. Then they set the big jib and hauled the stern anchor and Ashley took the wheel as the wind on their beam filled the jib and wind and current started to move the big sharpie out.

Martin looked over at the boatmen's shanty and they were all watching him. He waved to them, and they all looked worried with a frowns on their faces, instead of the usual beautiful smile showing their white teeth. They were worried that Martin and Henry were about to go out to sea. They were all familiar and comfortable on the river, which had plenty of its own dangers, but the ocean they had only their imaginations to believe, and the unknown was to be feared. Jacob was the most worried and he waved back at Martin as if it was the last he would ever see of him.

The Captain came on deck to check on things. It was almost low tide and between them and the Tybee lighthouse was a lot of shallow water. Oddly, the deepest water was along close to the beach, inside a huge mud bar that stretched for half a mile out. With only the big jib flying and the centerboard still up in the trunk, and only a slight current moving out, Ashley scanned the water's surface to discern the deeper water as the beach looked only a rocks throw away.

The wind was favorable out of the same direction as yesterday and the Captain hoped that it would continue like that for the rest of day and make their passage easy. A northwest wind usually ushered in cooling temperatures and blew for only a couple days, and it had started a day and a half ago. In these conditions, there was little danger of running aground because they could simply wait for the tide to finish going out and then to come back in enough to float them off but the delay could stop them from reaching the inlet to Darien before the wind changed and their trip could require an additional day or more if it started coming from the south.

After a slow passage over the shallow water and coming up on the north point of Tybee, the Captain relieved Ashley and he and Ken, with the windless, hoisted the huge mainsail, then the foresail, but left the centerboard up, and under full sail, with the wind mostly behind them, the sharpie surged and they flew out past the lighthouse and Henry and Martin gazed closely as they passed it, with their minds on different subjects. Henry was thinking about some major maintenance that was going to take a lot of time and money starting soon. Martin was looking for Captain Jones who was alone, sitting in his usual spot out in front of his driftwood shanty. Martin waived even though he knew the Captain couldn't see.

Once they were about a mile out from Tybee, the Captain warned Martin and Henry that they were about to head south and change their point off the wind and that the boat would be laid over a bit, unlike anything they had experienced yesterday and not to be frightened.

With Ashley at the helm, Ken lowered the huge centerboard with a clunk at the end and Ashley changed their heading from east to south and the sharpie healed over, with all sails up, and it was the most exhilarating feeling on the water Martin had ever had. By the smiles on Ashley and Ken's faces, you would think it was their first outing instead of a few hundred. Even Henry smiled ear to ear at the wind and waves, as the sharpie plunged into each swell.

Captain Ben said that it was not always this fun and easy. There were many days that were miserable and made a man have doubts and think of other things he might could do but then good days would always come back and made that same man glad of his job and dream of nothing else.

They sailed by the south end of Tybee and for a few minutes, Martin studied the low profile of each of the Indian Islands as they passed. He vowed to himself that soon he would explore each one. For now, he was satisfied to just gaze at each one from about two miles out. After a while, Henry went below to study his business journals, but Martin stayed on deck. Ken was at the wheel and the Captain gave a slight hand motion and Ken altered his course very slightly to move a little further offshore and Ashley let out all sails very slightly. They were a good crew that was attuned to the Captain's slightest directions and Martin was seeing why the Captain had said the crew was the most important part of the ship.

This was the first time Martin had been where tides and high river banks did not matter much and only wind mattered. A couple hours went by, and Ashley went below for a little while and came up with a big tin bowl for each person filled with a potato and carrot soup with little pieces of salted pork in it and a hunk of bread slathered in lard and a large spoon. After eating, Ashley went back below and came back with a wash pan and a bucket with a line attached and fished some sea water up and poured it in the pan and with a cake of lye soup cleaned up the bowls and pot and utensils and rinsed them in fresh ocean water and stowed it all back below.

The islands south of the Indian Islands were bigger and longer and had higher profiles. They would go by one for about five to ten miles, then a large inlet or sound then start by another island and then another sound. At about midafternoon, Captain Ben headed below and motioned for Martin to follow. He brought a rolled up nautical chart from his cabin and lifted up a leaf, hinged on one edge of the narrow tabletop and reached under to slide out a support piece and rolled out the chart.

He looked down on the chart and asked Martin if he knew the most important thing about understanding a chart and Martin said no, and he said, while looking him square in the eyes; To know where you are at, and he put his finger on a spot and said that they were right there. Martin said his father had given him a chart that he had memorized and knew that they had gone east from Savannah and then turned south once outside, but the chart only went to Ossabaw Sound, which he knew they had passed already. Captain Ben smiled at Martin. From Ossabaw Sound, he slid his finger southward on the chart and read the name of each island and sound they would pass. Martin said he had noticed the different shapes of the islands formed by their tree line and how the Indian Islands were lower than the big ones they were going by now. Then, the Captain moved his finger over to where they were going and to the inlet or sound that was where a large river that was named on the chart as the Altamaha, and then pointed out Darien at the inland shore and upriver a bit. He said they would anchor for the night just inside the sound and catch the incoming tide the next morning and whatever wind there was and make Darien either early or late in the day depending on wind direction. He told Martin that winds came from all directions but tides only went in or out.

Captain Ben and Martin went back out on deck. Ashley had taken Ken's place at the wheel and called Martin over and moved so Martin could steer, with Ashley by his side. Tybee is the westernmost spot on the east coast. From there, going south, the coastline goes slightly eastward to the tip of Florida and going north from Tybee, it goes north but slightly eastward to the outer banks of North Carolina. Following the coast at about two miles out, there was no distant point to steer for, so Ashley explained to Martin to watch their distance to the land and at the same time, feel the balance between the sails, the boat, and the rudder and the angle they were at of the incoming ocean swells.

About then, Henry came out and was surprised to see his brother at the helm. Henry had heard the many stories of his father, younger than Martin, going to sea. For an hour Martin stayed at the helm, enjoying every second and he noticed the wind calming slightly and shifting just a little to the west and Ashley put down his rope splicing to adjust the sails, then the Captain motioned his arm toward the coast and Ashley took over and nodded an approval to Martin and said they were an hour out and, as predicted, the northwest wind, after a couple days was shifting around more to the west and if their luck continued, it would be blowing out of the south or southwest by morning. They had come closer to the coast now and in the distance were two sets of tall bare masts and the Captain said they would have company tonight and said those two ships were anchored, waiting for a pilot and the incoming tide in the morning like them.

The Captain directed Ken much closer inside the sound than the two ships, because the sharpies draft, with the board up, was less than one fourth as deep as the big lumber freighters. Most inlets along the coast had two or three shoal lines separated by deeper water and without dropping a lead line an experienced sailor could read the surface to find the deeper water and the Captain directed the hook to drop much closer in than the two ships but between two shoals so they would have a calmer night because as the ocean swells went over the shoals, they rose up and could rock you out of your bunk. So, without any fuss, the sails were struck, and the big bow anchor dropped and the Captain went below to complete his logbook for the day.

In less than an hour, Ashley and Ken had the sails tucked and lashed, bilge pumped out, a few minor repairs done, and everything ready for the next, hopefully, short day to port because there was a tavern that they both liked that usually had some fair company. They had a sailor's life that was much easier than most; a good Captain, a good ship, short trips, and not long between taverns.

Super was leftover potato soup, eggs, and fried dough with the last of the plum preserves and a swig of rum for the Captain and crew, and Henry. After a little more rum, a sunset, and a few stories, it was time to turn in. It took a little while for Henry and Martin to get used to the boat rising and rocking with each swell, but slumber set in and they slept good.

In the morning, the Captain and crew were out on deck before Henry and Martin could muster themselves up. There was some urgency to get underway. The wind was light and had switched around to just a little west of south and the incoming tide was two hours away. With the sails set and headed for the Altamaha River entrance, against the current, the sharpie was making slow headway but that did not disappoint the Captain. A mile might take him an hour or more, but that was progress. He took the wheel and Ken adjusted the sails often to take full advantage of the wind that was variable.

Captain Ben knew that this south west breeze would be blocked by land mass as he got further within the river channel, and he would be relying more on the incoming tide than the wind. Ashley once again fried some dough in lard and made a big pot of tea. The Milam brothers were learning the simple diet of a sailor.

After two hours of very slow progress, they moved into the river channel and the wind would blow suddenly hard and heal the sharpie over and they would surge up the river for a few minutes, then the sails would stand straight up and luff. This was very different than the conditions they had been in for the two previous days, but the incoming tide was moving faster now that the ocean surge was pushing into the narrower river channel.

Sailing with only the occasional gust became more about keeping the sharpie in the middle of the river. Henry stayed below and Martin remained on deck. After another hour and within a few miles of the Darien wharf, three pulling boats, having recognized the Captain's boat, came out and attached lines to the bow and six men and six pair of oars went to work, with the tide, hauling the sharpie in to the wharf area in the spot that the Captain had been in many times before. While being pulled, the sails were struck, and Ashley and Ken prepared the boat for the next three or four days in port. The Darien riverfront was not near as big as Savannah but was busy like Savannah and now that the sharpie was tied up, there was no dock space left.

Henry talked to the Captain about the return trip and Captain Ben told him where the small inn was that he would be staying at and said Ashley and Ken would stay on the boat and take their baths at the inn. He said they would be here three nights and leave sometime in the morning after the third night. Henry agreed to see him the day before to confirm the schedule and gave him a piece of paper with John's address where they would be.

Captain Ben looked at Martin and asked him what direction the sharpie was pointed, and Martin answered quickly, due south Sir! and the Captain laughed loudly and said again that Martin was a survivor for sure. Next, Captain Ben asked one of the pulling boatmen, where a carriage and driver might be found to carry Henry and Martin to their friend's home. He said he would fetch one up right away and he hurried off.

Martin went back on the boat to watch what Ashley and Ken were attending to for the boat to be ready to leave when the time came. Martin told them both what a good trip it was. Ken said it was much better than most because the sharpie was her best with wind on her beam or stern quarter like it was coming from Tybee but that she wasn't fun going the least little bit to weather.

The carriage came and Martin said goodbye and he and Henry climbed on, and Henry gave him the location of John Wilcox's home and the driver said it was not too far.

John and Henry had gone to the College of Charleston together and had become good friends. Since Henry had started early, John was a few years older. His family was from Beaufort, South Carolina where his dad was a hardware merchant, operating a store in downtown Beaufort and had many connections in the businesses in the town. He made it his second business to keep up with all the latest trends in the booming economy, locally, and along the Georgia and South Carolina coasts.
Mechanization particularly interested him, and he was quick to notice news of a modern sawmill, using tidal power, being built in Darien, Georgia, which was the outlet for a vast virgin forest of Long Leaf Pine, just inland from there. He shared this news to his son John, who had been taking care of the accounting for his hardware store and several other Beaufort businesses. John corresponded with the London company that was building the mill and after they learned of his high marks and good references from the College of Charleston, he was immediately made a generous offer. They wanted John to relocate as soon as possible to Darien. This was a big change for John and his wife and two small children but the money and potential for advancement was huge and John decided to go alone to begin with and for his family to continue living in his parent's large home as they had been. Darien was only eighty miles south of Beaufort and within a month, he was in Darien and had bought a small but fine home, on the edge of town.

It was only a ten-minute ride to John's house, that was now home to him, his wife, Julia, and their two young daughters, Katherine (Katie) and Jamison (Jamie). Henry and Martin had felt funny walking when they first set foot off the boat onto the dock and Captain Ben saw them and said they would have their land legs back shortly, but they still felt a little awkward stepping off the carriage when they got to John's house.

The house was small, but quite nice, with an enclosed courtyard and a fence extending down the sides and surrounding a big rear yard as well.

John had heard the carriage and he and Julia came out on the porch to greet them. John and Henry were excited to see each other. Years had slipped by since they had left school and even though they were not far away from each other, they were both busy and had only visited a couple times early on, but they had stayed in touch regularly by mail.

Julia made tea and they sat and caught up with the things that they had been doing. This was an awkward age for Martin. He was included in the formal tea setting with the adults but didn't have much to add to the conversation until Henry talked about the trip down on the sharpie.

Martin mentioned the two lumber schooners that they had spent the previous night near and that they were probably still on their way in. John said they would probably be in by tomorrow and described how, instead of being secured along a wharf, the big ships came bow first onto the bank at the sawmill and after their ballast was unloaded, long, squared off timbers were lifted with the company boom and shoved through the big door in the bow and were laid into the belly of the ship, becoming both cargo and ballast for the return trip and said some ships hauled dimensional lumber and they were loaded at the wharf area.

He said that he worked in an office and for a break, he often walked down to watch the long timbers getting loaded into the ships on the bank by the sawmill and that is how he discovered what he wanted them to come see. This part of the conversation kept Martin rapt, and his comments were just as any adult might make, but when talk changed to accounting and business and Martin had to ask for more tea as he felt his eyelids getting heavy.

Thankfully, Julia suggested that John show them their room. Henry mentioned that both of them could really stand a bath and John showed them the accommodations. Afterwards, he said they could have an early supper and have a stroll to the waterfront. He said that he had arranged for most of the next day off to spend with them and show them around the huge sawmill operation and the particulars about what they had come to learn about.

The bath was very refreshing since it had been a few days since they had one at home. The supper was way different from Ashley's cooking, but for Martin, not as hardy as eating on the sharpie on the water with globs of lard on everything. He was amused at John's two young girls, and they stared at him as to not know what to expect. He made some funny faces until they laughed and from then on, they followed him about and they began doing the same at him and to each other, which was something they could do that had never occurred to them. Unfortunately, until Martin, the only company they had was their serious parents and a servant that came sometimes. Supper was followed by more sweet bread and tea and with an hour or so of daylight, they went for a stroll to the waterfront wharf area where the boat was docked.

John pointed out some of the historic buildings and told some of the history of the place. He said that the area was highly coveted by the Spanish, French, and British because of the good water access and abundance of natural resources. The British accomplished the first fort there called Fort King George, but because of the remoteness and danger, it was difficult to find able bodies to man it. England installed a "Regiment of Invalids" that were veterans who were physically challenged in their abilities. After a year, the fort burned and was rebuilt but abandoned after a couple years. Later, under the leadership of James Oglethorpe, Scottish Highlanders were imported, and the fort reestablished and the town of Darien with a nearby sawmill was built.

John skipped to more current times and said that Darien had become the foremost source of timber on the east coast and the Bank of Darien was one of the most prosperous in America. He explained that there were still profitable agricultural products grown at a profit and the fur industry was still going, but the mechanized sawmill was one of the biggest things to ever happen on the southeast coast.

The company hired three hundred slaves from local owners and employed another two hundred local whites. Also, in not to many years, steam engine power would probably replace the tidal power currently being used. He said that in the few short years he had been employed that he now had a room full of accountants that he supervised and that the money he was making was beyond anything he could have ever expected. He then added that although he had been able to pay for his home and had a sum of money saved, he and Julia were not that happy here. They missed their families and didn't see many possibilities for their children in Darien that would exist in Savannah.

Soon they were along the wharf and Martin looked close to see if any of the sharpie crew were about, but none were to be seen. They showed everyone the boat they had come on and John said that type of boat had become popular in Beaufort because of their shallow draft and inexpensive operating costs because of only requiring a small crew and low maintenance. John mentioned that if they would rather go back overland that he had used the coach to Savannah often when he had first come to Darien without his family and that it was one very long day trip. He added that in rainy weather it could take longer but that in good weather, they left at four in the morning and made two stops to change horses and could be in Savannah at eight that night. As they were turning to head back, Martin yelled out, startling the group, "Captain Ben!"

He ran ahead and received a hug from the Captain and presented him to John and his family. He had come down to check on the boat and particularly the bilge and everything had been shipshape. He said he was pleased to meet a local in the town that he frequently made trips to and when he learned that John was employed at the mill, he said that most of his cargo was always for them and that they had paid for his boat by all the business they gave him.

Martin then inquired about Ashley and Ken and Ben said that they were at the local tavern and wouldn't be back until much later. He added that he didn't care as long as they showed up in a condition to be a good hand and that they always did and that of all the crews he had over the years, they were the best. Martin added that Captain Ben was probably their best Captain as well. Henry, again, hearing Martin talk so maturely without as much Geechee dialect, was taken aback by the rapid growing up that had come over him. He smiled inwardly with pride.

John handed Captain Ben a small card and asked if he would join them for supper the next night and the Captain replied he would be honored to, and John said he could come about four, and the Captain looked happy and said he appreciated the invite and would look forward to the visit. Julia told the Captain to not spoil his appetite tomorrow because they were having a big supper and John said he would be preparing a special treat that he bet he nor Henry or Martin had never had. The Captain was noticeably delighted with the big supper and treat idea and again expressed his gratitude.

When they returned home, Julia put the girls to bed and she and John chatted with Henry and Martin a bit and Julia saw how tired they looked and suggested they get some rest and Henry said he was tired but didn't want to be dull and John said not to worry and that their visit was the most exciting thing for them in quite some time. Julia said she had set them some water by their beds and for them to sleep as long as they wanted in the morning.

Martin lay in bed thinking about his last two nights on the sharpie. He had liked the first night at the Lazaretto landing. They were in the lee, and it was calm. The next night in Altamaha sound, it was calm but there was nothing to block the ocean swells. Even in the deeper water between the shoals, there was a lot of motion as the sharpie rose up and down and rocked side to side.

He then thought about the things Alice had warned him about again and wondered if it was necessary but he had come to trust her wisdom and he would remember the things she had said. He knew the Milam place was different but, he had not been anywhere much except an on River Street in Savannah and once to Charleston and once to Tybee. He did see some rough looking characters on River Street.

Henry lay thinking about accounting and gross income amounts after thinking about how much money the sawmill might make with five hundred workers plus probably another fifty clericals and managers. It was the biggest business he had ever heard of. They were both soon asleep.

The brothers came downstairs in the morning and found Julia and the kids, but John had left early to supervise his office so that he could come home and spend the day with Henry and Martin. Julia, graciously, made them breakfast. The two girls followed Martin everywhere and made faces at him. They heard the front gate and John came through the door and was noticeably excited about the day ahead. He had thought a lot about what he was going to talk to them about. John enjoyed the success and good money he was making but had a pretty boring life and this could be a new chapter for him and his family. They lingered just a little, eating sweet bread with yaupon tea, and then they set out.

The first place they went to was at the bluff on the river in front of the sawmill. John explained what they were seeing and what was going on. The bluff was solid sawdust thirty or more feet high. A huge timber freighter ship had come in the day before and was pulled up, bow first, into the sawdust bank. Up on one side of the bow of the ship was a hole about three feet by three feet. When at sea, a heavy-duty door covered the hole. Some of the highest quality timber the world has ever seen was shoved through the bow hole and laid in the bottom of the ship and was both valuable cargo and ballast.

The huge virgin growth Long Leaf Pine trees grew tall and straight with no branches for eighty or more feet up the trunk. The logs were left thirty to sixty feet long and thick slabs were cut off four sides, leaving nothing but squared off heartwood. It was strong wood that could span a long distance, was rot and bug resistant and very stable and a superior building material for ship planking and decking, timber framing, and bridge building and more. It was in high demand all over the world and sold for high prices.

Much of it went to the northern states where the industrial revolution was in full swing and there was a steady growth and demand for building large warehouses for manufacturing. The ships hauling dimensional lumber were loaded at the wharfs and bundles of lumber were set down into the hull of ship through openings in the deck, which were covered when under way. John explained that most ships come in to Darien with stone ballast, most often picked up from creeks and riverbeds where they are the most easily available. Before they come here or to the wharf, the stones are off loaded onto a bank nearby and the timbers or lumber becomes their freight and ballast. He added that several of the small islands that they had passed coming in were actually formed by unloaded ballast stones from all over the world. John said that our timing was perfect and explained what was happening. This ship is full of long chunks of ice sawn from frozen lakes up north and used for ballast. River stone was the preferred ship ballast but difficult to get sometimes, especially in winter the rivers are frozen. Surprisingly, the thick wooden ship hulls insulate the ice and not a lot of it melted on the two-week trip down there. John said they had been setting things up to start unloading the ice and they would start soon.

He had the group back up because when they started there would be a lot of noise and it was hard to hear a conversation. There was a huge, long boom, set on top of a huge upright timber that John said was deep in the ground below the sawdust they were standing on. It must have had several thousand feet of rope and a hundred blocks and tackles and big sharp hooks for grappling timbers or ice and seventy men working everything.

A few men were walking up a plank and handing a rope to some men inside the belly of the ship and the rope had a scissors like clinching tool and shortly after it disappeared into the ship there was a yell and the rope coming from the big boom was hauled in and a huge long chunk of ice with the clinching tool attached slid out the opening in the ships bow and lifted up and more ropes pulled the boom over to the side and the long ice chunk was dropped on the river's edge and when the rope slacked, the clinch tool was removed and quickly sent back for another piece of ice.

All this was happening in a cacophony of men shouting and squeaking mechanical winches and all sorts of noises. John had them walk back more away from the noise and saw that Henry and Martin were without words and were not prepared for what they were seeing. John laughed and said he never tired of walking down here and watching all this for a break from his office work.

He pointed as another chunk of ice was being set down on the bank and said that in a few hours, there will be fifty chunks of ice down on the bank and it will take a week or so to melt away and locals will come and break it into smaller pieces and take it away to use to keep their drinks cold and preserve their dairy and meat in wooden boxes. He pointed to a big pile of timbers on the bank near the ship and said that when the ice ballast is all out, the boom will swing over and those timbers will go into the belly of the ship where the ice had been.

Then, John got a shovel and walked about ten feet down the hill of the sawdust bank and began, enthusiastically digging. This too added to the strangeness because they had not seen John be so animated and that he was doing something odd that they couldn't guess what it was about. Within a couple minutes, John had dug five feet into the sawdust of the hill and tapped the shovel onto an uncovered chunk of ice and told the brothers that it had been buried there two weeks ago. They went over to where John was and he moved away more of the loose sawdust hill and revealed more of the squared off chunks of ice, similar in size to the ones being set out on the other side of the boat. John noted to them that it was a little smaller now but not much and it was put there two weeks ago and if it were buried deeper, even less would have melted away.

Things were not sinking in yet to Henry and much less to Martin, but this was something John had been thinking about for a while. He quickly covered the ice blocks back up and ushered them to go so he could show them the next place. They followed him but each kept looking back at what he had just shown them. John led them about a quarter mile up to the main building and went inside the entrance to a large well-lit room with big windows on three sides and about a dozen finely crafted desks and a man at each one with stacks of papers and all were very busy studying or writing and shuffling papers. A man at a slightly larger desk stood up at their entrance and smiled at John as he introduced Henry and Martin and he bowed respectfully to them, and obviously, respecting John a great deal.

John said this was where he had begun a few years ago when the company first started. At that time, it was only him and two other accountants for a while because it was very difficult to find enough qualified people to come to a remote place like this. The other two with him were brought from London and Bernard, here, is one of them.

His mate had allergic reactions to the mosquitos and gnats and had to return to England. It was just us two and as the business grew, they were able to get more accountants and it is still growing. Early on, I had not brought my family yet and was able and willing to work very long hours to get things organized and begin accounting for all the new business and set things up to be able to manage growth of the business. What is happening here now is the accounting for all expenditures, receivables, billing, and profits for thousands of logs, timbers, and lumber. Accounts are maintained with hundreds of customers here in America and internationally. This is the biggest lumber operation on the east coast and maybe America. Next, John showed them his office and his desk was the finest they had ever seen. He said that they would tour the sawmilling operation another day because it was huge and took a while and he had told Julia they would be back for lunch.

So, the brothers, impressed with their new knowledge of ice for ballast and the grand success of John and the biggest business they had ever seen, followed John back outside. Carriages usually availed themselves near the mill for rides into town, a short ride but a long walk.

John hailed one and while riding, Henry asked what would become of the big chunks of ice in the sawdust hill. John said he had buried it there simply as an experiment to see how long it would last before melting away. He said he had witnessed the big piles of thirty or forty chunks dropped on the river bank taking a week or so before melting away but was curious how long one piece buried in the sawdust would last. He added that he had not dug any further but a little ways over he had put two pieces together and a bit further still he had buried three pieces together and planned to check on how long they lasted.

The two brothers were yet amazed again at John's enthusiasm and experimentation. John saw their consternation and said he was born to be an accountant and he liked accounting in ice and laughed. He added that he had plans for ice making them rich.

They arrived back at the house and saw that Julia and the kids were in the front courtyard expecting them. It had become a hot day and John suggested they sit for a spell on the porch since the bugs were not out and he said he would get some drinks. Martin sensed something unusual about John's manner and a little with Julia too but said nothing.

John returned with big platter with drinks and sliced lemon. Each of the four tall glasses was filled with yaupon tea and had a slice of lemon and were filled with ice chunks and frosted on the outside. John smiled broadly and said surprise! He served everyone and went back in and brought out two small mugs for the kids. All sat holding the cold glass and staring at the suspended ice. John handed out each a napkin to keep hands from being cold. They all sat and sipped sweet, iced yaupon tea with lemon and were amused at John.

When they had enjoyed and finished their iced tea, John said he had one more thing to show them. The day, thus far, had been quite an impressive surprise from the unloading of tons of ice to the biggest office and mill operation in America and then the most refreshing cold drink they had ever had. What could be next?

John asked that they follow him, and he proceeded to a small room in the back of the house, entered from a door off the back porch. They entered and there was an odd looking tall and wide bulky looking cabinet standing against the wall. John opened the unusual looking door to it, which was about five inches thick but didn't seem heavy. When he opened it, they felt a rush of cold air spill out and inside was a large chunk of ice in a metal pan on the floor of the cabinet. There were shelves and John pointed to some cheeses and a few jugs of water and a couple bottles of wine and some cutlets of chicken, some eggs, and a glass jug of milk. He lifted a covered dish and said that it was a leftover casserole from two days ago that was still good, and they might have it warmed later for supper.

As he began to close the door, he showed them the double rope gasket that sealed the door to keep the warm air out of the "icebox" he called it and smiled proudly. They went back out to the porch and John explained that he had been working on this project for a while but hadn't mentioned it to Henry because he wasn't sure if he was being crazy or if he was doing something worthwhile. He said he believes that when the public learned how they could preserve their food, many would want an icebox in their home and they would need a one hundred pound block delivered every week.

He went on to describe having the icebox made by a local cabinet maker and a how they had thought about what to use for insulation and had settled on ramming in dried Spanish moss down into the prebuilt building panels and door and then sealing the wooden sheathing on the panels with whale oil, then assembling the floor, ceiling, and wall panels and caulking the joints with boat hull calking material, then hang the door to fit as tightly as possible with a double gasket all around.

He had been using one large block of ice every week and thought that might be less in the wintertime. He had done some research and storing ice and using it for practical purposes was something that had been being done up north for a long time, similar to how powering a sawmill by impounding tidal cycles had also been done for seventy-five years up north before the highly successful one was built here. He said that there were plans available up north for building icehouses that could store large quantities of ice all winter.

At school, Henry had told John about the Milam place and the weekly supply trips to Tybee and he thought this could be something that might be practical for them and other similar operations. He thought the larger cities could be big consumers of ice. Large fishing boats could stay out longer if there catch was kept in ice. Everybody needed to preserve food. He thought it could be a great business venture and had been almost obsessed with the possibilities. Henry questioned why, with all his success he would think of doing something else. John acknowledged that the money he had made was ten times what he ever thought was possible and he had worked very hard to get to where he was, but he and Julia missed their relatives and wanted more for their children that a bigger, more diverse town could offer. He said that he had saved a considerable amount of money and that if Henry would be a partner, he would invest most of his savings in starting an ice business, and he would move his family to Savannah.

The brothers listened to John and could not help but feel his enthusiasm. Henry admitted that it was worth further discussion and then, he and John were taken aback at a comment that Martin made. He suggested that since Captain Ben may not have cargo to haul back to Savannah, why not have him haul a few thousand pounds of ice back and they could bury it in the big sawdust pile at the sawpit at their place and see what might be done with it there and he could add some to the next supply boat to Tybee for the lighthouse keepers to try out.

John and Henry stared at Martin in disbelief at what a simple but brilliant idea that was. Martin blushed at their attention. He said that he would talk to the Captain tomorrow, and again the two older men were shocked but pleased at Martin's simple and guileless confidence. All three shook hands in at least an agreement that there were real possibilities for them and ice. John said he had one more small surprise in the form of an edible that he would serve after supper.

They went back and joined Julia and the kids who were restless and bored and were happy to see their new friend who was at least closer to their age and much sillier than their parents. Julia had with her a servant who regularly helped her five days a week and lived with her brother nearby. Julia, proudly, presented Mable to the brothers and them to Mable, who was quite shy and managed only a quick glance at them. They both smiled broadly at her and said how glad they were to meet her.

John made the brothers some more iced yaupon tea with lemon, and they went out on the front porch. John initiated a topic to them about the black servant that was helping Julia and said it was quite interesting. He said that when James Oglethorpe established this town for the Crown with Scottish Highlanders, they declared that it would prohibit slavery and were the first to sign that into law and it applied to all of Georgia.

However, after a dozen years or so, politics changed and the majority that had voted in that law became the minority and the laws were reversed, allowing the importation of slaves. The initial push for that change had arisen in Savannah because neighboring South Carolina's economy surged further ahead of Georgia because of the thousands of enslaved African people to produce the valuable agricultural products such as cotton, rice, and indigo. So, economic reasons outweighed moral reasons and the laws were changed. Here, most of the population was white but there were some black people too. The question came up as to what to do with them after the laws were changed. Should they, after living free like everyone else be branded overnight as slaves? Should they be free, but their children be slaves? There was enough people still left here who opposed slavery to see that a special and lawful provision be made for them. They and their direct descendants were to be classified as free in perpetuity. John saw the look on Martin's face like he didn't understand what perpetuity meant and explained it to him. Mable and her brother, James, were the last of their family. The other black families protected by the special provision of freedom left or were taxed off their land or just died out.

 John went on to say that he and Julia grew up in a slave culture, but they had decided that they did not want to carry on the tradition and that they did not share their convictions to everyone. When he and Julia had heard about the unusual social status of Mable and her brother, who were the only two remaining from their family with the inherited freedom, they sought out and met Mable and hired her immediately after learning that she was in great need. Mable and her brother were shunned and were barely able to pay the taxes on the property that had been passed down to them. Most of it had been sold off to pay past tax debts and all that was left was a house in much need of repair and a few acres. Mable's job with them had enabled her to pay up their past debts and her brother grew a few vegetables for sale and caught and sold some seafood which is where most of the supper came from.

He also said that there were a few in town that did not favor he and Julia for what they were doing but that the town was so busy that people didn't take the time to do anything about much but talk and because the mill was such a force in the town and John had such a high up job, they were mostly overlooked. Henry had come to learn of John's sentiments while at college and was not surprised at his story.

As they finished discussing Mable, Captain Ben came to the front gate and John went out to welcome him in. Julia came out and all were happy to see him, especially Martin. The Captain had his best change of clothes on, was cleaned up, and his face shined in a hearty smile and he expressed his gratitude for their hospitality.

The mill was his biggest customer, and he came here often and usually spent a night or two but had never been a guest of anyone. His days and nights were spent mostly resting and he was quite often a bit lonely. His crew enjoyed the pub, and he liked an occasional drink of liquor, but didn't much like going to the pub.

John excused himself and said he would return with beverages. Again, he came back with yaupon, sweetened with honey and with a slice of lemon and chock full of ice and this time he had a bottle of rum to add if requested. The Captain was surprised at the ice and said he had heard of such on one of his trips to Charleston but didn't think much of it. He also said he liked rum. John went on to add some to everyone's glass, but Martin's, and they toasted to their new friend the Captain.

After a while, John asked the Captain if he would like to see his "icebox" and he said yes, and they all went again and the Captain was much impressed and said that he could use something like that on his sharpie and they could have cold rum drinks and Ashley and Ken would love it. About then, Julia announced that supper was ready, and they all sat to a great meal of a variety of things made possible by having the "icebox" and fresh fish from Mable's brother James. At the end of the meal, John requested that they all, including the kids and Mable go wait out on the porch while he fixed a surprise desert that he had learned about.

Henry and Martin had been seeing John do unusual things all day and were puzzled once again. John disappeared for a moment and came back with various things and set them on a work table. There was two big pots, one of them was extra big. A third pot had been in the icebox and was full of a sweetened creamy milk mixture of things, and a big box of coarse salt. He sat the big pot down into the bigger pot and added crushed ice in the space between the two pots, sprinkling the salt as he added the ice. Next he added the creamy mix and began stirring it with ta long wooden spoon. He began stirring the mix and after about ten minutes, the mix began to thicken and in five more minutes of stirring, it became too thick to stir and John looked at the group and said,
"Ice cream!"

All were transfixed by his performance and stared into the contents. Then, he began serving the frosty mix in bowls to everyone, including Mable, and said that this might be the first ever "ice cream" served in Georgia or at least the first ice cream served by him in Georgia. The girls were the first to try it and proclaimed how much they liked it. Everyone else did as well and there were few words but a lot of "mmmmm" sounds. The children finished first and asked for another spoonful and bowls were refilled for all until it was gone.

He said that the mill was a London company and his boss had newspapers sent to him from home and shared them with others and John said how much he enjoyed reading them and learning of new things trending, and one particular article was about a world exhibition in Paris, France and some of the new foods that were presented, and ice cream was one and they included a recipe and instructions, so it was one of the first things that came to mind when he saw the ballast ice being discarded by the ships.

He was worried that he had not tried it beforehand but happy that it turned out a success and said there was an apparatus, sold in Europe, called a churn, made especially for making ice cream and he was working on getting one. Martin noticed how happy Mable looked and thought about what John had told about her.

After the meal and desert, the Captain said there was something that he needed to tell the brothers. He said that a strong northeast wind had begun today and that it was typical for it to blow four, five, or six days and he would not attempt a return in that. He said he didn't like it a bit but no one could change the weather. So, if they didn't want to wait as much as a week, they should take the overland coach back to Savannah. Henry liked this news but it disappointed Martin. Henry replied immediately that they would plan for the coach and thanked the Captain for telling them right away.

Martin asked the Captain if he would like him to show him the big piles of ice tomorrow and he said he had nothing else to do and he would be delighted so they decided to meet at the boat, first thing in the morning. The Captain thanked John and Julia several times and said good night. Everyone took their dishes to the kitchen and John asked
Henry and Martin to take the girls out in the back yard while he cleaned up his ice cream things and after he and Julia got things clean and put away they would join them. Henry asked Martin what he thought about their trip so far and Martin said that it was the best adventure he had ever had and he had met more new people than ever before. He named Captain Ben, Ashley, Ken, John, Julia, the two girls, and Mable.
Plus, the boat trip and learning all about ballast ice and seeing at least part of the mill and John's important job was all interesting. All this so far in less than a week was very something to remember. Henry was pleased that Martin's experience was so good and was pleased that they had this time together. Martin had been born fifteen years after him at about the time he was leaving for college and so they had missed being around each other, early on. John and Julia came outside and said that Mable had gone home and what a good day it had been. They lingered until it started getting dark and Julia said it was time to get the kids ready for bed and all agreed that they were also ready to turn in.

The next morning, Martin was up before anyone else and went downstairs and was surprised to see Mable in the kitchen preparing a few things for breakfast. He had not heard her come in and she had gone about her work quietly. In a low voice, not to wake the rest, he said hello, and she managed a slight smile. She immediately cracked two eggs in the hot skillet and in less than two minutes, served him eggs with a big pile of grits, drizzled with lard, a thick slice of bacon, a cup of tea and a piece of last night's cornbread. She kept her back to Martin as she worked at the cook stove in her quiet way. Mable left the kitchen and went out to the back porch and into the room with the icebox, quiet as a cat, and returned with a jar of blackberry preserves and spooned a big glob on another piece of cornbread and put it down on Martin's plate.

With a full stomach and high spirits, Martin left the house, conscious of the house facing north and his walk to the wharf would be to the east, where the sun was coming up. He also was aware that it was mostly downhill. He could see the smoke from the Captain's pipe drifting out of the sharpies companionway as he approached. He stepped over the rail onto the deck, causing the slightest movement and immediately the Captain yelled he would be right up.

Martin looked over the boat while he waited and thought back about the trip down. He wished he were going back the same way instead of in a coach following the poop end of six horses. He also noticed one of the pulling boats, that had assisted them in their arrival, rowing toward them. The Captain came out and said that there were only a couple gallons of water in the bilge and that this was the driest boat he had ever captained. The pulling boat came up and the Captain told Martin that he had arranged this transportation late yesterday when he had come by to check on things after leaving John's house.

He said he much preferred a boat ride to a carriage ride any day. They stepped down into the smaller boat and the Captain said to go to the mill area where there was ice on the bank. The boatman knew right away what he was talking about because he regularly took pieces home with him, like many others around town. It was less than a mile.

Coming around the first bend, Martin saw the two big timber freighters that had been moored out with them. They were pulled up onto a bank and the boatman said that they were unloading their stone ballast in order to take on timber. He said that the whole island they were pulled up onto was created by ballast stone from all over America and the world. Martin said that ice ballast seemed like a better idea because it simply melted into the river and the boatman said he had never thought much of it.

Soon they were at the sawdust bank and Martin pointed out the two piles of ice. One made up of the large pieces set out by the boom and the other smaller piece pile chunked out by hand. The Captain said he had seen a lot in his shipping all over, but all that ice piled up beat most things he had seen. He shook his head and said the book of what he didn't know stayed bigger than the book of what he did know.

Martin told the boatman to pull into the bank and told the Captain to follow him to see more of what he didn't know of. Martin jumped out and clambered over and up the pile and found a short board and started digging while the Captain was still gazing at the peculiarity of all the ice. He yelled for the Captain to come over. He exposed the corner of the huge thick slab of ice. The Captain had a dumfounded look because he could not understand the reason why ice would be buried in that hill like that. Martin said these two were about twelve feet long and John said they weighed about thirty-five hundred pounds each and there was more buried nearby. With that he quickly covered them back up and told the Captain to come with him up on the top of the hill and they could sit a spell and he would tell him all about it.

The boatman had been listening and he was curious and followed them to a comfortable spot and Martin told the story he had heard from John and the proposal and instructions from John, if the Captain was interested. After hearing about it all, the Captain said that he didn't see why he couldn't do it. He said they may have to make each big piece into four pieces so heavy to lift with his boom. He said they could pack sawdust all around it to keep it from melting fast and to keep it from shifting. Lastly he added that with over three or four thousand pounds on each side, the sharpie would behave well, and he could stop by their place to unload on the way into Savannah and also, with the items he already had shipped down, and ice to ship back, this might be a profitable job after all. For the first time in his young life, Martin initiated a handshake. It was weak but was no less a bond of honor that seemed to come very naturally, and this would not be the last time Martin shook hands on a deal with the Captain.

They loaded up and enjoyed the boat ride back. The Captain told Martin that he probably wouldn't be seeing him until he got to their place with the ice because he knew that the coach to Savannah left the next day and that his brother didn't seem to be inclined to stay until the next one left three days later. Martin said they would have everything ready when he came and how he regretted not going back on the sharpie and the Captain said he would miss his company too but there would probably be other times and other trips that he may go on. So, they said good-bye and Martin headed back feeling good that he knew the Captain.

Martin got back just in time for lunch of a table spread out with leftovers from last night's big supper, all of which had been stored in the ice box. Everyone had just finished serving their plates and finding a place to sit. Julia and Mable went to the back porch with the kids and Henry and John went to the front porch with their food and Martin got himself some and joined them.

They had been discussing several things; one was how they might promote the ice business in Savannah. The other thing that John was talking about was a subject his father had pointed out to him the last time he had visited. He said that yaupon tea had gotten so popular that the local Indians were hauling a wagonload into Beaufort every week and selling out in a few days. People visiting relatives from other states had taken some home and shared it and boxes of it are getting sent on the stagecoaches as far as New England. He said that most all the people living in Savannah and Charleston and in between got their yaupon from a group of mostly Yamacraw and other remnants of displaced natives that lived in an area of South Carolina not far from Savannah. The animal hide business was mostly gone because most of the animals had been wiped out, but they still traded in hides some and they gathered yaupon, dried it and traveled to the markets in Savannah and Charleston and a few cities in between including Beaufort. It was cheaper than the British import teas and had as much or more of the stimulating effect.

John said his father paid attention to trends and said there may be something to it. Their conversation went back to the possibilities of ice. John gave Henry the information on icehouse construction by George Washington at Mount Vernon in 1770 and some from Thomas Jefferson at Monticello.

Having heard from Martin about the deal he had struck with Captain Ben Graham, they decided to store the ice in the large sawdust pile at their sawpit and try out a few things with it first, then decide where to go with it from there. Henry looked at his brother and inwardly was in awe. It seemed like just a short time ago, he was a kid, running around the Milam place, having fun and now he was involved in a business scheme with he and John. He smiled openly and asked Martin if he was having fun and Martin said the most fun of his life. Martin then said something that totally surprised Henry. He asked what time they were leaving tomorrow and since Henry had only made arrangements that morning he was shocked that Martin already knew. Martin revealed his informer and Henry laughed and said at four in the morning. They had lingered on the porch all afternoon until it had gotten dark and Henry suggested that he and Martin needed to turn in because they were soon to get up and leave. They walked out to the back porch and saw that Mable had quietly left before dark. Julia had lit a lantern and the kids had fallen asleep on a long bench. They sat to have a quiet moment with Julia and express their gratitude for her hospitality. She said they were welcome anytime and that they had few visitors and minimal social life but said they were happy. She thanked them for coming and said she hoped to see them in the fall when they usually visited their relatives in Beaufort.

John shook both brothers' hands and told Martin he was especially happy that he had accompanied his brother and that he was glad to know them both now and thanked him for entertaining the kids a little. He said that he had arranged a carriage to be there at three thirty and the trip to where the stage coach left was only a fifteen-minute ride. Mable had packed them a big basket of snacks and two bottles of water and it was sitting in the icebox. He said how refreshing their visit was and looked forward to seeing them soon and said he looked forward to news of what they were able to do with the ice.

Morning came quick and the two brothers were up and ready to go and they heard the carriage arrive. Martin went outback and grabbed the basket from the icebox and joined Henry going out the front door. It was very dark, and the carriage had a small lantern that didn't seem to help much but the sandy roads were light and he went slow. Martin sensed that they were going west and that seemed right because he had seen the Old Kings Highway barely within the chart that Captain Ben had shown him. It was just west of the vast marsh and low country that bordered the Georgia coast. They would be traveling mostly due north the whole way on it to Savannah.

In a few miles, the road veered off a little to the north and soon after that some dim lights were visible and an odor of livestock was strong. As they got closer, there was a long house with a half dozen or more lanterns on posts out front and a few shadowy figures milling around. Their carriage pulled up along the row of lanterns and the driver got down and swung the carriage door open and bowed slightly and told Henry that the fare had been taken care of. He helped them with their bags and told them that the coach house had some warm beverages, and a toilet was available. He said he was going in for a hot tea himself. They followed him in and were greeted by an old man that said they must be the brothers going to Savannah he had been paid and they nodded. He said they were running a little behind but not to worry because the road to Savannah was dry and they would still arrive on schedule and for them to make themselves comfortable on the benches outside and handed each a clay cup of hot yaupon.

They sat and watched as another carriage came up and a young couple got out and were directed inside. After a few more minutes, another carriage came, and one man got out and the stationmaster said that he was whom they were waiting for, and they could get loaded up now. He told Martin that there was plenty of room inside, but young people often liked to ride up top with Jehu, and that he was welcome to do so if he liked. Martin looked at Henry and Henry shrugged, and Martin said he would like that because he liked to see in all directions. Henry took the basket in with him, and Martin climbed up with the driver.

Jehu was a middle-aged black man with silver white hair on his head and face. The coach had a lantern set behind the seat to cast a small amount of light forward but not be in the driver's eyes. He said something and the horses leaned into their harness and the coach moved forward slowly. Martin noticed that the driver let the reins lie down in his lap without any tension and the horses seemed to be on their own control and going very slowly with visibility less than a twenty feet ahead.

Martin suspected that the horses weren't going by sight but by feel of the ruts in the road. They continued at that speed for an hour and the sun was not up, but close enough to the horizon that the white sandy ruts in the road became visible and Jehu said another word that Martin didn't understand but the horses did, and they launched into a clip somewhere between walking and galloping with Jehu now holding the reins. He glanced at Martin's interest and smiled. The first of the sun's rays hit Jehu's face as he looked at Martin and lit up his smiling white teeth and white hair in a sudden brilliance.

Martin found himself staring at him in awe. He felt a knock and looked down and toward the back and Henry was leaning out the window to check on him. A big smile let Henry know that everything was fine. This medium speed reminded Martin of the speed of Captain Ben's sharpie going south from Savannah to Darien in the good breeze a few days before and Martin thought to himself about all that had happened in just those few days.

Soon the sun was fully up, and Martin could see their surroundings. By habit he was already oriented, aware that the carriage ride from John's house was westward to the station and from there they continued west a little ways and turned right which was northward then crossed over a bridge made with cedar poles like the ones at Tybee and then back east to the edge of the trees, then northward again.

Now he could see the lay of the land. Martin could hardly look away from the beauty of it as he felt the gusts of wind in his face from the northeaster, which was the reason he was on this coach instead of the sharpie. The roadway was just above the top of the marsh on the edge of an oak forest of trees, wind-swept and leaning inward, shaped that way by the ocean winds like were blowing today. The harder gusts blew the horse's mane and tails side wards and rocked the coach occasionally. Jehu finally said his first words in a strong Geechee dialect that only Martin would understand. He jabbered about what a good day it was because all the mosquitos were blown to the other side of the land. Martin jabbered back the same thing but included that it was even better that the gnats were blew there too. Jehu looked at Martin in semi shock that this young white boy talked in his language and smiled again bigger and longer than his first smile.

Jehu veered the coach to the west and the road went deep into the oak forest and the trees formed a tunnel over the road that was still somewhat dark inside and after about five miles they came to a ferry landing and the ferry was waiting and expecting them. The horses, without any hesitation clopped onto the flat wooden barge as the coach passengers looked out at their first ferry crossing. A long rope stretched across the river where an attendant and a horse waited for a signal and began pulling the barge over, leaving a rope attached and trailing out so it could be retrieved by another horse on the nearside. This was the first of four ferries that would be waiting for them, and they had already crossed the first of seven cedar pole bridges.

Inside the coach, Henry was studying his business papers and the three other riders were sleeping. Henry mused to himself how glad he was to be going back by coach but at least on the sharpie, he could use his quill to write. The coach was a much rougher ride and especially with the windy conditions. Two more hours and two more bridges and another ferry crossing and maybe twenty-five miles or so and Jehu made a strange sound and the coach slowed. They were nearing the first way station and Jehu had slowed a mile before to the slow pace they had begun at to let the horses gradually cool off before they stopped. All the passengers in the coach were now awake and exchanged pleasantries for the first time because they had been mostly sleeping early on. This last slow mile or so gave them the chance to introduce themselves.

Henry was first to give him and his brothers names and who their father and mother was and where they lived. The couple said their names and their mother and father's names but that his father had died recently and they had traveled to Darien to settle his estate and were on their way back to Walterboro, South Carolina where she was from and where his mother was living with her family since her husband had passed. Condolences were given.

The lone gentleman began by apologizing for his tardiness to the station that morning because his carriage was late to pick him up. He said that he was traveling to Savannah where he had been visiting often for the past year but was from Boston Massachusetts. He was an engineer and had gone to Darien to meet with the sawmill owners about converting to steam power and had also been working on a steam powered mill to be built on the Savannah River outside of Savannah. A soft command from Jehu and the coach stopped.

It had been almost four hours since the coach had left Darien and they may have gone twenty five miles or so. Martin climbed down and the passengers got out and Jehu spoke, and the horses pulled the coach to the back of the station to change teams. The riders all walked around a bit to loosen up and circulate their blood and a lady came out of the station and said there were some snacks and tea inside.

Henry had the basket that Mable had packed, and he and Martin found a bench outside to have a snack. Henry opened the basket and was surprised that it felt cool inside, then reached to the bottom and found a chunk of ice wrapped in a cloth and laughed while showing Martin. They found some cornbread, bacon and cheese and some preserves. Henry got up and went inside and came back with some tea.

It was a good meal and they both talked about their trip and stay at John's house and his family including Mable. Martin mentioned that Alice had talked to him before he left, about how he might meet people that had different ideas about black people than his own family, but he said so far nothing much had changed. Henry was surprised and pleased that Alice had done that because he would have never thought about it.

He told Martin that she was right, but they had only met friends of his or in the case of the Captain, a friend of their father and friends usually have similar ways. He said to always remember what Alice had told him because as he traveled more he would be around all types. Martin got a few things out of the basket and wrapped it in a fresh cloth that was in there and walked around back to look for Jehu. He saw him in the horse barn relaxing on a bench with a clay jug of water and walked over and handed him the snack.

Jehu looked surprised that a passenger had come around back and that he was given something. He smiled in appreciation and Martin sat by him on the bench. Just after he sat, he thought of something and jumped up, startling Jehu a little and uttered "bribak" which meant that he would be right back and ran back around the front where Henry was still sitting and reached in the basket and grabbed the cloth with the shard of ice and, holding the loose ends of the cloth tightly, banged the bundle on the bench breaking the shard in a few pieces. Then he took one piece and put the rest back and told Henry that he would be right back and went back to Jehu, who was happily enjoying his food.

Martin picked up his clay jug and put the chunk of ice in it and handed it to Jehu, who didn't know what to think. Martin motioned for him to drink and Jehu, trusting Martin, put the jug to his mouth but hesitated as he felt the coldness and looking at Martin, slightly dubious, as Martin gestured again for him to drink. He did, slowly at first, then a big drink and put it down and smiled at Martin.

The station master came around just then with a stick in his hand, cursing and looking for Jehu and when he saw him, said that he had work to do, and raised the stick but Martin said quickly that it was his fault that Jehu had lingered, and the man lowered the stick but the scowl stayed on his face. He told Jehu that if he had to come search for him again, he would be beaten. Martin was shocked and trembling, but Jehu seemed accustomed to the man's way.

Martin said again that it was his fault because he had given him some leftovers and he had only been sitting down for a few minutes. Since Martin was white and a paying customer, it diffused the man's anger slightly but he raised the stick again as Jehu got up to go to the coach that had just been harnessed to a fresh team. Rather than go back with Henry, Martin followed Jehu thinking that it might stop the angry man from using his stick. They climbed aboard the coach and Jehu said something to the horses and they perked and began to move and walked slowly around front and stopped without Jehu using the reins.

Henry and the rest, now refreshed, boarded and they set off, slowly to begin with as before, then increased to a medium pace, not slow and not fast. Jehu did not seem fazed a bit by the encounter with the stationmaster, but Martin could think of nothing else. He felt an uneasiness that he had never felt, and his breathing was still a bit rapid. He felt furrows in his brow that he had never experienced. He couldn't get the image out of his head of the hateful look on the man's face as he raised the stick to strike. He remembered that he had gathered up the food that Jehu had not finished in the cloth and brought it up on the coach and set it behind the seat, so he took it out and handed it to Jehu. He tucked one rein under each leg and finished it off, smiling broadly in appreciation at Martin.

After an hour or so, Martin could begin to enjoy the ride again and he began thinking of how a simple sail rig could be attached to the coach and in an east or southeast or southern breeze, help the stage along but quickly realized that it would only work if there was room overhead for a sail and the oaks hung so low that they often had to duck down. He ceased that idea and when the road came along the edge of the tree line again, Martin looked out at a long expanse of marsh and the back side of a long island between them and the ocean.

They continued along the edge of the trees for another five miles or so and turned west again and Martin figured it was to cross another bridge or another ferry ride. He thought about the trip down in the sharpie and the chart that the Captain had shown him and wondered which island he had just seen between them and the ocean. He vowed to see if his father had a chart of the area between Savannah and Darien and if so to study it until he could remember the name of every island and sound in the order they were in.

This caused him to start thinking about his trip to Tybee coming up in a couple weeks or so. It would be the longest time away from home he had ever been, but he had no thoughts of how that might be. He wondered if he should be afraid to go into the Indian Islands, but he didn't feel any fear, just excitement. He thought about the islands north of Tybee that Charles Dyer had mentioned. There was Turtle Island where the huge snakes and pirates and other desperate sorts were and Daufuskie where Alice and her family had made their last stop before Tybee. He hadn't heard much about Hilton Head, except it having been a frequent area for British ships to moor at during the war. He wondered what English people were like. His father was English, but he wasn't sure if he was still like English people. He knew that the English were first to quit the slave trade and still patrolled the seas to stop ships from continuing in it. Then he thought about Charles Dyer saying that there was a lot of coming and going in Tybee Roads at night and wondered what happened at night that couldn't happen in the day. He regretted that he hadn't seen Ashley and Ken again before he left. All this and more occupied Martin's mind as the miles and hours went by. They came to another ferry, and they crossed like before. They continued inland over two more bridges and another ferry before going back out to the edge of the land where the road followed the slight bluff that continually bordered the edge of the marsh.

Inside the coach, Henry was explaining to the gentleman from Boston what his family did, and he seemed particularly interested in the lighthouse and the parabolic reflector and special lamp and how it made a beam of light and the signaling systems they used. It was no longer secret information and Henry talked freely about it. He told Henry the area near Savannah where the steam powered sawmill was planned and about the steam powered mill conversion in Darien. Henry invited him out to meet his family while he was working in Savannah next time and he said he would like that.

There couldn't be a private conversation in the coach so the couple from Walterboro entered, off and on, in the talk. He said that his great grandfather was one of the original Scottish Highlanders that came to settle Darien and he regretted not staying to continue the line, but he had joined the American Navy during the war against England and was sent to Charleston and was a junior officer and had met his wife there. Her father was a planter near there and he had met his daughter at a fundraiser ball for veterans of the war. Her parents, like many of their friends spent summers in Walterboro for better health and her mom got sick every time after they went back to the coast, so they sold the plantation and moved to Walterboro permanently.

Joseph said when the war ended for a few years he got out of the Navy, which had been his dad's idea, not his, and asked and received permission to marry Sarah. Now that his father had passed, his mother was to live with them. He added that he had not yet found a real career opportunity to his liking, but that Sarah's family had been generous and that her father had unfinished businesses in the Charleston area that he had been handling for him.

He said they were happy, and that Sarah was very early on with their first child and they were glad about that. He mentioned the inn they were staying in for the night in Savannah and Henry said his father was friends with the owner and to be sure to mention that they were now friends of Henry, eldest son of Captain Walter Milam. This made Joseph and Sarah quite happy, and they felt a warmth about their plans that they had not felt before meeting Henry. Thomas, the engineer from Boston lit up and asked if he could give the same honorable reference because he was staying in the same establishment, and Henry said of course, and they all laughed. Henry and Martin were very different in their talents and personalities, but both had the Milam good humor and generosity that enhanced the lives of all they met.

They felt the speed slow and knew that they were soon to be at the second way station and in about fifteen minutes heard the low deep sound of Jehu's voice and everything stopped. The cabin group got out and were spry from the pleasant conversations and Martin noticed it right away. He jabbered something to Jehu which was asking if he could stay on and go around back with the coach and Jehu nodded and just like before, circled around back and left the rig to have the team replaced and Jehu found the place he usually rested at, and Martin followed.

Just as they had sat, the stationmaster came back and Martin tensed up, not knowing what to expect. However, he relaxed when he heard the man say the first few words, which were kind, as he handed Jehu a wooden platter with an assortment of food items and a clay jug of tea. He looked at Martin and said he had more food if he wanted some, but Martin said they had brought some from Darien. The man asked Martin how his trip was so far, and Martin said that for the most part it had been fun. Martin talked slower and made an extra effort to speak more proper English and he mentioned how mean the man at the last station had been."Oh, that was Eunice Jenkins; he is like that a lot. He can be quite unpleasant. He's the only Jenkins left of the plantation that his family and ancestors had been at for a hundred years. That's where Jehu came from before I brought him here." said the stationmaster.

Martin said that he had ridden up top with Jehu from the start and was glad he had. He said he was impressed at how little Jehu had to do or say to control the horses and what a pleasant fellow to be around he was. The man sensed that he might have a captive listener and he was the type that liked to tell a story. Meeting the travelers and sharing his stories was the favorite part of his job.

He told Martin that he needed a break, and he would just take it here with them while his help was changing out horses and he would tell the whole story about Jehu. Martin said he would like to hear but wanted to get his lunch first and would be right back. He went around front where Henry and the others were sitting at a table outside, and the couple from Walterboro had brought food and were sharing with the engineer, and Henry was eating out of the basket they had and Martin grabbed a piece of cornbread and some cold bacon, and told Henry where he would be, got a jar of yaupon from inside, and hurried back to hear the story about Jehu.

When he got back, the stationmaster introduced himself as Lancy Simmons and Martin said who he was and who his father was. Lancy said he had heard of his father, and it was good words. Lancy went on to say that when Jenkins mother and father passed, Jenkins took over the plantation which had been profitable most years, but like most all the rest, had some very lean years too. When old man Jenkins had it, he had thirty slaves, including Jehu's mother and father, and grew cotton, indigo, sugar cane, corn and whatever he could, and cotton and sugar cane were his moneymakers plus chickens, pigs and some cows. He had a dozen horses and Jehu's father and mother had the job of taking care of them. The stable in the barn was in better repair than their slave cabin so they took to staying in it all the time. Old man Jenkins didn't care as long as they performed their tasks.

Other than getting a small ration of corn, sweet potatoes, and some meat, they became somewhat independent from the other farm activities and had a garden of their own and chickens and a pig or two. Old man Jenkins liked that he didn't have to worry with them, and he was very happy at how well they took care of the horses, which were a very valuable asset because of the fieldwork they did. They had a child, and this is him, Jehu, who was born literally right in a stall on a bed of hay beside a horse. His mother and father and the horses heard Jehu's first cry for life.

Before he could walk, he crawled over, around, under, and in between horses and somehow managed to not get rolled or stepped on. Jehu grew up in the care of his mother and father and the horses. When Jehu was about seven, there came a very lean year, worst in fifty years some said. Old man Jenkins crops failed including his moneymakers, cotton and sugar cane. He was desperate, having no food for his family, animals, and slaves. He was forced to sell half his land, most of his horses and whatever else he could.

He took his slaves to the slave market in Savannah, including little Jehu and his mother and father, and sold all he could. Jehu's mother sold to one bidder and his father to another, but Jehu was such a scraggly poor looking thing, he was left with a few others to take back. Jehu instinctively returned to the barn with the two remaining horses that were too old to be sold, and he was pretty much forgotten about by Jenkins. It came a cold hard winter and old man Jenkins and his wife barely survived but lost their daughter, but Eunice, their son, managed to hang on.

Jehu only survived the cold nights by laying almost under the old mare when she laid down at night. In the day, he would spend hours in the woods looking for acorns from a certain oak tree that he had learned about from his father who had regularly brought them back and boiled them until they were tender, and the bitterness was gone. He couldn't make a fire, so he crushed them with a rock and removed the shell and put the crushed nut in his mouth until it softened and swallowed it. A half dozen of the big meaty acorns a day kept something in his mouth and sustained him. Most of what he gathered he gave to the two horses. He remembered going with his father to the edge of the marsh nearby and gathering marsh grass for the horses and he did that too. The hard part of winter is only about eight weeks and soon spring furnished more edibles to gather. The horse's favorite that came out early, and something Jehu chewed on too, was the wild grape vines, another lesson from his father. In the early spring, the new growth is tender and juicy.

Old man Jenkins managed to get a large crop of collard greens going early, several weeks before the last frost and kill a few deer and a few turkeys and he and those left lived to labor another year. He was left now with a wife and a twelve year old son (Eunice) and eight slaves who were what no one had bid on and were in even worse shape after the hard winter. He didn't even count Jehu, who he had left and not gone back to check on him or the old horses all winter. When he finally went to check he was surprised to find Jehu alive and was overcome with guilt of leaving the child there to fend for himself.

Spring came on strong and the unusually cold winter had killed all the bug eggs in the ground and old man Jenkins was able to have a small but good crop of cotton and sugar cane, corn and sweet potatoes. It was enough to survive and even get ahead a bit. He was able to purchase a couple more slaves and a few more horses for Jehu to take care of. To get back from his low point, he had begun to use part of his sugar cane crop to make liquor and with a nearby market in Savannah was able to do quite well, despite his small operation, and in a few years, caught up and got more ahead. By his early twenties, Eunice learned the process and was able to deliver the goods, in the night, to cash buyers at the wharfs in Savannah. Unfortunately, Eunice developed a liking for the spirits and on many of his trips back home, he passed out in the wagon and the horses led themselves back to the barn where Jehu helped Eunice to his bed and took care of the horses. His father disapproved of his drinking but was unable to stop him because he had no one else to deliver his liquor.

A few more years went by, and old man Jenkins and his wife passed and left the place to Eunice but his drinking increased until he let things run down. One cold morning, being hung over sick and impatient to get the fireplace started, he put three big pieces of fat lighter in and lit it. It blazed up furiously and out of the firebox so big that he couldn't stop it and within a few minutes it was too late and all the keepsakes that had been accumulated over the last hundred years of the Jenkins family became ashes, except for Eunice who was able to get outside, and with the few remaining slaves, including Jehu, watched and cried as it all went up.

This was a much more dire situation than even the hard winter years before. Eunice had to sell all the land, animals, and slaves, except two acres out near the road. Lancy interrupted himself and said that he had only about five minutes before he had to attend to the coach getting back on the road but said that would be time enough to finish the story but he would need to leave out some of the smaller things. Martin was all ears. Lancy said that he needed to back the story up a bit to tell something he left out. It concerns some details of when old man Jenkins fell ill when he checked on Jehu, after the really bad year old man Jenkins suffered through and had left little Jehu on his own with the two old horses, not caring if he died. When he finally did check on him, after neglecting and abandoning him to probably die of cold and starvation, he saw him all skinny and puny with his belly swollen, he fainted from deep guilt and grief and exhaustion from all his losses and lay like dead for a day and when he woke, told his wife that an angel had visited him and told him to grant Jehu his freedom upon his death. He remained true to the vision and made the legal arrangements, as part of his will, for Jehu to be a free man.

Later, Eunice straightened out and flew right a bit and was able to, with the proceeds from the sale of what was left of the place, to get a small house built on the remaining two acres out by the road. Jehu was free but had no place to go. Eunice let him build a shanty out back for himself and together, they were able to get a garden going and hunt squirrels and rabbits and deer and eventually buy a plow horse and a few more acres and grow a few crops and survive for fifteen years or so, but Eunice still looked on Jehu as a slave.

An opportunity came along when the coach company from Darien was looking for another way station on the road to Savannah, and Eunice, in his better self, seized it and mortgaged his house and land to get enough to build a barn and corral to maintain a team of horses to be used to refresh the team from Darien, coming and going. The company in Darien supplied the horses and he had the best horseman in Jehu, so it was quick to become a small success, despite Eunice having an ill temperament. One day he became so irate over nothing that he beat Jehu savagely and the next day, Jehu was gone and Eunice had to hire someone but they couldn't make the horses behave like they did for Jehu.

After the beating, Jehu had headed to Savannah. He had never been, but he had heard talk of it. On his way, he showed up at my place looking hungry and I gave him some biscuits and lard. His dialect was so strong that I could barely understand him but finally he showed me his terrible injuries from the beating, and I doctored him up and I thought I should let him stay in the barn that night.

When he walked in, he saw the horses and made a strange sound and they all perked up and he walked over to the stalls where we kept them until time to harness up to the coach. They hung their heads over the top rail to sniff him like they acted when I had a piece of cane for them. As this was happening, it dawned on me about who this thin, humble man was and what probably happened.

People had talked about him and what a miracle he was with horses and how he was raised with them. For years I had heard about a slave on the Jenkins place that had been born and raised by horses and could talk to them. Also, it was well known of what an awful and cruel man Eunice Jenkins could be. People said he had quit drinking but had become mean and that he had been more tolerable when he drank.

I went out and got one of my slaves that I had bought that had been a house slave and talked more proper but could still understand Geechee and brought him in the barn to help me understand the strong dialect of this man. I brought with me a big pot of yaupon and some sweet bread and for the next two hours, I heard the story I have just told you. I had to fill in some hard to interpret spots, but I got the gist of it. To my grand surprise, Jehu pulled some papers out of his pocket, and they were signed by Mr. Joseph Adler Jenkins and pronounced Jehu a free man and had been prepared by a prominent lawyer in Savannah. He was, in fact, a free man.

What an amazing day that was. While I had my man with me in the barn, I let Jehu know that he was welcome to stay here as long as he wanted and that he could go to work with me or if he chose, or he could go to the main stage depot in Savannah after he healed from his beating.

Lancy stood up suddenly and Martin was so entranced in the story that the sudden movement startled him back into the moment. Lancy said he had overshot the time and was past the normal time to have gotten them and the coach back on the road. He said he didn't have time to finish the story completely but said that things worked out just fine for Jehu because he was now the best driver for the coach company in Darien and that he came and stayed here in my barn often. He sometimes stayed at the coach depot in Savannah, but that station master is somewhat ill tempered too. He never goes back to Jenkins place.

With that Lancy pardoned himself and went around front and apologized to the travelers but Henry assured him that they would not have wanted it any different because they were enjoying the extended break. They loaded up and Martin went and gave a big handshake to Lancy. It wasn't the kind of handshake about an agreement that he had made lately, but it was the kind of handshake that expressed gratitude. The story had touched Martin deeply and when he looked at Jehu beside him up on the coach seat, he was in awe and amazed by his story and his simple elegance.

Martin looked at the new team of horses and then Jehu made that sound and they leaned into the load and moved slowly for the first mile, just as the other team had, and then he picked up the reins from his knees, and they picked up the pace to that medium speed. The road came close to the edge of the land and Martin looked once again out over the marsh and a gust of that same northeaster blew against him and the coach and he felt an intense gratitude for the wind itself for changing their plans so he could meet Jehu. A momentary experience of clarity came over him, not of any thought, but of a feeling of something more perfect than words or thoughts could describe. He could feel the life inside of him and each breath seemed like magic.

Inside the coach had become more casual, as the group had gotten to know each other during the ride. The extended break at the last stop and their long, shared lunch, and conversation made them seem like longer friends than eight or so hours. Henry had given up trying to work on his business papers and even began to enjoy the view out over the marsh since he was on that side by the window.

Thomas, the engineer, was talking to Joseph about his experiences in the Navy while Sarah napped. Henry was listening in while looking out and then a grog came over them from their lunch and all fell into a nap as the coach rocked and rolled from the wind and road. They awoke as the coach pulled onto the next ferry on the bank of a small river.

After the ferry crossing, the road never went back out to the edge of the land but continued inland over several more bridges and finally over on the last ferry that crossed the Ogeechee River. The coach went around and came into the west side of the city and arrived a little late after fifteen hours of travel. The passengers got out and were awkward a bit at first until they became adjusted to the solid ground. Henry asked the station-master for two carriages, one for him and Martin and one for the others.

He welcomed them to Savannah and once again mentioned the inn-keeper's first name and reminded them to mention his name. They had already exchanged each other's addresses and they were ready to board the carriage as soon as it got there because they had suddenly felt the weariness of their journey.

Martin and Henry both saw them onto their carriage and bid them farewell after Henry paid the driver for them. Martin told Henry that he wanted to talk to Jehu before he left and went to the back of the station to find him. They talked in deep Geechee for a few minutes. Martin told him that he would be gone for a while to Tybee but when he got back, he would check with the station master to find out when his next trip was and come see him and that when he got a day off, he wanted him to visit him at his and Henry's home. Their conversation had drawn a few onlookers, surprised to hear a young white boy so intensely involved in a conversation with who they assumed was a slave. Instead of shaking Jehu's hand, Martin embraced him in a hug and the onlookers were taken aback. Martin was aware of their looks but ignored them and said goodbye to Jehu. He and Henry climbed into the carriage and the driver recognized Henry and knew where to go. They got home very late but everyone except the kids was awake and they stayed up past midnight to talk about the trip. Martin had not napped like the others but the excitement of being home and all kept him going but he was dog tired when he finally did get to bed.

12.
MILAM ICE

The next morning, both brothers were off catching up on their work that they had left. Martin went straight to Alice's house and told her about his experiences. She noticed that even in that short time away, Martin had gained a certain air of maturity and the little boy she had raised was changing. He told her that there were some things that he was gonna be needing to do before the trip to Tybee and Henry suggested that Johnny continue in the job of seeing that the supply boat was loaded with everything needed and that maybe that could become part of his regular tasks.

Alice said that she was helping Johnny with the checklist that Martin had made and that she was determined that she would teach him to read before the year was over. Martin pointed to her stomach and asked her how that was, and she laughed and said fine. He told her about all the good people he had met and the run in with Eunice Jenkins and Jehu and she had been right in warning him. This made Alice feel especially good. He added a little about Jehu's story and that he had particularly liked him and hoped that he could visit sometime and meet her. When he asked about Maggie, Alice said she was just fine and that she had just brought her a new book to read and she had said what a good visit y'all had before you left.

Next, Martin went to the boathouse where he was welcomed back heartily. After seeing him leave the Lazaretto landing and heading out toward the ocean, they were sure they would never see him again and had been worried day and night until they heard that they were back. They begged that he shouldn't do that anymore or else they would die worrying. Martin laughed and said that one day before long he was gonna have his own sharpie like Captain Ben and go all over. Johnny said he had something to show Martin and left the room and returned with a notebook that had the checklist of items and quantities for the supply boat and read the list slowly. Next he opened a small notebook with a very worn cover. Alice had written about ten words in big letters on several pages and Johnny pronounced each one proudly. Martin said that he was learning to read faster than he had been able to and added that they both had a good teacher.

Henry had asked Martin to meet him at the school that they had both attended, with the buckboard wagon without saying what there was to do. Martin went to get the horses hitched to the wagon and soon was on his way to town. He wondered what it was, but Henry had only left him a note in the morning and didn't explain. He got to the school and Henry was already there. Martin asked what the buckboard was for, and Henry said that there was a sawpit back toward home where there was a big sawdust pile and he had realized that their pile was not enough and even if they added what was at the wood shop, there still may not be enough to keep the ice from melting. He obtained permission to have all we wanted for free from the sawpit. Henry said that after he had shown Martin the sawdust, he was going to a cabinet maker in town and get him started on the icebox for their home similar to John's icebox. He added that he had thought a lot about ice and all the things John said it could be used for, and he was convinced that it was something that could improve people's lives and the business of it could possibly insure the future prosperity of the Milam place.

So, both started out back in the direction of home and in a mile they veered off toward the river on a little used wagon road with Martin following, and in a quarter mile came up to a small bluff near the river and a long narrow pit dug deep into the ground. There was a huge sixty-foot pine log shored up above the pit. It was being squared up with men below and above, pulling the long saw blade up and down. They were singing a chantey in rhythm with their work.

There was a big pile of sawdust about thirty yards from the end of the pit where the men had been carting it out from the pit. Henry told Martin they were gonna need about eight or ten heaped up wagons full to add to what they. He said he had planned with the sawpit owner for the men there to load the wagon and for someone to help him unload it back home.

At the sawpit, Henry said something to one of the men and headed off back to Savannah. Martin pulled the wagon over to the pile and two men came over with big wooden shovels and in a few minutes had the wagon heaped up and Martin was off with his first load.

Back home he pulled along the side of the big pile of sawdust at their sawpit that they only used a few times a year. It seemed like it was plenty to do the job, but he would do as Henry asked. Rather than wait for a helper, Martin set to work on unloading the wagon himself. In a half hour, he had shoved and shoveled the sawdust out and took the rig back for more and they heaped the wagon up again but said they were leaving, and he said he would be back the next day.

Martin had done what Henry had asked and there was some daylight left and he felt a little breeze on his ears and decided to go for a quick sail on the river, so he headed back to the boathouse where his boat was. After saying hello to the men, he drug his boat out from under the building. Within minutes he had it by the edge of the river and soon after that, had the mast set up and with paddle and life float on board, shoved the little craft out in the river which was extra full because of the full moon that would be coming up shortly.

The tide was dead still, finished coming in but not yet starting out, Martin's favorite time on the river. Once his paddle was in place for a rudder, he was full tilt in just a minute and enjoying every second, clipping along swiftly. He went from one side of the wide river to the other and imagined what it would be like when he had his own sharpie. He decided that when he did, he would keep this boat on board for trips to shore or just for fun. Johnny had really done a good job. The hull was now thin and light and sealed, so it didn't soak up water and get heavy. Occasionally, when a good long gust would come, Martin could feel the hull lift up and plane across the top of the water for a quarter mile or so. Each time this happened, Martin got better at shifting his weight, as the wind came near blowing the boat over.

In half an hour, he was near the wharf area of Savannah, and two ships with eight pulling boats each were out in the river to catch the outgoing tide toward the ocean. He flew by the first pulling boat and ship within twenty feet then circled around the next ship and came about and rolled the sail around the mast and laid it in the boat and began paddling home as the tide was shifting to go out.

He soon passed the ships and pulling boats he had sailed by and said hello. He had become a familiar sight to the men in the pulling boats and they liked seeing him and waved. The full moon had the tide extra high, and Martin drifted until he got to the Wilmington River and had to paddle the rest of the way against the outgoing tide. He thought about how many times he had made that trip to Savannah and back and how big a world that had seemed, but now after his recent travels, it seemed small.

The sun was casting long shadows as he returned to the bank at the boathouse. Martin paused and looked at the moon rising up over the marsh to the east. Just as the sun was sinking on one side of the earth, the moon was rising on the other. On this day, darkness would not fully come because as the sun sunk lower, the moon rose higher and the two of them remained in sight of each other for a short time, reflecting a twilight over this side of the earth.

Back home, Martin cleaned up, and sat with his mother and father at supper. Henry and his family were having their dinner together in their end of the house, which was like a separate home but under the same roof. His parents asked him more about his trip and Martin went into further detail than he had the night before. They were particularly interested to hear about the run in with Eunice Jenkins and were glad to hear how Martin had handled himself and he told them about the long talk Alice had with him about things like that before he left, and they looked at each other in a way that acknowledged the wisdom and appreciation of Alice. Martha said they both had many encounters with people that had different views on race than them, especially Walter.

Martha said her acquaintances were more delicate about their different views and maintained sensibilities, but she said sometimes Walter's did not, and said it had been especially hard for him when he first came to Savannah, before he had established so many friends and allies. More than once, angry confrontations could have ended in a duel, which was not an uncommon way for differences to be settled. Walter, with his wisdom and wit had deftly avoided them all without compromising his beliefs or appearing afraid. Martin had never heard that about his father and he would not forget it. Again, he realized what a sheltered and different world he had been raised in and what a different and dangerous world there was outside of the Milam place.

Walter said that the work crew and barge would be leaving next week and that the Dyers were expecting and looking forward to his visit which could be a couple months or so. He said that he wanted Martin to be in charge of seeing that the entire material list was loaded on the barge so the workmen would have everything they needed. He also didn't expect Martin to be at the job on Tybee all the time but wanted him there enough to get an idea of how it was done. Also, that Henry had the list of materials and that in addition to the bridge and road work, there was repair work to be done on the brick of the lighthouse and Henry had hired a crew from Savannah to do that work. Jacob and a few men from the Milam place were to work on the road and bridges and additional accommodations were being handled by Charles Dyer.

If the bugs get intolerable, they may move the work camp to the south end of Tybee where the breeze keeps them away. They would also be sending both supply boats every week for work crew provisions and additional supplies that might be needed. Martha told Martin that she was sure he was gonna be all over everywhere since he would be having his boat there but to be careful and always have the life float with him that his father had given him. He assured her that he would be careful and do what she said. Martin said that when he got through with what Henry had wanted him to do, he would start on the barge materials. They had their supper and went to bed.

Martin was up early, had his breakfast and was back at the horse barn early. Henry stopped by and saw that he was about to head out for more sawdust. He was pleased to see that Martin had hastily fastened some boards to extend the sides of the wagon up higher so he could carry a lot more and make fewer trips. He said that he had settled with the cabinet maker, and he would have it done in a several days. He also said that the cabinetmaker had suggested stuffing cotton in the icebox walls instead of moss like John did and that might be an improvement. They went their separate ways.

The sawyers were singing their chantey louder early in the morning than they had been in the afternoon before, and Martin could hear them as soon as he pulled onto the road to the sawpit. He thought to himself that he had not ever witnessed any task harder than their work. The oarsman on the supply boat worked hard but pulling two oars through the water didn't seem near as hard as pulling a big heavy blade through a big tree trunk. The handle on both ends stuck out on both sides for two men to be on each end and Martin wondered if the two down in the pit had it better or worse than the two up top. He pulled in as close to the pile as possible and two workers with shovels came over and loaded him and he was soon on his way back with a bigger load than the day before. Henry had planned for a worker today to help him unload and he had seen Martin coming and came over to help. They were familiar with each other but had never worked together and knew each other's names but hadn't been around each other much.

Izak had been picking small light colored melons and brought one for them to eat and it was perfectly ripe and sweet and still cool from the night. Martin motioned for Izak to come along and said he would like to get a few more of the melons, so they walked out in the field and picked a dozen melons, loaded them on the wagon, and Martin headed back out for his next load, telling Izak that he would be back in about an hour and need his help again.

As before, he pulled up close to the pile and the two workers came out and Martin had jumped down and with a large knife began quartering the melons and scraping out the seeds and told the two helpers to call the rest of the crew and they came over and ate it all in a short time, thanked him, and went back to work. He got loaded and headed back.

Izak had picked all the melons and went with Martin the rest of the trips and they had quite a pile of sawdust by the end of the day. They actually had made two large piles, leaving a space between them so they could slide the ice chunks off the wagon and in between the two piles then shove the sawdust from each side over the ice. John had said that the deeper the ice was in the sawdust, the longer it would last. Martin knew he couldn't get it as thick as it was on the riverbank in Darien but the pit was seven feet deep and full of sawdust and up level with the ground and he had enough piled on each side to get six feet over the top of the ice and six feet deep on the sides.

They laid wide pine planks down to slide the ice on. Henry happened along about then and said he thought that would be more than enough and was impressed at how they had made two piles and a wood slide. Martin said good it was done because he could get started tomorrow on loading the barge. Also, he expected to see Captain Ben any day. Henry said that would be just fine and that many of the materials had already been delivered and stacked well above the high water mark near the boathouse.

Henry told Martin that it was very important to keep the bags of mortar for repairing the lighthouse brickwork dry and that there were oil cloths over it now and to place short timbers under it, so it is up off the deck and secure the oil cloths back over it carefully. Also, don't load anything over the bilge access because the barge leaked and had to be bailed out a couple times a day. Johnny had been doing it but when it gets loaded it might need it done more often.

Henry pulled the papers with the material list out of his satchel and handed them to Martin. He then told Izak that he would need him to help Martin all day tomorrow and maybe the next day too. Izak smiled to himself because he had not liked working in the gardens, picking vegetables and hoeing weeds, however he was always afraid of the river because he couldn't swim but he didn't tell Martin that because anything to him was better than working in the gardens. They planned to meet at the boathouse, where the barge was anchored out at, in the morning.

There was still some daylight and Martin went by to see Maggie. Her family was outside, as usual at the end of the day with a few friends, watching and laughing at the chickens and gossiping. Maggie's face lit up when she saw Martin and her little brother ran up to Martin, who was holding two of the melons up against his chest and handed one to the younger boy and he ran with it to his mom and ran back to get the other one. He and Maggie joined her mom and dad and they all said how he had gone across the ocean and back and it was a miracle that he survived.

Martin laughed and said that Jacob had told them a story bigger than it was and made Jacob laugh. He told them about Darien and the big sawmill that had a machine that cut logs up faster than two hundred men could and the nice friends of Henry that they stayed with and a little about

Mable and her brother James. Also, about the coach ride back and his new friend Jehu and all the rivers they had to cross and how they changed horses two times and how he had met a mean man that tried to beat his new friend with a stick.

Martin told just a few things about Jehu but said it was a longer story than he had time for and Ellie made him promise to tell it another time. They were all wide eyed and astonished about what he did tell of his and Henry's trip. To them it was a much bigger story than it was, and they thought surely that it was a true miracle that Martin had survived and they felt blessed that he was telling them.

They would tell the same story to their friends and them to their friends and the tale would have grown many times its real size to great epic proportions of Martin crossing the oceans and all that went on. Maggie listened with interest but was not taken away by it as her family. She had been devouring a book or two a week that Alice had been bringing from the Milam library. Maggie's known world had gotten bigger from all the books she had been reading.

Another morning came and Martin saw a note left on the kitchen table by Henry. The friends he had traveled with in the coach trip had sent it to them. They thanked us for making their trip enjoyable and especially thanked Henry for telling them to tell the inn owner that they were his friends. They said they felt like they got special treatment and they were told what a great debt the people of Savannah owed their father. The couple said that they would welcome us for a visit to Walterboro and the Boston engineer said he would see us when he returned to Savannah.

Izak was waiting at the boathouse for Martin and was excited about his new work. There was a rope tied to one of the cedar columns supporting the boathouse and going out in the river about seventy five feet and attached to the front of the wooden barge which was about fifty feet long and about fifteen feet wide. It was squared off on both ends and had a big open flat bottom that slanted up on both ends. It was as deep as Martin was tall. The hull was made of cypress planks that had been applied dry when it was built and after it was slid into the river, swelled tight to keep out the water. It had loose decking boards covering the bottom to stack cargo on.

Martin started pulling on the rope and Izak helped. They both pulled and the front of the barge where the rope was tied, slowly started turning toward them and then the whole barge began coming in. When it bumped onto the bottom, Martin loosened the knot on the column and pulled the slack out of the line and tied it again. Martin and his new helper pulled two long wide pine planks out from under the boathouse and they leaned one up on the front edge of the barge for a ramp up and the other on the inside for another ramp down.

The tide was going out, so the barge would soon be sitting on the bank. Then Martin got out the list of materials that Henry gave him and began to study the multiple items stacked up at the top of the riverbank where it was flat. Izak was a few years older than Martin and a good bit stronger and Martin was impressed at how easily he lifted the long cedar poles they began to carry onto the barge. He had counted how many so that he could stack half on one side and the other half on the other side to keep the barge balanced.

While they were working, Izak asked Martin if he knew how to swim and Martin said he did and Izak asked if it was difficult and Martin said it was easy and that the boatmen taught him how when he was only three years old. Izak had watched curiously when Martin had studied the list of materials and asked Martin about learning to read. Martin said it was not as easy as swimming and he had been a slow learner at it but it was easier for most people. They continued checking and loading until lunchtime and went inside the boathouse where the men were about to break for lunch too. Jacob told Martin that he and Izak could eat with them since they could never eat all the food that was sent to them from the kitchen house and that was exactly what Martin had hoped he would hear from Jacob. They had a long table set up to eat outside when the weather was good and it was today.

Everybody knew everybody on the Milam place, but Izak was kind of shy and he was a little awkward to talk, especially in a group. Jacob asked him how he got with Martin and he didn't say anything at first but Jacob, seeing he was shy, encouraged him a bit and he told them that he had been picking those same melons that was part of today's lunch and Mr. Henry had asked him to help Martin haul sawdust.

Jacob asked Martin what the sawdust was for and Martin was now the one to not answer right off. Martin hesitated because he wasn't quite sure how to describe something to the crew of boatmen that they had never seen anything like it before. He was finally about to say something and the man from the kitchen with the food and utensils in a long push cart came up and everyone's, including Jacob's, attention switched to eating.

There were several pots that were set on the table with beans, potatoes, stew, and grits. Also, a long dough bowl full of the sliced melon that Izak had been picking and another dough bowl full of biscuits and a pot and ladle with hot lard for the biscuits. The food at Martin's house was more refined, but the boathouse food always tasted good and there was always plenty of it.

While they were eating, two more delivery wagons came from Savannah and supplies were set off. When the meal was finished, dishes and utensils were stacked on the cart and Jacob and Johnny followed Martin over to the barge and Jacob asked Martin again about the sawdust he had been hauling. Martin said that it was part of something that Henry was working on and he couldn't say exactly what it was and that part of it was being brought by boat in a few days and he would show it to him when it got there. Jacobs's curiosity was not satisfied but he was okay with Martin's answer for now.

He and Johnny went back to their work and Martin and Izak did to theirs. The delivery that had just come was boxes of long metal spikes and bags of mortar with new oil clothes Henry had mentioned. The mortar was very heavy and Martin was glad he had Izak to help. Martin was very careful to stack the mortar up on short timbers up off the deck and cover and bind the oil cloth securely to keep it dry.

Just as they had that finished, three more wagons came, loaded high with milled boards, all the same width and thickness for the new bridge decking. The tide had gone out and the barge was high and dry.

Martin moved the loading plank over so a wagon could be backed up to the barge so the hundreds of decking boards could slide off and in. This kept them busy the rest of the day. They were about to leave and Johnny came. The barge leaked and he was in charge of bailing it out every day and while it was slanted like this on the bank, it was easier to do because the water was all gathered up at the low end and it needed bailing before the tide came back in. Martin told Johnny that Izak wanted to learn how to swim and read and that he might be a good one to learn how to be a boatman. Johnny said that might work because Jacob had told him that Henry said they might need another man. Martin said he would talk to Henry about it and maybe Izak could start training soon because it took a full year at least to learn all that a boatman had to do, which included not only how to row, but swimming and rescue skills, and boat maintenance and more.

Izak heard Martin's words and that it could be about him. He had never imagined anything more about himself beyond what he was doing. He asked Martin if he was talking about him and Martin said he was and took Isak's hand and led him out in the water just knee high. Martin could tell how afraid he was and told him to stand there and he dove head first into the river and swam out a ways and then back. He told Izak that he would soon be able to do that and Izak smiled real big. With them both standing in the water, Martin told him that all people were made to swim and laid back in the water and floated a few moments. He said they just forgot they could and only had to be reminded that it was something they already knew how to do. Martin then led him a little deeper and took one of his hands and told him to hold his hand open with his fingers tight together like the fins on a fish and paddle the water. Izak thrashed at the water and Martin had him stop and told him that fish didn't splash the water like that. Martin showed him how to hold his hand flat and pull on the water. He had Izak squat down in waist high water with his back to the bank and told him to keep his hands under the water and to lay back and relax and try to paddle himself back to the edge of the river without using his feet to walk.

Martin said he would stay by his side and not to be afraid. Izak paddled hard and was able to move a few feet and then stood up and saw he had moved some and Martin said he did good and that was all for the day and they walked out. Martin told him that he would get a little bit better every time that he tried and soon he would be able to swim across the river. Martin told him to remember what he had said about everybody was born to know how to swim, they just had to remember it.

Izak was in disbelief of himself. He had actually felt himself moved by paddling his hands. He told Martin that he had only ever been taught tasks, and Martin said training to be a boatman or being a boatman was a task. He said that resting or eating good meals and taking care of oneself was all tasks for a boatman, so they could be ready and strong to row the supply boat every week. Izak, said he had really never thought much about himself or what he might do, until the last few days of helping him. Martin said he would see him there again tomorrow.

Martin got home and saw that Henry's horse was there and went around to his side of the house and told him of their progress and Henry was pleased and said that perhaps Ben would be in tomorrow. Martin said they still had things to load on the barge and he told Henry about his idea of Izak becoming a boatman. Henry agreed that it might be time for Jacob to have an easier job and not to tell Johnny yet but he may be the one to be the new helmsman. Martin agreed and went around the outside to the front of the house where Walter and Martha were on the porch having tea. Martin was surprised, not at his mother having tea but his father was usually not home from Savannah by now. He sat and could tell there was an unusual air about them and he asked if everything was ok. There was a bit of a silence and his mom said that Walter had come home early because he had a sick spell today in Savannah while having lunch with friends. They called in the doctor, who happened to be nearby, and he said that Walters's heartbeat was a little irregular and he gave him some medicine and said he should rest a few days and he would come check on him every day until he was certain that he was ok. Walter said that he just had indigestion and that his friends, the doctor, and Martha were just being silly and that he was fine. Martin was accustomed to believing everything his father said and was convinced now that he was fine. He told them about his day and checking off and loading the barge and eating with the boatmen and his new helper and the swimming lesson. They listened with pride, aware of the struggles Martin had in school and how he had grown and embraced his work.

Martin excused himself to go get cleaned up and hugged them both. He noticed that his mother's brow was a bit furrowed but didn't think much about it. She told him that they had eaten early and were going to bed early and there was a plate of food left out for him and good night.

There was more to the story about Walters's health than even Martha knew. This wasn't the first time that he had felt ill but it had been worse this time. It had begun months before. Only his doctor and Walters's two oldest friends and lawyers, Sidney Perkins and Hulbert Adkins knew. Instead of going to the pubs and taverns as much, Walter began meeting with them to discuss something that was very important. He didn't even want to tell Henry about it yet. It was about all the people that did the work on the Milam place, who he considered his extended family. He knew that the way he had operated would no longer be tolerated when he was gone and what might happen to them if the Milam place was not there for them.

The next morning, Izak was waiting again, when Martin got to the boathouse. There had already been another delivery to go on the barge. They only had about a half days work, so Martin motioned Izak to come on and he would help him remember how to swim some more. Izak was less afraid today and Martin led him a little deeper and had him repeat what he had done the day before and he was able to move himself a little better and was eager to try again. They repeated it a half dozen times and each time Izak moved through the water a little smoother as he relaxed more and floated better. Martin encouraged him every time and urged him to relax and let his feet float up off the bottom. Martin told him how happy he was that he had improved so much. He told him that the next thing to learn was how to use his feet and legs like a frog along with his hands like a fish. In the shallow water, Martin laid back and pulled his legs up and then kicked them out and had Izak lay beside him and do it over and over and told him to lay back and hold his hands at his side and, like a fish, paddle his flat hands without bending his arms and at the same time pull his legs in and kick them out like a frog.

Then they went out in the water almost chest deep and Martin told him to watch as he laid back and did what they had just done in the shallow water. Martin paddled and kicked and moved swiftly across the water. Izak was amazed and told Martin that he looked like a fish and a frog both and Martin told him to try it. Isak struggled to do both together at first, but by the fourth time managed to coordinate enough to move toward shore better than ever. His excitement about his success empowered him to try harder and over and over until he was almost as good as Martin at it. Martin praised Izak about how good he did and told him that the next lesson would be about how to turn over on his stomach and asked Izak if he had ever seen a frog or a fish swim on its back and they both laughed and couldn't hardly stop and when they did and looked at each other they would start laughing again.

When they managed to control themselves, they got out and shook the water off a bit and Martin said he wanted to show Izak inside the boat-house. The boatmen were all sitting around the woodstove even though it was warm weather and it was not lit. The conversations were about storms and winds and real high tides and about giant black wild hogs on the South Carolina side of the Savannah River. Martin and Izak listened as each man took a turn telling what he knew of the subject. The talk got loud and excited and the waves and hogs grew bigger and bigger as each man added their own special flavor to the stories. Martin had heard many of these animated conversations and was still moved and convinced of their exaggerated dangers, but Izak was totally mesmerized by the stories. He hadn't heard such things before. Jacob, who sat listening and didn't say much saw the look on Izak's face and smiled and said boatmen were the biggest story tellers.

Jacob asked Martin if he had any word yet on the special cargo that Henry had ordered. Martin said he hoped soon because he and Izak need-ed to help with it in time for him to leave for Tybee this coming week. Jacob asked if Izak was going to Tybee and Martin said he hadn't thought about it but that he was a good hand. Jacob said that most of the crew Henry had hired out but that there were a few from here going and were gonna stay in the shanty at the Lazaretto landing.

Izak heard their talk but in light of the wild stories about the area he had just heard, he was a bit leery. Martin said he would talk to Henry about it and he still didn't know if he was to go on the barge with his boat or go in one of the supply boats and Jacob said it would be a quick trip on the boat but a two or three day trip on the barge.

It was time to get back to loading the barge and Martin pulled his check list out and began double checking the items that they had loaded and noting what was there and what items were still left to go on. Izak, while Martin was studying his list, and without being told, had untied the rope and pulled the barge slowly up to the bank, tied it off and set the walk boards in place. Then they set about loading the rest of the items and balancing the load and by lunchtime, everything that was there was loaded and accounted for and the tide had gone out from under the barge.

Meanwhile, Captain Ben and crew were waiting for that same tide to finish going out so they could begin their trip up the river when it began coming in again. It would be midafternoon before he would set out but decided he could get a good ways up river by dark, and then anchor in the river for half the night, then, very, very, early in the morning, catch the tide, and by moonlight, counting on no wind at all, drift up to where the Wilmington River branched off to the Milam's by mid-morning.

Martin and Izak joined Jacob and his crew for lunch again and afterwards, Martin showed Izak more things around the boathouse and they watched as a few men were carefully putting on a thin coat of whale oil to the entire supply boat after it had been drying from the rinse a few days before. Then they watched as two more men were replacing a couple cedar posts under the boat rails leading to the river. After a while, Martin said they were done for the day and he was going by to see Alice and Maggie and he could go along if he liked. They found Alice in the yard and as usual, she was happy to see Martin and smiled big at Izak too. She ushered them into the house where she had a pot of yaupon hot and sat them down with a big cup full and cold biscuits and blackberry jam.

Izak listened as Martin and Alice talked about the latest news. Martin said he was excited about going to Tybee for a month or more and he was gonna see if Izak could go too. Alice gave Martin some motherly advice and reminded him about her request concerning her family and he said a day didn't go by without him thinking about that. She beamed at him in appreciation of his concern. Izak was quiet but touched by their intimacy. They finished the tea and biscuits and Martin said they were next going to see Maggie and Alice said she was growing up quickly but not as quickly as he had been lately and that made Martin feel good.

Being Saturday, workday ended at noon, and friends were over a little earlier and out in the yard at Maggie's house as they usually were at the end of the day, watching chickens, and laughing and yacking loudly, and some were sipping a popular beverage of plum wine. They saw the two of them coming and carried on at how big Martin was getting. Maggie came over and said how glad she was that he came by and she knew, like everyone else, that he was leaving for Tybee and she was worried about him being gone. He assured her that he would be fine and one day before too long he was gonna have his own ship and be going much further. She liked Martin's adventurist spirit but worried about him at the same time.

She looked at Izak and smiled real big. She had always seen him around but had never spoken to him much because of his shyness and she was glad to see him up close. Martin told her that Izak might learn how to be a boatman if an opening came up and that he might even be going to Tybee.

He told her about the swimming lessons and how quick he was learning and what a good worker he was. He said he had even thought, while they were going over the list of things to go on the barge, how good it would be if he could learn to read and he thought maybe she could teach him. Maggie said she had never taught anyone but she could try and she mentioned that her father wanted to learn too.

Izak found himself speechless while being near Maggie and barely managed a smile. It was completely new territory for him to be the subject of any conversation and was a bit uncomfortable but, he had wished, while watching Martin go over the checklist of the things for the barge, that he could understand and read like Martin. Maggie and Martin chatted for some time with Izak mostly nodding at what was being said. When they were leaving, Maggie told Izak to come by anytime late in the day because they were most always outside and he nodded and managed a thank you.

Captain Ben, Ashley, and Ken drifted and anchored as planned and set out in the middle of the night by a bright but waning moon with an unexpected southeast breeze that moved them in excess of the tide speed and with the moon getting low in the west, they were at the Wilmington river and with sails down drifted the last mile. Ashley got in the skiff, with a rope attached, and pulled the sharpie a little over, close to the Milam side of the river and they anchored near the barge.

It was an early Sunday morning and Martin, anxious to check for Captain Ben's arrival, slipped out of bed and out of the house quietly and walked to the boathouse where he knew a half crew would be there and he could have his morning yaupon and bread with them. The roosters from every back yard were trying to outdo each in volume and style and the air was crisp and cool and felt good to breath.

When Martin saw the tall mast of the sharpie, he got excited and quickened his pace. Johnny and a couple of crew were already sitting outside, having tea and gazing at the river with the sharpie in it. Martin had told them that it would be coming soon. He sat with Johnny who had brought out some tea and biscuits for him.

Martin wanted to see them but told Johnny he would not disturb them because it was no telling how long they had been up to get there so early. Johnny said they could launch a boat when they woke and bring them in for tea and biscuits and not long after, they heard the cabin hatch slide and Ashley came out, sleepy headed and rolled himself a smoke, looked around and Martin yelled out. Ken followed shortly, looking wide awake and hyper in his movements, even though he had just got up. Such was the difference in the two. They both relieved themselves over the far side of the boat and then the Captain popped out and Martin yelled at him, in a way not much different than the roosters had sounded. Johnny and crew set out to get them.

Once on shore, the Captain and crew were served tea and biscuits and blackberry preserves. Martin asked them about their trip. Ken, being the most lively still, said it was OK but not as swift as the trip that Martin and Henry had been on. He said that the wind had been the most favorable on the trip down with he and Henry aboard than any trip he had ever been on, and there had been many. Martin said that he had regretted not being able to travel back with them but was glad things worked out the way they had because his trip back on the coach had been very interesting.

He asked if there had been any problem with having ice as cargo and Ashley said non except having to pump out the bilge more often due to melting. Johnny was in a query about their talk of ice and Martin assured him that he would show him later what they were talking about. Martin suggested that he show them around the place a little and let them get their land legs back on the way to his house where Ashley and Ken could meet his parents and see Henry and his family and have a hot bath and see where they were to stay the night and have a good meal later. The Captain said that sounded good but they needed to get a few things from the boat, so Johnny rowed them back out and in again with their ditty bags. Before they started out for the big house, Martin took the Captain and crew in the boathouse and pointed out the other boat and told them about the weekly procedure and about how long it took. They were impressed at the fine condition the boats were kept in and the launch and retrieve ramp. Going back outside he showed them his boat under the house and said he was taking it with him to Tybee for a couple months and explained to them what work they were doing there and pointed to the barge he had been loading to take with all the construction materials and about the lighthouse improvements.

As they walked toward the house he pointed out the buildings and what they were for, including the metal and woodworking shop, the horse barn and grain storage building, the brick lamp oil building, and the homes of Johnny and Jacob and explained that the other workers houses were scattered about the place.

Also, he pointed in the direction of where the sawpit and sawdust pile was where they would be storing the ice. When they were near the big house, he pointed out the upper level that faced east where they could get signals from and send signals to the lighthouse on Tybee and explained on the opposite side, on that same upper floor and facing west, there was a direct line of sight to the bluff in Savannah where they could send and receive signals also.

He told them about the rest of the place that they hadn't passed by and briefly explained how the place had to sustain itself and the lighthouse operation. Ken said they were guided by the lighthouse all the time but he had never thought much about how things worked.

Martha and Walter and Henry were all at the table in the kitchen. They had gotten news of the Captain coming that morning and Martha had gotten some help to prepare for a big Sunday dinner with their guest they had heard so many good things about. Walter had known Captain Ben from a pub that they both were regulars at and from seeing him at the wharfs often but Ben had never thought he would come there until the deal he had shook on with young Martin. Everything, except Martin and Henry was a new surprise to Ashley and Ken and they were full of gratitude for it, and especially when they were shown their quarters. Their room was nice with two single beds and off the back porch where they could sit out if they wanted.

Off the porch was another room that was used by everyone in the house and it had the copper tub and a porcelain flush toilet, also from England, with a tank mounted on the wall to create a flush to the toilet, which was piped to an underground tank and then spilled through a long and deep field of oyster shells four feet below ground level and two hundred feet long.

Water came by gravity from a tank mounted high on posts next to the roof eve to collect rainwater and piped to the lavatory sink and the tub and toilet tank. Martin led them out over a short brick sidewalk to a separate small building that was an outside kitchen with a big wood stove and big copper sink and big worktable. On the edge of the sink was a mechanical hand pump attached to a pipe going through the floor into the ground below. Martin showed them how to prime the pump and fill the bucket and pour it into a water jacket that was part of the stove and in a short time have very hot water to carry in and dump in the tub to take the chill off.

He asked them to show the Captain how things worked and said the Captain was staying in Henry's old room he had before he moved to the new area they had added for his family and they said they would make his bath ready for him when it was time. Martin said they could carry on as they pleased and that dinner would be in a couple hours and he would leave them at it to do what they wanted. They said a bath was what they

wanted first. They thanked Martin for accommodating them so completely and Martin said they had done equally well on the sharpie for him and
Henry, and he would never forget that trip.

Martin left them and went looking for Captain Ben. He found him
having a rum with his father and talking about Martin's least favorite subject, politics. It was something that was, of all things, the furthest from his
understanding. He told his father that he had settled Ashley and Ken and
they would draw the Captain a hot bath when he was ready. Walter said he
would show Ben to his room himself when they finished up their talk and
drink.

It was a happy day on the Milam place. The entire Milam family and
Captain Ben and Ashley and Ken were on the front porch all cleaned up
and bright. Captain Ben and crew had met everyone except Henry's family, who had been in their end of the house while they were getting cleaned
up.

Henry presented his wife, Claudia, and his oldest at nine, Louisa, and
his son, Henry Junior, at seven. Ellie had come to bring a special dish she
made when she heard they were having the company who had been in the
stories that Martin had told about. She set it in the kitchen and Martha
introduced her to the visitors and told that she was Jacob, the head boatman's wife. Martha gave her some sweet treats to take home as she left.

Next came Alice with another dish and she was introduced and when
they were told that Johnny was her husband, they said he was kind enough
to fetch them from their boat this morning before they were fully awake.
Captain Ben knew the story of Alice and the massacre and how she was
raised by Walter and Martha and had told Ashley and Ken. Martha asked
how she was feeling and since Johnny was at work, would she eat dinner
with them. Alice said she would like that.

Martha went in the kitchen and brought out another big pitcher of
Yaupon and filled everyone's cup and all sat and chatted. There were still
a few roosters crowing and another noise that Ken was the first to ask
about. Martha said that it was some of the people here who were at the
shout and praise house and Martin said it was one of the small outbuildings he had shown them. Ken still looked quizzical and Alice explained
that it was church and her people praised in voice and song. Ken thought
to himself that he had never had tea with a slave that was treated like family by his hosts. It added to the awe and mystery of his morning.

Dinner was served and deserts and more yaupon and everyone became
content. Walter and Captain Ben went off for some more talk of politics
and drink and Henry and his family to their end of the house. Martin suggested he show Ashley and Ken around a little more and they left Martha

and Alice and Henry and Claudia together on the porch.

Martin took Ashley and Ken to the back of the place, were the garden and grain crops were grown and the horse barn and sawpit. He showed them the big pile of sawdust where they would be taking the ice tomorrow and to the tack room in the barn. Ashley was reminded of his leatherworking at the tack shop before he went to work with Ben and Ken. Next they saw the chicken house where Ellie, who they had met, was in charge of.

They sat down to take a break and Ashley commented that he didn't understand how their place was able to operate so differently. Martin said that his father's family in England did not believe in slavery but Walter was thrust into this situation by his Navy assignment. He did the best he could do with it and treated the slaves he was given by the British Governor Wright with respect and like servants. Martin told him how some resented their ways but Walter was allowed a lot of leeway because of who he was and all the goodwill he had achieved and our important support for the lighthouse which is critical to the safety and prosperity of the city and state. He didn't know that Ben had told them about Alice and he felt confident enough to tell them how Alice, who they had met, was a survivor of a runaway slave massacre on Tybee and how his parents took her in and raised her like their own child and she had practically raised him and she was very literate and knew about the history of the world and spoke the Queens English and the Geechee slang of her people.

He could tell that Ashley and Ken were both touched and impressed by his story, but he didn't know that they knew it already but they were truly touched by Martin's telling of it and they didn't know the part of her raising him. Martin asked about where they were from and Ken said he was from Orangeburg, in South Carolina, which was an inland town about a hundred or so miles from there and he hadn't liked farming but wasn't sure what he did like and had some relatives in Charleston and went to visit them. He liked wandering the docks and met a fisherman with a boat that needed a helper so he tried it out for a while. He liked it but didn't make enough money and then he saw Captain Ben at a dock near them and liked the look of his boat and asked if he needed a hand. The Captain told him not then but maybe later.

About a month later, Captain Ben was in Charleston again and happened to be walking down the dock by the boat Ken was on and saw him and the Captain simply nodded and he understood it meant something and the next day grabbed his ditty bag and went to work with him. He said he was always treated fair and the Captain was pleasant to be around. Ken said they didn't go far offshore and usually it was only a couple or three days sailing and a day or two in port and he liked working on a delivery boat better than smelling like fish all the time and not being paid much at all.

Ashley said he was from South Carolina too but further upstate and had come to Savannah looking for work and got a job in the sail loft doing leather work on Bay Street and Captain Ben came in one day and wanted someone to rework the clews on his sails with leather and they sent him. He said it took him almost a week and while he was there, one mate left and the Captain asked him if he wanted to work with them. Ashley said he told him he knew how to do leather work but didn't know anything about sailing and the Captain said it was easier to teach a man that didn't know anything than a man that did, so he joined up with Ken and the Captain and he was glad he did.

Martin announced to them that he was gonna have a sharpie one day and they had no reason to doubt him. He said he didn't know how he could make it pay but thought about it a lot. Right now, he said he was excited about going to Tybee for a couple months and taking his little sailboat on the barge and exploring the islands north and south of Tybee. Ken said to be careful because of wild Indians to the south and pirates to the north. Martin said he didn't have any fear of the Indians but Charles Dyer, the lighthouse keeper, had warned him about the bad people to the north on Turtle Island. He said Charles Dyer said the Indians helped people who wandered into their area if they had boating problems or accidents and instead of eating them, like everybody was sure of, they rescued and helped them get to Tybee and pointed them to the lighthouse for help. He said Alice had told him of the Indians bringing her and the group of runaways food and teaching them how to survive before the massacre.

They returned to the big house and Ashley and Ken excused themselves to rest up. Martin went to talk to Henry about moving the ice from the sharpie to the sawdust pile the next day. They settled on a plan with Izak helping him and Captain Ben had said that Ashley and Ken would help. The big pieces could be set on the wagon with the sharpie boom and then slid into the middle of the two heaps of sawdust on the boards Martin and Izak had laid down. Ashley and Ken, having been up most of the night before, never got up from their nap. Martin and the Captain and Walter and Martha had leftovers for supper and went to bed early.

Martin was up early the next morning and found Ashley and Ken up and on the back porch. He quietly fixed some tea and leftovers and afterwards, they walked to the boathouse. He had planned to go get Izak but found him already there. Martin said he would go get the wagon if they could get the sharpie up to the edge of the riverbank while he was gone. Martin returned and brought two shovels to dig away the sawdust around

149

the ice and when they did, they noticed that much ice had melted away. Ashley said there was at least four thousand pounds left and Martin said that would be enough to experiment with for maybe a month if they buried it deep in the sawdust.

With two ice tongs, they used the long boom and lifted one of the big chunks out and set it in the wagon. The boathouse crew was out looking at what was going on and Martin picked a broken shard of ice from the wagon and handed it to Jacob and the others crowded around and they carried on about it to each other. Another big piece was lifted out and set in the wagon and Izak drove the wagon and the rest walked behind to the sawpit.

Once there, Martin and Izak propped up one end of a long plank onto the wagon and slid the ice out and down the plank onto another one laid between the two piles and they were pleased with how easy the two heavy chunks slid along the top of the wood planks. They put two sail canvases over it temporarily and went and got the other two pieces. Once it was placed with the other ice, they all shoveled and shoved the two heaps into one big heap and covered it with a big sail canvas as John had suggested to keep the sawdust dry from rain. He said dry sawdust insulated much better than wet sawdust. They didn't linger because they wanted to get the sharpie back out in deep water and Ashley and Ken saw to that when they got back to the river.

After the sharpie was anchored out, Martin took Izak up to the boathouse and asked Jacob if he would let Izak do some tasks around there. Jacob had heard that Izak might be interested in being a boatman and he said he had plenty of things he could do and Martin looked at Izak and saw that he was pleased with that idea.

Martin and Ashley and Ken returned to the house and found Walter and Martha and the Captain on the porch and sat with them for a while. They were talking about the modern steamship named Savannah that had recently come to town to stay for a few weeks before its maiden voyage to Charleston and how everyone thought that it was on fire because of all the smoke coming from its burner. Walter and Ben had planned to meet the next day to tour it.

Ben and crew were gonna stay until the last hour of outgoing tide and drift out the Wilmington River the mile to the Savannah River and be at the big river as the tide began in and drift into Savannah and get in late but be there to be loaded tomorrow for another trip. They were going to Port Royal with some farming hardware then they would return to Savannah with their holds full and decks stacked high with cotton. Ben said he didn't like hauling cotton because it didn't provide much ballast down in the holds and was cumbersome and in the way on deck but it was better than sailing back to Savannah without a load and only making money one way.

Later, when Walter said that Ben and crew were about to leave, Henry said he needed to settle up with Ben on his shipping charges. He asked Ben and Martin to come to his office. Ben gave him a written statement of his shipping charge and Henry wrote out a bank note for his bank in Savannah and handed it to him. He told Martin that he had asked him to come along because it was he who had thought of and struck the deal with Captain Ben and he wanted him to see it through. Martin was a little sheepish and didn't know exactly how to act but extended his hand to Ben and shook heartily bringing a large smile to Bens face and a proud one to Henrys.

Henry said he and John intended to make a business of ice and may need his services again. Ben thanked Henry for the business and the hospitality of his family and Henry said they were happy to have him and his crew and now that he was familiar with where they were he was welcome to visit anytime for pleasure or in need. They went back around to the porch where Martha had packed the rest of the leftovers from yesterday's big meal and some fresh deserts to go with it and a jug of yaupon. They all exchanged pleasantries and said good bye and Martin walked with them back to the boathouse.

With a line attached, Ashley and Ken paddled out in Martin's boat and Martin pulled it back. The Captain looked at Martin closely with the love of a father and good friend and thought to himself that Martin was the youngest friend he had ever had. Martin extended his hand to the Captain for a farewell shake before he boarded the little boat and paddled out to the sharpie. Martin had sent a couple of shovels for them to empty out the remaining sawdust and in a few minutes they sent them back with the boat.

They set the sharpie sails first, and then hauled in the bow anchor and the big sharpie swung around, with a light southeast wind mostly behind it and the last of the outgoing tide pushing it and glided off, to Martin and the boathouse crews delight. Martin watched as the sharpie rounded a slight bend in the Wilmington River and then only the sails were visible, gliding past the marsh.

Next morning, early, a wagon arrived with the new ice box parts and two of the workers who had built them. They had put the whole thing together in the shop to make sure all the parts fit and took it apart to deliver it. Henry was excited and directed them around back where he had made space in a room off the porch for it to go. They first cut a hole in the floor for a drain pipe to go, then set the floor component down and aligned the hole in the middle of it with the hole in the floor.

Next they set a wall panel and fastened it down and it was so thick that it stood on its own. Then went on the two side panels, which were fastened to the back panel and then the top went on and the big box with an open front, all fastened together stood firm. The two side panels had some hardware pre-fastened to them. On one side there were two heavy duty looking bronze half hinges and on the other side panel was half of a heavy duty door catch. Next came the door and it had the other half of the hinges and catch and they handed the two hinge pins to Henry and asked if he would drop the hinge pins in when they had the hinges aligned and he did.

After the door was on, they shut the door but the catch had to be adjusted slightly but when it was, the big thick door shut snugly against the side panels. There was a double rope gasket around the inside of the door that sealed things with the door shut. Next, one carpenter came in the door with a beautifully made copper deep pan with a drainpipe about a foot long sticking out the bottom. The pan was soldered at all joints and the drainpipe was soldered into the bottom. Both carpenters picked up the pan and it was just slightly smaller than the inside of the assembled ice box and they set it in and lowered it down with the drain pipe going through the bottom and the house floor so melted ice water would drain to the ground. Last were three shelves that fit between slats fastened on the panels.

Henry asked Martin to take the two carpenters to the sawdust pile to get a piece of ice and one carpenter took a few thin measuring sticks they had brought and cut one at the width of the copper pan and one at the length and the other at the height and they went off with Martin to get the ice. They came back shortly and set the ice in the pan.

Martin noticed how pleased Henry looked and thought he had never seen him so happy about something other than accounting work and smiled to himself. He told them he would be right back and went to get Claudia and the kids and Walter and Martha, who he had asked to stay away until he had it completed. When they were all there, Henry announced that this was the first icebox in Savannah and it would be the future prosperity of all on the Milam place and many outside the Milam place. He opened the door and when he did, everybody crowded around could feel the whoosh of cold air as the door swung open.

Henry said that he wasn't sure yet how often the ice would have to be replaced but John's in Darien lasted about five days in the summertime and longer in winter. He said that John's was insulated with moss but he had this one insulated with cotton and had the walls made thicker than John's. Henry said that the next icebox was to be for the Tybee lighthouse and a block of ice every week would be going on the supply boat and it was his intent to have an icebox in most houses in Savannah and Charleston and Beaufort and Walterboro. He said John had even bigger ideas that included inns and taverns, and fishing boats, fish houses, and big storage icehouses for tons of ice to be kept.

13.
BACK TO TYBEE

The next couple days were very busy for Martin and Henry, checking everything to go on the barge to Tybee and planning for the workers from the Milam place and the contract workers doing the masonry on the lighthouse. Also, the regular supply boat run had to be fitted in as usual and the extra Milam boat along with two hired boats were needed to take workers and supplies.

Charles and Daniel Dyer, on Tybee, and his guards, for the last month, had erected three small shanty houses by the guard house at Lazaretto landing with simple sleeping arrangements with one shanty having cooking utilities and utensils and food storage. They also dug an additional shallow well for washing. Drinking water was to be hauled in from the deep well at the lighthouse to prevent sickness. Also, latrines were built for adequate sanitation. It was no small task to accomplish all this but Henry was a good planner and starting three weeks ahead, and had three carpenters supplied with materials, staying at Lazaretto to assist Charles Dyer.

Martin made his rounds to say good-bye to Alice and Maggie and her family and got a lot of warnings about being safe from his mother and father and Henry and Alice. Henry was coming the following week to inspect work and accommodations and spend the night at the Dyers with Martin. Martin packed camping gear and the marine chart his father had given him and clothes and a present for Daniel and Mary.

The barge and three hired boatmen, plus a pulling boat, left out two days before the rest. The barge could only drift and the pulling boat was just for keeping it out of the eddies and in the channel and a little movement once they got there.

Time to leave came and the four boats, loaded with men, tied up in a line end to end were ready to leave. The tide was slack and about to start out with more people on the bank than usual to see them off. Jacob started the chantey by singing a verse and everyone on the boats and on the riverbank sang the chorus and then Jacob another verse and another chorus of many voices. The rhythm was set by twelve pair of oars lifting and dipping into the water and a grunt by the twelve rowers as they pulled hard on each stroke. This continued and was eerie, as the voices on the boats and voices on the land separated slowly.

Martin was in the back of the front boat by Jacob, where he had ridden before and he was full of excitement. He had wanted to do this sooner but had gotten involved in his work at the various projects for a couple years. He was satisfied, though, because he felt a lot more grown up and had a mission and purpose to the trip now. He felt half boy and half grown up. The boy just wanted to have fun and sail and explore, the grown up wanted to fulfill Alice's wish about seeing if her family might still be alive. The oarsmen didn't seem to be pulling as hard as usual but they were moving at a good speed. Martin had seen slaves passing by the boathouse like this with three or four bateaus tied end to end, rowing to and from Savannah from Wilmington Island. He wondered if they would catch the barge that had left early.

About half way to Tybee and on the South Carolina side of the river, he noticed some smoke several times, probably from cooking fires, and wondered if they were outlaws. There were no boats on the river bank but may have been hidden. This stretch of land from Savannah to Tybee, on both sides, was "no man's land," as described by most, and especially on the South Carolina side. It was mostly narrow strips of low lying land and flood water and marsh grass that was different than the marsh grass closer to the coast. It was eight to ten feet tall growing in watery brackish mud and flood water and stalks almost as big around as a cornstalk and it grew so thick a man could hardly walk through it. In it were giant alligators, giant wild hogs, and big rattlesnakes. These things kept ordinary people away but was a haven for outlaws. Jacob yelled and it made Martin jump when all his attention and imagination that was spread over the area re-entered his body. Jacob had turned around to look back and the oarsman in the last boat were being lazy and had their oars lade across the boat, being pulled by the other three boats. Everybody laughed and the men in the next to last boat put their oars down when Jacob turned back looking forward again. They were about two hours into the trip and the current was moving fast and the riverbank passed by quickly. Jacob steered the string of boats out into the middle of the channel and motioned for a break and the boats drifted freely.

Packed food was brought out and a lot of lively jive talking took place between the Milam plantation men and the outside help men. Martin saw Izak in the second boat and asked him how he was doing and he smiled big and said it beat hoeing weeds and spreading manure. After a break, the lead boat only rowed until the other three lined up behind, then everyone pulled on the oars. Rowing a line of boats like this takes some skill to get it right. Rowing to hard, and you push against the boat in front and, row to easy and you don't do your share.

They came up on a ship, anchored, waiting for the tide to turn back toward Savannah and Jacob steered close and told Martin to stand and ask how long since a barge had drifted by and the sailor on the deck yelled back about two hours ago. The sailors on the deck came over to their side and leaned over the rail to watch this odd caravan of boats pass. They passed two more ships in the next hour, one from Holland and one from Italy. After the second one, they saw the barge up ahead and by the time they closed in on it, Lazaretto was only a mile away. After entering Lazaretto Creek, they stopped and separated the boats and rowed up to the bank to where the two long timbers were for hauling the supply boat up each week.

One boat at a time was hauled up and supplies and gear were set out. Once unloaded, the regular supply boat was hauled out and unloaded and let back down the ramp. Then, both Milam supply boats were tied end to end and with Johnny at the helm, instead of Jacob, and six boatmen, began the trip back. The other two boats were winched up the rails and men drug them above the high water line and flipped them upside down until time to go home in a month or two.

Jacob wasn't too happy about staying away from his family but he had worked on the road and bridges the most over the years and had experience, plus he was a good leader and knew how to tell men what to do in an agreeable way. He showed the hired men their shanties and they were pleased, probably because they were nicer than what they were used to. They were loosely built so they could be taken down when the work was over so the lumber could be reused but they were new and clean and smelled good of fresh sawn pine. The men from the Milam place moved into the regular shanty. Three men began organizing the small kitchen shanty and stowing the food supplies and pots and utensils and the others searched along the river bank and drug in a big pile of driftwood for the cooking fire, enough for at least a week. Then Jacob said there wasn't anything else for them to do the rest of the day and they could sleep or if they wanted to, catch some fish for supper. About half did one and half did the other.

The wagon from the lighthouse was not there yet and Martin began wandering around the area over where the quarantine station had been years before. The main building and the dock were almost all rotted away. He walked a ways behind the building in some overgrown thickets and saw rows and rows of ballast stones, half buried, about two feet apart and knew they were grave markers. He tried to imagine how awful it must have been having hundreds of sick and famished people cooped up here on this little low lying spit of land, waiting until death or until they healed enough to be permitted to leave and being tormented by the gnats and mosquitos in the dreadful heat or the bitter damp cold that blew in from the northwest in the winter. A loud yelp, and again, Martin jumped as his wandering attention and imagination sprung back into his body. It was Charles Dyer coming to pick him up and he ran back over to the landing.

The two tacky horses pulled the wagon with Charles and Daniel and Mary. It had been three years since Martin had seen them. Daniel was bigger than him and had a slight beard and Mary was altogether different looking and they were both sun tanned. They laughed together at each other and were a pretty sight to see.

Jacob came over to say hey to Charles, who he had known for a long time, and they shook hands and Jacob told Charles to try and keep Martin from crossing the ocean while he was here because that was all he talked about and to please not let him go to Turtle Island. Charles laughed and said he would try.

After the supplies were loaded, Martin got his stuff and climbed on the wagon and they headed toward the lighthouse. Martin noticed how the narrow oyster shell road was sunk down in places and needed more shells and both bridges were rickety and had gaps in the decking where boards had rotted. The tackies were hesitant and hard to get them to go over the bridges, especially the longer bridge.

The road left the marsh and went along the back of the sand dunes and Martin heard the surf and between the dunes, could see Turtle Island, Daufuskie and Hilton Head, to the north. Charles looked back and saw Martin straining to see more of the ocean and steered the wagon toward the beach at the passage between the dunes. He said if they got out and lightened the load so the wheels would not sink in the sand, they could go down on the beach. They hopped out and Daniel got behind the wagon and pushed until they were through the dunes and on the hard beach, then they got back on.

Martin was mesmerized at the view and Charles stopped the wagon for a moment to let him take it all in. He had studied the chart that he had gotten from his father many times and now looked at Turtle island and followed the low profile eastward until he saw Daufuskie beyond and then, ever so slightly saw a separation, which was Calibogue Sound, and then Hilton Head and then the Atlantic. He remembered it from his first trip but it was like seeing it again for the first time, having studied it since on the chart and knowing what island each was.

Daniel and Mary were silent as they saw him so intensely staring. They saw these places and the ocean every day, but never looked so closely. Martin came out of his momentary trance to see them looking at him and pardoned himself and Charles continued on down the beach to the point. Martin smiled big when he saw the pilot shack and Captain Jones sitting out front and a few pilot crewmen sitting around.

Charles was enjoying this little trip almost as much as Martin because he seldom ventured out of the lighthouse compound. He pulled up close and Martin jumped out and went straight to Captain Jones and told him who he was and he grinned real big and was happy and said he thought of him often and had been hoping he would come again. Martin sensed that the Captain could not see at all now.

Charles got down and went over and touched his shoulder and said hello to him and the Captain said how glad that he had come to visit and how long it had been since he had. Charles said that he had gotten fat and it wasn't easy anymore to walk over the high dunes between the lighthouse and here but he was glad to send Daniel or Mary over with his food bucket every day. Yes, said the Captain, that keeps me alive and I can't thank you enough. That and these crewmen here keep wood cut for my little ship stove and bring a few things I need from Savannah and overall, I'm in good care. My only dread are the northeasters when they blow for a week so hard and I can't sit outside and these fellows aren't around. After a few hours of being outside the sand starts drifting up on me and fills my hair and ears and nose holes until I have to go inside for a few days until it quits and even though I can't see, I hate to be indoors except to sleep. Charles said that perhaps, on the next blow, he could come fetch him up in the wagon and bring him up to the lighthouse, but the Captain said not to worry. Charles told the crewmen sitting around how much he appreciated them looking after the Captain and if they ever needed anything to come straight up and ask him.

They laughed and said they had been calling him Captain Sandy after finding him half buried in drifting sand one day during a hard northeaster. They said they had to have the old man around or else they wouldn't know what kind of wind and weather was coming and went on to say how uncanny it was that he could sometimes tell a week ahead what to expect and as his eyesight had gone bad, his weather telling had gotten better and how they relied on his weather forecasts. Charles thought a minute and said if the Captain ever sees any big weather coming, come tell him and he could signal it to Savannah from the lighthouse. They agreed and said they would let him know about approaching rainy spells or northeasters or cold fronts or anything big. The Captain heard this talk and was pleased that he might be useful to Charles who had been a good friend and fed him every day these last six years since his eyes had gone bad and mentioned that it would be cool and clear for the next few days and the winds would be out of the northwest.

Charles touched the old man's shoulder again and said he needed to go and he was sure that he would be hearing more from Martin and his kids, since Martin was gonna be here for a for a month or two. Having made an old man the happiest he had been in a while, they loaded up and Charles headed back to the place they had come through the dunes and then doubled back toward the lighthouse.

They pulled up to the stockade fence surrounding the lighthouse compound and were met by one of the guards that had been expecting them for some time and said that Mrs. Dyer had almost sent him out looking for them. Charles said they had taken Martin on a tour. The guard followed them to the house and after they got out, the other guard joined him and they unloaded the supplies. Mrs. Dyer came out and hugged Martin and said how glad she was that he had finally come back. He said he was too. Charles said it was almost signal time and he wanted to let Walter know Martin had arrived safely along with the regular news and for the first time, Captain Sandy's weather and tide report. This was normally Daniels job every afternoon but Charles said he would do it so Daniel could be here with Martin.

Martin took his stuff up in Daniels loft area and got out the two presents he had brought and climbed back down the ladder. He had mostly been looking at the beach and islands and water and everything around him but now studied Mary and Daniel closely. He thought to himself, whereas Captain Jones and Charles and his wife, Margo, had waned a bit, Daniel and Mary had waxed a lot. Mary had grown and blossomed and was radiant and beautiful and Daniel a sturdy and mature young man with a beard and a little taller than his father.

Both were a golden brown, tan color. He thought he must have grown and looked different too, but it was much more obvious about them. He handed Mary her present first and said that his mother had chosen it for him to give her because he was at a loss to what she might like. She smiled big and her eyes lit up with excitement as she unwrapped the fine thin paper his mother had used, careful not to tear it so it could be used again. When she could see what it was, she couldn't help herself and let out a shrill scream that shocked and surprised everyone. Her first reaction after that was to instinctively hug and give Martin a kiss, which caused him to blush red and have an unusual feeling. She then held it by the beautifully gilded handle and looked at herself in the small mirror and then held it for her mother to see herself. Her excited emotion was like a wave that affected everyone.

Martin handed Daniel his present, wrapped in coarse brown paper. Daniel opened it and smiled broadly at Martin, thanking him and showed the rest the finely made pocket knife that Martin had gotten him from his favorite hardware store in Savannah. Daniel first opened the big blade and admired it for a moment, then opened the smaller blade and showed everybody. He hadn't screamed with the emotion of his sister but he was clearly overwhelmed and grateful. Martin told him to clean the sand out often and add a few drops of oil or else it would rust.

Daniel and Mary seldom left the lighthouse and gifts and visitors were rare. This was a big and exciting day for them. Margo said she had an early supper with their favorite things including pie and for them to get washed up and they could eat when Charles came back. Then she remembered the food she had made for Captain Jones and told Daniel to run it down to the beach to him.

Daniel was back shortly and soon after, Charles returned, and everyone sat down to a platter of deviled crab in crab shells and potatoes and beans. She had worked all morning, boiling crabs and picking crabmeat. The pilot crew on the beach had traps set and had brought her a bushel. Deviled crab was everybody's favorite but they took a lot of work. The desert was blackberry pie.

Mrs. Dyer brought a cup of yaupon to everybody and they went out on the front porch. Martin could hear the surf but the high dunes blocked the beach view but not the view of the upper part of the ocean and horizon. Behind the sixty foot dunes was why the lighthouse location was chosen after previous towers had been washed away by hurricanes.

They all asked Martin questions about his home and Savannah. He told them as briefly as he could about his failure and bad school experience and getting real sick and how he finally learned to read from Alice and how his father wanted him to learn how everything operated and so he worked in every department of the place, starting with the chickens and egg houses and after four or five months there he went to something else and lastly he was in charge of seeing that the supply boat was loaded with everything each week. He told about his sailboat that was on the barge. Also, he told them a lot about his recent trip to Darien and tried to explain about ice and how they learned about it and had some now in the sawdust pile and Henry was gonna have them an icebox made and how he said it was gonna change the way they do stuff with food. They had seen thin ice sheets on puddles before when it had gotten real cold a few times, but it was hard for them to imagine huge chunks of it. The whole family was glued to Martin's stories and wanted him to go on and on.

The guards, Captain Jones, and a few pilot boat crewmen were all they had to talk to besides each other. Light keepers and their families had a very isolated life. He also told them about what Alice had asked him to do while he was here. Of course, they were familiar with her since Charles had brought her there after finding her in the pluff mud the day of the massacre. Daniel was very young then and Mary was a toddler. They bathed and comforted Alice until she was able to go back with Walter. They had kept up with her story through Walter as the years went along. Martin said Alice believes that her family may still be alive because her experience with the Indians was that they were good and kind people because they had mercy for the runaways and brought food and showed them how to live more comfortable from bugs and disease and how the Indian lady had come, unafraid, to teach them those things and how she could speak English. Charles said he believed they were harmless because of the people they had rescued from boating mishaps and guided them there.

Martin said he wasn't sure how he could go about contacting them because they were quite shy and stayed within their islands and marsh and beach areas. Charles said that if you were in their area you were sure to be seen because they were very wary and kept a constant look out for intruders. He had heard that years ago they had traded with whites but had quit, probably because they may have been cheated, but he didn't know the particulars. He added that he wasn't worried about Martin over there in the Indian Islands but wished he would stay away from Turtle Island. The pilot crewmen said that there were two kinds of shipping in and out of Tybee Roads, daytime shipping and nighttime shipping and both times were busy but the nighttime shipping involved desperate characters that didn't think twice about killing. There were plantations on Daufuskie and Hilton Head and that only left Turtle Island, as a place to hide and do business and it was the center of every kind of contraband including the human sort. Although it was now against the law to bring slaves in from Africa, it was still regular business on Turtle Island. Martin said he wanted to sail to Daufuskie and Hilton Head but would steer clear of Turtle Island. He had hoped that Daniel could go with him and he would take Mary for a ride if she wanted but his boat would only hold two, and he added that the boat was sealed and wouldn't sink even if filled with water and described the floating safety device his father had given him, made from a special tree bark that floated and could keep two men up and made him promise that he would have it on the boat at all times.

Charles said Walter had told him what a good sailor he was and he wasn't worried. He also mentioned that Captain Jones had wanted Daniel to have his old pilot boat that he hadn't used in six years since his eye-sight had gone bad but it needed a lot of work and Daniel didn't think he had the skill to fix it. In its time, it was the fastest boat on the beach and Captain Jones success was because he would usually win the race to the ship needing a pilot. It had been built in England but the Captain had gotten it off a ship coming from the Caribbean of questionable origin. It has been stowed upside down to prevent any standing water and rot but the keel looked hogged a bit. You might look at it and if you like, you could have it and ship it back on the barge and restore it. Martin had noticed the boat and said he would think about it and that they were bringing the barge around on the beach closer to where the big bridge was so it would be closer to haul the materials from and that was to happen at the top of the tide on Monday and he would get his boat off and bring it around and drag it up to Captain Jones shanty. He added that his father wanted him to check in on the bridge construction occasionally just to get familiar with it while he was here. Charles told Martin that he could put a saddle on and use a tacky anytime he needed to. Also, one of the guards could fill in for Daniels signaling duties. We don't get company much so while you are here, y'all can come and go as you please, but just let us know where in case we need to find you. Mary suggested that they walk down to the beach before it got dark and so that's what they did.

At the top of the tall dunes between the lighthouse and beach, Martin stopped to look out over the beach and ocean in all directions. He thought to himself, for a moment, about his position. He was on a point of land facing the ocean to the east, and behind him, to the west, was Lazaret-to Landing and Savannah. To his left and north was looking across the mouth of the Savannah River and Hilton Head beyond, and to his right and south was the far south end of Tybee and what was called on the chart, the Back River, and across that were the Indian Islands.

Mary was watching him swing his arm out in different directions and asked him what he was doing and he said he was understanding where he was. She laughed at him and said he was on a big sand dune on Tybee acting silly and laughed some more. He smiled and said he knew that but it had become a habit for him to think about where he was in terms of the four directions of east, west, north, and south and said that he was practicing because he was going to be a captain and have his own ship one day.

She laughed and called him Captain Martin. Daniel said he could give them both a head start and still beat them to Captain Jones shanty. Martin and Mary took off and Daniel followed a few moments behind. Martin wasn't accustomed to running down a sand dune and fell forward after a few steps. In his hast to win, Daniel fell too. Captain Jones hadn't gone in yet and was happy for the company since both pilot crews were gone.

Martin asked him about the boat and the Captain had a lot to say about it. He asked Daniel to help him up and move his chair over close to the boat. He said that this boat looked a lot like the other pilot boats but if you looked close, there were some important differences. The subject excited him so that he got up out of his chair and put his hand out on the hull and felt the lapped planks deftly and ran his hand up to the keel, which would normally be the bottom, but the boat was upside down. Then he ran his hand down the length of the keel and said that its weight had been on the stem and stern so long that the keel had hogged down a half foot and caused the gunwales to flare out. Martin could see the swag in the bottom. The Captain said that could be fixed easy enough if the boat was set upright and blocked up at the ends and added about a foot of water. Then heat up four or five ballast stones and put them down in the middle. The stones will heat up the water and soften the wood and the weight of the stones will flatten out the keel slowly and be back straight when it dried, naturally bringing the gunwales back in place. It may have to be repeated three or four times but he had seen it work. He said this boat was the same dimensions of the other boats being used here on the beach but there were two differences. The planking on his was thinner but just as strong but lighter. Also, if you looked real close, you could see a difference in the bow angle because his had a sharper angle like a knife and cut through the water easier. He said those simple differences got him out to a ship ahead of the others and he got more piloting jobs than anybody. He said it was too fine a boat to be driftwood and he wished he or Daniel would take it. Daniel said Martin was better able to do something with it than he was and if he got it going again, he could bring it back and take him and Mary out and teach them to sail. Martin didn't have to think long on it and told the Captain he would take it and bring it back and do what Daniel said, in the spring.

The Captain let his fingers run from the keel over each strake to the gunwale once more and reached out to find Martin's shoulder and asked him to get him back over to his spot by his shanty. Daniel got the chair and Martin helped the Captain. Mary was touched to see to how kind and carefully Martin assisted the old man. Right then and there she fell for Martin.

They asked if they could do anything more for the Captain and he said he was fine and to tell their mother how much he liked the deviled crabs and blackberry pie and that she already knew that it was his favorite. They walked down the beach toward the south end a little then turned back to get home before dark. Daniel asked if they wanted to race again and Mary told him to race himself and made Martin laugh. Once at the top of the sand dune, the setting sun was entirely blocked out by the lighthouse and it cast a long shadow, contrasted in the light colored sand.

When they got back there were two washtubs of cold water on the front porch for Daniel and Martin and one on the back porch for Mary. After cold baths, they had a snack of leftovers and the boys went up to the loft for the night and Mary sat up with her mother a bit and told her about their visit with Captain Jones and how he said how much he liked the crabs but she was worried that he wasn't moving about so easy and how much he liked Martin and how kind and gentle Martin was to him. She went and got her new mirror and they took turns looking at themselves and laughing at each other.

Once up in the loft, Martin said he had a question he had been thinking about and Daniel said to go ahead and ask. Why do they have guards here? Daniel said that nothing hardly ever happened here to need guards anymore, but because they were so far away from anyone and the lighthouse was so important that it was better to err on the side of safety.

During the last war with England, there was an encampment of fifty soldiers here full time. Now the whole Georgia coast is full of Americans and the Indian wars are about done and my father says that America is about to add Florida and Spain would be gone from it too. Although there may be a few Tories left on Daufuskie, the war is over and British merchant ships are coming and going, peacefully trading again. What the guards are here for now is more about outlaws and smugglers, but smugglers steered clear of most everywhere and everybody, but he guessed that there was always a slight chance of a desperate outlaw or two but there hadn't been one during his lifetime.

People came mostly who had boating problems or accidents or an occasional person or two rescued by the Indians and sent here. He said that there were still a runaway or two hiding out on the south end occasionally but they too wanted to stay out of sight. He said he had a cousin come from Savannah last year for a few weeks and they camped out on the south end and didn't see anything except an occasional Indian dugout and a few Indians on the other side of the river.

Martin asked Daniel if he wanted to go with him to look for Alice's family. Daniel thought about it and said he didn't know an answer to that and they probably needed to talk to his father about it. He said he wouldn't be afraid because of what his father had always said about them but it could be better for Martin to go alone. Daniel asked Martin what he wanted to do tomorrow and Martin said he didn't know and that they could go sailing but it would be after the barge is up on the beach to get the boat off. Daniel said maybe they could saddle up the two tackies and ride to the beach and all around the island if you like. Martin said that sounded like fun. They quit talking and went to sleep.

Sunday morning came and began as most days with yaupon, coffee, eggs and grits and bacon and a leftover piece of blackberry pie. Daniel told Mary that he had thought he would take Martin around the island on the tackies but if she wanted to go he could hitch up the wagon so the three of them could go. She said for them to go and she could go with Martin on the horses another time and thanked him for offering.

They grabbed a sack of bread and some hard cheese and a jug of water and said they would be home well before dark and hurried out to get the horses ready. Daniel had ridden a lot more than Martin but Martin was not a beginner. They went behind the dunes toward the south end until the dunes were low enough for the horses to cross over to the beach easily then galloped at the edge of the water where the sand was hard and in a few minutes slowed to a walk the rest of the way to the southern point of Tybee where he Back River comes and goes.

Daniel said that at a very low tide, he could go out a mile on the bar that extended out from where they were. He pointed out that the river split into two channels entering the ocean leaving a large sand bar in between. The smaller channel followed the Tybee beach around to the north back toward the lighthouse but was only ankle deep at low tide and the bigger one went south along the beach of the Indian Islands a ways before dumping out into the ocean and it was not deep at low tide but deeper than the other one. He said he had made the mistake of riding out to the end of the sand bar at low tide and lingering to long until the tide had risen in the small channel between him and Tybee beach. Had he been a little later and it deeper, he thinks that the tacky may not have been able to walk through the strong current to get back and swimming would have been difficult and they may have been swept out. He said he was lucky that day.

They continued around and headed west on the edge of the Back River until the sandy beach ended and marsh began and a creek entered the island, then they looked across the river for any signs of life but saw nothing. Martin reminded Daniel that they were exactly on the spot of the massacre that Alice and maybe her family survived. He nodded and said that there were some old shallow wells that those runaways had dug and he usually let the horses have a drink and it had never sickened them. They took them to drink a little and Daniel said they could go across the middle of the island back on the trail that they used when the supply boats used this landing, on rare occasions. They let the horses walk since they had just drunk water and Martin noticed how different this inland part of the island looked than the other parts he had been on.

They were about a half-mile from the beach and followed the ridge northward. It was higher ground but not very high ground. Nothing much was high ground on Tybee but the dunes on the north end starting about a half mile before the lighthouse and wrapped around the north point and continued for about a little more than a half mile past there. There was one more high area just inside the dunes about half way to Lazaretto where you could go up on and see over the dunes toward Daufuskie.

About halfway home, they crossed over a marsh area and a small creek that had a giant old Longleaf resinous pine log across it that had been there since Indian times. The sun had turned it silver and Daniel said it was so full of resin that it wouldn't rot. He also said this creek was the same one that they had seen at the Back River landing earlier, but smaller and that it almost split the island in two and his father had said that it had washed through in a big hurricanes.

They got off and walked the log over the creek and let the tackies walk and they sunk in the mud as they went down the bank and into the creek bottom. Daniel said the tide was low now and harder to go through the creek mud but at high tide the tackies simply swam across. He said the tackies were better than anything for going in marsh mud because of how big their feet were in proportion to their body and that's why they used them. Daniel said they had left the wagon route that continues just behind the sand dunes around to the lighthouse but this was another way to the Lazaretto Landing.

A little way past there, Martin recognized the bigger of the two bridges they came to repair that he had crossed over before. The tackies didn't like walking on the bridge planks and Daniel suggested they get off and walk them over. He said he was glad the bridge would be repaired soon. In a bit, they came to the smaller bridge and got off again and walked the horses over again. Martin told Daniel about exploring the old quarantine station and the ballast stone grave markers when he first came. Daniel said the pilot boatmen said there were ghosts there but they said there were ghosts everywhere.

A slight breeze blew smoke over them from the morning cooking fire at the shanties and Martin thought to himself that the wind was out of the northwest, like Captain Jones said it would be. Jacob and a few others were sitting around smoking and relaxing. Work wouldn't start until the next day and a half dozen men had taken the pulling boat out to the anchored barge and were fishing off of it and a few had walked out to the point and were fishing off the bank.

Jacob smiled big and was happy to see them, especially Martin, who reminded him of his family and the older he got, the less he liked to be away from his family but he was a loyal worker and didn't complain. Martin asked how they were and Jacob said the night had been a good one. Lots of fresh fish and crabs and clams, all cooked together in one big pot. There were no bugs but there might be some soon if the wind switched around. Martin asked him what the plan was for tomorrow.

Jacob said that they would catch the outgoing tide in the morning and tow the barge around to where the beach started and anchor it out until the tide was fullest late in the afternoon and pull it up high on the beach and tie it to a cedar where it could stay until all the work was done. Martin said he might be there to get his boat off, but if he wasn't, could he have some men set it off above the high water line and tie it off and Jacob smiled and nodded. He said that he was gonna be taking Captain Jone's old pilot boat back to the boathouse to repair and sometime later he would get it there and would need some help loading it and Jacob nodded again.

Martin asked if they were in need of anything and he said that Henry had thought of everything, as he always did, and all he could want for was his family. Martin thought to himself that this should be the last time Jacob should have to stay away this long. One night a week on the supply run was probably okay but this was too much. Martin went to his horse and took a small package out of his lunch sack and handed it to Jacob privately and Jacob saw the burgundy stain on the wrap and slipped it in his pocket smiling in appreciation of Martin bringing him a piece of left-over blackberry pie. Some excited hollering came from the barge and they looked and a worker was pulling a hand line up with a huge drum fish. Supper says Jacob. Martin asked Daniel if he wanted to go see the graves he had found and he said ok. Jacob said not to be disturbing those poor folks, they may get up and come over here in the night. Martin laughed and said they would be quiet and step easy.

Lazaretto Landing was nothing much but a large hammock, only a few feet above sea level, with layers and layers of discarded oyster shells that had sunk down and made the surface hard and blazing hot in the summer and the northwest winds were freezing in the winter. But the worst thing about Lazaretto Landing was the gnats. It was northwest of Tybee and the prevailing southeasterlies blew clouds of gnats over to there and at times they were almost impossible to tolerate. The best thing about the Lazaretto landing was its location. It was less than a quarter mile from the South Channel and had deep enough water for ships coming into the South channel from the Atlantic to the quarantine station to leave the sick and infirmed. Most was human cargo of the African slave trade up until the quarantine station was moved to Cockspur. It was the only deep water access and egress to and from Tybee, particularly critical in supplying the lighthouse with all its needs.

Martin and Daniel walked past the rotted remains of the old quarantine station to the small patch of land behind it. Within the dense yaupon and briar thickets, Martin pointed out the rows of ballast stone grave markers and Daniel said it was spooky and was hesitant to go further. Martin went a little further along than he had the first time he was there and noticed something curious. There was a small opening hollowed out in the thickets with a fire spot in the middle that was not warm but had been used recently. The ground was tamped flat from someone staying there and some rags of cloth strewn around. Martin whispered that someone must have been there and left when all the men came to stay in the shanties, the day before. Daniel whispered he had seen all he wanted and headed out. Martin hesitated and looked around for any clues about who had been staying there. He didn't and followed Daniel out. They went straight back to the shanties and Martin said he wouldn't tell Jacob because they might be spooked about it. Daniel said he was spooked already and was ready to continue their ride.

Martin had been thinking on something all morning pertaining to his talk last night with Daniel about Alice's family and how best to approach the Indians about it and he thought he might ask Jacob about an idea he had about it so when they got back to the shanties, he saw Jacob in the same place, but now alone and asked him if he could talk a minute and Jacob nodded. He didn't know if Jacob knew what Alice asked him to do here and asked him if he did and Jacob nodded again and Martin was glad he did. Martin explained to Jacob about how Alice thought that her family might still be alive and how he had told her that, while on Tybee, he would go over to the Indian Islands and see if he could find out anything about them. He said that he had thought a lot about the best way to go about it and he had an idea that he wasn't sure about and again Jacob nodded. He said that he was thinking about asking if Alice could come and go with him since she was somewhat familiar with the lady that was their leader that had come over and helped her family and all the runaways. Jacob nodded again and touched Martin's shoulder tenderly and said that everyone knew what Martin's intentions were and he had been thinking about it a lot himself and that he also thought Alice going with him was a good idea. Martin felt good having Jacob's approval and would ask Henry the same question when he came down the next week.

They continued their ride and Daniel said one of his favorite places was where he figured they would bring the barge up on the beach where it was the closest they could get it to the bridge work. His father called it the wash through because in hurricanes when the water came up high, it was another place where the salt water would wash through the island. It was a low place and parts had standing brackish water. He wasn't sure why he liked it but it had different looking marsh grass in it and always had a few otters and they were fun to watch.

They cut over to the beach right where the marsh ended and got down and left the horses and went back into the low woods quietly looking for otters in the brackish marsh but didn't see any. They saw where they had made trails through the mud and decided to come back early one morning and look again. They got their lunch sacks and sat and ate while the horses ate some sea oats.

Daniel said he really liked someone to do stuff with besides his sister and he often wished he didn't live away from everything like they do but most of the time he liked it. He pretty much figured that he would be a light keeper like his father and grandfather had been but his father said that even if he did, he needed to go off to Savannah or Charleston for a year or so to see if he might prefer a different life. Martin said, to begin with, he could come to his house for a few weeks or a month or more whenever he wanted. The supply boat was available every week for him to come and go if he preferred. Martin said he might ought to do it before long because he expected to have his own boat in a couple years and he knew he wanted a sharpie like his friend Captain Ben. Daniel had seen Captain Ben and crew many times come into the south channel, following the shallow channel right off the beach near where they were sitting. He said they were so close to shore sometimes he could throw an oyster shell and hit them. Martin said that if he were gonna do the signals from the lighthouse today, he would like to go with him and Daniel said sure and it would be time to do it in about an hour or so.

They finished up and got the tackies from the dunes and made their way back to the lighthouse, tended the horses and went inside. Daniel told his father he would do the signals today and got a charcoal pencil and paper with a list of messages about tides and ship comings and goings and the new thing of Captain Sandy's weather and tide forecast. He got Martin and said they could go on up a little early and wait for three o'clock and look for the first signal coming from the Milam plantation.

Martin followed Daniel up the lighthouse stairs, remembering how afraid he was years before when he first did this. He was much more confident now and looked out each small window as the climbed to the top and out on the circular balcony. Daniel got his signaling box with the mirror and shutter and got it all set up while Martin studied the surroundings. He had wanted to see the spot that the supply crew had seen the group of Indians on the oyster midden a while back. He had been thinking this might be his best chance at seeing them again. He could see the big white splotch of the oyster shell mounds because the sun angle lit it up brighter than the dark mud bank and green marsh grass.

Daniel had his apparatus all set and he saw the first flash come from the Milam plantation. He looked at the message from his father once more and then started his messages and Martin was again, as he was the first time he heard it, mesmerized by the thin wood shutter tapping as Daniel, skillfully slid it up and down at rapid and hesitated flashes of light to convey the messages. He finished in less than three minutes and waited to receive a message of the number of ships making it to the wharf that day and wrote it down on the paper. He sent another message about Captain Sandy's weather and tides and he was done for the day.

While he was setting up he had seen Martin peering out and even leaning forward over the balcony rail to get a closed look and thought of something. He took his equipment back inside and came back out with another wooden box and called Martin over and opened it and took out a finely made monocular. It had a clamp like hardware attached to the bottom with which Daniel affixed it to the balcony rail and motioned Martin to have a look and showed him the simple focus adjustment.

Martin had seen one in his father's study when he was a small child but this was much larger and much more powerful. Daniel said his father had gotten it recently to better identify ships, coming and going. Daniel had it set up looking out toward a ship sailing out of the river and told Martin to take a look. He did and could hardly believe how clearly he could see the details of the ship. Daniel showed him how to loosen the pivot knob and swing it over or down and tighten it back and refocus at a different distance. He swung it down to Captain Jones shanty and particularly on the Captain and exclaimed that he could see his pipe stem. Next, Daniel moved it on the west side and told Martin to look for his home and he did and could only make out the bluff with a barely visible small white splotch of their house.

He asked Daniel to move it around so he could look toward the southwest and when he did, Martin looked for the big oyster shell mound on the river and was amazed at how close and detailed it looked but there was no one around. He remembered that this was where Jacob had seen the Indian children and the one that was black. He moved it to the island closest to the midden and saw nothing and then to the next island further out in the marsh and saw nothing, then without the instrument he looked at the other islands out in the marsh and studied their profile shaped by the top of the tree lines and noticed one island that had a slightly higher looking profile and figured it had higher ground and it was longer than the rest. He focused the instrument on one end of that island and saw a hint of smoke coming up out of the trees. He moved the monocular over to see the middle of the island and saw nothing and then a little more to see the other end and saw another hint of smoke. He looked again to see if any tidal creeks came close, but the tide was not high enough in the creeks to see them clearly.

Next he had Daniel move it to see southward and he focused on the far southern point he had studied with his bare eyes earlier and exclaimed that he could see two canoes just coming into narrow split in the point. He hadn't been able to see earlier that the long point was actually a double point with a narrow sleuth of water separating the tip with a strip of beach on each side.

He watched intensely as the men drug the boats up a little on the beach and the four of them each pick up a basket and walked up into the edge of the woods and set them down, then go back and all four men, two on each side up toward the front, drag a canoe up into the woods and go back and get the other one and do the same, then pick up the baskets and disappear into the woods.

Martin was so excited that he was shaking and Daniel noticed. Martin thought about what he had just seen and asked Daniel if he could come back later in the afternoon when the tide was high so he could see what creeks came up near the long island and Daniel said they could. Martin thought to himself about how much he had already learned without even going out in his boat. They went back down the stairs and Daniel let his father know he was done and gave him the ship information he had written down on the paper with the messages. Charles studied it for a moment and put it in a box on his desk.

He told Daniel his mother had something for the three of them to do so they found her and she gave them a large metal pan and told Daniel to find his sister and for them to go pick some plums before they got to ripe and to watch out for snakes. They found Mary outside and they went through the gate and around to the south side of the compound where the wild plum trees were thickest and were loaded with plums, some still green and some turning yellow and some fully ripened and deep pinkish red.

Daniel said to watch for snakes. The ones in the branches are just Black Racers and were there waiting on a small bird coming for a plum and they were not to worry about. But the snakes on the ground could be rattlers and watch out for them. They bent down under the low canopy of plum trees and reached up to pick the ripe ones. Without having to move much they were piling the plums up in the pan because there were so many.

Mary saw the first Black snake and pointed it out to Martin. She showed no sign of alarm and he sensed it was ok. They watched it and it didn't move until they were quite close, then it showed why it was called a Black Racer and stretched out to five feet and raced across the midst of the thick plum tree canopy. Daniel and Mary had seen this a hundred times but were thrilled as always. Watching carefully before they stepped further into the thicket, they moved a couple more times and the pan was so full it was quite heavy for Daniel to lift.

They took them into Mrs. Dyer and she was thrilled and immediately emptied some into another pan and said they were for Captain Jones and the pilot crewman next time they went down to the beach and they said they would go now and left out the door. They found the Captain and one crew who had lost a coin flip to see who got to go out and meet the incoming ship. The other crew had just left and Captain Jones pointed to them as if he could see with his blind eyes, just getting past the surf with the ship in the distance. The Captain could smell the ripe plums and smiled and he said to set the pan in the shanty and there was a bowl they could pour some in to give to the pilot crew.

Martin held the pan out and let the top plums touch the Captains hand and he got a handful then he took them inside and poured some in the bowl and took them to the crew. They were all smoking little white clay pipes with thin stems and playing cards on a big shard of driftwood and thanked him.

Martin went back and started telling the Captain all he had done in the short time he had been there and particularly about seeing his first Indians and looking at the islands with the monocular and seeing him and his pipe just a little while before. The Captain may have had a blank stare out into the ocean but all his other senses were attuned to Martin's excitement as he puffed the pipe out of the corner of his mouth. Martin told him he had made arrangements for taking his boat back on the barge and thanked him again and promised to do a thorough and fine job of restoring it and take him and Daniel and Mary out in it next spring.

The old captain told Martin that he had spent time on the point of land that he had seen the Indians on starting about ten years before the War of Independence. He said he was quite young at that time. The British strictly controlled and levied fees on everything, coming and going into the Savannah River, but there was a lot of back door shipping happening in Warsaw Sound and loading and unloading at Wilmington Island. Ships were few and far between and passage could only happen at full tide and was tricky and he spent weeks sometime in between ships, camped on that point. He said it was a rough life, but he was young and it was an adventure and that point was a nice place most days, winter and summer, with the prevailing southeasterlies keeping the bugs away and moderating the temperatures. The boat right there that is now yours, I traded for off a ship of plundered goods that I piloted into Warsaw Sound. Their story was they had traded for it in the Caribbean but who knows, but it is a finely made English pilot boat, that's for sure. Back then, I was both an oarsman and the pilot. There were only three of us, not like now with a pilot and three crew. The Indians there didn't care that my two mates and me were around and we stayed out of their way. They camped and gathered and processed seafood there. The onshore ocean breeze blew almost every day and they must have had fifty drying racks with fish and conch meat drying and every week or so they loaded up their canoes and left for a few days, I guess to trade or take it to a village or something.

Occasionally, they brought some fish or conchs to us but we couldn't understand each other much but we understood that they were friendly and generous. They smiled and said a word, "gereg" or something like that and it must have been a greeting of some sort because it felt friendly and they said it over and over. We were there for a few years, until the Brits tightened up and kept a ship anchored in the Wilmington river close to where it dumps into the sound to restrict comings and goings, then me and my mates went legal and brought my new boat here and I have been here since.

Martin enjoyed the story and remembered he had wanted to look again with the monocular at high tide. Daniel got the now empty bowl from the crew and dumped the rest of the plums in it and took a handful more to the Captain and they said good night to the Captain and crew still playing cards who were staying the night expecting to get a job in the morning on a ship they could see now, far out on the horizon and coming their way.

Once again, Martin, Daniel, and Mary climbed to the top of the high sand dune between the beach and the lighthouse. They were earlier today and the long shadow of the lighthouse hadn't quite reached the bottom of the sand dune but it was still four or five times longer than the lighthouse was tall. Mary played walking with one foot inside the shadow and one foot outside on the light colored sand, all the way to the compound gate. They stopped at the house to clean the sand off their feet. Once inside, Mary went her way, and Daniel found his father in the small brick lamp oil building, filling two copper jugs with handles with lamp oil. Daniel said he was taking Martin up top to look through the monocular and his father said his timing was perfect and handed each an oil jug, checking that the small top was screwed on tightly. Off you go, he said.

Once up on the lighthouse balcony, Daniel asked Martin where he wanted to start and he said west so he attached it on the Savannah side of the balcony. Martin could see the barge without the monocular but wanted to see it better. He looked with it and saw the barge at anchor, where they had drifted it out from Lazaretto earlier with the outgoing tide and drifted along in the channel close to the beach a little less than a mile from the landing and anchored it to wait until the tide got high.

Now, a few hundred yards away from the barge, he saw the pulling boat with two men on the oars and two more seated, approaching the barge. The tide was about at its peak and way up on the beach and he continued to watch as two men climbed onto the barge and pulling up the anchor, preparing to move the barge way up on the beach with the tide at its highest. He saw his boat on the barge. He asked Daniel to move he monocular again but this time to let him assist so he could get some practice doing it himself. Daniel said that the most important thing was to keep one hand holding it at all times and with the other hand loosen or tighten the clamp.

Next, they moved over to the south side and Martin looked at the double pointed island and didn't see any smoke or activity. He looked at how he would go there from Tybee and saw that going outside in the ocean along the beach and coming in at Warsaw Sound would be the shortest way if the weather were not rough and the tide high enough and then another way through a shallow inlet a little way south of the Back River and snake his way to the little inlet that split the point.

Then he looked at how he might get to the long island where he had seen the smoke. He looked more closely at the long island and let out a scream that startled Daniel. He said there were two canoes coming from the direction of the double point island and about three fourths of the way to the long island and they were not in a creek but poling the canoes directly across the marsh to the island. The tide was extra high and only the tips of the grass were above the water. Martin said that the canoes had baskets heaped up in the middle, probably with seafood. He let Daniel watch for a few minutes and Daniel said they were across the main part of the marsh and were now in a creek and had switched to paddles. He let Martin watch again and he looked ahead to see if there might be a place they were headed for. He saw a place where he creek came up close to the island and a little bluff and exclaimed that there was a group of people on the edge of the bank with smoke drifting up nearby.

He switched back to the canoes that were very close to the island now and watched as they nosed into the bank. He couldn't tell if it was men or women or children on the bank, but they crowded around both sides of the boats and the baskets were carried up on the bluff to the edge of the woods. Martin said he couldn't count but it may have been a dozen or more people. Then to his surprise, he saw two men go back to one canoe and push off and continue on further down the creek with a couple baskets still inside. In about a hundred feet, the creek veered away from the island in a hard curve, headed back out toward the middle of the marsh. As it first began to curve, the canoe forked off left on a tiny creek, not much more than a ditch, but plenty full enough now at high tide for the canoe to swiftly follow it along the edge of the island a forth of a mile or so. Just barely at the tip of the island, the canoe pulled up on the bank but all Martin could see was the last foot of it sticking out of the brambles. It stayed only a minute or two and then was backed out and the men simply faced the other way and paddled back to the first camp without the baskets of whatever it was.

Martin looked back at the tip where they had just dropped off the two baskets and saw smoke going up out of the tree line. He let Daniel look and told him what he had just seen. He looked again and watched the two men return to the other canoe, and more people came down and dragged both boats up in the woods and out of sight. Martin looked at Daniel and asked, why would they have two cooking fires? Daniel said he didn't know but most of the cooking was at the first spot because that's where most of the baskets were off loaded. Martin looked again at the area of the second stop to see if there was a creek to access it from another direction and he was surprised to not see one. He guessed there would be one around the tip of the island near there but could not see that side. It was getting late so they put things away and headed back down. Martin thought about what he had seen on the way down and onto the front porch where he almost tripped over one of the two washtubs sat out for their baths. They didn't have any water this time and Daniel said they would have to haul their own from the kitchen pump. Martin, still going over in his mind's eye, what he had seen of the Indians, almost stumbled again over the other tub. Daniel asked him if he was okay and he said yes and began paying a little more attention to what he was doing.

After supper, Martin told Charles and his wife about his idea of taking Alice with him to the Indian Islands to talk to the lady who he assumed was still the chief or leader. He said that if they thought it was okay, she could come on the supply boat next week. He said also that he would speak to Henry about it when he came in a couple days on the supply boat to check on things. They thought for a bit and Margo told Martin that they both loved Alice and how Charles had picked her up from the pluff mud and brought her back here and cared and prayed for her to survive that first day that they had brought her back. She added how they had kept up with her all these years and were so happy for her.

Of course, they would want her to find her parents if they were still alive and would do anything in their power to help that happen and she said she was sure she was speaking for Charles too and he nodded in agreement. She had heard the whole story from his mother several times, about the kind Indian lady helping Alice and her family and the group of runaways. She said she hoped that the lady was still alive and couldn't imagine how y'all would go about contacting them.

Martin said he didn't know himself and told them what they had seen a little while ago. Charles said that from what he had heard, they were extremely shy and private and had heard the story from Jacob about seeing a group at the big oyster midden on the Back river but that was highly unusual because most people that saw them, saw them going away to the woods. He said they would go along with anything he and Henry decided on.

Daniel and Mary hadn't said anything but Mary was touched by Martin's efforts to do something so noble and she was impressed at his maturity and earnest concern and his adult type of discussion with her parents. He normally didn't act like that and usually appeared rather absent-minded and a bit childlike. Charles added that the Indians may be less likely to run away, seeing a black woman and a young man approach rather than a white man or two. He said he didn't blame them because he knew local colonials had randomly taken pot shots at them and bragged about it later. He also knew that at one time there had been many more of them on Ossabaw and Warsaw islands until many died of disease and the rest were run off by land grabbers. He said legally, they were the rightful owners of those and the Indian Islands but no one cared. He said that at the rate they had been dying off, this might be about the last of them soon and that will be it. Martin didn't like hearing all that, the last part especially.

Meanwhile back at the Milam's, Henry had been checking on how the ice in the icebox was holding up. He had chipped a lot out to show people and couldn't really tell how long it would have lasted if left alone but there was only a small piece left after six days. He went to the boathouse for Johnny to help him uncover the stored ice in the sawdust pile. They removed the large canvas cover and shoveled away the sawdust to expose a chunk big enough to saw off a piece. The ice had melted some but there was plenty left. Johnny used the measure stick Henry had brought and sawed the length he needed, then sawed the width and they slid it out to the wagon and then shoveled the sawdust back and covered it up. Back at the house, they lowered the new chunk of ice in the copper tub after Henry had put the remaining pieces of ice in a big pot and took it to the kitchen and put in a big pot of yaupon that had been made. Next he sliced a half dozen oranges from the yard and squeezed them in the iced tea and stirred it, then handed the heavy pot to Johnny and said it was for him and the others at the boathouse and said he would ride him over in the buggy. He dropped Johnny off and the other men immediately surrounded him when they saw he had a treat.

Henry had been thinking on something since he and Johnny had been to get the ice. He was thinking about a bigger version of an icebox. Big enough to walk in and store many big chunks of ice, with a large door and a loading dock about the same height of a wagon bed. He was thinking of wall, ceiling, and floor panels, over a foot thick.

He thought it might be too big of a job for the cabinetmaker that built the icebox in the house. It would take a couple good carpenters and need to be built on sight or maybe the foundation and floor and roof built on site and the wall, ceiling panels, and the door be built in the shop and assembled on site. He also thought about the most practical location to make loading and unloading easy. He even thought about a new heavy duty insulated wagon design for deliveries. Henry liked all these new possibilities and decided to write to John about his ideas and while in town today, talk to Jason, the cabinet maker, about his involvement, and drop the letter to John off at the stage depot to be delivered to Darien on tomorrows run. He went back to his office and did a rough sketch of a building that was basically a very large icebox with thick insulated walls, floor, and ceiling with a loading porch and a simple gable roof. He would leave the details out to be discussed with Jason.

He was glad to get this done today because he knew he would be gone to Tybee for the next two days. He decided to go now to Savannah to talk to the cabinetmaker and drop off the letter so he could be back early enough to be with his family some before his trip to Tybee.

Henry stopped off at the stage depot first to send his letter to John. He was thrilled to see Jehu relaxing out front and went over to say hello. Jehu was a beautiful sight, especially when he smiled with his white hair and beard and white teeth and he had a pleasant way about him. He asked about Martin right off and Henry told him he was gone to Tybee for couple months and would come see him when he got back. He said that Lancy Jenkins wants to see him too.

Henry shook his hand and thought to himself what an amazing story about him and he may have never known it if Martin had ridden in the coach with him or he may not have met the couple from Walterboro or Thomas, the engineer from Boston if they had gone back by boat as planned. He said goodbye to Jehu and went inside to pay his postage and send the letter and left for Jason's shop nearby. He found Jason busy with his helper, repairing a large table, set upside downwards on his workbench.

Jason looked up and said he had been thinking about that icebox and wondered how it was working. Henry said it was working just fine and said he had another one for him to build, but a much bigger one and asked if he had time to sit with him a little while to talk about it. Jason said sure and told his helper to clean up the shop while he was with Henry. Jason swept off a small worktable and pulled up two stools. Henry showed him his rough plan and said it would be somewhere close to the river at the Milam plantation.

He explained that they were keeping the ice deep in a sawdust pile now but needed something that could hold much more. Henry told Jason he needed his help in designing the panels first, then build them in his shop, then to supervise their assembly on a foundation and floor that he would have built. Henry said he wanted to use cotton again for insulation and he thought the panel thickness should be a foot and a half or two feet thick. After the wall and roof panels are put together and the basic box is there, he would have carpenters build a simple gabled roof on it.

Also, he would be putting a tabby concrete mix on the floor, about three to four inches thick, sloped to a drain. Jason said it was a bigger job than he had ever done but he was willing to give it his best. He said he would need more help than just he and his helper because the panels would be heavy to build and move around. Henry said he would pay for whatever it took and if space was a problem, he could arrange to have the panels picked up as they were built.

Henry went on more and shared his ice business vision with Jason and told him that he could see many "ice houses" and "ice boxes" in the future and that's why he was willing to pay him to develop a system that could go together tightly and accurately and could be shipped to anywhere in the south and that he expected Savannah and Charleston to be the main areas of business and there would be a need to have a bigger shop and more workers.

Jason was a bit stunned at the idea because he could never have imagined making iceboxes, which he didn't even know such a thing existed until recently. He had always thought about tables, chairs, shelves, and cabinets for what he might be building in a small shop with a helper. Henry told him that he was gonna be gone to Tybee for a couple days and could come back at the end of the week to see what he had come up with. Henry had an envelope with a bank note inside and gave it to him and told

Jason it could get him started.

Jason saw the amount Henry had written on the outside and Jason said that was more than ample and turned to his helper and said he could have the rest of the day off and told Henry he would get started drawing the plans this afternoon. Henry told Jason that he wanted everything to be heavy duty and high quality so that future repairs would be minimized and a system that could be duplicated. Also, he didn't expect to get everything right the first time around but improve the system as they learned what they were doing. He mentioned that the inside and outside of his panels would be sheathed over again on site with cypress and sealed with oil to keep out moisture and that the door needed to have an extra tight seal when closed, like on the icebox he had built. He also mentioned that the cotton would need to be tamped down in the panels so there would not be any voids to compromise the insulating effects.

Henry said he needed to go be with his family before his trip and that he would see Jason on Friday and shook Jason's hand and said he had confidence in his ability and in the prosperity that was ahead for them both. Jason hadn't ever had a customer like Henry that was so sure of what he wanted and willing to pay for it handsomely.

Henry set out for home feeling good about his day. As he went along on the familiar way home, his mind wandered to many things. He thought to himself that he was enjoying this new business venture and hoped that soon his friend, John would be able to move his family up to Savannah. He didn't have that many friends that he considered confidants. He and his wife were well known around town, mainly because of his name and went to a few social events but were not that outgoing. He liked accomplishing things and making things go smoothly and spent most of his time doing that or being with his family.

Many of his Savannah friends would not understand it but he had meaningful relationships with the people on their place. Jacob, Johnny, Alice and every man, woman, and child there were important to him, like his own family, and he lived with a desire for their betterment. He had learned this from his parents. As he contemplated this, he felt gratitude welling up from inside and felt the richness of it. He realized that he could have been taught anything as a child and would have believed it to be so and not understand the things he does about the human rights and equality of all people.

He was aware that his father's good will supported the unique way that they ran their place and he thought about the time when his father would not be around and it would be on his shoulders to continue the protection of his family as well as his extended family of the workers that made the Milam place possible. He had some ideas about dealing with the changes that he knew were ahead and that was another reason he hoped John would come to live there, so he could have someone to talk confidently with to help refine his ideas and strategies. These thoughts of life without his father around had been coming to him more often, especially since hearing about his recent health issues. Henry didn't like thinking of these things but he felt a responsibility to the people of the Milam place like his father always had.

The carriage horse must have sensed his inattention and had slowed way down to a slow walk on its own. A big wagon loaded with the sawpit workers going home for the day, pulled up to the road ahead, waiting for him to pass. Henry's horse stopped suddenly waiting for a command and Henry came back from his absence of mind and waved the wagon to go ahead of them and jiggled the reins slightly and continued on.

He left his thoughts about his father and resumed his normal pace and was soon home. Claudia and his children were on the front porch with his mother and father and he pulled up and called his kids to go with him to put the horse up. They liked going to the horse barn and being with their father. Willy, the carriage driver, was at the barn and told Henry to go on home, and he would take care of the horse, so he and the kids walked home and onto the porch with Walter and Martha. Claudia had made some iced yaupon with orange juice and Alice had come over and they sat and had tea.

Alice knew Henry was leaving in the morning on the supply boat and had something to tell him and waited for the right time to say it. Everyone sipped and talked and Henry told about what he had done in Savannah. Henry said that he first went to the coach depot and was pleasantly surprised to see Jehu and chat with him a bit. He was doing just fine and was most interested about Martin's well-being. They hadn't met Jehu but he had become a familiar figure to everybody because of the stories that Martin had told about him.

Next, he told about going to the cabinetmakers shop and they went over a plan for a very large ice storage house and that went well and Jason was to draw some plans and he was to return on Friday to review them. He said he liked Jason. Everyone saw how enthusiastic Henry was when he discussed the ice business. Walter said he had skipped his Savannah visit today and hoped his friends were able to manage their rum without him but he doubted it and Martha said he had managed to make a mess at home but was glad to have him around anyway. She said that it was odd not having Martin around because he was so active.

Without him around, the pace of things had slowed. She said it would be quite odd when they were both gone the next couple days and mentioned that she had set out a box of things for him to take tomorrow for Martin and the Dyers. She asked him to remind Martin to be careful and not to do anything to worry the Dyers. She told Henry that Charles ended his messages to them every day that Martin was well and accounted for and it made her feel good that he was in good hands. Henry reminded her that Martin was often distracted but was sensible and an advanced boater and swimmer.

Alice had been quiet and Henry asked how she had been and she said just fine and had not noticed much difference since her pregnancy except that she was hungry a lot. She said she had something for Henry to tell Martin that she had recently remembered and that was the name of the Indian lady who had helped her family and the others on Tybee. She said she remembered it the morning after Martin left.

She said her name was "Ayana" and she thought Martin should know because it could be helpful. Henry went into his father's office and wrote it down on a scrap of paper so he would not forget and went back outside. Alice was pleased to have conveyed the message and said she hoped Martin had some success in his search. Martha thought to herself how much she wished Alice would find out something about her family, whether it is good or bad, so she could either rejoice or mourn, and at least it could be settled for her. Alice said she had said what she wanted to and was ready to go home and wished Henry well on his trip and said goodnight. Martha said to wait, because she had something for her and Johnny and left and came back with a still warm sweet potato soufflé. She said it was Henry's favorite and she had made one for him and Claudia too. Alice said it was Johnny's favorite too and everything was her favorite lately. She hugged them all and especially Henry and said to hug Martin for her.

When Henry heard about the pie he said it was time for his supper and hugged his parents and said goodnight. He went to his end of the house and had an extra special supper. Claudia was always worried when Henry or anybody went somewhere in a boat. She had been pleased when they had to return by coach on his recent trip to Darien. She was raised on nearby Wilmington Island with no bridge connecting it to the mainland and boats were used often. For some this may have made them more comfortable with boating but it had the opposite effect with Claudia. She remembered how often the mishaps had been, and some deaths by drowning, and was always nervous about boating. They had their supper and sent the kids off to bed and she and Henry enjoyed some quiet and intimate time together.

Back on Tybee, the day before Henry was to come, Martin and Daniel were up early thinking about what to do. Martin said he would like to look out over the Indian Islands at least once every day and also he wanted to teach Daniel how to sail. Maybe they could do both today and Daniel said there was no reason why not and that his mother and father had given him the whole time he was here off. Martin said that tomorrow he should go with Henry to check on the bridge and roadwork but Daniel was welcome to come along for that.

They had a quick breakfast and were at the top of the lighthouse just as the sun had risen. Daniel tied a small rope on the base of the monocular in case it was dropped while clamping it on and off the rail. Martin started by looking at Lazaretto and saw that the men were up and the crew that were working on the brickwork had just left to come to the lighthouse. The Milam carpenters were leaving for the barge on the beach at the same time the two guards and the wagon were leaving the lighthouse to meet them at the barge with the wagon to haul materials over to the big bridge. Next, Martin looked at what he now called Claw Island, the island with the point that looked split with a narrow inlet separating the point. It did not have a name on his chart. He yelped and startled Daniel and said there was a huge canoe near the end of the island. He looked closely and said there were nine men paddling the canoe that must be forty feet long and it was pulling up on the beach. He let Daniel look and Daniel said he had heard his father talk about big voyaging canoes that the Ogeechee Indians used for trading.

Martin looked again and the nine men had gotten out and appeared to be resting or waiting and were all looking over the marsh toward the long island. Martin swung the monocular over that way and yelped again and said there were four canoes with three men in two of them and two men in each of the others and it was difficult to tell for sure, but two of the men looked black. There were big baskets of something stacked in between the men. They watched for half an hour, as the four heavily loaded canoes slowly made their way to Claw Island where the big canoe was and pulled up beside it.

The men waiting on the beach came down to meet them and seemed to greet each other briefly and began to set the bundles from the big canoe onto the beach and load the baskets from the smaller canoes onto the large one. Then, they all put the bundles from the beach onto the four smaller canoes. They faced off and extended hands to each other's shoulders and the big canoe shoved off but with eleven men, two more than it had come with, and it was the two that were black that had come from the long island.

The four canoes followed with two fewer men than they had come with, and with the traded goods. The big canoe bridged the choppy waves and was much faster than the smaller boats. Martin and Daniel continued to take turns watching the boats go away from the point and then the smaller ones veered off to the right and into the flooded marsh grass and each put their paddles down and picked up a pole and with one poling on each side it was amazing how quickly they slid through the flooded marsh. Martin moved the monocular and swung it over to the long island and saw smoke at both ends of the island again.

It was obvious that the four canoes were headed back to the long island loaded with a different cargo and two less men who had looked black. They stopped watching after a few minutes and discussed what may be in the bundles but didn't have a good answer. Daniel said that the baskets that were loaded in the big canoe seemed heavy and he said it could be shells or salt but he knew the Indians traded salt but not as big a quantity as that.

Then he lit up and yelled that he knew what it was and had Martin's attention. He said it was crabs packed in wet moss to keep them alive. He said he had seen the pilot crews with a couple baskets full on the beach one day and said they cooked a dozen or so each night and kept the rest alive by adding a little seawater occasionally on top of the moss to keep it moist. He asked them how long they would stay alive like that and they told him a week or a little more if they were kept wet and it was an old Indian trick.

Daniel said the big canoe had probably come from inland Georgia somewhere. Martin said he remembered a river called the Ogeechee on one of his father's charts and it meandered for sixty or more miles inland and then Daniel lit up again and said that the bundles from the big canoe were probably skins or furs. Martin agreed instantly with him and was impressed at how clever Daniel had been and asked why the big canoe took back two black people, but Daniel didn't have an answer for that.

Martin looked again and the smaller canoes were already halfway across the marsh to Long Island. He remarked to Daniel that the reason they were able to go so swiftly was the water was smooth across the top of the grass and the Indians were in unison in their movements together with the poles. He also commented that they kept the poles at a low angle, probably so they would push against the lower part of the grass and not sink the pole down in the mud.

They were now out in the creek and had switched to the paddles and getting up close to the island and just as yesterday some people came out on the bank awaiting them at the first fire spot. Three boats pulled into the bank and the people started quickly unloading the bundles but the fourth canoe continued on and veered off on the ditch and continued to the tip of the island and pulled in again with only the end of the canoe exposed like yesterday, and in a few minutes, backed out and returned to the other three boats and people came down and pulled all four boats up into the woods. Other than the smoke, there was nothing else visible to let you know any-one was there.

Martin was silent and thinking to himself. Finally, he said that he and Alice should take his boat strait up to the first fire spot and talk to them. Daniel said they might act shy like his father had said, and then what? Martin said he didn't know what but maybe Alice would have some ideas. Daniel took the monocular off the rail and put it up and they went down from the lighthouse and went inside and saw Mary and Charles and Mar-go at the kitchen table. Martin told them what they had just seen. Charles said that was crabs and the Indians used to trade crabs and conchs packed in wet moss that could be kept alive for a week or more and hauled them up the Ogeechee to trade.

Charles said the most interesting part of what y'all saw was the two black men. I think they were runaways being aided and hidden in the big canoe and carried inland to make their way north. The Indians have a history of helping runaways. There has always been a steady stream of runaways coming here, hoping to get a ship or anyway out. The Savan-nah paper had rewards every week posted for capturing runaways that escaped. Martin went up to the loft and brought the chart of the area his father had given him and spread it out on the table. He showed them the island he called Claw island and the thin inlet separating the tip and then moved his finger across the marsh to Long island and to the two places where they had seen smoke and told how on both days they had looked, supplies were delivered to both spots. He asked Charles why they would have two cooking fires and Charles said he didn't really know but it may be a separate camp for runaways. Daniel told about most of the items each day went to the first spot and Charles said that there must be two groups, one bigger than the other.

These new ideas excited Martin because it seemed possible Alice's family might be there. Charles said he had to go meet the masonry repair crew at the gate who were walking from Lazaretto and left the table. Mary asked the boys what they were gonna do today and Martin said he thought he would give Daniel his first sailing lesson. She asked him when was hers and he was surprised that she was interested and he said soon after if she liked and she said she would. He said he would send Daniel up for her when they got back. They asked Mrs. Dyer for some leftovers for a lunch and she put some biscuits and bacon and hard cheese in a cloth bag and a canteen of water and they headed out for where the barge was.

Martin's boat was stowed well above the high water mark with the sail and paddle underneath along with the safety float. They turned it over and Martin put the mast in the slot with the sail rolled up on it and told Daniel that all he had to do was move from one side of the boat to the other when he was told. He said it was quite easy and he would understand it after a short while. He told him that if the boat turned over not to worry because it happened sometimes but could be righted easily and reminded him about the safety float and that the boat would not sink.

The tide was still high and they dragged the boat through the light surf and Martin told Daniel to get in and stay in the middle. Martin hopped in next and put the paddle through the hoop and out the back for a rudder and pulled the sail and it furled out from the mast. The wind was out of the south and was mostly blocked by the land until they got out a ways and Martin asked Daniel to move over to the right side and he tightened the sail up and the little narrow boat shot forward toward Daufuskie. The further out they got the better the breeze and Martin maintained his direction and Daniel stayed put.

He then told Daniel that they were going to do something called coming about and said to move to the other side when he said to. He pulled hard on the tiller paddle and the boat changed directions and the wind filled the other side of the sail. Martin said switch and Daniel moved over and again the little boat shot forward, this time back toward the west side of Tybee and toward Lazaretto, and Daniel was grinning real big. Just behind the breakers Martin came about again and told Daniel to move again and they were headed for Hilton Head, and they stayed in that direction for a few miles and passed Hilton Head and on out into the ocean about a mile and came about again to head back.

A strong gust came and the boat almost went over but they both hung out as far as possible and the little boat planed across the top of the water for a half mile. Daniel was still grinning and didn't understand how close they came to going over. Martin continued back and forth for a couple more times, then headed straight for Captain Jones shanty and landed on the beach there. The pilot crewmen had been watching them tack back and forth and a few came down to the edge as they came in.

The tide had started going out so there was no need to pull the boat up far and Martin pulled the mast out of the slot and left it lying in the boat. The men examined every part of the little boat and one picked up the bow to gauge its weight and said it was light as a feather. Martin and Daniel walked up to the Captain. A pilot was with him and had been describing the little sailboat with the two boys, as it had tacked back and forth. Martin said hello and touched the Captain's shoulder. He was very happy about them being there. Martin told Daniel if he would go get Mary, he would take her out and he could visit with the Captain until they got back. Daniel was happy with the idea of Mary having the fun he had and said sure he would go get her.

Captain Jones asked Martin to walk him down to the little boat so his hands could see it for him. Martin agreed and took hold of his arm and the old man lifted himself up and Martin guided him to the boat and stopped and told him that they were a foot away. He inched closer until his shin slightly touched the hull then bent down and felt it with his hand. One of the men brought his chair and he sat close and let his hand clasp the edge of the bow area and he felt the thickness and then got up and bent down and asked to have his chair moved a few feet and felt more of the hull and got up again and asked for his chair to be moved again until he had felt all along the boat hull.

He told Martin that it had the thinnest hull of any dugout he had ever seen and it must be a good sailor and Martin said it was and the only boat he had ever sailed except being a passenger on Captain Ben's sharpie. The Captain told him that he was gonna have a fun time with his old boat when he got it finished. He said it was only twice as long but ten times as big and that boats were that way. Martin picked up the safety float his father got him and put it in the Captains hand and explained what it was and where he got it and the Captain complimented his father and said how something like that could have saved a few lives in his time. He got up and put his arm out and Martin took it and walked him up to his spot by the shanty and a crewman put his chair in place and he felt it with his leg and seated himself.

Daniel and Mary yelled from the top of the sand dunes and ran down and out to the shanty and up to the Captain, breathing heavily. The Captain smiled in their direction and said, well if it isn't Anne Bonny about to go out on Captain Calico Jack's ship! Daniel and Martin didn't know what he was talking about but Mary did and told the Captain that she would be needing a haircut and some trousers and a jerkin soon. She and the Captain laughed loudly but not the boys because they didn't understand what they were talking about.

Daniel told Mary to relax and simply do what Martin said and she would be fine. Mary reacted and said she would be able to do as good or better than Daniel had done and her quick answer surprised Martin and made him smile to himself. They went down to the boat and Daniel grabbed the bow and swung it around and pulled it out about knee deep. Mary got in and Martin told her where to sit and to simply switch sides when he said to. The boat was headed in the direction of Hilton Head and

Martin hopped in and pulled on the sail and the mast spun as the sail un-furled and at the same time he pulled hard on the paddle(rudder) and the boat shot out with him and Mary side by side.

He could see a few hundred yards away where the ocean waves were choppy from the wind having fetched up around Tybee and came about before getting there. He didn't want to blow over, especially on Mary's first sail. He told her to switch as he came about and they headed toward Turtle Island and he steered the boat so the wind was from mostly behind them and stayed on that coarse for fifteen minutes until he could see the beach and the sand dunes more clearly and told Mary to look for pirates because that was Turtle Island ahead.

She had heard the stories about Turtle Island and looked as he had said, then saw his smirk and knew he was kidding her. He came about again and he thought to himself how quickly she caught on and how smoothly and in unison with him she had moved without him having to say anything. Now, Martin headed for the sound that separated Daufuskie and Hilton Head.

His thoughts went to Alice's story of her family's last leg of their es-cape, waiting on two boats, and proper tides, and leaving in the night to be rowed across to Tybee beach. He pictured two boats with the twelve runaways in them landing on Tybee at night and young little Alice with her family and how brave they were. Mary noticed his blank look and nudged him and he snapped out of his stupor. This wasn't the first time Mary had seen him daydreaming or whatever it was that he drifted into and wondered about him being like this and wondered if there might be something wrong with him.

A crewman was on his knees beside the Captain, telling every detail of Martin and Mary in the little boat. He described their direction, toward what island and how far or how close to each island and from what angle they were to the wind. The Captain was enjoying every minute of it and in his mind's eye was a perfect vision of all the sights again that he had seen more than a thousand times. Martin came about again and headed toward where the barge was pulled up on Tybee and just outside of the breakers, came about again and ran along the length of the beach until he got to the Captain and went in and grounded.

Daniel was awaiting them in the water and pulled the mast out and wound the sail up while a couple crewmen drug the boat up on the beach. Martin said to keep going and when they had gotten well above the high water line he said that was enough. Mary had gone over and stood by the Captain. He could feel her excitement as she carried on about how thrill-ing it was. Martin and Daniel turned the boat upside down and stowed the few loose things under it and went over to Mary and the Captain. The Captain said that this was his best day in a long time and squeezed their hands. Several of the crewmen looked on in pleasure of seeing him so happy. Martin told the Captain that they were gonna go now and be back as soon as he could and the Captain laughed and said he would keep an eye on his boat. Before they could leave, he told Daniel to give a message to his father that there was word from the crewmen that there was to be a duel sometime in the next week or two on Tybee. Someone in Savannah had arranged for two pilot boats to bring the two participants and their witnesses to Tybee for their meeting. They were traveling from Virginia now and a day was to be set once both parties were in Savannah. Daniel was not surprised because this had been happening a few times a year for as long as he could remember and many years before that, but it was always a serious matter and Charles would be glad to know about it. Daniel thanked the Captain and said he would tell him as soon as he got back.

The three of them climbed to the top of the dunes and the sun cast a shadow of the lighthouse across the light sand and Daniel commented that by the length of the shadow, it must be three o'clock. Daniel liked to do this and was usually close in his guess. When they went through the gate five minutes later, Charles was just coming down from the lighthouse and asked them how they had done. Mary was first to say how much fun she had sailing and wanted to do it more. Daniel said the same thing, but with less excitement. Martin said it was much more fun than sailing in the Savannah and Wilmington rivers and added how the crewmen had described the event to Captain Jones and he had said it was his best day in a long time.

Daniel passed on what the Captain said about the duel, and Charles took a deep breath and said he was tired of that and it was time for Georgia to outlaw it. He added that all the other states around had and that is why people from all over came there to do it. He said he hated it more that it might happen while Martin was here. Mary went to find her mother to tell her about her sailing adventure. She suggested they go pick some more plums and Martin asked for two pans so he could take some to the men at the landing.

She said that was a thoughtful idea and handed them two large pans, one extra-large and they headed for the plum trees, which grew so thick that they created a continuous canopy. They picked plums for the next two hours, until both pans were heaped up and took them back to the house to Margo. She was surprised to see how many they picked in such a short time and Daniel said the trees were full and they were easy to pick. She poured most of the large pan into a big pot on the wood stove and the rest into a big clay dish on the table for everyone to eat when they wanted and had Daniel take the other pan down in the root cellar where they would stay cool until tomorrow.

It was getting late and they got their own wash tubs out and Daniel took Mary's to her and they took turns hauling buckets of water to fill Mary's tub, then filled their own and got cleaned up a little while before dark. Daniel asked Martin if he wanted to go up top and look through the monocular and he said he would, so they first found Charles and had him fill two cans of lamp oil to save him the trouble the next day and went up the stairs to the lighthouse balcony. Martin set the monocular up to look south but saw nothing and then to look at Long Island and saw some smoke from the same places but no canoes or people anywhere. Daniel suggested Turtle Island and Martin was surprised at himself for not having searched it before because he had been obsessed with the Indian Islands. He moved the rig over to the northwest side of the balcony and set up to look at Turtle Island.

There was a sloop anchored in the Harbor River, next to Turtle Island and two longboats had just left it and were loaded with something and headed for the island. The tide was low and they pulled up to an oyster midden bank where they could avoid walking up in mud. A narrow strip of land with scrub cedars came out from the island to where they had landed. The men got out of the boats and walked up the oyster bank and followed the strip of land to the woods and disappeared. Martin was excited and let Daniel take a look at the two longboats. They waited a while and kept looking for the men to return to the longboats but darkness was coming so they put the monocular up and went down.

Margo called them to the supper table, where she had grits, fish, and biscuits set out. Charles asked if they had seen anything new and Martin told about the sloop and the two longboats and said it got dark before they could see anything else. Charles said that there is no telling what the rest of the story may be but it was probably nothing about it legal. Martin asked if there were so many big snakes and alligators there, why didn't the outlaws get bitten or eaten?

Charles said that they probably did but when you are a desperate outlaw, the risk of snakes and alligators are less than the risk of hanging and those big rattlesnakes and alligators represented safety to them because even the law stayed away. He looked at both Daniel and Martin and told them firmly not to be getting any ideas about going over there. They both nodded in agreement.

Mary said she hoped that all the outlaws stayed on Turtle Island and didn't come over to Tybee. Martin thought to himself that when he got a little older he might go to Turtle Island because all this talk about it made him want to go. Charles said that Henry would not be in until low tide in the late afternoon tomorrow and he wanted them to take the wagon and pick him up. They happily agreed.

Margo reminded them about their supper and talking stopped and eating took over. For desert, Margo served bowls of the still hot plums she had cooked down with sugar. She gave each a biscuit to go with it and they ate it up heartily. Mary said she hadn't forgotten about taking Martin on the tabby horses and would one day soon when they weren't being used. He said he looked forward to that. Charles told everyone to come out on the porch to sit a while and they did.

The sound of the waves and their full stomachs made the three drowsy and excused themselves shortly and went to bed while Charles and his wife lingered a while. Lying in bed before they went to sleep, Martin asked if Daniel would go with him very early up top to look again at Turtle Island. Daniel said sure and he liked to watch the sunrise from there.

The next thing Martin knew was the tapping of the broom stick on their floor by Margo as she did every morning. They went down and Daniel said he was taking Martin up top to see the sunrise and Charles said he had filled two cans of lamp oil and he would appreciate it if they would take them up. He said his trip up without carrying them was much easier. They ate their grits and eggs and bacon quickly and hurried out and got the cans of oil and went up top.

The sun was just about to peek over the horizon as Martin got the monocular set up and peered through it to Turtle Island, but the longboats and the sloop were gone. He was a bit disappointed but not much because the Indian Islands and Alice's parents were his main concern. He moved the rig over to the south side and looked at Long island first and saw some smoke at the usual spots and then swung the rig over to look at the claw pointed island and saw nothing there.

Daniel was looking east at the half risen sun and Martin joined him. He told Daniel something his father had told him was important and to never forget because it was helpful in understanding how to navigate by the heavenly bodies. Martin said, no, the sun is not coming up and thought to himself this was fun and he would lead Daniel on a little more before he revealed the truth of the matter. He said again, no, Daniel, it may look like it but the sun is definitely not coming up and I will bet you a half-dime it is not.

Daniel was getting a bit heated and said he would take the bet but Martin, knowing he was right, called off the bet and then explained the facts. Daniel, he said, I too thought the sun came up every morning, until my father explained that the sun does not come up but that we, here on earth, were rolling over toward the sun and because of the giant size of things, it only appears the sun is rising.

At about noon we will be right under it and then as we spin some more we will be in the earth's shadow or what we call nighttime, then we will spin around more until it will look again like the sun is rising. Daniel had a look of recognition and cracked a slight smile and thanked Martin for not taking his money and sharing his father's knowledge. Daniel said he had a few things to do inside and told Martin that he could look with the monocular for a bit.

Martin set up the monocular on the west side and looked back toward Lazaretto and noticed two pilot boats, one behind the other, moving swiftly with the outgoing tide toward Tybee. They were well past Lazaretto Creek and not far from where the barge had been left up at the top of the beach. There were two oarsmen and two passengers in each boat. They passed the barge a few hundred yards and pulled up on the beach about a half mile before Captain Jones' shanty.

Martin called Daniel to come look and when he did, he said immediately that it was the duel that Captain Jones had told them about, but Martin said it was to be in a week or two and that they were on their way from Virginia. Daniel said he guessed that the Captain had only general information and it was happening sooner because that was about to be a duel for sure and had seen this before. Daniel looked out over the rail for his father but didn't see him because he would like to know what was happening.

Martin asked if they should go find him and Daniel said the duel would be done by the time they got back with him, if they found him. Martin moved for Daniel to look through the instrument and Daniel said he could see them pretty good with only his eyes. Daniel said this is how it always happened, two duelers plus two witnesses and a couple pilot boatmen to bring them down to Tybee. They don't mess around about it and its over before you know it. Already, the boats were nudged up on the beach and two men were getting out of each boat and the two that were witnesses came together and were talking and one had a case with the weapons.

The two who were to duel were standing at a distance. After the witnesses talked for a moment, the men dueling approached and there was a short conversation and one of the witnesses opened the case and presented it to the two men and said something and one man reached out and picked out a pistol and the other man took the one left in the case. The two witnesses walked up the beach away and not in the line of fire. The two with the guns had a brief conversation and then with back to back, started taking paces away and after nine steps, turned and fired. Both men slumped down on the hard sand and the witnesses called to the oarsmen and they all came up and picked up a wounded or dead man and carried them down to the boats and laid them in.

A witness picked up the guns and put them in the case and each got back on their boat and as the tide was at that point where it was neither coming nor going, both boats headed back west toward Savannah.

Martin and Daniel looked at each other, stunned at what had just happened so quickly from when Martin had called Daniel to come look. The silence was broken by a yell from Charles below on the ground asking what was going on because he had heard gunfire coming from the beach.

Daniel yelled, "Duel!," and hurried to put the monocular away and get down the stairs. Martin had a head start and reached the ground first where Charles was waiting. He began telling the story and Daniel came out the door and Martin hesitated a moment and then kept telling what they saw. Charles said he hated that Martin had to see such a thing. Martin said it was okay he saw it but he hated that one or both of those men are dead and they didn't have the sense to settle their differences another way. Charles was a bit relieved at Martin's clarity.

Mrs. Dyer sensed something going on and came out but Mary hadn't heard anything and was still in her room. Daniel told the story when his mother came out and she wept and held Daniel and then hugged Martin. She then changed to being mad and said that she was tired of this happening and the law should be changed so it wouldn't happen again. She said that they should go in the house. Mary had come to the door wondering what was going on. They told her and she was horrified and wished it had never happened and that people were crazy to do such a thing. She asked why people did that.

Charles said some did it over disagreements over politics or business and some did it for romantic reasons or jealousy. He went on to say that the law did not enforce matters of honor, and men took honor seriously enough to be their own enforcers. She then asked why it was illegal in other states but legal in Georgia and that she remembered the last time this happened, the two men were from South Carolina and had traveled from Beaufort to Tybee because it was illegal there. Her father said that he didn't know the answer to that but he wished it wasn't so.

Mrs. Dyer said that other than the slave massacre, it was the worst thing that ever happened there. Martin and Daniel were upset about it all but Martin noticed how much more Mary was upset and didn't know what to make of it. She had not seen it in person like them but was more affected. Daniel suggested they go down and see the Captain and see if he heard the gunfire. Charles reminded Daniel about picking up Henry that afternoon as they were leaving.

They were silent on their walk to the beach and finally Mary said something that surprised them both. She said that women must be smarter than men because they had as much or more honor than men but didn't shoot each other over it. Daniel and Martin both had no answer to that and were silent. Mary wished they had something to say about it. They ran down the ocean side of the dune to the shanty and went straight up to the Captain and two pilot crews sitting near him.

Martin asked him if he had heard the gunfire and duel earlier and he and Daniel had seen the whole thing from the top of the lighthouse. The Captain said they had heard and the whole thing was over in less than five minutes. The pilot crews were more interested in their card game and cared less about the ordeal of the duel.

Daniel asked the Captain how many duels he had witnessed over the years. He said there had been more than he liked to remember but this one was a little different. They asked how so? He said most of the time, there was a shot fired then a pause and another shot but this morning, both shots were at the same moment. He said he waited to hear a second shot but didn't, then figured that it was two shots at the same time because it was so loud. He said that years ago, his shanty was closer to where the duel was but he had it moved a few hundred yards toward the point and around the bend a little to be out of the line of fire.

He said that in a few days, the Savannah newspaper would have the particulars about the event. He added that dueling was a custom brought over from Europe and that in America, in a big disagreement, men had simply fought with their fists or sometimes with guns but did it right away. He said he wasn't sure which was more or less civilized. On one hand, the American way seemed the least civilized but on the other hand, having a vow of murder and death and setting a date and following through seemed worse. Mary said that dueling was worse because it was premeditated. She said it with such strength and clarity that she surprised them and the Captain. Martin and Daniel had not ever heard the word, "premeditated" and didn't know what it meant but the Captain told Mary that she was perfectly correct. They thanked the Captain and decided to walk down the beach to the spot. When they got there, the footprints and blood was still fresh and they recounted the event, starting with the prints closest to the water's edge. Daniel pointed to the two separate sets as the one man got out of each boat and walked up higher on the beach and the group of prints as they met and the guns were taken by the two and the prints where the two witnesses walked higher up and waited and watched.

Next and the most dramatic of their reconstruction of the events was the place where two sets of prints, close but heading in opposite directions and then they counted, first one side then the other, nine steps and a reversal of direction and most awful, the blood on the beach, still red in the sand and the full body print. There was two sets of foot prints from the witnesses from up on the beach, one leading to each spot where the men had laid bleeding. These prints were deeper and spread wide because they were running.

Finally, they saw the multiple prints where the two oarsmen from each boat had run up and they and the witnesses prints as each group took their man to the boat, with a trail of blood mixed in. This review shook up Martin and Daniel more than seeing it from the lighthouse when it happened. Their voices trembled as they pointed at the prints and told Mary the story and before they finished, they both were in tears.

After they settled down they were awkward from their crying spell and shy to look at Mary, who, surprisingly, was in control and had quite a serious and mature look. She had been the most upset back at the lighthouse, but she was calm here where they had broken up. Mary looked out at the water and said that the same tide that was carrying the men back to Savannah would soon wash away the prints and blood here on the beach. Martin, surprised that he could speak, said that he doubted either man would be alive by the time they got there. Daniel said they would not know the details until the next supply boat came a week from today and learn about it in the newspaper they always brought for his father. They walked, without saying much, back to the lighthouse.

Margo had a lunch made early and Charles came in and there was less chat than usual. Daniel told about what the Captain had said but didn't tell about him and Martin and Mary going to see the footprints and blood. Margo reminded them to get the plums they had picked and take them with them as planned to Lazaretto. Martin and Mary finished and went outside.

Mary told Martin that he didn't have to feel bad about crying about the duel and that she liked that he had feelings enough to do that. She said that they were much more affected because they had actually seen the event as it happened and she didn't, and then seeing all the blood and all was too much. Martin was shocked that Mary was so smart and pleased that what she said made him comfortable with having cried so hard. He said back to her that yes, the ordeal had happened so fast while they were up on the lighthouse that it didn't seem real but going back to the spot was more powerful.

Martin and Daniel were silent on the ride to go pick up Henry. Martin thought that even the tackies seemed to be holding their heads low and ears pent back, with a sad sense of what had happened. The hammering got louder and louder, as they got closer to the first bridge. There were timbers and materials and workers on the bridge that had to move for them to cross over. They were using the old bridge as a platform to sink new support posts for a newer structure but had to do it so the bridge would remain serviceable. Everything was shoved aside and they passed over with hesitant but obedient horses. Jacob smiled real big at Martin and Martin said he would be back with Henry in a little while. They continued on to the small bridge and the horses were again nervous but crossed over to the oyster shell path over the marsh and through three more small hammocks and to the big hammock, which was Lazaretto landing.

They had come earlier than when the boat was expected, probably because they were restless from the day's events and Martin was anxious to hear what Henry would have to say about the duel. The cook and his helper were busy making supper for the group and Martin said hello. Daniel carried the big pan of plums to the cook and he was happy to have them and said they would have plum pudding for desert tonight. Martin asked Daniel if he wanted to walk over where all the graves were and see if there was any fresh signs of whoever was staying in the thicket and Daniel said he had all the excitement he wanted for the day and he would rather walk out to the point.

They walked through the low marsh grass and mud flats here and there, with thousands of fiddler crabs, hustling around to do whatever they do while the tide is out, running and going down their holes in the mud, as the boys walked over their territory. They walked out to the high white bank of oyster shells that formed the point where the Milam boatmen liked to fish. Martin looked over at Turtle Island and said he wondered where the sloop had gone that they had seen the day before.

Daniel had been staring across the South Channel and Martin asked him what he was studying and Daniel said it was about something his father often said and Martin asked what. He said his father said there should be another lighthouse built on that eastern tip of Cockspur Island. He always said that entering into the south channel was one of the most hazardous places on the entire coast to come into from the ocean when certain conditions happened. He said a northeaster with the tide going out of the Savannah river was the worst possible conditions because the wind had the whole Atlantic to fetch up and blow with tremendous force on shore there and the strong current going out of the river over the shoals caused steep waves that the wind blew and raised them up even more and blew the tops off and made tall and steep waves that made a dangerous seaway, especially at night.

He said a small lighthouse over there would save lives and ships. Martin said that sounded correct and maybe if Charles told his father, he might could help see that one could be built.

The grizzly duel and seeing the blood and all on the beach, left the boys somewhat melancholy. After a bit, Martin looked back toward Savannah and saw the supply boat in the distance moving quickly by oar and sail and current toward them. He yelped and said they were way early and Daniel asked how that could be. Martin said he guessed Henry may have had them leave a bit early before the tide started out and maybe the boatmen were showing off and wanted to please Henry and rowed faster and maybe because of the northwest breeze and the sail or maybe all those things but here they were. They watched them turn right into Lazaretto creek directly across from them and lower the small sail and Martin yelled and Johnny, at the helm in Jacobs normal spot, looked and saw it was Martin and yelled back causing all the oarsmen and Henry to look and smile. Johnny steered the boat over to their side of the creek and they walked back to the landing with the boat, just twenty yards away. They had been going with the outgoing tide in the south channel but once they had pulled into Lazaretto creek, they were going against the outgoing tide and their speed slowed to about the walking speed of the boys. Martin always marveled at the rhythm and unison of the oarsmen's work. All six of the long oars lifted up and sank down and pulled in perfect harmony and rhythm and a grunt by each man as he dipped the oars in the water and pulled hard. As always, the last of their trip was heightened by a chantey, timed by those grunts. Usually it was Jacob, but today it was Johnny that would sing a verse alone, then the rest would sing a kind of chorus and then Johnny again and it was a beautiful thing to hear. This was the first time Daniel had been this close and heard a good chantey and he was smiling big. Johnny upped the volume more than usual, probably because Henry was aboard and they all loved seeing Martin right there on the bank.

They were so loud that the cook and his helper came to look and started in on the chantey from where they were. Martin ran ahead and pulled the rope down from the windless and Johnny steered the boat up to the long timber rails that ran down below the low water line. Four oarsmen got out and went up and cranked the winch and the boat slowly slid up the rails with the rest still in the boat. Henry jumped out and hugged Martin and Daniel and said what a swift trip it had been. He said Johnny had told him the wind was out of the northwest and they could start out early and buck the tide with the sail up.

Johnny came over and smiled his pleasure of seeing them and asked how the old man (Jacob) was and Martin said fine and it was past quitting time and he should be here in a minute. Daniel brought the wagon in closer and the supplies for the lighthouse were loaded on it. Henry told Johnny what a good job he did steering clear of the eddies and always going the most direct way to save time and effort and Johnny said he had a great teacher in Jacob and today the oarsmen had wanted to show off to Henry and poured it on more than usual and it may have been one of the fastest trips ever with the sail.

Daniel had the horses ready and Henry rode up front with Daniel and Martin road in the back with the supplies. Jacob and crew were returning from work and Daniel stopped for Henry to speak to Jacob. He was happy to see Jacob and Jacob was him and Henry asked how it was going and Jacob said very well with all sun and no rain but Captain Jones had said there was rain coming in a day or two. Henry said he would be there first thing in the morning to talk and look things over and said good night.

When they started back, Martin said he had sensed from talking to Jacob a couple times that he was a bit sad and missed his family and Henry said yes, he wasn't going to have Jacob do this anymore and that he had some different plans for Jacob soon so that he wouldn't even have to be away the two days a week on the supply run anymore and it wasn't retirement but just a change of duties that would make life easier for him and his family. Martin liked hearing that.

Martin didn't want to tell Henry about the duel before he saw Jacob, so, shortly after he blurted out that he and Daniel, using his father's monocular from up on the lighthouse balcony, had seen two pilot boats pull up on the beach and four men get out and two of them dueled and shot each other and then were carried to the boats and headed back toward Savannah. Henry said that was awful news and hated that they had to see that, but it was no surprise because, unfortunately, Tybee Lighthouse had become the most popular place on the east coast for duels to be held at because it was the only place it was still legal and an easy place to plan a meeting because everyone knew where the Tybee lighthouse was.

He thought a minute and said it was odd because they had passed two pilot boats on the way, pulled up on the riverbank and he had wondered what they were doing. Martin told the rest of the story and Henry said he understood now why the pilot boats were there. It is customary, in a duel, for anyone killed, to be buried not far from the location of the duel. However, Henry continued, from your story, both men may have still been alive but died along the way and that would necessitate them stopping to bury one or probably both of them.

Daniel said that if Henry was correct, then there must be a lot of bodies buried around their house and along the river back to Savannah. Henry said, unfortunately yes, and especially when the duels used to take place up close to the lighthouse as he had heard. Daniel said that is just what Captain Jones said. He said he hadn't seen any but there must be plenty of ghosts around the lighthouse and Henry said if there were such a thing, that would probably be where they would be, and now, maybe a couple more along the river. Daniel didn't say anymore but his brow was furrowed in many wrinkles, because he didn't like hearing that there might be a lot of ghosts around the lighthouse.

Henry said the witnesses would make a statement to the authorities when they got to Savannah and they would find out the details soon enough. Martin told Henry what he had observed of the Indians over the last few days with the monocular and Henry commented that they sure had been having plenty of excitement. Martin said he had also gotten to know Captain Jones better and he had given him his old pilot boat and he wanted to load it on the barge and take it back and restore it. He also told him about taking Mary and Daniel sailing. Henry commented again what a busy time he was having.

Daniel pulled into the low place across the dunes over to the beach. The Milam crew had laid planks down in the soft sand for the wagon wheels, while hauling the materials from the barge to the bridge site, so they didn't have to get out and push to help the horses. Once on the hard beach sand Henry saw where the barge was and they went a ways more and Daniel stopped at the spot where the duel took place. Henry got out and Martin told the story again referring to the footprints.

Blood was still there but the sun had dried it. Henry shook his head and said it was time for Georgia to end this practice. They went on down to Captain Jones spot and stopped and Martin introduced Henry to the Captain and they were surprised that the Captain said he had met Henry once before when Henry was just a pup. He said that Captain Milam had come to visit the Captain of a ship he had piloted up the river and had little Henry with him. Henry said it was nice to meet him again and apologized for not remembering that first introduction and said how much Martin had talked about him and he had heard his prediction of rain and he hoped it didn't hamper their bridgework too much. He said not to worry, fall was the best weather of the year. Martin suggested that he and Henry get out and walk across the big dune to the lighthouse while Daniel took the wagon back up the beach and around. Henry said that was exactly what he needed because he had been sitting in the boat and the exercise would do him good. They got out and walked to the top of the dune and stopped to look around.

Martin pointed to and named the islands across the water and added about the big sloop they had observed by Turtle Island and the two loaded longboats. Then when they turned and started down the dune to the lighthouse, he pointed out the long shadow of the lighthouse and how Daniel could tell the time by where the shadow was in the afternoon.

They got to the lighthouse before Daniel and Martin said they needed to clean the sand off their feet first, then went up the porch stairs. Charles and his wife and Mary had been waiting on them and Martin said Daniel had dropped them off for Henry to walk over the dunes to get his land legs back and just then they heard Daniel coming through the back gate and go to the barn where the two guards helped him unload what went there and then they came and unloaded the rest onto the back porch of the house to be put up in a bit.

The Dyers welcomed Henry and handed him some yaupon and showed him a seat. Charles said the work was going fine and the weather had been perfect but they were expecting some rain. He asked if Martin had told him of the mornings event and Henry said yes and how they took him to see the footprints and blood on the beach where it had happened. Henry told him about seeing the two pilot boats on the riverbank. Charles said he would hear the rest of the story from the pilots on the beach after they had been to Savannah and back.

He suspected their story would have more details, having gotten it directly from the crew who had been there, than what would be in the Savannah newsprint. Henry said Martin sure had been busy since he had been there and he had heard all about things on the wagon ride back. Charles said yes and his children had enjoyed his company and he was glad of it because they got tired of each other and Daniel said that wasn't so but Mary said it was so and they laughed.

Martin said he had left out one thing that he had wanted to tell him and Henry was surprised that there could be more. Martin went over again what he had observed of the Indians and how he had not been able to be quite sure about how to approach them to inquire about Alice's family. He finally considered the idea of Alice going with him, since she had met the kind lady when she had come to help the whole group of runaways and mostly because she had such a good way with people.

He said he had mentioned the idea to Charles and his wife and to Jacob and they thought it was a good idea. Henry thought a minute and said that actually it was odd but just before he had left, Alice had come to him and told him about her dream where she had remembered the kind lady's name, which was "Ayana," and she wanted him to tell Martin. He thought a moment more and said that if the Dyers didn't mind putting up another Milam, he thought it a good idea. Charles said they would be pleased to have Alice come and would help in any way they could. Henry said he could send a boat with her the very next day if that needed to be but Martin said next week's supply boat would be fine because that would give him time to study things more. Charles asked Henry if he wanted to go look at the masonry repairs that had been going on before it got dark and he said yes, so they left to do that.

Margo asked the others if they would take some plum pudding down to the Captain before dark and they agreed. She asked how many crewmen were there and they said one crew had left and one was still there so she sent the rest of the pot to feed them all and reminded Daniel to bring her pot back.

The next morning came and Daniel had declined the night before to go with Henry and Martin to check on construction so he could catch up on a few things he had to do. At breakfast, Henry said he had gone to sleep listening to the ocean and how well he slept. Margo said she wished he could stay longer but understood how busy he always was.

Henry commented that he would soon have a surprise for her that would let her keep leftovers a week or more without them spoiling, and she laughed, thinking Henry was making some kind of joke she didn't understand but then she remembered Martin's story of ice and an icebox for them coming, but it didn't seem real and she had not given it much thought. Henry thought to himself that if he asked Jason the day he got back, he could have another icebox for the Dyers here soon. Henry said her surprise would be there in a week or two and Margo said all improvements were welcome and appreciated.

Daniel went with Henry and Charles and Martin to help get the wagon hitched for them. The two guards were at the gate, waiting for the masonry crew to arrive and Henry stopped a moment to talk with them about some things he had observed with Charles the day before. The guards had been given the job of seeing that the masonry crew had what they needed. He spoke with them for a moment and then thanked them for their work and then he and Martin went on to the big bridge. They could already hear the hammering from the bridge and Martin said Jacob liked to get an early start before the day heated up.

They got there and work ceased for Henry and Jacob to look over things and Martin followed to learn what he could. Jacob had maintained this bridge for many years and had gradually improved it over the years and now was making it even better. Martin had only one thing to say and that was about how spooky the tackies were crossing over the bridge and if the decking was placed closer, they may be less hesitant to walk over. Jacob said that would take extra decking but they had brought extra and probably had enough. They talked about the smaller bridge and Jacob assured Henry he was gonna make it just fine.

Henry told Jacob that he wanted him to work with the carpenters and teach them all he could and let him know which one knew the work best so he could be in charge next time because he wasn't going to ask him to come there again so he wouldn't have to leave his family anymore. Jacob's eyes welled up and thanked Henry and Henry said, no, thank you for all your good work. He added that when the small bridge was done, he could come home and didn't have to wait for the road way to be reworked with more oyster shells because that didn't require much supervision. Izak heard that and asked if he could be part of that crew and Henry said he didn't see why not.

Jacob added that Izak had been a very good hand. They talked a little about the oyster shell roadway and Henry shook Jacobs hand and touched his shoulder at the same time and Martin was looking and learning, not just about bridge building but how to be respectful with men doing work. As they were about to leave, Henry remembered something and told Jacob about the icebox he hoped to send next week and how heavy it was and where to put it and told him to not lift any part of it himself but to just be a good boss man.

Jacob said he would try and said they had plenty of men to help. Jacob had the men move materials off the bridge so the brothers could cross over and the tackies were hesitant to go but finally did and after they had both crossed, Henry told Martin what a good idea he had about installing the decking closer together. They road on down to the small bridge and again had a little trouble coaxing the tackies over and then on to the landing where the cook and his helper were still cleaning up from the big breakfast. Johnny and all the oarsmen were out on the point fishing with hand lines, killing a little time, waiting for the tide to change back toward Savannah.

Henry had asked him if they could leave a little late this morning because he had things to do and Johnny said that was fine but they would have some tide to buck on the way back. Henry talked to the cook about how things were going and what could make things better and made a list of additional things to send on next week's boat. He then inspected the latrine and the well and the inside of the shanties, telling Martin the things he saw that were good and a few that were not and why. He told Martin that sanitary conditions were very important because a sick crew was an unhappy crew and work was hard enough and everybody deserved to be as well as possible. He said that their father had taught them to treat all the help as crewmen on a ship and their safety and well-being was of the most importance. After they had looked over everything at the landing, Henry said he was done with his work for the trip and wanted to go on back to have a little time to visit with the Dyers before leaving.

When they got back, Charles and Henry got in serious conversation about something and Daniel asked what they were talking about. Charles said that there was going to be a small fort built out in front of the light-house, between the bottom of the sand dunes and Captain Jones' shanty. Daniel asked what for and Charles said it was to guard the river entrance. Henry said a lot of people thought it was a folly because there are several entrances into Savannah and most would be out of canon range from here but as security for the lighthouse it will be great. There was a need for something like it during the recent war with the British, but that was over and done with. They kept ships over near Hilton Head several years and if they had wanted to destroy the lighthouse, they could have easily done it, but they expected to retake America and they wanted this lighthouse in good working order with it. We will probably, in the next ten years or so, have a small fort between us and the ocean and we will do what we can to cooperate. He added that it was called a Martello Tower and is to be part of a string of small forts every fifty miles along the coast. Margo Dyer changed the subject and said she had been thinking about Alice and what would happen if she did find her family. Henry said he had thought of that too but guessed it would be best to think about that when and if it happened. He added that Alice was seldom without good understanding and clarity and he trusted her wisdom more than his own in anything other than business matters. Charles said that if they did find her family, it wouldn't be good for that news to get out. Henry said everyone on the Milam place knows that Martin is down here looking for her family, but they all know it shouldn't be told to outsiders.

Daniel and Martin had gone out to get the horses hitched to the wagon to take Henry. Henry told Charles and Margo how thankful they were to them for all their good work and for having Martin visit and taking care of him. They both said that Martin was a joy to have and it had been good for their whole family and in some ways he seemed older and more mature than them, especially how he had been so determined to help find Alice's family. Henry said that Martin had promised Alice when he was only ten that he would do that. He said that Alice had practically raised Martin and she was somewhat like his second mother and that Martin had a strong will like their father. He added that their father went to sea when he was only fourteen and Martin talks about having his own boat and going soon.

His mother and I have done all we could to keep him busy doing other things but it probably won't work much longer.

Daniel and Martin came in the wagon to get Henry. Mary asked to go, so she and Martin road in the back and Henry was up front with Daniel. The Dyers walked out with them and told Henry that his visit was too short and to say hey to everybody. Henry said they needed to do something so they could come visit them, and Margo said Charles didn't like to leave but when Daniel was a couple years older maybe he would reconsider things. Daniel said he knew everything now and he and the guards would be fine without them for a few days. Charles said to go because they were late leaving already and Daniel spoke to the horses and they headed at a quicker pace than usual to the landing. Jacob had the rest of the new bridge decking complete and everything cleared and the horses hesitated at first but after a few yards on the new solid decking, resumed their gate.

Johnny and crew had the boat pointed toward Savannah when the wagon arrived at the landing and Henry quickly said goodbye to Martin and said that unless Alice objected, she would be on the supply boat next week. He told Mary and Daniel goodbye and they would have to come visit soon. Henry, with his one bag, walked down one of the rails and climbed in and they shoved off a couple hours after the tide had begun in and they sang and bucked it until they went the short distance out of Lazaretto creek and then were swept toward Savannah by the power of current and oars.

Henry was glad he had come and glad to be going. There were many things waiting for him to do at home and in Savannah. Foremost on his mind was his favorite professor from college was in Savannah for a few days and wanted to visit Henry while he was there. He wished he could put one or two of the things on his list off but couldn't. The professor was there for a few days only and he wanted to do a few things with the ice he had in the sawdust pile before it melted and order an ice box for the lighthouse, and the Milam operation always required attention and his family definitely couldn't be left out and he needed to talk with Alice. It all seemed too much to do, but once they were well under way, he got a piece of paper and a pen and managed, even with the motion of the boat, to make a list of his tasks. When he was finished, he felt better that it was all listed out and now seemed doable and he decided to enjoy the ride. He turned to see Johnny and thought to himself how Johnny had taken more of a leader type role since he had married Alice and had begun to learn how to read by taking over Martin's job of checking that everything was loaded and accounted for each week on the supply boat.

He wondered how Johnny was going to take to the idea of Alice going to Tybee and the Indian Islands. He was confident that Alice would want to go and he knew she would explain it to Johnny in a way that he would feel good about her going. Alice had a way that whatever she did happened with grace and benefited everyone involved and the way for her to proceed always opened up for her. He thought about the other boatmen and what he could do for their betterment and remembered that Izak might be a good new boatman trainee. Henry knew there were a lot of changes ahead for the Milam place. He remembered something his mother had said often about worrying about how to attend to everything; "Water the root and the rest of the tree will do fine."

He would water the roots and trust that all would be served. He thought about the duel that Martin and his friends had witnessed and how things like this and the recent trip to Darien were making Martin grow up.

Henry watched the riverbank go by and they passed two ships, each with their own pulling boats, keeping them in the river channel, as they drifted toward Savannah. Sails hung slack on the ships because there was no wind today but the current was taking them along at about a mile or two an hour. The supply boat passed the ships swiftly and Henry marveled at the strength and coordination of the oarsmen. They knew they had left late and they were trying to catch up a bit plus they wanted to put on a little showboat for Henry. Usually, three men would row for about an hour, then the resting three would take over, but today, they were switching up every thirty minutes because they were pushing it a little harder so they would be further up the river when the tide changed direction. Henry enjoyed watching them switch so quickly that the boat speed hardly changed. They were pulling very hard on the long oars but not one ever seemed to labor that hard. Each man was lean and muscular and fit for the task. While resting, they drank water and snacked and mostly joked with each other. Johnny listened and observed them while steering the boat and occasionally laughed with them. Henry could barely understand what they were saying. In a group, their Geechee dialect deepened and speeded up and became almost private to their group. Oddly, Henry could feel their humor and spirit without understanding a lot of their words and when a burst of laughter happened, he laughed along with them. The hours went by and they were soon turning into the Wilmington River, and only a mile away from home. Henry knew that the men had to work harder the last hour because the tide had turned and they were bucking it and he was the reason they were late leaving.

Once they turned off the Savannah River into the Wilmington River, they began their chantey song with a verse from Johnny and a chorus from the crew and the rowing set the rhythm and they chugged along gracefully in sound and sight. There were a few people at the boathouse waiting for their arrival and they picked up in perfect rhythm by seeing the movement of the six oars and their singing and the singing of the oarsmen merged when they got closer.

Henry had heard these chanteys, with the boats coming and going a hundred times, but every time was special and he smiled to himself at the pleasure of it. He noticed how much better and relaxed he felt after being on the river and in the company of the simple and pure joys of the boatmen. Even with all his education, and being the boss of the place, he felt on equal terms with them as human beings and loved them as he did his own family.

They pulled in and Henry stepped out and the chatter and banter of the oarsmen and the people waiting was loud and happy. He felt gratitude for his understanding and clarity of life as he nodded to Johnny and went straight away to the big house. Martha and Walter and Claudia and the kids were on the front porch. They had offered, before he left, to have the carriage waiting for him on his return, but he had declined because the short walk home got the circulation going in his legs from sitting so long in the boat. He was glad more than ever to return to his family. He briefly said the work was going just fine and then told all the things Martin was doing and observing and about the duel, which they had already heard about just a few hours before he arrived, but what they had no way of knowing was that Martin and Daniel had witnessed it first hand and Martha was horrified that they were so near to it all.

Walter said Martin would be fine and he had witnessed death at a younger age than Martin. This didn't lessen Martha's concern about Martin. The story that had rapidly gotten to them was just that a duel had taken place on Tybee, but there were no details. Henry told of seeing the two pilot boats not far from Savannah on the bank on his trip down. Walter said he would get the whole story tomorrow.

Alice came over and said she couldn't wait to hear if Martin had been able to find out anything about her family. Martha got her some tea and she sat down to listen to what Henry had to say. Henry first told her about the duel and all and she was like Martha and didn't like that Martin had to see that. Then Henry said there was no news of her parents but Martin had been busy learning about the Indians and he told her how he had been using a monocular up on the lighthouse to see what island the Indians were living on and observed their comings and goings. Henry said that Martin had thought about the best way to approach them and had decided to ask if she would go to Tybee and go with him. He thought that they would be less likely to shy away if they saw you with him coming up. This idea did not surprise Alice at all because she had thought of suggesting it herself because she had been near the woman when she had come those days to help the group before the massacre and she may even remember her and this relieved Henry and he thought to himself to never consider it a problem to talk to Alice about anything.

He told Alice that she could go on the supply boat next week. Henry said he hoped Johnny would be ok with the idea and she said she would talk to him and that he knew it was important to her. Martha asked her if she was sure she was up to it in her condition, with child, and Alice said it was not a problem. She had gained a little weight but felt better than ever. Henry said the Dyers were happy to hear she might come and stay and were like us, hopeful to learn of her family.

Alice thanked Henry and said she wanted to go home now and talk to Johnny. She hugged them all and Henry was in awe at the glow about her and he could feel it when she embraced him. He thought to himself what an amazing gift Alice had been to his family and how he could never explain this to some of his friends. He hugged his parents and thanked them and he and his family went to their end of the big house. Henry was glad to be with his family again and thought about Jacob being away from his.

Next morning, Henry was up and off to Savannah early and at Jason's shop as he and his helper were just getting there. Jason was glad to see him and showed him the drawings for the icehouse. Henry liked what he saw and told Jason he approved of the plans and wanted him to get started on it, but he had another project he needed done right away if he could manage it. He told him about needing another icebox like the one he had built for his home but this one was for the lighthouse at Tybee. Jason said the second one would be easier and better than the first because he had learned a few things.

Henry said he first thought he would have it assembled at Tybee but was thinking now of having it put together here and shipped complete because he thought he could do a better job of it here in the shop and there were plenty of men on Tybee now to heft it up onto the back porch of the keepers house. He also wanted a simple ice chest to be a permanent fixture on the supply boat for taking a block of ice every week, big enough to hold a twenty-four by thirty inch block of ice and with the wall thickness added, fit perfectly in the width of the boat and secured. Jason said he would need to go take measurements of the inside of the boat to do that and it would be a few hundred extra pounds so he should talk to one of the boatmen about where in the boat it should go.

Henry said for him to talk to Johnny about that. Henry said to build the icebox for the house first so he could get it on Captain Bens next trip out and he would bring the wagon and men to load it and take it to the wharf and load it on the Captains boat and the ice chest for the boat could come later. Jason agreed to have the icebox done soon. Henry said the ice house panels didn't need to be done for a month or more because the carpenters needed to get back from Tybee and have time to have the foundation and floor in before the panels arrive. Jason said he might add a second helper, at least temporarily with all he had to do.

Henry shook his hand, gave him another a bank note payment and thanked him and felt good to have that task completed. Next he went to see if Captain Ben was in town or when he would be. He drove the buggy down to the wharf but didn't see the sharpie in its usual place and went to the warehouse that housed the sawmill hardware that he often shipped and asked the clerk if he expected him anytime soon and he said he had left this morning and gone to Darien and would be back in four or five days.

14.
PROFESSOR ALBERT MCWILLIAMSON

Next, Henry went to the inn, where his old professor was staying and found him having a late breakfast alone in the café. He saw Henry come in the door and leapt to his feet and embraced him. Albert said he thought he wouldn't see him until tomorrow. Henry said he had gotten back yesterday in the afternoon and had business in town early this morning and decided to see if he might catch up with him.

The innkeeper recognized Henry and came over to welcome him and Henry introduced him to his friend. He asked Henry what he would like and he said maybe a pastry and some tea. Henry told Albert that if he had other plans and didn't have time to talk now, he could come back later and Albert said this was a perfect time. Henry suggested they eat, then walk down to the riverfront and speak in a more private setting and Al nodded in approval. They finished up their food and walked down to the river and found a comfortable place to sit, overlooking the river.

Albert was a Professor of Ethics and had been educated as a Unitarian clergy but entered into teaching about business and law ethics instead. He was sought out by the College of Charleston and moved there and met his wife and they had one child that had married and started their own family near Charleston about the time that Henry had started school. Henry and John were in Alberts class together and he and John and Albert became good friends and spent a lot of time beyond the classroom talking of the many things going on in the world, particularly in the south and after some time, it became clear that they all three had similar feelings about the institution of slavery. Henry told about his family and how they operated and what they believed about things. Later, Henry confided in his father about his professor and John and the talks they had and how they now knew of the Milam's sentiments. Walter trusted Henry's judgment.

Albert asked about Martin, and Henry told about his difficult learning handicaps and failure at school. Henry glowed, telling about how he had excelled in his own ways and Alice had managed to get his attention oriented enough to teach him to read and how he had spent a few years working and learning by doing in every aspect of the Milam operation. Henry told of his obsession with becoming a ship captain at an early age like his father and where he was now and what he was doing there about searching for Alice's family. Albert was amazed at the story of Martin and then asked about John. Henry went on to tell about his recent visit he and Martin had and all about John's rapid success and his wife and family. He told him why John had asked them to come and all about the ice and about how they planned to make a business of it. Albert was surprised that John would leave his lucrative position in Darien and Henry told him how he had wanted more things for his daughters than Darien had to offer. Henry said he was surprised too about John wanting to move but then began telling about how they were both excited and in agreement about the huge potential of the ice business and John had accumulated some wealth to invest in it with Henry. Henry described the icebox at their home and the one he was having built for the lighthouse and the icehouse storage building that was being planned as they spoke.

Albert said his life was not as exciting as his and John's but he and his wife were happy and enjoyed a social life with his academic friends but their favorite thing to do was visiting with his daughter and husband and grandchild, who lived nearby.

He said he had two friends that he could speak with in confidence about things but Charleston had become even further entrenched in the system of enslavement of people of color and the system was supported by the three major powers of business, politics, and religion and everyone was afraid to vary from the status quo because it might mean losing the huge wave of wealth and prosperity that maintained the social sensibilities of the elite and supported a working class. There was no time to listen to conscience and if it was ever heard, the social habit of church going was there to distract any discomfort by having well thought out concepts, carefully crafted by comfortable and high living religious leaders, that made out slavery as a service and mandate by God and the Bible.

Henry said that his father had slowed down and recently been in less than his normal good health and he was running the whole operation now and knew that when his father was gone, most of the goodwill and leniency toward them would be gone too and he loved and cared for every person on the place and wanted to do something to insure their betterment, prosperity, and security. With his father not around, they may no longer be guaranteed the new lighthouse contract every year and this had prompted his interest in the ice business with John.

They may or may not lose the lighthouse contract but he wanted to have more than that to depend on if they did. His biggest goal would be to set all the workers free but knew that was not as easy as it sounded because he wanted it to be done in a way that would ensure their health and welfare, once freed. It was perplexing because he wasn't sure that they would be any better off and possibly less better off if they left the Milam place. He said everybody there was made aware that the door was always open and they would be given money to get a start, if they chose to go and any support they needed. He said that it was not a bed of roses for a free black around Savannah. They were stigmatized and reproached so that they often lived in poverty worse than many slaves. He said that many were intimidated so much that they had left to go someplace else. People were afraid that if they had any success, it would encourage slaves to aspire freedom and that was a threat to the status quo. He said that everyone on the Milam place now had plenty of good food, clothing, and decent shelter, and a doctor if they were sick, and support in old age. They had free time to be with their family and friends and lived a life isolated from the normal slave life of the south, where beatings were often, and family separations could happen at any time and all the other atrocities that were common. Henry said that he needed help in understanding how best to move forward in his leadership of the Milam place and he was reaching out for any advice that Albert might have.

Albert listened to Henry intently and when Henry finished and asked him for his help, his brow furrowed deeply and he breathed a deep sigh. Henry, you are correct in your concerns and I admire yours and your family's adherence to conscience and heart instead of greater profit and the immoral custom and practice of human bondage. Having known you, I am not surprised to hear of what you want to do but I fear that you will bear the brunt of powerful institutional and personal prejudice beyond anything you have ever experienced. The choices you make could bring about changes to your family that could be very unpleasant and possibly make things turn out less than good for all the people you want to protect. You are wise beyond your years to seek guidance in these matters before acting. Albert said he would advise him as best he could but that may not be enough. He said there were a few new progressives in Charleston but any talk about anything that went against tradition was most often frowned on. Albert thought a minute and told Henry that there were laws that he was probably aware of called " manumission laws" to deal directly with granting freedom to slaves.

These laws were different in every state and generally stacked against the process and getting more and more difficult. He said that it was easier thirty years ago to manumit a slave than it is now. Currently, Georgia followed the guidelines of South Carolina and in South Carolina, a freed slave could not own property in that state, so if you had in mind to give your people a piece of property, this would not be possible. In most states, a slave, when freed, had to leave that state for a year and pay a fee to return and an annual fee thereafter. In South Carolina and probably in Georgia, application for freeing a slave has to be reviewed by a committee appointed by local authorities and people of prejudice filled them and made certain restrictions that made things difficult and their decision was final. One of the things that was a legitimate reason for a review was that some slave owners were pretending to be humanitarian but were actually freeing themselves of the responsibility and cost of providing for an old slave that could no longer work and was trying to leave it to the state to take care of him or her in their last days.

He also said that application for one or two slaves to be freed was one thing but asking about all the ones on the Milam place at once would cause a stir and resistance and probably a negative decision by the review group. Albert said that one state had a legal arrangement where an owner could release his slaves if he signed an agreement to take back and support them if they were infirmed for any reason. Albert reiterated that what Henry wanted was something that was stacked against him by the institutions of southern state governments to make things about manumission difficult, but he would look further into it with utmost sincerity and confidentiality and if there was a way, he would find it. He added that the manumission laws and restrictions on free blacks had gotten worse because of the recent slave revolts and with the slave population as much or greater than the white population, everyone feared a revolt.

Henry was thoroughly sobered by what Albert had laid out for him, but not deterred from his mission but simply understood that it was a bigger task than he may have considered. He felt fortunate to get such solid advice and thanked Albert and Albert said that Henry was one of his favorite students and now a dear friend and he admired what he was trying to do. He said that when John came he would plan on coming back to Savannah and all three could meet and in the meantime he would dig up what more he could on the subject and perhaps he and John could visit him in Charleston. Henry walked Albert back to the inn and shook his hand and expressed how grateful he was to him for his help and Albert said he appreciated being involved in such a meaningful and noble endeavor. They vowed to meet again soon, so Albert could tell of what he had learned about slave manumission.

Henry was surprised and pleased that his list was being checked off so efficiently and his most important task of meeting with Albert was accomplished and that Albert had agreed to help. He made his way to his home and office where another list of things awaited him about the everyday and ongoing management of the Milam place. He was surprised to see Walter home again today. For several weeks he had been at home more days than he was in town and that was not like him. What could be going on and how could the pubs in Savannah be managing without such a major patron and character as Walter? It was nice having his character around home too. His children liked being around both grandparents and it gave Claudia a break with the kids.

There was a letter waiting for Henry from Thomas Smith, the engineer from Boston he had ridden with on the coach from Darien. He said he would be in Savannah in a week or two on business and wanted to visit the Milam place like Henry had offered. Henry was delighted to hear from him. Henry wrote a quick letter saying that he would like that very much and had business matters to discuss with him as well. He went and asked his father when he was going to town next and he said in the morning and Henry asked him to take his letter to the mail house and Walter said he would. Also, he asked him to include in the afternoon messages to the Tybee light that Charles was to have the visitor on next week's boat as planned, without saying who the visitor was and Walter understood his intent. Walter said he would get the full story on the Tybee duel while he was in town as well and Henry returned to his office work.

Meanwhile on Tybee, Martin and Daniel and Mary were sent out again for plums and blackberries by Margo, while they were still ripe and ready. She liked to cook them down with sugar and fill up as many earthen jars, and seal the lids with wax as she could, to have some deserts over the winter. Her other annual ritual was making plum wine in three big clay crocks. This would take a lot of plums and she asked them to pick a big pan full every day for the next few days, and they agreed to it. Martin had a plan to look every day from up on the lighthouse at the Indian Islands to learn what he might about their comings and goings that could help when he and Alice went to see them. He also wanted to sail some more and use the chart his father had given him and the other thing was to get Captain Jones' boat to the barge and loaded to go back. They could look with the monocular every day early, then pick plums and have the rest of the day to do as they pleased.

So, with two pans, one for plums and one for blackberries, they went outside the compound and straight out into the nearest area of plum trees. Blackberries had begun to ripen since their last time out and they grew all under the plum trees. Daniel said, since he was taller and plums were bigger and faster to fill the pan, he would pick plums if they would stoop and pick blackberries and they agreed. Mary told Martin that she might take him riding with her on the tackies this week if he wanted, and he said he would like that. She said her favorite ride was down the beach to the south end and around on the narrow beach of the Back River until the beach ended and that many afternoons the sky would have brilliant colors as the sun set and it was prettiest from there.

Martin said that he liked that end of the island because it was near the Indian Islands. Mary asked him if he was afraid of going to see the Indians and he said no because of what he had heard from her father and from Alice's story. Daniel asked what would happen if he found her parents alive and Martin said that would be up to them and Alice and he hadn't really thought about that. He said he was thinking about taking his boat down to the Back River this week and leaving it so he could quickly cross over the river when he wanted and become familiar with the area. He said he could drag the boat up into the woods and he asked Daniel if he thought anyone might steal it.

Daniel said he didn't think so because there was hardly anybody there except the Indians across the river and they seldom came over to this side. He said maybe Martin could take it tomorrow and Mary could ride one tacky and lead the other and y'all could ride back on the beach. Mary thought that to be a great idea and Martin said perhaps so. The plum pan was filling faster than the berry pan and Daniel started picking berries too.

Martin said he also needed to get the Captains boat down to the barge and had been thinking about how to do that. It was too big for the wagon but he thought he knew how to do it. He asked Daniel if the tackies would walk in the ocean a little over ankle deep and Daniel said they loved it especially when it was hot. Well, Martin said, he thought that if the pilot crewmen would help him drag it over to one of the tide pools left on the beach and let it soak in the water so the planks would swell, he was thinking that on a calm day, it could be dragged down in the ocean at about a foot deep and then pulled along toward the barge with a long rope hooked to a tacky. Daniel said that one of them may have to stay inside the boat and bail water if it still leaked a lot. They picked berries while they talked and the pan was full and all three stood up and picked plums until that pan was finished filling and they went back to the house as the sun was getting close to setting.

The big pans were heaped up and heavy, especially for Martin, who was not as big as Daniel. Margo was delighted with how many they got and said she would start cooking the berries and if they could do that a couple more times this week, she would have enough for wine. She told Martin that they had heard that Alice would be there on next week's supply boat and Martin breathed a sigh of relief because he had worried about going alone and didn't want to ask Daniel or anyone else. He wasn't afraid to go alone but was not sure about saying the right thing and Alice was the best at saying and doing the right thing and her presence always made whatever was going on better. He would spend the week doing whatever he could to be prepared for going with Alice.

Martin asked Charles if he thought his boat would be safe, left on the south end in the woods and he told him why he was asking. Charles said he didn't see why not and reminded him to be back before dark each day so they wouldn't worry. Martin said that he would take it and leave it tomorrow and Mary said she would bring both tackies and they could ride back home together. He told Charles the things he wanted to do this week before Alice came but he didn't have a clear plan yet about how to go about things, once she was here. All he knew now was that they appeared to be living on the long island, maybe in two different encampments and there were regular trips to and from the pointed island with the split that he called Claw Island. It appears they trade with other Indians from somewhere up the Ogeechee River and may be helping some runaways. Martin said he wondered if there might be a better day or time to go see them and if Charles or anyone had any ideas, he would listen. Charles said the tide would be high in the morning for a few days after Alice was here and if y'all left on the high tide early, you would have a high tide late in the afternoon to return on. Martin agreed and thanked him for his advice. He should have thought of that but hadn't because he had been thinking of the actual meeting.

Charles said the Indians were not childish, but childlike and they loved gifts and a gift was a token of good will and intentions and a basket of plumbs or oranges from their tree in the yard might be good. Martin liked that idea too, and thanked Charles again. Margo brought everyone some egg custard and Martin ate some and thought to himself that he hadn't had anything that good since John had made the iced cream in Darien. Mary and Daniel and Martin excused themselves and went outside and walked around the inside of the compound until dark, peeling and eating oranges from the tree growing against the lighthouse, and talking about the last week.

Mary said that so many more things had happened since Martin came and she couldn't imagine what would happen when Alice came and she didn't know what to think. She had heard about people trading with the Indians years ago but not in her lifetime and no one had anything to do with them anymore. Daniel said he believed it was possible for Alice's family to be there without anyone ever knowing because no one ever went around there except a few lost drunks from Savannah and they wouldn't notice anything. Martin said he hoped Daniel was right and perhaps in a week they would know, one way or the other. He said he hoped that the lady chief was still alive because Alice said she spoke English and was very kind. Mary said she was going to her room to read some and go to bed. Both boys were tired and they went in too.

Daniel and Martin were up on the lighthouse balcony before the sun had fully come up the next morning. Martin had brought his chart to compare the creeks and islands to what they could see with the monocular. They first looked Claw Island as Martin had been calling it and saw two canoes about to enter the little inlet at the point and watched them pull up to the bank and drag the canoes up in the woods but didn't see them anymore after waiting a while, so he swung the monocular over a bit so he could see Long Island. He saw nothing more than the smoke rising from the two places and moved the monocular around to the west side to view Lazaretto Landing.

He saw men leaving the landing in two groups, one for the lighthouse and one for the bridge. He took out his chart and found the landing on it and then looked at it through the monocular and then he looked how Lazaretto creek went north a short distance from the landing and merged into the south channel and he stared at his chart affirming what he had just saw. Then he scanned the short distance of the marsh, toward the lighthouse and where the marsh ended and beach began and saw the barge up at the top of the beach there. On further was a slight bend and then on down at the point was Captain Jones' shanty and the lighthouse. He was already pretty familiar with that part of the island so he swung the monocular back to Lazaretto landing and from there he looked southwest to where Lazaretto Creek merged into the Back River, then looked at his chart at what he had just seen, trying to fix it in his memory. He continued doing that, following the river to the south end of Tybee with the Indian Islands and the huge oyster midden on the right. First with the monocular he looked at things, then his chart, then the monocular again until the rivers and islands were fixed in his mind's eye. There was not much to remember about the wide stretch of beach from the Back River to the lighthouse so he swung back around to study the Indian Islands and creeks to think about how he might go with Alice. He looked along the beach south to Warsaw Sound. He looked at Warsaw Sound on the map and saw a big river circling around behind the islands and a small river that went off it and became the west end of the Back River, so he had completed a study around Tybee and the Indian Islands and hoped he could remember it all without the chart, even though he would have the chart with him.

His chart didn't show many of the small creeks within the Indian Islands much and Martin figured that whoever made the chart didn't want to venture in there. He realized that Daniel was waiting for him all this time and apologized for leaving him out but Daniel said there was no problem. He said he had been mesmerized, watching the sun and trying to imagine them atop the lighthouse at the edge of the ocean, spinning toward the sun like Martin had talked about and they both laughed and Martin took a break and let Daniel look a bit through the monocular.

Martin shared some more knowledge his father had told him. He said that the sun was a star, just as the ones we saw at night were but it was our star and we would freeze to death without it. He also explained that us and our moon and some planets were circling around it and it took one year for the earth to get around the sun and while it was traveling around, it was spinning and it spun three hundred and sixty five times during that passage and that was the number of days in a year. Daniel liked these talks about the earth and heavenly bodies.

Martin said he had seen enough for the day and they needed to go pick plums and blackberries because he was taking his boat to the back river and Mary was to pick him up, and they were gonna have that horse ride she had promised. They put things away and went down the stairs. The earth, moon, and stars were spinning around in Daniels head and he tripped up going down the stairs a few times and Martin asked if he was ok.

Mary was waiting with the two pans and after the boys got a drink, they went picking again. Mary was more of an eager picker this morning because she had some purpose to her day. Martin sensed her hurry and quickened his pace and Daniel seemed a bit still dazed, thinking about the things Martin had taught him. In two hours, both pans were full and Martin and Daniel each carried them to Margo who was again delighted and she said she had a special treat and reached way up and behind on a shelf and pulled out a small clay jar and with a spoon, dipped some golden honey on a biscuit for each one of them. The honey was a very coveted item that one of the pilot crew had brought her and it was only used at special occasions or when someone was sick.

Mary asked Martin how long it would take him to sail to the south end. He thought a moment and said that if Daniel would help him get the boat down to the water he could be leaving the beach in about half hour or a little more and go out in the ocean and follow the beach to the Back River. He said a couple hours or so from then should put him at the Back River landing. Mary said she would bring them a bag of lunch. Martin told Margo that they would be back in the afternoon plenty before dark and he and Daniel left for the beach.

They stopped to say hello and chat with Captain Jones. He said one of the pilot crew had told him already this morning that both the two men from Virginia in the duel had been alive when first loaded on the boats but had died before they got to Savannah and were buried on the South Carolina side of the river, next to each other. Martin asked why they had dueled and the Captain simply said politics and honor. Neither of them understood politics and just shook their heads. Daniel commented how odd it was that they had so seriously disagreed in this life but were now buried beside each other in death. The Captain said that politics was a scourge and could divide friends and even brothers. Martin then told the Captain his idea about putting his boat in a tide pool to swell up the planks and then using a tacky to pull it to the barge in shallow water.

The Captain said if they did that for several days, they might have to bale a bit but they could probably row it there and not have to fool with the horse. Martin said if he had time and if there were still some crew left on the beach to help him, he might soak it some this afternoon. The Captain looked pleased that Martin was serious about doing something that he was no longer able to do with his old boat. It had pained him to see it just lay there on the beach. He told the Captain where he was going and said he hoped to see him later in the day.

Daniel grabbed the little boat by the bow and alone, drug it down the beach and into the water and held it until Martin had it rigged and off he shot toward Hilton Head for a half mile then came about and with an east wind on his beam followed the Tybee beach south just outside the breakers and realized that his trip was gonna take less time than he had told Mary and he could sail on past Tybee to look at the little inlet between Tybee and Warsaw that led into the islands. In a short time, he was doing just that and in fifteen minutes was out in front of the inlet. This would be the easiest way to Long Island if the wind and tide was right and on a good high tide, he could go right across the marsh as he had seen the Indian canoes do.

He came about and through the wind and headed back toward Tybee with the wind on his other beam and followed along the beach and turned west into the Tybee inlet with the wind at his back and then crossed over to the Tybee side of the river and pulled up on the bank just before the sandy beach ended and the marsh began at the creek. He took the mast and sail and paddle out and walked them up the bank and into the edge of the woods and then went back for the boat and grabbed it by the bow like Daniel had done and pulled it a short way and stopped to rest before pulling it some more and then rest again and then into the edge of the woods.

He went back and sat near the water and looked across the river but didn't see anything. He looked down the beach toward the ocean and saw Mary and the two tackies coming around the point. He thought about her and Daniel and how different they were and how lucky they were to have each other and how lonely they would be if either were an only child. It was pretty much certain that Daniel would be the next light keeper but what would Mary do? Would she get sent off to school? She knew a lot already from what her mother had taught her and all the books she read. His next thought surprised him and it was he wished she were his sister. He liked being around her and hearing what she would say. She was kind of perky like Maggie and next he thought that she and Maggie would enjoy each other's company and probably would get to one day before too long. Maggie was older, but they both liked reading.

Mary was getting close now and Martin smiled at seeing her with the two horses. She came near and asked where the boat was and Martin pointed up to the woods. He took the reins of his horse and got on and asked her where to. She said she wanted to go back to the point she had just come from because it was her favorite place on the island, so they turned and let the horses walk slowly back.

Martin asked her why she liked the point so much and she said because the beach was the widest there and at low tide it extended more than a mile out and she liked all the tide pools left when the tide was out and the contours in the sand left by the tidal current. Martin said he liked it because the Indian Islands were just across the river and she asked him why he liked the Indian Islands so much and he said he wasn't quite sure, but maybe it had something to do with it being one of the last areas around there that was mostly untouched and less tamed and civilized.

Mary said that it would be better to wait an hour or so for the tide to go out all the way before they went out on the big sand bar but she would take him to another one of her favorite places while they waited. He said he would follow wherever she went. She headed back down the beach toward the lighthouse and at the big bend turned inland over the dunes and over the marshy spot where he had been before with Daniel but, instead of continuing straight and going over the big bridge she turned right and went about a quarter mile and the undergrowth opened up to a place where about a dozen huge pine trees were. The group of them were much taller than the surrounding trees.

She got off her horse and took off her shoes and told him to do the same. There was no undergrowth under the pines and nothing but a thick layer of long pine needles in between the giant trees and Mary said she loved the feel of walking here with bare feet. Martin remembered the profile of these tall trees when he was out in Captain Ben's sharpie. They grew higher than the other trees and made a bump in the island profile and easy to spot from sea. Each tree was thicker than Martin was tall.

Mary said it was her favorite place to come. She said it seemed ancient and magical. Martin walked up close to one of the big trees and looked up and the first branches were probably seventy feet up. There were a half dozen huge stumps and Mary saw him looking at them and she said that when her father had first showed her the place, he said that every ten years or so the Indians had come and cut one to make a trading canoe and Martin thought of the long canoe he and Daniel had seen recently.

She motioned for him to follow and she went a ways and pointed to a hole in the ground, full to the edge with water, about five feet across and it looked black. She bent down and cupped her hand and dipped it in the water and showed him and the water was perfectly clear but the hole looked black and the water oozed up and a small rivulet flowed down from it to the edge of the marsh.

She cupped her hand again and drank some and nodded for Martin to do the same. He did and the water was cool and sweeter than he had ever tasted. She said her father said this was a ceremonial meeting place and Indians had been coming here to meet each year from many miles away, for hundreds of years, and that the water comes from deep in the earth and had healing powers. He said it would be an easy place to give directions to. Just go to where the Savannah river dumps out into the ocean, look south at Tybee and look for the clump of trees that stuck up much higher than the rest. After they drank their fill, she went and brought the tackies over and they sucked up the cool water.

She said that if you followed this out, it was the same marshy area that he and Daniel had just crossed over and if you followed it further, it became the creek that emptied out in the Back River beside the landing. Martin remembered the marsh and creek going up into the island and thought that he would one day go back in it at high tide. Mary asked Martin if he was ready to have some lunch and he said he was, and she got the sack from her horse.

They found a spot in the middle of the big pines layered thick with long pine needles and she set out biscuits and bacon and sweet potatoes. She had also brought some oranges and peeled one for Martin and one for herself. They finished the food and a wave of relaxation came over them both. Martin laid back on the soft bed of pine needles and looked up at the giant pines and Mary did too.

The tops of the dozen or so pines formed a canopy, but unlike a hardwood canopy, it allowed filtered sun to reach the needle covered ground, allowing shade with a sprinkling of warm sunlight and there was a slight pungency of pine sap about the needles and was quite pleasant and relaxing. They both drifted into a nap and Mary woke first and touched Martin's shoulder and he woke, surprised that he had dozed and his first sight was Mary smiling at him from above with an outstretched hand for his. He took it and pulled himself up and was struck for a moment by her prettiness and the soft warmth of her hand as he had touched it. She laughed and said what a good sleeper he was and he said he seldom took naps but when he had laid down after their snack, he had felt almost spellbound and the next thing he knew was her touching him.

She laughed again and said he was a dreamer, but Martin didn't understand what that meant, but laughed at himself with her. He did, however, manage to think to himself what a difference it was to be around Mary, compared to being around her brother.

Mary said they had lingered there so long that the tide was already coming in over the point on the south end and they would have to ride out on it another day but they could ride up to the Lazaretto landing. Mary said she liked riding on the oyster shell path through the marsh and hammocks to Lazaretto. Martin said he did too and that would give him a chance to look at the bridge construction like his father had wanted him to do.

They got on the tackies and road the short distance to the big bridge. Jacob saw them and had the men clear the bridge for them to pass and Martin got off his horse after he crossed and walked back to look at what was going on. Jacob met him and walked with him back across and explained what they were doing. They had first driven down the new cedar pilings with a device made with a piece of oak log as a big hammer with two handles fastened to the sides and it was set on top of the piling and two men stood on the bridge and lifted the rig up and slammed it down on top of the new piling, driving it down into the mud until it reached harder ground, then driving it down some more until it had good bearing.

All the new pilings had been put in and braced and now they were adding new cross framing and then new decking, spaced closer together than before. He showed Martin how they were replacing the new framing and decking, one section at a time, using the existing bridge to work off of, so the bridge could still be used every day. Martin got the gist of it in his mind and thanked Jacob and went back with Mary and they continued on to the landing. Mary said she liked the oyster shell trail because she had always wanted to walk across the marsh but no one could do that because of sinking in mud. Martin then told her about the burial area near there that he had taken Daniel to and she said she wanted to go. He told her about the little clearing where someone had been hiding and she said she still wanted to see and Martin said he would take her.

They took the horses to the landing and tied them. Martin said hello to the cook and his helper and said they were gonna leave the horses there and go for a walk. The cook told Martin he would be better to walk out toward the point overlooking the south channel and Martin thought it odd that he would mention that but he had told Mary that he would show her the area beyond the old quarantine station. Martin asked Mary if she knew about the quarantine station that had been there and she said she had heard her father talk about it and how terrible it was. Martin said it was probably worse than anything they could imagine. He began to point out a few ballast stones here and there then came to the spot where there were rows and rows spaced closely and Mary said there must be hundreds and Martin said there are probably more that are unmarked than are marked. He put his finger to his lips to tell her to be silent as he headed toward the little hollowed out spot in the thicket that he and Daniel had found. Martin could feel his heart pounding and he looked back at Mary and she didn't seem afraid. Martin slowed down, watching that each step was on a sandy place to not make any noise.

As they came close to the spot, he looked back and pointed ahead to Mary and they slowed even more to avoid any noise. When they were close enough to see in the little clearing Martin gasped and put his hand over his mouth to seal any sound of it. There was a man lying on a blanket asleep. Martin recognized the blanket to be like the ones they had brought for the men at the landings. He also noticed a bowl and utensils like the ones they had brought. He looked at Mary and her eyes were wide and he motioned for them to go back and Martin followed Mary back, looking over his shoulder often to see if they were being followed. When they were about a hundred feet away, they ran and Martin could barely keep up with Mary and they didn't stop until they were back at the landing.

After they caught their breath, Martin said that he didn't think they needed to be afraid but he had let fear over rule his reason. The bowl and utensils and blanket were what they had brought from the Milam place and had to have been given to whoever that was because the cook and his helper were always there during the day and many men were around at night and it wouldn't be possible for someone to come and steal anything and not be seen or heard. He said Jacob would know and he would ask him on their way back. They didn't let on to the cook about what they had seen and left for home.

When they got to the bridge construction, Jacob had the men move the materials off the bridge and Martin saw that they had finished a section of the new decking and noticed that the horses were less hesitant walking over it but when they got to the part that had the old decking, they slowed and were uneasy. When they got to the other side, he motioned to Jacob to come over and asked him about the man they had seen and Jacob said he had come up last night, half starved, and begged for food. He had run away from a city way up the river from Savannah and hid on a ship and shortly after leaving the port of Savannah, was discovered and was let off there by the ship captain. Jacob said he was terribly worried about it because helping him could bring trouble to everyone. Martin told Jacob not to worry and that he had done the right thing to feed the man and touched Jacobs shoulder affectionately, but Jacob still had a worried look. They headed home down the oyster shell trail a ways and Martin stopped to talk with Mary. He told her that harboring a runaway was against the law and they should tell Charles and Margo.

When they got home, Charles and Daniel were up in the lighthouse, signaling Savannah. Margo was there but Mary told Martin that they should wait until everyone was together. Margo sensed something was astir and asked Mary what was going on and she said something was going on but she wanted to wait until her father and Daniel were there. Margo asked if something was wrong with Captain Jones and Mary said no and Margo asked what it was again. As Mary was about to say something, she heard Daniel come in the back door and Margo relented and said she had some tea ready and Mary met her father as he was coming in and told him that she needed to talk with him and her mother. Margo poured tea and they sat at the kitchen table and Mary told of her and Martin finding the runaway and what Jacob had done and said. Charles had a look of seriousness that Martin had not seen before and his brow was furrowed deeply. He told them that they did the right thing to come and tell them because it was a very serious matter, because if slave hunters came and caught him, he could be frightened into telling about Jacob helping him and Jacob could be taken away to jail and maybe other things worse than that. Mary said she had heard about slave hunters and their dogs and how about half the time the dogs chewed a runaway to death before they could be stopped. Charles said that was possible but slave hunters didn't get paid for a dead slave, so they wanted them kept alive. Margo said they should at least get him away from Lazaretto, because that would be the first place a slave hunter boat would stop.

Martin said that would be good because Jacob had looked terribly worried about what to do and if he had done the wrong thing by helping him. Charles said he did need to move from Lazaretto and that the south end would probably be best because it would be less likely to look like we were helping by harboring him. He said he wasn't sure what to do after that but he would be best to wait there until we came up with something, but the thing to remember is that helping him is against the law and again, if he were caught and frightened into telling what happened, he could go to jail and lose the lighthouse position, and that would be the end of the Dyers at the Tybee lighthouse.

So, whatever we do, once we start, has to work. Jacob needs to give him directions to the wooded area near the Back River landing and let him walk alone so there is no trace of anyone else's scent with him, then burn off the place he has been sleeping at and he needs some food for a few days, and we will see if we can find him a way to get off the island. Daniel said maybe a pilot or crewman down on the beach might know of something and Charles said not to talk to any of them, but it would be safe to talk to Captain Jones because he was like family. Martin asked if it might be possible for him to go across the river and the Indians helping him, and Charles said that could be another possibility, in light of what y'all saw recently, and said he wouldn't be surprised if Alice's family was still alive because of help from the Indians. Charles said, looking at Daniel, you need to go now and tell Jacob what the plan is and tell him to tell the runaway what you and Martin look like so he won't run if you have to go for him for any reason.

Jacob and crew were just leaving the bridgework and Daniel called Jacob back to the bridge and said that there was something that Charles had wanted him to attend to about the old pilings they were pulling out. Jacob looked surprised and then saw a slight wink from Daniel and knew there was something he needed to tell him without the others hearing. When Jacob got there Daniel told him what the plan was and Jacob was somewhat relieved after worrying all day if he had done something dangerously wrong which could cause trouble for the Dyers and himself. He said he would see to everything that he said as soon as he got back to Lazaretto.

Next morning, Martin and Daniel were up early as usual and had some breakfast and were up top before it was totally light so they could look over things for anything new. Martin looked out to Long Island first and saw the usual two different cooking fires and then over at Claw Island and saw smoke from a fire there. He didn't know what to make of that, other than it was another place for them to stay sometimes. Martin said he hadn't looked over to the Lazaretto landing yet as he always did and set up on that side and looked and was surprised to see an extra boat there and showed Daniel and he said he didn't know who it could be. They put the monocular away and went down and told Charles about the extra boat and he said they should go right away and see who it was in case it had something to do with the runaway. Mary heard them and said she would stay so they could go on the horses instead of the wagon. They hurried on out and got the horses ready and left.

Martin and Daniel slowed the horses down a few hundred yards before the landing to talk. Martin said that he was worried that this boat might be slave hunters and was glad they had sent the runaway to the south end yesterday. Daniel said that if these were slave hunters, they could tell them that they needed to look on the south end where runways usually went and it would take them a couple hours to get there by boat and they could ride there in twenty minutes and take him somewhere else. It would not look good for them to see where he had been staying so close to the landing. As they had slowed, a swarm of gnats came over them and the horses got restless and they broke out in a gallop to escape them. As they approached the landing, they saw a man with a gun on his shoulder talking to Jacob and both were busy trying to keep the gnats away from their faces. Jacob was showing him the special permit papers he had been given, with a list of names of the Milam crew and the sub contract crew. Normally, no more than seven slaves were allowed to be off together, but Henry had made special arrangements for this situation.

The rest of the bridge crew were bunched up in the smoke coming off the cooking fire to ward off the gnats. There were three men in the boat, battling the bugs and yelling for the man with the gun to come on or they were gonna leave him. The man saw the boys and said that he had barely been able to understand Jacob and didn't think Jacob understood him but that the permit looked in order. He went on to say that the reason they were there was because a runaway slave was found hiding on a ship leaving Savannah and had stopped and sent him ashore to this landing before departing the river. The pilot had reported it when he had returned to Savannah recently, but it had happened some time ago.

The slave hunter said there was an unusually large reward posted in the Savannah paper and they aimed to find the runaway and get it. The workers had cut some green palmetto frons and heaped them up on the fire to make more smoke and Daniel nodded for the man to follow him over to the smoke to try and escape the gnats. Daniel said most runaways went to the south end where British ships, still to this day, sometimes sent long boats ashore to fetch runaways. Between coughing fits from the smoke, Daniel said he was welcome to search the area.

The men in the boat were yelling and the man said he guessed they would go around to the south end of Tybee and Daniel told them where the shallow well was in case they needed water and he mentioned that they kept a small boat there, pulled up in the woods. The headman was pleased, thinking he was helped out by Daniel and given good information.

They shoved off and the three oarsmen rowed as hard as they could but a cloud of gnats, not slowed by tide, stayed swarmed over them. Daniel and Martin watched as they were barely making forward progress against the tide and the men would let go of their oar to clear the gnats off their face and the loose oar would be clanked by a working oar beside it and they were dropping oars right and left. The boss man that Daniel had talked to was at the helm and yelling every time a man stopped rowing to beat the gnats off his face. Their slow progress enabled the gnats even more time to feast and stay with them. Then, after a loud burst of yelling and cursing, the boat turned back and headed toward the landing again.

Daniel and Martin walked over close to the creek bank and heard one man yelling that he never wanted to come back to this place. As the boat passed the landing, the head man saw Daniel and said they would try again tomorrow and the yelling continued as the boat left the creek and stopped at the point at the entrance to the South Channel where there was enough of an ocean breeze coming in to keep the gnats off. Martin and Daniel and the men on the landing were coughing but were free from the bugs while engulfed in smoke.

Although they didn't like the men, they couldn't help but feel some small amount of pity for them. Meanwhile the cook had a pot on the fire and had filled it with water and had some of the men strip a lot of myrtle branches of leaves and was boiling the leaves to make an ointment for the bridge crew to coat their exposed flesh to ward off the gnats. This was the first time since they had gotten there that the gnats were unbearable.

Martin told Jacob he had done a good job with the slave hunters and Jacob told him that Daniel was the one that told the best lie to get them gone. Jacob said he had never in his long life been glad for gnats and said he might change his mind before the day was done and they all felt some relief and laughed and coughed at the same time while still in the smoke. Daniel walked out of the smoke to see where the slavers had gotten to and saw them down on the point and saw that they were making camp to be there for the night and felt some relief that at least they were where an eye could be kept on them. Daniel told Jacob that they would go on down to the Back River and take the runaway to another place and Jacob said they were late getting started but would go on to work. Because of all that was going on they had forgotten the poor tackies who were constantly swishing the bugs off their face with their tail and more than ready to run when they were mounted and shot down the oyster trail to outrun the swarms.

The boys didn't slow down until halfway through the island and stopped to see if there were any more bugs. There were no more and they breathed another sigh of relief. The whole ordeal had seemed like a long time but was less than an hour and they continued on to the south end.

When they rode out of the woods into the small dunes along the Back River, they felt the wind in their faces and were glad of it because bugs and an onshore breeze couldn't be in the same place at the same time and what was onshore there was offshore at the Lazaretto landing and why the bugs were so bad there that morning.

They looked around to see if the runaway was anywhere and didn't see anything and took everything off the horses and walked them to the shallow well and let them drink. They didn't know what to do so they sat on top of a dune and watched the edge of the woods trying to think of how they might get his attention without scaring him. What they didn't know was that they were being watched by who they were trying to see. He was certain who they were according to what he had been told, but scared and sad and famished. Not famished from lack of food because he had plenty of food from Jacob lately but famished of spirit from his ordeal of the last few weeks. He had been so tired that he had walked into the work camp at the landing to give himself up, expecting to be returned into his life of bondage, but was instead fed and encouraged by Jacob. Now, seeing the two white boys, with in mind a lifelong understanding of what most white people were about, he was hesitant, even though Jacob had told him that if he saw them, to not be afraid. He saw the smaller of the two stand up and cup his hands to his mouth and yell something. He didn't understand the word he yelled but felt the tone and saw something in the boy's body movements that helped him overcome his fear and yell back and it made both boys jump up and wave their arms and he walked out of the edge of the woods to be seen.

With head hung down, the young man walked toward the boys, slowly and looking up briefly every few moments to watch the language of their body movements. He was trembling and ready to bolt away but at the same time remembering the face of Jacob and the feeling he had when Jacob was talking and now it was the faith in that feeling that kept him from running. When he was about twenty paces away, Martin said something that he didn't understand, but he felt the same thing in his words that was in Jacobs and he collapsed to his knees in the sand, unafraid but overcome with his stresses. Martin hurried over and instinctively reached down and tried to lift him up but he was bigger and couldn't until he felt Daniel with him and they stood him up and together managed to walk down by the river bank and sit him down.

The tackies had been watching and came over and nuzzled Daniel, ready to go home. Martin sensed the exhausted spirit of the man and the only words he could say was, was "Its all good," and he repeated it every few minutes and was shocked when the man repeated it back to him in a proper English dialect and Martin was relieved that he was coming out of his distressed state enough to talk. Martin repeated the same words again and they were said back with a head raised up a bit. Martin said they were there to help and that they were gonna take him to a safe place and help him all they could. Martin didn't know what else to say but finally said as he pointed to his chest, "Martin" and touched Daniel and said," Daniel." Still feeble, the man said, "Mallie," and for the first time raised his head up and looked into Martin's eyes only for a quick glance.

They stood quiet for a little longer and Martin felt a small perk in Mallie and he looked up again and their eyes met and Martin bumped him with his shoulder slightly and smiled and he felt Mallie come a little more to life. Then again, the boys were shocked by him saying, "Thank you" several times and "I'm Sorry," as if he needed to apologize for his sunken state. Martin got the water and they all took a long swig and again another perk came over him and they stood and looked each other over and Mallie held his head up more normal and let them both see into his eyes and he into theirs. Mallie spoke first and said that Jacob was right in saying that he need not be afraid of them and had said that Martin was not like any man he had ever met and could feel the spirit of a man no matter what color and his father and family were the same way. He said he didn't understand then but could see and feel now what he was saying. Martin and Daniel continued to be amazed at what good language and clarity Mallie spoke with and how he had woken from his dejected state so quickly. Martin told him about the slave hunters and how they would be coming there to look for him but they wanted to take him to a safe place where he could rest without worry of being found until something was done more permanently. He also said they could talk more after they went there and said they needed to pick up any provisions or anything that might show that he had been there. Mallie led them to where he had been and they picked up the few things he had and then took some leafy myrtle branches and swept his prints from the sandy area outside the woods. Daniel saddled the two horses while Martin stood with Mallie, then with Martin and Mallie on one horse and Daniel on the other, they headed for Mallie's next hiding place.

Once at the big pine area, Martin showed him the well hole with the water bubbling up and gave him the lunch bag they had with a few remaining snacks. Then Martin suggested they sit and talk because he was interested in how Mallie came to be there and he wanted to tell about him and Daniel and the lighthouse at Tybee. They got some water and sat down on the thick bed of pine needles and Martin wanted to tell Mallie about them to put any fears away he might have and as simply and general as he could he explained about his family and the lighthouse and Daniels family.

Martin noticed how Mallie's overall look had changed since he had first seen him when he walked up to them. His desperate look was gone and a more normal way was about him after Martin had finished telling about his side of the story. Martin asked Mallie to tell them how he came to be there and learn such good English and all and said they had heard a little from the slave hunters. Mallie took a deep breath and said he had thought about his life some but not much because he was always busy with the many everyday tasks he had and when he wasn't, he only thought about how he would run away one day.

He said that he had been a slave of an important and well known lawyer in Augusta, named Thomas Waters, for as long as he could remember. He had become his personal attendant, which meant he followed him everywhere and did whatever needed doing. His master was very smart, but kept everything a mess and was disorganized, so most of his time was spent looking for what his frustrated master couldn't find in his mess of papers and books. He would print a few simple words and I looked for what matched them and some were repeated enough that I learned a few words.

After a few years I could read a little and from that I was able to read a few books then it just became easier and easier. I even began looking up different things for him in his law books and was always around him in his meetings and learned more and more about the law and how it worked. After many years I had learned more than many lawyers.

He got plenty to eat and a roof over his head but he was miserable. He had the most unpleasant master who hit him with his walking stick if he couldn't find something he wanted fast enough and cursed him awful. He said he thought about a way to escape every day. He said his master had always done good in his law practice but not hugely good because he was always so disorganized. Mallie said when he had become familiar with the law, he was able to organize things and his master won all his cases and became wealthy and well known. He was still just as mean as ever, though, but acted nice to him when other people were around. The mayor of Augusta died suddenly and there weren't many people that were qualified enough to take his place until they could hold an election, so he was asked to fill in temporarily. Before the mayor had died, he had been invited on a ceremonial maiden trip on the steamship Savannah to Charleston from Savannah and he was obligated to go, instead of the deceased mayor. He was a certain kind of smart but couldn't remember names, keep up with any of his important papers or even find his shoes, so that meant that

Mallie would have to go.

Mallie said his master knew he had to have him all the time or else he could face embarrassment or worse if he was left to his own to take care of things. So, they went to Savannah and there was a delay for a few days in the departure of the new ship to Charleston because of the weather, and they stayed in Savannah for a while and he followed his ill-humored master everywhere he went and he mostly paced the riverfront. I had read about the city and the lighthouse at Tybee and how the ships came in and out of the city, by tidal current and saw that the departures, from the city, were when the tide started out.

I saw several ships with cotton bails loaded on the decks with canvas covers over them, making preparations for departure one afternoon, and figured one might be leaving on the high tide during the night. It seemed crazy but I didn't think I would ever be that near a place of departure again so I decided to go for it.

Mallie said his master had gotten special permission for him to stay in his room and that night, when he passed out from drinking rum, with one bag and a few clothes and a loaf of bread and a water bottle, he left. I knew I would probably get caught during the voyage but wasn't afraid they would throw me overboard because I was a young slave with value because I could read and speak proper English. It wasn't a well thought out plan but desperation can make a man act rash.

I was discovered just before we got to Tybee but the Captain didn't want to turn back and the river pilot said they could drop me off at Tybee and he would tell the authorities when he returned to Savannah. I was taken ashore and left with some bread and a little dried meat, where I almost died of hunger and bug bites and then the work crew showed up a few days later. I was so desperate and miserable I walked into their camp one night expecting to be returned to my evil owner who would have beaten me severely, but here I am in my third location and I must say my accommodations are improving, thanks to y'all.

Martin and Daniel were impressed at how well Mallie talked and at his courage to stowaway on a ship and Mallie saw their astonishment. He asked them if they would have not done the same and then said it was an unfair question because they had no way of knowing what a life of bondage was like. Martin said he had often thought about that very thing, especially after meeting his new ex slave friend, Jehu, he had met recently, who had been severely treated. Mallie said he had found only one book at his owners home that spoke against slavery and the movement of a group in New England to abolish it and that is why he had wanted to go there and pulled a scrap of paper from his pocket with the name of that organization and an address in Philadelphia, Pennsylvania.

Martin said this had been a big day and they should be going. Mallie looked at the two of them and his voice broke as he said how he owed his life to them and Jacob. His emotion struck them both and they both reached out and touched his back. They said they were fortunate enough to have been taught well and were going to help him the best they could. When they got to the place with the big pines, Martin assured him that it was a safe place for him to be would be and showed him the fresh water hole. He pulled a thin round wooden tube from his pocket and twisted a bung out of the end and showed Mallie three stick matches and told him to use them carefully and put the bung back in and gave it to him. He assured him again of this being a safe place and he could rest in peace and with their leftover lunch and the food Jacob had given him and water, he was good for two or three days but they would be back sooner than that and for him to keep an eye out for them and to keep out of sight of anyone else.

They got back to the lighthouse a little before dark and got cleaned up for supper and sat down with everyone and told the story of their day and everyone's food got cold on their plates from listening instead of eating. Finally, Charles said they had done the right thing but he was unsure what to do next with Mallie and the longer they waited, the greater the risk was for them and him and he would think about it and it was a serious thing and if not handled right, could make a lot of things very difficult. Martin said that the place with the big pines and fresh water was his favorite place on Tybee. Charles said it was not only his favorite place but in years past was the favorite place for Indians to come from all over for about a month or so in December, starting many years before colonials began coming to Tybee. His grandfather told him they came and stayed in the big pines to socialize and tell stories and happenings of things in their villages. Some drank yaupon in a ceremonial way to gain clarity about the coming year. Margo knew about making yaupon that way but Martin didn't and neither did Daniel or Mary.

Charles went on to say that drinking yaupon for a ceremony was different than how they drank yaupon and he could see the quizzical look on their faces. He said they put a lot of yaupon leaves in a big pot with water and cooked it slowly for a few days until it cooked down to a thick black almost syrupy drink. He said the purpose of the ceremony was in search of clarity to make important decisions. A few of them would get together and swallow some and it would cause them to vomit and they would swallow some more and vomit again and after three or so times they would become purged and achieve clarity of thought and make decisions about matters of importance.

Charles said he hadn't tried that but knew the Indians had great knowledge of natural things and it was probably a good thing. He added that the Indians also brewed yaupon a weaker way for everyday use and taught the colonials and now, at least in the south, it is a regular drink and getting more popular, plus it is free for the picking, unlike the tea brought over by the Brits from the Far East. He said there was another thing that they came to the big pines for but it was not often but maybe every ten years or so. He said that those pines, for some reason, grew larger and straighter than anywhere else and they would come and cut one and spend a long time making a voyaging canoe with it.

Martin said he had seen a few old stumps and Charles shook his head in agreement. Mary said what would happen if they were all cut and Charles said he didn't know but that probably wouldn't happen now that only a few old Indians came anymore. Charles said there were a few last year and Martin said he would sure like to meet them and added that when he went by Tybee on Captain Ben's boat, the big pines were easy to spot because they were clumped together and were much higher than the other trees and made a bump in the shape of the island.

Charles said that now people look for the lighthouse to know it is Tybee but before that they must have looked for the bump of the tall pines, and they laughed, but it was true. Mary said since Martin had come to the island of the tall pines, more exciting things had happened in a few weeks than had happened in ten years and that the books she had been reading had seemed exciting until all these goings on and she might should write her own book and they laughed at Mary's reaction to things. Martin really enjoyed hearing about all that and thanked Charles for telling about it.

Margo saw Daniel yawning while Charles was talking and suggested the boys go on to bed because they had such a long and stressful day. Mary said she was stressed and tired from just hearing about what had gone on at the Lazaretto landing. She said slave hunters on Tybee were as bad or worse than a duel on Tybee. The boys excused themselves and went up to bed.

As Martin lay to sleep, his thoughts were that he still had Alice and going over to the Indian islands to be concerned about. It worried him at first, then he remembered how things always were when he was with Alice. It seemed like the world was always waiting and opened up for her and his concerns ended and the next thing he knew was Margo's broom handle tapping on the floor in the morning.

Back in Savannah, every hour of Henry's time was planned and filled with his family, the Milam place goings on, and his new ice business. Today his first stop was down at the riverfront to see if Captain Ben was back and he was, so Henry pulled beside his boat and Ben stuck his head out and when he saw who it was, came out with his usual smile and asked how Martin was doing on Tybee. Henry said he was busy and there had been a lot of excitement. He said he was here to hire him for two things when he was available. First, to deliver a wooden item about three and a half feet wide by two and a half feet deep by seven feet tall and about five hundred pounds, to Lazaretto and second, bring another load of ice from Darien like before. Ben said he could take the first item to Tybee in a few days but wouldn't be going to Darien again for another week and be coming back in about a week after that.

Henry said that would work if he could get the first item done in time and the Captain said he could hold up for a day if that would help. Henry said if he could do that he would go ahead and commit to it, thinking the extra day would work. He said if there was any change to that plan, he would let him know before the day was out. Henry said that it looked like the ice business was something that was going to continue and grow and if so they might need to think of a way to better insulate his holds but not interfere with his other cargo capacity. Ben said he had been thinking about that to and had an idea already. Henry asked what and Ben said that early on as a young sailor on a merchant vessel he was laid over in Portugal for a few weeks, waiting for a load of cork. The village port we were in had been exporting cork for wine and champagne bottles for over a hundred years. He said the cork was the bark of a tree that grew there and big pieces were peeled off trees and the trees grew more back. There had been so much around that scrapes were nailed up on house walls and layered on roofs to keep them cool in the summer and warm in the winter. He said he saw large pieces of it about two inches thick by six or eight feet long and about three feet wide, stacked up everywhere, waiting to be shipped out.

Anyhow, He said he never thought about it again until they were shoveling out the wet sawdust from the hold after they had unloaded the ice at the Milam plantation. It was wet and soggy and probably didn't insulate very good when it was wet and we saw that a good portion of the ice had melted from what we had loaded up in Darien. I remembered the houses in Portugal, with big flat pieces nailed up on their outside walls and roof and it held up to rain and sun and sea spray and kept the houses cool in the summer and warm in winter. The fact that it doesn't absorb moisture is one of the reasons it works to seal a bottle of wine. I figured about four inches could be nailed up to the walls of my hold and left without being a hindrance for other kinds of cargo and be there when I had ice to haul.

Henry said he appreciated him mentioning that because it could be better than the cotton they were using now which was better than the moss that John had used and he asked Ben how he might find the source of cork. Ben said he didn't know but he knew who could find it out and said Walter Milam. Henry said he would ask him and said if he would see him in a couple days with the icebox and men to help load it, if he hadn't heard different from him by days end.

Next, Henry went to see Jason to see how the icebox was coming and found him and his helper hard at work on it. Jason said it would be all put together by tomorrow and Henry said he would be there the morning after that with men and a wagon. Jason said he would be done with the ice chest for the supply boat a few days after that but wanted to go and measure the inside of one of the supply boats before he started.

Henry said for him to hire a carriage to get there and back and he would pay for it. He also told Jason that they eventually would need an ice chest in both boats since they alternated the boats each week but they could use the same boat until they had tried out this first ice chest in case there needed to be any improvements. Henry mentioned the cork idea that Ben had suggested and Jason said cork sounded better and maybe they wouldn't have to make the walls so thick and he had been concerned that cotton might not be good if it got soaked with water but he would build it to keep water out as best he could.

Henry said he would like to try the cork on the boat as soon as he was able to get some. Jason said to bring six men because the new icebox was so heavy and Henry said he would and headed back to the Milam place. He went first to the boathouse and went in looking for Johnny and found him doing some boat maintenance and asked him to come outside to talk. They walked outside and Henry reached out and touched Johnny's shoulder and said he knew he must be worried about Alice going to Tybee to look for her parents. Johnny said he worried about it every minute and would worry about it every minute until she got back but the same thing that made him worry about her wanted her to go. Henry smiled at Johnny and was struck with his answer. He told Johnny how Alice was as dear to his parents as he and Martin were and they worried too but what Alice did and said was usually right and she had said how kind the Indian lady was and Charles and Jacob thought it was best if she went and Martin thought so to.

Johnny's eyes welled up and thanked Henry for coming and talking to him about it because it made him feel some better already, but he would still worry every minute. Henry said they had asked Charles to include in the messages every day about how Martin and Alice were doing and he could walk up to the house every afternoon to check. Johnny said he would. Henry went from there to the sawdust pile to get some ice for the icebox on their porch and saw that it was getting low. It had been a bit more than a week and he figured he would have enough to take today and in a few days to go in the new icebox going to the lighthouse and if he was lucky some to go on the supply boat in the new ice chest the following week, then shortly after that, Ben should be back with more.

He didn't have any help so instead of sawing one big piece off, he sawed two smaller pieces that he could lift and sat them on the buggy floor. At home he saw there was a small piece left still and set the new pieces in the pan. Henry liked messing about with ice and enjoyed planning and doing the things needed to get started in the ice business. He liked it because he liked business but more so because it was an entirely new kind of business and they didn't have anything much to go on and had to invent most everything, as they went along. He also liked it because he believed it could be very profitable. His family depended on a contract with the federal government every year and he was glad to have something to fall back on in case that didn't happen for some reason. It was unlikely that would happen but he wanted to be prepared if it did.

Alice was both happy and a worried about her trip to Tybee in a few days. She had thought about this for a long time and knew that she may find out that they were still alive or that they had died. And, if they were alive, what would happen? Would they stay or would they come to the Milam place. They were still runaways and belonged to the evil owner they had run away from. This last possibility unnerved even Alice. She was still a runaway and belonged to him too. She had always felt secure with the Milam's but some people in Savannah knew her story and she was a legend in slave cultures of Georgia and South Carolina. Walter was to powerful a character for anyone to do anything to harm her or change her status, but if her family was alive and the story was known, it would be newsworthy and the Savannah paper would publish it and something bad could come of it all. What could become of Johnny and who might the baby in her belly belong to if they had to return to South Carolina? If it came down to it, she would do about anything to keep her baby and Johnny.

Since Alice survived the awful massacre ordeal, nothing had ever come close to matching what she had gone through. This was the first time she had felt the grip of fear in her life after that. At the height of her fear and nervousness, a knock came to the door and Henry's voice called out her name. She told him to come in and when he did he saw the tears and the sad look about her and was surprised because he had never seen Alice anyway but perky and positive with a shining face and smile. He reached out to touch her shoulder and she sobbed uncontrollably. Henry pulled her to him and she felt limp and sobbed his shoulder wet for a while before she could speak. When she could, she told Henry of her concerns and Henry assured her that she had the whole Milam family to support her, whatever the outcome came to be, and reminded her of the wisdom of Walter and how he and Martha loved her as they did him and Martin. He said she was not going to need to run away again and no one was to have her baby or Johnny. He told her that the worst that could happen was that he would pay their wretched owner for her and her family.

First, he said, they need to know if they are in fact alive and then act according to what that outcome is. Alice gained control of herself and apologized to Henry for being so needy and Henry said that she had always been a giver and there was no shame in receiving. Alice said what she needed was some tea and went and poured some for them both and they went outside and sat on the little porch. She said she had lost her hope from fear of what might happen instead of gaining hope and happiness for possibly seeing her family again and thanked Henry for his support and encouragement. Henry said he shouldn't have waited just before she left to come talk to her and she said he came at the perfect time because her cup was empty but now was full again and she was ready for whatever happened. They finished their tea and Alice thanked Henry again and Henry said no that it was him that thanked her for all she had done for him and his family and the whole Milam place.

Next morning, the tide was high early when the supply boat was about to leave with Alice, sitting near Johnny at the helm. Everyone on the place knew by now about her trip and many were on the bank to see her off including Walter, Martha, and Henry and his family. As they shoved off the bank and the oars began dipping and pulling, Johnny started the chantey with a verse and the oarsmen and all those on the bank did the chorus, this repeated until Johnny's lead verse could no longer be heard on the bank. It was somewhat of an eerie departure.

Henry set about his tasks, one of which was to go to town to make sure the icebox was completed to be picked up and shipped the next day. Also, he had gotten two letters the day before, one from John Wilcox about his moving plans and one from Thomas, the engineer from Boston about his upcoming visit. On his trip to town, he thought to himself about his visit with Alice and what may become of her search for her parents and thought about the valor of his little brother in his helping her.

Jason had the icebox ready and it looked good and Jason showed Henry a few improvements he had made over the first one he had built. Henry paid him and went from there to check to see if Ben was still on schedule to leave the next day. He was surprised to see Ashley and Ken there with him. Captain Ben said they were doing some maintenance this morning and would load their cargo today and be ready to leave with the outgoing tide early the next day after loading Henry's icebox. Henry had given the Captain the dimensions and they had made some adjustments on the deck of the sharpie for it to set and be tied down. Henry said he would be there at daylight and he would signal Charles today on Tybee to meet him with extra men to unload at the high tide the following day.

He also said he had spoken to his father about getting some cork and he knew immediately who in Savannah that had some. Henry had much to do and told Captain Ben he would see him in the morning and headed out to finish his tasks before going home.

15.
ALICE AND THE INDIAN ISLANDS

Meanwhile on Tybee everyone had been waiting for the day Alice would get there. Even with everything else going on, Martin had been up on the lighthouse and had made a detailed chart of all the creeks he could see leading up to Long Island where the main Indian camp appeared to be. He went over and over them until he memorized them in his mind's eye.

He had two plans to get there. One was through the creeks and the other was to sail directly across the marsh, but that would have to be at the very top of the tide. Daniel had helped him fashion two special push sticks with a small fork on the bottom to push against the bottom of the marsh grass. He did not know what to expect and how long they might be but figured that if they needed to be there all day, with the moon full, and the high tide at the end of the day, he could sail or push back across the marsh directly toward the lighthouse and across the back river. If they had to leave shortly after they got there, he could follow the outgoing tide in the creek to the small inlet to the ocean, only, if he left soon enough after high tide.

Charles and Martin took the wagon down to the landing to wait for the boat to come and they stopped to talk to Jacob for a few minutes on their way. Once at the landing, they waited in the wagon and Martin talked about what he had planned about him and Alice going to look for her family. Charles said he would send Daniel with them in the wagon and have him wait all day and into the night if need be. Martin pointed to the supply boat in the distance and on schedule. Martin found himself nervous and trembling slightly. This is something he had been thinking about since he was ten.

He hadn't known how but had told her then that he would do this, and he still didn't know how. He had studied the creeks and islands and what he could of the Indians and where they were and Alice had become part of the plan to go with him, which he never would have imagined. He reckoned that the biggest moments were to happen in the next few days and there were still some big questions about that, and he had the business with Mallie to do something about and he wished that he could put off Mallie but knew that couldn't be done. In his mind's eye, he could see them sailing up to the spot on Long Island where the bigger camp seemed to be. What he would say or how they might react or if the lady named Ayana was there and if Alice's family was there or if they were not, what then? After worrying about all that, he remembered that in the beginning, he was gonna be alone in his boat or maybe with Daniel to approach the island and now, Alice was gonna be there and that calmed him down. He heard his name called from what seemed like far away and then again and realized it was Charles right beside him.

Martin had been in one of those trances that Mary had caught him in and Charles asked him if he was all right, and Martin said he was fine, and was just doing a little thinking. Charles put his arm over Martin's shoulder and said he was still yet a boy but was doing things fit for a man and a good man at that. Martin didn't know what to say to that but it made him feel good and said thanks and called him Uncle Charles. This took Charles by surprise and he found himself welled up slightly and squeezed Martin's shoulder.

The boat was turning into Lazaretto creek now and they could see Alice back by Johnny and heard Johnny start the chantey with a verse and Alice and the crew followed with the chorus and the cook and his helper, on the bank, joined in. Charles got the biggest kick out of it because he usually missed hearing the chanteys. Johnny steered the boat perfectly up to the rails and stayed with Alice in the boat and had the crew winch the boat up and then got out and helped Alice out. Charles watched and thought to himself and remembered Alice being loaded onto the supply boat as a child years ago after they had brought her home covered with pluff mud and in shock.

Again, he welled up and couldn't stop a few tears from flooding over. He quickly recovered himself and went over and hugged Alice and congratulated her and Johnny about the baby and said he was gonna take them home and send the guards back with the wagon to pick up the supplies. Johnny looked surprised because he had reckoned he would be staying at the boatmen's shanty.

Charles noticed this and said he was not about to have them separate for the night. He said it would be rough enough that Johnny may not see her until next week. He said they had been working and sprucing up a small room they had been using for storage and it had a window and was comfortable. Johnny was dumbfounded and didn't know what to say because he had never stayed at a white man's house and even though he was accustomed to the fair and equal treatment by the Milams, he was still unprepared for what was happening. Alice felt close to Charles and Margo because they had rescued her. She had always thought of her time after the massacre as her second life. Charles and Margo were the first faces she saw when she came back around after being picked up out of the mud, unconscious but alive and taken to the lighthouse. Seeing their faces and the love she felt was her first experience when she had awakened.

At the time, she had no recollection of what had happened, not just at the massacre but anything of her whole earlier life and the situation was akin to a newborn seeing its parents for the first time. These were the thoughts and feelings in Alice as she told Johnny in the most pleasant way that everything was fine about him being with her and he just had to forget what he thought he knew about things and squeezed his hand assuringly. Martin had kept quiet at their greetings but at a break he said hey to Alice and she hugged him and thanked him and Charles for what they were doing for her. Charles said that Martin had been the one to thank because he had been on a mission to make this all happen.

Martin was sheepish about the compliments and steered the attention away from himself by grabbing Johnny's hand and shaking it and telling him how crazy and exciting sailing the boat in the ocean had been, and he now had another bigger boat that Captain Jones had given him and he hoped that Johnny would help him with that too. Charles said they needed to go because after they got home, he was sending the guards back to pick up the supplies from today's delivery and he didn't want them sitting too long. He helped Alice up in front and Martin and Johnny got in the back.

They stopped for only a moment to say hey to Jacob and when he saw Alice, his smile almost got bigger than his face and Johnny barely managed to tell Jacob that he was staying at the lighthouse tonight and would be there tomorrow in plenty of time to leave with the tide. Jacob was a little surprised but no one saw the wink that Alice did to Jacob, that made him smile again. They hurried on to the lighthouse and got out and sent the guards back with the wagon.

Alice looked around. She felt a connection to the place but couldn't remember being there after the massacre, but she had been told about it. They walked over to the house and Margo was waiting and hugged her and smiled and cried at the same time. She hugged Johnny too and said how proud she was of him. They went in the house and she showed them the room where they were to stay and where to wash up and refresh and said to come out on the porch and have some tea when they were finished.

Margo squeezed a dozen oranges in a big jug and added a pot of yaupon and some honey and Daniel and Mary took the mugs and tea outside and brought a few extra chairs. Johnny and Alice came out and sat down. Margo asked Alice if she felt alright and Alice said she felt better than ever but was having a mix of feelings and thoughts about going over to the islands with Martin. Charles said he needed to get ready for his afternoon trip up top with lamp oil and to signal Savannah and Daniel said he would go with him but Charles said he would take one of the guards, when they got back.

Martin said he was thinking about taking Johnny down to the beach to meet Captain Jones and maybe walk down to the barge and show him his new boat and Daniel could go with them and he thought they might help pick some oranges for his trip. Johnny looked at Alice and she said to go on with them and she would be fine. Martin was ready to go, because sitting and chatting often made him fidget after only a short time. He asked Margo if she had a big basket he could use to pick some oranges and she told Daniel where to go get one and Martin nodded for Johnny to come on.

They went with Daniel out to the orange tree that was growing on the south side of the lighthouse. Martin commented at how big and lush it was and Daniel said his father had planted it there because this was the sunny side and it stayed warmer here in winter because the bricks soaked up the heat from the sun and kept the tree warm during the cold months. He said most of the oranges are at the top because the crew working on the lighthouse bricks have been picking the ones within easy reach. He told Martin he would boost him up so he could climb up and pick at the top and drop them down to them. Martin did and was soon dropping the big oranges down to them and the basket filled much quicker than the plums and blackberries did.

Martin jumped down and looked at the basket and said it was colorful and would be easy to spot in the front of his boat by the Indians. They carried the basket over to the horse barn and then headed for the beach. Martin told Johnny about Captain Jones on the way and retold the story of the duel and Johnny said he hoped there would be none of that while his Alice was here and Daniel said it only happened a time or two a year and not to worry. Johnny said he would worry every minute until she was back.

They stopped at the top of the dune and Martin pointed out to Johnny the different directions and what things were. Johnny was fascinated seeing Daufuskie and Hilton head so good from the top of the big dune and said he had heard stories of a lot of his people there and how they were mostly on their own a lot because their owners left for half the year. Martin pointed south and told Johnny that the Back River was about a mile and a half down that way.

They went on down to the shanty and found the Captain in his usual spot and he perked up when he heard Martin's voice. Martin had brought a sack of oranges and handed one to the Captain and he felt the roundness and softness of it and smelled it and said he would have it tonight. Martin took the rest of the bag to the three crewmen and pilot, doing their usual thing of smoking and playing cards. He walked back up and told the Captain that he had brought his friend, Johnny, the helmsman on the supply boat down to visit and the Captain reached out to shake hands.

He told the Captain that Johnny was the one who had helped him fix up his little dug out and he was gonna help him fix up the boat he had gotten from him and they were gonna walk down to see it. The Captain was glad to hear about that and told Johnny that it was a fine boat and happy it had found a new home. Martin said Johnny was the husband of Alice who he had spoken to the Captain about a few days before and said he had one more question and that was about the weather over the next couple days. The Captain answered quickly that he expected some showers tonight and maybe some cooler weather tomorrow with a northwest wind for a few days but he could be off by a bit but that was what he thought. Martin thanked him and touched the Captain's shoulder affectionately and they headed off for the barge and he saw the orange peels scattered around the crewmen as they left.

Johnny saw the boat hull on the beach and said to Martin that it was sweet. He looked over the shape and particularly the fine entry of the bow and the graceful sweep of the gunnel as it connected both ends of the boat. He said it was close in shape and size of the supply boat. Johnny hefted the bow up and said it might be slightly lighter than their boat and Martin said the Captain said it was particularly light and sharp and was faster than anything around. Daniel said he hoped it didn't leak as bad as it did when they brought it here and Johnny said getting the keel back to where it belonged would make the lap strakes tighter. Martin said this was gonna be his winter project and he didn't want Johnny to do anything but tell him how to do it. Johnny said he would help some and Martin said no, because he was gonna be busy being a big daddy soon and they laughed together.

Martin reached under the boat and pulled out an old sail and carefully spread it out on the beach and it was rotted and split in places and Johnny said that was no good and Martin said he knew that but had kept it to use for a pattern for the new sail and the same for that old mast, which needed some work. He said the oars are still good because they were stored in the shanty. Johnny said he wanted to go back to spend some time with Alice because he wouldn't see her again until next week and Martin said sure.

At the top of the dune, Daniel announced what time it was and it puzzled Johnny. Daniel showed him the sun and the long shadow and how he could closely guess the time by its length. Johnny was impressed and said he did something like that except he used the tides. They stopped at the bottom of the steps and stomped and shook the sand off their bare feet before going in and Daniel showed his mother his feet and she approved.

She, Mary and Alice had been looking at old keepsake things that had been discarded and then discovered when they had cleaned and fixed up the room for Alice. Margo wanted to give Alice something for her child even though it was six months away. She didn't know if it was to be a boy or girl so she gave her some of Mary's and Daniel's baby clothes. Alice was pleased and overwhelmed because she had never expected anything like this. The Dyers had kept up with Alice through Walter and Martha and knew she had become part of their family. Mary was having a lot of fun seeing all her little clothes and especially seeing her mother have so much fun. When Johnny saw Alice, he was surprised at how happy and giddy she was. He had never seen her this happy and all three of them were laughing and carrying on like he had never seen. He didn't understand but was glad to see Alice the way she was. He sat down and Alice showed him the two sets of clothes she was given. Alice said she was told that be it a girl or boy, she would have a second set that might work for the next baby and Johnny didn't know what to think about that.

Neither Martin nor Daniel liked hearing the talk about baby clothes and decided to go up on the lighthouse to have a look around so they went to see if Charles had set out any lamp oil containers for them to carry and there was and they grabbed them and went up. Once on top, Daniel set up the monocular for Martin to have a look toward Lazaretto and Martin swung it around and looked at the oyster midden spot but didn't see anything then swung around to the Back River landing and yelled that the slave hunters boat was up on the beach and told Daniel to take a look.

Daniel looked and said he saw the boat but no men and that must mean they are probably out searching the island and they needed to go right away and see what was going on. He told Martin to go tell his mother where they were going but not what they had seen and to grab a couple of leftover biscuits while he saddled the horses. Martin went and told Margo they were going to ride the horses to the south end. He asked her for the biscuits and she put them and a few other leftovers in a sack and Martin left. Daniel had the horses ready and they left and ran the horses hard.

First they went to where they had left Mallie and found him safe and gave him the sack of food, then to the Back River landing. Daniel said to let him do the talking. They rode out over the small dunes and to the river's edge and saw the group down by the boat and rode straight over to them. The headman who had talked to Daniel before said he was glad to see them because they might could help him and if they could, they might help themselves.

He said he thought sure the runaway was still around here somewhere on this island because he had no way of getting off. He said they looked in the woods over there and saw where he probably stayed and saw where he had tried to sweep away his prints. He's a smart devil according to the big ad in the Savannah paper that told all about him and his escape. He can read and write and speaks the Queens English. His owner is a lawyer and the temporary mayor of Augusta and wants him back bad enough to offer the biggest reward that me or anybody else has ever seen for one slave.

He said they had spread out and walked almost to the lighthouse looking but didn't see any more signs of him but the island was too big for men to find him, especially as smart as he is but the island wasn't too big for a pack of dogs to find him and he was going back to Savannah and get the best pack there was. He went on to say that if they caught him while he was gone, he would give them one quarter of the reward and that was a lot of money but he would like handing it over. He said they needed to go because the sooner they got gone, the sooner they could be back.

Daniel asked how long he thought it would take them to get back and he said that they should get back to Savannah by tomorrow night and he needed a day to get the dogs and resupply and would leave the day after that and be back that night so about three days he reckoned. He reminded the boys of the reward money and left thinking the boys were on his side.

Talking with the slave hunters had animated Daniel more than Martin had seen him ever be. He told Daniel he was glad he didn't have to say anything because he was so nervous they would have suspected something but somehow they considered Daniel a friend and ally. Daniel said he would talk to his father tonight but didn't think he wanted to tell Johnny or Alice or Mallie just yet about what had happened.

Martin agreed and said Johnny was already worried enough and knowing that there were slave hunters around might put him over the edge. Daniel said the most important thing now was to get Martin ready to go and then to figure out what to do with Mallie before the slave hunters got back. Martin said there wasn't much to him getting ready and wouldn't mind going tomorrow instead of the day after. Daniel said it would be best to wait for Johnny to be gone tomorrow, and then go the next day. They left for home and when they got there found everyone else on the porch. They took care of the horses and went around to the porch with the others.

Margo said they were having a big supper and hoped they were hungry and they said they were very hungry. Martin could tell Johnny had relaxed some and was the picture of happiness sitting with Alice. Martin thought to himself how nice Charles and Margo were to welcome him and then to help him feel comfortable. After some tea, Margo told Daniel to go get the food she had packed for Captain Jones and take it to him and not to tarry, because they would be waiting for him to come back before eating. Martin said he would go too and Margo said for them not to dally and come straight back. They got the food and took it down and the Captain was alone because both crews had taken out their captains to ships and were following them into Savannah. They asked the Captain if he would like some help getting up and in the shanty to have his supper and he said he would like that. Martin helped him up and into the shanty and got him to sit down to his little table. He worried how he would get up on his own and as if the Captain heard his thoughts and concerns, he told Martin it was only hard for him to get up after he had been sitting for a long spell and he would be fine now. Martin felt relieved at hearing that and they bid the Captain good night and they went back home to their own supper. It was another one of those best suppers from Margo. She had two casseroles and cornbread and gravy and chicken and dumplings, then blackberry pie.

After supper, Daniel nodded to his father and he understood it meant that they needed to talk so he followed Daniel out to the yard and they walked over to the horse barn. Daniel told him about what had happened and all and said he didn't know what to do with Mallie. Charles thought a bit and said he was glad Daniel had talked to the slaver so they knew what his plans were. He said that there was no place on the island they could hide him that a good pack of slave dogs wouldn't find and Turtle Island was out and that just left Daufuskie or Hilton Head or the Indian Islands. He said they should wait until Martin got back from his trip and see if any possibilities came of it. He said he didn't know what but it was certain that something had to be done before the slavers got back. He said they had tomorrow to come up with something and they would do whatever was needed.

Charles told Daniel that he would be having a long day when Martin and Alice went across the river. Daniel said he knew and wished there was something he could do but it was all up to them and all he could do was wait all day and into the night until they got back. Charles said they could bring a boat there and keep it ready if he thought it would be helpful and Daniel said he didn't think it would. He said he was confident in Martin getting Alice there and confident in Alice once they were there but that is all he could be sure of. Charles said he wasn't concerned about their safety and was glad the mystery of her family might finally be solved. He also mentioned to Daniel that Captain Ben would probably be in to Laza- retto tomorrow while Martin is gone and he is delivering the new ice box

Henry had made for us and Jacob will bring a crew to load it up on the back porch and that he ought to be more excited about it but there were so many urgent things going on that he would rather it came another time but Henry didn't know about us dealing with the runaway and all. They will probably get in late and unload it the next day so they will need the wagon then. Daniel said yes there was a lot to think about and do.

While Daniel was with his father, Mary and Martin walked out to the dune looking over the beach. Martin told her about them seeing and talking to the slave hunters and that was what Daniel had gone to talk to their father about now, and they didn't want Johnny to know about the slave hunters being there and coming back. He said he felt terribly uncomfortable when the slavers were on the island and that he was terrified while he and Daniel were with them and could barely contain himself but Daniel was just the opposite. He wasn't nervous a bit and acted perfectly in control and didn't cause any suspicion and was so convincing that they thought they had found a true friend and helper. Mary said she would be glad when they were gone and when Alice's search was finished and maybe Martin and them could just have some fun without so many things going on all the time. Martin said he would like that too but he couldn't rest until he had completed the vow he had made to Alice about her family and the slave hunters were far away. When Mary heard Martin say that she thought to herself that she wanted to be with Martin more than anything and suddenly hugged him and kissed his cheek. Martin was taken by surprise and felt a flush come over him. Mary glowed and smiled real big at Martin's innocence and was pleased with herself. Martin managed a little smile back and didn't say it but felt great pleasure from Mary's advance. He said they better get back and looked at Mary's beautiful face and they both burst out laughing with each other and couldn't stop for a bit and when they finally did, they headed back to the house. Mary's mother noticed the extra glow about Mary when she came in and smiled to herself.

Daniel had finished talking to his father and he and Martin went to bed early because they were exhausted and they both slept deeply. It seemed like little time passed before Martin heard Margo's broom stick tapping on the floor to wake them up to start another day. They were to take Johnny to Lazaretto to go back to Savannah and Alice was going along to see Johnny off. Margo fed them biscuits and gravy and had already packed a biscuit for Jacob and had Daniel go for the wagon. She told Johnny not to worry and that they would signal Walter as soon as she was back. He said again that he would worry every minute until then, and Alice smiled at him.

Johnny thanked Margo for everything and said he hoped it didn't bring any trouble for them because of him being there. Margo said the rest of the world knew nothing about them and what they did and that is her favorite thing about being there by themselves and what happens on Tybee stays on Tybee. She said she liked doing what she thought fit for herself even if it didn't fit elsewhere. She hugged Johnny and told them not to forget the biscuit for Jacob and couldn't hold back a few tears as they left.

They were crossing the big bridge and Martin noticed how the horses were more comfortable on the new decking planks that were close together and was pleased with himself for suggesting it. They got to the landing early and the crews all had just finished breakfast. Martin handed Jacob his biscuit and Johnny hopped off and helped Alice down and Alice reached out to hug him once more.

Daniel told Jacob about Captain Ben coming the next day and Jacob said he knew about what needed doing but hadn't known when and said he would need the wagon and Daniel said he would bring it. He said the Captain would anchor in Lazaretto creek tomorrow night and be ready to unload the next morning and said he had hoped to be able to set the big box directly onto the wagon with the boats boom because it was heavy. Jacob saw the troubled look on Johnny's face and put his arm on his shoulder and told him everything was gonna be fine and that Martin was young but had the wisdom of his father and the Indians were peaceful. The boatmen had the boat ready and waiting for Johnny, with the place at the helm left open for him. He took his spot and they shoved off for the trip back. Johnny's mood was blue and the verse he sang to start the chantey was blue and so was the chorus. It brought tears to the eyes of Martin, Daniel, Jacob, and most to Alice.

Martin said he wanted them to first go to the Back River landing and make sure the boat was fine and let Alice see the area again after all this time. Alice had been quiet and Martin asked her what was on her mind. She said in the front of her mind, the same thing, wanting to find her family and the last she saw of them, going away in the canoe, but beyond that was the memories of their journey from where they ran away from to finally get here and walking down the beach in the darkness, feeling both afraid and glad to be where they had set out for.

She said the horror of the final day was there but what she had been thinking most about was the kind Indian lady that had come for a few days to help them, as the whole group of runaways were on the brink of giving up and going back to what they had run away from. Alice said she didn't think about it then but wondered now how the lady had learned to speak English and why she bothered to help them. She said she also remembered the Indians in the canoes coming a few times a week bringing fish and crabs and conchs and clams and how shy they seemed and wouldn't look you in the eye and were in a great hurry to unload their seafood and leave quickly, but how they hesitated for a moment after the shooting began for her family to get in the boat.

Martin said he wanted to bring her here today to see the place they were going to in the morning. Martin pointed to Long Island way across the marsh and told her that it was where they were going. He said it could take three hours to paddle there following the creeks but there was a full moon and the tide would be high enough for them to sail across the top of the marsh, directly to the island. They got off the wagon and walked up in the edge of the woods and saw that the boat was there and headed back home.

On the ride back, Martin told Alice the story about the slavers looking for Mallie and why he hadn't said anything earlier because he didn't want to make Johnny any more afraid. Alice asked if they needed to stop by to see the runaway but Daniel said he had enough food and he would bring some more over tomorrow while they were across the river. Martin told Alice about the large canoe and the two black passengers and that Charles said it was probably Indians helping runaways escape the area and that could be a possibility for Mallie.

That possibility made Daniel sigh a breath of relief because he had been worrying about Mallie and their involvement and he didn't want Mallie to be hunted down and bitten up by slave dogs and returned, nor did he want his father to lose his job if things didn't work out. Mallie could be forced to tell of his being helped by them and it could mean some serious trouble for them and the Milam family. There was a lot at stake and he had known it from the beginning. He didn't regret what they had done, but, like his sister, longed for a little less excitement and would feel better when Mallie was taken care of and Martin and Alice had gone and come back. They got back and told the Dyers of their morning and Margo said they should not do much the rest of the day so they would be more rested for their trip tomorrow and said she would make a good supper for them to sleep on. Mary asked Alice if she would look at the books she had and make a list of some she would recommend and Alice said she would like that and went to Mary's room and began discussing the ones they had both read.

This had little interest for Martin and Daniel and they decided to walk down to the beach and Margo said lunch would be ready in about an hour and she had a snack packed for Captain Jones and to take it with them. Charles said he had some things to do but he wanted to sit and talk to Martin and Alice one more time today about their trip. Martin and Daniel got the sack for the Captain and walked over the dune and down to the beach. Both crews were gone and the Captain had the whole beach to himself and was glad to hear the boys come up. He smelled of the sack and said God bless Margo Dyer. Martin told the Captain about going the next day and asked if he had any advice. He told Martin to be as calm and confident as he could because the Indians had more sensitive feelings than us and they could sense fear. Martin told him about talking to the slave hunters and he asked what that was about and they ended up telling him about Mallie. He said they were taking a big chance helping him but he would have done the same thing. He said the slave hunters were the worst of the worst.

Martin told of how Daniel had been so confident and convincing and how he had been a nervous wreck. He said he wouldn't be that way around the Indians tomorrow because he was not afraid and respected them. The Captain said they would sense that and he would not have a problem. The Captain said that, in his younger days, he heard stories about the chief of that band of Indians. It was known that he was wise and spoke English and carried on a prosperous trade with the colonials in Savannah and the other Indians from up the Ogeechee. He had even sent his daughter to Savannah to be educated by a private tutor.

When her father died, her mother became the leader and when her mother died, the daughter became the leader. After the chief died, they quit trading with the colonials. Martin soaked up every word that the Captain said and told the Captain the name of the lady according to Alice's story. The Captain told Martin that he was a "little big man" for helping Alice. As he was leaving, Martin asked the Captain again about the wind and weather the next day and the Captain said pretty much like today, clear with a cool breeze out of the northwest like he had said before and Martin said that would work good because he could sail straight across to Long Island without coming about. They said goodbye to the Captain and headed home.

Margo had fried grits and fish for lunch and biscuits and orange rind jelly for dessert. Alice complimented her on her cooking and Margo said that they missed a lot of things being there on an island, but good food wasn't one of them, thanks to all the good things sent from the Milam plantation and fresh seafood brought by some of the pilot crews sometimes. Martin said she was gonna like her new icebox.

After lunch, Charles suggested they have some yaupon on the porch and talk about their trip across the river. A cool breeze was making the porch just right. Charles commented that it was rare that a tropical storm had not been their way this year and Margo said the year was not over yet.

She brought out the honey jar and put a spoonful in each cup of tea.

Martin began by saying he hoped it was ok to tell the Captain about Mallie earlier and Charles said that the Captain was family and that was fine. Martin said he wanted to hear anything more that the Captain might say about his trip that could be helpful. He told what Captain Jones said about the Indian lady and her mother and father and how her father had her stay in Savannah and get educated. Alice was particularly interested to hear about her. Charles said that he had heard bits and pieces of that but the Captain was a closer source and it was good to know as much as possible. Martin retold the story of the Captain getting his start on the "Claw Island" beach and the Indians being peaceful and generous and the word they said to the Captain and his crew, "gereg," which the Captain understood to mean a greeting of some sort. Martin said he intended to go directly across the marsh at the peak of high tide with the big pan of oranges with Alice standing in the front and hope for the best. He said he had thought of many things but a direct and quick approach was what he intended and hoped that Alice and providence would handle the rest. He said that if things went well, he would come back across the marsh twelve hours later when the tide was high again. The moon was full so the tide would be higher and he would be able to see and Daniel had told him he would keep a fire going on the beach, plus, all he had to do was head directly toward the lighthouse and that would put him at the landing.

Charles was pleased and impressed to see young Martin with such maturity, clarity and confidence. He asked Alice if she had any doubts or fears and she said she was ready to know the truth, whether it be good news or bad and thanked Charles for accommodating them and especially how they had made Johnny feel welcome and comfortable and for finding her in the pluff mud and saving and comforting her all those years ago. Charles said she had been a blessing for them and the Milam's and an inspiration to many others.

Margo said she would give them a sack of food for tomorrow and the big pan of oranges was already setting out and ready for them to take and a couple jugs of water too and a separate sack for Daniel and Mallie. Mary asked if she could go with them in the morning and wait with Daniel tomorrow and Charles said if her mother approved, it was ok with him and Margo said it was fine with her and she would put more food in Daniels sack.

Charles said it was time for his daily lamp maintenance and signaling with Savannah and Daniel said he would help and Charles said the guards had been helping him and he was fine and Daniel should have a restful day because they would be up early and have a big day tomorrow. He left and said they could talk more after supper.

Margo said she had an easy task for the three of them if they were up to it and that was to pick plums and blackberries one more time because she had found a few more clay pots while cleaning out the storage room for Alice. Daniel said they were just about all gone now but they may be able to get the last of them and he went and got two small pans from the kitchen and they left. Margo asked Alice if there was anything she would like to do and Alice said she was a bit tired and wouldn't mind a nap and Margo said she could manage one herself.

The plums were few and far between and those left were either a little rotten or very ripe and red. The blackberries were similar but extra sweet and tasty and had to be picked gently so they wouldn't smush in your fingers. Daniel mentioned he had talked to his father about staying a few months at the Milam place and Martin said that would be fun. He said he may go to his aunt and uncles home in Charleston after that but wasn't particularly excited about that. Martin said that if he did, he might be able to go there on Captain Bens sharpie because he often had trips to Charleston and he might could go along. Mary said she was ready for a trip herself but said she didn't know where she wanted to go. She said she could go to the same relatives in Charleston or to relatives in Savannah and if Daniel went to Charleston, she might prefer Savannah, however, she thought to herself that Savannah would be best because she could be near Martin. She said she was just as ready as Daniel to go off but she probably wouldn't be allowed for yet another year at least but she would start asking now every few weeks so it could be sooner rather than later. Daniel asked her what she wanted to go off for so much and she said there were lots of things that he couldn't understand even though he was older and he scoffed at that. The real reason she wanted to go off bumped into her as he jumped back from a blacksnake in the plum tree branches.

They filled the two pans and took them back to the house. Margo had just woken up from a nap and told them to be quiet because Alice was sleeping. She looked at what they had picked and was pleased and whispered that these were very ripe and would make the very best preserves and thanked them. They went outside and walked to the top of the big dune and sat in the sand, looking out over the beach. The Captain was in his usual spot. Martin said he would miss the Captain when he left and hoped he would be around for many more years. Daniel said his wits were still sharp but his body was worn and rusted and getting up was hard for him. Mary said she wondered if he knew about the new tower coming that Charles and Henry had spoken about and Daniel said he got most of the news from the pilots and he probably did know.

He said one of the crewmen had told him recently that people in Savannah were always asking about him and wondered if he was real or just one of the many tall tales that the crewmen had a reputation for telling. They had come to hear of him because people were always asking the crewmen when they got in what weather was coming and they always started their reply, "Captain Sandy says" and sometimes sing a little jingle about him and his pet seagull and clam down in Davy Jones locker. They told how he was blind and how he sat every day in the same spot and lived in the little shanty and how he had gotten his name from when they found him half buried in sand after sitting out on the beach in a northeaster.

Mary said it sounded like good material for a book and she should start writing some of those pilot crew tales down and Daniel said she would have plenty to work with. Mary said just the last few weeks since Martin had been here was more exciting than most people had in a lifetime and the next few days would probably be a bigger story than the rest. She said, in a matter of fact way that she would write her own book and looked at Martin and Daniel and said she was sure that she would look back on this moment of them sitting here in the sand and her first vision of herself becoming writer. The boys were surprised at Mary's sudden conviction of her future and didn't dare express any doubt of its certainty. She added that Daniel didn't have to worry about her taking his light keeper job, now that she was to be a book writer. She said she would start as soon as Martin left and begin with the things that happened while he was here and then with the stories from her mother and father and then Captain Jones and the pilots and crewmen and the Milam's and more. That's it she said, now I know what I intend to do with my life. Martin said he was ready to go so he could get his few things together for tomorrow. They turned back to the house and as usual, Daniel looked at how long the lighthouse shadow was and announced the time. Margo yelled for them to leave the sand outside before they came in as they had already begun to remove their shoes and shake the sand off their clothes. The bath pans were on the porch and the boys filled theirs and carried water to Mary's on the back porch.

Before supper, Martin loaded the basket of oranges on the wagon and a sack of a few essentials like matches and a hand axe and a length of rope and a folding knife and an extra change of clothes and a bed roll. He asked Alice if she had what she needed and she said she was only taking a few extra clothes and a bed roll and a pencil and a few pieces of paper. Margo said she would have that sack of food for them and one for Mallie and Daniel and Mary.

The whole house smelled good from the plums and blackberries that had been cooking. Margo had set them on the back porch to cool and the northwest breeze was blowing the smell of them throughout the house. She called everyone to supper and again had the best supper ever. It was a simple meal of two heavily crusted pies with chicken and potatoes and carrots and onions inside on top of a thick bottom crust and underneath a golden brown top crust. She cut through the top and bottom crusts and served it with a big, almost flat spoon, carefully including both bottom and top crusts with semi soupy chicken bits and vegetables in between. Everyone had extra servings and Margo sent Daniel to the beach with the pie pan with the last two servings plus a bowl of cooked plums to Captain Jones and told him to hurry back and to leave the sand outside, and they would wait to have desert when he got back.

Daniel was back as they had settled down and was hurrying up the stairs but sent back to do a better job of cleaning sand off his feet. Margo said she spent half her life trying to keep sand out of the house and said she loved having that big sand dune between them and the ocean but she was sure that if she had not been here to sweep it out all these years, it would have taken over and it would be higher than the house. Daniel had only the cooked plums in mind and not his sandy feet. Margo said the plums were picked within a day of turning bad but were just right because they were the sweetest at that time. She served everyone a bowl full and a biscuit and Alice and Martin did what the Dyers did, which was to break up the crispy biscuit into the bowl of cooked plums and eat it with a spoon.

When they finished the meal, Charles asked if there was anything Martin or Alice could think of that he could do for them. Martin said he couldn't think of anything that they needed. We have favorable wind and a high tide and the light of the full moon. We have oranges for a gift and I have Alice to do all the talking and Daniel and Mary waiting on my return. Charles said he would watch them go over with the monocular from atop the lighthouse and look some during the day. Charles said there was something he didn't want to have to say but thought he should and looked at Alice and asked her if she was prepared for whatever they found out, be it good or bad. Alice said she had thought often of all the possibilities and thanked Charles for his concern and all that he did to make this happen. Charles said this was something that had been on his mind all these years and thanks to Martin, they would know some answers soon. Mary noticed Martin squirming uncomfortably at the attention and felt a warm affection for him. Margo said she would wake them early and have them a good meal before they left and they should go now and get to bed.

Before leaving the porch, Margo pointed to the glow of the moon behind the tall dune between them and the ocean. The full moon had risen above the ocean but not above the dune. Margo said it was her favorite moment every month. She told Mary to hurry and show Alice and Martin the lighthouse. Mary motioned them to come down to the end of the porch so they could look up at the lighthouse and they both gasped. The house and the whole compound was still in the shadow of the dune, cast by the bright moon, but the top of the lighthouse was above the shadow and was illuminated almost bright as day, with a dark sky beyond.

Daniel was standing there and said he had looked at this every month that the weather was clear as long as he could remember and was always in awe. The thing is, he said, is that this is a double reflection. The lighthouse is reflecting the light of the moon, which is reflecting the light of the sun, which has barely set. As they watched, the light moved down the lighthouse until the moon peaked over the dune and moonlight flooded the whole compound. Margo said this sight every month was one of the many rewards for their isolated life.

Although Martin had slept plenty, it seemed almost like no time had passed until he heard the tapping of Margo's broom stick on the floor and he was awake in an instant, fully aware of what he was about for the day. He was already on his feet, pulling on his pants as Daniel was slowly waking up. He made sure he was awake and went on down the ladder and found Charles and Margo and Alice already up and finishing a cup of yaupon. The table was set and grits and bacon was made and the pan was hot and eggs set out ready to be cracked and fried. Margo poured Martin some tea and began frying eggs and by the time Mary and Daniel came, she had fried a dozen and served them and started some more and poured Daniel some coffee. She had prepared so thoroughly that she was able to sit and eat with everyone. Daniel finished up and went out to get the wagon and horses ready and brought it over to the house. Martin heard the horses and thanked Margo and got up to go. She handed him the food sacks and Alice said she would take a moment for herself and be right back.

Charles and Margo hugged Martin and told him how proud they were of him and hugged Mary and when Alice came back, they hugged her too. They went downstairs and Martin got in the back of the wagon with the big pan of oranges and Mary and Alice sat in front with Daniel and they left before the sun was up but had begun to lighten up the sky a bit and in a half hour, they road over the small dunes at the Back River landing.

The sun was barely up and the tide was within a half hour of full but had already reached the height of a normal high tide. The marsh was flooded and the air was cool and crisp with a steady wind, still out of the northwest. Daniel and Martin went to get the boat and drug it down on the beach and near the edge of the river while Mary and Alice, together, carried the big pan of oranges from the wagon. Martin told Alice which side of the boat she would need to be on and said that she would stay there because he wouldn't have to come about at all.

She had watched him in the river so much that she understood what he was saying. He explained to her that if the grass slowed them down, he had the special poles with a small fork in the end to push with but from how high the tide was looking, he didn't think it would be necessary. Once they had everything prepared, Martin said they could kill a few minutes before they left to let the tide reach the highest. Already, just the tips of the marsh grass were showing.

Martin took out the small monocular his father had given him and looked over at Long Island and saw a small amount of smoke rising from both ends of the island. He handed it to Alice and told her which smoke rise they would be going to, then Daniel and Mary took a look. They waited, mostly in silence for a while longer until Martin announced that the tide had gone slack and would be still for the next half hour and it was the time to go.

Daniel drug the boat down into the water, set the mast and rudder in place and Martin let Alice get settled, and he pulled the sail and it rolled out from the mast and filled with wind. Daniel shoved them out and they moved out onto the river at a medium speed.

Martin loved the slack water that happened every six hours at the bottom and top of the tides. The water was high and would just stay there before turning to go the other way in about thirty minutes. He looked across the river and set his sight on the east end of Long Island and they were soon to the other side of the river and entered over the top of the marsh and the small waves that there had been in the river were dampened by the tips of the grass and they glided along, just a little slower than in crossing the river as the grass brushed the boat bottom.

They were about halfway across the marsh and Martin hadn't needed to use the push pole because the water was so high. As they neared the island, Alice said she could see a couple of people at the edge of the island looking out at them. A little further, they saw two canoes being pulled from the woods with two men in each, coming out to meet them, keeping a distance and turning and going along with them, one on each side. As they got closer, Martin's boat began to slow in marsh grass that was slightly taller and he rolled up the sail and began using the pole.

One canoe shot out quickly ahead to the little bluff where the people had gathered and Martin could see, even at a distance, they were talking to a small person. He hadn't known what to expect but being led in by canoes and having a group await his arrival was not what he would have imagined. As they got closer, they entered the creek that led to the small bluff of what he had been calling the first landing.

As they came near the bluff, all the people except one left into the woods and out of sight. The one person standing was a little older lady watching them closely and Martin heard Alice say that it was her. She seemed to be expecting them and Martin wondered how she would know they were coming and why the others had left her alone and vulnerable even though she wasn't.

He nosed the boat up onto the bank and she smiled and said, you must be Alice. Both Alice and Martin were already surprised by how things had happened but shocked at her knowing Alice. The next thing she said was even more shocking when the little lady said he must be Captain Milam's son. Martin could not speak even if he knew what to say and Alice was first to talk. She said that she must be Ayana and the lady smiled broadly and nodded yes. She said she had been expecting her for years and when she was told that a sailboat was coming across the river, she suspected it was them.

They got out and Martin pulled the little boat up and still didn't see anyone else around and wondered where they all went. He had last seen the other canoe going to the other end of the island and they seemed alone on the island with the lady. She led them to a spot where a large oak was growing out over the marsh and the fresh morning breeze was blowing over them. This was a frequented spot with some logs to sit on and even though it was mostly oaks there were pine needles spread on the ground, that must have been brought there from the pines nearby. She sat and motioned to a spot for them to sit.

She sat quiet for a few minutes and stared out across the marsh, not seeming to look at anything particular but maybe thinking or feeling the moment. She was a small woman and her skin was wrinkled and dark with a hint of red. Her eyes were dark and piercing and very much alive. Martin or Alice had nothing to say but there was no awkwardness in the silence. Finally, she spoke, and what she said was that Alice need not worry anymore because her family was there and well.

Alice went limp and knelt on the pine needles and wept and tears streamed down Martin's face and he remembered the promise he had made to Alice years before. The little lady's gaze returned out across the marsh for a while until Alice quieted and then she began to speak to them again. She said that she would take her to her family but first she needed to talk to them. Alice asked how she knew who they were and the lady said she would get to that in her story.

Alice said she remembered her name from when she had visited and helped her group and saved them from going back to where they had run away from. Ayana said she had been troubled about that for all these years and Alice was surprised and asked why. She said that had she not come, and they returned to slavery, the slaughter would not have happened. Alice said she had thought about that too but as awful as it was, they had all left a torturous hell and had known freedom for the first time in their life, and even if it was short lived, it was a good thing and that she had no way of knowing what lay ahead and the blame was all in the evil men who planned and carried out the act, and not in any way her fault. Ayana said it was good to hear her say that.

Ayana paused and looked out over the marsh again and then began to speak. She said what she was about to tell would help them understand her people and why they had helped her family. First she said that her whole story went back more than a thousand years and was passed down to her from more than a hundred generations back, but most of what she would tell this day started with the daughter of her grandmothers grandmother, who first fled north from the French, then the Spanish, then the English who all came in big boats and destroyed her people.

Before they came, my people, the Guale, lived from Tybee south to the town now called Darien. From the great river there to the great river in Savannah was where we lived for more than a hundred generations, peacefully and rich and thankful in abundance of all the things we needed with little effort and much time to enjoy life. We were healthy and prosperous.

We had a regular and healthy mix of other people following the big rivers from the inland areas to our coast and some staying and added to the variety of our culture and the health of our blood. We accepted all if they came in peace and humility. For a hundred generations, we migrated slowly every year for a few months to the higher ground a hundred miles inland. This annual journey was part of our life and we were away from the coast when the big storms came and when the bugs and heat were bad.

As I was told, some stayed behind every year but most went along, even the old could go because it was not a hurried journey. The first blackberries and plums to bloom signaled us to get ready to go. There was no hurry and our people were like a slow tide going west that took a month or so to reach the inland foothills. We followed the ripening blackberries and other fruits. Some days we traveled a few miles and some days we didn't travel and camped for a few days. We carried on an important custom of trading with the different tribes of people on our way and our valuable trade item was salt, which we gathered and processed from the salt ponds around here over the winter. One man could carry ten pounds of salt easily and trade for more skins, furs, tools, herbs, ornaments and other things that would require three men to carry back home, so, with what we traded for and the plentiful sea food and plants on our islands, we had all we needed with little effort and lived a life of abundance for many generations.

I was told it took my people about two months to reach where the flat land rose up into hills and we would spend a few weeks trading and socializing and then start the slow movement back toward the coast. We were like a great human tide that flowed in toward the higher ground, leaving things that we had there in trade for things we needed to take back. We developed allies with the different tribes and this provided security from wandering bands or possible enemies.

Friendships of families carried on for generations and the annual meetings were celebrated with much joy and happiness and was something for all to look forward to during the winter. Mating happened across the different tribes as young people met and loved and our blood stayed healthy. Some of us stayed and became them and some of them came back and became us. Peace, prosperity, and health reigned for more than a thousand years.

Ayana paused and said the reason she was telling this long story was to help them understand how things had been with her people and how things were now here with her people and hoped they did not tire of listening. She said when she finished, she would take Alice to her family. Alice said she wanted to hear and she would not be tired and had waited this long and could wait a little longer. Martin said he wanted to hear it all. Martin's ability to pay attention had seldom been this good. She continued and said that the good times came to an end when the big boats from France came, but not at first.

Our people welcomed them and fed them and nourished them back to health from their long journey. We showed them how to harvest the abundant seafoods and the acorns and other plentiful plants and fruits to eat and showed them how to escape most of the bugs. When we left for our first journey inland after they had arrived, they stayed here and when we got back, we were treated badly by them and forced to work for them and made to worship their god or be punished severely. Next came the Spanish and drove off the French and they were worse. They forced their religious ways on us and beat us if we didn't accept their teachings.

Most of us bent to their rules and some that didn't were whipped or shot and some fled. Some of us moved away and eventually there was a war. Many of my people were killed by them but most died of sickness. The sickness spread from the first island they came to and to the other islands and to the tribes we visited on our annual journey, and in one lifetime, most of our people had left or were dead. The ones that remained suffered in health from the food they were forced to grow instead of eating the healthy seafood diets they were accustomed to.

They preached a merciful god but were merciless in their punishments if we practiced our own traditions. After a war with them, some of our people fled south and some fled north and the leader of those going north was my ninth grandmother removed.

We were forced out of every island we tried to live on and this small group of islands are the last of our ancestral land and there are no empty islands to the north or south now to run away to. There are but eighteen of us left. No one knows what happened to those that went south.

Now, the Spanish are gone and the English are on our ancestral lands. These islands and the two big islands south of here, Ossabaw and Warsaw, were granted to us by General Oglethorpe about eighty years ago. We were forced off of the big islands and about one hundred of us came to these islands but many of us have died of disease. Of these islands, this is the only one that has thick dirt enough for us to grow a few things and stay above most storm waters and hold our waste without poisoning our drinking water.

We go often to the island across the marsh from here to catch fish and conchs and crabs for our food and enough to trade with the Ogeechee Indians. This island is only about a mile long and a half mile wide and there is eighteen of us now on this end and your family and a few others on the other end. You will understand why we live separately after I finish my story.

When my father was alive, we traded heavily with the colonials in Savannah. My father assimilated, learned to speak English, made contacts and friends, and was the first of my people to gain a small amount of wealth by trading in the seafood we gathered and processed. When I was old enough, he sent me to stay with an English family in Savannah. I had already learned English from him and I was taught the basics and exposed to the classics in a library of books from all around the world. I stayed in Savannah six months a year for five years but when my father got sick and died I moved back and helped my mother who became the leader of the remaining seventy of us. We both were sickened at times but managed to stay alive. She was not only the leader but had been what you would call the doctor of our people as her mother and grandmother had been.

My father had been the leader but she was the most powerful force and there would be none of us now without her tireless efforts to keep us alive. She could not stop the sickness but slowed it down. She learned that it was catching and warned against being around people from Savannah or even being near our own people that were sick or had been around colonials. She learned that breath could carry sickness.

Ayana pointed out a very small island out in the marsh between the beach island and us and said that her mother had required those that were sick to stay there until they were well or died and she went herself to nurse them every day. She wore a soft doeskin over her mouth and nose for protection from sickness. Our numbers continued to go down and she finally forbade all trading and contact with the people in Savannah. She was rebuked and laughed at for her efforts by many of her own people and thought to have gone crazy by some.

When our numbers continued to go down, most of the ones that were left were the ones that had listened to her and we shied away from outside contact and our numbers were few but held steady for the first time ever. When my mother died, I was looked to as the leader. Her mission to save our people from dying out became my mission. She had fought the sickness and death and taught us how to best avoid it.

That is why I brought you here to this spot where the ocean breeze carries away our breath before it can be mixed. That was the hardest thing for my people to believe but they did because they respected her. It was hard for them to accept for two reasons. They considered it a sign of weakness to avoid a sick person. The other reason is because we have a special word in our language that expresses the joy and happiness of being near enough to share the air and the very breath between us. It is a short word but its meaning is long and full because when it is said it holds an appreciation for closeness and gratitude for the breath of life that we first sucked in when we came out of our mother and the last one that we blow out when we finish this dream world we are in. Our language is like that, and unlike the English language, one word can have deep meaning by what it makes us feel more so than what it makes us think. If you only knew one word of our language and came amongst us it should be "Gereg." Martin about choked when he heard her say that as he thought of Captain Jones telling of what the kind and generous Indians had repeated to him when he had been on their island long ago. Martin had been so surprised and shocked when they got there that he had forgotten to say it. Ayana went on to say that, because of her mother's knowledge and wisdom, they stayed mostly to themselves, without any outside contact except to help runaways and trading with the Ogeechee Indians, which they always did in the ocean breezes, or with doeskin masks, and had no deaths from sickness for a dozen years or more.

The war came and that didn't affect us much except for a lot more runaway slaves coming around that had been freed by the war going on.

Most gathered on Tybee and some wandered over here. We believed in keeping ourselves free of outside contact but also recognized the evil of slavery and when we would see a runaway, often near death of drowning of hunger or disease, or from their beatings, we would try to help. Before the war and after we took fish and crabs and conchs to the large group of runaways that had learned to come to Tybee, hoping for a way out. After the war, less British ships came to carry runaways off and their numbers grew because there were less rescuers. When we dropped off food, we did it quickly to avoid contact and sickness and I made those that went to wash themselves in the saltwater before they could come back in with us. My people told me that they could see, even in their brief stop, that the people looked very sick and some could only crawl. From my mother's teaching about sickness, I knew what had happened when I heard this news.

Because we had always lived on islands, we had to learn about how to keep our waste separate from our source of drinking water and it was more important when we moved to these islands because they are smaller and don't have thick dirt like the big islands of Warsaw and Ossabaw and greater care has to be taken to prevent what goes out of us from poisoning what goes in us. Again, my mother was the powerful force and had learned about these things from her family and I learned about them from her. The runaways had been in the same spot for so many years until the shallow wells they were drinking from were poisoned and making everyone sick. That's when I went there for few days and showed them where to dig a new well and how important it was where they left their waste.

The young mulatto man there was very appreciative and was totally dedicated to helping his people. Also, I taught them about plants they could eat. Alice said she remembered how the people felt better almost overnight after drinking the better water. She also said she remembered Ayana refusing to sit and talk to them and instead stood at the edge of the river and they gathered on the riverbank to listen to her. Ayana told Alice she would not remember but she had always placed herself so that the ocean breeze was blowing away from her so she would not catch any sickness and take it back to her people.

Ayana took another one of her pauses and looked out over the marsh before saying that what she had to say next was difficult for her, and knew it had to be for Alice, because it was the darkest day she and her people had ever known, and they had known many dark times. She said that her people, as had become a habit, were delivering the baskets of seafood just before dawn and as the last baskets were unloaded, the attack started and gunshots and smoke erupted and people were falling dead all over the beach.

Her people told her that Alice and her family had been helping unload the baskets when the shooting started and they made room for her family and a couple others to get in and quickly left the riverbank. They came back, horrified and told of you being yanked from the canoe by a white man with buckskins and a painted face. We had heard all the gunfire and went to our beach, across from Tybee, and saw the carnage and learned the details from the men in the canoes and for the first time I saw your family. At the time, they could not even talk because they were in such shock. We took them to the small island that we had used for quarantine and took them food and drink every day. Your mother and father could not talk for weeks but your brother came around after a few days and tended to the others, which included your family plus a few more that had been near the canoes. Early the day after the massacre, we went to look across the river and saw the black mass of bodies and later watched as men came and burned the bodies and a land breeze carried the smoke and spirits out into the ocean. We were aware that we were just a river away from something like that and knew that most colonials despised us and wished we were gone and we had doubts about staying and thought we should leave. Everyone looked to me for some guidance but for the first time, I had no clear answer and was filled with doubt about being able to save my people.

I was deeply troubled and was unsure what to do and remembered a ritual my mother had taught me about how to attain clarity in a troubling time. She and my father had done it many times with a few other members of our family when it was difficult to decide on important matters. Ayana said the yaupon tea we were drinking was the plant used for the ceremony. Instead of a mild drink, a large quantity is cooked slowly for a few days down to a small amount that is thick like syrup and black. On the new moon, she said she went off alone and drank it and vomited just as she had seen her mother and father do and then she drank more and vomited again and did this until no vomit came and she just sat, alone in the night until all her senses turned within, and she became intimate with her life through her breath and bathed in it until the sun came up and woke with a deep purity and clarity. She said she knew what to do, and that was to listen to the voices of her people, and so, the next day we sat and I asked them what we should. Some said we should go and live with the Ogeechee people. They had been our friends for many generations and would accept us as them. Some said we should stay and be even more watchful of anyone coming across the river. After much discussion, I suggested we let the children decide and all agreed. We had always looked to children for guidance and especially the ones who dreamed and remembered their dreams and could tell them to us. We only had three children in our group, at that time, and each said we should stay.

Ayana told Alice that her mother and father began to come back around but remained in deep sorrow over having lost her to such a hideous devil and your mother cried off and on for months. After some time, we cleared a place on the other end of our island and made shelters for your family and the others. Until your family, we had never allowed anyone but our people on the island, not because we looked down on anyone but there was so few of us and we had learned that contact with the world beyond our island brought sickness and death.

We continued to take in runaways but used caution to keep a distance and left them on our little quarantine island and took care of them until they were refreshed and healthy. After they had been there for a few weeks we moved them to the end of our island with your family. The first two runaways after we had settled your family were a brother and sister in their teens. They had run away with their mother and father, who had drowned when the old boat they used sank. Your mother took to them and that began to awaken her from the deep melancholy she had been in. Helping others helped her recover her own sense of self and she took a special interest in helping runaways from then on and still does to this day. Our lives and lives of others depend on the secrecy of us helping runaway slaves. We have carried on a link in the passage of runaways from around Savannah and nearby South Carolina islands for over seventy years. We help them recover and renourish, then send them up the Ogeechee to where they are guided north from there by others.

My grandfather started this not long after we came to these small islands. When the Ogeechee people come in their large trading canoes here to us every month, they bring furs and other trade items for seafood and we send two and sometimes three runaways with them, hidden under the baskets of fresh seafood. The colonials never suspected them and they travel freely as they always have. When they are up the river a ways, they are carried in smaller canoes at night for sixty miles inland where they meet their next link to continue overland to more links that eventually end up north where they are aided by abolitionists.

Ayana looked at Alice and told her that her mother and father and brother and the two others embraced their role in helping the runaways, especially her mother, and over the many years, she has helped hundreds, mostly from around Savannah. She looked at Alice and said it would be a surprise to her that her family had learned that she had survived and much about her life since the massacre and both Alice and Martin were stunned at that statement. After the runaways were quarantined and nursed back to health, and brought to her end of the island, she would always ask where they were from. Over time, and from many runaways she learned a tremendous amount about the local news and happenings within the slave communities around Savannah and beyond. Ayana looked at Alice and said how her mother learned how she was saved by the light keeper and raised by a kind plantation owner and his wife, as their own child and how she became a legend from having survived the great massacre and her enlightened ways and attendance in the underground meetings. She told her that she was a legend and we were told by the runaways of all you did to keep the light of freedom alive in the minds and hearts of your people. The Milam place itself was known about and the kind master and his son who spoke and understood Geechee talk and the Geechee ways. From all these things I learned to expect you to come looking one day and here you are.

From a hundred thousand of us on the Georgia coast, there is but eighteen of us now. I don't know what future there is for us but it was my vow to my mother to keep our story and us alive and to continue to help our African brothers and sisters escape the tyranny they suffer. For security, we blocked all the creeks that had come close to the other end of the island to prevent any boats from coming up that way and dug a small creek to get there from this end. This makes any boat coming to this island have to pass by our end and we keep a watch out all day starting at sun up and saw your sail come into the marsh today. We have been left mostly alone for many years but we know that will end as it has on every island my people have ever been on. These islands we have left to us do not have thick dirt and are not thought to have value for crowing crops, so the colonials have little interest in them. This one has a little thicker dirt, but is small and does not have easy access, therefore it has remained to us, but we know that could change at any time. We are left alone mostly because the colonials are afraid of what they think we are like. Even back to my grandfather's time, whenever colonials go missing, it is said that the Indians ate them. This is far from the truth but probably works in our favor because it keeps some away.

So, Ayana said, this is a little of the story of my people and how we are here now and about your family. She said they could go now and see Alice's family and that she had left off one surprise for Alice to learn from them when she got there. She then looked at Martin and said what a brave young man he was for bringing Alice and that he was now like family and could return and be welcomed but to keep it a secret. Alice thanked Ayana for telling them all this before she saw her parents, so she and Martin would have better understanding. Martin said he had something to ask of Ayana before they finished their talk and she nodded. He briefly told the story of Mallie and the slave hunters and how they were to return with dogs to hunt him down. He asked if he could bring Mallie here and if they would help him escape. He added that he knew a way to make the slavers believe that he had gone north in the direction of Turtle Island so they would not want to come here looking for him. Ayana said he could do that if he was sure that he could do it in such a way that the slave hunters were deceived and not come there looking. She reached in a sack and handed Martin a doeskin mask and told him to feel the breeze blowing from her to him and told him that when he came to wear the mask and position himself downwind to prevent the spread of disease to her people. Martin said he understood and would do what she said. He thought of Daniel, on the other side of the river, and wished he could be there.

Ayana got up and motioned for them to follow. She tied a doeskin mask over her mouth and nose and sang a little song out loudly and people began appearing out from behind the trees and bushes as they could feel all was well by her tune but maintained a distance. She led them through a narrow well-worn path with dense undergrowth of saw palmettos. Then they came into a large, clear opening in the canopy that extended over to near the edge of the island on both sides. There were sand oaks on the edge of the opening on both sides so that from out in the marsh the opening was not obvious, and the outline of the island was not interrupted.

It was cleared and the soil was rich and black and there were dried and spent corn stalks with bean vines clinging to them and hundreds of big brown squash scattered about on long vines. Only a bird from up above could see that this large opening in the middle of the island was there. They continued to the far end of the garden area and then down a narrow path through yaupon for a few hundred yards and into another open but fully canopied area with four palm covered shelters with an open area and fire pit. Ayana had sent someone ahead to let them know she was coming with special visitors and to not be afraid. Ayana nodded for them to stop and she walked ahead and stopped at a distance from the group of adults and one child, all looking curious at what this unusual visit was about. They had gotten the message to not be afraid and they trusted Ayana completely, but there had never been visitors, other than the regular stream of runaways coming in and going out. They saw the mask on Ayana and knew she was bringing outsiders.

Alice saw the two oldest ones and recognized her mother and father and then looked at the others for her brother and didn't see him at first and then looked over them again and settled on a tall man standing particularly close to an Indian woman with a skinny dark boy at her side and then she understood what Ayana had said about a surprise. It was her brother and he had taken an Indian mate and it was their child and he was who Jacob had seen and told her about. All this reckoning to Alice happened in just a few moments as she watched Ayana speaking to the group and a swoon of happy shrieks and then tearful wails and Ayana moved further away and Alice rushed forth and hugged and happily cried with her mother and father. After a few minutes, she pulled away and found her brother and cried with him and hugged his mate and child and then hugged everyone in the group.

She was the lost child to an awful ending to her family at first but they had learned of her rescue and survival from runaways they had helped over the years. She had done more than just survived but had become a legend and inspiration in South Carolina and Georgia. After things settled a bit, Alice's mother looked at Martin and said she had gotten enough bits and pieces of stories to know who he was and some about his whole family. He shied away from the attention and said Alice had been like his second mother and like his sister and a member of his family.

Alice turned her attention to her brother and his mate and child. She looked closely at him while remembering him when they were children. He said his wife's name was Pua and their sons name was Mica after his wife's father. She next hugged her father who had been watching, with flooded eyes. When they hugged, he asked about the bump in her stomach and she said she was a long time in finally getting one and a new round of happy weeping came over them and Alice's mother felt her belly and asked who the father was and Alice was said it was Johnny and he was a good man and maybe he could come soon.

Daniel and Mary waited around a little while after Martin and Alice had left and then got in the wagon and went to find Mallie. Although this latest hideaway was the most secure yet, Mallie kept an ear out and heard them coming and stayed hidden until he was sure it was them. It was still hard for him to grasp the fact that these white people had saved his life and were bent on helping him.

Daniel handed him the food sack and told him to be ready early the next day because there were some plans in the works for him and that he wasn't sure yet what they were but it would be tomorrow for sure because of the slavers coming back. Mallie said he liked this place better than the other two places he had hidden out and was curious about what was next and he could never thank them enough. Mary told him not to worry because something would be done about his escape from Tybee soon. Daniel told Mary they may as well eat here with Mallie and went and got their food sack and they sat on the thick layers of pine needles and had their lunch of leftovers. Mallie complimented their mothers cooking and asked for them to please extend his gratitude to both their parents for helping him.

They lingered in the warm filtered rays of the sun for only a few minutes and Daniel said he could take a nap but needed to go and reminded Mallie to be on the lookout for them coming early tomorrow. While riding back, Daniel said if he took a nap, he would rather do it down by the Back River in case something came up with Martin. Mary said she didn't know what could come up since he would have to wait on the tide to come up before he could leave, and Daniel said he knew that but still wanted to be there for him. They got back and unhitched the horses so they could drink and eat sea oats, then found themselves a comfortable place to wait.

Martin had mostly been watching as Alice and her family settled down to serious talk. The other people living there told their stories to Alice and everyone kept cups full of yaupon and the talking and laughing and sometimes crying, was nonstop. Alice stepped away and spoke with Martin for a minute and she was glowing with such happiness like he had never seen her before. He thought about how happy his mother and father would be when they heard this good news and especially his mother.

Alice told Martin that she would be spending the night and probably a few days there but that he would need to go back today and Martin said he had been thinking about that and wished that he could go back sooner than waiting for the high tide which wouldn't be until about dark. He said he thought about asking Ayana's help by having some of her people help him drag his boat out through the creek, then he could go around the ocean way back to Tybee and be able to get started on what was to be done with Mallie.

Alice said for him to go and ask and not to worry about her. He said he would and if he left now, he would just see her tomorrow when he brought Mallie . Alice hugged him tightly and said how she loved him and how he had made the best day of her life come about. Martin could feel how happy she was and he was happy with her and himself in the best kind of way. He told everyone that he might be leaving and would be back tomorrow and they all praised him for bringing Alice.

There was only one path to follow back and Martin thought to himself if he might ought to whistle or something so he didn't frighten or surprise anyone but decided not to and as he approached the main encampment, Ayana was waiting for him as he came into the opening and he noticed a few young men emerging from the woods and realized that they had been following along near him and he hadn't even noticed and one must have gone ahead quickly and told Ayana he was coming.

He noticed how she kept her distance like when she had taken them to the other encampment and understood her reason for doing it. He asked her if he could talk to her at the breezy spot they had used before and she said they could. Once there, Martin asked if she thought he could get out of the creek to the sound so he wouldn't have to wait longer for high tide to go across the marsh. He told her about Alice staying and him returning with the runaway tomorrow and it would be better for him to get back early rather than late.

He was glad to hear her say that he could leave even at low tide because she would send a few men to lead him and carry his little boat out to the deeper creek that led to Warsaw Sound. She said he could leave now if he wanted to. Martin said that would be good because he had a lot to do to prepare for tomorrow. He told her about how he had been thinking about the story of her people and how he had always dreamed about these islands and hoped that he would come more and that he would help them in any way he could if there was ever a need. He told her that he didn't know if it would be any help to them, but he planned on being a captain on his own small trading ship in a few years.

She told Martin that she didn't know what the future was but there would, as always, be changes. She said her life's goal was to preserve her people and they had been pushed from one island to the next and were now as far north as they could be pushed. If they got pushed again, and if there were still some of them alive, they would have to go by boat south to the southern part of Florida where she heard was not yet overrun by colonials or go live with the people of the Ogeechee River, but she didn't know how long before they would be forced out. Martin said that his father was a powerful figure in Savannah and if there was ever a need, he was there to ask.

Ayana thanked him and he said the thanks belonged to her for all she had done for her people and Alice's family and all the runaways that have been helped over the years. He said he should be going since he could and she got up and nodded for him to follow. Back at her camp, she spoke some indigenous language and in less than a minute, there were four men ready to go with instructions from Ayana. Each had a doe skin cover over their face.

Martin walked over to the boat and saw that the big pan of oranges was still there and told Ayana that they were for them and set them out on the bank. The Indians helping him had leather sandals tightly strapped to their feet to keep their feet from getting cut by oysters and they dragged the boat in the shallow water, staying in the middle of the creek because the bottom was firmer there. Whenever Martin struggled a bit, he was quickly helped. After about an hour they got to the sound where the water was deep and Martin set the sail and climbed in. He wished he could thank his helpers because he could have never made that alone but simply looked at them and smiled, then he remembered and said, "Gereg" and they laughed. He thought it was a better thing to say upon an arrival but it seemed to work for him leaving. He tightened the sail and the little boat shot out into the sound, with his helpers watching curiously.

Once he rounded the point at Claw Island and headed north, with a good breeze on his beam, he almost reached a planning speed as he stayed just out enough from shore to be behind the waves before they began to curl and break. It was Martin's favorite point of sail and location, on the edge of both the ocean and land.

The sailing was fun, but he couldn't help thinking about all he had to do to help Mallie tomorrow and somehow making sure that the slavers left Tybee for good. It was serious business and the slavers were experienced, crude and dangerous and he didn't want to take any chances with the Dyers life and livelihood or with Ayana and her people and Alice's family and the others. He had been thinking about how he could get Mallie off Tybee and over to Long Island with Alice's parents in a way that the slavers wouldn't know where he had gone. Just before coming to the Tybee Inlet, Martin was seized with a plan that made him smile with resolve and certainty about how to get Mallie away and fool the slavers.

The tide was swiftly coming in now but the wind was mostly against him so he rolled up the sail and paddled. In a bit, he could see Daniel and Mary on the river bank, just above the high water line where the sand was soft, and the two tackies grazing on the sea oats beyond. He didn't know it was coming, but he began to feel such a gratitude and gladness at this culmination of so many things. Tears came and at the same time a smile that stretched so wide that his cheek muscles ached.

Neither Daniel nor Mary had noticed Martin coming. Daniel had been napping off and on and Mary had occasionally looked out at the islands directly across the river and not back toward the ocean. Martin was close before Mary saw him and she shrieked and jumped up and woke Daniel and they went down to the edge.

Martin nudged onto the bank and got out with the big smile still on his face. Mary through her arms around him and kissed his cheek and made him uncomfortable but less than the first time she did it. Daniel was grinning and asked him what happened. Martin said he had much to tell and asked Daniel if he would help him carry the boat up and put it in the back of the wagon and Daniel looked surprised and asked why the wagon? Martin said he could talk while they were carrying the boat up and Mary and Daniel sensed his urgency and Mary carried the mast with the sail wrapped tightly around it and paddles.

Martin said, first, Alice is with her family and they are fine. Next, the Indian lady, Ayana, was there and was old but agile and very smart, wise, and gracious but most of her people have died off and she is doing all she can to preserve them. And, what your father said about the Indians helping runaways, after we told him what we saw on the beach with the big trading canoe, is truer than we thought. So, we have a solution to Mallie and that's what loading this boat on the wagon is about and why I can't quit smiling. Martin was speaking quicker and with greater confidence and clarity and authority than Mary and Daniel had ever heard him be.

Martin told about the four Indians dragging and carrying him and his boat out the creek at low tide so he would have time to get back and prepare for tomorrow. Martin said after they got the boat and all lashed onto the wagon, he would tell more on the way home, but he first needed to stop by and tell Mallie to be ready in the morning and what the plan was. Daniel said he had told Mallie already to expect to be picked up early and not to worry because something would be worked out for him and Martin said that was excellent, and he had told them the main things about what happened but he had a lot more to say and would rather wait and tell it to them and their parents together.

When they got back, Charles and his wife were both anxiously awaiting their return because Charles had seen, with the monocular from up on the lighthouse, Martin return alone and they wanted to know about Alice. Martin said right away that Alice was fine and with her family and he had a lot to tell and they should have some tea and sit down and he would tell everything to them all at once. They went to the front porch and Margo brought out some tea and Martin began by telling the high points of Ayana's story and about the layout and description of the island and the reunion with Alice and her family and her brother and his Indian wife and child.

Even though he only hit the high points, it was still a while before Martin finished and they were in awe at what had happened in only a half day. Martin said it was both sad and happy learning of everything. Sad about Ayana and how few of her people were left and all they had been through for so many years and happy about Alice finding her family. He said he was particularly happy that they had a way to help Mallie because he had been worried about any trouble that could come to them if they were suspected of helping him in any way and he wouldn't rest easy until Mallie was off Tybee and on his way up the Ogeechee, and the slavers had come and gone.

Then he told why he had brought his boat on the wagon. He said that if he left with Mallie from the Back River, the slavers and dogs could figure that out and suspect and guess that they had taken Mallie over to the Indian islands and go there with the dogs and wreak havoc. So, his plan was to make it look like a boat had picked Mallie up on this end and headed for Turtle Island but instead he would leave with Mallie and sail around Tybee and take him over to the Indian Islands for Alice's family to help him on his way up north, just like the other runaways they helped.

He said he would walk to get Mallie early and let him walk over to the north beach and leave a well scented trail. Daniel could meet us on the beach there with the wagon and boat. I will pound the edge of a board in the sand a few feet up from the high water line to look like a keelboat had been pulled up on the beach like they had picked someone up. He said that he could add some boot prints along with Mallie's shoe prints to make it more real.

Mary was impressed with how confident and mature Martin was being and what a creative plan he had come up with. She burst out that this all was better than any of her books. Daniel looked disgusted and told her this was serious and real and nobody could ever get hurt in a book. Mary told Daniel he was a clod. Charles had been listening intently with a furrowed brow. Martin finished up his recounting of everything and asked Charles what he was thinking. Charles said he thought his idea to fool the slavers was a good one but added that when he got back tomorrow from taking Mallie, to go swimming for a while, then put his clothes, mast, sail, poles and paddles in the boat, and put enough ballast stones to sink it to the bottom over night to wash any scent of Mallie off, then go back early the next morning before the slavers get there and put the boat back where it has been. One of us will leave you a fresh set of clothes up in the edge of the woods where you leave the boat.

Another thing, he said, was that Daniel should cross over to the beach down where the barge is pulled up because there is already a wagon trail there where the men have been hauling materials from the barge. And he said for Daniel to keep the wagon below the high water line so the next tide will wash away the tracks and for him to keep the wagon a good distance from Martin and Mallie to prevent any scent of them on it. He said they will need the wagon at the landing tomorrow to haul the ice box that Captain Ben was bringing but they should be through in plenty of time to get it there.

One other thing he said was that none of the sub contract work crew should know anything about this. They could go back and say something to the wrong people and perhaps we should only tell Jacob and let everyone else find out when they return home after the work is done here. He said he had also been thinking ahead of what Alice and her family might do now that they have reunited but live in different places. If her family tried to leave the islands, they were still runaways and if caught, could be returned, even after all this time, to their owners, including Alice's brother and son and possibly even Alice and her baby too.

Martin interrupted and said he had overheard Alice's mother say she would never leave the islands on her own because she had found a higher purpose in helping runaways escape, and she had a new family there now with the Indians and her grandson and his mother. Margo said those were all important considerations but could wait until this business with the runaway and slavers is over. Charles said that the sun was far enough over now and he wanted to signal Walter about what had happened. Margo told Daniel to go along so they could be done quicker because she had leftovers warming for an early supper. Martin said he was starved and her leftovers were better than most other people's first overs.

He was left sitting with Mary alone and she told him how smart and brave he had been. Martin asked Mary if she wanted to know a secret and she said of course she did. Martin said he had kept it a secret because he didn't want to be fused over but today was his fifteenth birthday. Mary was shocked and said her Mother could have made him a sweet cake like she did for them on their birthdays and she said she would go tell her now and she could make one tomorrow. Martin said it was a secret and if she didn't keep it, he would never tell her another one. Mary thought for a moment and said but if I don't tell, will you tell me any more secrets you have now and any you have later? Martin said he would and that made Mary very happy and kissed Martin's cheek and made him blush red in the face but he thought to himself that he liked it.

He reminded her that he would probably be going home in about a week. She said she had known it was coming soon from hearing her father talk about the work getting almost finished and said how boring things would be when he was gone. Martin said he was gonna be coming back more often because he didn't think Alice's family would leave the islands and that, after she had her baby, Alice would want to visit and he would probably be the one to take her and the baby and probably Johnny too and if he got his boat finished in a few months he wanted to bring it down to practice operating it and to show Captain Jones.

Margo called from the kitchen and said they could take the Captain his food while waiting on Charles and Daniel, but not to dally and to clean the sand off their feet before they came back in. She handed Martin a plate with left over sweet potatoes, string beans, and chicken and dumplings, and corn bread and they hurried out and returned just as Charles and Daniel came back and ate supper. Martin couldn't remember when food had tasted this good. He wondered what Alice was having to eat.

After supper, they went, like most of the time, on the porch and had tea. Martin and Daniel talked about their plan for the next day. Martin would leave to go get Mallie, let him walk alone, over to north beach, staying off the beaten path, like a runaway might do, and purposely brush up against bushes to leave a good scent trail for the dogs and then split off, and go across the dunes to north beach, leaving a set of prints across the dunes and onto the beach. Martin would stay on the wagon trail past north beach and cross over to the beach where the barge was and walk in the edge of the water, back to where Mallie is.

Daniel said he would wait a bit after Martin had left and take the wagon and boat through the dunes by the barge and stay below the high water line too and set the boat off on the edge of the water and wait for them. Martin asked Charles if he had some old boots to make some prints in the sand and a board to make a keel mark as if a boat had been pulled up and he said he did and he would put them in the boat in a little while.

Charles said for Daniel not to forget to keep a distance with the wagon from Martin and Mallie to not spread any scent of Mallie or any he may have gotten on Martin. Martin said he would do the fake boot prints and keel imprint and sail back around to the south end of Tybee and over to Long Island with Mallie. The slavers would see Mallie's prints over the dunes and the boot prints around the keel mark and think someone had come and picked up Mallie. Margo said she wished this was all over and Charles said it would be soon but he was more worried than he let show. He told the boys it was a good plan if they followed it carefully because slavers and their dogs were relentless.

Charles said the bridge work and the brick repair on the lighthouse was within a couple days of being done and most all the crews would be leaving soon except a few people to haul oyster shells onto the path over the marsh for a few weeks and he guessed Martin was about ready to go back home. Martin said he missed his home but this trip had been way more than what he had ever imagined and his vow to help Alice was completed and his curiosity about the Indian Islands was answered a lot and as soon as he could get his new boat rebuilt he would be back again. Margo said he could come as often as he liked and stay as long as he wanted. Not long after supper, everyone was ready for bed after a big day, especially Martin.

Knock, knock, knock was the sound of Margo's broom handle on the ceiling below him. Martin lifted out of his bed quickly and it seemed like only minutes since he had laid down to sleep the night before, but he felt rested and woke with the urgency of his things to do for the day. He made sure that Daniel was stirring before he went downstairs. Mary was up and said she wanted to give Martin a small gift for Mallie and handed him a small wool scarf. She said she wanted to go with Martin this morning but didn't want to risk spreading any scent and she didn't want to change clothes and let the ocean wash her old ones and anyhow his boat only held two. She said she wanted Martin to tell Mallie that she was impressed by his desire for freedom and courage to go for it and she wished him the best and she told Martin to tell him why she didn't come.

Daniel came in and they had a big hot biscuit with a little lard and three eggs and bacon inside with a heap of blackberry preserves on the side. Charles had come in and Martin said he intended to be back by mid-morning because of the slavers coming. He said Ayana and everyone there was expecting him with Mallie and he intended to leave when the tide was still almost full and go straight across and return quickly while the tide was at its fullest. Charles said he would be watching with the monocular for him and the slavers. Charles also added that by the time Martin finished his new boat and returned to Tybee, he and Daniel would have a signaling device that was small and he could take it to the islands and they could signal back and forth from the lighthouse. It would be smaller and simple without the box but suitable for basic messaging. He said he had been thinking about it since he and Daniel had first gone over there last week and would send an order for the small mirror on the next supply boat. This idea perked Daniel's interest and Martin said it was a great idea. Martin said he needed to go and Mary gave him the package for Mallie and Margo handed him a food sack and a jug of water.

The sun was about halfway above the horizon as Martin left the lighthouse compound. As he walked, he thought of his tasks and the amount of time each would take and when he should be back and done. He thought to himself to be very careful about any trace of scent that slave dogs might catch and raise suspicion. He had gone over this before he went to sleep last night and was doing it again in case there was something he hadn't thought of in his plan. He walked to the big pines and Mallie was already standing and waiting for him.

He stopped about twenty-five feet from him and Mallie looked afraid and looked around. Martin quickly told him to not be afraid and then explained briefly about what he had found out the day before and they were going across to the Indian Islands this morning before the slavers came with the dogs and how they were gonna make it look like he had left Tybee on a boat from north beach, probably to Turtle Island. Martin said he would explain the rest of the details on the boat ride but now he didn't have time and for him to follow him off to the side alone so he would leave only one set of prints and to purposely brush up against a bush every ten feet or so to leave a good scent trail and if they got separated to callout. Martin started down the wagon trail and Mallie followed but off to the side and into the woods a bit. Martin stopped often for him to catch up and to make sure they didn't get separated.

They passed near the lighthouse and continued a little ways further and Martin told Mallie to turn right and walk over the dunes and just onto the beach and stand there and wait for him to go down a ways further and cross over and come back to where he was standing. He said that Daniel would be there but to stay away so no scent would get on him or the wagon. Martin ran on down another half mile and crossed over the dunes and saw Daniel down by the water's edge. He had unloaded the boat and was holding it by a rope in the shallow water. He had set the mast, the oar for a rudder, put in the cork safety float and had it ready to go.

Mallie was at the top of the beach waiting and Martin told Daniel to leave the boots and board on the beach and pull the boat up on the beach a little and back off with the wagon a way. Martin called Mallie down and said they didn't have to worry now about mixing scents and told him what he planned to do with his clothes and boat when he came back to Tybee later and gave him the gift from Mary and told him what she said. He then took the board up above the high water line, near where Mallie had come across the dunes and pounded the edge of it, making a narrow groove like a boat keel being drug up out of the water would make, then took the old boots and made a few prints and brushed away his and told Mallie to walk over and leave some more of his prints.

Martin nodded for Mallie to come on and he put the board and boots in his boat and told Mallie to sit in the middle and just move from one side to the other when he told him and he shoved off and was under way. Mallie didn't look very comfortable and Martin said not to worry. The wind had moved around during the night and was out of the north and made an easy sail down the beach and they passed Captain Jones and his shanty and the lighthouse. Both pilot crews had left together and Martin could see that they were headed for two ships that had come in during the night and anchored.

Martin headed east with the wind on his beam and rounded the north point of Tybee and with the wind behind him sailed down the beach, just outside the breakers, then followed the shallow channel along the beach into the Back River, all the while telling Mallie the story of Ayana and her people and of Alice's family and how they had helped hundreds of runaways. With the wind still mostly behind, Martin angled across the Back River and with the tide almost high and marsh grass showing he headed straight at the east end of Long Island and with the tide not fully high, he rolled the sail up and showed Mallie a pole and how to use it and he was awkward with it at first but got better quickly when he learned to hold the end of the pole down low and to push the fork at the bottom of the pole against the lower part of the marsh grass.

With both of them poling, they made their way, not as fast as yesterday's trip when the water was higher, but much faster than following the creeks, which would have taken hours. When they got to the creek near the island, Martin handed Mallie a paddle and he saw some people out on the first landing, looking at them. He recognized Ayana there and when he got near, she motioned for him to go on to the small creek that led to the second landing. They did and in a few minutes they were pulled up on the bank by Alice's brother and his young son.

Martin jumped out and told Mallie that this was Zach and his son Mika and they welcomed Mallie and Zach helped him out of the boat and up and into the clearing where their small palm houses were and he received a welcome by the rest of the group and Alice stood up and stepped forward and hugged him and pointed to her mother and father first and said they were Abe and Lucie and went on and pointed to the rest and gave their names. Lucie stood and told him that they welcomed all runaways but he was special because he had come at the time of their reunion with Alice and by way of Martin and it was the happiest of all times.

She said he could stay as long or as short a time as he wanted and when and if he wanted to go, they had a way to send him up the Ogeechee that would put him with another connection to continue north. Mallie was overcome with the joy. He was given some tea and a corn bread and a place to sit with them as if he was a family member. Martin finished his tea and biscuit quickly and told Alice that he had to go while the tide was high and why and asked if everything was ok and she said, thanks to him, things were beyond what she could have ever dreamed or imagined and hugged him tightly. He said he would be back tomorrow or the next day at the latest and was there anything that he could bring and she said to bring more oranges because they didn't get much fruit. He said ok and turned to the rest of the group and said goodbye and he and Zach went back to the boat with little Mica following along.

He got in and Zach pushed him out and he paddled out the narrow creek to the bigger creek and passed by the first landing and waved to Ayana and paddled and poled out over the marsh grass. The tide was higher going back and only him in the boat and poling was easier. The wind was against him so he kept the sail rolled up on the mast and paddled across the Back River in the slack of the tide to the landing. Once on the bank, he pulled the boat up a little and took the mast out and laid it in the bottom of the boat.

Next, he dove under the water and swam a long ways out before coming up, then dove back under and swam back in, to rid himself of any scent of Mallie. Then, he took his clothes off and put them in the boat with all the other things. He then gathered a few ballast stones from the bank and after pushing the boat out knee deep set the large stones in the bottom on top of the mast, sail, poles, and paddles, and clothes and all, and pushed it out and tilted it a little and it filled with water and sank like a rock to the bottom, then swam around a bit and splashed more to wash any remaining scent off of himself. He looked across the river and smiled to himself thinking of the good change of fortune Mallie was having and then remembered the slavers coming and ran up to find his clothes.

He expected the slavers would be either starting from Savannah about now that the tide was starting out or from some place along the way that they may have stopped at to wait for a tide change, but he would have a look with the monocular when he got back.

Martin ran the whole way back to the lighthouse compound and he heard Charles call him from up on the lighthouse balcony. He looked up and Charles was motioning for him to come up. He hurried up the stairs and out on the balcony and Charles had the monocular set up looking back toward Savannah and Martin looked and saw the slavers boat way up the south channel, headed for Lazaretto several miles away. He said that they would probably set up camp for the night and start their hunt in the morning but that they should take a look every hour at them and what they were doing. Martin said good, and he would go down in an hour or so and drag his boat up in the woods.

He told Martin to swing around and look toward north beach and he did and saw Captain Ben and his sharpie with Ashley and Ken. The channel comes close to the beach there and they were pulled up in the shallow water and Daniel was standing in the water with the wagon and horses and the water was above his knees. They had the huge boom with a set of blocks and tackle about to lift the icebox up and onto the wagon. Jacob and his crew were out in the water, waiting for the icebox to get swung around to the wagon. Martin said he wished he were there and Charles told him that he was where he needed to be and had plenty to do on his own and Jacob and his crew and Daniel could manage on their own and they would be up here with it in a bit. Martin said he was right and said he was actually hungry and might go down and look for a snack.

Margo and Mary were outside on the porch when Martin went down and they asked about his trip with Mallie. He told them that it went just fine and everyone treated Mallie very kindly and Alice was happy and her family and the others were all still celebrating her return. Margo said it was a shame that Johnny could not be there and Martin said he had thought of that too. Margo asked why Johnny couldn't stay for a week when he came on the supply boat and go back with Alice on the next weeks boat. Martin said he didn't see why not because the work here is almost done.

Margo asked Martin if he would like a biscuit and he said he had come down to ask if he might have a snack. She said she didn't ever want anybody hungry and went to fix him something. Mary asked Martin what he had to do for the rest of the day and he said he only had to go put the boat up and he had thought he might pick some more oranges for the people over on the island. She said she would help if he liked and he said he would like that.

Margo came with tea and biscuits and preserves and shelled pecans and a cold piece of leftover bacon. Martin seldom noticed that he was hungry but did today and felt much better after the food. He thanked her and said he and Mary were gonna go pick some oranges for the people on the islands and he still had the pan he had used before but wanted another one so he could take more. She said good because the oranges would just rot on the tree otherwise. She gave him the pan and they went out to the barn and got the other pan and went to the orange tree. Martin climbed up in the tree where there were still plenty left and dropped them down to Mary one at a time till the pans were full.

Just as they finished the oranges, Daniel came with the wagon and Jacob and crew. Martin and Mary went to watch them unload the big wooden icebox. Margo was up on the porch where it was to go and didn't quite know what to think about it. Daniel pulled a paper from his pocket that Henry had sent. He read it aloud and it said there was two heavy chunks of ice inside and they could be removed to make it easier to get the icebox up the stairs and in place and to be careful to not damage the copper drainpipe coming out the bottom that drained the water from melted ice and about the hole needed in the porch for it to drain through to the sandy ground.

Jacob had a couple men remove the ice chunks and set them up on the porch and Daniel shut the door and the men laid the big box back and with ten men it was an easy task to set it up on the porch and put the ice back in. Charles said if they could just set it near where it was going he and Daniel could measure and cut the hole and slide it over in place themselves later.

Margo had made two pans of egg and bacon biscuits extra, knowing that the men would be there and brought out a platter full and told Daniel to get them some mugs of fresh well water. While they were eating, Margo talked to Charles about Johnny staying for the week and Jacob going back early. He said he would signal a message about that to Henry this afternoon and he didn't see why that couldn't happen.

Martin saw Daniel and said he and Mary were going to haul up his boat and didn't know if the horses had too big of a day for them to saddle them up and take them. Daniel said they were fine but not to run them. He said they loved going down there because their favorite food was sea oats. Mary went to tell her mother she was going with Martin and when she came back he was helping Daniel and her father with the icebox. They had slid the icebox over some and were cutting a hole slowly through the hard pine porch floor. Martin told them he was going and would be back soon. Charles said they needed to talk tonight after supper about the slavers who would probably be at it with their dogs at dawn. He said when he last looked, they were setting up camp over near the Lazaretto landing. Martin asked if the slave dogs would smell anything of where Mallie had been staying in the woods down at Lazaretto and Charles said he had Jacob burn that area off where he had slept and the rain we had since then would have washed away his trail from there to the Back River.

Martin and Mary left and Daniel and Charles watched as they walked together toward the barn. Charles looked at Daniel and smiled and said he thought Mary had decided on her husband but Martin didn't know it. Daniel said Mary may have a life at sea if she goes with Martin because all he thinks about is becoming a boat captain with his own boat. Charles said he would be proud to have Martin in the family but didn't like to think of Mary living on a boat. Charles said he wanted Daniel to help him messaging today because it was long and he was so quick and good at it.

Martin and Mary rode the horses to the Back River and as they got close to the south end, both horses perked up noticeably and Mary said they always did this because they loved sea oats and knew they were near. They set them out in the small dunes to eat and they went down to get the boat. The tide had gone out a ways but was still washing over the little boat and the bottom had a half-foot of sand inside. Martin took a paddle from under a stone and sloshed a lot of the sand out and set the stones out and took out the mast and other stuff including his clothes. He then rolled the boat over and dumped the rest of the sand out and drug it out of the water and rolled it back up right. He and Mary drug it up to the edge of the woods and went back for the mast and paddles.

Afterwards, Martin was wet already and went for a swim and nodded for Mary to come in. He said they should dally a bit so the horses could get their fill. Mary, clothes and all, swam out to Martin and they played like kids for a while and got out and walked a ways to drip off. Martin couldn't help noticing how beautiful Mary looked, especially when she smiled and her face lit up. He liked being with her and realized he would miss her when he went home. They rode the horses back home.

Mary and Martin were putting up the horses in the barn as Charles and Daniel were just coming down from the lighthouse and Charles said Henry had thought it a good idea about Johnny staying until next week and Jacob leaving early. Martin said he didn't know which of the two would be the most pleased to hear that. They all walked to the back porch where Margo was putting something in the new icebox. She said she had put a large crock in, filled with fresh water to cool for drinking. Martin said it took them some time to learn what they could use theirs for. He said that he liked having the butter and cheese and milk all the time. He said that now theirs stayed full of things. She asked what if we miss getting ice one week and Martin said that hadn't happened yet for them since they had ice buried right there but it would be some trouble and food would have to be thrown out and then restocked when there was more ice. He said Henry was working on a plan to build an ice storage building so he could have thousands of pounds of ice all the time and a special insulated box built into both supply boats to bring ice there every week. Daniel said that Captain Ben said he was bringing a load of ice back from his trip to Darien this week and Henry had asked him to stop at Lazaretto on his way back to leave some for here and he should have the supply boats set up to deliver it weekly after that.

Margo said it sure seemed like a lot of work. Martin said Henry had big ideas about it and his best friend from college is quitting his good job in Darien and moving to Savannah to help establish the Milam Ice Company. They want to build lots of iceboxes for people and businesses and deliver ice to them regularly. Henry thinks it will become very popular. He even wants to haul ice to Beaufort and Charleston. Our icebox is insulated with moss but yours is better with cotton but he is already looking into improving it more by using cork from Portugal. Daniel asked like wine bottle cork and Martin said yes and like the lifesaving float that I keep in the boat.

Martin said y'all will wonder, like we did, how you managed without an icebox. He said that on his next trip, when he finished his new boat, he promised to make them a treat that John in Darien had made them and it was the tastiest thing he had ever had. Margo told Martin they would miss him when he was gone. She said she had made a good supper and asked if they would take Captain Jones his down now before they ate in a little while and they said sure. She gave them a bowl of fish chowder with potatoes and carrots and a small sack of still warm biscuits.

Both the crews were gone and the Captain was all alone and perked up noticeably when he heard them coming and smelled the hot chowder and biscuits. He told them to put it in the shanty and while it cooled he would hear of their latest goings on. Martin told of his trip with Alice and finding her family and Ayana, the Indian lady and the trip earlier with Mallie and the slavers being back at Lazaretto and starting with their dogs tomorrow and all they had done to throw them off with the fake boot prints and a keel mark just down the beach a bit and he was delighted. The Captain commented on how busy they had been and Martin said he hoped things would settle down a bit for the last week he had here before going home. The Captain said he hated to hear that and Martin said he would be back when he got the boat done. The Captain said he would have something to look forward to and he had Daniel and Mary and their family and was the luckiest captain in the world. Now, he said, if Daniel would get me onto my feet, I think I will go enjoy my supper and turn in. He added that he would look for those slavers tomorrow and laughed at his blind self.

After shaking the sand off their bare feet, the three of them went to the supper table, where Margo had a huge bowl of fish chowder and a pan of biscuits. Daniel said the Captain was excited about his chowder and he told how he had joked about looking for the slavers tomorrow. When they were having their desert of blackberry preserves on biscuits, Charles mentioned the slavers coming and he was hoping they would come to the conclusion early on that Mallie had gone off the island so they would leave. Martin said he did too and wouldn't feel good again until they were gone and said he would be like Johnny was about Alice and worry every minute till they were gone. Margo asked Daniel to put the leftover bowl of chowder in the icebox but corrected herself and said maybe it would be better to let it cool first and then she would put it in. They went to the porch to have some yaupon tea and Martin told everyone about what Ayana had said about where they might have to go if they are run off the islands like they had been run off other islands.

She said they could go up the Ogeechee and become part of the Ogeechee people or she mentioned going out in the ocean to somewhere in Florida. Charles said there had been recent talk of the government shipping other Indians to central Florida to a huge reservation that had been set up there. Martin asked why would she say ocean then? Charles said she may have been thinking of south Florida where many Indians still live somewhat undisturbed in the swamplands and maybe she would prefer that to a reservation but it would be a long and dangerous trip to get there. Maybe she knows of a boat that could take them. Martin said she was very smart and keeping her people alive and together was always her biggest concern and he didn't think she would take them to a reservation.

The next day came and after an early breakfast, Daniel, Martin and Charles went up to the lighthouse balcony and looked with the monocular at what the slavers were up to. They must have left before daylight because they had already gotten to the Back River landing and were just headed over the small dunes toward the woods with the dogs tugging at their leashes with such vigor that the men could hardly hold them back and when they were let go, they frantically began barking and going back and forth, where the runaway had stayed.

There were two sets of dogs and handlers and they scoured the width of the island as they moved toward the north end, where the lighthouse was. When one group got to the big pines area, their dogs started to really get excited and the men with them blew on a small horn which meant for the others to come there. The men looked around and saw where someone had stayed and the well and all and put all the dogs together on that scent trail which had been marked by Mallie very heavily.

The men were as excited as the dogs that this was the runaway for sure and their excitement was picked up by the dogs and the barking turned to howling that could be heard from anywhere on the island. Martin and Daniel and Charles heard it and smiled at each other. They couldn't see them but followed their sound as they came just west of the lighthouse a ways and then burst out of the woods dragging the men by their leashes into the dunes. Martin said he thought they would have just let the dogs go and Charles said they wanted their runaway alive and in good health because he had such a large reward and that many dogs would surely kill a man in minutes if they caught up to him.

The loud, wild and frantic group of them crossed over the dunes and stopped abruptly at where the keel mark was just above the high water line and they could see them, even without the monocular now, and tell by their body movement at their disappointment at what they assumed to be the runaways escape to the islands beyond. The headman could be seen stomping his feet and was like a dog, barking and cursing his men. They could hear him from where they were.

After a lot of stomping and cursing by the headman at his crew, they split up and half the men and dogs went toward Lazaretto and the other half went toward the Captain's shanty. Charles and the boys were in a high state of anxious excitement and could barely contain themselves as they saw the one group stop and talk to the Captain and then to the one pilot crew that was on the beach. Charles had the boys walk back around on the balcony so they wouldn't be seen and put his finger to his mouth for them to be quiet because the sound traveled so well and they didn't want to let the slavers know they were watching.

The headman was in this group and was loud and animated. Right in front of the Captain, he turned and yelled at the men again and they cowered back from him and even the dogs did too. He said a few things to the Captain and the Captain said a few things and pointed up the beach where the keel mark and boot prints were left and then spoke more and he pointed across to Turtle Island. The headman started yelling and cursing again and men and dogs cowered down. He walked back to the keel mark again with the men and dogs following. He looked over the boot prints some more and stared out across the water. They were soon joined by the rest of the group who got yelled at some more and then they all went through the dunes and headed back toward the south end of the island.

Martin and Daniel could hardly contain themselves over the drama they had just seen. Martin remembered the duel they had seen from the same place but this lasted longer and although the action was not deadly, there was more of it. Charles was even taken aback over all the excitement and all, unlike his normal way that was always calm and steady. Martin told Daniel he wanted to run down and ask the Captain what the men said and Daniel asked his father if that was all right. Charles said it was ok but not to let on to the pilot crew that they knew anything about all this. Charles said he wanted to stay here and keep an eye on the slavers and Martin said they would come back shortly and both hurried down the stairs to the bottom and ran across the dunes and down on the beach. Daniel said to Martin to let him do the talking to the crew.

They ran up to the crew and Daniel said they had been up in the lighthouse helping clean the lens glass and had heard a bunch of dogs barking from the other end of the island and listened as they came our way and then saw the dogs and men come on the beach and a lot of shouting and then saw them come here and we could hear the one man yelling.

My father sent us down to see what was going on. Martin thought to himself what a great liar Daniel was. He had heard him lie to the slavers and now to the pilot crew and was surprised at his confidence and how believable he made himself to be. They were all laughing and less serious about it than Martin thought they should have been, but when the pilot explained, Martin and Daniel were laughing about it too.

He said the head slaver had asked the Captain if he had seen a boat come up and pick up a runaway and leave and the Captain told him that he did see the boat and two men come ashore and sit and wait on the beach for a couple hours and then he saw a runaway in rags come over the dunes and join them and they drug the boat down to the water and went off toward Turtle Island. He said he went and got his monocular and watched until they pulled up on the beach at Turtle Island and let the runaway out and then they set out toward Daufuskie.

The pilot stopped his story a few times because his laughter prevented him from being able to talk and he and the whole crew were wiping the tears of laughter from their eyes. The pilot went on to say that their tears was mostly from laughter but partly because they hadn't seen the Captain lie like that since before he was blind, when he was known from all over for his convincing way of telling tall tales and it struck their hearts to hear him lie so vividly again and the stupid slavers never doubted a spec of what he was saying nor did they guess that he was blind.

Again, they laughed loudly and Charles could hear them from up where he was. Martin thought to himself how very funny all these lies and deceptions were. First, all the trouble they had been through to deceive the slavers into thinking Mallie had gotten away to Turtle Island, then Daniel's convincing lie to the pilots about them wanting to know what the commotion was about and the best lie of all, that had the pilot and crew in such hysterics that they were wallowing in the sand laughing so hard, was the one told to the slavers by the Captain about all he had seen.

From up on the lighthouse, Charles watched the boys go and see the Captain and pilot crew and from hearing all the laughter, suspected some tall tales and he got a big laugh out of it too, without even knowing the details. Next the boys went over to the Captain, who had been sitting alone and enjoying what he had been hearing and he reached up and touched both boys and told them quietly that all this merriment was because of the good they had done by that poor runaway and he was touched by their deed. Martin said he hoped their deeds ended soon with the slavers leaving the island. Martin whispered to him that he and Daniel and Charles had been watching from up on the lighthouse and he had to come down and hear what they said.

The Captain said that when he told the head man that the boat had come and gone with the runaway, he went crazy and said he should shoot them all because they had gotten so drunk the night before they were supposed to return and were so sick that he had to put off coming for a day and had he come the day before as planned, he surely would have collected the biggest reward that had ever been offered for one runaway. He wanted them to go get the boat and go over to Turtle Island and they left here arguing about that. His men said the snakes would kill all their dogs for sure and maybe a few of them and things worse than snakes might get the rest of them.

The three crewmen and the pilot got up and walked down to where the fake boat keel mark and boot prints were and the Captain and the boys could talk normal without being overheard. Martin told the Captain that he was amazed at how convincingly Daniel could lie so good and when he tried, he stuttered and couldn't get his words to come out normal and anybody would suspect him. The Captain said it was important to understand the difference between telling an untruth and a tall tale. An untruth disturbed your conscience and a tall tale didn't bother it a bit. He said in every ship he piloted into Savannah and other places, he never told anything untrue about the river channel or weather or anything that could have an ill effect on anyone but he sure as hell told them some tall tales that had no consequence and entertained them to the point that they asked for him every time they returned.

He said that telling tall tales was a common man's opportunity to be on a stage that might never happen for him otherwise. He said he wasn't sure why but sailors, fishermen, pilots and crewmen or anyone working on or around the water seemed to like to tell stories that were larger than life. Martin said that included lighthouse keepers and looked at Daniel and they laughed some more.

Then Martin remembered that they needed to go back up and see what had become of the slavers and they thanked the Captain and he said the thanks belonged to them and they ran up and over the dune and went to the oil building and each got a can of oil and then up the lighthouse stairs and found Charles still looking through the monocular. He said the slavers had just gotten underway and headed back to Lazaretto and he guessed to Savannah but he wouldn't be relieved until he saw them going up the south channel.

The boys told him of what they had learned from the Captain and the pilot and his crew. Charles said they could either be headed back to Savannah or making a big mistake and going to Turtle Island. When they told how the pilot and crew had to say about the Captain and his reputation for tall tales and how he had lied so convincingly to the slavers and they never caught on to the fact that he was blind and it made Charles laugh again until he cried. He said it was true about the Captain being famous for his exaggerated stories but he was one of the few men he trusted to tell the real truth when it mattered because the Captain knew when it mattered.

He added that he needed to check on the slavers every hour to see where they were and where they might be headed. He thanked them for remembering to bring up the oil because his legs were getting worn out from so many years of climbing lighthouse stairs and carting those three gallon cans of oil made it harder to climb.

The boys went down from the lighthouse and told about the morning's events to Mary and Margo. Mary said she was getting more and more exciting material for her forthcoming book and Martin carried on about what a good liar Daniel was and Mary said she already knew that and Margo wasn't so happy to hear it but was overall proud of her family. Charles came down and said it would be a couple hours before the slavers got to Lazaretto and instead of staying to watch he would just let the boys go up and check on them after a while.

Everyone else was having tea so Charles got him some and joined the conversation. They had been talking about what had happened on the beach but Mary said she had been thinking about Ayana and her people and Alice's mother and all the hundreds of runaways she had helped and how that had helped her get over what she thought was the loss of Alice and now Alice was back. She realized that the Indians were runaways too and didn't have to but reached out to help runaway slaves at the risk of their own lives and culture and in a way, we are runaways, here on this island and are compelled to help both the runaway Indians and slaves. Charles said that Mary was right and he was proud that she understood the big picture and she was right about them even though he and his wife had never discussed why they liked the isolation of what they do.

Charles looked at Mary and said his great grandfather was a runaway from Darien right outside Savannah but that's a long story. Mary said he had never told about all that and asked for him to please tell it now. Daniel and Martin were attentive and Daniel said they had plenty of time to get to the Lazaretto landing before the slavers and Margo told him to go ahead, since we were already talking about runaways. Charles said ok he would.

He looked at Mary like she was the only one he was talking to and said that when his great grandfather came to New Inverness, which is now the town of Darien, slavery was forbidden because it went against what he and the rest of the Scotts with him believed about all men being equal before God. However, in about twenty years, for economic reasons, slavery, by law, was allowed in the whole state, and slave ships began arriving in Darien. When your great grandfather died, his son, ran away or left Darien with his family to go to a place called New Ebenezer, near Savannah. It was a town started by religious refugees from Germany that didn't believe in slavery.

After a few years there his wife stayed sick all the time and the doctors said she might improve with ocean air so he hired a boat to take him, his wife and small kids and enough supplies and a tent and spent a month on

Tybee. My grandmother's health improved greatly but they had to return to Ebenezer because they ran out of supplies and food. After a week back she got sick again and almost died this time.

My grandfather took more supplies and the tent back to Tybee and again his wife's health improved. They were staying about half way between here and the south end just inside the dunes and should have been afraid but were not. There were still a few Indians left on the island and they were never a problem but there were some outlaws and pirates that hid out here. There was a shanty at the day marker here where the town of Savannah tried to maintain a few people to watch out over the river entrance but supplies and food were irregular and most didn't hold up to the lonely isolation and unreliable food supplies and after a month or two they would quit and leave.

My grandfather got to know a man and his wife who had stayed at the tower for six months but couldn't take it any longer and left but told my grandfather he should apply for the job and he did and being the only applicant, he got it. The supply boats were inconsistent but they planted some things and fished and hunted and even traded some with the few Indians to supplement the food sent from Savannah once and a while. All they had to do was to keep a daily report of ship sightings and anything unusual they might see and whenever the supply boat did come, send the report back with them. Their pay was not much but they were able to save it all because they didn't have anywhere to spend it. My grandmother's health remained good and she and my grandfather lived a long life.

They had three children, my father and two sisters. The girls grew up and one married a pilot and the other a crewman that they met here on the beach and one ended up in Charleston with a family and the other in Savannah with a family and when my grandparents died, my father stayed here alone for some years until his sister brought a women she knew from Savannah down to meet him and they were married soon after by one of the pilots right there on the beach.

My two sisters came first, then me. My father salvaged washed up lumber and logs from the beach and added on to the shanty and we all lived there together for the next six years. Things were very primitive then and supplies limited and my parents thought my sisters could have a better life in the city so they sent one sister to Savannah with her aunt and the other to Charleston with the other aunt, where they married and settled.

When I was eighteen, my father died and my mother went to Savannah with her sister in law and daughter, and I stayed alone. A message came on the supply boat and I had to leave the island temporarily and go back to Ebenezer where my father had a small piece of inherited property that had not sold but a willing buyer had come up and I had to sign the papers. I met your mother there and we were married within a week, right there in Ebenezer. She returned with me to Tybee and we continued our job as keepers.

Of course, there was no light to keep burning and our job continued to log all ships coming and going and anything unusual. Then, the big storm came that blew down most of the lighthouse and destroyed our shanty and nearly killed us but we fortunately had a strong tabby foundation with a root cellar and holed up in it till the storm blew over. It was almost a year before the reconstruction of the lighthouse began.

There was an encampment of a hundred workers and slaves and lots of supply boats, coming and going, hauling hundreds of thousands of bricks and other building supplies. We had rebuilt our shanty but left because all the commotion and ruckus of the work crews. Every night there was drinking and fights and all, so we moved away.

A couple years later, a messenger came and told us that the director of the new lighthouse and operation was coming in a week to inspect things and wanted to meet with us, so we moved back. He and a small group came from Savannah in a sloop and stayed at the Lazaretto landing for a week. That was Martin's father, Captain Walter Milam. He came every day and I was his guide to all things about Tybee. He was, except for the governor, the highest-ranking Brit in the city and state, and actually was more popular and favored than the governor, but you wouldn't know it by how common and gracious he was. He came every day to our shanty with all kinds of food and wines and deserts.

We got to know each other quit well and quickly became good friends. We were surprised to learn that we had common ideas about the equal rights of all men, regardless of color or origin, even though he had been granted ownership of slaves by the governor. We hit it off right away and he told us that there were big plans for the lighthouse and he had in mind for us to be part of it all but didn't go into the details.

Our isolation kept us from knowing a lot about the divisions between American patriots and those loyal to the crown. We knew very little of what went on in Savannah and much less with the rest of the colonies. We had witnessed the fights amongst some of the workers over their different views but stayed out of things. Walter had confided in us the changing times and confessed his liking of America but kept all his attention on his assignment.

Then, one day, Walter came and told us what his assignments were about. We could hardly believe our good fortune after hearing Walter's overall plan, which included us and of a special support farm and trained boatmen and boats and a boathouse to insure regular weekly supply runs of food and oil and maintenance of the new lighting equipment that could make a light beam that could be seen six miles out. We wouldn't know until after the war about the intended equipment, which had been hidden as war seemed likely, that would make a light beam that could be seen sixteen miles out.

The war came and went and Walter became an American and retrieved the new lighting equipment from where he had it hidden and finally set it up. We finally felt confident and settled into our new light keepers house and compound. We had the most advanced lighthouse in America with a light beam that could be seen from sixteen miles out and a signaling system to communicate to the Milam place and Savannah. The lighthouse switched from state to Federal control but that didn't change things much except the weekly reports were more complicated and took longer and we got paid a little more.

We were a little late starting a family but we managed having you and your brother, and here we are. Mary said she had never heard the whole story at one sitting and Charles said that her saying they were runaways too, provoked his thoughts and the yaupon was particularly strong and stimulating today. He said there was a lot of providence in how so many things had happened and worked out the last week with Martin meeting up with the Indians across the river and the runaway and Alice's family and all and he didn't know if it was the providence of Mallie, or the Indians, or Alice's family. Martin was in one of his fogs while listening to the story and asked how there could be more than one providence. Margo was struck with the clarity and truth in Martin's question and said there was but one providence and she thought to herself that they were fortunate in having met Walter and now to have the guileless words of pure truth coming from his son. Charles said he loved it here and hoped his family could continue in the tradition but more than that he wanted them to be guided by their own choices. Margo said amen to that.

Daniel suggested that he and Mary and Martin take the wagon to Lazaretto to watch for the slavers coming by and see if they headed for Savannah or Turtle Island. Charles said he could do that from up on the lighthouse but if they do go, to tell Jacob that he could go on back on the supply boat tomorrow and not have to wait to go back with the rest of the crew in a couple weeks. He told Martin to tell Jacob what had been going on but not anyone else.

The bridge crew was finishing up on the small bridge when they arrived and Jacob had the men clear some scrap materials so they could cross. The horses didn't hesitate walking on the new decking that was installed without a wide space in between like before. Martin asked Jacob if they could talk for a minute and he said they could talk all day because he was getting close to done and running out of things to do. Martin and Jacob walked off a ways and Martin told Jacob of all the latest things that had happened and all and him going home early. Jacob liked everything he was told, especially the last part. He reminded Martin that if the rest of the crew was gonna be working on hauling oyster shells for the roadway, they would need the wagon all week. Martin said he would tell Charles that.

Martin said there was one other thing and reached in his pocket and pulled out one of Margo's big biscuits with blackberry preserves wrapped in a clean kitchen rag and handed it over and Jacob put it quickly in his pocket like it was contraband. Jacob told Martin that he knew he must have a birthday soon because he remembered his mother having him in the early fall and here we are in early fall again and Martin said he was right but not to tell anyone because he didn't want the Dyers making a fuss over him. Martin hugged Jacob and told him that this was the last time he would be asked to go off from his family and Jacob said he liked hearing that and said that Walter sure had two fine sons.

The cooking fire was about out but there was a big pot of leftover grits or something from breakfast still simmering and they could smell it a hundred yards before getting to the landing. The cook and his helper were fishing for big drum fish out on the point. Although they had already eaten, the grits smelled especially good and Martin looked around in the shanty and got three bowls and spoons and served him and Daniel and Mary each a bowl full. When they began eating it, they saw that it had crabmeat in it that made it taste so good. As they were eating, they heard yelling and screaming and they jumped up, thinking something terrible had happened because they were so keyed up from the earlier events of the day, but saw, out on the point, the cook hauling in a big drum fish about three feet long.

Martin and Daniel went back and filled their bowls again and said how good it was and they had never had grits with crab cooked in them. The cook and his helper came back with the big drum with the head on but they had gutted it out by the river. They moved the pot of grits off and set a huge pot over the coals and put the fish in it and it was so long that its tail stuck up on one side. The helper made several trips with buckets of water until the big pot was over half full of water, then began cutting potatoes and onions in half and tossing them in. The cook smiled and said that one fish was gonna feed all the men supper tonight and breakfast tomorrow and his helper could do the cleaning up and he was done with cooking for now.

After their grits, Martin asked the others if they wanted to walk over and see all the graves marked with ballast stones and they said ok. Mary said the last time she was here she ended up running away after seeing Mallie's hiding spot. They walked past the graves and saw where Jacob had burned off the hiding spot, to get rid of any scent, in case the slavers came there. They were looking around when they heard some dogs barking in the distance. Martin asked Daniel to give him a boost up a small pine tree nearby so he could look out over the river to the south. Daniel put his hands together and Martin put his foot in them and Daniel heaved and Martin got to the first branch and was able to climb up branches from there to the top and looked out and saw the slavers rowing with the tide toward the landing about a half mile away as the seagull would fly but about two miles away in the river.

Some of the crab grits smell must have drifted in the wind and got the dogs excited but he could also hear the men shouting at each other. Martin then shimmied down from the tree and said they should go back to the landing. They did and could hear the men arguing, as they got closer and the dogs barking at either the food they smelled or because of the disturbance of all the men shouting at each other. When they got to the landing, it was obvious that part of them wanted to go straight over to Turtle Island and catch the runaway and part, which must have included the dog's owner, yelling something about his dogs getting killed by snakes. The arguing and barking continued as the boat went by and at the point where they either had to go left toward Savannah or right toward Turtle Island, they turned left toward Savannah. Martin was relieved. Had they continued their search over to Turtle Island, it would delay their going home another day or so, and he would feel sorry for the dogs that surely would have gotten snake bit and maybe even worse things to them all. He didn't like them but he didn't wish them death.

Supper at the lighthouse was an especially happy one that night. Everyone was relieved that the slavers were gone and Mallie was in good hands and on his way to freedom and Alice was with her family. Martin was especially relieved because he somehow thought the whole thing would not have happened if he had not come and he had been very afraid that if things had gone wrong, the Dyers would have had a life-changing problem and maybe the Milam's too. He wished he had the things it took to make ice cream like John had made them in Darien. He thought about how good it would be with the blackberry preserves and biscuits they were having for desert. He thought to himself that he would do that on his next trip.

The supply boat came early the next morning and Martin, Mary, and Daniel were there waiting, along with Jacob, who was cleaned up and ready for his return home. They heard the chantey start as the boat turned into Lazaretto Creek from the south channel. Martin could hear Johnny's voice, particularly loud, above the rest because he was so happy to be coming to see his Alice and he was smiling big as he steered the boat up to the rails at the landing. The crew climbed out and walked up the rails and winched the boat up with Johnny in it. The cook had them all bowls of leftover fish stew and they ate it before they started unloading the supplies.

Martin told Johnny how good Alice was doing and how happy she was and he could take him over on the high tide this afternoon and he liked hearing that. Johnny saw the big smile on Jacobs face and said that he wasn't the only man ready to see his woman that day and hugged Jacob. When the crew finished eating, they loaded the supplies on the wagon. Martin and Mary and Daniel said goodbye to Jacob, and headed back to the lighthouse with Johnny, and as the tide turned and began to flow back toward Savannah the supply boat, with Jacob at the helm again, was swept back toward Savannah.

Johnny noticed how happy Martin was and Martin told him the story about Mallie and the slavers during their ride back and how nervous it had made everybody. Martin said he didn't tell him last week because he didn't want to worry him any more than he was already worried about Alice being gone. Johnny's brow furrowed real deep for a few moments before saying anything and then told Martin that he probably did the right thing and it was over and Alice was safe but it was still troubling. Johnny said how everybody missed Martin back home and Jacob and Alice too. Martin said he missed home but there had been so many things going on here, he hadn't been homesick but would be glad to be back next week. He said that Daniel might be coming to visit and Mary may be staying for a while with her relatives in Savannah. Also, he wanted to get back and start working on his new boat.

They pulled into the compound and stopped to leave off some supplies in the barn and a barrel of lamp oil in the small brick building, before loading the rest into the house. Daniel said he would take care of the horses. Charles and his wife welcomed Johnny back and said how good Alice was doing and what a good man he was to go along with her in all this. He said Alice could do no wrong and she was everything to him, but he had still worried about her every minute since she left and would until he could see and hold her again. Martin said he knew that and that's why he hadn't told him about Mallie and the slavers coming because he didn't want him to be overcome with worry. He told Johnny to relax and rest because before the days end he would be with Alice and have the whole week to do with her as he pleased. He said he wanted to take Johnny up on the lighthouse to show him the island Alice was on and Johnny said he didn't care about going up high like that but if he could see where his Alice was, he would do it. Margo told them to go on the porch and she would bring some tea and biscuits. Charles brought out the big pot of tea and poured everyone a mug full and Margo served the biscuits and plum preserves as Daniel and Mary came up from the barn.

Johnny said all the talk at the Milam place this last week was about Alice and the Indians and her family being alive and all and how Johnny was going over to see her. He said the stories had gone around about three times and there wasn't much left of the truth in it. He said had they known what he knew now of the runaway and the slavers, some would have surely passed on from worry, including him. He also said everybody was crazy about all the good things Mrs. Dyer cooked and were asking him how she made things and he said he couldn't say because he hadn't watched her do it. He said they all wanted to know how she cooked those big biscuits that she always fixed for the boatmen. Margo was modest and said it was the salt air that made things taste better. Daniel mentioned the grits with crab they had at the landing and how good it was and she said she would try that next time someone brought a mess of crabs. Mary suddenly looked animated and said they made her have a great idea and it was to include her mother's recipes in her book!

Charles said he thought that was an excellent idea. Mary said she had stayed up most all the night rewriting her notes about the things her father had told them about his family and the early days here. She said she had been writing about all the things that had happened since Martin was here too, and already had fifty pages of notes. A deadly duel, runaways, Captain Jones stories, Indian Islands, Alice and her family and what she survived and all her family went through, and slavers and Mallie, and Ayana and her people, and this was just the beginning. She said she hadn't even started making notes about Walter Milam and all that he did and his family, and the story about Martin's friend Jehu, and so much more that she thought of every day.

She thought she would work on those things and more when she went to stay with her relatives in Savannah and she could visit with the Milam's and ask Walter to tell all and Martha too. Charles and his wife were seeing something bloom about Mary and were quite pleased. Charles was particularly happy that Mary saw fit to record the history of their family and all the things that had happened. Daniel told his father that they were gonna take Johnny up on the lighthouse and they would carry some oil up and Charles said good. He and Martin and Johnny got up to leave and Johnny thanked Margo and Charles for everything again.

They picked up some lamp oil and Daniel was first up the stairs, then Johnny, then Martin to help Johnny feel more comfortable between them. Martin told Johnny not to worry and had him look out the small windows, as they got higher so he wouldn't be shocked at the top. He remembered looking out the little windows his first time going up. Johnny was more interested in seeing where Alice was than he was afraid but like everyone else, going up for the first time, he was quite taken aback when he walked out onto the balcony.

Johnny had climbed a large oak shade tree when he was about ten and could see out over a field of cotton but this was too much to take in. Martin saw the astonishment and fear on Johnny's face and pointed to the long island way out in the middle of the marsh and said that was where Alice was. He told him to look closely and he could see a little smoke coming up above the trees in two places and said Alice was at the west end where the smaller amount of smoke was. Daniel fastened the monocular to the rail and focused it in on the west end of the island and told Johnny to take a look. When he did, he yelled and said he was ready to go now and Martin said they could when the tide came in and flooded the marsh later in the day.

Martin began telling about what else there was to see but Johnny remained glued to the monocular. When he did look up, Martin turned the device around and focused it on the landing at Lazaretto and had him look at that and he was amazed and said he could see the cook and his helper and Martin told him to gently move the monocular and look up the south channel toward Savannah. Then Daniel moved the instrument around to the north so they could see Turtle Island, Daufuskie, and Hilton Head and then Daniel moved it some more so they could see to the east out over the ocean and Johnny yelled when he saw two ships, with all their sails set, sailing toward each other, one coming in to Savannah and one leaving, with the wind on their opposite beams.

Johnny said he saw another boat that might be Captain Ben and told Martin to look and he did and said it was him and he would probably stop at Lazaretto for the night and catch the tide to Savannah in the morning and he was returning from a delivery to Darien and was supposed to bring a load of ice back to the Milam's and drop off a chunk for the Dyers new ice box and they will need to pick it up in the morning. Martin had Johnny step inside and showed him the lantern and parabolic reflector and the mechanization that rotated the whole works at night. Martin then took him outside again and walked with him around the balcony and showed him the Back River where his boat was and where they would be leaving from.

Johnny said he wished the tide would hurry up and come on in so he could go see Alice and Martin said it would only be a few more hours and they could go pick some oranges to take and have some lunch and then it would be time to leave. Johnny took one more look through the monocular before Daniel put it away and they went down.

Martin climbed up the orange tree and dropped down the last of the oranges left on the tree and almost filled the large pan and they took them to the wagon. Martin said they still had an hour before they needed to leave and maybe they could walk down to see Captain Jones. Johnny said everyone called him Captain Sandy at home. Martin told him how the blind captain had told the slavers he had seen the boat that picked up Mallie and head for Turtle Island and Johnny got a kick out of that.

They stopped by the house to get some food for the Captain before going down on the beach. Martin told Johnny that they confided everything to the Captain but not any of the pilots or the crewmen because they told everything to everybody in Savannah. When they got down on the beach, Johnny walked behind Daniel and Martin like a good slave would do, to avoid raising suspicion by the crewmen. They asked Martin why they hadn't seen his little boat lately and Martin said he had been keeping it at the Back River because he had been doing a lot of fishing there lately. He told them he was going home next week but would be back in a few months when he got the Captains old boat rebuilt and looked forward to a little racing with wagers and the pilot said that would be easy money. They all laughed and he said he would hate to take his money but would, just to teach him a lesson. Martin said talk is cheap and they laughed more at that. Once over by the Captain and out of hearing distance, Martin told the Captain they had brought Johnny, the boatman and Alice's husband. Johnny asked the Captain if he had seen any more runaways being picked up lately and the Captain said no, but he was always on the lookout and they all laughed again. Martin pulled a couple oranges from his pocket and placed them on the Captains lap and the Captain said he was gonna miss Martin when he was gone and Martin said he would miss being here too but would be back soon.

Daniel said there was Captain Ben and his sharpie now and in close and not far beyond the breakers and Captain Jones said he could get away with that because of the sharpies shallow draft and he could save a couple hours by following the shallow channel in close instead of staying out in the main channel. Daniel and Martin walked down close to the water's edge and Martin yelled and Ashley and Ken both waved. Captain Ben emerged from the cabin when he heard the yelling and smiled big when he saw what was happening. Captain Jones knew of Martin's wanting to be a ship captain as soon as he could and he told Martin that he should see if Captain Ben would take him on.

A pilot crewman, standing near them, mentioned that it was getting time soon that Captain Ben might retire, and let his crew take over. The Captain told Martin that all captains and crews were not necessarily nice and being on a boat with ill-humored mates or a bad captain, in such close quarters, could be very unpleasant and he didn't want Martin to have to deal with anything like that. And, safety was important, even for coastal deliveries and he sure didn't want anything to happen to him, and he hoped he could get on with Captain Ben, because he was the best, and he wouldn't be having a crew that were not of high standards. Martin listened closely to Captain Jones and said he would ask Captain Ben about things tomorrow morning when he went to pick up the ice.

They told the Captain goodbye and walked back over the dune to the house, cleaned the sand off their feet and Margo had set out leftovers from the icebox for them to have a meal before leaving. Daniel grabbed a biscuit and went out to hitch the horses while Johnny and Martin finished eating. Johnny told Margo again how thankful he was for them and all they did for him and Alice and she said they were glad to do what they could. They heard the wagon outside and hurried out and loaded up. Mary and Margo watched them leave from the porch. Margo saw the look on Mary's face as she waved to Martin and it made her feel good and she remembered the feeling she had for Charles when he came to Ebenezer and she knew they would be together right after they met.

On the ride down to the Back River landing, Martin told Johnny more about Ayana and her people and how they had all died off from disease and how careful Ayana was now about new people coming to the island and because of this, kept two separate camps on the island. He told him the camp where Alice's family was had several runaways every month coming in and several runaways leaving on the big trading canoe with the Ogeechee Indians and how they were taken sixty miles inland where they were helped by others for the next leg of their flight to the north.

He explained how Ayana's mother had discovered how her people were sickened by contact with colonials and often died from it. Johnny asked Martin why the Indians helped runaways and Martin said he didn't know but they had been doing it for as long as there were runaways. He thought a minute and told Johnny they, and their people, for hundreds of years had been runaways themselves from the colonials and they were not savages like everybody says. Johnny said most all slaves believed that they were like wild animals and their favorite food was people and particularly dark skinned people and nobody liked to go off from their plantation. Martin said those were lies told by the owners so slaves would be afraid to run away. He told Johnny how sometimes the local colonials around here, would drink whiskey and shoot at the group of them like their lives had no value and didn't matter, same as black folks. He said Alice had told him that a hundred years ago, the Indians were used as slaves but their owners couldn't keep them from running away into the woods because they knew how to survive in the wild. She said they shipped thousands to some islands where they were made to work at sugar plantations. Johnny asked Martin if he thought things would ever be different and Martin said he thought so because his father was taught that all men were Gods children and even though he was given the Milam plantation and the slaves, he believes all your lives matter and he doesn't think he owns you and does all he can for you to be happy and have a life of your own, and he thinks that the truth will eventually be known and is afraid it might cause a civil war with Americans against Americans.

Johnny said he owed his life to Alice, who owed her life to Charles for picking her up out of the mud after the massacre, and Walter and Martha for raising her like their own and teaching her how to read about the world and her helping him to see himself as something more than property. Martin said yeah, that's how it works. It's like my boat that I found, rotten and waterlogged and you teaching me how to make it better than new and adding a sail and then teaching me how to sail it. Johnny liked hearing this from Martin, not for pride, but for his feeling of self-worth, which was a new experience for him. Martin told Johnny that Alice gave a lot of others the kind of gift she had given him. It wasn't the kind of gift that you could hold in your hand or sail over the water. It was a gift of knowledge and understanding, and whoever she gave it to was able to give some of it to someone else. Martin said that's why he thought it might take a while but things would change for the better when more people got that kind of knowledge. Daniel had been listening to them talk and he felt clarified inside about things that had never been sorted and he felt a sense of gratitude. He didn't say it but he thought to himself that he felt more grown up or something different since Martin had come.

As they rode over the small dunes and to the landing, the tackies became noticeably perky because they were near sea oats. Martin told Daniel he would be back in less than two hours and he could walk back but Daniel said he would wait and could take a nap or do a little fishing. While he unhitched the horses to let them eat sea oats, Martin and Johnny carried the boat down and loaded the big pan of oranges and Johnny's bag and headed out across the river.

Martin showed Johnny the poles and explained how to use them to push the boat through the marsh and said they would need to do a lot of pushing today because the southeast breeze was not favorable for sailing that way but would be good for him coming back and they were going just a little before the peak of the tide so he would have a little more time on the island before having to come back. Martin steered the boat out of the river and toward the ocean, away from the direction they needed to go.

Johnny had not taken his eyes off the long island, where Alice was, way out across the marsh, but was not surprised by Martin going away from it. Instead, he was pleased at what a good sailor he had become and knew he would come about at the mouth of the Back River so that he would have the wind on his beam and have the still incoming tide with him and pick up speed to head across the marsh toward the long island.

The tide was not full up and after a short distance into the marsh, they rolled up the sail and the two of them poled the boat from there. Johnny was so excited that he, alone, had the little boat shooting over the flooded marsh grass, sometimes sliding on the mud bottom, and they were soon to the creek and switched to paddles. Martin saw people out at the first camp, who had become familiar with his coming and going and were less shy or afraid.

Ayana came out and as Martin steered the boat up to the bank Johnny set out the pan of oranges. Martin was aware that the southeast breeze was blowing from Ayana to them and he knew that Ayana was aware of that and was why she didn't hesitate to step close enough to Johnny to get the basket of oranges. Johnny had heard about Ayana and smiled broadly at her in appreciation. She could feel the warmth and thankfulness from him. Martin poled the boat off the bank and paddled it into the small creek and around to the tip of the island where the other camp was. The whole group was waiting, having been told by a lookout that they were coming.

From where Alice was standing, she could see that it was Johnny with Martin but the rest didn't know who it was. Johnny saw Alice and leapt from the boat before it bumped the bank to Alice with her family looking on in tears, having understood by then who he was. He hugged her for a few moments and then felt her stomach and she smiled real big. Then she grabbed Martin and hugged him.

Martin said he had time for a cup of tea but needed to go soon to be able to stop and talk to Ayana and get back across the marsh while it was still flooded. He wished that he had planned to spend the night and maybe he could come back during the week and do that. Martin asked how things had gone for Mallie. They said Mallie was determined to be on his way and was taken away this morning on the big canoe with two other runaways. Lucie said that's why she could never leave this island because nothing had ever made her feel so good as helping the runaways.

Martin said he liked helping too and told them to never forget the debt they owed the Indians for sheltering and hiding and supporting them so they could help. Alice took note of the wisdom coming from Martin and was reminded of his father. She saw that she was not alone in admiration, as she saw how closely the whole group hung on his words and when he got up to leave, everyone hugged him. Johnny said he had put the safety float back in his boat that he had left from his last trip. Martin said that he would be back no later than the day before the supply boat next week to pick them up. Johnny had only been there fifteen minutes but fit in perfectly. He thought to himself that Johnny and Alice may not want to go back and if so, he would understand why and he knew Henry and his father would be surprised but would understand.

Martin paddled the boat back around to the other landing where Ayana was waiting. He was glad they had come across the marsh a little before peak high tide so he would have the time to talk with Ayana. He could never have been able to pole through the marsh grass with the tide not full up had it not been for the strength of Johnny, then he smiled to himself as he thought that Johnny, being so excited to see Alice, could have probably poled them across the marsh with no water in it at all.

He pulled up on the bank and hopped out, and Ayana nodded for him to follow her around to a different spot than before because the wind was blowing from a different way this time. Today, the breeze was coming across the marsh from the ocean and bathing that edge of the east side of the island in fresh ocean air. As Martin felt the breeze in his face, he understood how it kept his breath from going toward Ayana. A young man, with a doeskin mask on, followed them with a pot of tea and two gourds and set them down and left. Ayana thanked Martin for the oranges.

Martin thanked her for all she did to help the runaways on top of helping her own people, and Alice's family. She said it was what she was taught. Martin said he wanted to tell her that he would be going back home next week and probably Alice and Johnny would be too. He wanted to tell her that Charles had said he was there to help if anything ever came up. Then he tried to explain how Charles sent messages by using a mirror to reflect the sun in flashes to the Milam plantation and they relayed the messages to Savannah. He had ordered a small mirror to be left with her and Daniel would teach her how to use it. It was easier than Martin had imagined explaining how the mirror worked for signaling because Ayana was so bright. She said that she felt that changes may be coming for them in a few years and this signaling could be helpful. Martin said he felt good about it because she could communicate with Charles and Charles could communicate with them. He said he hadn't told Daniel yet but had decided to give him his little boat, so he could come across when he wanted to, and that Daniel understands about protecting her and her people from sickness by keeping a distance or wearing a mask. He said he would speak to his father about everything so that they may be able to help in any way if the need should arise.

Ayana handed a piece of folded doeskin to Martin. It was about twice as big as his hand and was covered with small red beads out to the edges. It had a thin leather strap in a loop and she told him to put it over his head. He did and it lay on his chest. She told him to look closely at a simple design in the middle. The whole piece was covered in red beads but there was one white bead in the middle and four black beads around it. She said the white bead was him and the black beads were Alice and her family and the red beads were the thousands of her people that had come before her.

She said to only wear it on special occasions and to keep it safe and give it to his first-born child before he died. She handed him a simple leather purse to keep it in. Martin didn't know what to say and looked into Ayana's eyes and for a few moments their feelings merged and Martin could see and feel the pulse of life in him and Ayana and in the trees and ground around them. It was an unusual feeling and they sat in silence for a few minutes and Martin felt a sense of peace and calm and gratitude.

Ayana spoke first and told Martin that what he was feeling inside and outside was what they worshipped. We live to feel and see it in ourselves and in our surroundings. We see it begins with the first inward breath of a baby at birth and see it end with the last breath out of an old person. We honor it in all things, especially in each other and is the origin of the word we say when we meet, "Gereg." Martin thought to himself how different this was than what the colonials thought of the Indians. He was staring out over the marsh and remembered that he needed to go. He gulped down he rest of his yaupon and thanked Ayana for the gift and said he would be back to get Johnny and Alice a day or two before the supply boat came again.

Martin had to work extra hard to get across the top of the marsh because he had lingered with Ayana but was glad he did. It was the same feeling the times he had special conversations with Alice. Had the wind not been out of the southeast and filling his sail, he could not have been able to make it across the marsh by pushing only. After almost an hour of hard work, Martin made it directly across the marsh to the Back River. He realized how lucky he was to have made it because he would have had to stay there in the marsh for almost twelve hours for the tide to go out and come back in. It would have been impossible for him to walk and drag his boat because he would sink to his knees or further with each step. He pushed hard one last time and the little boat eased past the edge of the grass and then lunged forward in the river with the wind on his stern quarter. The little dugout planed across the Back River faster than ever. He saw Daniel walking down to meet him and sailed up onto the riverbank. Daniel knew the routine and rolled the sail up on the mast and set it inside and grabbed the bow and started dragging it up into the woods. Martin was glad because he was exhausted from the slow hard trip back over the marsh. Daniel had seen Martin's sail and had the wagon rigged and ready and they were soon on the way back to the lighthouse and went through the gate at dusk.

Margo had supper waiting and the boys cleaned up a bit and went in and they were waiting to hear about his short trip to take Johnny. He began by saying how Johnny had shoved the boat so hard and fast across the marsh and how happy he and Alice were to see each other again and how Johnny fit right in like they had known him forever. Mallie's arrival happened to be the day before the big trading canoe came and so he only spent one night and was sent on his way. Everyone liked him and wanted him to stay but he was determined to go. Martin said he told Ayana about the new signaling mirror devise and she caught on to how it worked easily. I told her that I would discuss their situation with my father and that he would help all he could if help was ever needed. I also told her that I was leaving my little boat for Daniel when I left so that he could come and go there if needed. They were all surprised to hear this and Daniel was especially surprised. Martin said he had a new boat and would be spending all his spare time getting it rebuilt so he could come back in it. No one had touched their food while listening to Martin and when he said that was all he had to say, they started eating. Margo said for them to save room for the blackberry pie, because it was extra good because it was made from the last berries that they picked and they were just shy of being overripe and extra sweet and tasty. Martin again wished he could make them ice cream and vowed again to himself to do it on the next trip.

Margo brought one of the two pies to the table and said it was cooled down enough to get whole slices out and divided it into five sections and served it up. She said the other pie was for Captain Jones and Captain Ben and crew tomorrow when y'all go down to pick up the ice he has for us. Charles poured tea and they lingered at the table and talked a bit.
Charles said he enjoyed not having slavers and runaways to think about and commented on the huge reward that was offered for Mallie. Daniel

told how Mallie had learned to read and learned about law so thoroughly and it helped his owner so much that his law business boomed and he made a lot of money. Mallie had said that because the regular mayor died, his master was asked to be mayor, until they could have an election. Charles said he was probably worried that he couldn't sustain his recent success without Mallie and had offered such a high reward.

Mary said she wasn't sure why, but wouldn't be surprised if after some time, Mallie came back. Margo said that would be fine in a few years but she had hoped for a little less excitement for a while. Mary said she found it particularly interesting how Ayana learned that sickness was catching by breath. Martin said that from what Ayana said, her mother saw so many of her people get sick, with many dying from the sickness that she made it her life's work to care for and prevent sickness. She made the connection that her people were getting sick when they traded with the colonials and when her mate (Ayana's father) died, she became the leader and stopped all trading and sickness went down. When someone did get sick, she used a small island for a quarantine place and covered her nose and mouth for protection and cleaned herself before coming back. She passed on her life's work and knowledge about sickness to Ayana.

Mary said that the story of Ayana and her people would be a big part of her book if Ayana would tell it all to her. Martin said she would. He said that a connection to the past through their ancestors was very important to her people and the story of it was carefully told from one generation to the next by mothers to daughters. He said it was sad, but Ayana was worried that her people may be nearing their end and she would want their story told, even if was in writing. Martin said he would take her when he came back next time or maybe Daniel could take her sooner.

Margo said that Daniel needed to go off the island soon like they had always thought should happen so he can decide if he wants to be the next light keeper or do something else. Daniel both dreaded and liked hearing about this. He liked it here on Tybee but sometimes got a little bored. He could skip the whole idea of going away but it was his parent's idea and they had insisted that he go. Margo said he could go this year and had mentioned him wanting to start out staying at the Milam's for a while and then go and stay with his aunt in Savannah or his aunt in Charleston. Mary said that she could go this year too. She had gone for a short visit with her aunt in Charleston but she was to young then to know anything. Margo said she didn't know if they could have them both gone at the same time and Charles said it might be better than having one here while the other is gone. Margo said it was something to think about.

She asked Martin what he wanted to do here his last week and if he told her his favorite food or dessert, she would fix it. Martin said everything she made was his favorite but his favorite was her blackberry pie and her chicken potpie. Martin said he wanted to let Daniel have a little more sailing practice before he left him on his own and he would like to take Mary out again. He also wanted to spend some time up on the lighthouse and study the Indian Islands more with the monocular and add some details to his chart about some of the creeks and islands. There was a lot of details left out, he guessed, because the people making it didn't want to venture in that area much. Also, he said he wanted to see Captain Jones a little each day for the rest of his days there. He and Daniel had intended to go look at the otters in area over behind where the barge was but never got around to it. The only other thing he could think of was the big pines and how good it felt there when the sun filtered down onto the thick bed of long pine needles on the ground.

Charles said that after they had talked about that place recently he remembered the last time the Indians had come and cut one of the big pines and made a trading canoe. It was fifteen years ago or so, a year or two after Daniel was born. He said they were here a month and they carved out the inside by first burning, then scraping and burning and scraping over and over until it was hollowed out and used small axes, traded from the colonials, to shape the outside. He said it took a dozen of them two months, then they waited on the next full moon high tide to drag it to the marsh area and then out through the creek that comes out by the Back River landing. He said it could be the same trading canoe that the runaways are being carried off in.

Martin asked Mary if she wanted to go with him and Daniel in the morning to get some ice from Captain Ben and she said she would. Margo said to remember the pie for them and Captain Jones, and she had cut out the piece for Captain Jones separately. Martin said they would go to Lazaretto first because Captain Ben may want to, with the strong southeaster, leave early and buck the tide and head to Savannah.

Knock, knock, knock, came from Margo's broom handle on the ceiling below Martin. He sat up but Daniel didn't move. He found his pants and socks and jacket and went downstairs and found Charles, Margo, and Mary at the kitchen table. Margo knocked on the ceiling again and a creak in the floor was heard when Daniel got up. Margo smiled and put here broom away. Martin asked what the smell was coming from the stove area. He said it smelled good but was not familiar.

Margo said it came on last week's supply boat and she had meant to fix it sooner and said that it was something called "coffee" that had come in on a boat to Savannah from South America and Henry thought we might

305

like it. She poured a few swallows in everyone's cup to taste. Charles said it was interesting but would take some getting used to. Daniel came down and was drowsy and Margo handed him some coffee and Daniel gulped it down without thinking and asked what it was and Mary said coffee and Daniel looked puzzled but asked for some more. Everyone else asked for some of the usual, which was yaupon.

Next came a platter of fried eggs and bacon and a pot of grits set on the table and warmed up biscuits from last night's supper. Margo managed to fry a dozen eggs in just a few minutes and have all the food ready and still have time to sit and eat with everybody. She never seemed in a hurry but always got a lot done quickly.

Charles finished up first and said he and the two guards were doing maintenance work on the lighthouse lamp and reflector today and he heard the door slam shut to the lighthouse and that meant that the guards were on the way up and he needed to go. Daniel was accustomed to helping and asked his father if he wanted him to help today and Charles said he was still on vacation because he had company but his vacation ended after this week and to enjoy it while he could. Daniel jumped up and said his father was right and they should go on to Lazaretto and get the ice so they could have some time afterwards to do some more fun things.

Mary looked quizzically at Daniel because he usually didn't fully wake up for an hour after he got up and here he was only a short time from coming down, telling of all they should get done for the day. Margo noticed it too and said that Henry had sent a note with the coffee about how it was a very stimulating drink and she could see it working that way for Daniel. Martin saw that Daniel was different too and Daniel was the only one that didn't notice the difference in himself. He said he would go get the horses and wagon ready and would be ready for them to go in a jiffy.

Martin and Mary looked at each other, not knowing what had gotten into Daniel and Margo saw them and said it was that new drink that Henry had sent and she would ask for more because she liked seeing Daniel good and woke up. While they were talking, Margo had a basket with the pie and three large bacon and egg biscuits for Captain Ben and Ashley and Ken. She said they could take Captain Jones his later. In only a few minutes, they heard Daniel with the wagon and Martin took the basket and they left for Lazaretto. The big bridge was done and everything cleaned up and the tackies crossed over without any hesitation because of the new decking. Martin noticed the finished work and thought about what it was like before and wondered how long before it would need repair again.

The cook and his helper had finished breakfast and were sitting by the cooking fire. The brick crew had already left to go back to Savannah. The Milam crew was finished with the bridgework and were out at the point fishing. Martin looked out and saw Ashley and Ken sitting on the sharpie deck having tea. Captain Ben came out and Martin yelled at him and the Captain smiled when he saw Martin. They had the pulling boat out, from using it the night before when they came in, and Ken was already climbing in to come pick them up and bring them out.

It was a standard thing for Margo to send them breakfast when they stayed at Lazaretto and they, and especially Ashley, were happy to see the wagon come this morning. Martin and Daniel and Mary walked down to the bottom of the ramp and climbed in the boat and Ken rowed back out to the sharpie. They passed the basket up and Ashley was giddy, as usual, when he was handed the basket of food with the pie and big egg and bacon biscuits. Martin asked how the trip was and Ben said it was almost perfect because they had gone down with a northwester and come back on a southeaster and if it stays the same, we will be anchored at the Milam place by midafternoon and time enough for Henry to unload this ice before dark, even bucking a tide part of the way. He told Martin to have Charles message Henry so he can be ready with the wagon and have the sawdust pile opened up. He added that they had put four small chunks on top of the load for them this morning so it would be easier to load than one big chunk and they had allowed for some melting to have an adequate amount.

They started in on the biscuits and Ben said it was the best biscuit he had ever had. Martin said to save room for the blackberry pie. Ben said that Margo was always at her sweetest and somehow managed to put her sweetness in everything she cooked. He instructed Martin to make it clear to Margo how much they appreciated the meal she sent every time they came into Lazaretto Landing. It was always delicious plus it gave them something to look forward to. Ashley and Ken shook their heads in agreement with Ben.

Martin told Ben how everything worked out with Mallie and the slavers and the Indians. Ben reminded Ashley and Ken that this was a subject of total secrecy and they nodded in agreement. Ken said that they would hear the slavers version of that adventure because it would still be current waterfront news by the time they got back but may have gotten far from the truth by then. Martin told Ben that he had turned fifteen while he was on Tybee. Daniel was surprised to hear that and asked why he hadn't told them and Martin said because there was so much stuff going on that he didn't want a fuss made over him but he had told Mary but made her promise not to tell.

Martin went on talking, directing his talk to Captain Ben. I was thinking that since my father went to sea when he was fourteen, I should be able to at fifteen and I was wondering if you could use an extra hand occasionally. Ben listened intently to what Martin was saying and didn't answer for a few moments, and then he answered carefully. He said that there may be some possibilities but he should talk to his mother and father first, because he didn't want them to think that ole Ben was putting any ideas in his head.

Martin answered back quickly that they would not think that because he had made it clear often that it was his intention to go as soon as possible and his father would know that you would not do anything like that. Ben thought to himself that Martin was young but had better understanding about things than most grown men. Ben thought a few long moments again, before he spoke, and said that his back was wore out and that he probably was gonna call it quits in about a year or sooner and his intent was to let Ashley and Ken buy his boat and let them pay him over time as they were able to make some money hauling cargo.

Martin noticed how surprised Ashley and Ken looked and realized that this was something that Ben had thought about but had not told them yet. Ben said that if they accepted, they could use an extra hand and in a year, he would be bigger and stronger and have that new boat restored and know a lot more about sailing than he does now. He looked at Ken and Ashley and asked what they had to say about that and they were both a bit dumbfounded over the news and couldn't answer quickly but Ken managed to say he would be all in and Ashley nodded his approval and said that he couldn't think of a better hand than Martin could be.

Captain Ben repeated what he said earlier and said for Martin to make it clear to his mother and father that this was his idea and not old Ben making the suggestion. Martin was both delighted and disappointed. He had imagined himself, in about a month, making trips on Bens sharpie but also the idea of waiting a year and being bigger and having more experience sounded good too and the idea of taking a few months and restoring the boat, then spend the rest of the year sailing it further off than he was able to with his dugout boat sounded good too.

Ben thought to himself what a fine lad Martin was and what a fine crew Ashley and Ken were and told them so. Martin noticed that Ben looked a little sad. Ben changed the subject and said that ice was the first cargo he had ever hauled that could disappear and they needed to be on their way so they would have something when they got there. Ashley and Ken were a little absent minded because they were still in deep thought about what Ben had said about handing over the boat and business to them. They came back to the present and Ken climbed into the pulling boat as Ashley went to the hold and lifted out one of the four chunks of ice and handed it to Ken. When he finished loading the rest, Ken held out his hand to Mary and she got in and the boys jumped in. Ken rowed to the bank at the bottom of the rails and Ken and Daniel loaded the ice onto the wagon.

Martin wanted to stay and watch them get under way, but Daniel reminded him of what Ben had said about ice cargo disappearing so they should get on back and put this in the icebox, so they left for home. Captain Ben and his crew left out of Lazaretto Creek with the tide and into the south channel while the tide was against them but they had a strong southeaster on their stern quarter and made good headway and when they reached the South channel, the wind and the current was with them and Martin and Daniel and Mary watched as the big sails of the sharpie fly west toward Savannah.

Ashley and Ken were still thinking about what the Captain had said, three and a half hours later when they steered south into the Wilmington River, still with the tide and eased out on the sails and grounded into the soft mud of the riverbank at the Milam place to hold the boat long enough to unload their ice before the still rising tide would float the boat again. Once the sail was secured, Ashley and Ken set up the blocks and tackle and ice tongs onto the boom for lifting the ice out. Henry had gotten the signal from Tybee that Ben was on his way and saw his sails coming up the river and had two wagons ready and waiting near the bank.

The long sharpie was on the river's edge and the wagon was pulled down on the river bank, staying toward the top where the sand was firm but within reach of the long sharpie boom and they began, with the ice tongs, lifting the ice chunks out of the holds and swinging out and over to the wagon and setting it down. The sharpie was perfect for loading and off-loading on a river bank because when the boom was out with a load, the hard chine of the hull bared down on the bank and was a stable platform. Two trips for each wagon to the sawdust pile, and it was all done and all the boatmen who had been watching from the boathouse went on the last wagon loads and helped slide the last chunks down the flat boards into the middle of the sawdust pile and pushed and shoveled and heaped up the pile over the ice so that it was mounded up six feet over the ice chunks and spread the sail cloth over it. Back at the river, Ashley and Ken, with the pulling boat, hauled the sharpie out a ways and set both hooks so it wouldn't swing with the tides and they came ashore.

Henry had told the Captain that he and crew were expected for supper and he would have a check for his ice hauling. Captain Ben looked at

Ashley and Ken and said that the shipping business seldom gets any better than this but it could get a lot worse. He said they left with a favorable northwester going south to Darien, and while there a day getting loaded, the wind shifted around to a southeaster and they came back north on favorable wind and had a wonderful meal in the morning and now were about to have another great meal and with good friends.

Up at the house, Henry said he had some good news. He said that his father inquired about getting cork from Portugal and one of his friends told him about an old warehouse in Savannah that was full of it and had been left there for years. The story is that a Portuguese ship loaded with slabs of cork got out of control coming into the south channel during a bad northeaster and grounded out and broke up. The cork floated out and the northeaster blew it up the river and the next incoming tide carried it further up and some salvers gathered it and stored it in a warehouse where it had been sitting for five years. Walter went ahead and paid the salvers for all of it and this made his friend, who owned the warehouse, happy because they paid him the back rent and he said he would be glad to get it out of the way and agreed to haul it to the Milam place. So, we can, when you have time, help you get it put on the walls of all your holds. Ben said how about starting tomorrow and surprised Henry with his quick decision. Henry told Ben he could get the cork and carpenters there by day after tomorrow and he would pay for the labor and materials because it would save him over time by keeping his ice from melting away. Ben said that would work out fine because he could spend a few nights in Savannah and take care of some business and Ashley and Ken always liked time on the hill.

Ben asked if they missed Martin and Martha said the whole place missed Martin and Alice and Johnny and Jacob too. Ken said from what he knew about human nature, there was a certain very pretty and smart young lady on Tybee that was going to miss him when he left there. Martha looked shocked but not unpleased. She said that something like that would have never occurred to her. Walter smiled. Ken said that it was easy to tell after they had been together on the sharpie, just this morning, that she is more advanced in those areas but Martin was not completely oblivious. They were both smiling big at each other. Henry said he had been surprised several times, since Martin went with him to see John in Darien, at how big he had gotten and how mature he was, and Charles Dyer had said that he had gone there and had fun but was on a mission like a grown up about Alice and her family and never wavered in his determination.

Walter and Ben went into another room for some rum and Claudia and the kids came over to the porch with Henry and Ken and Ashley and the kids played outside. Henry said he overheard Ben tell Walter that he was retiring from shipping in a year or less. Ashley said he had told them that, just this morning, and he wants us to take over. The whole conversation started when Martin asked Ben if he could go to work on the sharpie and Ben said not now but maybe when he quit in about a year, and he could be a mate with us. Ben had never mentioned to us before that he was quitting or that he would let us take over and pay for the boat as we went along. We were surprised and it hadn't even sunk in yet but of course our answer was yes.

Martha said they had tried to keep Martin busy with other things to keep his mind off going off to sea. His father went at fourteen and he thinks it would be a good thing for Martin but I am afraid for him. Claudia said she didn't like boats because there was always accidents and mishaps on them while she was growing up on Wilmington Island. She said trips to Savannah were often an adventure and sometimes people lost their lives. Ken said Martin wouldn't exactly be going to sea because their trips are not that far out in the ocean and we seldom go out beyond the sight of land. It's not without adventure and rough weather but if things look bad, we wait until they calm down. Also, the sharpie is well built and we keep it in good shape. Henry said that he knew how Martin was about having his mind set on something and he would a lot rather him go off with Ashley and Ken than someone they didn't know anything about. Martha said she may have to go along with the idea but that a lot could change in a year. She said it was time to eat and Ashley noticeably perked at the suggestion. She said it was such a nice day and there were no bugs out so they should eat at the porch table. Ken and Ashley offered to help serve and Martha said that would be nice. She told Henry to sit and watch his kids because he was always so busy that he didn't do that enough. After they got everything out, Martha called Walter and Ben and they all enjoyed string bean casserole and turkey and pie and tea.

It was getting near dark and Ben said they should be going back to the boat. Walter said he wished Ben had stayed there but Ben said he had stayed there before but didn't want to wear out his welcome and Walter said he couldn't do that. Ben said he would like for them to be able to come there in the morning and get bathed before they went to Savannah and Walter said fine and Henry said he would give them a ride in when he went to make arrangements to get the cork and nails for the sharpie work. He said he could give them a ride back to the boat and Ben said they would rather walk. He said they would be around in the morning to get cleaned up and thanked Martha for the good food and hospitality. She told them to not bother fixing any food on the boat in the morning because she needed them to help eat the supper left overs.

Walter and Martha and Henry and his family lingered a little longer and Martha brought up the subject of Ben retiring and Martin going off. Walter said he and Ben had talked about that too and he couldn't think of a better way for Martin to learn about boats and the sea. Martha said she thought that too but it seemed that such a short time ago Martin was a small boy and now he would be going away. Walter reminded her that it would be a year and not now. Ben told him that Ashley and Ken were first rate and they would take extra care with Martin. He said he shuttered to think of Martin going off with just any old crew at such a young age or any age for that matter.

Henry said that he agreed with Walter and he had liked everything he saw in Ashley and Ken on the trip to Darien. He said that he expected that in a year when Martin would start, they would have enough ice business to keep them busy and would even have to get another boat.

Henry said he had gotten a letter from John today and he has given the sawmill notice of resignation and will stay on a month to get things in order and asked me to find them a townhome in Savannah. They want to move and get the girls in school here as soon as they can. He said the townhome may be temporary until they find something more to their liking. Henry said he would be glad to have John here as a partner, because their combined effort would get things moving in their new ice business quicker. Walter said he liked what they were doing and that Henry had a good partner that he shared common values with. Claudia said she liked that John and his family were moving there too, because they had friends around town and had a lot of invitations to things but few intimate friends that they could be comfortable having come over and all. Martha said she knew what she meant.

Morning came and so did Ben and crew. They knew how to use the bath facilities and when they had cleaned up, Claudia had come to the big kitchen and had eggs and grits and warmed some of the supper left overs. Ben told Henry they had hauled the boat up on the bank at the top of the tide and tied it off and he would wait to hear from him when it was ready and they would come take it in to Savannah to load for another trip.

Martha told Ben that she and Walter had talked about Martin working with Ashley and Ken and she was concerned but they thought it was the perfect start for him and she looked at Ashley and Ken and said she was confident in their judgment. Ken said he was sure that Martin would hold up his end and that he probably would have his own boat before too long from what he could see of how Martin was. She congratulated them on becoming owners of a shipping company. They both were uneasy with this new prospect and didn't know how to respond but thanked her. She told them that they and the Captain were always welcome in their home.

Henry came around with the carriage and picked them up and they were off to Savannah. Henry had brought a bank note and given it to Captain Ben and told him how happy he was to be giving him that and hoped that he would be handing him much more in the future and Ben reminded him that after a year he would be giving it to Ken and Ashley and smiled and said they would be giving some of that back to him. Henry dropped them and their things off at the inn and headed first to Jason's shop. Jason saw him and said he was planning to go out today to the boathouse and measure the ice storage in the supply boat and Henry said he was glad he got here before he left. He told him about finding the cork and said it would be better than the cotton on the boat because it didn't absorb water and was probably a better insulator. He said he was going today to make arrangements to have it sent out to their place. Jason said that all sounded good and he thought the cork would work better too. Henry told him to expect the cork either today or first thing in the morning and to talk to Jacob at the boathouse when he came out to measure because Johnny was not back from Tybee yet.

From there Henry went to see his father's friend who owned the warehouse where the cork was stored. He knew where Fred Johnson lived in a fine townhome near Oglethorpe Square and found him in his courtyard trying to see what kind of bug had been feasting on his camellias. Henry said hello to him through the gate and announced who he was. Mr. Johnson was pleased to see him and opened the gate and told Henry that the last time he had seen him he must have been about six years old and he was in a carriage with his mother and father who had come to town to watch the Independence Day celebrations.

Henry said he remembered that trip to town but couldn't recall meeting him, but he did know something that might save his camellias. Mr. Johnson said that if it worked, that it would make him even happier than his father helping him get the back rent and getting that big pile of cork out of his warehouse. Henry said his mother had him go down to the river when the tide was coming in strong and fill a jug of river water and she would sprinkle it all over her camellias every day for a week and the salt water killed the bugs.

Sometimes she had me sprinkle it and always said to cover the buds and leaves but not enough that it would drip down on the ground because if the salt got in the roots, it would kill the plant. A gold piece would not have made Mr. Johnson happier. He said that it shouldn't, but it depressed him that his flowers died in the bud from insect infestation. Henry repeated to get the water on the incoming tide because it had more salt in it and don't let it get on the ground because if a ruined bud depressed him, a dead plant might do him in. Mr. Johnson exclaimed that the Milam's were always about good news and that he guessed Henry was here about getting the cork. Henry said yes sir and if tomorrow were possible he would be most delighted. Mr. Johnson said that since he had delighted him this morning, he would be happy to delight him by bringing it tomorrow. By the way, are the Milam's making wine? Henry said no but he would be hearing soon enough what they were doing with the cork and he promised that once again he would be delighted with what they were up to. Mr. Johnson said he would have his men have the first load there early tomorrow and it would take a few trips and a few days to move it all. Henry thanked him and said he was glad to have met him. Mr. Johnson said he hoped he would see him again sooner than it had been since he last saw him and then asked Henry if he knew if the tide was coming or going because he wanted some salt water for his camellias today. Henry told him to go down to the river at about three or four this afternoon and shook Mr. Johnson's hand and said it was nice seeing him.

Henry decided that he didn't know what size nails to get and he would wait until they had the cork and Jacob looked over it and where it went in the boat and then go and get the size that was needed. He was glad to be able to head back home and be done with his trip before noon. He regretted that he didn't ask Mr. Johnson if he knew of any townhouses near him for sale that might work for John, but he could do that later.

Henry did arrive home before noon. He went past the house to the boathouse and talked to Jacob about his plans and about the nails and needing two carpenters to help him. Jacob reminded him that he had a supply run to Tybee in a few days and they would be back with Alice and Martin and Johnny. Henry said once he got the carpenters properly instructed he could leave it to them. He told Jacob that when the first load of cork came in the morning, he would come get him and they could take a piece out to the boat and him look at it and tell him what else was needed. Jacob said he had never done anything with cork and he didn't even know what it looked like or how to cut it. Henry said he didn't know much more than him but it was thick bark that came off a tree way across the ocean and it was very light to pick up. Jacob said if it was from a tree then it might be like wood and he didn't think it would be a problem.

Jacob said he was sure glad Martin and Alice, and Johnny were coming home because the place was not the same without them. Henry said he was right and it wasn't like the same place when he was gone either. Jacob smiled at that and said Henry was just carrying on and Henry said no, he wasn't. He told Jacob that he was as important to the Milam place as he was. This was the kind of thing to understand and say that Henry had learned by being around his father and it ennobled the people they were around because it was sincere. Henry was his own kind of special because he was all about business but stayed close in touch with his heart. He touched Jacobs shoulder and told him he would see him in the morning.

Back at home, Henry went looking for his father and found him in the library. He asked if he had a minute and he said he hoped he had a lot more than that and asked what he could do for him. Henry said he wanted his recommendation for a lawyer to set up the ice business for him and John, one that he could trust to keep their business affairs completely private and one that had knowledge of the laws of business and constitutional law too. Walter said it sounded like he might need more than one to cover both of those things and all in between. Henry said probably so. He told his father about his meeting with Albert, his professor from school, and Walter was familiar with him from Henry's references to him in the past. Henry, as carefully as he could, told his father about the things they had discussed about their unorthodox plantation system and how they treated their slaves and how to ensure those policies into the future when things might change. Walter saw how Henry was carefully choosing his words and he said that Henry was concerned about how things might be different when he was no longer around, and how he was the one that would be left with the responsibility of the lives of these people that have worked and supported us and become our extended family.

Walters' frank response and acknowledgement ushered in a higher level of clarity to the conversation. Walter went on to say that he was fully aware that his presence and influence maintained the freedom they had in the way they operated and he and the friends he had in high places in the community were all getting old and the Savannah they knew now would be different when he and them are gone. Walter said he had for some time been in conversations with his most trusted allies about the very thing Henry was talking about. Henry said he was relieved to hear that. He said now we can combine our resources and hopefully make a plan that will ensure, as best we can, the continued betterment of these people that have become like family to us.

Walter said he had wrestled with slave ownership every day from the very beginning when he was granted the whole setup. He said it was a difficult situation to reconcile because their safety and wellbeing was at stake. Henry told his father the things Albert told him how the laws of manumission were getting more and more stacked against setting slaves free. Each state formed their own laws and Georgia had adopted the laws from South Carolina, since they had slavery before Georgia. If a slave is freed, he cannot own property and he has to leave the state for a year and when and if he comes back, he has to pay an annual fee.

There are manumission review boards to look at each application for freeing a slave that are selected by local leaders and they are slanted against the process. An application for one slave is difficult and an application for multiple slaves is almost impossible. Walter told Henry that if ever they were able to free the people on the Milam place, they would first need to teach them to read and write and the basics of how the law works and what few rights they have by law and they need some money to get a start on things. Walter said that if a free black could not take care of himself and came under the care of the state, he or she could be auctioned back into slavery.

It's sad but that's how it is and whatever we do, we need to think it through, carefully and thoroughly. Walter said that he was proud of Henry for thinking ahead about things when he was gone because it could get difficult for him and everybody and that he was wise to broaden their possibilities and to seek out knowledge of the law in preparation of changes that were coming. Walter wrote two names on a piece of paper and handed it to Henry and said that he would let them know that Henry would be in touch. Henry looked at the names and remembered their visits and thanked his father.

Walter said he would suggest that Henry work in two directions; one in the direction that they had been discussing here today, by seeking legal advice and becoming armed by knowledge of the law, and secondly, begin to educate all the people on the plantation so if changes come about, they are better prepared. Walter went on to say that, as Henry well knew, he would have to be careful because the powers of business, political, and religious institutions would perceive educating a group of slaves as sacrilegious and seditious, and against the status quo.

Also, he was concerned about the possibility of his new business merging with the Milam place and becoming so big that it drew a lot of attention and scrutiny. People are often jealous of success and envy can breed enemies. So, don't hide but be subtle and modest in your growth and prosperity. He said to keep his ice business separate because even though their contract with the government to maintain the lighthouse was solid, a change in administrations could change things, but probably not while he was alive. He said that if that was ever taken away, it should not be able to affect your new business.

Walter said he had one last thought and that pertained to educating the people of the Milam place. He said to enlist the help of Alice because she had a great gift of understanding and it was powerful. Henry said she had already started with a few, and Walter said to be careful as you go. Henry thanked his father and Walter told him not to worry, he still had some years left.

Henry went to his office and shut the door and sat quietly and let the thoughts and ideas of his talk with his father sink in. The task ahead of him, considered all at once was too much to handle, but he knew better, and made a list of his overall goals and tasks and the manageable and practical steps to take to get them done. He really liked how his father had broken down things into two fronts: a strategy from within the Milam place and one from without. From within he had Alice to help educate. He had seen the effect of Alice and how she used her lit candle to light the un-lit candle in others and how they were able to do the same after they were lit. From without, he had John, Albert, and Walter's friends to help him set things up properly and move in a direction that stable and secure and was best for everybody. Then he thought of his mother and how she was her own self but supported Walter and then his own wife, Claudia, who was very independent too, and supported him and then there was Martin who was a force himself that Henry was certain of but didn't fully understand how Martin could help. Then, the Dyers who were way off on Tybee but their convictions were a pillar of strength. Then he realized that the workers, like he had just told Jacob, were as important as he was. Then Henry had a moment of clarity followed by a feeling of gratitude. He felt a power of Providence that was helping the workers of the Milam place through him and had the simple feeling of being only an instrument and he liked that feeling best because it made all things seem possible and gave him confidence in himself and his country. He hoped that he could save some of this confidence he was having today for when doubts might come later. He remembered that his father had always said his greatest ally was "good understanding" and what he was having was the best understanding he had ever had and to insure that it lasted he would do best to seek help from his allies, trust in the knowledge within himself, and feel that power and force that was using him for the betterment of others.

Claudia came in his office and told him that she and the kids and Martha had some lunch a while ago and she had come to tell him and Walter but could feel how they were intent in their conversation and left them to themselves but Walter had come now and he could too if he liked. Henry often did not know he was hungry and decided to go with her suggestion and stop and eat. He saw his father leaving the kitchen table as he was arriving and said he had forgotten to mention that he had met Mr. Johnson this morning about the cork. Walter said good, and Henry said he was so happy that I had wanted, of all things, all that cork taking up his ware-house and all he could say was that I was a Godsend, especially because I told him how to rid his camellias of bugs and Walter laughed as he left the table. Claudia set a plate of food in front of Henry and after a few bites he said he was actually starved and Claudia just shook her head slowly at him. Henry finished up his late lunch and had a cup of tea and worked a little more in his office and then spent the last thirty minutes of daylight watching his kids play.

About an hour after daylight the next morning, everybody's dogs were barking and Henry guessed that it was very early but that must be Mr. Johnsons men with the cork and sure enough it was and when they pulled up to the big house Henry went out and was surprised to see Mr. Johnson in his carriage right behind the big wagon. He told Henry that he had always wanted to come out here and decided this was a good reason to do it. Henry said he could go show his men the barn and he could visit with Walter if he liked and Mr. Johnson said he would like that and just as he said it Walter came out and they laughed at each other. Fred said that Walter looked a lot younger and better in the low light of the tavern they usually were together at and Walter said he was a bit too heavy for a one horse carriage and they laughed at themselves and traded a few more insults and laughed some more. Walter asked him to come in and when he got down and walked toward the house, he noticed their camellias and complemented on their beauty and health with no bugs and told Henry he had started the salt water treatment on his yesterday afternoon and had already noticed that he was less depressed.

Henry said good and that he had forgotten to ask him something while he was there and Mr. Johnson looked eager to know what it was and Henry told him about his friend and family wanting to move to Savannah and looking for a townhome to buy. Mr. Johnson said the Milam's were solving yet another of his problems and Henry asked how that was? He said that he lived alone in his home since his wife had passed and his daughter and her family had wanted him to move in with them and it was probably best because the stairs at his home were getting to be too much for him to climb and he had put it off because he didn't want to bother with selling but here you came with a buyer. He said he would have to dig up and take his camellias if he did go. Henry asked him to tell the details of a sale to his father if he was certain that he wanted to move and he would pass the information along to his friend.

Henry showed the men where to unload and stayed to look at what a big piece of cork looked like. The wagon looked like it was overloaded because it was piled up about eight feet high, but after they untied the ropes holding it down, and slid some off, Henry picked up a piece about the size of a big table top, and he realized that it was lightweight for its size. It had some weight to it but not near as heavy as a similar size piece of wood. He tried to split it and found it quite tough because it did not have a grain in any particular direction like wood. Also, it had been stacked flat for years, and most of the curve of the tree trunk was gone.

He took a piece with him and went off to find Jacob at the boathouse and asked him to come with him to the sharpie and look the work over. He showed Jacob the cork and Jacob felt it and tried to bend and tear it to feel what it was like and left for a minute and came back with a handsaw and sawed the big piece in half to get a feel for it. Henry nodded for Jacob to go up on the sharpie, which was right out in front of the boathouse sitting on the riverbank with the tide out.

Once on the boat, Henry removed the boards covering one of the holds and showed Jacob the space. Jacob took his pocketknife out and opened the blade and stuck it in the cork to see how hard it was. Next he used a stick and measured the wall and cork thickness and then told Henry the two sizes of nails to get and to get a keg of each. Jacob said he would find his carpenters and they would start squaring off the big pieces of cork and haul it down to the boat for tomorrow. Henry admired Jacob's mild and easy way and trusted he would do a fine job. Jacob went looking for his help and Henry went back to his office.

He could hear Fredrick Johnson and Walter talking loudly because neither could hear as well as they used to. They were talking about England, where they were both born, and how the people did things there different than how they did things here. Fortunately, they were in agreement about where things were done best. Henry noticed that they each had a cup of rum and shook his head at his father as he went by and Walter knew Henry was thinking it was too early for them to be into the rum and Walter told him it was Johnsons fault that he had come there for the first time ever and it was bad luck for a man not to have a drink on his first visit. Henry kept shaking his head and went into his office.

He found a piece of paper on his desk with the details about the sale of Mr. Johnson's house. He sat down right away and wrote John a letter and put it with the paper from Mr. Johnson and put more paper around it and bound it and added John's name and address and tucked it under his arm to take by the stage depot to go to John in the morning. He could do that after picking up the nails.

In the next few days, the holds on the sharpie got lined of cork on the sides and bottom and the walls of the hold were now almost six inches thick after adding the cork but the overall storage space was reduced very little. Jacob had added a layer under the boards that covered the holds too. When Captain Ben and crew came back to pick up the sharpie, Ben approved of the work. Jason had been out and he and Jacob looked at the supply boats and Jason took measurements and picked up a big pile of cork slabs to take back to his shop.

The next week, Henry went to see his father's lawyer friends. Henry had heard his father speak about Sidney and Hulbert before and they received Henry like a family member. Much of what they had gone over with Walter was similar to what Henry had been thinking on his own and what Albert had told about. Henry told them about his concerns for the people of the Milam place in the event of social changes and they said that was his father's main concerns too plus he wanted to ensure their welfare when he was gone. Hulbert added that Walter had great confidence in Henry but knew his adversaries would be emboldened when he was no longer around.

Both gentlemen assured Henry that there was no greater friend to them than his father and he had asked them for assistance in these matters and to do it through Henry from now on out and that they would be there for him, same as they had been for his father. Henry told them about his friend and professor, Doctor Albert McWilliamson, and where his sympathies were and all about John too. Walter had made it clear to them about Henry's discretion and good judgment and they trusted that they could trust his friends and associates. It was agreed that, when convenient, they should all meet together, in total privacy, to better understand how best to proceed.

Meanwhile, back on Tybee things had smoothed out a lot. Martin took Daniel out on the little boat a few more times and then let him go alone until he felt comfortable and then he took Mary out and they sailed, like before, over close to Turtle Island and Martin wished he could go there and look around but knew he shouldn't and then they sailed by Daufuskie and Hilton Head and he thought that he would visit those two islands when he came back with his new boat. He visited a little everyday with Captain Jones before he left. One of the pilot crews told all the wild tales that were being circulating around Savannah about the runaway slave chase and his escape to the no man's land of Turtle Island. They said that between the stories of the recent dueling deaths and the runaway slave, that Tybee was what everyone had been talking about for weeks. Martin also spent some time up on the lighthouse balcony with the monocular, adding to the details on his chart. Also, there was conversation with Charles and Margo about Daniel and maybe Mary, both, coming to stay in Savannah for up to a year, with Daniel first coming to the Milam place and then to either

Savannah or Charleston. Mary said she wanted to stay in Savannah the whole time.

The day came to go pick up Alice and Johnny and Martin knew he would have to make two trips because his boat could only carry two people, so he decided that he would ask if he could use one of the Indian canoes and let Johnny and Alice follow him back in it and leave it at the landing to be picked up later. Martin wished that he would have more time to be with Ayana but would do that on the next trip to Tybee, in a few months.

Daniel and Mary took him down in the wagon and he set out about an hour before high tide but had to wait a bit on the other side until the tide got up high enough to set out across the top of the marsh. Ayana was out at the edge of the first landing on Long Island because she knew the supply boat day and had expected Martin the day before and had her people keep a lookout for his sail. Martin stopped for only a moment to tell her thanks for all she did and that he was coming back in a few months and that Daniel would be coming over with the signaling mirror soon.

Her entire group of people were standing around her and Martin thought to himself that this was all that was left of them and he made one of those solemn vows to himself that he would do all he could to protect and preserve what was left of them. Ayana told him that she had thought he would need another canoe and had sent it around already to the other landing. Martin was glad and not surprised at how gracious she was. He continued on to the other camp and was surprised to see that whole group, standing on the bank around Alice and Johnny. Alice's mother hugged him right away and then every one of the others did the same. It was both a sad and happy time.

Alice told him how grateful she and everyone was to him for what he had done to discover and reunite them and to bring her and Johnny over. Martin told Alice's brother about the signal mirror and Daniel coming over to show Ayana how to use it and how the Dyers were like his family in sympathizing with them and the Indians and they did not have to worry about word getting out of them being there and that this new device would help insure their safety. He said he would be back in a few months and probably again a few months after that to bring Alice for a visit after she had her baby.

When they passed the next landing and Ayana was standing out with her small group of people. The wind was blowing from them to the group, so Martin stayed out a ways and Ayana understood why Martin kept a distance and smiled to herself. She placed her hand at her heart as the two boats passed. Martin did the same and repeated the vow within himself about protecting Ayana and her people.

The tide had just reached fully in and Martin passed a rope to Johnny, in the canoe, and unrolled his sail and without paddling or poling, both boats glided slowly across the top of the marsh and finally out into the Back River. It was Martin's favorite part of the tide cycle when it was not coming or going and stood still for a half hour and the east wind blew both boats, still attached, across the river where Daniel and Mary were waiting with the wagon. Martin suggested that Daniel take the sailboat, that was now his, around to north beach and they could drag the Indian canoe up above the high water line and drive the wagon back. He grinned and thanked Martin and Martin told him that they would wait and watch until he had managed to tack back and forth a few times to get around the point, where the east wind would then sweep him home quickly. Daniel shoved off and tacked back across the river again and back and forth a few times until he rounded the point, then they set off in the wagon for the lighthouse. Daniel was waiting when they got there and Martin asked him how he did and he said he did good and was glad Martin had suggested he go alone. He told them that they could go on in and he would take care of the horses and wagon.

Charles and Margo hugged Alice and Johnny and Margo said she had an early supper made and they wanted to know all about their week across the river. She said she knew they probably wanted to get cleaned up and refreshed and there was no hurry and they would wait until they were done to start supper. She told Martin that he and Mary could take Captain Jones his supper and had it ready to go. She handed them a basket and Martin smelled it and grinned and thanked Margo for fixing his two favorite things the night before he had to go home. She said she was more than glad to do it for him. He and Mary left together and crossed over the dune and down onto the beach and found the Captain alone in his spot. He was happy to hear them coming and knew that Martin was leaving the next day. He asked Martin to put the food in his shanty and sit a minute and tell him all that had gone on.

Martin and Mary sat on the sand by the Captain and Martin told of his trip and about talking to Ayana and Alice's mother and father and brother. The Captain said he had talked to Daniel just a bit ago when he had come up in the boat and he told about you giving him your boat and I thought that was very big of you. Martin said it was big of the Captain to give him his boat and the Captain said he was glad it had a new life. He said that he would miss him.

Mary was quiet and listened and watched Martin try to fend off the compliments in his shy way. She felt like she knew Martin better than anyone and would miss him more than anyone when he went away. He and Mary sat a while longer, mostly watching across the river at Turtle, Daufuskie, and Hilton Head islands and Martin said he would miss Tybee and the lighthouse and all the islands around. He told the Captain that the next time he came, it would be in his old boat and he would come straight to this spot, but now he had to go and would help him up if he liked and the Captain said he would like that. Martin gently lifted up on the Captain and felt his feebleness and hoped that he would be there when he returned but knew it may not be so. Mary watched and admired how carefully Martin helped the Captain to his shanty.

They walked up and over the big dune and Martin thought of Daniel always guessing at the time according to the length of the lighthouse shadow and smiled to himself. He felt Mary's hand hold onto his and as he turned to face her, she kissed him full on his lips for more than a moment. He couldn't say how long the kiss lasted but it was the longest kiss he had ever had and it awakened a yearning that would stay with him the whole time he was away from her.

At the house they cleaned the sand off their feet and walked into the kitchen where Alice and Johnny were sitting with Charles and Margo and Alice was telling about their week. Margo saw the glow in her daughter and smiled to herself. She asked Martin to go get Daniel for supper and he went out and found him in the horse barn and came back with him. The Dyers weren't the type to pray at every meal but never lacked in expressing gratitude in everyday life, but tonight Charles said a few things before supper.

He expressed thankfulness and said how they appreciated all that they had and how much they were thankful for each other and Martin and Alice and Johnny and Alice's family and Ayana and her people and for the whole world and especially for Martin coming. Margo set out several hot chicken pot pies and big bowls and they all ate. Then she set one of two big blackberry pies and they ate it, then, as usual, they all went out on the porch and had cups of yaupon. Daniel asked about the new coffee drink and Margo said she would make some more in the morning early when they got up to get Martin down to the landing.

Mary wished it wasn't so that Martin was leaving and wished she could somehow go with him but knew that wasn't possible. She knew she would be going to Savannah soon but she wished he could stay until the day came for her to go, so she wouldn't have to miss a day of seeing him. Martin asked Daniel about his first trip alone in his new boat and Daniel said it was more fun once he had managed to tack back and forth and get out of the Back River and head north along Tybee beach with the wind in his favor. He said he went so fast that he was at the north beach in no time and a couple times he felt the boat slide across the top of the water. This made Martin feel good that he had been able to teach Daniel to sail and that he had given the boat to him. Martin told him to put a coat of oil on the entire boat and the mast occasionally so it won't soak up any water and Johnny smiled to himself, remembering how Martin had worked so hard scraping the soft wood away from the boat when they first started working on it and then he remembered the awkward but wonderful feelings he had when Alice would come and get Martin. Charles asked Johnny if he was the new helmsman now and Johnny said he wasn't sure but he was happy to do whatever he was needed at. Martin said that he thought he would be because Henry had some new work plans for Jacob and he hoped it was so because he wanted his friend Izak to get to start training to be a boatman and that he had already started Izak's training by teaching him how to swim. Alice had been quiet and Margo asked her how she was feeling and Alice said she was fine but was just thinking about her family and Ayana and her people. She said she had gone out to the breezy place with Ayana a couple times during the week and talked with her for several hours and came to understand better how much she and her people had suffered and how smart and dedicated Ayana was to not only her people but to the runaways too. She said that they risked their own safety every time they helped a runaway, even though Ayana had taught them to keep a distance and to wear a deerskin mask when they were close. She said her family's lives depended on the lives of the Indians and she was worried about it. Charles said she was right to be concerned but added that once Daniel had taught Ayana to use the signaling mirror, they will know how they are regularly and can pass on the messages, in code, to the Milam place. Alice said that would be a big help.

Margo said she had wondered if it would be possible that the plantation owner that her and her family had belonged to was still around and if so could he be paid off so that if they had to leave the island, at least there would be no chance of them being caught and sent back. Alice said she had often thought about all those and other possibilities and she had planned to talk to Henry about it. Martin was amazed and surprised to hear about all this. The idea that Alice and her family could still be hunted down and captured by someone from South Carolina should have occurred to him but it never had until now.

Next day, low tide was midmorning, so Martin had some time to be around before leaving and he was glad about that. They got up early and had a big breakfast and had time to chat and another trip up on the lighthouse balcony and a last visit with Captain Jones. Daniel pulled the wagon around and Margo and Charles hugged Martin and told him how happy they were that he had come and they hugged Alice and Johnny too and Margo couldn't hold back the tears. Alice sat up front with Daniel and Johnny and Martin and Mary got in back.

Martin studied both bridges one more time as they crossed over and once again was pleased at how the horses never hesitated as they walked over the new bridge decking. Daniel complimented Martin on his idea of placing the decking boards closed together. Martin loved this little narrow roadbed of white oysters, connecting the small hammocks, and spanning across the marsh from Tybee to the Lazaretto landing.

The supply boat was at the landing when they got there, probably because the crew knew they were picking up Martin and Johnny and Alice and pulled a little harder on the oars and Jacob had particularly guided them on the shortest possible passages from bend to bend in the river, avoiding all the eddies that could slow them down. They were all sitting around the cooking fire with the cook and his helper who had a lot of spare time now that most of the crew had left. Everyone was particularly glad to see Alice and Johnny because there had been a flurry of talk and speculation about how they might stay with the Indians and never come back.

Jacob had the biggest smile of all and hugged Alice and felt the bump in her stomach and laughed out loud with Johnny. Daniel showed Jacob the big basket of his mother's lighthouse egg and bacon biscuits and Jacob said they could eat them on the way home instead of eating them there because there were a lot of people waiting to see them come back home and he wanted to get underway.

They all unloaded the supplies onto the wagon and Jacob nodded for Johnny to take the helmsman seat and this made Johnny feel good because he wasn't sure if Jacob was ready to give up his job just yet. Alice came and hugged Daniel and Mary and went and sat with Jacob in back of the boat near Johnny. Martin turned to Mary and Daniel and told them how much he would miss them and thanked them for everything and said he would be back soon but they may even be coming to Savannah before that. Martin hugged Daniel and then hugged Mary and was struck by the sweet smell and softness of Mary and saw the tears well up in her and, for the first time, Daniel noticed the tenderness that happened between Martin and Mary. He didn't know what to think about it but the moment shifted and Martin was loading up to go.

They stood and watched and listened with the cook and his helper, as the boat pulled away and Jacob started a chantey verse and then the crew sang the chorus and then another verse and another chorus until they rounded the point and headed up the south channel. Daniel said they needed to get the wagonload of supplies with the ice back to the lighthouse so they left. Mary was quiet riding back and oddly Daniel sensed her melancholy and tried to say something to shift her attention by talking about how nice the new oyster shell road was. That didn't faze her and she just stared out across the marsh. He knew what was bothering her but didn't know how to talk about it, but finally blurted out something stupid about liking Martin. Daniels words seemed to knock the dam down that was holding back Mary's emotions and she

burst into tears and told Daniel that she loved Martin and wanted to spend her whole life with him. The flood of emotion shocked Daniel and even caused the two horses to stop and they just sat there for a few minutes. Daniel was partly choked up from Mary's state and unable to know what to say but finally said something else stupid about him being only fifteen and that was too young for them to get married and said another stupid thing about Martin being a mate on the sharpie and being gone all the time.

Mary knew that the horses understood more about her situation than Daniel did but he was all she had to talk to about it now and told him that age didn't matter because she was certain about what she wanted when she was near Martin and knew he felt it too. She said her mother and aunts married when they were sixteen and she would be sixteen in less than a year. Daniel realized that he hadn't been able so far to say anything that could shift the conversation and he didn't know what to say so he coaxed the horses to go and Mary remained silent the rest of the way home. Daniel and the guards unloaded the supplies and Mary went to her room.

Meanwhile, as soon as the supply boat left Lazaretto Creek and started up the south channel toward Savannah, Jacob broke out the mast and sail and with the wind and tide going the same way, all the oars were laid aside. The big basket of Margo's biscuits was opened and cups were filled with yaupon, and for the next three hours, it became a pleasure cruise for everybody. Only Johnny at the helm had anything to do. Some slept, some laughed and carried on and some just watched the riverbank go by. These easy trips happened occasionally and were relished because there were many rough trips, especially in the winter.

Alice and Johnny were both absorbed in thoughts about the past week. Alice, more so, because it was as if she had caught up on so many years she had missed with her family and things had changed so much for her and them but their love for each other had been there every day since they were separated. It was different for her family than it was for her because they had learned that Alice was alive and well because they had begun to get bits and pieces of information from runaways that they had helped.

It was the first thing that her mother asked about when they took in another runaway and from the hundreds that they helped, they had not only learned about Alice's legendary status in the secret and underworld slave culture of Georgia and South Carolina, but of where she lived and the child, Martin, she raised. Alice, on the other hand, knew nothing of what had gone on with her parents. It was the opinion of most that they died in the massacre and if they were taken away by Indians, they were eaten by the Indians. However, Alice had experienced, first hand, the Indians kindness and she always held hope that her family was alive and she had Martin who believed her and had vowed, at such a young age, to go and search for them. Johnny was simply feeling gladness to have Alice near again. Having met Alice's family made him feel meaningful like he was part of a family for the first time in his life, having been raised on a slave production farm like livestock, and not ever knowing a mother or father or brothers or sisters.

A nod from Jacob to Martin and the sail and mast came down and stowed and the oarsmen took their places and began their chantey earlier than usual as they turned onto the Wilmington River still a mile away from home. There was a crowd waiting on the riverbank and it was a truly beautiful and unique experience of the sounds of the singing in two places getting closer and closer and finally all together at the riverbank.

It was a special occasion for everyone standing on the bank as they welcomed back their family members. Walter and Martha and Henry and his family were there. The singing stopped and a loud and excited jabber started with everyone going at it at once. A bystander would not understand a single word but there would be no mistake in the joyful nature of it all. Martin found Walter and Martha and Henry and his family and everybody hugged and they lingered a bit to say hello to everybody. Jacob and Ellie and Maggie and Thomas came over to hug Martin and Henry's kids and then found Alice and Johnny. Ellie inspected Alice's tummy and patted it and laughed. Alice couldn't wait to show her the baby clothes that Margo had given her and began pulling out a few from her bag and Ellie screamed with delight when she saw that she had clothes for a boy and girl and screamed some more when Alice told her about Margo saying that she would be needing another set for her next one. Martin told Henry he had a lot to tell about his trip and Henry told him he had a lot to tell about things that happened while he was gone and one was that John had resigned from his job and was moving to Savannah and coming soon to look at a townhouse to buy. Martin said, great because he can teach me how to make ice cream.

The Milams began walking back toward their house and Alice and

Johnny and Jacob and Ellie walked with them a way until they split off to go to their homes. Not much work got done on the Milam place that day or the next few days and Walter and Henry didn't care. There were often days like this that were undeclared holidays besides Sundays and times like Christmas and Easter and Thanksgiving and some birthdays. Sometimes it was a marriage or a birth or a death, but holidays were regular, and not far in between.

Once at the house and on the porch and yaupon was poured, Martin talked for two hours about his trip to Tybee. He could have kept on but Martha said it was time to eat. Claudia and Henry helped Martha set out big bowls of food on the table and Walter said a prayer of thankfulness. Martin continued his stories while they ate and everyone was highly entertained and thrilled, especially about the duel and Mallie and the slavers and how good a liar Daniel was but not as good a liar as the blind Captain Jones telling how he had seen the boat with the two men come up and then take the runaways over to Turtle Island and all the stories of Ayana and her people and her mother and father. He continued when they had finished supper and went out on the porch for more tea. All were amazed at how much Martin seemed to grow up and mature in the short time he was away.

He said he was finally getting tired then added how Margo woke them up by tapping on the ceiling early every morning and said how much Daniel had liked the new coffee drink that Henry had added on the supply boat. Everyone was tired from the days celebrating and somewhat worn out by all the stories that Martin told. Henry smiled to himself, thinking how Martin was animated like his father when telling stories and he had enjoyed seeing his father listen to Martin.

Martin's first day back began with Henry. He woke early like he had been accustomed to at the lighthouse. His first thought was of Margo and her way of tapping on the floor to wake them up. Walter and Martha were not up yet but he heard some slight sounds from Henry's end of the house and went around and saw Henry in the window motioning him to come in. He went to their small kitchen table and could smell the new coffee drink that Henry had sent to the lighthouse for the Dyers to try. Henry poured Martin a cup and nodded for Martin to follow him into his office where he had a small sitting area. Martin sipped the coffee and Henry said it took some getting used to and he liked it in the mornings but still liked yaupon in the afternoons. He said the coffee had a little more kick to it. Martin said that he had noticed how it had kicked Daniel out of his morning stupor.

Henry said he wanted to talk to him about what his new jobs could be

328

for the coming year and tell him what had been happening since he was gone. Martin said he was glad Henry was thinking about that because he had been wondering about it himself and trusted that Henry would have the better understanding of the things that needed doing the most. He said he also had some things he had questions about that he hoped Henry would have some answers for. Henry said the biggest new thing was John and his family coming and getting the ice business going and he explained the importance of having something else to sustain the Milam plantation in case things ever changed.

Henry told Martin more about their father's health issues. This was a bit much for Martin and Henry saw that and said it was difficult to talk about and he had been worrying about how to discuss it but he needed to know. Martin was taken back a bit and they heard a tap on the door and Claudia said she had made some breakfast for them. It was a good time to break from their conversation because Martin was unsettled about what Henry had told him about their father. They went into the kitchen and sat and had some eggs and grits and bacon and biscuits with Claudia. The kids were not up yet and it was just the three of them.

Claudia mentioned that the kids and Walter and Martha were on the same schedule and she had come to like the time she and Henry had been having alone in the early mornings before they got up, but Martin was welcome to join them anytime. Henry asked Martin what he had wanted to talk about that he had mentioned earlier and said maybe Claudia would like to hear too.

He told Henry and Claudia about how Ayana and her people supported and provided cover for Alice's family and helped get the runaways, once they were healthy, to the Ogeechee people who hid them in their big trading canoe and took them inland. Alice's mother had said that she would never want to leave because she wanted to keep helping the regular flow of runaways that came to them and how she had helped hundreds of them during her time there and how it had helped her overcome the grief about the massacre and what they had thought happened to Alice when she was yanked from the canoe that morning. Martin went on to say that experiencing the slavers was the worst fear he had ever had in his life.

He told how that Ayana and her people were squeezed as far as they could go now, after having been forced to leave the larger islands to the south and how there were not many of them left because of disease. Martin said he loved Ayana and her people and realized that they were also runaways and wanted to do all he could to help them and the future of Alice's family was tied to the future of Ayana and them. He said that when he was in the midst of helping Mallie and was thinking about taking him to the Indian Islands so they could help him escape to up north, he realized that if the slavers had seen through his trickery, they could have easily gone right across the Back River with their dogs and not only catch Mallie but Alice's family too and when they learned from where they had run away from, they would seek a reward from the owner or sell them at the auction. If the South Carolina owner came forth, the story would probably be news in the Savannah paper and Alice could become connected. Martin apologized for all the fear and concern he had but it almost became too much for him to think about, especially when he thought about what might become of Alice and her new child and Johnny too if their story got out. He said he could not fathom the horror of Alice and her family being taken back to the evil master in South Carolina that they had escaped from and without Johnny, but with her new child, which would legally be the property of the owner of Alice. He said, equally disturbing is what could happen with Ayana and her people if word got out about them helping the runaways and where they would go if they were run off.

Claudia and Henry were struck with the intense feelings of Martin. Claudia asked Henry what could be done about all that and Henry said he had thought some about Alice still being a runaway and her story somehow being connected to her escape and old master but didn't think it would happen. Most owners at the time of the massacre that had slaves missing assumed that they had died in the massacre there or the one that happened soon after that on Sullivans Island in South Carolina.

Henry's brow furrowed deeply and he was silent for a bit and Claudia saw how deep in thought and stress he was in and suggested they have some more coffee. Martin's concerns and conversation had stirred up some other things Henry wanted to discuss. He said he would need some time to think about it all and Martin said he had thought about it and asked why not find out where the plantation was in South Carolina and go and offer the owner an amount he couldn't refuse for Alice and her family and the two friends that stayed with them.

Martin's simple clarity caused the wrinkles in Henry's brow to get even deeper. Henry said it may not be as simple as Martin had put it but it may be a good general plan. He said from what he understood, she was from a plantation on a very big island somewhere not too far north in South Carolina. Henry thought to himself that he had so many things that he had planned to do and he really didn't want to have something to slow his progress but his heart reigned over his minds objections and he couldn't help himself and told Martin how glad he was to have these things brought up.

He found himself telling Martin that these things concerning Alice and her family were the most important things their family had to take care of. He said even the ice business could wait. Henry said that he needed some legal advice about this and other things concerning the future of the Milam place and all the people on it. He said he had thought a meeting of the Milam's and their most trusted friends and advisors might be a good idea. He would want John to be there and he was already coming and he would want his and John's favorite professor of business and ethics (Albert McWilliamson) and Walter's two old Lawyer friends and John's father, and Alice of course to be there. He would want Charles and Margo Dyer to be there but he knew Charles would not leave the lighthouse. Henry said having a meeting of all those would help him feel more confident and see more clearly about decisions that needed to be made that could have important consequences to the whole Milam place including what they were now discussing about Alice and family, and it needed to be soon. He said he wasn't sure what to do about Ayana and her people. Martin told him about the new signaling device that Charles was getting for Ayana so they could stay better in touch. Their breakfast had sat, half eaten, and gotten cold and Claudia scraped it on a plate for the dog and got them each a warm egg and bacon biscuit from the stove and some jam and more coffee.

Henry's kids were up and were surprised to see Martin there when they came in sleepy eyed to the kitchen and hugged him. Martin could hear Walter and Martha stirring about the same time and Henry suggested they go back to his office and continue their discussions. Claudia filled Henry's cup with coffee and Martin declined more and said he would be right back after he had told his parents where he was. He went around and found them at the kitchen table and said he had been at breakfast with Henry and would be there a while longer and Martha thanked him for telling them. She said Walter had needed the extra rest lately and she had adjusted their time getting up a bit.

As Martin walked around to Henry's end of the house, he thought of what his mother had just said in light of what Henry had told him about his father's health.

Martin found Henry in his office and Henry said he was almost afraid to ask him if he had any more things to ask about and Martin said that there was one other thing that he would like to discuss that had been on his mind and Henry said to please tell him. Martin said that he knew Henry had his hands full with a lot of new things and with his regular work load and was glad to hear that John was coming and could help him with the new ice business and all but he wanted to soon be doing what he needed to do to become a boat captain and went over again what Captain Ben proposed to him starting in about a year.

He was hoping to make that come sooner than later and wanted to let Henry know in regard to what plans he might have for him. Henry said that was a lot easier to think about than what he had brought up earlier. After a few moments pause, he said that he had gone away to school for his education at fifteen and realized that Martin's education would mean him going away too and he wished for him to be there but wished more for him to have the education that most suited him and they had found out most assuredly that it was not the same type of learning that had suited him. Martin was pleased at Henry's agreeable understanding and said that he knew his father would approve but knew his mother would not like him going off to sea and wished that Henry would assure her if he got the chance and Henry said he would. Martin added that it wasn't like he would be going off for months or years like his father had done at a younger age than him, but he would be going for a week or two at the most and would still be around to help when he could.

Henry said he suspected that they would be needing to ship ice to places that boats could access easier than wagons anyhow and maybe he was aspiring to do something that would fit right in. He said he had already been thinking about a specially designed wagon for hauling ice and Martin could be thinking about a specially designed sharpie for hauling ice and they had already found out about cork and would soon be learning how well it worked from Captain Bens boat that now had cork lining the holds and from what Jason was building in on the supply boats for a weekly supply of ice to the lighthouse. The idea of a special sharpie ice-boat took hold of Martin's entire attention and he had to make an effort to listen to the other things Henry wanted to tell him about.

Henry went on to say they would probably be advised to separate the ice business from the lighthouse management and provisioning and probably be purchasing a piece of property close by for the things they needed which included an ice house for storage and a large barn, pasture, and corral for horses and an area for all things related to building and maintaining heavy duty insulated wagons for hauling ice, and other things he hadn't been able to think of because it was all new.

He said he was thinking that Jehu would be a useful employee and could include him a small but adequate living space in the barn. Martin lit up at that idea and said that would be perfect and Henry said he thought Martin would like it and wanted him to bring Jehu out after the barn was started and maybe even before, now that he thought about it because Jehu could have some ideas for some things that would be best for the horses. Martin said he would go ahead and bring him out as soon as he could. Henry said he didn't want to make enemies of the stage outfit for luring away Jehu so they would need to do it in a way if possible that would not cause them to feel a loss.

Martin marveled at Henry's thoughtfulness and business knowledge and was glad that the Milam operation was in his hands. Next, Henry asked Martin what he thought about the bridge and road rebuilding and the brick repairs on the lighthouse. Martin said he hadn't looked a lot at the bricks but they looked better and he had noticed that the crew worked steady. He said he had paid more attention to the bridge and roadway because their father had said for him to and Martin told Henry about how the horses were always hesitant to walk over the widely spaced decking boards but now Jacob had placed them closer together and the horses were more secure and didn't hesitate anymore and Daniel or whoever was driving the wagon did not have to get out and coax and lead them over. Henry said that was good and was probably one of the things that took the project longer than he had expected and Martin said that he thought they may have had to add more cedar pilings than was planned and that meant replacing the frames between them too. Henry said it was no problem and he said it was better that it was done properly because the bridges were important. They could, if they had to, use the Back River landing but it took a lot longer to get there and back.

Martin said he had told Jacob about him not being asked to stay away from his family again and he had liked that idea and Martin said if there was another boatman needed, he had hoped that Izak could start training to be one. He had already taught him to swim. Martin added that he was smart and he had taken him with him to see Jacob's family and had the idea that Maggie could teach him to read and he could help with checking the lists for loading the boats and maybe other things. Henry said that Alice was teaching Johnny to read and he had been loading the supply boats with her help. He thought Izak could start his official training and one thing that he wanted to do was teach everyone on the place, that was willing, to read and write. If Maggie could teach Izak, maybe she could help Alice teach reading and writing to others.

Martin said that would be good because Maggie didn't like taking care of chickens with her mother. Henry added that he didn't think that he needed to say it but they needed to be extra careful that they were secretive about the reading and writing lessons because they could be accused and charged with sedition to upset the government. Martin said he was aware of that and feared it would eventually come to light. He also said that if he was able to learn to read, anybody could. Henry told Martin to go ahead and tell Izak about him training to be a boatman only if it was what he was sure that he wanted because it was a hard and dangerous job. Martin said he was certain he would say he would because he hated working in the gardens. Henry said he wasn't sure yet what he had planned for Jacob but had some ideas. Martin said Jacob really liked the boathouse and the water and all but he really liked building things too and maybe he would like to work on the new icehouse. Henry said that was an excellent idea but said they had plans to make the ice business operate with only paid employees, eventually, and there was some legal planning yet to be done concerning those matters. Henry said that they had used almost the whole morning but considered it to be very well spent time and would make their early morning meetings a regular thing.

He said it wouldn't have to be for as long as they talked today but he would like it at least once a week. He told Martin that he valued his outlook and understanding about things. He said that he tended to overthink and make things more complicated than they needed to be and he appreciated Martin's simple clarity. Martin was surprised that Henry could need him because he thought of him as so much smarter than himself. Martin sensed that Henry felt he had other things to attend to and said he didn't want to hold him up but there was one more thing and he had just now, this morning thought about it. Anyhow, he said he knew that it was Saint Helena Island that Alice and her family had run away from and it was east of Beaufort, where John was from. He said that what he thought of was that they could hire the sharpie with Ashley and Ken to take them there to pay off their owner. He said the accommodations would not be that great but better than trying to hire a boat everyday back and forth from Beaufort, which could take all day or more depending on the weather. He added that they could try and find a place to stay there but that could be difficult. Henry said that in light of what they were going to do and who they were dealing with, staying on a boat could be more secure. To begin with, they needed a written account of all Alice could remember of names and places and then maybe he could ask John's father in Beaufort to help find out more about the place and the owner that they needed to see. Anyhow, they would probably be seeing Johns father soon and could ask him about those things.

Henry said he still didn't know what to tell Martin about any assigned duties for him but he could start by finishing Izak's swim lessons and arrange a visit from Jehu and talk to Captain Ben when he comes back through again about his sharpie and the trip to South Carolina. He added that he might spend some time with their father too and then he remembered that their barge would be back in a day or two and it always needed maintenance and to get with Jacob about how and what to do to it and let

Izak help as part of his training. He said that in a week he would have a better plan for him. Henry told Martin how proud he was of him and all and how he had done so good and how much he was a help to him. Martin felt good about the compliments but thought them over generous.

Back on Tybee at the lighthouse, Daniel fell back to the routine of his duties helping his father. One of the biggest tasks was keeping the huge glass lens with all its angles clean. The ocean breezes deposited a salt spray that cut back on how far the light could be seen from out at sea. Fresh buckets of water had to be hauled up on a pulley system set up on the balcony rail and rags wetted to wipe off the salt film and then rinsed and wiped again. It was worse during a northeaster because of the strong wind off the ocean and all the salt spray that the wind kicked up, and that was also the time that seeing the light from afar was most important so it had to be done daily for as long as the northeaster blew, which was sometimes as much as a week but usually four or five days.

Daniel liked the winds from the northwest and west and southwest because the lens stayed clean much longer. Mary had things to do, helping Margo but not as much was expected of her because she was younger and it was expected that Daniel would become the next keeper and needed to get accustomed to the work of it. She read some but now spent a lot of time making notes and planning her book that she had become determined to write. Charles and Margo had started a family late and it wouldn't be long before Charles would need Daniel to take over if that was what he was inclined to do.

Being a lighthouse keeper was a big and unique commitment to a life with not much social interaction and few could stay with it. Charles was hoping it would be Daniels choice but was wise and knew not to expect it. Daniel was mostly sure that he would do it but had been told from early on that he would be sent off to the mainland, for a stay, so he could better decide for himself what he wanted.

It was, in those times, expected that girls would be sent to seek a life on the mainland. There were exceptions, however, where daughters were without brothers and assumed the role when their parents got too old or when they would marry and their husbands would become the keeper or when a husband would die and the wife would carry on. For a man or woman, it was a hard life but it had its riches and rewards in the beauty and independence from the outside world, if that is what a person liked.

The first day after Martin left, Daniel had some coffee and started right into his duties just like before Martin had come, but Mary was in a melancholy way and it was obvious to Margo. She made some yaupon and asked Mary to join her on the porch. Before Margo could say anything,

Mary blurted out that she had never felt so good as she did with Martin, then she burst into tears. After she sobbed for a few minutes, and regained her composure some, Margo hugged her and told her that she was proud of her for having such strong feelings and was glad she could let her feelings out. She told her that Martin was not far away and that she and Charles had talked about her and Daniel going to the mainland together and she could stay with her aunt in Savannah and see Martin often if she liked. Mary said she wanted to go now and Margo was surprised at how deeply smitten Mary was. She had never had to console Mary for anything more than a minor argument with Daniel or something small and she felt at a loss for what to say that could make her feel better. She told her that she had put some honey in her tea and to try and drink a little. Mary did and felt some better. The hard cry seemed to have helped. They sat quietly for a while, and then Margo was surprised that she thought of something to say to Mary that might help her. She reminded Mary of the notes she had been taking about a book she said she would write and said that it could make her feel better to work on that regularly until it was time for her to go to stay with her aunt in Savannah. She added that just getting the story of Ayana and her people could keep her busy for a month or more. Daniel could take you over in his boat he got from Martin and you could sit and talk to Ayana on the breezy spot that Martin talked about. Margo's ideas lifted Mary's spirit and she cried on her shoulder again but this time out of gratitude.

When she pulled back she told her mother that she knew that it might be a couple of years but she would be Martin's wife. Margo knew that a lot could happen in two years but could only say that she hoped so. She added that girls learned things about life sooner than boys and she was ahead of Martin on things but understand that and be patient with things. She said she shouldn't be able to say anything about patience because she had married her father within a week after they had met but she was sixteen and not fifteen like her and Mary laughed a little and said ok she only had to wait less than a year.

Margo said they will have to wait and see how things went. They heard Charles and Daniel coming and Margo went in the kitchen and wet a soft rag and wiped Mary's face until she was refreshed before Daniel burst in and said he was done for a few hours and was gonna take out his new boat before he forgot the things Martin had taught him and asked Mary if she wanted to go. Margo answered for her and said she would love to. She told him to never go without the safety float and he said he wouldn't and she added that they could take the Captains food down as they went. She thought to herself that Daniel had seemed spryer lately and wondered if it was the new coffee drink he had been having. They grabbed a biscuit and water for themselves and the Captain's food and were out the door in a few minutes.

Margo sat with some more tea with Charles and told him how upset Mary had been. He didn't seem to fully understand the full drama of it but tried to act like he did. Margo asked him what he would do if Daniel went to the mainland and decided to choose a different career there instead of taking over here. Charles thought a minute and said they would have to think about that when the time came and he wanted both him and Mary to choose for themselves what they wanted, like he had done. He told Margo he couldn't imagine having chosen any other thing to do besides being a light keeper but his best choice was choosing her. Margo was still somewhat on the edge from talking to Mary and probably seemed to be overreacting to Charles when she hugged him and let out a few sobs and he tried but couldn't think of what he might have said to upset her.

Daniel and Mary took the Captain his food and he expressed so much thanks that it was like the first time they had done it instead of having done it every day for years. He said he missed their good buddy Martin and they said they did too. He told Daniel it was mighty big of him to give you that boat and Daniel said he knew that and that the Captain was good to give Martin his boat. He told the Captain that he and Mary were gonna be going off to the mainland for six months or so in a few months and they would miss him but the guards would keep bringing him his food. The Captain said he would miss them and Daniel said he hoped Martin would get back before they left and the Captain agreed.

Daniel drug the boat down to the water's edge, set the mast down through the hole in the thwart and one oar through the steel "U" shaped piece on the transom for a rudder and pulled on the sail and the mast spun around letting out the sail and they headed out to the eastern tip of Hilton Head on a fresh southerly breeze.

Although Mary was still a bit down from missing Martin, the thrill of the water and breeze and all made her feel better. She thought to herself that her mother's suggestion was good. If she couldn't be with Martin, she would feel better writing about him and she knew how absorbed she could get reading and in the little she had done in taking notes about her book, she had even gotten more taken up with it than reading. She realized that she might escape her misery for a few months if she could lose herself in her research and note taking. She was startled back to the moment when she felt the boat hull shift by Daniel coming about and moved her weight to the other side like Martin had taught her.

They were now headed to the west side of Tybee and when they had passed the north point a ways, the high dunes of Tybee blocked the wind and the sail slackened and they sat still just outside the breakers. Mary asked Daniel what next and Daniel said he didn't know and as he reached for a paddle, a wind swooped down from over the dunes and caught them by surprise and almost knocked them over. Daniel barely let the sail out in time and they blew out a way and came about again and headed back toward South Carolina.

When they were a mile or so out from Tybee, Daniel came about again and stayed on that tack until they went ashore near where the barge had been tied up at the top of the beach, but now was out in the shallow channel that was close in to the beach. There were two men with oars in the pulling boat keeping it in the channel and four men on the barge with fishing poles, as it drifted toward Savannah. Daniel told Mary that he pulled up here so she could have a turn and she was surprised. He told her that she should get comfortable operating the boat because there could come a time when she may need to and also because it was fun. They both got out and watched the barge for a few minutes moving slowly in the current toward the mouth of the south channel, then Daniel let Mary get in and he pointed the boat toward Daufuskie and when Mary was set, got in himself and they shot out and through the small breakers.

They went out about a mile toward Daufuskie, then came about and headed for Tybee and then again for Daufuskie several times until Mary got the feel of it. On the third time going back toward Tybee, she steered a little more west and they passed the slow moving barge and saw Izak and waved. Daniel said they were going home and it would probably take them two more days of drifting with the incoming tides, and anchoring during the outgoing tides, to reach the Milam place. They had a long pole set up on two temporary posts and a big canvas stretched across it with half the canvas to each side and tied off for shade and shelter from rain. Outside the canvas was some smoke drifting up from a cooking fire on top of a big pile of fresh beach sand they had loaded on before they left. Mary steered back toward South Carolina again, but this time straight toward Turtle Island.

On the way toward it, she told Daniel the things about it that Martin had told her. She said Martin said he was going there one day and he probably would but she wished he wouldn't. Daniel said he usually did what he set out to do and Mary just said "ugg." When they had gotten closer, Daniel pointed to a boat high up on the beach of Turtle Island. Daniel said he wondered what they were up to and Mary said probably nothing good and came about again and said she was ready to go in. Daniel told her to tighten the sail up and steer toward the Captain's shanty. It was slow going because the high dunes of the north end of Tybee blocked the wind but a breeze would swoop down and they would go fast for a way and then lay still until another one came and they came up on the beach at the shanty.

Mary thanked Daniel for letting her take the helm. Daniel said they both had a lot to learn and they would do it often so they could get good at it and she agreed. Daniel drug the little boat up and Mary carried the small mast and things up above the high water line and turned the boat over with everything tucked underneath. They went back to see the Captain who was alone because both pilot crews were gone. He complimented them both, as if he had been watching and Daniel said they had nearly gone over once in the lee of Tybee when a gust caught them unprepared. Captain Jones told Daniel that they should go over on purpose a few times so they both could learn to get the boat back up right again. Daniel said Martin had said he would do that with him but things got busy and he didn't. Captain Jones said not to worry and told them that the little boat was sealed up real good and wouldn't sink and the first thing to do was to pull the mast out and roll the sail up, then from one side, reach over the hull and grab the gunwale and use your body weight to roll it over and while still in the water, swoosh as much water out as you can then get in from the bow or stern, not the side, and swoosh out the rest of the water.

He said that it could be dangerous in the winter when the water was cold and y'all should not venture far from shore then. He said even the strongest swimmers could not be in cold water long before their limbs got numb and death often came shortly after that. He told them to, in the winter, put some matches in a small jar, and seal the lid with hot wax and secure it in the boat so you can start a fire and dry out and warm yourself if you needed to. He said just knowing how to swim was not enough to save yourself sometimes and you had to use your head. He said Walter had used his head to get y'all that safety float and he was sure glad he did.

Daniel and Mary did not expect to get the lecture from the Captain but appreciated it. They told him that the food basket was the leftovers from Martin's favorite food and he thanked them again. Daniel asked him if he would be all right getting up without any crew there and he said he would and thanked him. They left and headed up and over the big dune to the lighthouse, carefully removed the sand from themselves before going up on the porch to eat the snacks they had taken but not eaten.

Over in the Indian Islands, Alice's family was both happy and sad. Sad a little because Alice had gone but very happy that she had come. Her mother had gone the morning after Alice left and sat at the breezy point and talked to Ayana and drank strong yaupon for hours. She had become Ayana's closest friend over the years and they were even closer than sisters. They were the co-matriarchs of the little island refuge and each of their lives was made more pleasant by the other. It is almost unthinkable how they were so content, being cut off from the world, but if you think of where they came from and how they got there, it is understandable. For Lucie, anything was an improvement from the place she ran away from in South Carolina and then the escape from the bloody carnage of the massacre and the grief over what appeared to happen to Alice made her wish she had died too. Two things kept Lucie from dying of grief. First it was Ayana, who had her and her family and the others taken to the small quarantine island her mother had used, then, at the risk of sickness, paddled a canoe alone and brought food and turtle egg soup and healing herbs every day. Lucie and the others were still shaken up and traumatized from the massacre and when they saw Ayana first come with a doeskin mask over most of her face to protect her from sickness, they didn't know what to think. She came every day for a few weeks until they were all nourished better than they ever had been, even before their stay on Tybee. Ayana began to talk to them, but Lucie and her husband were too much in grief to talk, but Ayana continued and talked to the others and Alice's father and brother began to talk some and Ayana told them about other runaways they helped and kept them here until they were healthy. She told them they were gonna be moving them to their own camp on the big island she lived on and her people had built them shelters. After they moved, Ayana began to bring Lucie to the breezy spot every few days and told her about her people and all and her melancholy began to lift a bit.

Then one day, Ayana brought two runaways to Lucie, after they had been quarantined, and told her their routine of sending them with other Indians up the Ogeechee where others met them that helped them on their way to freedom. She said she thought she might try leaving them there for a few days before they had to go. The two runaways were a brother and sister in their late teens and Lucie took to them and they to her. Ayana saw the improvement in her from helping the two runaways and continued bringing more, after their quarantine, and she helped them get adjusted and ready for the next leg of their trip. Most were in a bad way and greatly afraid and some quite traumatized from beatings and their escape. Helping the runaways reach freedom, helped Lucie escape her trauma. After a few years, when talking to the runaways, Lucie began to hear bits and pieces of news and information from around Savannah and parts of South Carolina and she heard the story of the little girl that survived the massacre, buried in the pluff mud on Tybee. This was joyful news to Alice's family and Ayana and her people too because the canoe people had seen little Alice get yanked out of the canoe. Hundreds more runaways came over the years and Lucie continued to help them, and now, after seeing Alice and her good husband and a grandchild on the way, heaven had become on earth for her and she was the happiest she had ever been.

Ayana was happy too but she knew, based on what had happened to her people that there time there was limited and the next move would be a difficult choice. Lucie was happy but quite aware that hell and the devil were not that far away, just across the rivers and marshes. She was reminded of the hell, regularly, by the stories of terror she heard from all the runaways. They used the healing remedies of the Indians to sooth and repair the wounds on their backs from beatings that had prompted their running away and she had seen the poorly healed broken bones on their hands and arms from trying to shield themselves from the beatings. The stories they told were worse than any hell and brimstone preaching and was real, not an imagination by a preacher. A real hell on earth existed for many, right in the midst of the Christian south.

For Ayana, the refuge of the small island was not something that was new. Her people had sought the islands for security long before the colonials came. The separation from the mainland by rivers and vast stretches of marsh and mud isolated them from the sometimes warring that went on amongst tribes and let them feel at peace and have freedom from fear. It is unimaginable, however, the death and devastation when their culture of thousands of years in the making was taken away in less than a hundred years and all that remained of them was eighteen and the stories that Ayana knew and told. She had some satisfaction and hope, though, because her mother had learned and taught her how sickness was spread and their numbers had leveled off and they had not had any unnatural deaths since when they had been exposed by helping the large group of runaways that had gathered just before the massacre. She was still, after knowing of all that had happened, mostly content and at peace with herself. Her lamp inside remained lit and with it she had lit the lamp of Lucie.

Today, after they had sat for a long time on the breezy point, feeling and appreciating the peace within themselves and each other, Ayana handed Lucie a piece of leather with all red beadwork except six black beads and one white bead in the middle, similar to what she had made for Martin. Sylvie put it around her neck and she yearned to go over and hug Ayana but had learned to keep a distance, however, there was no loss of intimacy as they and the trees and the ground and the air between them came alive to their senses, as it often did when they sat and talked. Ayana always began their talks by recognizing the gift of breath that was filling them and giving them life and in all things around them too. From Ayana, Lucie came to tangibly feel that life and began slowly to have a greater sense of her own true self. This was not easy for someone brought up in slavery from birth when there is a wrong sense of oneself belonging to a master and there is no self-worth but only a sense of worth to a master. But over time, the light came on inside Lucie, reborn from something that had always been with her, brought to light by the clarity and understanding of Ayana. This enlightenment and rebirth of Lucie, spilled to the others in her camp and in some ways, despite the conditions they were brought together in and the cruel world not far away, this small island with co- matriarchs was a peaceful sanctuary for both groups.

A few days after Martin got back, he got up early as usual, and quietly got dressed so he wouldn't wake his parents and slipped outside. He saw lamplight in Henry's end of the house but remembered that Claudia had said she liked the time she and Henry had early in the morning before everybody else was up, so he didn't go around to their door but went where he went more than any other place, to the boathouse. Jacob and Johnny were already there and to his surprise, the barge was anchored out front. The sun was just beginning to peak over the marsh to the east and Martin could see they had a cooking fire going on the mound of sand and men were around it. He went up and inside the boathouse and Johnny and Jacob were drinking yaupon by the woodstove.

They were happy to see him and Johnny poured him some tea and pointed to some biscuits they had warming on top of the stove. Jacob said he thought he would see him this morning because he knew he would be looking for the barge with his boat on it. Martin said yes he was glad to get his boat but mostly wanted to see Izak to tell him the good news about Henry saying he could begin training to become a boatman. Jacob said he reckoned that Izak would take Johnny's place and Johnny would take his place and he wondered what was in store for him. Martin told Jacob not to worry because, Henry had some plans going on with the new ice business that he and John were working on. Martin told Jacob that Henry didn't want him to have to be away from his family every week and had some big ideas and Jacob was in them and would probably be talking to him about it all. Martin added that Henry knew Jacob liked building things and he had several buildings planned. Jacob said Henry had always done him good and wasn't worried a bit about things and he did like the boathouse but he liked spending every night at home the most and building things was always easy for him. He said Johnny would make a good helmsman and a good boathouse boss. They heard some noise outside and Martin said it was probably the men coming in from the barge and he went to see.

Izak and two others were stepping out of the pulling boat onto the bank and one man headed back out to get the rest. Martin yelled to Izak to come over and that he wanted to talk to him. He nodded for Izak to come on back to the woodstove with Johnny and Jacob and he poured him a cup of yaupon. Johnny asked about the trip from Tybee and Izak said he didn't think he would ever tire of fishing but he had fished so much the last three days, slowly drifting or while anchored waiting for the tide to shift back toward home, that he was through with fishing for a while. Johnny said it looked like he was gonna have more time on the water coming up and not for fishing.

Izak didn't get it and Martin said Henry had said that he could begin training to be a boatman if he was sure he really wanted to do it. Martin added that it would mean that he wouldn't be able to spend time weeding and hoeing in the gardens and laughed. Jacob told Izak not to speak to quick because there were some things more unpleasant about being on the river than hoeing dirt. Izak asked what could be worse, and Jacob said cold, windy and wet days pulling on oars for hours or being called out to a ship sinking on the river and lifting up drowned sailors into the boat or worse is finding some a few days later and they be ate up by crabs and swollen way up and hauling them in the boat and the smell when the rotten air lets out.

As Jacob went on to describe the bad things a boatman had to do sometimes, Martin looked closely at Izak to see if he faltered in doubt but didn't see him flinch a bit. After Jacob finished, Izak said he was ready for it all and Martin said there was one more thing that might make him change his mind and it was a new thing that other boatmen before him were not asked to do. Johnny and Jacob and Izak all wondered what Martin was talking about. Martin said that Henry had thought that Izak should learn to read and write. He said that Johnny was learning and even Jacob would need to. Izak lit up and said that he had wanted to read ever since he had seen Martin checking off the things on the lists when they had been loading the barge with all the materials to take to Tybee.

Martin asked Izak if he understood that a lot of white people didn't like black people to learn to read because they might forget their place and it was actually against the law and he and his family could lose everything and worse if it was found out that they encouraged and taught their workers to read and write. Izak said he knew all about that and knew how to act dumb as a log when he needed to and asked Martin if he would be his teacher. Martin said no, because he was not a very good reader but he was hoping that Maggie could like they had talked about on the last visit. Izak didn't say anything but could hardly stop himself from jumping up in joy because he had remembered how beautiful Maggie had looked when Martin had taken him over to see her and her family. He was too shy to say anything then but wished he could have. Martin said that Henry said that he still had to finish the swim lessons and Izak said he had practiced on his own at the beach on Tybee and gotten the hang of it.

Martin said he would need to see him swim and he needed to be able to swim good enough to pull a man that couldn't swim for his rescue training. He also told Izak that part of his training was taking care of and fixing boats and Henry had said they could work on the barge to start and he looked at Jacob and said he needed him to show them what to do and how to do it and what to do it with.

Jacob nodded in agreement and said that the barge needed to be hauled up and then the bottom scraped and some basic repair and cleaning out the mud to look for any rotted wood. He told Martin to go ahead and shovel out the big pile of sand they had put in for a cooking fire and there were a couple shovels onboard. He added that the moon was full in a few days and the tide will be high so we can get the barge way up on the bank and set some blocks under it so when the tide drops, y'all can scrape the bottom, then we will have to turn it around on the next high tide and block up the other side so you can get to it. Jacob said scraping off barnacles was a rough job and it could take a couple days per side and Martin said they could handle it but he didn't know anything about blocking it up and Jacob said he and the boatmen would do that and he would tell him when it was ready. Martin told Jacob that he and Izak would be over to his house this afternoon to talk to Maggie about teaching Izak to read and write and Jacob nodded ok.

Martin told Izak they could shovel out the sand from the barge, then set his new boat off and set it up on the bank above the high water line so work could start on it. They took the pulling boat out to the barge and found the shovels and started in on the sand pile. There was still a thick pile of hot coals from the fire and they shoveled them into the river first and Martin noticed that the sand was warm under them and shoveled some off and felt the sand and it was barely warm and a little more down and the sand was cool. He thought to himself what a good idea this was to be able to safely have a coking fire on a wooden barge. It took them all morning to shovel the sand and Martin said they could eat lunch with the boatmen and he could tell them about him learning to be a boatman. They were just finishing up when Martin saw the meal cart being brought over to the boathouse and told Izak that one of the best things about being a boatman was the lunch that was cooked in the outdoor kitchen and brought in every day. He said it wasn't fancy but very good.

They went and sat down and Martin told the men about Izak joining up with them and all and they all nodded in approval. Jacob mentioned that, once his training was over and him being the new man, he would be getting the jobs nobody else liked to do like scrubbing floors and latrine work and Izak, looking at all the good food being set out on the table, said it was fine with him to do whatever he was given to do and several of the men laughed a little, and one said he may change his mind when the food was not in front of him but the latrine was.

After lunch, several of the men wanted Martin to tell them the story of the duel on Tybee beach. They had been hearing of it from others but wanted to hear it straight from him. He said he didn't like much to think about it but said he would tell it if they really wanted to hear and they said to tell about the slavers then and Martin said he loved telling about that and said he would tell about the slavers. He went on to say that some of what he was gonna tell about was witnessed by Jacob here and Jacob nodded.

First he told how awful and mean the slavers were and all and how they were only one step ahead of them with moving the runaway, Mallie, from one hiding place on the island to the other, but what he wanted to tell was how the big swarm of gnats had been more than they could handle and they were hardly able to row their boat and swat away the gnats and the oars were bumping in to each other and falling in the water. He told of how mad their boss man was and all the cussing he did and said he outa shoot them all. Jacob shook his head and said how much worse and all it was than Martin was telling but he never thought he would be so happy for gnats to show up.

They all laughed and wanted Martin to tell more and he looked at Jacob and Jacob nodded and Martin said he would tell his favorite part of the slavers on Tybee and it was about how they had fooled them to think Mallie the runaway had gone to Turtle island instead of the Indian Islands and he went on longer than the first part about the details of weighting his boat and clothes down in the water so the dogs couldn't smell that the runaway was around him and using the edge of a board to make an imprint to look like a boat had been brought up on the beach to take the runaway off and the two different size boots he had used to make footprints in the sand around the boat.

Martin watched the men as they reacted to the different things he was saying and dwelled longer on the ones that got their attention the most. He remembered how Captain Jones had done that. Martin said he had forgot one of the worst and frightening things and that was how big and mean and ferocious the dogs were and how they practically drug the men holding them. He told them how the reward for Mallie was higher than any reward ever offered for one runaway and how the head slaver had told them that he didn't want the dogs loose because he wouldn't get any money for a dead slave.

They really liked hearing how Mallie had brushed up against all the bushes to make a good trail for the dogs to follow and all and how Daniel had his little boat ready and in the water nearby for him and Mallie to sail around the other side of Tybee and over to the Indian Islands. He paused a minute and saw that all the men were mesmerized and then said he was about to get to the best part of the story. He told how the slavers and dogs had followed Mallie's trail over the dunes and when they saw the groove in the sand he had made with a board to look like a boat had been pulled up and the boot prints and Millie's foot prints and figured that Mallie had escaped them and gone, and how awful the slaver boss was, but he said he was still not to the best part and paused again and the men's attention was on Martin's every breath.

Then he told of the slavers, after looking up the beach to the west toward Lazaretto, then walking back to the north point and asking the Captain Jones if he had seen anything of a boat and two men and a runaway. The blind Captain exclaimed in the most truthful and convincing voice how he had seen two men pull a boat up on the beach, get out and walk around a bit and wait and then the runaway come running over the dunes and down on to the beach and them leave in the boat and go across to Turtle Island and how the slavers had believed what a blind man had seen. The men all knew about Captain Jones being blind and they laughed until some fell to the ground and rolled around. When the laughing stopped for a moment, one would repeat one of Martin's words and the laughing would come again and when it stopped, someone would say another key word and it would start again, Izak included.

When things finally settled down, Martin said the tide had dropped until one side of the barge was part on the bank and the other side was in waste deep water. Jacob sent some men down to chock up the side that was in the water so that when the tide went out further, Martin and Izak could crawl under and scrape the barnacles off half the bottom. While they waited on the tide to go out, they set up a walk board to the edge of the barge and began removing tools and tarps and all that was taken to Tybee for the work.

Then, when the tide was all the way out, they got under the barge and scraped barnacles for a couple hours. It was the hardest work that either of them had ever done and they were covered by mud and barnacle bits. Martin said they needed to go for a swim. He said the day was about over and after a swimming lesson, they could walk home with Jacob and see Maggie about his reading lessons. Izak said that sounded good to him, especially the part about seeing Maggie.

They waded out into the water and Izak went out over his head and swam back to where he could stand and did it several times and Martin said he really did practice at Tybee and Izak said he did several times until he got comfortable and then did it for fun. Martin said the real test was if he could swim and pull another person and told him to wait here in the shallow water and when he called, to come get him, then swam a few hundred feet out and yelled for Izak to come. He yelled and told him to walk up the edge of the river a way, allowing for the current and Izak ran, then swam out ahead to allow for the current and got to Martin a little behind him and had to swim to catch up. Martin told him to swim around back of him and put his arm around his shoulder, across his chest and to kick with his feet and swim with his one arm and Izak did it instinctively.

The current had drifted them a way down the river and Martin told him to not try to buck the current back, but to go straight toward the bank. When they got to the edge, they were a quarter mile from where they had started. Martin was amazed at how strong and what a natural swimmer Izak was. Martin told Izak that there was something very important that he needed to hear and remember. He had heard Jacob tell the other boatmen this and that was if you were rescuing a person in the water that sometimes, in a panic, they would try to climb on top of you. Jacob said that in order to save yourself, to take a breath and swim down under the water so the person you were helping would let go because under was not where they wanted to go, then try again to get behind them and pull them in. He said that the boatmen practiced every month, even when the water got pretty cold. He said that rescues didn't happen much but when they did it could get pretty crazy and it was their job to be prepared for the worse. They walked up to the boathouse and sat outside to drip off and wait for Jacob to go with him home.

When they got to Jacobs house, some others had come over, as they usually did in the afternoon and all wanted Martin to tell some stories and Martin retold the story he had told earlier and there was again much laughter and carrying on. Afterwards, he found Maggie and he and her and Izak sat and Martin asked her about teaching Izak to read and write again because it was official that he was in training to be a boatman now and Henry said he wants everyone that wants to learn to read to be taught for their own betterment and he wanted Izak to learn so he could go over the check list of things going on the boat every week and other things too.

Maggie asked Izak what he thought of it and after stammering a bit, he said he didn't exactly know what betterment meant, but he had been excited about the idea since they first talked about it. Maggie looked at

Izak and he looked away quickly because he had been staring at her and she asked him when he wanted to start and he said whenever she wanted him to and she told Martin to get her a pen and paper and maybe a few simple books from their library and she could say a time to start after she had those in hand. She said she would see how it went teaching Izak and then think about helping Alice to teach others. Izak did his best to hide his feelings for fear of being to forward but managed to thank Maggie. Maggie complimented Martin on his story telling and said he must have heard a lot of stories while at Tybee because he was getting better at it. Martin said he guessed she was right and he had listened to his favorite storyteller and it was Captain Jones and he had not only told some good stories but told him a story about telling stories. Maggie didn't say it but noticed how Martin had grown up a lot from his trip to Tybee.

Maggie said it was getting late and she had some storytelling to do to her little brother before he went to bed. Martin said good night and Maggie smiled at Izak and he managed a small smile back. Martin went and found Jacob and told him he reckoned he and Izak would be back to work on the barge in the morning but he didn't know what to do and Jacob said he would show them when they got there.

Jacob looked at Izak and told him his boatman training was to stick with Martin and help him on the barge until it's done and find him and he would put him to something else. Martin said Maggie was gonna be teaching him to read and write like Henry had wanted. Jacob paused a moment and smiled to himself and said he reckoned that was good and he could use some teaching himself. Martin said good night then he and Izak headed home. Izak could think of nothing but the picture in his mind of Maggie smiling at him.

Next morning, the boys were at the boathouse early and had tea and biscuits with the boatmen. Jacob told Martin they needed to turn the barge around while the tide was high so when the tide dropped some later, they could chock up the other side and scrape off the other half of the bottom and pointed to the short logs that had been used before and said when the time came to come get a few of the men to help do the chocking. He said they had shoveled out some mud the day before but today, you can pull up the deck boards and set them to one side and clean out all the mud and junk on top of the bottom planking. He said he would send a man with them to help until they got the hang of it.

Martin asked Jacob where the best place would be to put his new boat to work on it and Jacob said anywhere at the top of the riverbank where there is a flat spot, and after we have taken the hog out of the bottom, it needs to go in the boathouse and dry out a week or so, then you can do all the other work to it in there. He told Martin that Izak could help him on his boat as part of his training and Martin said he hadn't counted on that but it would get him done sooner. Jacob called the boatman to help them get started and he handed Martin a short-handled shovel and two claw hammers and a small hoe to Izak and he laughed and said he thought he had seen the last of a hoe but here one was again.

The boatman told him that after a few days of scraping barnacles he might want to work in the field again. The boatman carried a steel bar with one end flattened a bit and they took the pulling boat out to the barge. Once inside, the boatman began by sticking the flattened end of the bar in a crack between two deck boards and prying up one board then pulling it up off the thick hull framing. He said there were only a few nails in each decking board, just enough to hold it down, and took a claw hammer and beat the nails back out and pulled them and told them to save the nails that weren't rusted to bad. He pried up a few more boards and Martin and Izak pulled them up by the end and backed out and pulled the nails.

Then the boatman showed them the mud that had accumulated on top of the hull planks and in between the thick hull framing and showed them how to use the shovel and hoe to scrape and dig the mud out. He explained that if the mud is left there, after a long time it would cause the planks to rot. He told them he would go and bring back some nails so they could put the decking back as they went along after they cleaned out the mud. He said he had helped do this the last time and told them he would be up in the boathouse if they had any problems.

For the next week, the boys worked on the barge and it was the hardest work that Martin had ever done but probably not the same for Izak, but it even had him shaking his head about it occasionally. The scraping off the thick layer of barnacles was the worst because it was lying on your back on the riverbank, underneath the barge that was blocked up. It was slow going and the scraped off barnacles fell down on them and all, but they got it done. Each day at the lunch with the boatmen, Izak was kidded about if he was ready to go back out in the fields and he may have had doubts but didn't show any.

To Martin's surprise, one day a few of the boatmen said Jacob had told them to get the hog out of the bottom of his boat. Martin didn't have to explain how Captain Jones said to do it because they had done it before and after a week of water and hot rocks, the keel was straight and the gunnels pushed back into place and the graceful shape was restored. Martin was getting much more help than he had expected but all the boatmen were interested in seeing it done. They moved a lot of stuff around in the boathouse to make room for it and blocked it up level and plumb to dry out. That same day, Jason came from town with the icebox for one of the supply boats and Martin and Izak helped him lift it into place and out again a few times to make some adjustments until it fit snuggly and then he installed the lid.

He showed Johnny how the block of ice for the lighthouse every week was to fit in the middle, leaving some room on each side for milk or other things to be kept cool during the trip. He said he was concerned about the added weight throwing off the balance of the boat and Johnny said they could shift other supply things to even it out. Martin admired the skillful work Jason had done. He used two layers of two inch slabs of cork to make the box with very little wood framing to keep the weight down but the whole thing was sturdy and after a few adjustments, it fit perfectly from one side of the boat to the other and with the lid on, was like another thwart to sit on. Jason said he would install the other one after they had tried this one out in case he needed to move it forward or back or anything and Johnny said they could use the same boat until they had the other ice chest done.

Martin had other things to do for a few weeks while his boat dried out good and left with Izak still coming every day to the boathouse, sweeping and cleaning and learning from mostly Johnny and Jacob about being a boatman and a reading lesson every few days from Maggie. Johnny gave Izak his first regular job getting and putting the block of ice on the boat every week. First they took a measuring stick and measured the inside of the new icebox in the boat then went to the sawdust hill and sawed two pieces because one big piece was to heavy and brought them back and set them in place. Johnny told Izak that he was the first ever official iceman and it was his job every week to saw it and have it in the boat and to do it not a long time before the boat left. He explained that the area on each side of the blocks of ice, inside the box, was for things that had to be kept cold for the trip, like dairy or meat.

The boat left that week with Johnny as the new helmsman. Jacob and Martin stood together on the bank and watched and listened to the chantey as they left and Martin asked Jacob if he wished he were going and Jacob said yes and no. He said he would miss being with the boatman on the trip to Tybee and seeing the Dyers and all but liked being with his family every day more. He said something that Martin didn't understand about his family might be changing soon and smiled slightly at Martin.

After watching the supply boat leave early, Martin walked home and saw that Henry and Claudia were up and went around to their door and went in. Henry said he was just who he wanted to see and he had good news that John had set a date for his coming to look at Mr. Johnsons townhome and they were planning on staying there and their mother and father were coming over from Beaufort for a couple days to see them while they were here. Martin saw how excited Henry was and asked where they were gonna stay and Henry said his kids were going to stay in his and Claudia's bedroom and John and Julia were staying in his kids bedroom with their kids and John's mother and father would stay in the guest room in the main area with Walter and Martha.

Henry said there was a lot to do to get ready for them and then a lot to do once they were here and Martin said he could help if he were needed and Henry said most things were things he had to do himself and thanked Martin for offering. Martin mentioned that they could ask John's father about the plantation that Alice and her family had run away from and Henry said it was his plan and asked if Martin would be in charge of that and Martin said he would. He said he would talk to Alice first and get as much information from her as he could, then talk to John's father about what he might know that could help them. Henry told Martin two things about John's father. Most importantly, he shared their views about anti-slavery and the other thing was that he knew most all the planters within fifty miles of Beaufort because they all had accounts at his Hardware store and were in every month. Henry told Martin that things were going to be very busy the next year or two, almost as busy as things were when their father first came over and started this whole thing. Martin told him that he had gone down early and watched the boat leave with Jacob and Henry was reminded that he needed to talk with Jacob about some things concerning the new ice house that Jason was building the parts for.

Claudia came in and told them she had some breakfast ready and they joined her at the small kitchen table. Martin didn't know he was hungry until he started eating and finished ahead of the others and Claudia gave him another biscuit and two more eggs. He said the work on the barge had given him a huge appetite lately. Henry added that he was also growing and had already gotten taller than him and they had been the same height before he went to Tybee.

Martin left Henry and went straight to Alice's house and asked if she had time to talk to him a while and she said she did and poured them both some tea. Martin saw that the bump in Alice's belly was easy to notice now and asked how she was doing and Alice said she was fine and thanks to Martin, the pain and emptiness she had felt inside about her family was gone and her days were full of thankfulness about it. She said she wasn't sure what was to become of it all and Martin said that he was here to talk about that. He explained that Henry was worried that if slavers ever found your family that the story of them and you could cause y'all to have to be returned to where you came from and you could have to go with your new child and without Johnny. He is intent on finding your owner and making him an offer to buy y'all that he couldn't refuse. He has asked me to set up the whole trip to do all that and I plan on finding out about him, if he is still around, and where his place is. He told her that John and his family were coming soon to make plans for their move to Savannah and his parents from Beaufort were coming to stay while they are here and that John's father knows all the plantation owners through his hardware business and that He hoped he could get some information from him to help them know how to go about things. Martin went on to say that he needed her to tell him what she could remember about the plantation and the owner. Martin added that she had already told him the name of the island but it was huge and even twice as big as Wilmington Island.

Alice said while she had just visited her parents, she had tried to talk to them about that time but they became very upset so she didn't continue but she did talk some to her brother and he remembered a lot more than her because he was older then. He talked about the fun time we had when our father would take us off the plantation in the wagon every month to a place called Tombee. His task was to drive the wagon and pick up the supplies there every month. I was very little but remember how much fun it was. The big creek came right up to that place and a supply boat would come from Beaufort and the Tombee plantation master would let us pick up our supplies there since it was closer for us than going to the landing on the other side of the island.

She said her brother said their place was about five miles north of Tombee. The master there and our old master were friends. Our father took us in the wagon with him and we played with the children there while he waited for the boat to come from Beaufort and it took all day and into the next day if the winds and tides were not favorable, and we would have to spend the night sometimes. Martin said that should help him find out what he needed from John's father and then he asked for the names of the two others who escaped with your family that were still with them on the island. Alice got a scrap of paper and wrote down what she had told Martin plus the names of the two others still with her family and "Mr. Mac. , their master, and the first names of the ones that ran away with them but had been killed at the massacre.

Alice asked when they were going and Martin said that Henry wanted to do it as soon as John and his family had come and gone and he reckoned that would be in about a month and there was gonna be a big meeting with everybody including you and Walter's lawyer friends while John and his family were here. He also told her about Maggie teaching Izak to read and write and how Henry wanted more people to learn how and probably was planning on asking her to help with that after your baby came. Alice told him that she would be glad to do it now and was glad Maggie would help. Martin was happy to have the information he needed from Alice and thanked her. He added that he would probably be taking her and the new baby to see her family, when the time came, and was already getting his new boat restored to do that with. He also reminded her that before that time, Ayana would be able to signal Charles with the new reflecting mirror that Daniel would be taking to her and showing her how to use. They could tell them when the baby comes and if they have a grandson or granddaughter or if there was ever a problem and this made Alice very happy. He took the paper and said goodbye and he would see her soon. While walking back home, Martin thought he would need to talk to John's father next, before he talked to Captain Ben about his boat and that may be a few weeks yet.

Henry was going out the door when Martin got home and he showed him the paper with the names and places that Alice had given him and Henry nodded in approval and then said his next thing was to talk to John's father when he came. Henry said he was going to see the man that owns the property next to the Milam plantation about buying fifty acres for the ice business and he would be back in the afternoon. Martin said he would be at the boathouse the rest of the day if Henry needed him and Henry said he wanted him and Jacob to go with him to town and see Jason at his shop because he wanted Jacob to supervise the ice house construction and he wanted him to see how things went together. He said he would have three carpenters to do most of the work and Jacob to be boss man and he was planning on going first thing in the morning and Martin could tell Jacob when he went to the boat house. Martin asked if they could stop by the stage depot while they were in town and see if Jehu was there and Henry said that was a great idea. Henry said he needed to go and if he didn't see him later, he would see him and Jacob in the morning.

Martin went inside to see his mother and father who were on the porch and his mother brought out tea and they sat for a little while. Martha said she was glad he stopped because it seemed almost like he lived someplace else because he was gone when they got up and gone somewhere or the other most of the time. Martin said he liked home but liked to go places too and he hoped to be going off regularly as a new crew member on Captain Ben's sharpie in less than a year or so and Martha said she wished he would wait a few more years. Walter said he would be sixteen then and that he had gone to sea when he was only fourteen and stayed away for years.

Martin said he liked that he would have the best of both worlds, home some helping Henry and off some learning about boats and the sea with Ashley and Ken. Martha said she wished he would help Henry all the time and forget the boat captain idea but she knew that Martin had his mind set on it and she wanted him to do for himself what he wanted, not what she wanted. Walter smiled at both Martha and Martin. Martha changed the subject and asked what about Daniel and Mary coming and Martin said they needed to come soon because Captain Ben could want him to start sooner. He said their father wanted Daniel to be away for almost a year so he could decide for himself if he wanted to be a light keeper or live on the mainland. Mary was a couple years younger and didn't have to decide so soon what she wanted, even though she seemed to know already and Martha asked what that was. Martin said she wanted to be the writer of books and decided her first to be about the history of hers and our families and Tybee and Savannah and the Milam place and the lighthouse and all the characters and events, starting from her great grandfather coming to Georgia from Scotland and Our father and his family in England. Martha said she sounded like she was like he was about boats and being a captain and Martin said he had not thought of that but she was right. Martin said she had read him the list of things she wanted to take notes about and it was a long list. Besides what he had already said, it included Ayana, the massacre and the story of Alice and her family in South Carolina, the duel, and the story and adventure of Mallie and his and our runaway and slaver chase and all that happened while he had been on Tybee, the ice business that Henry and John are starting and all the stories of the pilots and crews out on Tybee beach, and Martin said he couldn't remember the rest but she was really into it and she thinks she will be doing it for the next year or so. Martin said she had told him something that was a little hard for him to understand. She said it might be ten years or longer till she could publish a finished book about it all because what would be in the book could get them all in a heap of trouble. She has always read the newspapers from northern cities that Walter gets from ships that come into Savannah and send to her father and she thinks slavery will be eventually outlawed through the courts and slave days will be over.

He said she wanted to talk with you and father and all the people on the Milam place and some people from Savannah. She said it was going to be about the real things that happened. Martha said that was awfully ambitious of her and Martin said she was even as ambitious as Henry. Martin said he had only been around two girls near his age, Maggie and Mary, and both were ambitious. Maggie was a couple years older than him and she was practically like his sister since he was there a lot starting when he wasn't even a year old when Alice was taking care of him all the time. He said Mary was his age but knew a lot more about things than he did but he liked being around her and she seemed to like being around him. Martha smiled to herself because she had heard about what Margo had seen how things were when they were together. Martin also smiled to himself because he remembered what he felt when he was around Mary and he knew he was at least part of the reason she had wanted to come when Daniel came instead of waiting a year or so and he hadn't said so then but was glad of it and hoped she would.

Martin suggested that she and Walter should go on the supply boat and visit Charles and Margo for a week. This idea shocked both his mother and father and Martin went on to say that his father was home more now and he should see what he had done with the lighthouse and all and said they both would probably like the trip and the fresh sea air would be good for them both. Martin saw that what he said had surprised them. He asked his father if maybe they could ride together to his sailmaker friend in Savannah and take his old sail as a pattern to have a new one made and to ask him if he thought it possible to add a small jib sail. Walter said he would very much like to do that and he would be ready to do it whenever Martin wanted and added that a jib was an excellent idea. Martin hugged them both and walked out to go to the boathouse.

He left Walter and Martha with something to talk about, in having mentioned that they should go on a visit to Tybee. It was the furthest thing from their minds but was a fresh idea that stirred them both. Walter smiled and said that Martin's suggestion sounded like it was coming from a parent rather than a son and Martha laughed. She said maybe they should go for a visit. They always wanted Charles and Margo to come there but it was probably easier for them to go there, since Charles didn't have a "Henry" to run things, even though he would soon have Daniel to run things in a few years. Walter was still smiling, thinking about Martin's guileless wisdom that came out sometimes and said he thought his doctor would highly approve of him spending a week in fresh ocean air and that Martha would probably like a change of scenery too. Martha hadn't thought it all through but liked the idea of the good it might do Walter's health so she said that she would go if the Dyers would have them. She said there was some busy times ahead with John and his family and mother and father coming and the meeting they were planning and maybe after all that would be a good time to go off.

Martin found Jacob and Johnny at the boathouse doing a little repair work on the supply boat. Izak was sweeping and cleaning and looked up and smiled at Martin when he saw him. Jacob said that if Izak could op-

355

erate a pair of oars as good as he operated a broom, he would make a fine boatman and they laughed. Martin had gotten there at his favorite time, which was lunchtime. The food was always good and the conversation lively and a lot of laughing and carrying on. Lately a lot of the laughing and carrying on was at Izak, but he was smart and took it properly and laughed with them at himself. Martin told Jacob that Henry had wanted them to go with him to Savannah for about half the day tomorrow and Jacob said that would work for him and he hadn't been to Savannah for a while and would like that. Martin said they were going to see Jason, who was building the parts for the new icehouse and Henry wanted him to see how it will work because Jason is building thick panels, filled with cotton, kinda like a big icebox like we put on the back porch at Tybee, except a lot bigger so you could walk in and it would hold thousands of pounds of ice.

Martin said he had some time today and thought he would work on his boat. Johnny said he would help Martin get set up and show him a couple things and Martin said he didn't expect that but he would like it. The lunch cart was there and they sat and ate. One of the men asked Martin to tell a Tybee story and Martin said he could do a better job of it when his belly was full and he had a cup of strong yaupon and several men pushed the serving bowl toward Martin to be first served and one filled his cup with tea and told him to eat and drink and then tell his story and grinned at him.

While Martin was eating, he thought to himself what story he would tell them. There were several that they would enjoy. They liked hearing about the Indians and he had told about the slavers getting eaten up by gnats and they always liked to hear anything about Turtle Island. He knew what they would really like but it might take a little extra time but he thought Jacob would be ok with that, so while he was eating, he thought the story through a bit.

Martin finished up a little ahead of the rest and asked Jacob if he told a story that lasted a bit long would it be ok and Jacob said it would be fine. He told Martin to wait until they all had finished and got the table cleared and Martin had his cup filled again with yaupon. When everybody was finished and the table was cleared and cups refilled with tea, Martin started on a somber note by saying this was the most terrible of all that happened on Tybee and he wished that the laws were changed so it couldn't happen again and several men knew what he was about to tell about because they had heard it second hand. Martin went off subject some to explain the Indian word "Gereg" and all that this one word meant to the Indians and explained how it was just what they were doing now which was sharing air and how the Indians often started a story with thankfulness for the air that they were breathing that kept them alive and he wanted to take just a moment to feel the breath coming in them all and getting shared between them and be thankful for the breath and each other to share it with.

They listened to that and there was an air of clarity and reverence in understanding the magic of the moment and feeling it. Then he began to tell how he and Daniel had climbed up to the top of the lighthouse just about every day to look around at all the islands and rivers and to carry the heavy cans of lamp oil up for Charles. He told how Daniel was working on the lamp and he was looking out over the rivers and marsh and saw the two boats coming with the tide and having past Lazaretto and heading for Tybee and called for Daniel to come look. Many duels had happened on Tybee and Daniel knew right away what was happening, and in just ten minutes they landed on the beach not far from where Captain Jones' shanty is.

Then he told every detail about what happened from there on. Martin told nothing but the truth but spun each part of the story out a bit until it took about half an hour to tell it all. Unlike the story of the slavers and gnats that had everyone rolling around in laughter, this story had everyone in a different way. Martin told it with respect for the dead but also in a way that spoke against needless killing and the stupidity of a man's pride. He told of taking Henry and how the tide had washed away the blood but left the boot prints of the witnesses above the high water line and how that was where he had gotten the idea of fooling the slavers with the fake keel mark and the fake boot prints. He told them that they passed the spot every week where the men were buried after dying on the trip back to Savannah. It turned out to be a story he didn't enjoy telling as much as other stories because of the outcome but all at the table were mesmerized and thankful for hearing about it directly from Martin.

Johnny got up and nodded for Martin to follow him and they went inside and set up a place to work on his boat. Martin told Johnny he wanted to show him the old sail and got it and unfolded it out on the floor. He told Johnny that it was at least six times bigger than his other boats sail and he was planning on asking the sailmaker about a small jib sail and asked Johnny what he thought about that and he said it would work but he may need a sprit off the bow and explained to Martin how that would extend the length of the boat so he could have room in front of the mast for a jib sail. He walked over to the boats bow and held his arm out and said it would be a flat hardwood board about five feet long with about half fixed to the boat and about half sticking out and a piece of hardware at the end to fasten the foot of the jib sail to. Johnny said he thought a jib sail would work if it was not to big so it didn't get fouled up in the mainsail.

Johnny laid the mast out on the floor and the old sail by it like it would be set up and a stick where the bow sprit would be and measured with a stick how far the added bowsprit would stick out and how much room there would be for a jib. Johnny broke the stick off to what length the bottom of the jib could be and then from a point about two feet down from the top of the mast he laid a thin rope from there to the end of where the end of the bow sprit would be and cut the rope off at that length and gave Martin the rope and told him that was the longest length of the jib and handed him the stick and told him that was the length of the jib foot and then another piece of rope the length of the third side of the sail. Then, Johnny gave Martin a few pieces of glass shards and showed him how to scrape away the old surface of the wood along the gunwales of his boat and Martin spent the rest of the day doing that.

When Martin got home his mother was outside in the garden pulling some onions. She told Martin right away that she and Walter decided to take his advice and go to Tybee for a week. She said Walter couldn't signal today because it was too cloudy but would just wait and send a letter on next week's boat. She told Martin how glad she was that he had suggested it because it was just what they needed and what the doctor would want for his father. Martin said that if the salt air helped his father that they should go regularly and his mother agreed. She said she was a bit uneasy about being in the Dyers way and all but her worries were not as important as Walters health. She told him she had made his favorite tonight and he asked if it was chicken potpie and she said it was.

The next morning Martin quietly left the house and walked around to Henry's end and saw the lamp light in the kitchen and went in and Claudia said they had been waiting on him and she had breakfast ready. The stove was hot and the eggs sizzled when she cracked open a half dozen for Henry and Martin. She had already cooked the bacon and had it laid out on big biscuits that had been sliced in half and put three eggs on each and added a handful of green onions and put the biscuits back together and served it up. She had made some coffee and asked Martin if coffee was ok instead of yaupon and he said that was fine.

They were about done and Jacob came to the door and Claudia motioned for him to come on in and asked if he wanted a biscuit and he said Ellie had filled him up good but he asked what that smell was and Claudia said it was a new drink called coffee and asked if he would like to try some and he said it sure smelled good and she poured him a cup full. Henry said he liked it in the morning but still preferred yaupon in the afternoon. Jacob sipped some and made a funny face but sipped it again and said it was ok. They finished up breakfast and Willy had the carriage outside for them to take and they left as the sun was just beginning to light the sky. In a little less than an hour they were at Jason's shop and heard him and two helpers hammering and saw the big thick panels stacked up high in the shop.

Jason stopped when he saw them and told his helpers to clean up a bit while he talked with them. Jason knew Martin and had met Jacob when he was out to put the cork ice chest in the supply boat. He asked Jacob how it worked and Jacob said he didn't go on that trip but Johnny said it worked very good. He said the ice didn't melt hardly at all. Jason said he would get started on the second one as soon as he finished these panels. Henry told him that Jacob would be building the foundation and floor and then setting the panels and door, then building the roof and that he wanted Jacob to see what the panels were like. Jason got the two sheets of plans he had drawn and Henry asked him how many of the panels he had made and Jason said he wished he had more done but it was slow going.

Henry said that was good because he wanted to make the icehouse a little smaller than planned and went on to tell Jason that they were going to set up the ice business on a separate piece of property next to the Milam place and build an even bigger ice house there. He said this ice house would be for the Milam place's own use but in the beginning for their customers too, until they had the bigger one built. Jason said he had about half the panels done and Henry looked at the plan and said they could shorten the length of the building by four panels and the width by four panels so that would mean eight less panels and Jason said that was no problem. Jason showed the floor plan to Jacob and Jason put an "x" on the eight panels to leave off.

Jacob asked Jason for a stick to measure the panels with and Jason went to a pile of scrapes, knowing what Jacob would do and handed it to him with a charcoal marker and Jacob marked the stick at the width of a panel and Jason had a handsaw ready for him to cut it to length and then Jacob put the same stick down on a panel and marked the end and then moved the stick up and marked the end again and moved it up and marked it where it met the top edge.

After the width and length were measured, he marked the thickness of the panel on the back of the stick. Jason told Jacob that the floor he built could be a little too big and they could measure and make a filler panel after all the panels were set and standing. Jacob understood what he meant. Jason did a little sketch and said that a thick red cedar sill all around the floor that the panels would sit on would be good so the concrete floor would go against it and the cedar wont rot and it would be good if the floor joist and decking was made from red cedar too. Next, Jacob went over to a finished panel and hefted one end to check its weight and Jason said two men could pick it up but four men would be better. He said it was cumbersome because they were a foot and a half thick. Henry added that he would get cypress boards for sheathing the outside and the materials for the roof framing and decking and shingles. Jason called his helpers and asked them to show how they were filling the panels with cotton.

The two men started shoving arm loads of cotton from a big cotton bale into a panel that was all put together except for the top piece and then tamping it down with a pole with a flat board on the end. Jason said these were easy to build but the only problem was how much space it took up in his shop. Henry said he could go ahead and have the panels he had made taken out to the site and cover them to free up some space for him. Jason said that it was a good idea and Henry said he would send for the panels. He asked Jacob if he had any questions and Jacob said he didn't and Henry said they would be going then and thanked Jason.

Next, they headed for the stage depot, hoping to find Jehu. Henry told Martin that if Jehu was there to invite him to visit in a couple weeks after John and his family had come and gone. As they got close, Martin was the first to see Jehu sitting out front of the station. He jumped down from the carriage and went and shook Jehu's hand, who lit up when he saw Martin. Henry and Jacob came over and Jehu shook Henry's hand and Martin introduced Jacob. First, Martin and Jehu started jabbering in strong Geechee dialect. Martin said something to Jacob and the three of them jabbered and laughed so loud that the stationmaster came out to see what was going on.

He recognized Henry and asked if anything was wrong and Henry said quite the contrary and said that his younger brother had gotten to know Jehu on their trip from Darien on the stage and the man remained a bit puzzled at a young white boy was carrying on so with two black men. One he assumed was a slave of Henry's and Jehu, who was a freeman, but who he considered no more than a slave. Henry saw the furrowed brow of the stationmaster and assured him that they were okay and then handed him two sealed letters to be sent on the next stage to Charleston for Professor Albert McWilliamson and John in Darien. He was inviting Albert to come while John was here, leaving off anything about a meeting. The station master calmed a bit but told Henry that he didn't like Jehu carousing with his customers and that his job was with the horses and he cursed at Jehu and went back inside.

Henry and Martin exchanged a glance of understanding about Jehu's situation and Henry said they should help Jehu find a place where he was appreciated. Martin went back to talking to Jehu and told about them needing a good man for their horses and asked if he could come out to see them in a couple weeks. Jehu glanced to see if the station master was not coming and told Martin that he would come and Martin asked him what days he was usually here at the station and Jehu said every Sunday.

Martin told him that he would pick him up on the fourth Sunday from then in the morning and Jehu shook his head in understanding. The stationmaster came back out and told Jehu that he had more to do than stand around all day and Henry said they were just leaving. Martin looked at Jehu and nodded and Jehu nodded back and smiled and followed the stationmaster back inside. Henry and Jacob and Martin left for home.

Henry wanted their trusted professor from college to come while John was there and he wanted Walter's old lawyer friends out to meet him while he was there and he wanted council from them all together. Henry was extra busy the next few days with getting things ready for John and his family. He let Mr. Johnson know that John was coming to look at his townhome and also set up a time that John and Julia could visit with the teacher at the school that he and Martin had gone to and where his kids were going to. He went by to see Walters's old friends to see if they would come to the meeting at the Milam's. They said they would come to the meeting. Henry had also gotten a letter from Thomas, the engineer from Boston, that he would be coming the week John was there and wanted to meet with him about the new ice business.

362

16.
VISITORS

John had booked the whole stagecoach for his family and they arrived late in the day and worn out and sore from the trip that had started at three-thirty in the morning. Henry picked them up at the depot and by the time Henry got them back to the Milam plantation, it was late and by the time they got cleaned up a bit and had some food it was near midnight and they were travel weary and went to bed without much talk and visiting.

Morning came and Henry and Claudia were up early and Martin had come around to have breakfast with them and they talked quietly so John and Julia could sleep on a bit. After an hour or so, they got up and Claudia made tea. John asked what the unusual smell was and Henry said it was a new drink from South America called coffee and offered him some and John said he would try a bit. Henry said he had come to like it. John tasted it and wasn't sure if he liked it but asked for some more.

After breakfast, Henry asked John and Martin to go for a walk and so they walked over to the horse barn. Henry wanted to talk with John about the week without waking their kids and he wanted to show John some things. He told Martin that he didn't think he would want to come to the meeting but that he was welcome but he wanted him to go along so he could hear and learn about what would be happening because he should know. Henry added that he valued Martin's understanding on things because it was usually simpler than his. Martin said he didn't think he could know more than Henry and Henry said that ever since their trip to Darien, he had begun to learn some important things from him and John said he too was impressed with Martin's ideas. When they got to the barn, Henry showed John the huge pile of cork slabs and told how good it had worked keeping the ice from melting in their first time trying it out on the supply boat ice chest and the current plan was to make ice boxes with it. He also showed John the huge pile of sawdust where the current supply of ice was buried and said soon they would have an icehouse, with walls a foot and a half thick, and stuffed tight with cotton for insulation and walked over to the shed roof coming off the barn and showed John one of the panels he had just brought over from Jason's shop.

He said the plan he had was for this to be the icehouse for the Milam place, as well as ice storage for their new ice business, temporarily. He added that Jason would start on the panels for the big icehouse as soon as the purchase was finalized on their new property next door. Both John and Martin were impressed with all Henry had done and planned to do and his enthusiasm for it. Then he asked John if they wanted to go and see the townhouse today and that Mr. Johnson said he would stay home, so they could come by anytime and he had told him that it probably would be today or tomorrow. John said he would like to do it today if Julia did and he suspected she would because she was quite curious about it, even more than him.

John had got in so late that Henry had not mentioned that Albert was coming to the meeting and John was most happy to hear that. He also mentioned that Thomas just happened to be coming during the week and he wanted to meet with Henry about some things and Henry said he was glad John was there to be involved in that. Martin said he was glad that Henry and John were doing such great things and also glad he didn't have to go to any meetings because it was hard for him to sit and listen to business talk. Henry laughed and told John that all Martin could sit and listen to was about boats. They walked back to the house and found everybody up and much talk and good cheer going on and kids playing outside.

Alice had come over and it was just now showing good that she was pregnant. Martin noticed that she glowed even more than usual and asked if she had decided on a name yet and Alice said she hadn't but she would like suggestions if he had any. Martin asked John if he would make ice cream while he was here and John said he would if they had milk and sugar and eggs and Martin said they had enough of those things to make ice cream for the whole place and once he had learned the recipe from John, he intended on doing just that and then on his next trip to Tybee, do it for the Dyers too. Henry said he hoped that everybody in the south would soon have ice for ice cream. John's daughters, just outside in the yard, heard the word ice cream and began screaming ice cream, ice cream, because they loved it so much and it was always a celebratory time when they had it. Henry's kids hadn't had it but were curious about it since it sounded like fun.

John told Julia that Henry had said that they could look at the townhome today or tomorrow and he wasn't surprised that she said today. Henry said they could have some lunch first and he had already asked his mother if she and Walter could watch the kids. Henry reminded them that Mr. Johnson said he would stay home today and tomorrow so if they wanted to go back and look again tomorrow, that would be fine. Julia said she just wanted something that had been kept up and clean and she and

John wanted to build a new home in a year or two but didn't know where or what and this was to be something for them until they got a better understanding of the area.

She told Henry that there was one thing that she had been worrying about concerning the move, even more than what house they would live in and that was about Mable and her brother James. She said that Mable wanted to come with them and from what Henry had told them, there could be accommodation for her in the townhome at street level. Henry said the main level had the living room and kitchen and a water closet and a room that Mr. Johnson was using for his bedroom which could be an office for John and the two bedrooms upstairs for them in one and the two girls in the other.

Henry said that the street level would need a little work to be livable but had two windows on the front and back and a small window on each side and could be, with only a few things done be made quite comfortable for Mable and James. Julia said it was more than the accommodations that worried Mable. Mable was more than ready to leave Darien because she had struggled there for so long to keep the taxes paid and the house up and all, but she was worried about James. Mable said he was shy and had never gotten out much and when he did, it was out in the river. Julia said he did anything Mable asked him to do and followed her lead in things but she knew he would be uncomfortable in a new town and settings because he didn't get on with people well. He was quite shy.

Claudia asked Henry if there might be a place for him here and Henry said he could find him something. Julia said she didn't know if he could do without Mable. Martin had been listening in to the conversation and told Henry that Jehu would be needing a helper at the new place. Julia asked who was Jehu and Martin said he was a freed slave that had been the coach driver on their trip back from Darien and they wanted him to come work in the new ice business. Henry said that Martin's suggestion was a good one and the story of Jehu was a long one and he would tell them about it on the carriage ride to Savannah later, but that could be a perfect paring.

Walter had been watching the children play outside and Martha prepared an early lunch so Henry and Claudia and John and Julia could go to Savannah to look at the townhouse. While they were eating, Martin went for the carriage and had it out front and waiting. After the ladies freshened up, they left for Savannah. Henry went slowly while he told the story of Jehu and how they had visited him a few days ago and his boss man was mean spirited and ugly to him. Julia said she had learned that free blacks were given a hard time because their freedom might unsettle the traditional system of enslavement and opportunity was rare for a free black in the south and they were treated badly.

She said that in Darien, Mable and her brother were the last of the descendants of black families that were living there that had been guaranteed their freedom after the prohibition of slavery was lifted. Since then, most families that had been part of that decree were shut out and taxed off their land because they could not adapt in a society and economy that discriminated heavily against them and used slave labor. She said that Mable and James came close to losing what was left of their home place. Henry asked what would become of the place after they left and Julia said she didn't know but Mable said that most of her memories were of hard times but she would hate to see it go because her family had worked so hard to keep it. Henry said that she should keep it and make sure the taxes are paid in full so that it couldn't be taken away. He said that he would try to work something out on the new place for James to help Jehu and have a place to stay there and he would get a payday every week. Then, Henry told Jehu's background story and his and Martin's trip from Darien. Julia said that James and Jehu might be the perfect companions for each other.

Mr. Johnson was in the same place he was when Henry first met him, standing by and inspecting his camellias. He didn't hear them until they were close, then was startled and recognized Henry and was happy. He welcomed them into the courtyard and Henry introduced John and Julia. He had met Claudia when he had come out with the cork delivery. He told Henry to look at how good his camellias had been doing since he had been sprinkling them lightly with the incoming tidewater from the river like he had recommended.

He said that he had thought that if he sold his place he would dig up the camellias and take them with him but he decided that he would just ask whoever bought the place if he could come by sometimes and see them, because he was worried about them surviving the transplant. Julia answered quickly that if they became the new owners that she would hope he came by often and she would look with him. Mr. Johnson said that the Milam's had always been good luck for him and it would seem that by her comments that it would continue. He asked them in. After the first flight of stairs up, he was out of breath and had to stop for a few moments. He said the stairs were why he needed to move as far as he was concerned but his children had other reasons.

He led them in and they saw the study that he was using for his bedroom and the living room and kitchen and water closet and dining room. The rooms were smaller than their house in Darien but Julia was expecting that. What she liked was that it smelled fresh and clean. He said he liked that it was just across from Wright Square and he enjoyed it like it was his yard that the city kept it up and beautified. Next they went upstairs, and Julia was surprised that those rooms were similar in size to their current bedrooms. Julia was pleased with what she had seen but still had to see the ground floor, but Mr. Johnson didn't need to go down any more stairs but should rest on the main level. He said that was fine and he sat and rested.

One odd thing was that there were two steps down from the courtyard level to the interior floor level, so the home was set down below the side walk and street level about two feet. Henry said a lot of the homes were built like that because it helped them stay cool in the hot summer months. John liked that the lower part of the walls were a combination of ballast stone and brick and said they were doing that in Darien now because they were getting so much ballast stone from the ships coming to pick up timber. He also commented that this lower level was plenty big enough for Mable to have a living area and room for them to store some things. He asked Julia what she thought about the whole place and she said it wasn't the home of her dreams but she would be happy with it and John said he would be too.

Mr. Johnson was at the dining room table when they came back up and had the property deed laid out on the table. He smiled at Julia and said with pleasant confidence that he knew this was right for them. He was so jovial and certain about it all that it made the four of them smile at his forth rightness. John said they did want it and were pleased with the property and him. Mr. Johnson said he had checked on similar sales in the past year to ascertain a fair market price and had a list with seven townhomes and their addresses and their selling prices. In more of his forth rightness he showed them the formula of how he decided on a price and that was to add the seven selling prices together and then dividing by seven and then adding five percent for his location across from the square. John was impressed with the fairness of his method and reached out to shake on the deal.

John told him that he would move his holdings from the bank in Darien to the bank here and could pay him their agreed sum in about a month and give him a security deposit for now. Henry said they could probably do something now from his bank here in Savannah. Mr. Johnson said that he had the same bank and would leave the deed there for them to draw up the contract and attend to all the details to finalize things. He repeated that everything the Milam's had anything to do with turned out good for him. Henry said he appreciated that and the cork they purchased from him was premium value and worked out just right for them. He also said that he should come out to see them more often and Mr. Johnson said that he might need to do that to see Walter because he hadn't seen much of him at their favorite tavern lately.

John wrote down the payment information and asked Henry what else he would need to secure a bank note for the amount he showed him written on the paper and Henry said that since John hadn't begun using that bank yet, he would vouch for the total amount until he got his holdings moved into the bank after he got moved up. Mr. Johnson was impressed with Henry's actions and said everyone needed friends like him. They all thanked Mr. Johnson and Henry said they would go by the bank today and do their part. Mr. Johnson said he would walk with them down because he wanted to have a few more words with his camellias and they laughed but knew he meant it.

Henry asked if they wanted to walk across the street to the square and they said it would be nice. Henry pointed out the British Governor Wrights tall statue and said that he administered the orders from King Charles himself for the establishment of the Milam place and the finance of the properties and picked the slaves from his own place and granted them to Walter. He and Walter were best of friends and when the patriots arrested Governor Wright during a temporary takeover, Walter saw that he was released from a dirty jail and kept under his own house arrest instead. Henry said there were still many alive here who remembered his fair and generous ways with the people of the city before the war. When the British soon regained control of the city, Governor Wright extended many favors to Walter. They remained friends and regularly exchanged letters, even after the war and even after Walter changed and pledged his loyalty to America. Next, Henry pointed to a large piece of granite rock and said that it marked the final resting place of a man that was more important to Savannah than Governor Wright and Walter or anybody else and that was the great Yamacraw leader, Tomochichi. He went on to tell of how he moved his village over for Oglethorpe to set up and layout Savannah on this high bluff. Henry went on and on about the many times and ways that Tomochichi had saved the new immigrants from starvation and times when the natives were ready and willing to kill them all over disputes. He said that Walter had a couple favorite stories about Tomochichi but he couldn't tell them as good as Walter but would ask him to tell them after John's Mother and father and Albert were here. John and Julia were quite entertained and impressed at the rich history of the spot they would soon be living near and by Henry's knowledge of it and told him so.

Henry admitted that he was almost all business but still had a sense of place and pride and Claudia said she liked hearing that from him. Julia said this had sure happened fast and she was glad of it and she thought they would really like the square, especially the girls. Henry said they could go to the bank next because it was close and then stop by the school on the way back home.

Henry took John into the bank while the ladies walked to another square near the bank. Everyone in the bank paused and said hello to Henry and when Malden Peterson, the president, heard the talk, he came out of his office and when he saw who it was he invited them in. Henry introduced John to the bank president and told of them being at the College of Charleston together and John and his family moving to Savannah in a few weeks and he and John being business partners in a new business coming soon but were not ready to announce what it was yet. Mr. Peterson said they had plenty of room for money and Henry said he was there to make some more room and showed him the figures John had written down and who the note was to be payable to and that it was to come from his account and he and John could settle up after John got moved up and opened his own account. Mr. Peters said that told him something about their friendship and that would be somewhat of a bridge loan and he would let him know when the paperwork would be ready for Henry to sign. He said Mr. Johnson had been a customer since the bank had opened and Walter Milam had been too and he already told me that he thought that he would be selling his townhome to a friend of yours. Henry smiled and said that John and his wife hadn't even looked at the place until just over an hour ago. Mr. Peters smiled back and said that Mr. Johnson had always been a man that was quite sure of himself and was seldom wrong. Henry thanked him and John told him he would be seeing him about his banking in a few weeks.

Claudia and Julia were just getting back from their walk as they left the bank and Henry said the school master, Mr. Peeler, had said that they could stop by anytime when Henry had told him about John and Julia coming and their kids starting school. Henry had told him then that he would be keeping his kids out of school that week while they were here. The first thing Mr. Peeler asked when he saw Henry was if his kids were doing the homework he had assigned them to do while they were out, and Henry said they were. He introduced John and Julia and Mr. Peeler asked them what their girls names were and what were their ages. He said they would have a full schoolhouse with two additional students but said there would be no less education because of that. Mr. Peeler told that Henry was one of the best students he had ever had and his brother was the biggest challenge he ever had, and quickly said he meant no harm by that and Henry said that Mr. Peeler should be just as proud or even more so with his effort to teach Martin as he was for him and that the Milam's were all grateful for his efforts. He told Mr. Peeler how his mother dealt with Martin's difficulties, not seeing things from the correct direction. She knew that Martin was obsessed with all things nautical (It was actually Alice but Henry didn't want to tell of her being Martin's teacher) and drew a compass rose on the chalk board and told Martin that words and sentences started in the east and went west and pages of words and sentences started in the north and went south and that helped him a lot. Mr. Peeler was astonished because he could still vividly remember Martin starting or trying to pronounce or write his words in the wrong way and he could not forget his frustration and sometimes anguish trying to correct him.

Henry said all Martin cared about was boats and learning to be a ship captain and had already been promised a position on a small trading vessel out of Savannah, captained by a friend of Walters. Mr. Peeler said everyone in Savannah was a friend of Walter including himself and he thought about it every cool morning when he lit the beautiful wood heater Walter had shipped in from England and given to the school. Mr. Peeler said how nice it was that they came by and he looked forward to their girls coming to the school but he needed to get back to his students. He told Henry to say hello to Martin and he wished he could have thought of the compass rose idea himself.

As they left, Julia thanked Henry for arranging that because it really made her feel good about their girls going there. She added that they were thankful as well for him helping with the townhome and school and all and Henry said they would do the same for him and his family. He said he knew it must be a lot of work to move and wanted to help in every way he could. John said Savannah was where he wanted to come right out of school but the job in Darien came up and it ended up being good because he made more money than he would have thought possible. Henry added that had he come to Savannah, they would not know about ice and he thought they would make a lot of money from it. Claudia said how much they liked them coming because they knew a lot of people in Savannah and were on many invitation lists but didn't have many really good friends at all.

Their town business was done with plenty of day left and Henry steered toward home. He said he had seen the basket of sweet potatoes in his mother's kitchen and that usually meant sweet potato casserole and it was his favorite and he heard Alice mention something about Ellie bringing something she cooked over and everything Ellie made was delicious. John said he hoped his parents would get in early today from Beaufort and Henry said there was no rain in the forecast and hadn't been much, so the roads are in good shape, so they should be in well before dark. He said Willy has instructions to be there, waiting to bring them out as soon as they get in. Henry said that Martin was almost as excited about John teaching him how to make ice cream as he is about boats and that's a lot. John said he wrote out the recipe for him as Henry had requested and that he had a surprise for Martin. Henry said he wanted it for now but was mostly interested in making it for the Dyers at the lighthouse and he didn't tell them what it was but promised them a very special treat when he came back.

Julia asked Henry how he felt about Martin going off on a ship when he was barely sixteen and Henry said that was Martin's passion and had always heard of his father going at only fourteen and he was a determined and capable young man. He said Walter went off on a war ship with a hundred men for a year or two or more, into and over the vast oceans, but Martin will only be going on short trips up and down the coast on a fifty five foot boat with only two other sailors. He will sleep more than half his nights tied to a dock. Claudia said he would be safer on the nights in the ocean because a seaport can be a rough place. Henry said he would be a lot more concerned if he didn't know the skill and character of the two sailors he would be with and probably would have advised him to wait until later otherwise. He will be at home, in between trips, and that will be good for him and all of us because the Milam place always seems better with Martin around.

He went on to say there was something else happening in Martin's life that he hadn't spoken to any of us about, but Margo Dyer, in a letter to Martha, talked about how special things happened between Martin and their daughter Mary while he was at Tybee. Her and her brother are coming for a long visit soon, partly to stay with us and then to stay with their relatives in Savannah. Claudia said that might be interesting and then said that in a letter, Margo said that all Mary could think about was this book she was writing about Savannah, the Milam plantation, and the lighthouse and the last of the Guale Indians across the river and the story of Alice and the story of her own light keeper parents and ancestors and the stories of the pilots and crews on the beach and some from our own blind weatherman, "Captain Sandy."

Julia said that was an ambitious project for anyone, especially a young girl and Henry said she was very bright and being in the isolated environment of the lighthouse on Tybee, she had read most of the books from their library that we would send down and pick up on the supply boat, plus books from the Savannah library. Henry said it was unusual because she knew she would have to keep all her documented notes hidden until years later when she was sure that slavery would be abolished. Julia said that from what they had said about Mary, she would look forward to meeting her. They were about a quarter mile from the house and Claudia said she could hear the children laughing and squealing and it really sounded good and she said she was very pleased that their kids would grow up knowing each other.

Walter and Martha and Alice and Ellie and Martin were out on the porch drinking ice yaupon, watching the children play when the carriage pulled up with the two couples. Ellie had brought her young son, Thomas, who was a regular playmate of Henry's kids. Walter said from the look on their faces, everything went as planned and John said that it went even better and said his friend, Mr. Johnson, was a fine fellow. Walter said he was even finer after some rum.

Julia told Martha she was happy with the house and they had gone by the school and met the schoolmaster and was happy with him. She added that she was particularly happy about the beautiful square across from the house and the brick street that was in front of their house and surrounded the square. She said they had walked through the square and Henry had given them a tour with history lessons and also said that Walter might tell us the story of Tomochichi, after he had pointed out his grave marked by the big rock.

Walter overheard that and said he would be glad to right now and John said if he didn't mind, could he wait until his parents and Albert got here. Walter said he liked a bigger audience and would gladly wait until the appropriate time. John went on about how smoothly the sale agreement went and said the price settled on was good for both them and Mr. Johnson and Henry had been generous to bridge the payment until they were moved up and he became a bank customer.

John and Julia had met Alice before, but not Ellie and Martha who introduced her to them. Julia said she had heard about Ellie being the best cook in Savannah and how she had made something special for their supper. Ellie said she had spent all day yesterday preparing it and brought it over this morning and it would need to be warmed for supper and was now in the Milam's icebox.

She said she wasn't going to say what it was but it was everybody's favorite and took a long time to prepare. John said that talking about favorite foods made him remember something and went back into his room and brought out a narrow but large box and set it down in front of Martin and handed him a folded paper.

Martin was surprised and John told him to read the paper first, and then open the box. The heading on the paper said, "Ice Cream Churn" and Martin laughed and studied the recipe written on the paper. He then pulled the top of the box open and lifted out a tall tin container and a crank and rod with blades that fit down in the tin container into a notch at the bottom. He remembered John telling about it when they were in Darien. John said he had conspired with Henry to make sure y'all had the right size container for this to go inside of and have enough room all around for ice and salt. Martin smiled at Henry and said he had wondered what Henry was doing with the big crock he had seen him bring into the house from the outside kitchen. John said he would help Martin the first time he did it and that it was easier to use and worked much better than the makeshift system he had used in Darien.

17.
THE MEETING

Henry asked his father if he would come with him and John to his office and talk about the next few days. Walter said he would like that. Once they were comfortable, Henry said that Albert was arriving from Charleston the next day and he planned to pick him up, take him to the inn, and ask him to come out the next day. He thought that his lawyer friends could come then too. Walter said they were waiting to hear his plans and he would send a message to let them know when to come. Walter thanked Henry for setting up the meeting. Henry said it was Martin had a lot to do with it. Walter said he knew and smiled, thinking of Martin.

The meeting would fulfill the hopes and intentions he had held since he had first come to Savannah, and that was for the betterment of all the people on the Milam plantation. He said he had some things to say but would wait until everyone was gathered. He said that he would preside over the upcoming gathering, but he would be taking a back seat in future meetings and it would be up to them to carry on. He wanted to spend more time with Martha and do some things he had put off. One was to spend time by the ocean and he and Martha had decided to spend a week at the lighthouse in a few weeks, and he wanted to do that as regularly as he could. His doctor had said that the ocean air would probably help him live longer.

He probably didn't have to say it, but he emphasized the importance of the meeting being a complete secret. Other than us and our families, only Johnny and Jacob will have any idea of what is going on. If our activities became known, it would be considered treasonous and we would charged with serious offences and face jail and expulsion. It would mean the end of the Milam place, and those we tried to help could be cast out into awful circumstances. Families would be separated and sent off to new owners. I would sooner die than have that happen because I love them as I love my own family. It would be the end of the Milam place and all that we have done right in the past and all that we could hope to do right in the future. Henry agreed and said that he was having Johnny and Jacob patrol the perimeter during the meeting. The sound of horses and the creaking of a wagon brakes caught their attention. Walter said that must be John's parents, and Henry said they had a fast trip.

John's mother and father climbed down from the wagon, and Martin helped Willy unload all the cases and boxes they had brought. They hadn't seen their grandkids for so long that, for a moment, they weren't sure which ones were theirs. Richard Wilcox was visibly stooped and said the long coach ride had stove his back up. Henry said they would go for a walk shortly. Walter said he had some fine rum that would make it feel better and reached out to shake hands with Richard. Helen Wilcox saw Martha and walked close and hugged her and thanked her for having them. She then found her two grandchildren and got down to their level and kissed and hugged them. Martha introduced the rest of the group including Alice and Ellie and her children. Walter told Richard to follow him and walk around the house once or twice to get loosened up. The whole group followed and came back around to the porch where Martha had brought out extra chairs and a small table and chair set for the children. Henry had a bucket of chipped ice waiting in the icebox ready for iced yaupon. He brought it out to the big table and enjoyed filling so many mugs with ice and tea and then squeezing some lemon from the yard into each one. The Wilcox's were highly impressed but not surprised because John had been telling them about ice, but they hadn't had any yet. Richard said that everybody around Beaufort was drinking yaupon now and he was selling boxes of it in his store and getting orders for it from all over. He didn't know why they just didn't pick it themselves because it grew everywhere. He sipped the yaupon with ice and smiled and said he hoped they all would be having ice in their tea soon, and Henry said they would. Henry had a big pitcher full of tea with sugar and lemon and ice and kept everyone's glass full. Martha and Helen were beaming at the whole gathering, particularly at the children. Martha said that in the excitement she had forgotten some appetizers that she had prepared. Claudia told her to stay seated and she would get them. She went to the kitchen and returned with a stack of small plates and then a big platter of very thin little yellow cheese biscuits with lightly browned crispy edges and a hint of finely ground red pepper over the tops; Julia helped her serve. They served Helen and Martha first, and Helen asked what they were. Martha said it was an old family recipe of just three ingredients - very thin buttermilk biscuits with some cheddar cheese mixed in and then baked and a sprinkle of red pepper added. Helen tasted one but didn't know what to think. She tried another one and said it was the best appetizer she had ever had and she had never had anything like it. The platter got emptied quickly, and Martha said that she had learned not to make too many because folks filled up on them before the main meal and that today's supper was something special that Ellie made. Walter suggested that they walk down to the river before supper, and all agreed it was a good idea. Ellie told them all to go but that she would stay and prepare what she had made for supper. She said she would have it all out on the table when they got back.

The whole group walked slowly, and Walter shared personal stories. He spoke about the first time he had come to the spot. He had been looking for a place to set up many years ago, and this was a perfect stretch of high ground, close to Tybee, with thick fertile soil. It had a bluff where from the third floor the new light beam in the Tybee lighthouse was visible in the east and the bluff on which Savannah sat visible in the west. And it was on a deep river just a short distance from the Savannah River so a supply boat could be rowed every week, four hours with the tide, to the Lazaretto Landing, on the west side of Tybee, to bring food and supplies to the lighthouse. He described how he and his senior officers had anchored and lived aboard their ship while the land was cleared, the buildings built, and the place was set up to support itself and the Tybee Lighthouse operation. He told about the changes to their plans that the war had brought and how they had to hide the new light beam equipment for the duration. He spoke about how he had decided to become an American and how he had met Martha. Everyone was mesmerized and highly entertained by his stories, even his family who had heard them many times. Martin thought to himself what a grand idea Mary had about writing this story and the many things and people surrounding it all. He saw Mary in his mind's eye and felt a longing to see her again. He remembered the last time they had walked down to the beach together and the long kiss afterwards. He snapped out of his daydreaming when he heard his father mention his name in his story.

Richard asked Walter what became of his ship. Walter said it was confiscated by the British and scuttled just a mile south of here to block Patriots from coming up the Wilmington River as a backway to Savannah. He said that after the war it was broken up and removed to open up navigation along the Wilmington River again.

Walter could have gone on and on, but Martha nodded at him, and he understood that it was time to head back to the house. When they got there, Ellie had outdone herself. The table had three big platters, full of deviled crabs, in their big, beautiful shells, now turned red from cooking. She had boiled the crabs the day before, and she and Alice had spent the whole day removing the meat. They had added all the tasty ingredients to the mix and stored it in two big bowls in the icebox. While the group was following Walter, she had filled sixty of the crab shells with the mix. While they baked in the oven, she had set the porch table with all the bowls of other things Martha had made. It was quite a presentation and impressed and amazed the group. Martha said she should have stayed to help, but Ellie said it was not that much work and she liked doing it. She said there were still a few things to do, but Martha told her in a stern but lighthearted way to just sit herself down and she and Claudia would finish up. Martha poured Ellie a cup of yaupon with a little rum and hugged her and said she was not to do another thing except eat. After a few more dishes were set out, everyone sat down and enjoyed the big meal. Henry's favorite was the sweet potato casserole, and everybody couldn't stop saying how good the deviled crabs were.

Henry finished up ahead of the others and made a big pot of coffee and a pot of yaupon to have with the two big blackberry pies. The Wilcox's were very full and impressed by the good cooking and could not say enough about how good it all was and how thankful they were for the Milam's having them there. Ellie and Alice said they needed to go, so Martha went to the kitchen to get bowls to fill with every different leftover to take home for their family's supper. Alice said she would miss Walter's Tomochichi story but had heard it and would probably hear it another time; she hugged Walter and everyone there. Ellie did the same and said they should, on another night, ask Martin to tell a Tybee story and that he had become such a good storyteller. Martin told her that Thomas probably would like to stay and play until dark with the other kids and he would walk him home. Ellie said that he could, and Thomas smiled big and happy, showing his white teeth. Martin smiled to himself, noticing how when Thomas smiled big, he looked like his father.

After dark and after everyone had taken a break and rested a bit, everyone gathered again on the porch for more tea, coffee, and a little more pie. Martha lit a few candles, and Henry asked his father to tell about Tomochichi. Walter said that everyone might be tired of listening to him, but Julia said it had only made her want to hear more, and Helen and Richard agreed.

Walter began slowly and said that some of what he was about to tell, he had learned in England as a boy before he went to sea. The exotic nature of the new America was very popular news and was much in their conversations and was the most exciting news of the century. He said that, when he had learned of his appointment and orders, he had studied everything he could find about Savannah. He was surprised at how the Yamacraw chief Tomochichi was involved in so many plans and decisions concerning the city, especially early on, and how much Oglethorpe relied on his advice and counsel. Walter said that when he got to America, Tomochichi had been dead for almost thirty years, but there was much written about him, and he had continued to learn what a long and impactful life he had in the city.

Walter described what led up to the English decisions to establish at Savannah. There had been difficult economic times in England, and many people were jailed for delinquent debts. Prisons became crowded, and when the edges of the "elite" started to become included in the prison population, there came a time that something had to be done. England had long desired to have a piece of the action and riches of the new America. So, the decision was made to relieve the prisons by sending some prisoners to set up an English city south of Charleston that would hopefully keep the Spanish from expanding their foothold from the southern Georgia coast and Florida. There was also concern about the French who had established a small fort not far from Richard and Helen's hometown of Beaufort. So, the logical place to settle was somewhere between Beaufort and the South Georgia coast. The first big river they went up was our Savannah River. They found it to be deep and wide and saw the high bluff and decided that it was a good place. Walter said that, typically, the people of his former country had assumed that God was on their side and that it didn't matter that the village of savages was there already, so they had sent word back that they had found the spot. Then came Oglethorpe, with people selected with varied skills to establish a city, most of whom were prison parolees. Oglethorpe had a vision to lay out a planned city of streets and squares that could be filled in as more parolees came. They were fortunate that the Indians were friendly and most lucky that their leader was Tomochichi, who welcomed them and moved his village over to allow the new arrivals the prime location, high on the bluff, overlooking the river. It wasn't long before difficulties began for both the newcomers and the Indians. The Indians suffered from many new sicknesses. The English also had new illnesses and suffered from the heat and bugs. Other problems for the English were that all the Indians of the region were not as hospitable as Tomochichi and wanted to kill them all, and there may have been a few that thought they might even be tasty. Had the wise and kind Indian Tomochichi not stayed near and defended the new white people, the people of this area would now be speaking French or Spanish. In every confrontation, the Indian leader was able, with wit, wisdom, and diplomacy to prevent an early end to the English settlers. The other specter that could have ended the city was starvation.

Enough food supplies had been brought on the ships to tide the settlers over until they could grow what they had grown in England, but that didn't happen, and the food ran out and much rotted from the heat and humidity, and varmints unknown to them had eaten a much of it. Tomochichi noticed how puny many of them looked so he brought from his village baskets of dried and busted-up corn and showed them how to boil it to make a mush that became known as grits. This was after the first year when their spindly crops had been eaten before they could be harvested by bugs and wild animals. When their efforts failed again the next year, Tomochichi was generous again with more dried corn. Since the seeds they had brought hadn't produced anything, the third year he gave them squash, corn, and bean seeds and showed them how to add fish for fertilizer to their crops so that they produced enough, even after the varmints got their share, for themselves to eat and store for later.

The newcomers didn't know what to make of Tomochichi. He and his tribe were forever on the watch for hostile Indians that would have probably killed them all. Tomochichi's magnanimity was especially surprising and providential because most settlers thought of the Indians as sub human and closer to animals than people. But, Tomochichi had learned the English language before they could even begin to learn his, which allowed him to better guide and counsel them.

Walter stopped for a moment, and Martin noticed that he looked at everyone on the porch to see if he had their full attention. This subtle detail that lasted only a couple seconds helped Martin to later become a good storyteller like his father. Walter said he would tell one more thing that happened that he thinks about often. He said that Tomochichi was so gracious and intelligent that they had sent word of him home, and they were asked to bring Tomochichi and a few of his relatives to England. They asked him, and he said he would go, even though he was getting up in age. They went on a ship and arrived with much fanfare because the stories about the Indians and the new world had been many and exotic. Tomochichi was brought before the highest officials, and the King asked many questions about his world. One of the questions was who their politicians were. Tomochichi said they didn't have politicians. An English politician told him that people could not survive without politicians. The chief repeated that they had no politicians, and he was asked how they selected their leaders. Tomochichi said that their grandmothers selected their leaders and did so by watching and listening to the village children and asking them about their dreams. The ones that could remember and tell about their dreams, even after they got older, were asked to lead. He went on to say that the dream world is where we go when this world ends, and they prefer those familiar with it to lead them in this world. Martin had heard his father talk about Tomochichi before but had not heard this information about the grandmothers selecting leaders. He was reminded of Ayana and her mother and how they wisely led their people and how she had relied on the final word from the children to decide to stay where they were.

Walter saw that Richard and Helen were still listening with interest but also that they looked weary from their journey. He said that there were many more stories to tell about Tomochichi but he would save some for another time. Julia and John thanked Walter and said they would want to hear all the Tomochichi stories. Richard got up and groaned, and John asked if he was all right, and he said that he would be after a good night's sleep. He and Helen Wilcox kissed their grandkids and went to bed early. Walter and Martha did too. Henry, John, and Martin stayed on the porch while Claudia and Julia got the kids settled in bed. Henry told John that he would like him to accompany him tomorrow to pick up Albert and John said that he would. Martin said he was available if Henry needed anything. Henry said that maybe he could speak with John's father tomorrow. Martin said he wanted to make ice cream in the afternoon, and John said he would teach him in the morning. Martin said good night and Henry said they might stay up talking a little longer.

When Martin quietly left his end of the house the next morning, he saw that Henry and Claudia were up and joined them at their kitchen table. Claudia asked if he preferred coffee like Henry or yaupon. He said yaupon, so she poured him a mugful and started frying eggs. In just minutes she had grits, eggs, and biscuits for the three of them. As they finished, John and Julia came in, and Claudia served them too. John asked Martin if this was a good time to go over the ice cream preparation. Martin said sure and set out the churn and the crock. John positioned the churn inside the crock and pointed to the space between them where the ice would go. He explained that the ice had to be crushed enough to fit but not too small and to add a couple cups of salt to the ice. He said that it was best to make the ice cream mixture, according to his recipe, ahead of time and to let it chill in the icebox. Then pour the mixture into the churn and let it sit fifteen minutes before beginning to crank the churn. He cautioned that none of the salty ice or melted ice water should get into the ice cream mix container itself. Turn it until the mix starts getting thick, then turn it some more, then serve. John showed Martin the churn fins inside the metal container that stirred the mix when it turned. Martin was surprised at how simple it was and said he should be able to do it. John said he could help if he was needed. Martin asked Claudia what time would be best to make the ice cream and she said after lunch. Martin said he would plan on that and thanked Claudia for the breakfast and said he was going over to the boathouse to work and would be back soon because he wanted to talk to Mr. Wilcox. Henry told John that Albert had left at 3:00 a. m. and was due in Savannah around 7:00 p. m. so they would need to leave about 6:00 to pick him up. . Henry said the Charleston trip was longer than the trip from Beaufort, but they stopped for fresh teams of horses three times, so were able to travel faster to get here in one long day. It was the coach company's most traveled route, and they maintained the roads for easy passage.

Once at the boathouse, Martin joined Jacob, Johnny, and Izak for another cup of yaupon, and they then went over to inspect the boat Martin had come to work on. Johnny opened his pocketknife and stuck the point in a dozen places and said it was dry and very hard because it was mahogany and had baked for so long in the sun. He said the supply boats were made of softer wood and the planks were thicker. He said that Martin's boat planks were very thin, but that the wood was stronger and that the boat was made by a very good builder. He found the box of glass shards that he had just broken and cautioned Martin that they were sharp and to be careful not to cut his fingers. He showed him the pieces of leather and how to hold the glass tight. Johnny made it look easy as the fresh wood showed as he scraped. Jacob told Izak that he could help Martin and that this was part of his training. Izak liked that because he hadn't been able to talk to Martin much lately and wanted to tell him about all the things he had been doing and learning. Martin said he could only stay for a little while because he had other things going on. They looked through the shards to find pieces with the straightest, sharpest edges and gripped them tightly with the leather, but the scraping took a while to get the hang of. Izak told Martin that he liked training to be a boatman and that, unlike when he was a field worker, he looked forward to every day. It didn't seem like work because he liked it. He said he wished that his reading lessons were as easy as scraping the boat and that he wasn't sure he would ever learn to read and write but that he liked seeing Maggie. She didn't seem very friendly at first but had warmed up. H said he thought about her all the time now and that is why he kept trying to learn. Martin told him not to worry because, if he could learn, anybody could and told him how slow he had been to catch on and the teacher told him that he was the most difficult student he had ever had. Martin said the other students laughed at him and after the teacher gave up on him, he had to learn at home from Alice. He said he still couldn't read fast but was better at writing. This made Izak feel better because, when he had first seen Martin read the list of materials when they were loading the barge, he had thought Martin was so smart. Izak said that Johnny and Jacob were strict around the boathouse, but he understood that they just wanted him to learn. The other boatmen liked to kid around and made it rough on him sometime. Martin said that would go away when he got more experience. Martin smiled to himself, recalling

Jacob saying that something new was going on at his house and now he was sure that it was about Maggie and Izak. He told Izak to keep at it and that the reading and writing would become easier. Izak said he was going to keep at it and hoped Maggie wouldn't give up on him because he was slow and Martin said he didn't think she would.

Izak asked Martin what was new with him. He told him about what Captain Ben had told him about quitting and asking if he wanted to work on the boat when he was gone and how his mother did not like the idea. Izak asked him when it might happen and Martin said maybe in a year but maybe sooner than that he hoped. He said that he would be gone a week or so at a time, then home for a few days, and then off again. While talking and scraping, they had managed to get the first two planks clean from end to end. Martin had to go and left Izak there still scrapping.

When Martin went home, Richard Wilcox saw him and said he had been waiting to talk and this was a perfect time. He said that Henry had said that they needed some of his local knowledge. They went to get comfortable in the library, and Martin brought some tea. From John, Richard knew the story of Alice, what had happened to her and all that she had become. Martin told him about finding her family and Alice seeing them and staying a week over on the island where the Indians helped keep them hidden. He told him about the recent slavers and their dogs on Tybee and what could happen if they came back and went across the river to the Indian Islands and caught Alice's family. They could all be sent back to the awful plantation and master that they had run away from. Alice and her baby, without Johnny, might have to go too. He said that Henry wanted to go there and buy them all, but they needed to find out where the place was, and thought that he could help, since he did business with almost everybody in the area. He handed Mr. Wilcox the piece of paper on which Alice had written what she knew and what her brother had told her. Richard studied the paper and looked thoughtful for a minute or two and said he knew exactly who it was and where it was, and he knew a lot about the owner from his hardware purchases over the years and what his other customers from that island had told him.

Richard told Martin to get comfortable because he had a lot to say about it all. He said that man was the meanest owner in the area and had at times come close to losing everything and how he now had to make him pay for his things when he got them rather than extending him credit. Richard said it was odd that he was so mean because his father had been one of the nicest plantation masters on the island. The son drank a lot and used laudanum too much, and his people were always running away, although they never got far because it was difficult to get off the island

and usually came back in a day or two. Martin said that Alice said they were able to get away because her father had been the carriage and wagon driver for the plantation and was familiar with all the plantations on the island and knew somebody that had a boat who helped them get across the water. Martin said that Henry should be hearing this, and Richard said he could go over it again when Henry had time. Martin rolled open a chart of the area and asked if he could show him the place on it. Mr. Wilcox pointed to Saint Helena Island and to a creek on its southeast side and to a place where the creek came close to the land. He moved his finger north and west a few miles from there and said this was Willoughby Plantation, started by a veteran, Colonel Mashburn Willoughby, just after the war with England. People called him Colonel Mac. When he died, his son Melvin took over. The plantation has a small amount of marsh front but no direct access to a creek or river. It has a very valuable natural asset of a deep artesian spring that spews fresh cold water day and night even during dry times. Because of the ample fresh water, it had been a large Indian settlement before colonials came. Colonel Willoughby had engineered an irrigation system to flood his fields with the water and was able to have good years even during droughts when most others suffered losses. Even more profitable than his crop irrigation system is the pond that Colonel Mac designed and dug, utilizing the cold artesian water. He is the only one on the island who can maintain a small herd of cattle, because they have plenty of cold clean water to drink and a place to cool off and survive the bugs and scorching heat of summer. His cattle sales alone is enough to pay his bills and then some.

Not having deep water access, Colonel Mac had used Tombee's landing for monthly supplies. When he died, his son Melvin continued using it, but because of his drunkenness and ill behavior, relations soured and he must now come and go to meet the supply boat across the island at Land's End. Martin asked how they might go about visiting Melvin to do their business, and Richard thought a bit. He said that finding a place to stay on the island would be difficult and traveling back and forth from Beaufort could take a whole day or more, depending on tides and weather. Martin explained his idea about Captain Ben's sharpie and Ken and Ashley. Richard said that would work but that, because Saint Helena was so big, land transportation would be needed. Their visit would require a landing, transportation, and privacy that could not be had at the busy landing at Lands End. After some silence Richard said he had an idea that might work. He pointed again to the place where the creek came close to the land at Tombee where Colonel Mac was allowed to pick up his supplies for years before his son took over and spoiled things. The owner, Thomas Benjamin Chaplin was a longtime friend of Colonel Mac. He and his young wife had died recently of the fever and left the place to their young son, Thomas. His uncle Benjamin Chaplin is running things there now. He said that Benjamin is likable and would welcome some extra money and could probably offer to rent them a carriage, provide some advice and directions, and allow use of his landing. Your boat would be a bit big and cumbersome to navigate Station creek but y'all could moor out in Trenchers, where you would be protected from the weather, and row a skiff to Tombee landing.

Martin said that if they left early from Tybee, and the wind was blowing from the southeast as usual, they could sail there in a day. Richard asked Martin when they wanted to go and Martin said soon, which would be in a couple weeks. Richard said that he would get a letter to Benjamin Chaplin as soon as he got back to Beaufort. He would ask if, for a fee, they could use his landing and a carriage. Martin said that, if Mr. Chaplin agreed to help, he would then talk to Captain Ben about his boat and crew and they could set a day to leave. Martin told Richard how thankful he was for all the helpful information and Richard said he was glad he was able to share what he knew.

After their talk, Richard and Martin sat a few more minutes to finish their tea. Richard thought to himself how serious and mature Martin could be after having seen him play with the kids the day before and remembered John had told him about Martin's part kid part adult nature. Changing the subject, Richard told Martin that Henry had described his aspirations about a life on the water before long. Martin said that he would start as a hand on the boat they were just talking about when Captain Ben retired soon. Richard said that he could keep a boat like that busy with his customers on the Sea Islands between Savannah and Charleston. He told Martin to talk to him about it when he could captain his own boat in a few years. Martin said that he would do that. He said that his first work would probably be delivering ice if John and Henry's expectations came to pass. Richard said that could work perfectly because it would need to be done on a regular basis and his other items could be added to the deliveries. Martin told Richard that he really appreciated his help and hoped that now that John and his family were here he would see him more often. Richard agreed, and Martin said that it was time for him to start working on the dessert that he had planned after lunch.

Martin went to find Henry and John. He heard them having a busy conversation in Henry's office and did not want to interrupt, so he went to get ice from the sawdust pile. It was time to bring a new chunk for the icebox too. He decided to mix ingredients together first and let them chill in the ice box. With list in hand he went to the pantry, got the metal container that John had given him, and set it on the table. Claudia and Julia came in, and Claudia asked if he wanted some help. Martin said that he did because he was a bit behind in his plan. Julia said that she had helped John several times so she would be glad to help. Martin said that, if she would prepare the mix, he would go get the ice. He told her that the milk and eggs were in the icebox and the sugar was in the sugar chest. She asked him what flavor he wanted to make and he said that he had not thought about that. Claudia said she had something new in her spices that she had been wanting to try. It was called "vanilla," and it was several long dark beans from South America that one of Walter's captain friends had sent home with him. She went and got it. When she opened the jar, a rich and wonderful aroma came out, and Julia said that might be good. She could make a sample cup with some vanilla to see how it taste. Martin was glad for their help and left to get ice.

In an hour he set a chunk of ice on the kitchen table in a large pan, chipped it into small pieces, and put the pan in the icebox. Julia told him to open his mouth, and she put a big spoonful of the ice cream mix into his mouth and asked what he thought. He said it might be the best thing he had ever tasted but that it was very sweet. Julia said it wouldn't taste as sweet after it was churned and frozen. Claudia said they could eat lunch soon and afterwards he would have time to make it and be done in time before Henry and John left. Martin said that was perfect and thanked them again for their help.

Martha and Helen had been on a walk with the kids and came back with Alice, Ellie, Maggie, and Thomas. Martha told them that Martin was making a special treat after lunch and asked them to come. Claudia and Julia had laid out leftovers on the table and they served the kids and left the rest for others to serve themselves. Claudia sent Martin to Henry's office to get him, Walter, John, and Richard. They were so involved in their discussions that they didn't know it was time for lunch. John asked Martin if he was still planning on ice cream. Martin said that he was and that everything was prepared and that Julia and Claudia had helped him get it all together. He asked what flavor he had made, and Martin said he couldn't remember its name but was something Claudia had. He said that he would have it done in time for them to have before they left to meet Albert.

Martin had a quick snack and left before the others had finished. He brought out the big clay crock, set the churn container inside it, and added the creamy mix that was slightly off-white from the eggs. He began filling the space between the two containers with ice, adding some salt as he did, and then started slowly turning the crank. All the kids lost interest in their food while watching Martin. Martha told them to eat their food or they wouldn't get any ice cream, so they all gobbled what was left on their plates, then got up to watch Martin. He opened the metal top for them to see and they had quizzical looks when they smelled it. Julia's oldest daughter Katherine, who had ice cream at home a half dozen times, told them that it would get hard in a few minutes. Martin kept cranking and churning and every few minutes looked to see if it was freezing, He added more ice and salt as the ice melted and turned into a slurry. The churn became difficult to turn and Martin took the lid off, and the mix had become almost solid. Julia came over and began filling bowls, serving the kids first. The kids had finished by the time she had served everybody, and she refilled their bowls. The grownups were delighted and acted a little like big kids. No one had ever tasted vanilla, but everyone liked it. Claudia went in the pantry, returned with a vanilla bean to show them the source of the flavor. Claudia filled Alice's bowl and laughed as she told her that she needed to eat for two. Ellie said that she would have trouble explaining this to Jacob and laughed at Thomas eating his third helping. She then scooped the rest of the ice cream into all the bowls that were held out. The kids were all as happy as if they were at a party. Not long afterward, everyone got a little sleepy headed as the rich cream settled them. Martin remembered the same feeling after eating ice cream in Darien. Martha suggested that the kids take a nap. Claudia laid a thick blanket on the floor for Thomas.

Henry told John that he could use a nap too but that, if they could leave an hour or so earlier than planned, he could show him the fifty acres of land he had looked at for the ice company works and then pick up Albert. John liked the idea, and Henry went to the kitchen and made them some coffee. Maggie went to tell Martin how good the ice cream had been and what a good job he had done. She said that, although they had both been so busy and not seen much of each other, her father had told her about all that was going on. Martin smiled and said her father had told him what was going on with her too. He searched her face for any sign that she knew what he was talking about, and when he saw the corners of her mouth turn up slightly, he knew that what Jacob had said was correct. He asked her how the reading and writing lessons were going with Izak, and she glowed when Martin said his name. She modestly said that it was going just fine and that she wanted to take a book back from the library for their lesson tomorrow.

The grownups went for a nap and Maggie went to the library. Martin rigged the carriage for Henry and John and saw them off. He decided to go scrape the boat for a while, since he wasn't feeling as nappy as the rest. When he got to the boathouse, Izak was painting its big front doors. He lit up when he saw Martin and stopped and followed Martin inside because he wanted to see his reaction when he looked at the boat. Martin yelped when he saw it, and Izak was extra pleased and laughed at Martin. The outside hull was totally scraped and it had been sealed with whale oil and looked beautiful. Martin asked how he had gotten so much work done. He said that he had help because the boatmen couldn't stop themselves from helping him, and with a dozen hands working, it was done quickly. He said that they could add another coat of oil now, and then get some help to turn it right side up if Martin liked. Martin said that would be great. Izak said that he would finish the door that he had started but Martin could put more oil on and then they could turn it over. He got Martin a rag and a bucket of oil and went back to finish his painting. Martin slathered the oil on and saw that it just lay on top of the wood in most places. This meant that the wood grain was mostly sealed, and he wiped away the excess. As he finished, Izak returned with a couple of boatmen who turned the boat over and propped it up nice and level. The boatmen stayed to help Martin and Izak scrape the inside. They spread out around the boat, reaching inside to start on the top strake and finished it in about a half hour and started on the next one. Jacob came by, and Martin said he hoped he wasn't keeping the three boatmen from their work. Jacob said that it was good work for them and that they might need a third boat sometime to borrow. Martin said it would be sitting around a lot when he started working on the sharpie. Jacob said it would need to be under a shed and he would see that one got put up on the side of the boathouse. They scraped two more strakes as the afternoon wore on. Martin said he needed to go home, and Izak said they would quit too. He said he would try to finish up the scraping in the next few days. Martin said the new sails were probably ready, and he would check on them. He couldn't remember the name of the thing on the bow for the jib sail, but it would need to be installed and then all that was left was a little hardware repair and new sails and lines. It would be ready to go in the water in a couple weeks or less. He thanked Izak and the others. and Izak thanked him again for helping him get on as a boatman.

Henry and John were at the depot a little bit before the coach arrived and when it did, they were glad to see Albert on it. As he stepped off, John shook one hand while Henry shook the other. Albert said it had been too long since the three of them were together and now that John would be in Savannah, they could get together more often. He said there was a lot to talk about and he had missed their long meetings into the night when they were both in school. They asked about his family and he said that they were nearby and all was well with him and his wife. He said that he was looking forward to the meeting and had done some research and learned a lot that he wanted to share. Henry asked how he felt after the trip. Albert said he had napped a lot and felt well rested but was a bit sore but his excitement at seeing them had made his pains disappear. Henry suggested that they ride down onto River Street and walk and chat a bit before going to the inn. Albert agreed, and Henry drove the short distance to the waterfront. They walked, caught up on what they all had been doing, then road to the inn. They carried Albert's bags inside. The owner saw Henry and walked over and Henry reintroduced Albert, and the owner said he remembered him from his last visit and welcomed him back and said his room was ready and had a view of the waterfront this time. Henry said he would need a carriage in the morning to take him out to the Milam place. The owner said he would arrange it and asked Albert what time he would like it there and Albert looked at Henry, and he said that about 9:00 would be fine. Albert said he was ready to get cleaned up and have an early supper and early bedtime because he had left at three in the morning. The innkeeper said that he knew he had come from Charleston and must be tired and sore and that he could have a hot bath ready for him in about half an hour and would have a helper carry his bags and take him up to his room and Albert said he would like that. He thanked Henry and John and said he would look forward to seeing them in the morning.

Henry and John got back home just before dark and the kids were still playing outside, and the rest of their families were on the porch. Martin had just returned from the boathouse and Alice had gone with Ellie and left Thomas to play some more and had asked Martha if Martin could bring him home again. Martha had made the biggest pot of chicken soup that Martin had ever seen, and he had worked up an appetite scraping the boat. Everyone had soup and various desserts and tea, and some had rum. Martin took Thomas home, and everyone was ready for an early bedtime.

When Martin got up the next morning and came around to have tea, Henry was not in their kitchen as usual. Claudia said he had gone to talk to Jacob. Martin knew that it was to talk to Jacob and Johnny about doing nothing all day but riding around the place keeping a watchful eye. He returned a few minutes after Martin had finished his first cup of tea. John and Julia were up and in the kitchen by then too. John said he would have coffee when Henry asked, and he said that the coffee yesterday had really kept him going when he felt like napping. They all had some breakfast and a little while afterwards they could hear Walter and Martha up having breakfast with Richard and Helen at their end of the house. Claudia commented that the kids must have been really tired last night because they were usually up by now, and Julia said she knew hers were because they never played that long and hard at home.

The first guest to arrive was Albert. Henry brought him onto the porch and introduced him. John's parents said how many good things they had heard about him. Martha said to him to bring his wife the next time he came. Albert said that his wife would like that but that it was too short a notice this time and, from what he had learned from Henry yesterday, they had a full house already. Alice arrived and had brought Thomas again to play. She had met everyone before except Albert, who said he felt like he knew her from all that Henry had told him and she said she had heard much about him too. A few minutes later another carriage arrived with Walters's two lawyer friends. They were introduced, and Walter said he thought they could sit a bit on the porch and have some tea before going into the library for their meeting. The two old friends were Sidney Perkins and Hulbert Adkins, and they sat and talked with Albert and Richard. Richard talked about what was going on in Beaufort, and Albert talked about the College of Charleston, and how it was growing, and how students were coming from all over. After a bit, Walter suggested that they go to the library where Martha had laid out snacks and said that she or Claudia would keep tea and coffee hot in the kitchen and have a lunch ready whenever they decided to take a break.

After everyone was comfortable, Walter welcomed them all again and said that he thought they could cover the things he wanted today and meet more casually tomorrow. He said he wanted to talk first and then have Alice speak and then open up the discussions. He said that he urged total secrecy about today and cautioned that any communication later about their meeting should only be done face to face in private. Being overheard speaking about such matters could bring a charges but doing it in writing and being discovered could bring much more serious charges of sedition against the state and would have much more serious consequences. Walter said they pretty much knew his story but that they might not have heard how his beliefs on equal rights for all people had been formed. He said it was from the early teachings by his parents and that his parents and grandparents were early members of the Society of Friends, known commonly as the Quakers. They believed that all men were equal before a common God and did not believe in slavery and were against the British government for supporting the slave trade and their countrymen for profiting by it. They believed that by clarity of understanding, empathy, and gratitude, the spark of every man or woman could be ignited, and peace and prosperity would follow. The golden rule was what they lived by. Enslavement of one human being over another or one race over another was intolerable and the opposite of the golden rule. They were a minority, but they campaigned against slavery, and eventually, twenty years ago, the transatlantic slave trade ended, due in great part to their efforts. It is against the law now to import slaves into this country. However, the institution of slavery is bigger now than ever and entrenched in the political, religious, and economic way of life. Walter said that all he had been able to do was to treat the people in his charge just as he would if they were sailors on a ship under his command. He was able to operate like that because of the importance of his mission to the safety and prosperity of the city. He said that Henry was the captain now and the reason for the meeting was for advice and guidance to do what would be best for the future of everyone on the Milam place in light of the changes that would happen when he was no longer around. He wanted everyone on the Milam place to be legally free and able to fend for themselves and their betterment assured. He said that the door had always been open to anyone on the place and a promise of financial support if they chose to leave and they would have the option to return at any time if things didn't work out.

Walter said he wanted to say one more thing about what was the darkest day he had ever had since coming to America. It was the day he went to Tybee the day after the massacre of the hundreds of runaways by the South Carolina militia group, disguised as Indians. A survivor, who most of you know or know about will speak next, She was raised as mine and Martha's daughter and has been a beacon of light and inspiration to us all. She is no less dear to us than our sons Henry and Martin. Walter told of the carnage and of returning to Savannah with eight year old Alice and a plan to return to England or go to Canada. He had doubts about everything except what his parents had instilled in him. He no longer wanted to be an American because it held a double standard about human rights. Walter pointed to Alice, who had survived the massacre, and said that, partly because of her, with the persuasion of Hulbert and Sidney, he had decided to stay in America and do all he could to make things better. He realized that he would not be able to change the system but made a solemn vow to do everything he could to make a single standard for all those around him and do everything in his power for their betterment. He said he broke the law to educate Alice and was currently breaking the law to teach everyone here, that wants, to read. He said that after they taught Alice to read and write, she had read everything in their library and most everything in the Savannah library. She had learned the history of the world and this country and about literature and the arts. Greater than her self-education, she carries within herself a lit candle and by clarity and understanding can light an unlit candle in someone else or brighten a dim one. She will be having what Martha and I understand as our grandchild and has married one of the boatmen here whom we consider our son-in-law. Walter said Alice was next.

Alice stood to address the people in the room and said that she was honored to be included and deeply grateful that they were here for such a noble cause. She said that she had been in hell the first eight years of her life and then in something worse than hell in the slaughter of hundreds of runaways on Tybee by the South Carolina militia. She said that she, more than anyone, understood the unusual position that Walter and his family were in. She went on to say that it was hard for a white man to grasp that the simple sense of the self was the most important thing for a human being, because they had never been denied it. She said her own husband had come from a human livestock farm. He had no knowledge of his self and self-worth because, from his earliest learning, his self and worth were owned by his master. When I was able to help him understand that there was something inside of him that was his unique birthright and couldn't be taken away, it was like life started over for him. The great Socrates, speaking before the Oracle, implored men to know themselves above and beyond all else, more than two thousand years before these words were vowed in Philadelphia. And Alice recited possibly the most important sentence from the Declaration of Independence.

"We hold these truths to be self-evident, that all men are created equal, that they are endowed by their creator with certain inalienable rights, that among these are life, liberty and the pursuit of happiness."

Alice paused for a moment to let the quote sink in and subtly scanned the room to see if she had everyone's attention and then said that perhaps if the Oracle had been in Philadelphia during this declaration, its double standard would have been obvious to the so called founders of democracy. All the men in the room who had not been around Alice were a bit taken aback at the strength and blunt truth that she spoke. It was not mean-spirited or remorseful. It simply made what they already knew more clear and more evident. Walter viewed the room and smiled to himself. Henry glanced at John and saw that his jaw had dropped a bit. Alice said that Walter had told her earlier that he would give up the Milam place and give freedom to everyone if he could do it and be confident that their lives would be improved. She had told him that she thought it could be terrible for them because according to the law they would have to leave the state, and none of them would want to leave because they had heard what life was like for a slave or even a free black outside of the Milam place. She said that everyone there knew that if they asked Walter or Henry for their freedom, they would not hesitate to give it to them, but where would they go, what would they do, and what may become of them? This is probably the only plantation in America where the door is always open to leave if you want. There are no overseers, and there are no beatings. There are no family separations, and marriage is a sacrament that is honored. There is work, but there is leisure time too. We are teaching anyone that wants to learn to read and write. I can see in one young girl now that has learned to read that she is looking beyond the Milam place for possibilities. Literacy has expanded her understanding of the world and all that is in it, and she naturally aspires to more than what is here. She also understands the risk involved and she understands that the Milam's will support her to do so with her safety and security a priority. This will happen more as we teach more to read and write, but most here are no longer young. I am here to-day to offer my help and to seek help to understand how best to go from here to accomplish Walter's wish for equal rights and opportunity and bet-terment for everyone here. Walter has established a sanctuary, surrounded by people and powerful institutions that oppose his ways, but, still, his ideals drive him to do more. He is aware that the lives of the people here depend on the choices he makes, and he and Henry have made this meet-ing happen to best understand how to move forward in the best interest and safety of the whole place. She said that she was always thinking of how best to help with things here but that she lamented the suffering of all the enslaved people in America. She said that the only good she could see in the problem was that man and not God created it. A problem created by God would be too much for men to do anything about, but one creat-ed by men should be able to be solved by men. She said she hoped that good understanding, not war, would prevail and that with every genera-tion, conscience and humanity would continue to emerge, until the light would chase out the darkness. She added that she was honored to be in their presence in a common endeavor of such a great cause. She said she had attended the underground slave meetings where people of color and bondage could openly discuss their sufferings and how it kept the light of freedom lit, even though it couldn't be brought out in the open. She said this was somewhat like the underground meetings except that you all are not in bondage but reaching out to help those that are and that she was touched deeply by your selfless efforts at the risks of your own freedom and safety. Alice thanked everyone for coming and sat.

Henry waited for a minute before introducing Albert for Alice's im-pact to linger. He then spoke about Albert. He told how Albert had been his teacher in a class about professional ethics at the College of Charles-ton, how he was impressed by his truth and fairness in all business and personal dealings, and how he and John often stayed after class for lengthy discussions about the state of affairs in local and national government and business. He said that he learned more from these meetings than he did in the classroom. He and John had confided in each other about their contempt for slavery, and eventually they were able to speak openly about it to Albert. Then he invited us to secret meetings with a few other like-minded friends. We were surprised that there was a small but devout underground movement in Charleston to rid the country of slavery. With Albert and his group, there is no lack of patriotism. They did not want to subvert the country but were concerned that the expansion of the economy in the south on the backs of a race of people was morally wrong and practically unsustainable and would lead to further division and civil war. Henry said he reached out to Albert for help in how best to continue in guiding the Milam place in the coming years of change. Henry said that Albert had come to Savannah recently and he had asked Albert for help and guidance and he said he would return to Charleston and learn all he could and now he has returned to share his understanding. He looked at Albert and thanked him.

Albert stood and thanked everyone for what they were doing and thanked Henry for inviting him. He said that he first wanted to share his understanding on a few things he had observed in his years in Charleston because a slave-based economy had started there fifty years before it had in Savannah and in many things Savannah had followed the lead of Charleston. He said that true ethics are impossible to commingle with an economy based on slavery, but the people of Charleston believe that their wealth and their way of life are dependent on that status quo. The political proponents of this thinking are getting the vast majority of the votes and deep financial backing. The churches have also become repositories of vast wealth and have educated their clergy to soothe the consciences of the people by using the Bible in ways that show African people are being helped by being delivered from the animalistic behaviors of a dark continent. These religious beliefs provide slave owners with godly justification for human bondage. Efforts to Christianize the slaves enable the owners to frame their power in moral terms. All these persuasions rationalize and cover up the murderous crime against Africans and enable society to flourish with delicate sensibilities on the surface, but with deep and dark underpinnings of inhumanity.

Albert said that Henry had told him about wanting to legally free everyone on the Milam place and that he had warned him about possible difficulties and repercussions for him, his family, and those being freed. I told him that I would research it, and I did, but first I would like to make a more general statement. Freedom is about being able to make choices.

The people here on the Milam place are given choices they would not be allowed to make at other similar places because of the culture we live in. Albert said he wanted to make something perfectly clear about what he just said. He was in no way trying to justify anything about the hideousness of slavery or any way excuse it. Henry's motives are pure and selfless, and he got them directly from his parents. Henry has made it clear that they all are willing to risk everything to do the best for the people under their care even if it means losing everything, but losing everything could jeopardize the well-being of the people here if they were thrust out into the world unprepared.

Things have gotten tougher for enslaved people in South Carolina, and Georgia generally follows South Carolina's lead. In South Carolina, the white population has a posture of confidence that they are in control, while underneath is an ever present fear of revolt by the slaves who outnumber the whites. This fear has long been there but has increased many fold after the several slave uprisings. More than ever, all manner of things are being done to maintain strict control over the slave population. Public beatings and militia groups are encouraged and are everywhere, patrolling the countryside, and anyone can make a legal detainment of any slave that they think has run off. Free blacks are looked down on and shunned from opportunity. A new law called the Negro Seamen's Act forces a captain from any ship coming into South Carolina, from any place in the world, to surrender any free black sailors into jail, to stay until the ship leaves. Free blacks scare people because they think they might incite those still enslaved. Banishment laws expel newly freed slaves from the state for a year, and they are charged an annual fee when they return, and, if they return early or can't pay the fee, they can become property of the state and be auctioned off as a slave again. One way or another the number of free blacks grew in the area, and the white population began to push back for an end to all pathways for blacks to freedom. So, just a few years back, the South Carolina Assembly passed, "An Act to Restrain the Emancipation of Slaves." We no longer have a manumission process that an average owner can exercise to free his slave. The process means that a "Gain of Sympathy" must be developed among the white conservative men that form the State General Assembly. So, the virtual absence of Georgia's manumission laws meant that Georgia had to devise its own laws now whereas in the past Georgia copied South Carolina's which sought to hinder the manumission process and now, Georgia's manumission laws are as restrictive as those in South Carolina.

Now, Albert said, he wanted to talk about what he considered the greatest force in Charleston against Africans and pure ethics. It is organized religion. To better describe what we are faced with, I want to tell you about a very popular Baptist preacher in Charleston. His name is Richard Furman, and he leads the largest church in the area and is the mainstay of the "Bible Defenses of Slavery Crowd" in all of South Carolina. He is a highly motivated leader and has a prescribed fundamental Old Testament interpretation of the Bible that makes slavery into the will of God and a blessing for those that go along with it. On the slave rebellion that is still fresh in people's minds, Mr. Richards had these things to say: "The rebellion was inspired by the dueling methods of interpreting scripture within American Christianity. Writers and many respected people in pro-moted positions are very unfriendly to the principles and practice of hold-ing slaves, and they write about and speak out and promote to the public their views. They do this to disturb the domestic peace. Their anti-slavery talks produce insubordination and rebellion. Most disturbing is that their opposition is born of the scriptures, but pro-slavers believe that support for slavery is synonymous with Christian orthodoxy. They say that if the Bible is wrong in sanctioning slavery, it might be untrustworthy on the nature of salvation itself." Albert added that, to support their racism, the book of Genesis is referenced as saying that the darker races are set aside by divine act as an inferior race, punished by their moral failures from the beginning of humanity.

Albert looked at Henry and said he had spent a lot of time thinking about his request for help. I wish there was an easy way to do what you asked about freeing the people of the Milam place, but an easy way could mean a steep downward slope in their quality of life. Ya'll have given them a sense of place and security, so moving up north to an abolitionist state is not a sure-fire solution. Even if they agreed to that, without being legally manumitted here, they could be picked up there and brought back and auctioned off into slavery again by one of the many slave patrols that make a living going up north capturing runaways, within the laws that protect their doing so.

In closing, Albert said that he had been having secret meetings for fifteen years with his most trusted friends in Charleston for support and better understanding of the times and trends and to keep the flame of free-dom burning, in hopes that the real ideals of America will emerge. He said that with all the intensified fervor of the pro slavery crowd that dominates his area, he was not able to do much directly to help the cause, so his meetings were like watering the root in hopes that the plant would remain alive. Albert said he wished he could have brought a packaged solution, but the Milam's had boxed themselves into a situation that wasn't bad but was difficult, with things how they were, to alter or change without sinking the ship and causing grave danger to all those onboard. Again, in light of the numerous slave rebellions, and the strong adherence to the status quo, things have gotten more difficult to free a slave in the south. He said he had wished that he could offer a clear and final solution, but he could not, but what he could do was to continue in a collaborated effort to help. Albert thanked everyone again for including him in this meeting of such a higher cause and hoped to continue to do what he could to make the American dream available to all. Albert sat and Henry suggested a break. He left to help Martha bring in tea and coffee and the thin crispy cheese biscuits that everybody had always loved.

After the break, Henry asked Walter's two old friends to speak. Mr. Hulbert Adkins stood and said his longtime friend and associate Sidney Perkins would speak for both of them. He sat, and Sidney Perkins stood and told Hulbert to speak up if he thought of anything more that should be said, and Hulbert nodded approval.

Sidney said he wanted to first say something about how long and how much he had had conversations with Walter about things of extreme confidence and secrecy, starting back before the revolution. Walter even confided in us where he had hidden the light beam apparatus that was originally intended to go in the Tybee lighthouse, in case something happened to him and two of his officers that were privy to everything. We had many talks about whether to switch our allegiance to America before we actually did. Probably our most difficult conversations were after the massacre at Tybee, when Walter wanted to weigh anchor and leave this place. Hulbert and I are glad we were able to help convince him to stay, but it was because of Alice that he stayed. He has long been conflicted in being the owner of slaves. Walter noticeably winced, and Alice, sitting next to him, noticed and reached out and held his hand."I can say this to all y'all, and I speak to Walter too, that there is no man with more empathy toward the plight of the African people at the hands of our countrymen than Walter Milam. In England, Walter would be Sir Walter now. His aspirations have always been for others. With that said, and if Hulbert has nothing to add, I want to talk about the specifics of what we came to discuss. Hulbert nodded his head in approval.

Sidney said that the law firm of Adkins and Perkins had been busy in the halls of justice in Savannah for the last thirty five years and were always close to the pulse of the city. He said that it was interesting to hear Professor McWilliams speak about things in Charleston and that there were similar things happening here. He said that Georgia does have its own manumission laws now but as Albert stated they were made to be difficult to navigate for even a veteran lawyer and impossible for an individual. Also, free blacks were stigmatized and shunted from opportunity. As in South Carolina, any slaves that could be manumitted had to leave the state for a year and to return, they had to pay an annual fee or tax to stay, and if they couldn't and didn't leave, were subject to be auctioned back into slavery, just as Albert said about South Carolina. An owner might be successful manumitting a single slave now and then but could not do more than one at a time and would raise suspicions if he tried to manumit too many times. With all the goodwill that Walter has, he would get away with more than most but never be able to free his whole group. He is already doing things that anyone else would be jailed for. Many people know and resent his fair treatment of his people because they think it is a type of sedition and makes the other slaves want more and destabilizes the practices of keeping them down and unheard from.

Back to what Albert was saying, we have been seeing a shift in attitudes of the people caused by a greater collusion of the churches and government and business interests to make slavery into a strong American institution. The popular belief is that the economy and welfare of the city and state depend on the status quo. We agree that the economy is enhanced by these things but not for the long term because there is a great moral divide happening in the country that will eventually cripple the economy and lead to war. As Albert said, a slave system is unsustainable.

Hulbert and I have talked many times to Walter, and it will be a difficult path to do what he wants without any peril to the people involved and the losses it would bring him and his family. I understand that reading and writing lessons, which is against the law, is being offered to all here who want to learn. All our previous meetings had been with Walter alone. We are glad to see that now Henry and Alice were involved because the future is more in their hands now than ours and Walters. By sharing what we have learned and know with them, we hope that the common cause we all have will continue and be enhanced. It is obvious that Walter is the head of the Milam place and that he has indicated that Henry is taking command, but we and they know that no one more than Alice is in touch with the people here that we are trying to protect. In trying to fulfill Walter's latest request for our help in these matters, we came out earlier to speak with her regarding our intent, to better understand things from her point of view. We have known Alice from when Walter and Martha first took her in as their own and came to know of her special gifts of human understanding and should not have been surprised at her brilliance when we sat with her for a few hours and asked for her help. She said that she had taken it upon herself to visit and sit with every worker at the place to share her understanding and to gain theirs of their place in the world and the world around them and to uncover their sense of self and freedom of choice. What surprised us was that she had been carrying on this process for the last ten years. She has made them aware that they had a choice and could leave if they wanted, but none wanted, and told her that knowing they could go if they wanted helped them feel free where they were. She said, however, she could see in one particular young girl who she had taught to read, that there was a yearning to see and learn, for herself, about the world beyond the Milam place. She said that there were only three other young people here that she suspected that may want to leave, if they had a clear and safe exit, after they learned to read and write and learn about the world beyond. Alice also expressed her concern for the older people here, not about their welfare because the Milam's guaranteed that. What she was concerned about was political changes that could cause the Milam place to no longer operate as it had always been. She was aware that Walters goodwill and strong alliances could not last forever and she was aware also that the fervor of a slave based society in Savannah was growing rather than diminishing. What she was seeing was what we also had seen and it was much like what Professor Albert was just talking about.

We feared that we would have to tell Walter that his hope of freeing all on his place would not be different from what we had told him in the past, so we broadened our investigations and learned of a situation in Philadelphia that is connected to the religion that Walter spoke of earlier " The Society of Friends," now called Quakers, that his parents were involved with. Through their efforts, in 1780 the Gradual Abolition Law was passed in Philadelphia. This didn't mean that slavery was ended there but that all those born there afterwards were free. This made that area a freedom zone surrounded by three states that still allowed slavery, and it became a haven for runaways and free blacks. This led to a big problem involving the "Runaway Slave Act" that allowed slave catchers, for high rewards, to come and track down runaways and take them back. A bigger problem evolved when the slave catchers began grabbing any person of color and taking them back and selling them. The Quakers acted again and passed the "Personal Liberty Law" so a slave catcher had to provide proof and evidence, in a courtroom, that the person was in fact the runaway and from whom and appear before a legally appointed "Vigilance Committee" to make their case. They could be fined or sent to jail if not fully justified, and the number of slave catchers went down considerably and the area then became an even greater haven for free and runaway Africans. In this free zone, the Quakers have even started schools from beginning education to higher learning that has never been available to free and runaway Africans. More important to our search of a solution to Walters and Alice's and Henry's wants, they also have a system where slaves can be manumitted there to avoid the newer restrictions and limitations on manumission laws and process in the south. We investigated these possibilities through longtime associates in Philadelphia that share our ideals of equal rights for all. Our goal once again was to find a process for anyone or all from the Milam place to be legally freed without local hindrances or consequences.

During and after the manumission process in Philadelphia, a place for the person to stay would have to be secured, and we have learned that the Quakers have people of the community that are sympathizers and willingly take in any runaway seeking manumission and afterwards while attending the Quaker school or for a period of time, simply help them to adjust to their new position in life. We were surprised to learn that the Quakers buy more slaves than anyone in the area, but not for the usual purpose. They do this when they hear of particularly cruel owners and they will send an agent as far away as the south states to make a purchase. The newly bought slave is brought to Philadelphia, manumitted, and gradually reintroduced into the world as a free black.

Sidney went on to say that the Quakers that make all these things possible, founded the "Philadelphia Abolitionist Society." They articulate a threefold mission: to fight against slavery politically and within the law, to provide free legal aid to free blacks and escapees, and to empower communities of color through education and financial support. Sidney added that Quakers considered it their life's work to end suffering. He said they were somewhat aware of the Quakers work from what Walter had told of his parents, but they did not know how dedicated and powerfully organized they were until they began studying what they were doing in Philadelphia.

Sidney went on to say that it would take a lot of money and effort simply to get a black man or woman from the Milam place to Philadelphia, and financial support would be needed for their care and for schooling. Fees are not mandatory but are expected for those that can pay. Traveling is not easy for a slave or free black. Stage lines won't carry them, and inns won't take them. Expensive private transportation may be the only way. Walters's instructions to us were to, at any cost, explore how he might free a few or every person on his place, and that is what we did. He could manumit one a year here, but it would still raise a lot of questions, and the process could be stopped after a few years. Technically, he could spend a lot of money and send everyone on the place to Philadelphia to be manumitted and acclimated, but that would halt the work of the Milam place, which would shut it down. Maybe three or four or five could go at a time every year and return and nobody would have to know. So, with some adjustment, work could carry on. There would be some fees that free blacks have to pay but those could be paid in arrears if the plan was discovered. Ideally, no one would know that the people here were legally free.

Sidney said that was the summary of their investigation at Walter's request into possible routes to freedom and personal betterment for all the folks at the Milam place. Sidney said how glad they were to be part of this meeting and to be among likeminded people against the atrocity of human bondage. He said he hoped that, without war, America would somehow amend the Constitution to include all people on equal terms.

Henry stood and thanked everyone and reminded them of the total secrecy that his father emphasized earlier. He said that Sidney and Hulbert and Albert were returning tomorrow for informal discussions and more good food and enjoyment. Claudia had been monitoring their progress and said that there were all sorts of delectable things on the porch and pots of yaupon and coffee too. Henry encouraged everyone to walk around outside if they liked. He went over to his father and Sidney. Walter was telling Sidney that it was encouraging to hear about such a strong abolitionist movement in Philadelphia and he suspected that it would grow to other areas. Sidney said the forces against abolition up north were mainly those with financial and manufacturing ties to the agricultural products of the south, made possible by the subjugation of Africans. He said that, except for the Quakers, organized religion was a small factor up north, but that it was a big factor in the south where slaves and slave life was everywhere. He said religion soothed the conscience of the Christian owners so that their sensibilities were not troubled and they did not think of their ownership as sinful. In fact, it was common religious doctrine that the enslaved were being served and it was for their own good and a blessing.

Walter saw Alice and asked her who was the young girl wanting to be manumitted. She said it was Jacob's daughter Maggie. Walter said he should have known but he had been a bit out of touch lately. Alice said Maggie had a bright future. Walter asked what Jacob and Ellie might think about her going off to school and Alice said they wouldn't like it but that they wanted what was best for her. She wasn't very happy or fulfilled tending chickens but had been helping teach Izak to read and write and teaching came natural to her. She smiled and added that there was an attraction developing between Maggie and Izak, which could either complicate the situation or make it easier. Alice said she was tired and was going home to rest. She turned to Sidney and thanked him for everything that he and Hulbert had done. She found Albert and thanked him too. The rest of the group was outside stretching their legs. As Claudia brought a few things from the kitchen, Alice told her that she was leaving, and Claudia said for her to take some food home for her and Johnny and some for Jacob and his family and she called Martin to carry it all for her and asked him to bring Thomas back to play. Alice protested that she could carry the food, but Claudia wouldn't hear it and filled two baskets with some of everything. She told Alice to tell the others she was leaving, and she would send Martin to find her when she had packed the baskets and to not plan any cooking for the next few days because of how much she had and to tell Ellie the same. She said that Martin could take the other basket to Ellie after he had taken hers. She hugged Alice and felt her swollen stomach and told her to look after herself, and Alice said she would.

The rest of the day was spent eating and drinking and in conversations both serious and lighthearted, with the noise of kids playing outside. When Martin had gone to Jacob's house with the food and got Thomas, Izak was there with Maggie, and they started right away to unpack all the food to see what each thing was. Martin noticed how Maggie's attention was on Izak and how she carried on with him so happily. He smiled to himself and asked Izak how his lessons were going and Izak just grinned at Martin and said he was learning a lot more than he had thought he ever would. Maggie laughed and said he thinks he knows more than he does. Martin saw Thomas fidgeting, ready to go play. He took his hand to head back to the house, and when they got outside and Martin released his hand, Thomas took off running to the house where the other kids were screaming and laughing. The rest of the day was spent eating snacks and desserts and drinking tea and coffee and a few had rum. Later in the afternoon Sidney offered Albert a ride back to the inn and to pick him up in the morning because it was just a few minutes out of their way. Albert said he would like that and it would give them more opportunity to get acquainted to discuss how they might collaborate on the Milam's behalf. Martin took Thomas home. It had been a long day, and all were ready for an early bedtime.

The next morning Martin walked to the boathouse because Izak had asked him to check on their progress on his boat. They had made some minor repairs, put the bowsprit on, scraped the rest down to bare wood, and wiped on a few coats of oil. With only the sails and a few lines, it would be ready for the water. He walked back to the house and had breakfast with Henry and Claudia before the rest of the house was stirring. Henry asked Martin to come with his tea to the office to talk about their upcoming trip to South Carolina. Henry was very organized and had prepared lists of tasks for himself and for Martin to do to get ready, but before they could get started, they heard a carriage and went outside to welcome Sidney, Hulbert, and Albert back.

The day was relaxed and a chance for everyone to get to know each other more. Walter, Sidney, and Hulbert entertained everyone describing their lives in England before they came to America. Martin told some Tybee stories and Henry and John talked about their big plans for the ice business. Richard Wilcox talked about all the new business and growth of Beaufort.

Martha, Claudia, Julia, Helen Wilcox, Alice, and Ellie talked about all things but politics. The morning slipped by, and a big lunch was served on the porch. Afterwards, kids and a few adults stopped for a nap, then more desserts, tea, and coffee in the early afternoon, Albert said he would be getting up at 3:00 the next morning for the coach ride back to Charleston so he should be going back to his room for a bath and an early bed time. Henry told Sidney that he and John wanted to take Albert back, and Albert spent nearly an hour exchanging pleasantries and telling everyone good-bye. Martha encouraged him to come back with his wife and stay there with them next time.

On the ride to town, Henry and John reminisced about their time in school, how the years since had been so full and seemed to have passed so quickly, and how good it was to be doing something together again. John told Albert that as soon as he got moved and settled a bit, he and Henry would be coming to Charleston for a visit. Albert said that he looked forward to returning the hospitality he had been shown the last few days. They both thanked Albert for all that he had taught them in and out of the classroom and for trusting them to engage in the secret meetings. Albert said that he enjoyed their youthful energy and looked forward to another meeting and visit. He said how impressed he was with Martin and how different he and Henry were. He said Martin was part guileless child and part adult, and Henry agreed. Albert said that he was glad that they would be living in the same city and just a long day's coach ride away from him. He added that he was curious about and wished them success in their new ice business and would be willing to help when they were ready to do business in Charleston. They went into the inn, and the owner came over to say hello to Henry and meet John, and how glad he was that Albert had stayed with them again. Albert shook hands and hugged Henry and John and told them how pleased and proud he was of them and pleased that he had been included in their endeavors.

About a mile from the city, Henry let go of the reins and the horses knew their way and walked slowly homeward. The men talked about the two days' events, and Henry reminded John that he wanted both of them to meet with Thomas, the engineer from Boston, who he expected him any day. John said that they had some serious planning to do and could get to it when his parents left. Henry agreed and said they should enjoy themselves for a few days while they could because they both had so much to do in the next six months. John said he would have more time to help once he got his family and Mable and her brother moved up.

As they came through the Milam gate, they saw Johnny on a horse, stopped, and Henry asked him how things were. Johnny said all he had seen the last couple days were turkeys, deer, and possums but no two-legged animals. They laughed, and Henry said that was good. Johnny said he was putting on weight from all the good food and sweets that Alice had been bringing home and in another few weeks he might be too heavy to get on this horse. They said they both had to loosen their belts. Henry said that maybe someone riding around the place a couple times a day might be a good routine all the time. Johnny said that Henry would be surprised at how everybody already watched out. He said that a black man or woman started watching out right after he or she came out of their mother's stomach. As though he knew what the meetings had been about, he said the people here know what a good thing they have. Henry said it was a good thing for all of us and he intended to keep it that way and make it even better. John asked Johnny what they were going to name their baby. Johnny said that, if it was a boy, they would name him John and call him "John John." He said that had been his idea and Alice wanted to let him have his way about it if it was a boy because she wanted her way about it if it was a girl. He said that Alice had gotten a name out of a book about Africa and the name is "Jochebed." Johnny said he didn't care if it was a boy or girl or what its name was, he just wanted it out of Alice and into this world alive. John said he believed "Jochebed" was a girl's version of "Jacob."

Johnny reminded Henry that he would be gone on the supply boat to Tybee tomorrow, but Jacob would be checking on things, and Henry said he had forgotten about that with all the company. Johnny added that they were low on ice, but they had enough for here and the lighthouse for one more week. He hoped that Captain Ben would come this week with ice, or some food might go bad. Henry said he hoped so too.

Back home, the porch was still full of food and people. Claudia and Julia had finished their work and were sitting with Martha, Helen, and Alice. They were enjoying themselves just watching the kids play. Walter and Richard were talking loudly about old times because both were hard of hearing.

Henry said the name "Jochebed" to Alice and she was surprised and said he must have been talking to Johnny. She said she wasn't sure at first about his choice to call him John John but that it had begun to sound alright after a little bit. She said that she would be happy with a boy or a girl and either name.

With the meeting over, the next few days were relaxed. Henry and Claudia spent time with each other, as did John and Julia, and the grandparents enjoyed time with the grandkids. Captain Ben and his crew showed up the day before Richard and Helen were to leave. He had delivered some hardware to Darien and brought back some ice. Captain Ben's presence always added fun and laughter. Martin told him that he deserved to retire soon because had worked so hard. Everyone laughed because they knew that Martin wanted to start his new adventure aboard the sharpie sooner than later. Henry asked about renting his boat and crew for a week and explained why and where they were going. Captain Ben said that there was no problem in that and that it would be a good excuse to do some thorough cleaning and maintenance work on it. He asked when Henry wanted the boat and Henry said he hoped in a couple weeks, and Ben said to let him know as soon as he could. On his father's chart Martin showed Ben their destination, and Ben said a southeaster would get them there from Tybee in less than a day, maybe not all the way up the creek to Tombee, but to Trenchards Inlet at Station Creek, where they could take a pulling boat to the landing. Martin said they could take his new boat, but the Captain said it was too big to haul onto the deck and in danger of getting damaged if they ran into bad weather while pulling it. Martin said he wouldn't like that. Martin asked if they would like to go see his new boat all fixed up. Ben said he had seen it many times while it was in use and later while it sat bottom-up by Captain Jones.

Ashley and Ken did go to see it and really liked it. Ken said it had the sweetest sheer he had ever seen. Martin said that, since he had only ever sailed his little dugout, he might need some help learning to sail this new boat, and they said they would be glad to teach him. Ken hefted the bow and said she was light. Jacob told them to keep an eye on Martin because he sometimes got ahead of himself. Ashley said he would be easier to look after than Captain Ben had been lately. Martin asked what he meant. Ashley said that they loved the Captain but that at age seventy five he was safer on land than on the water. He still had the skills in his head, but the years had taken their toll on his body, and they were concerned for him more than a few times. They were going to address it with him, but he let them know that he was aware of it himself. Their insights made Jacob feel good about them working with Martin. Jacob said, "Yes. Once a man, and twice a child," and all agreed. Martin said he would go with his father to

405

pick up the new sails and have the boat ready to go in a week but that it would likely be a couple weeks before they would head to South Carolina. Jacob told Ashley and Ken that Johnny would be leaving early with the supply boat in the morning but he would have some biscuits and tea ready when they got up. Ashley said they should go now and get Captain Ben back and on the boat before dark and let the folks from Beaufort get to bed because he had heard them talking about leaving at 3:00 in the morning.

Things were winding down at the house except for Thomas and the other kids who hadn't stopped playing for six days straight. It was still a buffet style set-up on the porch with Claudia adding something new and interesting every hour or two. Ben told Ashley and Ken that he had eaten while they were gone and for them to eat because he wanted to get back to the boat soon. Although Ashley and Ken could serve themselves, Claudia couldn't help herself and graciously helped them get their food and tea and made them feel well served and comfortable. Martin noticed that Ashley was so pleased that he was giddy, and Ken said he got that way when there was plenty of good food. Martin asked his father if he would take him to his friend the sailmaker to pick up his new sails, and Walter said he would be glad to. Martin said that Ashley and Ken wanted to go with him when he took the boat out for the first time, and Walter said that sounded like a good idea. Ben said he wanted to explain to Martin about different size boats, and that one boat could be only a third longer than another boat but be more than twice as big. Length, width, depth, and weight can add more than one might expect. He said that his new boat was a little less than twice the length of his dugout but probably ten times bigger. He said he had seen the math but he couldn't perform it himself. You will understand what I'm saying when you sail this new boat. Martin said he would remember that. Captain Ben added that his sharpie was two and a half times longer than Martin's new boat but was a hundred times bigger and heavier. Martin was a slow reader, but he understood math better than average. He didn't doubt what Ben was saying but needed to think about it to understand why it was that way. Ben said it was even more so as you went up in size. His sharpie was fifty-five feet long and a one-hundred-and-sixty foot clipper would only be about three times as long but seventy times heavier. He said that was the way it was with boats, and Walter agreed that what Ben was saying was true.

Henry said that their conversation gave him the idea that Jason could build an icebox for the sharpie before their trip and they could take a bigger variety of foods. Ashley was attentive because he did most of the cooking and food stocking for their trips, which were usually no more than two weeks, including time spent loading or unloading cargo. He said being able to preserve certain foods opened up interesting possibilities and he would be giving that some thought. Ben added that they would leave tomorrow afternoon on the incoming tide and be at their usual dock in Savannah before dark. Henry said he and John would be taking Henry and Helen tomorrow to the stage depot, and they would go see Jason to talk about measuring a spot for an icebox on the sharpie. Claudia saw that Ashley and Ken had finished and asked them whether they wanted blackberry pie or pound cake or both. Ken said they hadn't had food this good since the last time they were here. Martha said that she hoped to see them more often when Martin began going off with them. Martha said that, as shipmates, they were like family, and their visit had eased her worries about Martin going on boat trips because she felt he would be safe with them.

Ben thanked everyone and told Richard and Helen that he hoped to see them again soon and they said to come see them next time he was close by. He said he would like that. He told Martha and Walter that he would see them again tomorrow and told Henry he would look out for the cabinet man. Ashley and Ken thanked everyone and went with Captain Ben back to the boat for the night. Everyone else cleared the table, and Claudia sent Martin to Jacob's house with pie and cake and to take Thomas home. She called the other kids in to get ready for bed, and she, Henry, John, and Julia went to their end of the house, leaving Walter, Martha, Richard, and Helen alone on the porch. Martha said she knew they would probably stay with John and Julia in Savannah when they came again, but they were always welcome with them. Helen said they hoped to be back at Christmas. Richard thanked them for their hospitality and said he would have a lot to think about from their meeting. Martha said that she would be up to have some tea and a lunch packed for them but that Walter probably would not be up, so Walter said his farewells wished them a pleasant coach ride home. Richard said he had napped half the way coming and probably would do the same going.

In the morning, Henry was up before anybody and brought the carriage around to the house while Claudia made breakfast. After hugs and kisses, they hurried out so they wouldn't be late for the coach. Others were up because it was a supply run to Tybee day, and they could hear activity at the boathouse of supplies being loaded including the ice that Captain had just brought from Darien. On the way, Richard told Henry more about Melvin Willoughby, the plantation owner he was going to see. He said that he would probably not be easy to deal with, but that enough money could make him say yes to anything because he always seemed to be in a financial bind. He said that Benjamin Chapman, the manager of Tombee, was an agreeable fellow who he usually saw about once a month and since it had been almost a month, he might see him this week, and if he had missed his visit, he would send a letter over about renting the carriage and using his landing. He said his story to Benjamin Chaplin would be that Henry might buy some slaves from Willoughby, which would actually be the truth and would be believable because he was always saying that he needed to sell off half of his slaves. He was always complaining about how unfair life was and how he had to feed, shelter, and cloth so many slaves to get such a little bit of work done. Richard said his problems stemmed from his poor organization, poor planning, and his addiction to alcohol and laudanum. His land was some of the richest on Saint Helena with an unlimited amount of fresh water spewing up out of the ground, and he could be the richest planter around. He said that the locals knew him as the man that killed his disabled slave years ago, not long after he took over after his father, Colonel Mashburn Willoughby, died. Henry said he had heard that story from Alice.

With the lively conversation the trip to town went more than pleasant, and they got to the stage depot with time to spare. The depot manager told Henry that the other three passengers were here and boarded, so they could leave a little early if that suited them. Richard said he would like that because he had much to do back home. John helped his mother down and hugged her and then his father. They hugged Henry and told him what a nice time they had and how gracious his family was. Henry said they didn't have that many visitors and it was them who were thankful for their visit. Helen said that he and his family should come see them sometime, and Henry said they would but not soon because of all that he and John had to do in the next year or two.

18.
THE ICE BUSINESS

On one hand, Henry wished that all the events lately could have stretched over a longer period, but, on the other hand, task oriented as he was, he was pleased that the important meeting had taken place, that John had come and bought a house, that boats, iceboxes, and ice houses were equipped and built or being built, that a meeting with the engineer from Boston was planned, that there was time to spend with John to make plans, and most importantly, that the issues with Alice and her family were planned and about to get under way. It had been one of his busiest two weeks ever, and it wasn't over because with the trip to Saint Helena Island coming soon, he had things to finish up.

Next day before the sun up, Henry and John were off to Savannah. It was too early to go to Jason's shop, so Henry suggested they go to the inn for coffee or tea and maybe some pastries. John said he could go for the tea. The innkeeper welcomed them, and Henry asked if they might have a window seat, so they could watch River Street come alive. Henry said they would both like tea and they would take whatever sweet bread was fresh. It was still dark, but the riverfront was already busy and looked like two rows of lights from the lanterns on the wagons lined up, some coming with loads of goods and some leaving with loads of goods. Watching all the commerce made Henry excited to get their business up and running. John pulled out his papers and said he didn't expect to go into many working details this morning but wanted to review and prioritize general tasks. Henry said that he knew they hadn't officially set up their partnership but he had gone ahead and done some things already. John said he hoped to have moved from Darien in a month and to have things squared away at the bank soon after. Henry said that they had the land, a start on an icehouse, some supplies stored in the barn, and some expenses with Jason. The next projects would be the buildings on the new property, and the big icehouse would come first. Part of the barn would be a stable for the horses, and the other part would be a workspace with woodworking tools to service a fleet of wagons and a blacksmith shop for wagon parts and horse shoeing. He said these were just his initial thoughts and they

410

would probably be revised by Thomas. Henry said that the interesting thing about it all was that there was no roadmap to follow. We need draft horses, which are common, but we will need specially designed wagons that are extra heavy duty and insulated, and we need their beds at the same level as our ice house so the ice can slide in and out easily. We designed our icehouse walls, insulated with cotton insulation almost two feet thick. We will need to build special iceboxes for the people we will be selling ice to. We have already improved the iceboxes by changing our insulation from moss to cotton and now to cork. Another innovation that we have already made is insulating the holds on Captain Ben's sharpie with cork instead of the sawdust like we covered it with that first time. John said he was sorry to stick Henry with all the work, but Henry said not to worry, that they both would soon be in the thick of it. Henry said that he liked the setting up side more than the accounting side, and that, if things take off as they hoped, there will be plenty of accounting to do. John said that, because it's a totally new idea, there would be some selling to do. He said that his father would spread the news around Beaufort and everybody knows the Milam's around Savannah, so setting up business in those two places should be easy. Henry said that, after they got a few dozen customers, word would spread, and they might have more than they could keep up with. Every customer will need an icebox, and we could have a thousand customers in a year and that is a lot of ice every week or two, and it is a big project to build and deliver a thousand iceboxes. Plus, there is Charleston to the north and Jacksonville to the south and all in between. A new woodworking shop will need to be built right after the barn, and Jason will be our man to manage it. John said his father pointed out that if they had a boat delivering ice regularly to all the sea island plantations on the Georgia and South Carolina coast, they could take on delivering other cargo as well. As daylight came, they saw that there was hardly a cobblestone visible on River Street because of the many wagons. Henry said Jason should be at his shop, so they paid and left. Henry knew how crowded the riverfront got so he had left their wagon up on Bay Street and joked that they needed the exercise of walking up the hill.

Jason and two helpers were in the shop, and there was hardly room to walk because the thick insulated icehouse wall panels were stacked everywhere. Henry introduced John to Jason, and John said that he had heard good things about him from Henry. Jason told Henry that they would be finished with the last panel by the end of the day, and Henry said he would start hauling them out to the Milam place tomorrow to give him some room to work. He then asked him about building a small icebox into Captain Ben's sharpie sometime in the next week and told him where it was docked on River Street so he could take measurements and that captain and crew would be back late in the afternoon. Henry said he would send some more slabs of cork on the wagon that would be coming for the panels. He said that he would have the foundation and floor ready for the panels to be set in a few weeks and would like him and his helpers there to see what improvements they might make on the next set of panels for the next-to-be-built larger icehouse. Jason said that was a good idea because they had learned much as they fabricated these first panels. Henry told Jason that in six months he would have so much for him that he would need a half dozen helpers and a shop ten times bigger, so he should begin looking for more helpers. Jason said that suited him because he didn't care if he never repaired another broken chair or table leg or tried to make something out of wood to satisfy a fickle owner. They said their goodbyes, and Henry said he would have a wagon there in the morning to start hauling the panels.

A half mile from home, Henry and John could hear the kids screaming and playing. John said he was happy for his kids to be moving there because they didn't have many friends to play with in Darien. Henry said that he was glad too because, although he and Claudia knew a lot of people in Savannah, they had very few friends who they could share their private lives with like they could with John and Julia. The kids raced out to meet the carriage, and little Thomas was the fastest. Henry stopped and pulled him up onto his lap and put the reins in his hands, and Thomas smiled proudly at the other kids.

Claudia, Julia, and Alice were on the porch having tea, and Walter and Martha had gone for a nap. Claudia said that she was worried about Walter because of how tired he looked, and Martha had told her that all the company and conversation, much as he liked it, had worn him out. Henry asked if he should send for the doctor. Claudia said to wait and see how he was after his nap. John said that perhaps they should go back to Darien soon so things would be quieter for Walter. Henry said that they should stay and that Walter had just overdone himself and would probably be fine by tomorrow. He said that his doctor had recommended he spend some time at the ocean and he was going to Tybee for a week or so soon.

Claudia said that a message had come for Henry that morning and was on his desk. He got it and said it was from Thomas, the engineer from Boston, and he was to arrive in Savannah the next day and would come out to visit the day after that. Henry said that was perfect and that he would like John to be at the meeting. John said they could plan on going back to Darien soon after that. Julia said she enjoyed this trip but was overwhelmed as she thought of all the moving work ahead.

After a while, when Walter and Martha came out to the porch, everyone asked how Walter was feeling. Martha said that he was fine and that he was just tired from having a little too much fun. Walter added that he couldn't drink rum and carry on as he had always done. Martha said Walter wanted Henry to take care of their business concerning Alice and her family over in South Carolina, so that when he went to Tybee, he would not have to worry about it. Henry said he would do it and asked his mother what she thought. She said they would all feel better if they knew that Alice and her family were attended to. It had always been a fear in the backs of their minds and was even more important now that Alice had a family. She said that she and Walter were fine waiting to go to Tybee once those things were done. Henry said that he and Martin planned to leave in a week once they heard from Richard about being able to use a landing and a carriage. Henry asked where Martin was, and Martha said he had gotten his new sails and Ashley and Ken had come from Savannah and they were in the river trying out the new boat he had gotten from Captain Jones. Walter said he would like to see that, and Martha said that he could tomorrow because Ashley and Ken were staying the night, and they would be in the river again tomorrow. Alice said she needed to go fix some supper, and she went to hug Walter and said how lucky he was to have Martha because she had common sense enough for them both. He said he didn't admit it often enough, but she was right. She next hugged Henry and said how much she appreciated what he was doing for her, and Henry said it was little compared to all that she had done and meant to him and his family and the whole Milam place. Alice hugged everyone else and left for home. About dark Martin returned and everyone had finished supper and were on the porch watching and laughing at the kids playing outside. He was excited and told his father about how good a boat he had and how much Ashley and Ken had taught him in just a couple hours and how Ben had been right about how much bigger his new boat was than his dugout. Walter's face lit up as he shared Martin's excitement and said that he would be coming down to the river to watch him tomorrow, and Martin said he had hoped he would. Henry told Martin that they would be leaving for South Carolina in about a week and he would send word back with Ashley and Ken to make sure that it would be alright with Captain Ben. Martha handed a basket to Martin with supper to take to Ashley and Ken. She asked to take it and come right back for his own supper.

Henry was up early the next morning. He had Jacob carry some cork slabs to Jason's shop when they went for the icehouse wall panels. The barn was full of panels and cork, so they set them where the icehouse was to be built and covered them with oiled canvas. Henry and John were busy in preparation for Thomas's visit the next day. Martha and Walter had taken all the kids with them when they went to the river to watch Martin sail his new boat, so Claudia and Julia enjoyed the free time alone together without kids to watch over or people to attend to.

Julia talked about the things she had to do to get ready to move. She said she and John had never expected to spend their life in Darien, so had not accumulated that many things and had not gotten attached to the area. It was like they had been there for John's job and never really settled down and that made leaving easier. She said that strangely enough her biggest concern was that Mable and her brother James would like moving to Savannah. She knew that Mable liked the idea, but it was hard to tell about James because he was shy and didn't say much. She said her kids couldn't wait to move because they didn't have many friends in Darien. She and John were eager to move, but the task was a bit overwhelming. She said she shouldn't be worrying and was thankful that Mable and James could help pack and she knew that John would take care of selling the house and he said he would make sure that Mable's home place was free of debt and secure. Claudia said that she would help her get settled in and Julia said that it had helped a lot to have Claudia talk with because all John could think about was the business of ice. Claudia said Henry was like that too.

Jacob had brought some chairs to the river and set them up on the bluff. He sat with Walter and watched Ashley, Ken, and Martin in the new boat, tacking back and forth in the full tide. Jacob said that Martin would sure be a captain soon, and Walter said it was like watching himself sixty five years ago.

When Martin got in from sailing, Martin reminded Henry that the next day was when he had told Jehu that he would pick him up in town and take him out for the day. Henry said he and John would be busy with Thomas, the engineer from Boston, all day but that shouldn't make any difference. Martin said he had told Jacob about Jehu and asked if he would spend some time with him when he arrived. Henry said that Jacob could use a helper full time because he was about to start on the icehouse, but he didn't want to upset the stage depot owner by hiring Jehu away. Martin said he wouldn't say much when he went to pick Jehu up, but if pressed, he would say they wanted Jehu to look at their horses. Martin left early the next morning with the carriage to pick up Jehu. He found him sitting in front of the depot, and he smiled real big when he saw Martin. The depot owner came out and Martin had been rehearsing what he would say to the depot owner and was nervous because of how rude he had been before. Before Martin could speak, the stage owner saw Jehu in the carriage and told Martin that he didn't know where he was taking Jehu but he hoped that he wouldn't bring him back because he was tired of having him around. Martin was relieved to hear that. He simply said that he had some horses for Jehu to look at and that when they were done, he could take Jehu wherever the depot owner wanted, and he said he didn't care where he took him as long as it was not back there. Martin left with Jehu, glad that he did not have to lie, and Henry would be pleased because the stage manager felt like they were doing him a favor. He didn't know why the fellow was so tired of Jehu being around but was certain he was making a mistake because there was no one better than Jehu at caring for horses. Jehu said nothing but sensed that he was through with the depot and that good things were happening. He had felt something special about Martin right away when he had climbed onto the top of the coach on that trip from Darian many months ago and Martin shared the same feeling. When they had left the station behind, Martin asked Jehu if he had left anything behind. Jehu smiled and shook his head, and Martin smiled back. When they pulled into the Milam place, Martin told Jehu that this was his home and Jehu's new home, and Martin went straight to the boathouse to find Jacob. Jacob walked out to meet them. They jabbered in thick Geechee dialect for a few minutes, and then Jacob got in the carriage. Martin drove, and Jacob did most of the talking, telling Jehu everything about the Milam place. They decided that Jehu would live in the boathouse until the new barn was built, with accommodations for him and hopefully Mable's brother James. After touring the whole place, they headed back to the horse barn to leave the carriage. Willy, who was the carriage driver and who cared for the horses, was there. Martin introduced Jehu and said that he would be taking care of the horses in the new barn that Henry was building and that until then Jehu could help Willy when he wasn't helping Jacob. Willy welcomed Jehu and said that Martin had told him about how good he was with horses and that there was always plenty that needed doing with them. Jehu didn't know how to react very well to praise and just nodded. Martin asked Willy if he had time to unhitch the horse and Willy said all he had was time, so Martin, Jehu, and Jacob walked back. Martin went to his house while Jacob and Jehu went on back to the boathouse and Jacob introduced Jehu to the boatmen and told them that Jehu would be staying there for a few months until Henry's new barn was built. Jacob showed Jehu his bunk and told him that he would have his meals there every and that some days he could go home with him for supper. Other than the kindness of Lancy Jenkins and his mother and father, this was about the most kindness that Jehu had ever been shown.

At the house Martin found Henry in his office with John. He told Henry about the good fortune of the station manager thinking they were doing a favor by taking Jehu off his hands for good. They figured that he would probably have regrets eventually because nobody was as good with horses as Jehu. Martin told Henry that he had arranged for Jehu to stay in the boathouse bunk room, without asking him first. Henry said he was glad that he had because he was busy getting ready for their trip to South Carolina. He said that Ashley and Ken said that they didn't think Captain Ben had any trips planned, so it would be fine to leave the next week if they heard from Richard that he had made the arrangements for a landing and transportation. Henry asked Martin if he could take care of provisioning the trip so that he could do other things he needed to do. Martin told Henry he would and that all Henry would need to do was to get onboard the boat when it was time to go. Henry said he appreciated that and that he would pick up the legal papers from Sidney and some gold for the purchase. While they were talking, they heard a carriage pull up and Henry said that it must be Thomas. It was, and they brought him inside and introduced him to their families. Henry asked Martin to get Walter and Martha to come and meet Thomas and that they would be on the porch. Claudia had a big pot of yaupon and some snacks ready, and they all sat a while after Walter and Martha came. Thomas was fascinated with yaupon, having never heard of it. Claudia went to the kitchen and brought a small sack of it for Thomas to take home to Boston. Thomas smiled and said that he could have something of a tea party. After tea, Henry said that he, John, and Thomas had a lot to go over and would be in his office. Claudia said she would have some food ready in a while, and Henry thanked her.

Once in the office, Henry suggested that they talk for an hour or so until lunch, then they could take a break and eat and then show Thomas around the place a bit. Thomas said that would be fine and that he was curious about everything and added that the tea had been very stimulating and that he was glad to have learned of it. Henry said that it was getting more popular and grew wild there and in the Carolinas. Henry asked John to recount to Thomas how he had first seen the timber ships discarding their ballast ice on the river banks in Darien and how it sparked the idea of forming a business delivering ice in Savannah, Charleston, and the other sea islands. John told the story and said that someone from Maine had been testing the market in Charleston but that nothing had yet come of it. They explained that their first idea was to get ice from the boats coming to Darien, but when he heard of the steam sawmill coming to Savannah, their idea changed. Savannah was closer, and they expected that there would be plenty of timber freighters coming in like in Darien and many would be coming from Maine and other northern ports, which would mean plenty of ballast ice, but they expected that there would come a time soon when ice was not only ballast but paid for cargo specifically for them. Henry asked about the timeline for the sawmill, and Thomas said they hoped to be up and running in about six months. Henry said that would work for them, and, if they needed ice sooner, they could pick up eight tons at a time in Darien with the local shipper they had been using and that would be enough for a start. He added that once they really got going, they hoped to ship out, by wagon and boat, much more than that per day by the end of the first year, and if our business grows as much in Charleston as we think it will, we will need a setup there bigger than what we plan for here. He told Thomas that he wanted to hire him to help them plan the most efficient way to set things up and to handle the growth they expected and said that he knew that there was very little information out there about ice. Ice melts and is heavy and we have made some progress in learning how to slow the melting down a lot. He told him about the ice-boxes, the ice chests, and that building the first icehouse was in progress. He said that he would show him more after lunch. Henry told him how they had been storing the big ice blocks in a sawdust pile. He added that after today, Thomas would know everything that they had learned about ice, and that the three of them would be practically equal in ice knowl-edge, which was not that much.

Henry told Thomas that he was not expecting an answer today about whether he could or what capacity or how their business relationship might be. Thomas said that he currently was an independent business and had one helper and that the sawmill company had hired him to provide technical information about setting things up, not unlike what Henry was asking. He said that even though steam was relatively new technology, there were ample sources of information about it, but on the other hand, there was very little information about the business of ice and Henry said that he and John understood that. John said that they had the financing and the ability to manage and grow a business, but they needed help in planning the facilities to handle the thousands of tons of ice per year they expected to sell in a couple of years and developing the systems of opera-tions to efficiently handle it all. It's all new and there are a lot of questions. Does some ice weigh more per cubic foot than other ice? Should we build an icehouse near where the ships come in? What kind of wagon do we need to design that is heavy duty and insulated enough? What standard size and weights should we sell? Should we forget the ballast ice in favor of buying ice specifically made for us? What are the safest and most prac-tical ways to load and unload ice? How do we get ice that is free of dirt and debris? Henry said those were just a few of the questions that they knew to ask. Henry asked Thomas, if he were willing, would he have the time to do research? Thomas said that he had been working on the sawmill project for almost a year and that most of his work was done and that he would only need to check occasionally that construction was going properly. He told Henry that he was taken aback by their project since it was new and different from anything he had considered before. He admitted that he was no businessman but could see the huge benefit in being able to preserve food. Henry said that they visualized not only everyday food storage, but also the dessert possibilities for the growing affluent populations of Savannah and Charleston, and for fishing fleets to be able to keep their catch fresh. Henry reiterated that using and selling ice was entirely new, and that they had learned a little but anticipated many steps ahead to be able to supply thousands of homes and businesses. He told Thomas that they understood that there was a lot to learn and much trial and error ahead, but they believed the future gains would more than offset the early losses.

Before lunch, they took Thomas to see the icebox. Henry led the way to the rear of the house and into the storage room and pointed to the big wooden box and opened the door for Thomas to see, and they felt the cold air woosh out. He showed Thomas the big copper ice container with two big chunks of ice and the drain for melted water. There was cheese and butter inside and a crock full of milk. There were chicken parts cut up and ready to cook. On one shelf were containers of leftovers from supper the night before. On the top shelf Henry saw something unexpected. It was a beautiful lemon pie with a thick topping of meringue, beautifully and perfectly browned, showing finger pinch marks around the browned edges of crust. Henry said that it must be a surprise for Thomas and they would have to act like it was, so as not to disappoint Martha who had made it. Henry told them to hurry back to the office before they were discovered. As they exited, Thomas commented on the quality of the woodwork and how snuggly the door fit. Henry told him about the cabinet maker that they were working with and how he had participated in developing the first few iceboxes and the first icehouse, and they hoped to have one in every house in Savannah before long and to be delivering a hundred and fifty pounds of ice per week each one.

Back in the office Henry described how John's first icebox was insulated with Spanish moss, like Thomas had seen hanging from the trees coming from Savannah. Then they had switched to cotton but were about to switch again to cork. They felt that the cork seemed to work best because it need not be as thick and did not absorb moisture but they may learn that they both could work in different applications. Thomas was taken aback somewhat at all this new information and at the enthusiasm shown by Henry and John.

Henry explained that he had been doing most of the talking, not because John was shy, but because John was living in Darien and Henry had been the one dealing with the ice business so far and John would be moving there soon. It was John who had first noted the ice ballast being discarded and had observed the mill workers using it to keep their water and beer cold and had brought Henry there to see. Henry said they had all the insulated wall panels built for a small icehouse there on the Milam place, to serve temporarily until they built a bigger one on property they had acquired next door. There they were soon to build a large horse barn, corral, and pasture area and a carpentry and metal shop for wagon maintenance. Henry added that much might change if Thomas decided to work with them because of his insights as a professional engineer. We need a lot of wagons specifically designed for our ice purposes, some for local deliveries of small quantities, and some for more distant deliveries that can carry ten tons and be well insulated so that the ice does not melt in transit. He said all they had determined so far was that the bed level of the wagon should match the floor level of the icehouse because ice was heavy but would slide on a flat smooth surface very easily and that cork would probably work best as an insulator unless they discovered something a better. We could build wagons here but need specifications. So, again, we have something to design and build without any specific guidance. I suspect that people in Boston would know more about wagons than we do, since it is a more industrial area. Also, we will need a few more boats to deliver ice to the coastal communities and sea islands. One that can carry a load, sail well, and not draw much water because of our shoals and tidal flows. Claudia gave a soft knock at the door, peeked in, and said that lunch was ready. Henry said they would be right there, and after she left, reminded them that they knew nothing about a lemon pie.

Claudia had a fine lunch set out, and Walter and Martha joined them. Thomas was very impressed with the whole Milam place and the Milam family. He said that Boston just had its first dusting of snow and here he was eating on an outside porch and in shirtsleeves. Henry said the weather was nice for about ten months a year but there were some cold spells. He said, however, they had their problems, and he reached out and touched the screen fabric behind him which was made from thin copper wire. Without it, he said, there would be swarms of demonic little bugs sometimes that could make life miserable, and that some people from up north preferred the cold over being attacked by gnats. Thomas said that he was fortunate to have only battled gnats a few times on his trips to Savannah. After Claudia asked him, Henry fetched glasses of iced yaupon tea from the kitchen and she had mixed in some sour orange juice from a tree in the yard and had sweetened it with sugar. It was Thomas' first iced beverage, and everyone was waiting for his reaction. After a few careful sips, he smiled and pronounced "iced tea." He said that, for all the tea in Boston, he had never thought to try it cold. Beer was the only chilled beverage, and he had never thought about how it was made cold, but it looked like he might be researching that in the near future.

Henry noticed that Martin was missing and asked where he was. Martha said that he was probably at the boathouse or horse barn with Jehu. Henry explained briefly to Thomas how Martin had met Jehu on the trip back from Darien when he had gone to see the ballast ice situation that John had discovered. Just then Martin arrived and apologized for being late for lunch with their guest. He fetched his own tea as Claudia set him a place at the table. He was visibly excited at how the horses reacted to Jehu. He said that when Jehu entered the stalls and made a few murmurs, they came to him like pet dogs and that Jacob and the boatmen liked him to.

Thomas said that he had heard that Martin liked boats and the water. Martin said that he did and Thomas described the scene at Boston harbor. He said that fifty times all the ships in Savannah would almost equal the number of ships on Boston waterfront. He said there were ships of all sizes from around the world, and hundreds of trading vessels as small as thirty feet and as big as two hundred and fifty feet. He said that he was familiar with sharpies like Henry said y'all used because their design originated in Massachusetts and that he had seen one at the Savannah docks. Martin exclaimed that's the one Henry had meant and that was Captain Ben's sharpie and that they had sailed on it to Darien to see John and the ballast ice. Henry said that they had insulated the boat's holds with cork for bringing ice from Darien. Thomas said that he didn't know exactly where in New England the sharpie design had originated but that it was the most popular design for small trading vessels in Boston. He knew a man who had designed more than a hundred, and he could design one for the Milam ice business if they would specify their needs. That excited Martin and he said that he could make the list right away. Claudia said that could wait and that it was time for lunch. Martin agreed but his mind raced while he ate.

Thomas was impressed by the food that Claudia served, especially the string bean casserole and the sweet potato casserole. Afterwards, Claudia asked Henry to go to the icebox for a surprise dessert. Henry asked what the dessert was, and Claudia said that he would know as soon as he opened the icebox. John smiled at Henry's acting ability. Henry returned with the impressive pie, and the men acted surprised. Claudia carefully cut pieces for everyone. The icebox chill made the pie solid enough to be sliced into precise and beautiful large wedges. The crust was golden brown, its crispy edge pinched all around the filling was thick and yellow, and the delicate meringue topping perfectly browned. Claudia served a large piece to Thomas first and then the others; she asked Henry to put the remaining two-wedge serving back in the icebox to keep it cold to take to Alice and Johnny later. Thomas waited until all were served and said that it was the most beautiful dessert that he had ever seen. Martin said that his wedge reminded him of the bow of a sharpie and everyone laughed. Everyone waited for Thomas to try it first and he said how good it was. Henry finished and brought everyone coffee. Henry said that he and John were taking Thomas on a tour of the Milam place and asked Martin if he would like to go. Martin said he had things to do around the house.

After Henry left, Martin immediately got paper and charcoal pencil from Henry's office. He found his grandfather and asked if he would help do a rough design of a sharpie. Walter smiled at Martin's enthusiasm but said that he should wait to confer with Captain Ben, Ashley, and Ken. Martin was disappointed and said that he really wanted something to give to Thomas right away. Walter suggested he ride to town to see if he could find them that afternoon. Martin jumped up and went to get his horse. Martha looked at Walter and shook her head, and Walter said he was the same compulsive way about anything to do with boats when he was a boy.

Martin went to the barn to saddle up, and Henry and John were there showing Thomas the icehouse panels, the cork slabs, and the sawdust pile where they stored the ice. Henry saw how excited Martin was and Martin told Thomas that he would have him a rough design before he left for Boston. Thomas said he would be there for another week and said he would probably be back out to see them again. Martin said that would give him plenty of time and told Henry that he would be back around dark.

Thomas was very interested in how long the ice lasted when buried in the sawdust pile. He was also surprised at the stacks of cork slabs and said that he only knew cork from wine bottles. Henry added that his father had given Martin a three-foot long round piece about ten inches in diameter that was wrapped in canvas and had rope handles that could keep several people afloat. He said that they were kept on board ships to throw to men overboard because, oddly enough, many sailors couldn't swim. He said they had found this supply of cork abandoned in a warehouse and were lining up a source in Portugal for more. Thomas said that he would have to think about how thick to make the walls for the wagon Henry wanted. Henry said that the boat iceboxes they had made were four inches thick and they worked well for trips to Tybee. The one being built for food storage on Captain Ben's sharpie was to be four inches thick also, and hopefully it would keep things cold for a week. He said they had insulated the walls of the sharpie's hold slightly thicker. Thomas suggested they might build smaller wagons with thinner walls for local deliveries and bigger wagons with thicker insulation for longer distance deliveries. John said that, although they expected business year-round, most demand would be in the warmer months. He said that the long summers with sweltering heat and melting ice would mean melting profits.

Just as they were climbing onto the carriage to visit the site of the future icehouse, they were engulfed by a swarm of gnats. John cut a few small palmetto frons and handed one to Thomas so he could fan his face to keep them off. Henry snapped the reins, and with a little speed they escaped the swarm. Thomas said that he had experienced them once before but not as bad as this. Henry said no one, not even the indigenous people who had been here for thousands of years, could win against them. He said that with their eastern exposure and the prevailing winds from the southeast, the gnats were kept from them most of the time but the marsh grass was a breeding ground, and between them and Tybee there was a lot of marsh grass. They pulled up to the spot, on a small bluff by the river, and fortunately there was a breeze that kept the gnats away. Henry said they had picked this spot so they could offload ice directly to or from a boat and access it with a wagon. Their original plan was for a large icehouse there, but Walter's lawyers advised that the ice business be separate from the function of supporting the Tybee lighthouse, so, this would be temporary until the bigger icehouse could be completed on the new property. He added that their intention was to operate the ice business profitably without the use of slave labor, and to do that, every system needed to be practical and efficient, and that was why they needed his help.

Thomas said he liked that idea but imagined that it would be hard to do and be competitive and that the sawmill he had been working on required two hundred slaves. John said that was why they wanted to do the right engineering and smart business practices. He said that he had seen how the reliance on slave labor at the Darien sawmill could generate a profit but it sometimes stunted ingenuity. When a problem cropped up, management often just added more slave bodies instead of finding thoughtful solutions. He said that, since their business was new, they expected some loss but they intended to stay the course and make efficient adjustments until it became profitable. Thomas paused and looked at them both squarely and said, because of their positive attitude about thoughtful engineered solutions and their commitment to operate without slave labor, he wanted to commit, then and there, to work with them. Thomas said that he rather liked being part of a new, undiscovered business where growth would depend on creativity and invention. He cautioned that there would be mistakes, and they assured him that they were aware of that.

Henry then showed Thomas the boathouse just to give him an overview of the Milam operation. They then went to the new acreage they had bought for the new business. Henry explained that their initial thought was for a single large building with a barn for the horses and adjoining pasture and corral and another metal working and wood shop for wagon making, maintenance, and icebox production. He pointed to the area near the river where they visualized the large new icehouse. He told Thomas to use his own imagination and feel free to reimagine their plans. Thomas said that his first thought was that it would be better to have separate buildings because horses would not like the shop noises. Also, the woodworking shop would need to be the larger building to manufacture all the iceboxes and icehouse parts. Henry said that while they wanted to start as soon as possible, they would wait as long as necessary for a plan to be fully thought out. Thomas said that he would start on a rough site plan as soon as he got back to Savannah and visit them again to discuss possibilities before leaving for Boston. John said that he would be returning to Darien in two days but that he would feel comfortable with Thomas' professional ideas and Henry could keep him informed, as he had been doing by letters sent on the stage coach. Henry reminded Thomas to develop his own plan and not feel constrained by theirs. Thomas asked what materials were available locally for the building foundations and for road bases for the heavy wagon loads. Henry said they had an unlimited supply and easy access to tons of oyster shells. Thomas said they used gravel up north, but it was expensive. He said that sometimes clam shells were used but that they were not as abundant as the South's oyster shells that he had seen heaped up on the river banks. He said that a small mountain of oyster shells would be needed, and Henry said they would start piling them up as soon as they had the labor to do it. Thomas asked about the labor since they planned on not using slaves, and Henry said there was an abundance of labor with the influx of many skilled immigrants. He said they would probably set up a work camp on site, and Thomas said they could think about that on his next trip, after he had laid out the buildings. Thomas asked about water, and Henry said there was plenty of good water which was not that deep or difficult to get. Thomas said their flat terrain there would be easier to build on than Boston's hills full of rock and he would do more research before he came again. Henry and John expressed how pleased they were to have enlisted him, and Thomas said he was equally appreciative to have them as principal clients.

In Savannah, Martin found Captain Ben, Ashley, and Ken on the sharpie. Everyone was glad to see one another. Captain Ben was sitting on a bench on the wharf, and Ashley and Ken were doing maintenance on the boat. They took Martin's arrival as an excuse to take a break, and Ashley brought out mugs of tea. He asked what brought Martin to town. Martin said he wanted their input for Thomas on the design for a new sharpie, specifically designed for their ice business. Captain Ben said that his sharpie had been built in Boston, and that he had bought it there and sailed it down here. He said that most folks had not seen a boat like it then but there were many more here now, especially in the Carolinas. Martin said that Thomas had a friend in Boston who designed sharpies and who he would ask to design one for their needs and said that his father said to consult with y'all first. Captain Ben said that was an excellent idea. Give it some extra beam, and it can carry a heavy cargo but will only sail off the wind but being able to carry a lot may be more important and practical. Ben told Martin that he need not do a drawing, simply provide a list describing the boat's intended use, the waters it would work, how long the passages would be, the estimated weight and nature of the cargo. The designer would review the needs list and do the drawings. Ben asked Ashley and Ken what they thought. Ken said he preferred an unstayed mast, but that, since the boom would be used to load and unload heavy chunks of ice, the mast would need stays. But, he continued, it might be possible to attach stays halfway up the mast when the boom was in use and to detach them when lifting was done. He also said that he liked an easy-to-release anchor, so that the boat could be stopped quickly if things went wrong and a windlass that one man could operate alone if necessary. Ashley said it might be a more difficult build, but that, instead of a single large centerboard, he liked the idea of two easier-to-lift centerboards, one set in the cabin trunk and another in the cockpit. The design might reduce the drawback of sailing into the wind because of the wider beam and make the boat a little faster with only one down, sailing off the wind. Captain Ben said they would make a list of things to send along with Thomas. He said they would get it done in a few days and get it to the Milam place or to the inn where Thomas was staying. Martin told them how much he appreciated their help, and Ben asked about their planned trip to South Carolina.

Martin said he thought they would leave soon after Thomas left if arrangements had been made for a landing and a carriage on Saint Helena. Captain Ben showed Martin where Ashley planned for the icebox to be built and said that Jason should be there to install it soon. Martin asked if he needed to do anything regarding provisions, and Ashley said all he needed to do was pay for it. Martin said he didn't have any money with him, and Captain Ben said not to worry, he had accounts at all the necessary places and would include it all in the bill for the boat and crew.

Captain Ben said that his own sailing days would end soon and how did Martin's parents feel about him coming to work sooner. Martin said that his father would have him start the next day but his mother would rather him stay on land forever but had given her blessing. Ben said that the South Carolina trip would be a small introduction and that Ashley and Ken would need his help. Martin said he agreed with his father. Ben said that he had a trip to Darien planned as soon as they returned from South Carolina and hoped their ice supply would last until he was able to get back with more. Martin said that there was plenty when he had gotten some the week before and that he would pile sawdust higher and thicker and said that the last ice supply had lasted seven weeks and said he was heading home and would let them know when they heard from John's father in Beaufort.

On his way home Martin ran into John and Henry taking Thomas back to Savannah. He told Thomas that he would have information to him soon on their sharpie specifications. Thomas remarked at how quick that was, and Henry said that anything to do with boats happened quickly with Martin.

19.
THE WILLOUGHBY PLANTATION

The next day a message came from Richard. Henry was pleased that Richard had been careful not to mention names or places, but his message was clear. He said simply that everything requested was approved and would be ready whenever Henry provided him with their schedule. When Martin returned from the boathouse, he found Henry and John in Henry's office. Henry shared the information with him of how Richard had heard from Benjamin Chaplin and things were set for using his landing and carriage. He said that John and his family would be leaving the next day as would Thomas a few days later, then they could proceed. Martin said that he and Ashley and Ken could leave early and get the sharpie to Tybee because if the wind was against them, it could take a couple days and Henry could come on the regular supply boat, and they could all leave the next day for South Carolina. Henry said he liked that idea because he would much rather be home working than drifting a couple of days to get to Lazaretto. Martin said that he would take it from there and plan things so that Henry would be away from his work as little as possible, and if they were lucky and got back at the right time, Henry could ride the supply boat back home and save some time then to. Henry thanked Martin for the planning in a way that saved him time. Martin said for Henry just to get the legal paperwork from Sidney and the gold from the bank and he would handle the rest. For now, he could plan on going on the supply boat the next Wednesday and them all leaving Lazaretto early Thursday, arriving at Trenchers Inlet in the afternoon, and be at the Tombee landing by midmorning on Friday, but that all would depend on weather and wind. He added that tides were predictable but that winds were not. He looked at his tide chart again and told Henry that the supply boat would be leaving that day on the outgoing tide which started at noon. Martin said that things could change because they would need favorable winds to head out from Lazaretto north to Saint Helena Island and he would have Daniel check with Captain Jones about the forecast when their voyage got closer. Henry said that the weather was not the uncertainty that was most on his mind and said that it was the Willoughby character he was worried about.

From Richard's description, he didn't expect him to be an easy person to deal with, but there was something more that he had been thinking about. If he learned who we were, he might try some extortion or blackmail to expose the story of Alice and her family to get more money. We could all be vulnerable, including Ayana and her people. Martin said he didn't know how extortion or blackmail worked. Henry said that even after the purchase, Willoughby could threaten to go to the local newspaper and tell what he knew if we didn't agree to pay him more money. John had been silent but said that the talk of the newspaper made him wonder if there had been a reward posted by Willoughby when Alice and her family and the few friends had run away. Henry jumped up and said, "Brilliant," and startled Martin and John. He said the Savannah paper had archives back to 1802 and they could have Sidney and Hulbert check. Martin said that he had an idea but wasn't sure if it was possible. Henry and John were ready to listen because Martin's ideas were usually fresh and simple and less complicated than their own. They looked so intently at Martin that it made him stammer. He said that it might be better to ask if Ashley and Ken could talk to Willoughby instead of him and Henry. They could say they were coastal traders and had come across a small group of runaways starving on a remote island between there and Darien. The runaways had actually hailed them because they were starving to death and sick and wanted to be returned to where they had run away from years ago. John asked Martin when he had thought of the story, and Martin said just this very moment when you asked about a reward. Both were surprised, but John more so because Henry already knew how Martin had such a vivid imagination and his ideas were often different than most others. He and his family had learned that Martin had some shortcomings but had some extra comings that more than compensated. Martin paused a moment and gazed out Henry's office window and said that the runaways could have told Ashley and Ken where the place was that they ran away from and told that there had been a reward for their return. They could say that there were six in the group and that all were old except for two,
(meaning Alice and her brother) and they could take them all to the slave market in Savannah and make some money but would need proof of ownership, so they would prefer to bring them there and get the reward money instead. If Willoughby balked at paying the reward, Ashley could flash some gold and ask what Willoughby would take to sign ownership over to them, less the amount of the reward. Martin said that, from what Richard Wilcox had said, he would more likely be agreeable to get money than having to pay out money. If Willoughby hesitated, they could pretend to leave and say that they would just sell them on the underground market,

where they would not need proof of ownership. Martin said that, from what John's father said, Willoughby would not let the gold walk away. He would most likely agree to sign over ownership and would not tell anyone and he would probably not like to have any further dealings with coastal traders like them because they were often unsavory types. Henry interrupted to say that he didn't know if Ashley and Ken would agree to something like that and that he would feel awkward asking them. Martin said he was sure they would not only agree but also would be excited and feel special doing it. He said they wouldn't expect to be paid beyond what they were getting for the trip, but that it would be nice to give them some of the gold. The lawyer Sidney could draft an agreement with the slave names and let Ashley and Ken fill in their names as buyers and Willoughby sign as seller. Henry said that he could then, for the record, buy them from Ashley and Ken, if that was necessary. Henry took a long breath, leaned back and looked at Martin in amazement, and said he could have never guessed in a million years where this all was going. He exchanged a glance with John, and they both smiled at Martin. Martin said he had learned from Captain Jones that there was nothing wrong with telling a tall tale if it didn't harm anyone. Henry said that he would send a message to Richard about their schedule. After he saw John and his family off, he and Martin could talk with Ashley and Ken with Captain Ben also in on the conversation and he would also let his father know of their plan.

John said he needed to go get his family ready for the trip home tomorrow. He added that he was glad they had planned on stopping to spend the night at Lancy Jenkins' place on the way back because the long trip coming up had exhausted them. Henry said that he had Martin to thank because he had befriended Lancy, and he had agreed to have a nice clean place ready and food all fixed for supper and breakfast so you and Julia would have little to do when you got there. He also said he would send his best freight wagon to them for their furnishings when they were ready to leave next month, with two men to load things.

Because the trip back was for two travel days instead of one, and the coach was booked for them only, John and his family were able to start at 6:00 for the stage depot in the morning rather than 3:00 like before. Walter and Martha were there with Claudia and the kids, along with Alice and Johnny, and Jacob, Ellie, Thomas, Maggie, and even Izak, to see them off. Jacob had added a bench to the wagon for Henry and Martin, and the kids sat in the back with the luggage, with their legs hanging off. It was a happy farewell because everyone knew they were going to go home to pack and be back in a month.

At the depot the stationmaster helped them with their things. He thanked Henry for taking Jehu off his hands. Henry smiled and said he was glad to do it and caught a glance from Martin. Although they were going home to get ready to come back, Julia had tears on her cheeks and hugged Henry and Martin. They hugged the girls and helped them up into the coach. John said he would be anticipating news about their trip and any new developments. He said he had appreciated the regular messages that Henry had been sending. They all loaded up and the stage left.

Henry and Martin left the depot and headed for the waterfront to see Captain Ben and his crew. They went to Bay Street and down onto River Street and got in line with the other wagons coming to pick up freight from the row of ships at the wharf and went past the big boats to Captain Ben's regular. Ben was glad to see them and said he had something for them and something else to show them and asked them below. He pointed to the icebox that Jason had built and installed the day before. He said he wished they could have known and brought some ice and said what a good job Jason had done to fit it in like it had been built in originally. He lifted the lid and showed them the separate compartment for the ice and the storage area for food beside it. They were all like kids with a new toy. Martin said he would get some ice out soon and told them when they were planning to be ready to leave for South Carolina. Then Ben went to his berth and brought out a scrolled paper. He unrolled it to reveal that it was full of written descriptions and sketches of boat details. Ben said that they got carried away from simply making a list. They had begun to put a list together, all describing what they thought was important, and he began sketching. Ben said that he had learned early in his youth about drawing to scale and took some of their ideas and went into town and got some paper and a marker and a rule and set about drawing these and said they had a list to go with it and then read the list and pointed to his drawings. Martin looked over the drawings and noted the over fifty five foot length and the twelve-foot beam and the small centerboard trunk in the back of the cockpit. Ken said the man in Boston would probably laugh at some of their requests, like the detachable stays halfway up the main mast for extra lifting power when they would use the boom for lifting ice and all the storage holds were lined with a six inch thickness of cork. Ben said, "Anyhow, here it is." Henry thanked them and said he would take it with him and give it to Thomas when he came out tomorrow or the next day.

Martin told Ben when they planned to leave and how he, Ashley, and Ken could take the boat down to Lazaretto and how Henry could get on the supply boat. Henry said they had come to town to see John and his family off and also to discuss a matter of great importance that involved Ashley and Ken that they wanted Ben to hear. He said that he had talked to his father about it the night before and he had thought it was fine, but only if Ben and crew agreed. Henry said whatever they decided would in no way change his plans to go but would change how he had planned on going about things. He had the full attention and curiosity of the Captain and crew. They knew that Henry was all about getting things done, but always in a sensible and fair way, and idle talk was not his thing. Henry went on to remind them of what they knew about the character Willoughby who they were going to see and told them that they were among a small group of men that the Milam's trusted like family. As he described their original plan and their worry about it, Ken spoke up and asked why not let him and Ashley go and do the talking with Willoughby. Ben said quickly that Ken's idea was good. Henry and Martin looked at each other in astonishment, and Henry said that was exactly what they come to propose. Captain Ben said that now he wanted to go with them, and they all laughed hard for a few minutes. Henry said he had a hard time believing how this plan had come about only yesterday. Ashley said that Martin had already attained the rank of captain without having any sea time, and they laughed loudly. Ben said he was kidding about going but thought it was a good plan. He looked at Martin and said he was at least as salty as his old man, and more laughter came. A couple of sailors were walking by during the loud laughing, and one commented that they were starting on the rum quite early in the day and looked at Martin and said he was mighty young for that kind of behavior. When the laughing slowed down a bit, Henry stood and announced that he needed to be on his way because he had lots to do.

Henry and Martin were a happy pair on the ride home. Henry was relieved that Ken had suggested exactly what they were planning to ask, relieving him of the awkwardness of asking. Martin was simply happy. Ben and crew had been just as he expected, and he was getting excited about the trip. His first trip on the sharpie to Darien had been farther, but this trip was about more of an adventure about important matters that affected people's lives and there was much that remained unknown concerning the Willoughby character. Also, Captain Ben had said that they would need his help, so it would be his first trip as a crewman.

When they got home, Henry went straight to his father, told him about their talks, and how pleased he was. He noticed his father's eyes well up when he told how they said that Martin had become a captain without any sea time and was as salty as his father. Walter said he was proud of Henry accepting Martin's special ways, and Henry's eyes welled up too. Martha came in and asked how things were going, and Henry said much better than planned and told her when they expected to leave. She said that she was glad that Henry was going along with Martin, and Henry said that she should be glad that Martin was going along with him. Martha said she heard about the scallywag they were going to be dealing with and that worried her. Henry then told her that Ken had suggested that he and Ashley deal with the man, instead of him and Martin, and she said that made her feel better. She added that they were both tall and looked menacing even though they were quite the opposite. She said things are going to be a lot different the next month or so. First, you and Martin will be gone for a week then shortly afterward, Walter and I will be gone to Tybee, then she said, now that she thought of it, John and Julia and family will be moving up and soon after that we may have Daniel and Mary coming and that's not all and said Alice would be having her baby. Martha said she needed to lie down because just thinking of all that had made her tired.

The next day Thomas came, and they went to Henry's office. Thomas rolled out four pages of plans on Henry's desk. There was a site plan and three building plans. He said he had spent a couple of long contemplative nights about the project. He said he had said it before but this work was different from any other project he had done because most of what they were doing was unprecedented, whereas his work usually involved studying existing information and specifications. He said this was about imagining what the process would involve and then designing the buildings and site plan to match those thoughts and emphasized that there might be some trial and error, and that errors could be expensive, and that the real challenge was to set it all up to work and to minimize errors and oversights. Henry spoke up and very clearly told Thomas that he and John were fully aware of those uncertainties and they believed that by using his professional services, they would make less costly errors, but realized that even with his help, there would be some loss in the process. Thomas said he had kept the buildings simple and designed them so they could be added on to easily and have open spaces inside to easily adapt the work as they went along. The site plan had three buildings in one area and the icehouse set off a quarter mile away by the river. Thomas said he did not do a building plan for the icehouse, since that was already being built, but did indicate the elevation for the floor since they wanted to make the new wagons at the same height. He said the other buildings were the carpentry shop, the metal shop, and the large barn and corral for the horses. The extra-large barn had a big open area big enough for four wagons, separate corrals, food storage areas, harness and tack rooms, and an apartment for two workers, as they had asked. It was set a way off from the two shop buildings with a connecting fenced pasture beyond. The two shops were close together because there would probably be many projects involving wood and metal, particularly the wagons. All four buildings were connected by oyster-shell paving with additional paved areas for maneuvering horse teams and wagons. The carpentry shop was the biggest building and had open shed roofed areas on three sides so that cork and icehouse panel storage would be kept out of the weather. The inside was a clear span which Jason could adapt to as he saw fit and ample ventilation for the hot weather. Also on the site plan were two wells and sanitation waste fields, with the wells at the higher elevation.

Henry was impressed and, taskmaster that he was, became energized seeing it all. Thomas saw his excitement and said that they could stake out the buildings today, and Henry could start on site work as soon as he wanted, while the plans were being finalized. This made Henry somewhat giddy with pleasure and anxiety. He said he would send for Jacob to help stake things out, since he would be overseeing it all. Thomas added that he would have foundation and structural framing plans sent to him in a few weeks, but there was plenty of site work for them to get started on. He said he had just lately become familiar with a system of building with green, undried timber with special metal connector specifications and thought it would be a good fit for them. He said he would prepare a list of the sizes and quantity of beam material and other lumber needed, and John could probably get an order out quickly from the mill in Darien before he left, so it would arrive by the time the foundations were in. Thomas said his next planned trip down for the Savannah sawmill would be in about three months and he would have the wagon and boat plans and the specific characteristics of ice they had asked about and meet with them about the logistics of growing the business. Henry said he would find Jacob so that they could all go to the site.

Jacob, Thomas, and Henry finished up staking out the buildings by early afternoon. Henry asked Thomas if he wanted to stay for supper, but he declined because he had work to do for the sawmill before he left in a couple of days that he had put off so he could have what he just presented them. Henry gave him the folded plans that Ben had prepared. Thomas glanced at them and said his friend was a great sharpie designer and they would be pleased with what he would do for them. Henry told Thomas that he was welcome to stay with them when he came back, and Thomas thanked him but said that the inn in Savannah was convenient for his sawmill clients to stop by, but perhaps when that job was finished and he was working just with them that would be nice. Henry thanked him and they left to take Thomas back to the inn, and Jacob left for home. Later, on his own way home, Henry considered his involvement with Thomas.

Martin added a message to Daniel and Mary to the daily signaling to

Tybee that he may be there at Lazaretto for two nights on Ben's sharpie soon before leaving for Saint Helena Island. He had been very busy but had thought a lot about how they, especially Mary, were doing. He didn't let on to anybody, but he thought of her all the time. He wondered how Daniel was doing and if he had taught Ayana how to signal with the mirror, and he also thought a lot about Ayana and her people. It made him uncomfortable to think about things too much. He would be at Tybee in just a few days and get all his questions answered, and he looked forward beyond that to when Mary would be visiting for a few months.

Martin went to the boathouse to tell Jacob and Johnny about the trip and Johnny told Martin that he would be worried every minute that he and Henry were away making a deal with the devil, because Alice had told him stories about how mean their old master's son was. Martin said he didn't like going but that the man still owned Alice and her family and that Henry was hell-bent on making it so he would not have any claim on her, her family, or the new baby. He said he had seen Henry in some very determined moods but never like he was now to get this business taken care of. Johnny said that he couldn't, in all his time on this earth, thank Henry for risking his life to do that, and he said he thought the same of Martin and Ashley and Ken. Martin told him they had a good plan and John's father had fixed it all for them, so he didn't have to worry, and Johnny said worry was all he could do about it and he would sure look forward to seeing that boat coming back with them on it alive.

Later, Martin found Alice home, and Ellie was there after getting her work done early like she had been doing lately to be with and help Alice. Thomas was there and ran up and hugged Martin. Ellie held the screen door open for Martin and said they were just talking about him but he didn't have to worry because it was all good. She said they were talking about him going to South Carolina because they had just heard he was going soon, and Martin was amazed at how fast news got around. Seeing his surprise, Ellie smiled and said she also knew Henry had been over at that new land with a Yankee man, putting sticks in the ground for some buildings, and that nothing could go on around there without her knowing about it quick. She said she heard about things all around quicker than she did about some things in her own house. She said that Izak was arriving as she left, supposedly to do book work with Maggie, but she knew better than that. She got a laugh out of Alice and Martin, and Martin said Izak was a good man and Ellie agreed and said, "Yeah and the man part is what I'm worried about." Alice said she might be a grandmother soon, and Ellie jumped up and said she better go home and check on them now. Alice said no and for her to go fix some tea, and Ellie reluctantly went into the kitchen.

Alice said she was glad he had come by because she wanted to talk to him before he and Henry left and she had been expecting him. Martin said he wasn't worried but simply wanted to know everything he could that might be helpful. She said Melvin Willoughby was a hateful man and she didn't know what he might do or try but she was confident in Henry's abilities and she had been thinking of one thing that might could help. She said she was very young but remembered a woman that was her mother's and father's age and they had grown up there together and were dear friends. Her name was Prissy, and everybody liked her because of her good nature. Alice said she didn't know her whole story, but while she had been over at the Indian Islands seeing her parents, they told stories about her that she wouldn't have been able to understand when she was young. She just remembered that she was nice and everyone liked her. She said her mother said that Prissy was a very pretty child and only had a mother, and her mother died, and the good old Colonel Willoughby felt sorry for her, and one day he picked her up and sat her on his knee and gave her some candy from his pocket, but she wouldn't eat it, and he asked her what was wrong, and she said she didn't want to eat it because the other kids didn't have any. He waited, thinking she would change her mind, but she didn't, so he pulled some more candy out and gave it to the other children there watching, and Alice's mother and father were two of the four children there, and only when they ate the candy, did Prissy eat hers. Old man Willoughby was surprised and thought it curious how she had acted. The next day he came again and sat her on his lap and gave her candy, and again she wouldn't eat until the others got some, and he had come with extra, and he gave the others some, and from then on every day or two he would bring sweets, and she wouldn't eat any until he gave them all some. He got attached to her and to the joy that the children caused him, and when she got older, he treated her a little like his daughter instead of a slave and would bring her into the house and read her stories. This is when his son, Melvin, began to get jealous because of the attention she was getting, and she was so bright that she began to listen and follow the words in the book, until she could read them on her own and asked if she could teach the other kids to read. The Colonel wouldn't allow that but told her that she could read to the kids sometimes there on the house steps but had to give him back the book when she was finished. This led to other privileges that she always wanted to share with the others. When Colonel Willoughby died, and his son became the master, any and all privileges stopped, and everything got bad. He drank a lot and took something he got from town and would get delirious and talk crazy and he was as mean to Prissy as his father had been nice to her. She got beatings regularly for the smallest reasons and sometimes for no reason at all. Everybody loved Prissy, and they hated to see her getting treated worse than any of them. They began to manipulate the master when he was delirious on laudanum and whiskey, to believe that Prissy was in touch with spirits, and they carried on about it in front of him even when he was sober and said that she was able to talk to his father's spirit and sometimes the spirit of the old, crippled slave he had beaten and chained to the outhouse and let die. He tried to resist what they said, but the part about her talking to his dead father got under his skin, and they sensed that it made him afraid, and they took advantage of his fear and were able to control him somewhat and keep him from doing mean things to Prissy. Alice's mother said that she didn't know if Prissy was still alive and there was no telling what had gone on since they ran away. Alice said she didn't even know if this information would be helpful, but if there was a chance to find out if Prissy was still alive, her mother and father would like to know how she was because she had been the bright spot for them and everybody there. Even when things got very bad, she always had a smile and made people feel good. Martin said he didn't know if the information would help but it was good to know and he would find out what he could. Ellie had brought her tea in as Alice had begun her story and set it down but hadn't touched it and had become mesmerized listening and asked Alice why she hadn't told her the Miss Prissy story before, and Alice smiled and said she was waiting until the story needed telling. Martin knew that this would be the big story now all about the place and knew the true meaning would not be lost but the story would change a little with each telling. Then Martin told Alice how they planned to go about things, and Ellie was very surprised about Ashley and Ken sticking their necks out for people that were not even kinfolks and said they must be special. Martin said they were and that he would be taking a lot of boat trips with them before long. Ellie asked Martin why he couldn't be happy enough just working there because everything he needed was there. Martin couldn't answer for a few moments and then said he guessed he was going off so that this place would be able to stay here. He wasn't sure where that answer came from and wasn't even sure it was correct, but Ellie and Alice seemed to understand something about it because their eyes welled up but didn't drip.

After the story, the three of them sat and drank the tea. Alice told Martin that, when her memory came back of the massacre and her family and all, and she was first able to talk about it to his mother, he was in his mother's belly like her child was now. She said that she felt a closeness with his mother that was more than even the closeness she had ever felt with her own mother. She said that was then and here we are now and she took Martin's hand and put it on her belly, and he felt a slight movement and smiled at Alice. Martin wondered, be it boy or girl, if their life would be as close as his was to Alice. He looked at Ellie, and she was in a strange way, staring at Alice's belly, and all she could manage to say was that it was a little girl in there and she could see her. Martin hadn't known what he was in for coming to see Alice today, but he was sure glad that he had. She had told him the story of Prissy that interesting and might be useful, but more importantly, she had filled him with a feeling of strength and clarity and purpose and gratitude, as she always did. They sat a bit, then Martin stood and leaned down and hugged Alice and told her to sit tight, and Ellie got up and hugged Martin and told him that she was filled with the spirit from his visit and would be looking over the water for him to be back.

When Martin got home, he saw his mother and father on the porch. His father pointed at the floor, and Martin laughed out loud. There were two long canvas things about as big around and long as him, and he knew immediately what they were. Walter said he wished he could say that it was his idea, but it had been his mother's idea. He said these were made just like the lifesaving float he had gotten him for his dugout but bigger. He said that one was for his new boat and he was giving one to Captain Ben for his sharpie and they were solid cork and each one could keep four men afloat. Martha said that, if he promised to always have one when he was on his boat or when he was on the sharpie, she would give her full blessings to him going off in boats. Martin was still feeling warm and fuzzy from his visit at Alice's house and couldn't stop the tears from rolling down his checks, and he hugged them both. He told her that he would promise what she had asked. He sat with them and talked about his day and the story from Alice and about what Alice said about how close she had felt to Martha, and then he noticed that his mother's eyes were teared up, and he thought to himself that he couldn't remember a day of so many tears.

The next morning, Martin was up early and went around to Henry's end of the house and saw light in the kitchen window and went in to have tea. Henry was having coffee and had his list out. Martin said he had time to help, and Henry said he needed a message sent to Sidney in town to see if he could find the reward offered for Alice and her family in the Savannah newspaper archives and give him the list of the names and ages of Alice, her family, and the others that ran away with them. He asked him also to go to the bank and pick up the gold pieces that would be used to pay off Melvin Willoughby. He handed Martin the letter to Sidney, the bank note for the gold, and a heavy duty leather purse with a strap to go around his neck. Martin said he would go to Sidney first and then stop to tell Ashley and Ken to come there to stock up on produce for the trip, spend the night, and leave from there. He said he would go by the bank last so he could come straight home with the gold, and Henry said that was a good idea. He handed Martin another bank note and said he could also drop that off to Jason. Claudia set a plate of eggs and grits in front of Martin, and he said he would leave right after he ate. Henry thanked him and said he felt better now because he had been struggling about how he could get everything done and Martin would save him almost a day.

Martin enjoyed his early ride into town. He liked the smell of the marsh areas, and he particularly liked the riverfront smell that started as he entered the city. Sidney's home was near the townhome that John was moving to. Martin could tell that no one was awake yet, and he knocked on the door a while before Sidney's wife came. She recognized Martin through the peephole and opened the door with a smile. He apologized for coming so early but that he had an important message from Henry for Sidney, and he handed it to her. She said she would wake him and give him the message, and Martin thanked her and left to see Jason. Jason was just arriving at his shop as Martin approached. Without getting off his horse, Martin handed the envelope to Jason and told him what a good job he did on the icebox in the sharpie. Jason thanked him for bringing him the payment, and Martin left to see Ashley and Ken. He found them sitting on the sharpie deck having tea and asked where Ben was. They said that he had taken a room on the hill to stay while they were gone and had moved in early. Martin said they could come out to their place and get what supplies were needed, load up with ice, and leave from there the following morning. They said it was a good plan, and Martin said he had another errand and would look for them later. Ashley said he was glad he had gotten everything from Savannah for the trip yesterday, so they could get going right away and could catch the last of the outgoing tide and be at the Wilmington River when it changed and drift up to the Milam plantation and be there in a couple hours. Ken said he liked the idea because he was bored and was ready for moving and a change of scenery.

Martin was next at the bank just as it opened and he went in to find the man he had seen Henry speak with before. He had to remind the banker that he was Henry's brother because he had kept quiet and out of the way when he had gone to the bank with Henry. The banker pretended that he recognized Martin when he handed him the message and bank note from Henry. He looked at the bank note and was a little hesitant, and Martin asked if there was a problem. Just then Mr. Johnson walked into the bank, saw them, came directly over, and said that his luckiest days were when he saw any member of the Milam family. The banker was surprised that Mr. Johnson knew Martin, and since Mr. Johnson was one of his banks best and oldest customers, he changed his attitude and told Martin that he would be right back with what he wanted. Mr. Johnson chatted with Martin, and Martin said how glad he was that he had arrived and put the banker at ease. Mr. Johnson said that bankers were just natured funny. The banker handed Martin two tightly wrapped heavy rolls of coins, and he put them in the leather purse he had over his shoulder and head. Mr. Johnson boasted to the banker that Martin would be, before he was out of his teens, a captain well known in Georgia and South Carolina. He spoke quite loud, and Martin recalled that Mr. Johnson didn't hear well. Martin may not have been recognized when he came this time, but because of Mr. Johnson's loud praise of him, all the bank workers were looking to see what the talk was about. Martin thanked Mr. Johnson for bonifying who he was, and the banker tried to gracefully apologize for not recognizing him immediately and said they were not accustomed to customers as young as him and wished to himself that he could have said it better. Martin wished them a good day and left.

When Martin walked into Henry's office and handed him the gold, Henry was surprised to see him back so soon and thanked him for saving him the time. Martin said that everything had gone well and that Ashley and Ken were coming afterwhile to make preparations to leave on tomorrow's early tide for Tybee. That would give them an extra day in case the trip down the river was slow. Henry thanked him again for setting things up so he could go on the supply boat and have more time to do his work. Martin didn't say it but he was hoping the trip to Tybee would only take a day or even less so he would have a full day or more to do some things he wanted. He wanted to visit a bit with Captain Jones, the Dyers, and especially Mary. He wished he had time to visit Ayana and Alice's family, but that would have to wait until his return from South Carolina. He had noticed a slight breeze out of the south and if that kept up, they could set all the sails they could have a wind on their beam and get there as fast or faster than a supply boat trip. Henry asked if he had heard Captain Jones' weather forecast yet, and Martin said he probably would hear it from his father later. Henry said that if it wasn't good and he didn't come on the regular supply boat trip, he could just have the boatmen make a special trip to bring him when the wind was right, but that Martin might be stuck at Tybee for a while. Martin said he would be happy either way – leaving as planned or waiting at Tybee. Seeing Mary for a few days would be nice. Martin went to his room and packed his clothes and a few things and headed for the boathouse. He carried one of the long lifesaver floats on his shoulder, and its cork smell reminded him fondly of his little dugout boat, and he wondered if Daniel had become good at sailing it. When he got to the boathouse, the sharpie was a quarter mile away and drifting slowly towards the boathouse without any sails up and against the southerly breeze. He walked down to the water's edge and watched as they set the pulling boat over, got in it with a line attached and pulled the sharpie closer, got back on and set the big bow anchor, then got back in the small boat and rowed to shore. Martin greeted them ashore; he asked if they were hungry, but they had eaten while drifting from Savannah.

They walked to the barn and rigged the carriage. Martin said they would dig out the ice later when they had everything else, so the ice wouldn't be out long and would not melt much. They went to the chicken house, and when Ellie saw Ashley and Ken with Martin, she carried on about how thankful she was about what they were doing and how brave they must be. Martin asked her if she would dress out a half dozen chickens for them to take, and she said she could have them ready in about thirty minutes, and Martin said he would be back. They went to the small barn next to the vegetable plot that Izak had worked on and his mother filled a large tote with a variety of vegetables, including sweet and white potatoes, beans, carrots, and greens. They went back to the chicken house for the chicken and then to the sawdust pile. They dug into it and sawed off a large chunk of ice that they put in the carriage and covered with a large sail cloth. They piled the sawdust higher and thicker than they found it. Martin lifted the sail cloth and put the chicken under it to stay cool, and he said he had one other thing that he had gotten yesterday that was in their icebox at home. They pulled up to the back of the house, and Martin ran and came back with three jars of clabber, a big block of butter, and a big package of bacon and put them under the sail cloth too. Then they headed back to the boathouse.

Martin pulled the wagon close to the water's edge, and they loaded the food supplies into the pulling boat and rowed out to the sharpie. Once down in the sharpie, Martin marveled again at the job Jason had done. He had built a big wooden box, lined it with two layers of cork, lined with copper sheet with soldered joints, and added a small drain in the bottom that went out through the hull well above the waterline. The box had a partition to separate the ice and the food. There was a lid for each compartment, and they were insulated and copper-lined and fit snuggly to keep warm air out. The storage area was big and divided so that meat could be stored separately. He said he would be curious how long the ice would keep. Ashley and Ken set the big chunk in and closed the lid. Ken set the chicken and bacon on one side and everything else but the potatoes and carrots on the other side, and there was still plenty of room. Ashley said that they had enough for at least a few weeks before needing to re-supply. He said that they should eat the chicken within a few days because he didn't know how long chicken on ice would last, and it wouldn't be pleasant for them to all be sick with diarrhea, and Ken said that was sure right. Martin said they still had things that his mother had made for them. Ken rowed Martin in so he could take the carriage back, and Martin said his family was expecting them for supper and Ken said they had a few things to do first.

Martin took the horse and carriage to the barn and walked home. His father was on the porch and told Martin that the weather report from Captain Jones was that the wind would probably stay out of the south for a few days and then swing a little southwest for a few days, but there could be a northeaster on the way in a week or less. Martin said a northeaster would certainly get them home in record time but coming into Lazaretto could be a little rough, especially if the tide was running out strong. Walter said they could always go inside but that would take three days instead of a day on the outside, He added that, if the weather was clear and it was not too bad a northeaster and if they came in on the last of the high tide, it would be a rough ride but should be alright. Walter said he was confident that Ken and Ashley would do the right thing. Martha asked Martin if he had told them about supper, and he said he had. She said that she had baked them a sweet potato casserole to take and Ellie had cooked them a dozen deviled crabs that they could keep in the ice chest and warm up when they were ready. She had also made a pecan pie that was in the ice-box. Martin said they were certainly going to South Carolina first class. She said that Alice was coming to supper and had not told Johnny yet, but he was coming too.

A little before dark, Ashley and Ken showed up at the same time little Thomas did, running ahead of Alice and Johnny and he joined Henry's kids playing and screaming in the yard. Martha commented that Alice was getting big and said she thought it wouldn't be more than a month until her baby came, and Alice agreed. Claudia came onto the porch and said Henry would be right there. Yaupon was poured over ice, and Martha went around to each mug and added a little honey, which she always did on special occasions. Henry came in, and Walter asked him to add a little rum to all that would like a little, and all accepted a little including Martin. Walter stood and proposed a long toast to the success of the South Carolina trip and a special toast to Ashley and Ken, who were both un-comfortable with the attention and more interested in the wide variety of food spread before them.

After supper, Martha brought out another pie that Ellie had sent and served it up. Ashley and Ken said it was the best pie they had ever had, and Ken asked Martha to please tell Ellie that and to thank her for them. Soon after, Alice said she needed to go home because she was tired, and she hugged Martin, Henry, Ashley, and Ken and thanked them for what they were doing. Only after several attempts were they able to corral Thomas, who was having so much fun playing. After they had gone, Henry said he had something for Ashley and Ken and reached into his pocket. He handed five shiny eagle gold pieces to Ken and five to Ashley, and they were both shocked. Henry said that it was only gold and hardly compared to the deed they had so willingly offered to do for his family. Both of them were speechless, and Walter told them that they and Ben were like family now and they were always welcome there anytime. He asked Henry to pour them all a half dram more of rum, and he toasted to fair winds and a safe trip and success in dealing with Melvin Willoughby.

The next morning, instead of having tea with Henry and Claudia, Martin went to the boathouse and had tea with Ashley and Ken. Jacob was there with Johnny and had brought egg biscuits for them and a few more, thinking that Martin might be there. Martin was about to walk to the house to say good bye when he saw Henry, Claudia, Walter, and Martha coming in the carriage to see them off. They got out, and Henry was carrying a basket with the deviled crabs, the pecan pie, and a casserole. Martha said that Alice had wanted to come but was feeling tired. Jacob rowed Ashley and Ken out in the skiff while Martin was hugging and saying good-bye and listening to a list of warnings from his mother. Martin climbed in the skiff and rowed himself out, and Ken and Ashley had the sails hoisted by the time he climbed aboard. The south wind and tide were going the same way, and they hoisted the jib and let it out. When they weighed anchor, the long sharpie drifted backwards a bit before the big jib could swing her around. Then with the skiff in tow, the wind and tide behind them, the big boat glided toward the big Savannah River. Martin sat at the tiller and watched as Ken and Ashley skillfully set the fore and main sails. They were at the Savannah River in less than a half hour.

Captain Jones had been correct in his wind prediction, and as they steered east, once out of the Wilmington River, the wind was on their beam and sometimes slightly on their stern as the river zigged and zagged. Ashley mentioned to Martin that this trip down the river might even be faster than the first trip when he and Henry had gone with them. He added that it wasn't always this fast. Often they would be a couple days when they were leaving Savannah when the wind would be out of the east and slow their drift down to a mile every couple of hours, and they would have to anchor and wait for the tide to come back in and start back out, then weigh anchor and drift some more. He said it usually didn't take more than two days and usually took a half day, but a strong northeaster could cause them to just set the hook and wait it out for however many days it would blow, which was usually five or six days, then start again toward Tybee.

The sail handling was easy on the way down with little adjusting necessary, and Ken let Martin take the helm most of the way. The sharpie's long waterline with the centerboard down could go long stretches with very little steering, and when the river switched back, they only had to let the sails out a bit or tighten them up a little. It was a leisure trip, and Martin had plenty of time to think about things. He thought about Ayana and her people and Captain Jones and hoped he was alright because he seemed so frail when Martin had last seen him. He thought about Mallie and wondered if he had made it to Philadelphia and of the adventure of how things went with him. He thought about Turtle Island and one day going there. Maybe he could go when the winter came and the snakes were underground, but Charles said the two-legged snakes were around all year there and they were worse than the no-legged kind. He hadn't explored Daufuskie Island or Hilton Head yet and wanted to do that. When they passed the place where the duelers were buried together, he remembered seeing the two men shoot each other on the beach and he thought that, in a way, he had not felt the same since. Something had changed about him because of it. Then he thought about Mary and pictured her in his mind's eye and she had changed him too. She was so quick-witted and could think so much faster than him, but she never made him feel bad about his slower wits and thinking. He tried to think of all the things she said that he liked. He couldn't remember very many, but he could feel something within, inside himself, that he had never felt and could remember the sparkle in her smile and eyes when she talked to him. He was lost in that feeling and sparkle when he heard Ken's voice, with a little alarm in it, asking if he saw the ship they were coming up on quickly. He jumped back into the moment and steered clear and was honest and told Ken that he was distracted by his thoughts. Ken said that was ok, it happened to him sometimes too, but they both should be careful about that. He added that it's best not to daydream in the river because there were always other boats and a hill on both sides, but once out in the ocean daydreaming was safer. When the river went eastward before switching back, Martin saw the Tybee lighthouse for a few minutes before its view was blocked again, and he felt some excitement building. Ashley went below and looked at the pocket watch they kept in a small wooden box and said they would be at Lazaretto by one o'clock. He relieved Martin at the wheel, and Martin went below and brought out the monocular to have next time the lighthouse came into view. When it did, he looked, but the boat motion made it hard to see very good, and Ken said, yeah, that thing only works good when things are still.

As they got closer, the wind got stronger, not because it was blowing harder, but because there were fewer trees to the south and endless open marsh, where there was nothing to block it, and it could fetch up more. The boat speed increased and in an hour, they were closing in on Lazaretto Creek. Ashley pointed to the land to the north that was a narrow island called Cockspur between the north and south channels and said that Ben said there was talk of a huge fort being built there one day to guard the river and that it was supposed to be in an invincible position because it was surrounded by marsh and the closest place that cannons could be set up was on Tybee and that would be out of range. Martin mentioned another small fort Charles had talked about to be built between the lighthouse and the ocean; Ashley said he had heard about that too and that it was called a Martello tower. Martin asked Ashley what he knew about Daufuskie, and Ashley said not much except that he heard that the plantation owners there were Tories. Martin asked how that could be since the war with England was over. Ashley said that people could be American but still favor the Crown, and Martin said he didn't understand government or politics at all. Ken said there were a lot more important things to understand. Ashley told Ken that he would get up all the speed he could and go into Lazaretto Creek as close to the inside bank as possible where the outgoing current was not as strong, and if they pointed up as much as possible, they might be able to get a few hundred yards up and not too far from the landing. Ken said he would stand by to drop the hook when they came to a stop. Martin asked if he could do anything, and Ken said to just sit, watch, and learn. Martin watched as Ashley cut it close as he had said, and Ken tightened up on the sails. The boat slowly made headway up the creek until the current began to win and Ken dropped the anchor and they drifted back out only about a hundred yards down from the landing. Ken let out a lot of anchor line and then set the stern anchor and cranked in the bow line until the sharpie was anchored on both ends. Martin helped get the centerboard up and the sails down and secured.

Some yelling could be heard from the landing, and it was Daniel and Mary. Martin waved and yelled that they were coming over in a few minutes. Ken said he would row Martin over to see his friends and come back since he and Ashley had things to do on the boat. Martin said he could stay and help because he needed to learn those things. Ken said there would be plenty of time for him to learn everything and that he had heard how sweet Martin and Mary were on each other. He laughed, and Martin smiled and said okay. He said he could see a basket in the wagon and that it was probably supper, and Ashley said he loved Margo's cooking. Martin and Ken climbed in the boat. Ken rowed and Martin steered up the creek about a hundred yards and across to the landing. Ken used the oar like a paddle and eased the boat up to the two long rails that the boatmen used to slide the supply boat up the bank every week. He waved to Daniel and Mary and said they would be over in a bit. Martin stepped out onto one of the rails carefully because they were wet and slippery. He walked up on it to above the high-water mark and hugged Daniel and Mary at the same time. Daniel said that Martin looked different, and Mary said he looked bigger, and Martin said they looked different too. Mary said she had missed him and that things had been boring since he had gone. Daniel said that it had been boring for her because all she did was read books and write in her notebooks all the time. Martin said he hadn't been bored but he missed them, Tybee, the lighthouse, Charles and Margo, Captain Jones, Ayana and her people, Alice's family, and the Indian Islands. He asked how Captain Jones was, and Daniel said he was as good as ever from his shoulders up, except for his eyes, but rusty from his shoulders down. It was hard for him to get on his feet after sitting for a while."The pilot crews have taken it on themselves for at least one of them to stay with him when they left for Savannah."

A few gnats attacked Martin's ear, and he swatted at them. Daniel said they needed to walk out on the high oyster mound on the edge of the creek because it was too breezy there for them. Once there Daniel talked about the dugout that Martin had given him and how he had practiced a lot and learned how to sail it almost as good as Martin. Mary laughed and said he had learned how to capsize it better than Martin too. Daniel said that was true and that he had learned to right it easily also since he had so much practice. He said that he had been over often to see Ayana and that she had learned to signal with the little mirror device and they had been practicing a lot. He said they hadn't practiced today but he could take Martin up tomorrow and show him and that Ayana would be excited that he was here and Alice's family would be too. Mary asked him how long he was staying, and he said until day after tomorrow. He said that he was free tomorrow and Henry was coming on the supply boat and they would depart early the next day. He told them their plans, and Mary said that Martin had one adventure after another. She said they had gotten a coded letter from Mallie that she would show to him tomorrow. Martin asked if he was alright, and Mary said he seemed to be quite well, but she couldn't figure out everything he was saying in the letter, and maybe Martin could help with that. Martin was amazed to hear it. He told them about Captain Ben retiring and him becoming a mate on the sharpie before too long. Mary was wide-eyed and asked when because she hoped to herself that he would not be away when she and Daniel visited Savannah. She was relieved when he said that it would probably be in about six months. Martin said that they would probably come after his mother and father's visit to Tybee in about a month. Mary said she was looking forward to the trip. Daniel said that he didn't like to leave his father with all the work but was looking forward to time with Martin. Martin said the Milam place was busier than ever and told a bit about John coming and the ice business that he and Henry were starting. They heard Ashley yell and saw them coming over in the boat and walked to meet them. Mary told them that she had some food from her mother and asked if they were hungry, and Ashley said they hadn't eaten since breakfast. Mary said that, since the gnats were not so bad out on the oyster mound, that they should eat there. Daniel brought a blanket and the food basket over and spread the blanket on the top of the mound, and Mary laid everything out. She took the jug of yaupon and mugs from the basket and poured everyone some and she served the big biscuits. Each one had two fried eggs and a thick slice of bacon. Mary said she could only eat one biscuit if anyone was still hungry. Ashley and Ken both smiled and asked Mary to thank her mom and thanked her for bringing the food. Martin was unusually hungry and ate both of his biscuits. He had never eaten more than one of Margo's biscuits before and was full and satisfied when he was done, and so was Daniel. Mary took a knife from the basket and cut her extra biscuit and gave Ashley and Ken each a half. After the meal, Daniel asked Martin if he wanted to stay the night at the lighthouse and his parents were hoping he would. Martin said that he had planned on staying on the sharpie, but Ken told him to go to the lighthouse, and Martin said he reckoned he could. Ken said they had more to do on the boat and again thanked Margo and Mary for the meal and returned to the sharpie.

Martin, Mary, and Daniel lingered and chatted. Martin told the story of Prissy, and Mary said that she hadn't brought her notebook, so he would have to tell the story to her parents later and she could take notes. Daniel said that all Mary did was read and write in her notebook. Mary asked him what was wrong with that, and he said there was nothing wrong with it but that she should get outside more. Mary told Martin that she had almost two hundred pages of notes about her mother and father's stories about their parents and grandparents and about earlier times on Tybee.

She said that she had gotten some good stories from Captain Jones, and Martin said he bet she did. She said that Daniel had promised to take her over to visit Ayana to write whatever she had to say, and she hoped to do that before coming to Savannah. Martin said she could easily get another two hundred pages from Ayana because the Indians were more a story telling people than colonials were and she had a good memory. Mary said she had a hundred pages of notes from when he had come for the bridge-work. Daniel suggested they go back to the lighthouse, so they gathered up and walked back to the wagon.

The ride on the narrow oyster road over the marsh, connecting the small hammocks, was Martin's favorite. To the north he could see Turtle Island, Daufuskie, and Hilton Head. His favorite view, however, was to the south, out over the vast area of marsh with the Indian Islands scattered in it. Each island had a slightly different shape but most were higher on the north ends where the strong northeast winds had piled up sand and debris over the years. He looked mostly at the profile of the long island where Ayana and her people and Alice's family were.

He remembered clearly his first visit when he had come in the wagon and seen it all. He had been immediately enchanted with the Indian Islands, knowing only that he wanted to visit them. Now learning their mysteries, he felt somewhat satisfied but no less enchanted. The biggest mystery left was Turtle Island in South Carolina. He knew he wouldn't be satisfied until he had gotten there, and he wondered what mysteries were waiting to be discovered. Mary saw the distant look on Martin's face that she had come to recognize and she bumped him with her elbow, and he jumped back into his skin. She laughed and asked where he had been and he laughed back and said it was so easy to fly over to the Indian Islands and Turtle Island with his imagination. No mud to slog through; no boats to drag through the marsh and the big snakes and pirates on Turtle Island couldn't get to him. That got Daniel laughing and he said he had never traveled in his imagination and was often surprised at the things Martin said. He halted the horses on the oyster shell path in the middle of the marsh, and all three laughed uncontrollably. The laughter would stop, only to start up again as soon as one of them caught another's eye. When they reached bridge, the horses crossed with no hesitation, and Martin felt satisfied for having suggested nailing the decking boards close together so the horses were comfortable. He noticed that the cedar planks which had been so red at first had turned silver. Daniel asked Martin if he wanted to go the beach way or the other way, and Martin said the other way because he wanted to wait to see Captain Jones. Daniel continued behind the sand dunes and soon pulled through the gate into the lighthouse compound. He dropped Martin and Mary off at the house and went to the horse barn to put the horses away. Margo came out the back door and waited on stair stoop and hugged Martin when he came up. Charles heard the commotion and waited for Martin in the kitchen. He hugged him and said that things had been awfully dull since he left. Margo said she missed Martin but sort of liked the dullness for a change. They asked how everybody was and said they hadn't heard yet when Walter and Martha were coming. Martin said that it would be soon after he and Henry got back from the trip to South Carolina. Margo said she would bring tea and he could tell them about the trip because they had only heard vague things about it.

They sat inside since the air was a little cool. Martin said that he would let his parents tell them the details of the big meeting at their house, but he wanted Charles to know how many times his father had said that he wished Charles and Margo could have been there. Charles said he wished he could have been there too but had thought it best to stay even though Daniel would have been capable in his stead.

Next Martin told Margo he wished she could have seen how much Ashley and Ken enjoyed her biscuits and how he liked them too. He noticed Mary had her notebook and was waiting for him to get on topic. He explained how now that they knew where Alice's family was and after the ordeal with Mallie and the slave hunters, Henry worried that if they were ever caught and the story of Alice got out, it would probably be written about in the Savannah paper. And since the Savannah paper was the biggest around, it was delivered and read by the people in Beaufort and their old owner could get wind of it and make trouble. He could make a claim on them as legitimately his and they would have to return to him, including Alice's baby and her brothers son too. He said Henry couldn't sleep at night, worrying about those possibilities and had put this task ahead of everything. , even his and John's new ice business.

Martin explained what they planned to do and how they had learned from John's father about Benjamin Chaplin, Tombee landing, and the prospect of paying for use of the landing and a carriage. Charles asked if Richard Wilcox had told Chapman who was coming. Martin said that fortunately Richard had not mentioned any names, which would make it possible for Ken and Ashley to go in his and Henry's stead to deal with Melvin Willoughby, which they offered to do. He outlined the story they planned to tell about finding the half-starved slaves on an island between Savannah and Darien. He said that Henry had originally planned to deal with Willoughby himself, but then worried that if Willoughby discovered his identity, he might later demand more money with a threat of telling his story to the Savannah newspaper, which would stir up a big mess for everyone. He explained that Walter's old lawyer friend had found the Savannah newspaper copy from years ago, placed by Willoughby describing the slaves and the reward. The lawyer had drawn up a contract to purchase them if Willoughby elected not to pay the reward, which is what they hoped would happen. He said that Henry was coming tomorrow in the late afternoon and he might not have time to visit since they would leave early the next morning. Margo said she hoped he would have time. Mary asked what if Willoughby said he would pay the reward and demand the slaves be returned. Martin said that they were hoping that he wouldn't. They had gold enough to make a generous offer, and according to Richard Wilcox, Willoughby was always in a financial bind, and always needed money. Margo asked why Henry was going if Ashley and Ken were going to be dealing with Willoughby. Martin said that he had never seen Henry so determined about anything as much as this and he was prepared to go see Willoughby himself if things didn't go as planned with Ashley and Ken. Charles said he had liked Ashley and Ken before but and after hearing this he liked them more. Martin told how it had been their idea to go instead of him and Henry. He then told the story of Prissy that Alice had learned from her mother. Mary asked why Prissy hadn't run away when Alice's parents had, and Martin said he didn't know. Mary said she could ask Alice's mother about it when she went over to the Indian Islands.

When Martin finished, Margo said that there wasn't much new around there except that they had quit having guards. The guards were not needed any more like they may have been with all the British ships around during the war. She said that the guards were always quitting because the remote assignment on Tybee was not tolerable. Over the years there were only a few that they felt comfortable with but they tried to treat them well. They had been hired by the state and not part of Walter's Federal Government contract. She said they had fixed up the little guard quarters nicely for Walter and Martha to stay in so they wouldn't feel under foot in the house and she hoped that having their own little place would have them come and stay more often. She said that Daniel and Mary getting ready to go off was the biggest news around there lately.

Charles said that there was more talk about a new fort being built in front of them, but he didn't think they needed it any more than they had the guards, especially since there was a plan to build a huge fort on Cockspur. Martin said Ashley had mentioned that, and Charles said that was probably a few years down the road. He said what was most needed was a lighthouse to mark the south channel at Cockspur, and he hoped that it would come soon because it was so hazardous especially when the northeasters blew. Martin agreed and that they might be coming back in a northeaster according to Captain Jones. Charles said that Daniel had probably told him about the signaling from Ayana and Martin said he had and was glad to hear of it. Charles said he didn't like to think about the future, but that with all the people coming year after year looking for opportunity, they would eventually want the Indian islands even though the land wasn't very good for crops. He lamented that no one cared about the Indians. Martin said he worried too, especially if they saw all the squash and corn and beans that were growing in the middle of the long island. Charles said he hoped it would be a while before settlers found out about that. Martin said that there lied another of their worries, that Ayana's people helping the runaways could be used against them and serve as a reason to run them off . Martin said it made him feel better that they could now stay in touch with them and was particularly proud of Daniel for teaching Ayana to use the signaling mirror. Daniel laughed and said that Martin spoke today about how he traveled all over in his imagination. Margo and Charles didn't understand until Mary explained. Margo said she understood and admired Martin for being able to do that. Mary thought of how she had often seen Martin with a "not there" look and now understood that at those times he actually was not there. She thought of how she herself didn't have to imagine things to write because her notes were full of stories that were told to her by different people.

Margo said that she knew they had a late lunch, but she had a pot of catfish stew for supper if anyone was still hungry and a blackberry pie made from the preserves she had put up from the berries they had picked when Martin was here. Martin was surprised that he was a little hungry but Daniel was always hungry. Martin walked out to the front porch, took in the vista, and went back in. He smiled and said he was remembering the convincing story Captain Jones had told the slave hunters about what he had seen. Mary said she had that plus a half dozen other stories from him in her notes. Daniel asked what she was ever going to do with all her notes. She said she wasn't sure but expected to have over six hundred pages of them by the end of her trip to Savannah. She said she didn't know but she liked doing it and she was certain that it needed doing. Martin had noticed that Charles and Margo approved of and liked what she was doing. After stew and pie, Martin began to feel tired from the long day; Margo noticed and said they should get ready for bed. She said she had Daniel make him the same bedding on the floor in the loft as he had before and she would have breakfast as usual.

In the morning Martin heard the familiar tapping on the floor by Margo's broom handle. He was instantly awake, but Daniel had not stirred a bit. He pulled his pants on and went downstairs. Charles and Margo were at the kitchen table, and Margo poured him some tea. She tapped on the ceiling again, this time a little harder, until she heard the floor creak as Daniel got out of bed. She put some ground coffee in a big mug, poured hot water in, and the air filled with the coffee aroma.

She said that Daniel was the only one in the family that drank coffee because it was the only thing that got him going in the morning. He came down and Margo set the mug of coffee in front of him, but he still seemed partly asleep. Margo had a large pot of grits cooked and began frying eggs and served Charles and Martin some on top of their grits and added some thick slices of bacon. Mary came in and sat next to Martin, and they exchanged smiles. Mary said she had been awake a few hours working on her notes from yesterday's stories and was caught up and ready for some more. Martin said he didn't have more to tell now but should have plenty when he got back from South Carolina. Daniel had sipped some coffee and said that he would take her to see Ayana soon, and she looked at her mother and father for approval. Margo said it was fine with her but for them to plan it so they were back home before dark or shortly after. Charles reminded Daniel about the supply boat arriving in the afternoon with Henry and supplies, and Margo told Martin that she expected Henry to come there for supper. Martin said he would, and she suggested that Ashley and Ken could come too. Mary said that would be good because she didn't have anything in her notes yet about Ashley and Ken. Daniel had finished his coffee and was beginning to look awake, and Margo served him some breakfast.

Martin said he wanted to go see the Captain and asked if Mary and Daniel wanted to go, and Margo said she would make a food basket for the Captain. Once there, Martin could see that the Captain did indeed look frail and pale. When he heard Martin's voice, he grew animated, and color came back to his face. Martin told him that his old boat was done and that it was beautiful and sailed great, and that he had added a bowsprit and jib sail. The Captain said he had always thought about a jib but had never got around to it. He said he had enjoyed seeing Daniel often out in the boat Martin had given him, and he said he saw him go over a few times and laughed. Martin told him about Captain Ben retiring and him starting on the sharpie soon. Captain Jones said he was starting about the same age as he had but with more experience and that he would do just fine. Martin thanked him again for the boat, and the Captain said he thanked him because another six months of baking out in the sun on the beach, and his old boat would have been ready for the fire. Martin said that he would be down with it soon. He told the Captain, briefly, where they were going and why, thinking that he might have something to suggest. He said he didn't ever go north much but had seen Saint Helena on a chart and it was one of the biggest islands around. He said he couldn't say much about what they were doing except that it was the right thing to do and that there was probably a northeaster on the way and, if so, they should come in during daylight and at high tide. He added that if it was blowing too hard to come back on the inland waters. The Captain said he didn't know what to say about what they were off to do on Saint Helena, but he was confident that Walter Milam's two sons would handle the situation correctly.

Daniel said he had blackberry pie for him and that he could have it now or save for later with his other food. He said he would have it now and to send thanks to their mother. Daniel sat the covered bowl on the Captain's lap, lifted the cloth, and said the spoon was on the starboard side. The Captain liked that and said his starboard side operated best, and Daniel said his too. They talked a while, mostly about all the ships coming and going and where the new tower was to be built, just a hundred yards from the Captain's shanty. The Captain didn't have any new stories to tell Mary today, but she already had fifty pages of notes from him, and she knew he had a lot more that she could get later. After a while, Martin said they should be going and he hoped to come back later in the afternoon. He looked at the Captain and worried about him. He, Daniel, and Mary headed up the big sand dune between there and the lighthouse. The sun hadn't crossed over beyond the lighthouse yet to cast a shadow toward the east, so Daniel couldn't guess the time as usual. Mary told them to look up at the lighthouse, and they did and saw Ashley, Ken, and their father with the monocular attached to the rail. Martin yelled and waved, and they waved back. Once at the porch stairs, they all cleaned the sand from their feet and went into the kitchen. Margo asked how their visit went, and Mary said things went great and how the Captain was glad to see Martin and sent his thanks for the pie. She was setting out leftovers and asked Daniel to get a few things from the icebox. She asked him if there was still ice left from what was brought last week, and he said there was. Martin commented that theirs sometimes didn't last a full week and that the Dyers' cotton insulation must be better than their moss, but that they were switching to cork that might even be better than cotton. Daniel suggested they could go up in the lighthouse and signal with Ayana, and Martin said he would like that. Margo told Martin that, if he had time, she wanted to show him how they had cleaned and fixed up the guardhouse for his mother and father to stay in when they came in a couple weeks. Mary said she would take him after they ate. Margo asked Daniel to go into the cellar and bring up a crock of plum preserves. Once he did, she cut the wax seal with a knife, removed the top, and spooned some into a serving bowl for them to put on the cold leftover biscuits. Martin fondly remembered him, Mary, and Daniel picking the plums and blackberries, and he thought about the blacksnakes they had seen in the plum tree branches above the blackberry vines. He piled some preserves on his biscuit and told Margo that it was just about his favorite food. She said she remembered that and that sweet potato casserole was Henry's favorite and they were having that tonight, and she hoped Ashley and Ken liked it. Martin said they surely would. Charles came in and sat at the table. He said that Ashley and Ken enjoyed looking in every direction from the balcony with the monocular. He asked them to leave it out and tethered to the rail because he or Daniel would be up after a while to send the daily messages and they could put it away.

At the guardhouse, Mary told Martin that Daniel and her father worked on the guardhouse, off and on, since he had left, to make it comfortable, hoping that his mother and father would like it and come stay often. She said his mother had sent a letter, discussing Walter's health and the doctor's advice that he breathe some ocean air. She said that they had not told anyone except Henry about the guard house renovation, and he had sent them some materials they needed for the project on the supply boat several times. Martin had only seen the inside once briefly, and he was surprised when she opened the door to see how nice it was. Previously it was somewhat primitive with a couple of bunks and a washstand and an outside privy. Now, it was very clean and bright. There was fresh white paint on the ceilings, the cement floor was scrubbed and the white oyster shells of the tabby walls matched the white ceilings. There was a big bed, a chest of drawers, a vanity with a washbasin, and two rocking chairs and there were shelves that they had built and painted white on one wall. The only things not white were the bright color-print bedspread, pillow coverings, and curtains that Margo had made for the two windows. Martin was surprised at how nice it all looked. There was a small wood-burning ship's stove in one corner, with a neat stack of live oak blocks to burn on chilly mornings. Mary pointed to a door on one wall, and Martin asked what it was. Mary said it was what they had spent the most time working on. She opened the door and said it was an inside toilet with a water tank for flushing on the wall like they had in the big house. She pointed to a hand pump mounted on a small countertop. Martin asked where the water came from, and Mary said she didn't understand and to ask Daniel, but it had something to do with the equipment they had requested from Henry. Martin was impressed and said he could live there. Mary smiled and said he just might do that one day. They sat in the rocking chairs to wait for Daniel. After a few moments, Mary told Martin how sad she had been since he left, and how she didn't know what to do with herself because she missed him so much. Her mother had noticed and tried to talk her out of her suffering. She had poured herself into her notes to get her mind off missing him. Martin thought to himself that he felt the same way and wished he could admit it as openly as Mary just had. He managed to say that he had not been able to put her out of his mind and had an ache inside for her and his activities helped him like hers had. Mary glowed upon hearing his words. She stood and bent to kiss him, and she pressed her cheek against his cheek. She said that hearing how he felt would help her endure the time when he left again. Martin was surprised to hear himself say that they would be together all the time one day. Mary swooned, but Daniel's bursting in interrupted them. Without seeming flustered, Mary asked Daniel to explain to Martin how the water got to the toilet tank. Daniel said that his father had researched it and had Henry send it on the supply boat along with the toilet. He explained that it was a metal pipe with a point on one end that had slits in it and they drove it into the sand down to the water table. The pipe had extensions and a piece to put on the end to hit with a sledge hammer so as not to crush it. With two extensions they were able to go about twelve feet down to the water table. The water was ok to drink but not as good as the water from the deep well at the big house and it didn't produce as much water, but it was enough. They piped it to the hand pump and ran a line to the water flush tank above the toilet, along with a valve so that they could fill a jug there and carry water to the washbasin on the vanity in the other room. Drinking water could be brought from the big house. The toilet discharges to a small, buried brick tank with an underground sanitary field made of oyster shells. He said that his father wanted to make things easy and comfortable so that Walter and Martha would come often. Martin was impressed and said that maybe they could set up a well point and hand pump for Ayana over across the river too. Daniel said he had already talked to her about it, and they wanted one for them and one for Alice's family on the other end of the island. Martin asked how Ayana knew to look for his signals, and Daniel said he usually did it about two o'clock. But she had taught everyone to be watchful and get her when they saw a reflected flash signal. Daniel asked if they could go up and help him clean reflector mirrors, and Martin said he was fine with that.

Ashley and Ken were just coming out of the lighthouse, and Martin asked if they had seen anything new. Ken said they had seen a few Indians and really enjoyed the view from so high. Ashley said they had seen a very large canoe up on the beach to the south, and Martin said to remind him on their trip to tell them what the Indians did with it. Mary said that their mom had leftovers for them and that she had kept Daniel from eating all the plum preserves so they could have some. Climbing the lighthouse steps excited Martin, and he remembered how nervous he was the first time and how he looked out each small window on the way up to see how high he was. He wasn't afraid now but was thrilled, especially to walk on the balcony and see the Indian Islands to the south. Daniel got the signaling box which they used for signaling the Milam place each afternoon. With the monocular he looked south for the big canoe. It was no longer on the beach but was heading west into Warsaw Sound followed by two smaller canoes that he figured may have come out with two or three runaways. Daniel set the box up and fastened it at an angle pointed between the sun and the long island that Ayana was on; he lifted the shutter and closed it rapidly a few times and a few minutes later there were some flashes in reply from the east end of the long island. Martin grinned so big that it made his cheeks ache. Daniel sent a long message of flashes and pauses, and Martin was mesmerized again by the wooden shutter sounding like some kind of strange marching drum music. The messages he had heard sent from the Milam balcony did not sound as rhythmic as Daniel's. They waited a few moments until flashes of light began to come from the island. The flashes and pauses were much slower than Daniel's. Martin asked what they were saying. Daniel said that the routine was to ask if all was well and if there were any unusual sightings. Today she said that there were two new runaways picked up and taken to the small quarantine island and that three runaways had been shipped out today. Daniel said that Ayana's signaling was slow because she was still getting used to it, and her little hand mirror was not as quick to operate as his apparatus with a sliding shutter. His father was working on a small box with a shutter for her like the one here. Next Daniel sent a long message, and Martin was again amazed at the speed that he operated the shutter. He paused, and a message came back with much slower flashes. Martin asked what was being said. Daniel smiled and said he told her that Martin was there for a day, would be gone tomorrow, and be back in a few days. She replied to remind Martin not to forget his red brothers and sisters and to come see them. Martin told Daniel to signal back that he could never forget them, and he would come again soon. Next Daniel messaged that he was bringing Mary over to talk soon, and Ayana messaged back that she liked that. After that message, he moved the signal box around the balcony and set it up to point between the sun and the Milam plantation to the west. He sent a few rapid flashes and waited for flashes to come back. He said it was a bit early but that the two Milam guards that came from Savannah every day for messages usually arrived early. When they did, he transmitted the information that his father had written with Captain

Sandy's (Captain Jones) weather and tide information, and descriptions of the vessels coming and going and the flags they flew. Then they messaged back about ships leaving, and Daniel wrote that down on the back of the paper his father had sent. His father would store that paper with all the rest starting from years back. Martin said that they used the same system on their end and that he had seen the boxes of papers stacked in Henry's office. He said that Henry made a monthly report and gave it to the mayor's office, and it was published in the Savannah newspaper every month. He said that any urgent news was messaged to Savannah the same day from the Milam place, and that Captain Sandy's weather and tide report was signaled every day and published in the Savannah paper. It was called "Captain Sandy's Weather All Around" because that is what the pilot boat men had first called him. Henry said that twice as many people bought the paper after Captain Sandy's report began appearing, and each paper was shared more because everyone wanted to know what the weather would be and they learned the salty old blind captain on the north Tybee beach was usually right.

When they were back on the ground, Mary said that she wanted Martin to see the coded letter from Mallie. She said her father wasn't pleased that he had sent it but was comfortable that it couldn't be understood by anyone but them. He had studied the wax seal to note whether it had been opened and resealed and he was confident that it had not been, but he hoped it would be the last letter sent from Mallie. Before Mary read the letter to Martin, she showed him the fancy French name and artist title that Mallie was pretending to be. The letter was mostly about his gratitude for the help and hospitality they had shown him when he had visited from Philadelphia to paint the Tybee Lighthouse. He mentioned the other two lighthouses he had visited to paint afterward and that he had sent those paintings back to France to be part of an exhibition at a famous museum there. He said that Tybee and the Dyers were his most heartfelt experiences, and he mentioned other places they had shown him that remained in his mind's eye as fresh and clear as the day he had seen them. He said he liked the ruins of the old quarantine hospital at Lazaretto with its ballast stone grave markers; and second, the grove of magnificent pines with the thick layer of pine needles beneath them and the nearby pool of fresh water bubbling up. Martin was speechless, and Mary said she should have shown it to him as soon as he arrived but had not in all the excitement. She said she was curious about the parts of the letter where he says that he has decided to stay in America and become a citizen and had begun teaching art in Philadelphia. Martin said that he could not decipher the hidden meaning but was able to understand the clever fictitious name he had given himself. Mary looked at the name, "Lee Mal'Loray," and asked Martin what he saw. Martin smiled because there had never been a time when he understood something that Mary didn't, and she had always needed to explain things to him. He said it reminded him of some of his own worst days, and Mary was even more confused. Martin explained that, during his short, failed time in the little school in Savannah, his teacher Mr. Peeler had been so frustrated that Martin would see and read words backwards and the other kids would laugh at him for it. He then pronounced the name "Lee Mal'Loray." And then "Lee Mal." And then "Mal Lee." With the recognition, Mary shrieked so loud that it startled Margo and the others. She hugged and kissed Martin right there in front of everyone, and they all laughed as Martin turned red. Mary said that Mallie might be teaching at the Quaker school for runaways and free blacks that she had heard about. Charles said that Mary should read the letter one more time and they should destroy it. So, she read it aloud slowly and handed it to Margo who put it in the cook stove to burn.

Martin said that it was about time to pick up Henry. Charles said he thought he heard Ashley and Ken coming up from the beach. Martin stepped out to remind them to get the sand off their feet because Margo didn't like sandy floors, and they happily obliged. Ashley said they could bring the boat themselves from the landing in the morning and pick up Martin and Henry out front near the Captain. The tall dunes would block the southerly wind would keep the water flat and a make a beach landing easy and that way the brothers could have more time with the Dyers. Margo said that was gracious of them, and Ken said it was the Captain's idea and he hoped that everyone would come down to see them off. Daniel said he was going to rig the tackies to pick up Henry and the supplies. He asked Martin and Mary if they wanted to ride along, and they did.

The supply boat had just arrived when the wagon pulled up. The boatmen had already hauled it up, and Henry was walking around to get his land legs back. He hugged Daniel and Mary then socked Martin on the shoulder while asking how things had gone. Martin said better than he could have imagined, and he told Henry that they would stay the night at the lighthouse rather than on the boat. Henry was glad to hear that because if there ever was a choice between boat or land, he would always pick land. Martin told Johnny that he and Henry had been being fed by Margo and for him to get the deviled crabs that Ellie had made them out of the sharpie and have them for supper because he didn't want them to go bad. Johnny said that would go just right with the leftovers that Jacob had sent with them, which they had put in the ice chest. He laughed that they wouldn't have to do any cooking, just to do warming up which they were best at and it would give them more time to do some fishing before dark. Some of the boatmen were making things comfortable in the shanty for the night, while others loaded supplies onto the wagon. The last things to go on were two blocks of ice for the lighthouse icebox. Henry and Martin told all the boatmen goodbye, and they looked concerned because word had spread about what they were going to do. Johnny told Henry and Martin that he would be worried every minute until he saw them back home.

The wagon pulled through the gate into the lighthouse compound and Martin told Henry that he had a pleasant surprise coming that Charles and Margo would want to show him. Henry said he liked surprises but not the one they had shown him the last time he visited here. He was referring to seeing the site on the beach where the duel had occurred. Mary had been quiet and liked watching how well Henry and Martin got along. When they pulled up to the back door, Ashley and Ken came out to unload supplies. Daniel told Henry, Martin, and Mary to go inside while they did the unloading. Henry and Mary went inside, but Martin stayed to help. They unloaded most of the supplies there, then took the animal feed to the barn and the lamp oil to the brick house. Martin told Daniel that he was surprised to see a chunk of ice left in the ice box from the last week and that they could bring a little less next week. Daniel said it was because the weather was getting cooler.

Charles and Margo told Henry to follow them with his clothes bag to the guardhouse. Charles opened the door, and Henry was indeed surprised. Margo said they had done it especially for his parents but any Milam was welcome. Charles was most proud of the privy. Henry shouldn't have been completely surprised the invoices had come through his office, but he had been too busy to really study them. He never had reason to doubt anything that Charles ordered. Henry was thoroughly impressed, and his reaction was just what the Dyers had hoped. They wanted Walter and Martha to be so comfortable that they would come often, and that was just what Henry was thinking. Charles said they were still waiting for one thing, an elongated copper tub that would be placed near the stove so hot water could be drawn easily. Henry set his clothes bag down on the chest of drawers, bounced a little on the edge of the bed, and told them it was perfect. Margo said fixing it up had been fun and how they had found whiskey bottles that the guards had hidden in every nook and cranny inside and out. Speaking of whiskey, Charles said that he was ready for some rum and yaupon, and Margo said she might have some too. Henry said this all got him to thinking that, with his mother and father on Tybee and Martin soon away with Ashley and Ken, it would only be him and his family in the big house. Margo said that he would have Daniel and Mary visiting soon and John and his family close by, so he needn't worry about too little going on.

She said that she wouldn't be surprised if he had a sister-in-law there too in a couple of years. Henry didn't understand. Margo said that there was something special going on with Martin and Mary. Henry was shocked, and Charles said he saw it too but was not as convinced as Margo. Margo said that Martin had turned more into a man since he had been there last and Mary had already been a woman when he was here before. Henry said that Martin was young and not quite sixteen. Margo said that didn't matter because Martin was the type that knew what he wanted and waiting a few years wouldn't change his plans. Henry said she was right about that and that over the last year Martin had surprised him with his determination. When he was just ten, he had told Alice that he was going to look for her parents on the Indian Islands as soon as he had his own boat. When he was fourteen, he had told his mother and father he was going to be a boat captain and start real soon at it. His mother had begged him to find ways to delay him, especially since Walter had found that some captains on the Savannah wharf already wanted Martin to go to sea with them. Walter himself didn't see a problem because he had gone to sea at fourteen. Considering everything, Henry said he shouldn't be surprised if Martin had already planned a wife. Charles said a lot of thanks should go to Captain Ben for offering him something that wouldn't take him far. Henry chuckled and said, "It just occurred to me that a certain man named Walter may have had something to do with Captain Ben's story about back problems, even though he probably does have them." Charles and Margo laughed and said Henry's hunch could very well be true. Henry thanked them again for the accommodations, and Margo said she was ready for the rum.

Henry stood to go but paused. He said there was one more thing he wanted to tell them, and that was about the big meeting they had at the house. He said that Walter said numerous times that he missed them being there because they were like family and he valued their insight, but he understood why they couldn't come. Henry said he would rather leave the full story for his parents to tell but suffice it to say that Walter got what he wanted but not in the way that he had expected. It wasn't a quick fix but a thorough one. Charles said he knew well Walter's wishes but sometimes high ideals like his take time. Margo hugged Henry and said she knew he had a lot on his plate more so than ever these days.

Back at the house, everyone was on the porch. Mary had served Ashley and Ken iced yaupon and rum, sweetened with honey, and she had mugs more for her mother, father, and Henry. When they all arrived, she decided to serve herself, Daniel, and Martin a bit too. She had lately become quite a good speaker from all her reading and note writing, and she asked if she could propose a toast. All agreed, and she said that she wanted all to wish Henry, Martin, Ashley, and Ken fair weather, safety, and success on their trip to South Carolina. Everyone lifted their mugs and drank to it. Henry then said he wanted to especially toast Ashley and Ken for how they had willingly offered to deal with Willoughby, and mugs were raised again. Ashley said he and Ken wanted to toast the Dyers for the generous hospitality today and all the times they had overnighted at Lazaretto. Either the wind had wafted the smell of the food to the porch or the rum had ignited appetites, but everyone was ready to eat. Margo said to give her five minutes to set things up so they could serve themselves and take their plates back to the porch.

It was another memorable supper that seemed like the best ever. There were casseroles, seafood, chicken, vegetables, bread, and several desserts. Charles said that over the years, when people learned that he was a light keeper on Tybee Island, the most common question was, "How do you ever get food to eat?" He said they would never believe how much and how good the food was, so he would lie and say that it wasn't easy but that they survived on the basics, and they believed that. He said that it wasn't this good when they started out because supply boats only came every couple months at best. He said that King George had a splendid idea when he decided to send Walter and set up a first-class support system to the lighthouse. He said that many people thought then and many still think that the support is more than needed, but they don't understand the value and importance of a working lighthouse as critical to Savannah's security and wealth with ships arriving from all over the world.

After dessert and more yaupon, Daniel hitched the tackies again to take Ashley and Ken back to the sharpie at Lazaretto. Martin and Mary went along for the ride. Martin pointed out the Indian Islands to Ashley and Ken as they went over the oyster shell road to Lazaretto. He mentioned that the wind was still coming out of the south like Captain Jones had predicted, and Ken said he hoped it would continue through at least tomorrow afternoon so they could get blown over to Saint Helena easily. He mentioned the Captain's warning about a northeaster and said, "We all can talk about the weather, but none of us can do anything about it." Ashley pointed out that they could choose to go out in it or stay in.

When the wagon arrived at Lazaretto, the boatmen were sitting around a fire outside, laughing and talking and trying to avoid a few gnats. Johnny stood to greet them and thanked Martin for the deviled crabs. Martin told him to thank Ellie and tell her why he gave them. Johnny asked Ashley what time they were leaving in the morning. About daylight Ashley said and Johnny said that he would see them because they were leaving about then as well. Ashley and Ken thanked Daniel for the ride and said goodbye to him and Mary. Mary wished them well and thanked them again for what they were doing. She said that, when she first learned that Martin would be going away on boat voyages in a few months, she was worried but it eased her mind that he was going with them. Ashley said they had a few things to make ready on the boat for the trip tomorrow and told Martin they would see him and Henry early in the morning and he and Ken went out to the sharpie. Martin, Daniel, and Mary stood by the fire smoke with the others a few minutes to escape the gnats, and then said they should be going. All the boatmen followed them to the wagon, and Johnny told Martin that the talk of the Milam place all week long had been about their trip to South Carolina. Everyone knew what they were going for and had heard the stories of the evil master, and they were hoping the week would pass quickly with their safe return so they could all quit worrying. Martin said not to worry, they would be fine. Johnny said they knew how he was, and he would worry every minute until they returned. Mary was touched by Johnny's concern and the look on the men's faces as they stood by the wagon looking at Martin. It was a look of dread and admiration, and she hoped that she might somehow be able to describe the feeling of the moment in her notes later. Daniel barely moved the reins, and the tackies started back.

They were quiet on the ride back. Martin was thinking about the northeaster that the Captain had predicted. He had never been on a boat in one, but he had been in one before on the north Tybee beach and remembered its fury and how it blew day after day. The wind would blow the frothy top off the waves and make salty foam that was blown onto the beach and through the air, and in some places near the shore the froth was waist high. Sometimes a piece would hit his face. It didn't hurt because it was mostly air, but he remembered its unusual taste. It was saltier than plain sea water and had a slight earthy taste too, like the wind had blown the water away and left an essence of ocean and earth. He thought of what it would be like to be out in a boat in it.

Mary was thinking about what to write in her notes which was what she had been consumed with since Martin had left after his first trip. When she had started, her style was like a simple factual record of events, like a history book. But moments like the boatmen standing around the wagon with soulful worried looks, made her want to include more than just facts. She had begun to describe feelings and that was more difficult, but she liked it. She had to ponder her own feelings and then try to write so that, when the time came to write the book about all this, she could remember those feelings. At first she was worried that she might not be able to recapture a feeling, but then, as she looked back on things she had written a month or so, it was actually easier than she had imagined. She then thought about other things in her life before she became obsessed with note taking, and she could remember the feelings better than the facts. It was a breakthrough for her. She began to pay closer attention to those sorts of things, and, as she was told a story by her father or mother or Captain Jones, she paid attention to her feelings about it and let that guide what she wrote. Of the three people on the wagon, Daniel was the most grounded and brought the others back from their wandering thoughts when he said that he hoped that there was some more pie left because he wanted some before bed.

When the wagon pulled into the lighthouse compound, Martin noticed that the guard house door was open and asked Daniel to let him off there because he figured that Henry was inside. Mary got off with him and they walked in. Henry was sitting in one of the rockers and looked up as they walked in. Martin thought that his look was peculiar but not anything to mention. Henry was thinking about what Margo had said earlier about Martin and Mary and was seeing them in a new light. He beamed with a big smile. Martin always liked it when Henry smiled because he was so serious most of the time. He said that he had just come over to look one more time before dark. He asked Martin if he thought their parents would like it. Martin said that they might be a little uncomfortable at first, just because it was someplace different, but he thought the fresh air, the sound of the ocean, and warm times with Margo and Charles would win them over. And he thought his father would especially like visiting Captain Jones and it would do them both good. Again, Henry was surprised at Martin for such a mature reply. Martin said that he knew that Henry wouldn't want to do it but that he and Claudia should come for a week. Henry said that it probably wouldn't happen any time soon because he planned to be busier than ever for the next couple of years, getting the ice business going with John in addition to attending to all the Milam place goings on but maybe in a few years he would come stay if Claudia was for it.

Mary said that she hoped that Henry would not be too busy to sit and tell the story of the Milam place when she visited. Henry said he would consider that a list-worthy thing to do. She said, good, because he was high on her list, just after his father, his mother, and Alice, and just before Martin. She expected the notes from Alice to be the longest, and Martin's to be the next longest. Henry complimented Mary on her organization and goals. He asked how long her list was, and she said about twenty people now but that she expected it to grow a lot after she got there and made inquiries. Ashley, Ken, and Captain Ben were eighteen, nineteen, and twenty. Henry said it seemed that she would be as busy as he would. He thought to himself how he had never understood how Mary was so motivated about her writings, but now with new insight he likened it to Martin's desire to be a ship captain and to his own drive to accomplish things. He tried to imagine Martin and Mary as a couple, but he couldn't visualize that. Henry said he felt like visiting Charles and Margo before bedtime.

Margo had leftovers sitting out and a big pitcher of yaupon with orange juice and honey. She poured six mugs almost full and added a little rum to each one and told everyone to help themselves to the leftovers and invited them to join her on the porch. While they were eating, Mary said she had a question for Henry, and he asked what it was. Mary asked if the South Carolina trip went as planned and Alice and the others were then owned by Ashley and Ken, what was the next step? Henry said that it was a good question, but he didn't have a complete answer. Obviously it would be better for them to be owned by Ashley and Ken than their current legal owner, from whom they had escaped. Henry explained that there were several issues that had prompted the urgency of their trip, including Martin's discovery of Alice's family, the encounter with the slave hunters, and Mallie's situation. Also, Ayana and her people's situation was precarious given the increase of colonials in the area. The Indians' security affected the security of Alice, her family, and her baby since they all legally belonged to the old master. Henry said that all the uncertainty weighed heavily on him and he wanted to change Alice's enslaved status without delay. He repeated the process of finding out the location of the old owner and the decision to offer him gold beyond the reward amount to buy them all. But a concern persisted that if the owner discovered the Milam's' identities, he might make more demands later with a threaten of bringing publicity to the transaction. He said how Ashley and Ken offered to negotiate with the owner, even before Henry proposed it. He explained how Richard Wilcox had helped with information about the Tombee Plantation owner who could rent them a carriage and allow use of his landing. Summarizing, Henry told Mary that it was a long answer to a good question. He added that Ashley and Ken had no desire to own other human beings but they understood the reason for what they were doing. For the time being, their having proof of ownership was important lest Alice's family be captured by slave hunters. If Ashley and Ken were the owners, that was that, and slave hunters could not capture them. If instead the Milam's

became the legal owners and Alice's background story was revealed, they might be implicated for wrong
doing and possibly have to forfeit ownership. Then the slaves might be returned to their old owners or confiscated by the state for auction. So, it made the best sense for Ashley and Ken to own them.

Margo suggested an early bedtime since Henry and Martin had such a big day ahead, and Charles gave Henry a lantern for his walk to the little house. Margo said she would send Daniel to wake him in the morning. He thanked them and left. Mary asked what time they expected Ashley and Ken to arrive from Lazaretto, and Martin said it depended on how hard the wind was blowing and if it held from the south. Daniel said they could go up the lighthouse and watch their progress, and Martin said he would enjoy that. Mary said she was going to her room to write her notes on the day's conversations, and she hugged Martin good night. Their cheeks briefly touching and he could smell her scent, and it lingered with him for a while. He hugged Margo and Charles, thanked them, and went up to the loft with Daniel. Margo got her and Charles another rum drink, and they sat a little longer. Charles told her that she might be right about Martin and Mary because he had noticed how they glowed around each other, especially Mary. Margo said she had seen it within the first hour that Martin first had come and stayed six months ago. She said that Martin would be sixteen soon and lots of people got married at that age but she didn't expect that they would, but they sure would have plenty of opportunity to get more serious about each other while Mary was in Savannah. She said that she didn't think Martin would do anything in the near future because he had agreed to start work with Ashley and Ken on the sharpie. She said Mary's stay in Savannah would be good for her; she would meet new people, and it could change her thinking about Martin, but she didn't expect it to. Charles smiled and said Martin and Mary brought back memories of them when they met in Ebenezer. Margo said the love part was the same, but they got married only a week after they met.

The familiar knocking of Margo's broom handle on the floor woke Martin. He sat up and saw that Daniel was undisturbed. He went over and shook his shoulder until he rolled over and asked if it was morning already. Martin said to sit up and he would smell the coffee that his mother had going, and that motivated Daniel enough to lift up. Martin went down and told Margo that he would go wake Henry. On his way he saw the lantern light in the little house and found Henry up, dressed, and packed. He thanked Martin for coming for him and said he always woke up early. They walked back and into the kitchen where the whole Dyer family was now. Margo had been up for some time and had the woodstove hot, with the second load of biscuits in the oven and a big pot of grits vigorously boiling, and she was cracking eggs into the big cast iron pan. Daniel was nursing a big mug of coffee, and Mary and Charles were having tea. Mary asked them what they would like. Henry said coffee, and Mary knew Martin wanted tea. Margo served Daniel, Charles, and Mary the first batch of eggs and bacon, while Henry and Martin had a few minutes to drink something warm. Then she served them grits, eggs, and bacon and started some more biscuits for Ashley, Ken, and Captain Jones. Henry noticed that Margo did everything without the slightest wasted motion. She was the first to finish her breakfast even though she was the last to start, and she made three big egg and bacon biscuits for the Captain, Ashley, and Ken and a whole basket full of buttered biscuits for the two pilot crews on the beach. Martin looked at Daniel and wondered if he would someday be the light keeper and if he would find a good wife and partner like his father had. The sun was rising and Daniel said they could go up and see if the sharpie had started out of Lazaretto yet. Mary said she wanted to go too.

Once up on the lighthouse balcony, Daniel set up the monocular on the west side and focused on the lazaretto landing. He said that Ashley and Ken were doing something on the deck of the sharpie and moved so Martin could look. He looked and said they were getting ready to haul the bow anchor so the current would swing the boat around and be pointed out the creek toward the south channel. He said he had seen them do that maneuver several times before. He said the boat was slow to swing because the tide was getting toward dead low. He let Mary look and said the wind was light and out of the south, but when the tide started in, it would probably pick up. Mary said she could see the boatmen stirring and they had let the supply boat down into the water. Martin asked Daniel if they could look over at the Indian Islands while everybody at Lazaretto was getting under way, and Daniel moved the monocular. Martin saw the two familiar columns of smoke from both ends of the island and then looked out toward the beach at the point. He had named the spot Claw Island because it looked to him like a crab claw with a little inlet splitting the point. He didn't notice anything unusual but remembered the exciting times when he and Daniel had first started seeing signs of life there and what they had learned on that first uncertain trip when he went with Alice and met Ayana. He let Mary look, and she asked Daniel if he would take her there soon to meet Ayana and record her story. He said he would take her whenever she asked, and she said that would be soon after Martin and Henry got back from South Carolina. Daniel moved the monocular back and had Martin take a look. He did and said it was interesting that the sharpie sails were fully set but had not much wind in them. With the slight wind and slack tide, it was barely moving. The supply boat was alongside it, then it began to move ahead of the sharpie. He saw that there was a line attached, and the boatmen were leaning hard into the oars, pulling the sharpie out of the creek. He laughed and let Mary and Daniel each have a look. He said the tide would soon start moving in, and as they turned east out of the creek, the land would block the wind. He suspected that Johnny saw the situation and, instead of heading up the south channel with the tide to go home, he decided to get them out to the lighthouse before the tide started in strong. It would make it hard for them because they wouldn't get back home before the tide starts out, and they would have to buck it for the last hour or two. Mary asked how long he thought it would be until they got around to the lighthouse to pick them up, and Martin said maybe an hour. Daniel asked how the light wind would affect them getting to South Carolina. Martin said that the wind would probably pick up as the tide started in and, once they were out past the high dunes of Tybee, the wind would not be blocked, the current would be less in the deeper water, and they would make better progress. Mary was impressed with Martin's knowledge. Daniel said there were two pilot crews waiting for a ship on the beach near the Captain, and they were about to be surprised to see the supply boat pulling the sharpie around. They took turns watching until the two boats had left the creek and headed eastward toward the ocean. Martin said Johnny was steering further away from the land so they could catch a little more breeze. He said it would be nice to be a little early and watch them from the beach. Daniel put the monocular up and they went down.

Charles, Margo, and Henry were on the porch chatting. Mary told them what they had seen, and Martin said they should be out in front in maybe a half hour. Henry said he was ready, and Martin said he could be ready in five minutes. Charles said he would walk down to the beach to see them off and asked Margo if she would like to come. Mary was surprised that he asked her because she had only seen her mother go down on the beach a couple times in her life. She was even more surprised to hear her mother say she would like to go. Daniel was so excited that he let out such a loud whoop that probably carried to the Captain and pilot men on the beach. Margo told Daniel to get the basket of biscuits, and the Dyer family plus Henry and Martin went over the dune and down to the beach. The pilot crew was looking out over the ocean for a ship, and they didn't see the group approaching. When they were almost to them, Margo said good morning to the captain. He asked what brought her to the beach, and she said it was his idea about Henry and Martin being picked up there by the sharpie. She said that they decided to come see them off and Charles said it was perfect weather for a beach landing. She gave him a biscuit, a cloth napkin, and a mug of tea, then handed a basket of biscuits to the group of pilot crewmen. Each one thanked her no less than five times, not only for the biscuits, but also for visiting the Captain and making him so happy.

Martin pointed back toward Lazaretto at the sharpie about a half mile away being pulled by the supply boat. Mary described the scene to Captain Jones. As the boat got nearer, they could hear the chantey that the men were singing. On each hard pull on the oars, there was a grunt that set the rhythm of the chantey. Johnny sang a verse, and the men followed with a chorus. The whole group on the beach was mesmerized. When the boat was a few hundred yards away, the pilot captain told his crew to take their boat down to the water's edge. The four of them dragged it there and waited for Henry and Martin. All the Dyers hugged Henry and Martin and followed them down to the water. As they were rowed out, they sat facing back toward the beach, and Martin was focused on Mary the whole way out. They came close to the supply boat first, and all the boatmen were smiling real big. Martin told Johnny he better get on home, but Johnny said they weren't done yet. As soon as Martin and Henry climbed aboard the sharpie, he steered the supply boat away from the beach toward Hilton Head with the sharpie still in tow. Martin asked Ashley what was going on, and Ashley said Johnny had insisted on getting them a ways farther out, to where the southern breeze was not blocked by the tall dunes of Tybee. He pointed out another quarter mile where the surface of the water was choppy from the wind swooping down. Before they reached the rougher water, a wind swooped down and filled the sharpie sails and the tow rope from the supply boat went slack as the sharpie gained speed and Johnny set the tow rope free. He steered back west toward the south channel, and Ken steered the sharpie directly at the eastern tip of Hilton Head. The farther they got from Tybee, the more room the wind had to fetch up and they continued eastward for a few miles till they were out of the inward tidal flow and beyond the Hilton Head shoals. Martin watched Tybee get smaller and smaller and grinned at Henry. Henry told Martin that he had managed to get him on two boat trips in the past year, which was as many as he had been on the rest of his life. Ashley and Ken laughed at them. The sailing was smooth and easily handled, and even Henry seemed to be enjoying it a bit.

About an hour later, Ashley went below and added some wood to the stove. Hickory wood smoke wafted over the cockpit, and then the smell of sweet potato casserole. Soon Ashley reached out of the cabin and set four plates in the cockpit, each with a warmed up egg-and-bacon with a hearty portion of sweet potato casserole. Ashley took the helm from Ken to let him eat, and the sailing was so easy, he managed to eat while steering. The salt air had made Henry more hungry than usual, and Martin was surprised to see him eating with so much gusto. When they finished, Ken brought out a chart and laid it on the cockpit floor out of the wind, and pointed to where they were relative to the southern tip of Hilton Head. He moved his finger further north and pointed to the north end of Hilton Head and to Port Royal Sound. He said it was the mouth of a river much wider than the Savannah River. Because of its large width, it was called the Broad River and he and Ashley had been in and out of it many times with Captain Ben. Ken moved his finger north and across Port Royal Sound to Saint Helena Island. He said it was a huge island almost twenty-five miles long and had many plantations. He said there was a village where many plantation owners spent summers and it was used as a meeting place for a simple governing body represented by each plantation. He said it was also used year-round as a place to meet and trade livestock, food, fish, or anything one owner had more of than he needed. He said some owners allowed their slaves to bring fish or vegetables they caught or grew on their own to sell on Sundays, and some greedy owners insisted on a cut of the take. Occasionally a traveling preacher might come, and most owners let their slaves attend. Also, the village was a place where slaves could buy shine and share news and stories. Owners threatened to not let their slaves go to the village on Sundays if they didn't act right. Henry asked Ken how he knew all this. Ken said he, Ashley, and Captain Ben had often waited out the weather there during cold spells and northeasters. He said that Captain Ben never needed much of an excuse to stay for a few days because he had an old captain friend William "Bill" Farnsworth on the north end of the island. As his friend got older, he stayed home more than he went to sea and he lived alone with a paid servant couple and he and Ben could while away a few days easily. Ken said they liked going there too. He lets us use his horses when we stay, and we have gotten to know a lot of the island. We don't know the plantation owners, but we have ridden all over the island. If we are there on a Sunday, Captain Bill sends us to the village in his carriage to pick up fresh fish, produce, and shine, and we sometimes stay for a few hours and have met people and learned a lot about the place. Ben says he's coming here during winter months when he quits. That's what I know about the place, but we haven't been up Station Creek where Tombee is.

Henry and Martin were surprised that Ashley and Ken had spent so much time on Saint Helena. Next, Ken pointed to an island east of Saint

Helena, with a long beach, called Pritchard's Island. Then to an inlet called Trenchards Inlet, separating Pritchard's Island and Saint Helena Island. Then he pointed to a creek at the far end of the inlet called Station Creek. He traced how the creek went off the inlet and close to land and where the Tombee landing was. The creek then looped around back to the Broad River. Captain Ben had told him that a good place to moor out would be in Trenchards Inlet at where Station Creek branched off.

Ashley kept the sharpie far out from Hilton Head where the wind was stronger. With its long hull the sharpie moved swiftly along the length of the island, and after a couple hours, they were nearing the northern end of Hilton Head. Ashley and Ken talked about the best way to enter Port Royal Sound with its many shoals. Because it was high tide and they wanted to cross the sound before the tide started out, they decided to lift the centerboard and go directly across the shoals. Ashley steered into the wind, the boat came to a stop, and they cranked the centerboard up into its trunk. They then steered back off the wind, and Ken stood on the bow to watch the water ahead for shallow areas. He motioned Martin to come up with him, and for the next hour, Martin got his first lesson in watching the water for shoals. Several times, Ken would motion Ashley this way or the other, and he spoke to Martin almost the whole time pointing out the many different ways of estimating water depth by how waves and current acted. The tide began to shift before they reached the far side of the sound, but before it had strengthened, they were approaching the entrance to Trenchards Inlet in the early afternoon, still with a south-southwesterly mostly behind them. Ashley said he had hoped to get up the inlet and moor at the entrance to Station Creek but was happy and satisfied to have gotten to where they were. He said that, moored in the sound, they would rock a bit overnight, but it would not be bad unless the wind picked up. Ken suggested that they keep going, bucking the tide into Trenchards a bit until the current got too strong to make any headway. Ashley said that sounded good because they had plenty of daylight and nothing better to do. He steered to the middle of the inlet with the centerboard still up, against the outgoing tide, but with the wind. Ken and Martin stayed on the bow. Martin watched the edge of the marsh to gauge their progress. After about an hour, as the speed of outgoing current increased and the wind speed stayed the same, the sharpie slowed to a standstill, and Ken said it was time to drop the hook. He told Martin to stay clear but to watch what he was doing, and he and Ashley went through a smooth routine, and in a short time, the boat was secured in the middle of the inlet by an anchor on each end and the sails were dropped. Martin was anxious to help, and Ken let him and Henry help gather in the big sails. When the work was done,

Henry went below and made mugs of iced yaupon with a little rum for them all and had them waiting when everything was secured and Ashley and Ken could call it a day. Once seated in the long cockpit, Henry toasted to them and to a good day, even for him, on the water. Ashley said he had another toast in mind but was out of rum, so he went below and fixed another one for everyone. When he sat, he raised his mug and toasted to Johnny and the crew for pulling them out of Lazaretto Creek to the north beach and beyond. He said, without the pull, they could have plodded for a few hours trying to get to the outside. Henry added to the toast and raised his mug and said a toast of gratitude was the best kind. Martin had never had more than one drink of rum and felt a little queasy, so he finished only about half of his second mug.

Martin said he bet Johnny and his crew were not back home yet and he couldn't understand how they could row for so long. Henry said he often thought of that too. Ken said that they were strong and knew how to pace themselves and they had a good system where three men rowed for thirty minutes then rested while the other three took a turn and continued that rotation the whole trip. Martin said most trips were quick and easy but occasionally there were rough ones. Like when there was a strong east wind blowing up the Savannah River against the outgoing tide. Or when it was cold and rainy or both and they had to go the longer route the back way around Tybee to the Back River landing. Ashley said he had never been that way but would like to try it sometime. Martin said they should do it in his new boat, or they could just go from Lazaretto around Tybee to the landing some time and spend the night on the south end and come back with the tide the next day. Ashley said he would like that, but Ken said that between trips he liked to stay put on land when possible. Henry agreed that, unless it was for a very good reason like this trip, he always preferred to stay on the land. He said his parents had two sons, one that preferred the land and one that preferred the water. Ashley said he had some more boating experience for Martin to practice, and Martin's attention became keen. Ashley went below and returned with some potatoes, onions, a small knife, and a pot and handed it all to Martin. Everyone had a good laugh. He said they needed to be peeled and cut up small so they would cook faster. Martin took to it and got it done. Ashley added water and some bacon from the icebox to the pot and started it cooking.

Henry asked how much farther it was to Station Creek. Ken said just a few miles and, with the flood tide in the morning, they would be there quickly. He said that they could be anchored at the mouth of Station Creek a little before mid-morning and launch the skiff, and he and Ashley could be at Tombee landing before noon. Henry said that would not leave much time to find Benjamin Chaplin and get his carriage and then travel to Willoughby's plantation and find him. Ashley said that maybe they would just find Chaplin and plan the carriage for the next morning. Ken said that they could start earlier in the morning and gain another hour or two, and Henry liked that idea. They could just play things by ear when and if they found Chaplin at home. He might be away or busy; they would have to wait and see. Henry went below and came out with the leather satchel with the rolls of gold coins and the old Savannah newspaper that offered the reward for Alice's family and the others when they had run away. He showed the newspaper to Ashley and Ken. There was a large piece on the runaways, with their names, descriptions of their size, complexion, and skills, and the reward for each. The reward total for the ten of them was eight hundred dollars. Henry said this was all part of the background that he wanted them to be familiar with. Henry had thought it through, and he pulled out a list of names that included Alice, her family, and the others. He pulled out the sales contract that Sidney had prepared. It listed those six runaways that were left of the original escaped ten and a purchase price of twelve hundred dollars."So, y'all can tell him that you can go fetch them off the island and bring them back for the reward from him, or you can pay him in gold $1200 for all of them, less the reward amount. We hope that he doesn't want them back, and I don't think he will, from what Richard Wilcox has said about him always being strapped for cash. Remember to tell him you want them free and clear so you can sell them legally at the slave market for more money instead of selling them on the black market for less, which y'all will do if he won't pay the reward or take your offer." Henry said that there were 150 $20 gold pieces and he didn't care if they spent them all to get Willoughby to sign the sales contract. He said they could have offered more than the $1200 right off, but it would be so far over the going rates that Willoughby might get suspicious and back off. Richard Wilcox said he was paranoid and acted erratically, and Henry did not want him to get cross or strange and walk away from the deal. He would also give Benjamin Chaplin four gold pieces for accommodating them. He should be satisfied with that because the going rate in Savannah for a carriage and driver for a week is two gold pieces. Henry asked if they had any questions and they said that they did not but would sleep on it and may have some in the morning. The sun was setting, and the sky was all red in the west. Martin said Captain Jones always said that meant good weather for at least two more days. The stew was boiling, and they all could smell it coming out of the cabin. Henry said that, since he had been sitting most of the day, he wanted to serve supper. Ashley told him where the big tin bowls and spoons were, and Henry went in and handed out bowls full of soup. He asked for their mugs back and filled them about half full again, added a little honey and chipped ice, and squeezed a little lemon. Then he passed them out with a plate of four cold biscuits. They ate and watched the sun go down. Martin hadn't said much because he was tired, and the rum had gotten to him a bit. Henry saw that he looked worn out and suggested that they turn in. Ashley went below and lit a lantern in Ben's cabin; he told Henry that Ben's bunk was for him and the bedding on the floor was for Martin. He said he and Ken would be in shortly.

Martin and Henry were hard asleep within minutes of lying down. They didn't hear Ken and Ashley continue talking on deck or hear them when they came below. The next thing Martin knew was eight hours later, just before sunup, the smell of eggs, bacon, and coffee, and Ashley and Ken talking quietly. He got up from the floor, nudged Henry awake, and went out onto the deck. Ken wiped a place off for Martin to sit because everything was wet from a heavy dew. Saying Martin's name, Ashley stuck a cup of yaupon out the door, and Martin took the hot mug in both hands. Henry was next, and Ken dried a place for him to sit. Ashley passed out a cup of coffee for him, and he was pleasantly surprised that Ashley knew he was a coffee drinker. Next a tin plate for Ken came out the door with grits, eggs, bacon, and a fresh biscuit. A few minutes later two more tins came for Martin and Henry. Then Ashley emerged with a tin full for himself and said he would try some coffee for a change. He asked if they had slept well, and Henry said he couldn't remember when he had slept so solidly. Ken said they had been up about an hour and hoped that they had not woken them. He said there wasn't much wind yet but it would probably pick up in a bit. And the tide had a couple of hours yet before it turned but it would get slower and slower as it ebbed and they could set the sails and maybe get up the inlet a ways before it started in. Henry said not to worry too much about a late arrival today at Tombee; it would be enough to simply get things set this afternoon for an early start tomorrow.

After breakfast, the wind did pick up a little, and the tide had slowed. They set the sails, and the boat moved up the inlet slowly with the sun just above the horizon. After the tide went slack and then started in slowly, the boat moved a little faster, and in a little over an hour they were at the Station Creek entrance. Ashley and Ken set the anchors, and Henry and Martin helped them get the sails down. Then they set the skiff off. Ashley had packed a basket of food and a big jug of water. Henry put the satchel of gold and papers over Ken's head and shook both their hands. He and Martin watched them row into Station Creek in the still of the morning with the tide.

The Tombee big house was a beautiful two-story home on top of a high tabby foundation, with full-width screen porches on both floors. It faced southeast, the ideal direction to capture the prevailing breezes. It commanded a full uninterrupted view over the expanse of marshland to the east and south. The wind was out of the south still, and smoke from the slave houses and the kitchen for the big house could be seen blowing off to the north. There was no activity around the landing, but shouting could be heard from the back of the big house. There was a double row of silvered cedar posts from the bank into the creek, with sparsely placed planks to walk on and to serve as a dock. There was a small open sloop pulled a little above the high-water line. The tide was still somewhat low and barely reached the end of the dock. Ashley pulled the boat up and held it tight to let Ken climb up the few boards nailed on the posts for a ladder then he climbed up and tied the line off. They carefully walked on the sparse cross planks, not stepping on the middle of them because they looked a bit rotten. They looked around and still didn't see anyone and walked toward the back of the house to the outside kitchen where the voices were coming from. Before they got close, Ken hollered, hoping not to startle anyone. An older black woman looked out the open kitchen doorway and didn't look surprised to see them. Ashley said they were looking for Benjamin Chaplin; she smiled big and said he was out in the field overseeing. She said he told her somebody might be coming to see him and to call him if they did. She sent two children to go after Master Ben. They lit out running and screaming for him like he was already close by. The cook looked Ashley and Ken over and seemed to sum up instantly that they were good people and said her name was Mary. She told them that there was good water at the well if they wanted to help themselves to some.

In a little while, a man and a small boy came walking up. He said they must be who Richard Wilcox had said was coming. Ken said that they were and introduced themselves, by their first names only. He asked what they had come in, and Ashley told him they left their boat and crew out in Trenchers and rowed a smaller boat to his landing. He said he had a carriage for them to use as he had promised and asked what business they had with Willoughby. Ashley said slave business and that's all, and Chaplin said that was about all he got out of Wilcox too. Ken took out four gold pieces and handed two to Chaplin and showed him the other two and said he could have them when they were done. Chaplin was surprised at the amount and said he didn't need to know any more than they had told him but not much would surprise him about anything Willoughby might be up to. Ashley said they didn't think they would be done with him today but should be done tomorrow and asked if he would give them directions. Chaplin said he would after he brought the carriage around. He told them to wait out front and he would be right back. They walked toward the landing and sat on the bank. Ashley told Ken that Chaplin seemed nice enough, and Ken said that Richard Wilcox had told Henry that he was and that he treated his slaves better than most.

Chaplin and the boy came with the wagon and pulled around front by the landing. Ken reached into his pocket, pulled out a small wooden object, and handed it to the boy. It was a carved wooden dolphin, and the young boy looked at his uncle to see if he should take it, and received a nod, then took it and studied it carefully and managed to smile very slightly at Ken. That pleased Chaplin, and he said that Wilcox said that you two were not trouble, but because you had dealings with Willoughby, I had doubts. Ashley said that Wilcox had told them about him and his nephew. Chaplin was surprised. His tension toward them eased a bit, and he said that Thomas was the future of Tombee. He said that he didn't need to know what their dealings were with Willoughby but advised that they be wary because he was unpredictable. He said that his overseer was easier to deal with than him and that Willoughby pretty much let him run a lot of things there because he had made such a mess of things himself in the ten years after his father, Colonel Willoughby, died and left it all to him. He didn't manage things well and would have lost the place except that his slaves stepped up and saved it, in spite of him, and out of a great loyalty to his father who they all loved, plus they understood that they could be living under much worse conditions. He said it was odd that, even though Willoughby was the master of the place, his slaves gained a small amount of control of things. Before they did, a big group of them had run away years ago and never returned. He said there had been a massacre of hundreds of runaways on Tybee Island about that time. If they had made it that far alive, they were probably killed."Anyhow, I've probably said more than I should have."

He told them to take the harness and everything off the horse when they got back because he knew his way to the barn. They could leave the wagon there and just find him again in the morning. Ken looked at the sun and said they were further along than he thought they would be and they may as well look for Willoughby. Ashley said he would be lying if he said he was looking forward to it, but they should go and find him.

They left Tombee and headed south on the road along the edge of the woods and marsh a ways. They then turned west, toward the middle of the island as Chaplin had told them, and after about a mile, turned north on a road that seemed like the island ridge. They followed it four miles or so until they came to the huge shade oak out in a corn field that Chaplin said was on the Willoughby place. It was lunch time, and the field hands were under the shade of the big oak, and a lunch wagon was parked there with them. They all stared at the carriage. They recognized the Chaplin's horse and carriage but didn't recognize Ashley and Ken. After the big oak, they turned left onto a smaller road and went down from the ridge. Off to the left was a strange looking pond full of blue water. There was a pipe at one end with water shooting up about four feet and spilling into the pond. They could feel the coolness of the southerly breeze as it blew across the cool water and over them. Nearby, in a grove of oaks, was a big house like Chaplin had described. On the other side of the road to their right was another big shade oak with a small herd of cattle crowded in its shade. It was strange to see so many cattle on a coastal plantation. As they pulled up to the big house, a black man on a horse came out to meet them. Ken said the field hands had probably told them about two strange men coming. The man rode up to them before they got to the house and asked them what their business was. Ashley said they had some business to do with Melvin Willoughby. He told them that he had gone to the village on business and wouldn't be back until tomorrow. He saw the disappointment on their faces and told them that he was Abraham and had been the overseer for years and asked what their business was again. Ken said they were coastal traders and had some trading to do with Willoughby. Abraham asked what kind of trading, and Ken said they probably should only talk to Willoughby about that. During this small talk, both Ken and Ashley and Abraham had been sizing each other up. Ken and Ashley were thinking that they might like to start their business with Abraham, in light of what Benjamin Chaplin had said, but they wanted Abraham to make that opening.

After an uncomfortable silence, Abraham suggested they ride down to the big house and talk some more in the shade. This delighted Ken and Ashley, but they held their approval in check. Ken asked if they could let the horse drink some water, and Abraham said they would have to go to the mountains of South Carolina to get as good water as they had here. He motioned for them to follow him to the house. A pipe coming down from the pond fed a small stream of water into a trough. The area around it was wet and cool from the overflow. The horse stuck his head under and drank his fill while Abraham watched them. Ashley told Abraham that, since he had been the overseer for so long, he would know a lot about what they had come to do. Abraham, a bit wary of the two strangers, said he knew a lot about the place from way back when Colonel Mashburn Willoughby was alive. In light of Chaplin's information, Ashley ventured to say to Abraham that it might not hurt to say what their business was about. He asked Ken for the Savannah paper with the runaway rewards and showed it to Abraham "This was a long time ago, but we have access to these runaways." Abraham looked at the paper funny, and Ken realized that he couldn't read, but he had some idea of what it was because he recognized Willoughby's name and because runaway slave notices were common. He told them to wait there and he would be right back, and he rode off hurriedly. Ashley told Ken he hoped he would agree with him in trying to get as much out of Abraham as they could, and Ken said that if he hadn't said anything, he would have.

When Abraham returned, he had an older black woman seated behind him on the horse; he got off and helped her down. He brought her over, asked for the paper, handed it to her, and asked her to read it. She read it to herself first and was so shocked that her knees buckled and she slumped down onto the dirt. Abraham was startled and he put his hands under her arms, lifted her, and asked, "What is it, Prissy?" Ken and Ashley exchanged a quick glance as the woman gathered her strength and read the descriptions of the runaways aloud, and she and Abraham were in shock. He told her that these men have found them and want the reward. She looked at them, unsure how to react, and asked where the runaways were. Prissy said it sounded like Lucie and her man, as well as Alice and her brother, Abraham, who had been named after the overseer. She said she couldn't remember the names of the others in the group that fled when they heard that massa was going to sell them off in different directions and Abraham said he remembered. He said he mostly remembered how ill massa was for the longest time about it and he still rants and raves about it occasionally. Ashley took out the papers from Sidney and read the names on the sales contract. Abraham asked what did the paper mean and he handed it to Prissy, and she started reading. Ken thought to himself that Prissy could read better than him or Ashley. Abraham heard what Prissy was reading but didn't understand it. He asked her what it all meant, and she said it meant that these two wanted to buy all of them if they can't get the reward. Abraham was quiet, thinking how he might benefit from it all, when suddenly there was a loud noise from the cows in the field under the shade oak. Prissy reacted and said that a cow was calving, and from all her commotion, it sounded like she was about to die. Abraham said he better go because the calf might need to be pulled out. Prissy said, "Massa be crazy if he comes home and have one and maybe two dead cows." Abraham got on his horse and left quickly for the oak, leaving Prissy with Ashley and Ken. Ashley made a split-second decision, and believing that Ken would agree, told Prissy that Lucie had told them all about her and how they were there to buy the runaways from Willoughby, not for their benefit, but for their own welfare. He said that they were well and safe and in hiding on an island in Georgia. Prissy believed Ashley, but it was almost too much for her to take in. She put her hands up to cover her eyes to try to think it through. Ken noticed the scarred flesh of both her forearms and knew it was from trying to fend off beatings. On impulse and with compassion for Prissy, he said that they would buy her too and take her to where Lucie and her family was. Ashley raised his eyebrows and smiled at Ken's quick thinking. Ashley told Prissy to listen carefully and explained their plan and said he wasn't sure how to handle Abraham. Prissy answered immediately that gold could solve that problem. Ken and Ashley smiled slightly at each other, not in triumph, but in gratitude that things were working out well, and in a way that neither could have imagined. Ashley heard that all the cow commotion had settled down and figured that Abraham would be back soon. He quickly told Prissy how they were planning to demand the reward money or buy the runaways outright and what they would say they would do if Willoughby did not agree and that would be to sell them on the black market. Tears were rolling down Prissy's cheeks, but they weren't stopping her from thinking quickly. She told them that she would go behind the big house to act like she was doing something while Abraham was gone, so he wouldn't suspect anything. She said that Abraham was not a bad man but had to look out for himself, and that he had always gone along with the slaves to keep the massa from being mean to everyone. She said he was the best at acting like he was always looking out for the massa, but they all knew he was for them. She said that massa had come to understand that his own bad ways had almost lost him everything so he was afraid to do much without Abraham's help. She said that massa would return tomorrow and that he would be the most crazy. He wasn't at the village doing business like he said but was getting laudanum from the doctor and shine from white trash and sometimes would be acting crazy. This usually made him easy for them to manipulate because they knew the things to tell him about his father's spirit and about the bad things he did after his father died. It made him so afraid that he would do anything Abraham or even she asked, but sometimes he would just go in his room and not come out for days. Ashley said she better git and said they may not see her until tomorrow, and she hurried around to the other side of the big house just before Abraham got back. He asked where she was, and Ken said she had gone off as soon as he had left for the cows. Abraham said he would be right back with her, and Ashley said he wanted to give him something before she came back. That got Abraham's full attention. Ashley reached into his pocket and pulled out four of the new shiny gold pieces and told Abraham that they were his and that he had four more for him if he helped them get what they wanted from Willoughby. Abraham got down from his horse and took the coins. He studied them and bit down on one. He looked Ashley and Ken up and down, and there was an awkward spell of silence before he grinned and said he was with them but he didn't want any funny business. Ashley said he could be sure there wouldn't be because they knew that he could make the deal happen or stop it, but to remember that they could turn things back on him too if he wasn't straight with them. He would get his money when the deal was done. Ken suggested that he not bring Prissy back so it would only be between him and them, and Abraham liked that idea. Ken said that the reward was just eight hundred dollars and they figured they could sell the runaways for more than that, but they would take the reward if that was all Willoughby would do. Abraham said that massa didn't like paying out money, and Ken told him that they would pay him two thousand dollars, less what the reward money was. And they would pay three hundred more dollars for Prissy. And if Abraham could make the deal happen, they would gladly give him four more gold pieces on top of what they already had. Abraham could not read or write well but he understood math. He was hesitant and said he was going to get Prissy and didn't care what she knew because she was gonna be gone. He jumped on his horse and lit out to get her. While he was gone Ashley looked over the sales contract that Sidney had drawn up. Ken asked what they could do about Prissy. Ashley said that Henry could put a document together tonight for her sale. Abraham was back quickly with Prissy with him on the horse again. Ashley showed her the sales document. She read the list and the payment for them all. It was two thousand dollars, and then the reward was subtracted, leaving twelve hundred dollars. Ashley stated that they would also pay three hundred dollars for Prissy and would bring the document for her sale tomorrow. He then said to Prissy that they would give Abraham eighty more dollars on top of what they had given him. Prissy repeated everything slowly to Abraham, and he was satisfied. Prissy asked him what he was gonna do with all that money, and he said he was gonna put it with what he already had. He would buy his freedom soon and have enough money left to go to Canada, wherever that was. She asked him when, and he said he would wait for the right time to come up."Massa don't beat nobody no more, and he stays drunk half the time, and we are mostly on our own. All he does is collect some money for what we grow and the cattle we sell. He mostly forgets to pay any bills until they come looking for him, but now most make him pay up front." They all knew that they would do fine as long as that cold water kept coming up out of the ground. Ashley and Ken shook Abraham's hand and told them they would see them the next day.

Ashley and Ken were hungry but didn't want to stop and eat, so they ate while riding back to Tombee. They knew that Henry and Martin would be waiting, eager to know how it all went. There was no one about on the water side of Tombee, and they freed up the horse as Chaplin had said to do and left the carriage. It was midafternoon and the outgoing tide had started which made their trip back to the sharpie easy.

Martin saw them coming. Henry was below doing accounting work and came out when Martin called. They watched and waited as the boat got closer, and Martin took a line from Ken as it came alongside. He could tell from the look on their faces that they had good news and they came aboard and sat in the cockpit. Henry had made mugs of iced yaupon with honey and lemon and they drank it all down. Ken began telling what had happened, starting with Benjamin Chaplin and then about the Willoughby place. Ken would pause occasionally, and Ashley would talk. Ken told Henry that he had probably made a mistake in offering to buy Prissy and that he and Ashley had agreed to go in together and pay for her since that wasn't part of Henry's plan. He described how terrible the scars were on her arms and how he couldn't help himself, and Ashley backed him up. Henry said he wasn't hearing any of it about them paying with their own money and that he would have done the same. He would pay and was thankful to them for making a good decision. They also told Henry that they had offered more money than they had planned but wanted to make sure the deal was accepted. Ashley said they would need a sales document for Prissy, and Henry said he could easily do that. Martin said it was gonna be a real special moment when Prissy was reunited with Alice's family after all these years and after all these things had gone on. Ashley said that today was a great success, but the biggest test will be tomorrow when they meet Willoughby. Abraham had told them how bad and how long he had been crazy about the escape and Prissy said he would probably be acting crazy when he came home tomorrow, especially hearing about the runaways again. Henry agreed and said today's success was worth celebrating. Success tomorrow would be more difficult but hopefully even more rewarding. Ken said being finished tomorrow was not guaranteed and how Prissy had said that sometimes Willoughby would lock himself in his room for days when he came from town. Henry said they would have to wait and see, but hopefully the gold would be enough to bring Willoughby out of his room.

Martin asked Ken to tell him more about the pond of blue water. He said he had heard of something like, called "blue hole," north of Savannah on the river and had always wanted to see it. Ken said it was natural but didn't look natural because it was so different from anything he had ever seen. The water was cold like the ice in the icebox but not solid like ice, and it just came up night and day, and they piped some off for the cattle and some off for the house, and it looked clean and pure, not like swamp water. He said he would have asked more about it, but their visit wasn't the casual talk kind, and Martin said he understood that. Ashley said he had heard a little about water coming up out of the ground under pressure like that, and it was called "artesian" water, and it came from way deep in the ground, much deeper than the dug wells that are common. Martin said he wanted to see an artesian well but didn't much want to see that particular one.

Ashley said he wanted to fix a big supper, and Martin said he would peel potatoes or whatever needed doing. Ashley went below and handed out potatoes and carrots for Martin to start on. Henry said he had more accounting work to do. Ken said he had no intention of doing anything but a little whittling and went below and picked out a piece of stove wood, made himself comfortable and set to work. Martin filled the pan with cutup potatoes carrots and handed it back to Ashley who was busy making biscuits. Martin noticed the smoke coming out of the small stovepipe blowing back north and mentioned that the winds were shifting somewhat. Ken said that would make for a long sail back but not as long as it would if it changed to southeast, and Martin asked him to explain. Ken said if it were a south wind, they would sail out of Port Royal eastward for about thirty miles into the ocean and then come about. If they were lucky they could sail directly into Tybee Roads and if they were not lucky and couldn't point up into the wind enough, they would have to tack out again thirty miles and come back. Martin said he had never been out more than a few miles like they did going to Darien.

While whittling, Ken said that if the wind was out of the southeast, it might take three days to get back. Martin asked what about in a northeaster that Captain Jones said might blow. Ken said it depends on how strong it was. If it was real strong, they might just wait until it quit, which could be as long as a week, but was usually four or five days. Martin said he wouldn't mind that, but Henry wouldn't like it. He asked if they had enough food for a week, and Ken said Ashley always brought plenty of food and there was always fish and crabs to catch, or they could use Chaplin's carriage to go to the village to get some food. He added that if they did have to stay over, they could go see Captain Ben's friend on the north end of the island. Martin asked what if the northeaster was not that bad and Ken said they would have to consider that when the time came. Ashley called out that supper would be ready in about half hour, and Henry said he would fix the yaupon and filled mugs with tea, honey, ice, and a little rum. Ken had finished whittling and was tossing the wood chips over and showed Martin the little turtle he had carved, and Martin was impressed. Martin sipped his yaupon and thought to himself that he was going to pass on the second rum drink if it was offered because of how he had felt the night before. Ashley went below and handed out big tin bowls of stew and biscuits, and everybody was hungry. Henry was first to finish and said he was going for more and waited to serve seconds to everyone else. He complimented Ashley's cooking, and Ashley said it was just the salt air that made things taste better. After he finished, he went back and sent out some blackberry preserves and more biscuits for dessert.

After supper, the conversation was about what might happen tomorrow and what they might do under certain situations. Ken said they really didn't know what to expect and he was sure glad that they had an ally in Prissy and another that was almost certain in Abraham, and he hoped that with their help, they could have success. Ashley said Benjamin Chaplin had warmed up to them a bit, and he could be helpful too. Henry told them to be patient and not to worry if it took more days than tomorrow. He said they knew he didn't particularly like being on a boat but that this venture was more important to him than even the ice business and most everything else. He would have all the patience needed to get things done and done right and even if that meant more time and money, that was fine. He added that lives mattered most, and the knowledge of that was the greatest gift he had received from his parents. This made Ashley and Ken feel better because they were not sure how things might go or how long it would take and that they had offered so much money in the deal than was planned. Martin was listening and was proud of Henry for being the way he was. Ken said that they would have plenty of time in the morning because they didn't have to be at the Willoughby place until noon and the carriage was all set up, and Ashley said they may have time to catch a fish or two for breakfast.

It had been an early bedtime, and Ashley was up before the sun and had a half dozen fishing lines baited with bacon rinds over the side of the boat, and within a half hour had enough catfish for breakfast, and in another half hour had them cleaned and ready to fry. He had put the grits on and had coffee and tea going when Ken woke and came out on deck. They both had finished a coffee when Martin and then Henry came out. Ashley went below and handed out a coffee for Henry and a yaupon for Martin and began frying catfish slabs. He handed Ken the first tin, heaped with grits, two slabs of catfish, a big leftover biscuit, and blackberry preserves. In a few more minutes, he handed out tins for Martin and Henry, and then made one for himself. He announced that there were more grits and biscuits but no more fish and to serve themselves. Henry told Ashley what a good job he had done to catch, clean, and cook breakfast, and Ken said that Captain Ben was always saying that he didn't want to retire because he would miss Ashley's cooking. The praise from Henry and Ken made Ashley giddy.

After breakfast, Henry and Martin went below to clean up, allowing Ashley and Ken to relax and have some smokes before they left. When they were done, Henry came out and said that he had been thinking about what one of them had said last night about Benjamin Chaplin warming up, and he thought it might be a good idea to tell Chaplin what they were there to do, without telling him who him and Martin were. There would be no untruth in saying that they had found the runaways on an island in Georgia and wanted to buy them. That would provide a legitimate witness if ever Willoughby made any false claims. Henry's idea appealed to Ashley and Ken because they could tell that Chaplin was very curious about their endeavor, and they both had the impression that he was a good man. Henry added that whatever happened, they would hear about it later from Richard Wilcox because he was probably more in touch with every plantation owner on Saint Helena than anyone because they all visited his hardware store at least once a month. Also, he was easy to confide in, and everyone, once off the island, liked to talk. Ken said they should go early enough to have some time with Chaplin before going to see Willoughby.

With the satchel of gold and papers around Ken's neck and the additional document about Prissy, he and Ashley shoved off from the sharpie with optimism and guarded confidence. Henry and Martin wished them well. They both rowed and soon rounded the bend in Station Creek and before long they were tied off at the rickety dock at the Tombee landing. Ashley grabbed the food bag and water jug, and they climbed onto the dock, again being careful where they stepped on the deck boards. They heard the sounds of people around back of the big house, and when they walked up, the same lady looked out and yelled to the same two children playing in the dirt yard to go get massa, and in a half hour, Benjamin Chaplin and young Thomas Chaplin came on the same horse and carriage. When they got off, Ken reached into his pocket and handed young Thomas the turtle he had whittled the day before. The boy studied it closely and smiled. Ken asked him what had happened to the dolphin fish, and he pulled it from his pocket and showed it and put it back and continued his fascination with the turtle. Chaplin smiled and said that Thomas had three rooms full of expensive toys from all over the world but he had played with the dolphin fish all day yesterday and gone to sleep with it in his hand last night.

Then Chaplin's light-heartiness changed, and his brow furrowed. He said he didn't like to mind other people's business but he was curious about what their dealings were with Willoughby. He said the gold they had given him yesterday and the promise of more had at first eased his mind, but that later he had been troubled and had not been able to sleep well. Ashley said that if they could find a comfortable spot to sit, they would tell him because they surely didn't want him to think about things that were not so. Chaplin said they could go to the garden area on the south side of the house where there were some benches. He went to the kitchen outside and brought glasses of water. They sat, and Ashley began the story; parts were true, and parts were left out, but what he told was true. Chaplin's brow stayed furrowed as he listened. Ashley explained that they had found the runaways and had found the reward and showed him the old reward ad from the Savannah newspaper. He said they did not have the runaways with them, but they were being securely kept. They had come to see if the reward would be paid if they brought them back. Ashley was pleased with himself for not being untrue, since Alice and her family were in fact securely kept."The overseer said that Willoughby didn't like paying money out and he brought a slave named Prissy to read the paper we had, and we said we could just buy the runaways if we could deduct the reward from the cost. We will even buy the lady Prissy who read the reward paper for him." After a few moments of silence, Chaplin thanked them for telling him what was going on so he would not have to try and imagine what they were up to. He said that Willoughby was unpredictable and had acted rash often, so he didn't like to be in doubt about him any more than he needed to be. He said everybody knew Prissy from when the Colonel took her everywhere with him and she was so bright and happy and how good and cheerful she had made him feel. He said that he had heard of all the beating that went on after Colonel Willoughby died and how she got more beatings than others because young Willoughby was jealous of the affection that was shone her instead of him by his father. He said everyone on the island knew about the old cripple slave that he beat and let freeze and die, tied out all night to a post in the cold. Many of them wished he had been held accountable. He said that it was the largest group of runaways ever to get off the island and no one ever knew how they managed to do it without being picked up. He said he wouldn't let his own slaves know it, but he was secretly glad they got away. He said he remembered the family that ran off because they used to come and play with his slave children back when old man Willoughby was alive and used the landing once or twice a month. The father of the runaway family had been old man Willoughby's carriage driver for years. He said he purposely didn't get attached to his or anyone else's slaves because it could interfere with their proper management, but because of Willoughby and how bright Prissy was, he loved her like everyone else did, and when the beatings happened, he was deeply saddened. He was glad she was getting away from the place because anywhere else would have to be better. He added that her being able to read and write was both a blessing and a curse for her.

Chaplin said he didn't mean to be revealing so much of his feelings, but the poor night's sleep had left him without much composure. Ken said he would like to ask him about Abraham. Chaplin said everyone knew he ran the Willoughby place, and that Willoughby was crazy and miserable, living alone in the big house. Everyone was waiting for him to die, but he was to mean to die and carried on with the good fortune his father left.

"Anyhow, Abraham is a smart old bird, and the Willoughby place is unlike any other place on this big island because it doesn't need cotton or rain to make money. Abraham manages the slaves and most of all somehow manages Willoughby." Chaplin said he was being long-winded, but it was relieving his nerves to tell the story. He went on to say that after old man Willoughby died, young Willoughby demoted Abraham and brought in a new overseer that was in line with his thinking that brute force was the way to get the most from slaves and making a spectacle of beatings was a good way to keep the slaves in line. The new overseer was worried about his lack of success and told Willoughby that he needed to sell off his slaves and get new ones because they had been spoiled by his father's good treatment, which was the furthest thing from the truth. Old man Willoughby had things going so smooth with Abraham in charge that he didn't have to worry about a thing and had a hundred head of cattle and selling them regularly more than paid the bills. He sold food crops at the village and in Beaufort and added to his profits, and because of his unlimited water his crops came in every year no matter if there was a drought. Young Willoughby not just inherited a lot of money but a smooth operating plantation that was a moneymaker, and he came close to losing it all. When the slaves got wind of them being separated and sold off, the group of runaways took off, and darkness and near ruin came over the place. Willoughby drank more and started on laudanum, and maybe the laudanum numbed him enough or something happened that I don't know about, but Abraham was put back in charge. Somehow Willoughby didn't get any less mean but backed off for fear of losing everything. It is still different from all the other plantations, mainly because of the water, but also now because the overseer and the slaves seem to have gained control to a large extent. It's not a good example to the other slaves on the island when they hear about things there. It's always one of the things the slaves talk about at the village on Sundays.

Ashley said he wasn't looking forward to meeting Willoughby and hadn't quite decided how best to deal with him. Chaplin said, to be completely forthright with Abraham and give him a handful of those gold coins you have and let him deal with Willoughby because nobody else on the island can deal with him. Ken said they should be going. Chaplin said he needed to go too and he hadn't planned to carry on so, but he had thought most of the night about things and he thanked them because he now knew what was happening now and what they were about and could control his imagination. He said he should be less of a worrier like Thomas, who had been quietly playing with the little wooden fish and turtle. They thanked him and shook his hand.

Ashley and Ken maintained an even composure until they were well down the road. Ken stopped the horse and looked at Ashley in something like disbelief. He said he could never have imagined how things had played out, and Ashley just shook his head. He said their conversation with Chaplin should have eased his mind, but he was even more nervous now. Ken said that Chaplin was out of sorts from a rough night, and his nervousness had made him nervous too. He said they were still ahead of time and could have a snack now because they might not be able to later and it might calm their nerves a bit. Ashley agreed and said he would never think of Saint Helena Island the same again. Ken said they had bitten off a lot in volunteering to do this, but that he had no regrets. Ashley said he felt the same way. They ate some cold biscuits with lard and more blackberry preserves and drank some yaupon. It did settle and refresh them somewhat, and they started again on their way.

Again, they passed the field of corn with the big shade oak with all the hoes leaning up against it and the hands lined up at the food wagon. When they were seen by the group, a boy dashed away, probably doing as told and going to tell Abraham that they were coming. Sure enough, by the time they had gotten to the big house, Abraham and Prissy were out in the yard to meet them. Ashley asked if Willoughby was back, and Abraham said he was and he was in a bad way as usual. He told them that he wanted to see those papers again about the sale. Prissy read the sales contract, and when she had, Ashley handed her the sales document for her, and she read that to Abraham. Then Ashley took out a small purse of gold coins and said that it was his when the deal was done. Abraham said it was a deal and he would see to it being done, but it would probably take some time. Ashley and Ken didn't know how much time he was talking about but said they had time. He told them to wait there with Prissy and that Willoughby had shut himself in his room and he would go see if he would let him in. Prissy was nervous and didn't say anything but her being nervous made Ashley and Ken nervous and they didn't know what to expect. Prissy had witnessed how awful Willoughby had been when coming home from his town visits.

When Abraham entered the house and went upstairs to the bedroom, they could hear him knocking hard on the door. They heard a voice telling him to go away, then Abraham yelling back, and more yelling for him to go away. Abraham said something that they couldn't understand, and the door must have opened because they heard Willoughby's screams much louder. Some slaves from out back had heard the commotion, and a group had formed, looking and listening. Willoughby burst out the front door and down the stairs heading in their direction. Prissy cringed, and Ashley and Ken didn't know if they should leave or not. Then they saw Abraham hold Willingham back and talk to him, and it seemed to calm him a bit. The craziness of the situation was in the air and powerfully unsettling. Ken told Ashley that they should leave, and Prissy told them to hold on and that she had seen him act out many times and it was always frightening but she had seen Abraham do his magic before, and it had always worked. She saw the look of horror on Ashley and Ken's faces and pleaded with them to wait a bit longer. They were both so affected and wanted to leave but thought of Henry and Martin and waited. Ken said that this was unsettling him like nothing he had ever been around. He said the man's craziness was dark and dimming his own soul. They watched and saw Abraham coax Willoughby back up the stairs and inside, and heard them going up the stairs, and then saw Abraham come back out and come toward them. They were amazed that he looked somewhat calm and collected like he knew exactly what he was doing. He told them that when he told Willoughby that the runaways had been found, he went into a rage like he hadn't seen since when they ran away in the beginning. He said back then he was mad at first but wasn't worried because slaves almost never made it off the island, but after a week his rage began to grow, and it got so bad that it made everyone miserable to the point that they wished the runaways would be caught and returned. His rage grew and grew and never seemed to calm for almost a year, and the new overseer became so afraid that he left. Prissy added that when the new and mean overseer left, Willoughby saw that he better ask Abraham to be the overseer again.

Abraham said he wanted to hold the gold and take it to Willoughby and let him touch it so he might come around. Ken opened the satchel and counted out the coins to the right amount plus the amount for Prissy and put it in a sack they had brought, and Abraham left for the house again. Ashley said he has the gold, and we have nothing signed, but he felt sure that Henry would have done the same thing, and Ken agreed. They watched as Abraham entered the house and listened as he yelled and banged on the door and heard more of the Willoughby's crazy yelling. Ken wished that he was someplace else. He didn't think he would be shot or hurt, but he had never experienced that amount of misery from a human being, and it pained him in a way he had never felt. It was as if his inner self was being shut off like a candle being snuffed out, and he felt like he might die if he didn't run away. On the brink of running, he happened to glance at Prissy, and the little spark left in his candle flamed back, and he felt like he could last this thing out as long as he kept an eye on Prissy.

After a bit, the screaming stopped, and Abraham came back and calmly asked Ashley for the sales contract for the runaways and for Prissy. Ashley showed Abraham the places marked with an X where Willoughby had to sign his name, and Abraham headed back to the house. The three of them braced for the outburst they knew was coming, but it didn't come, and Abraham came right back after just a few minutes. They thought something must have gone wrong, but Abraham calmly handed them the signed contracts and held his hand out. Ashley looked over the signature and handed Abraham his purse of gold, and Abraham looked pleased. He looked at Prissy, and she told him that there was a secret she needed to tell him. She told him the names of three slaves that she had taught to read, so he would have someone to help him when she was gone. She said they will be surprised to learn that you know, and you better be nice to them, so they can help you when you need something to read. She told Abraham to tell the rest that she loved them, and that she had been sold to a good master in Georgia. Ashley and Ken thanked Abraham, and the three of them loaded up and started back. There were no hands in the field as they went by, and Prissy said they had all heard the commotion and gone back to the house to listen in, and usually when one of these kind of things happened, Abraham let them take the rest of the day off. A ways farther, Ashley stopped the horse and said he needed to take a few minutes and get back to his right senses, and Ken said he really needed that too but it might take him days or weeks. Prissy said again that those spells with Willoughby happened a lot, but they were never any easier to stand, and nobody on the place slept much the night after.

They continued on to Tombee and sent out for Benjamin Chaplin when they arrived. He and his young nephew came in a short time, and he said he was surprised to see them back so quickly. He looked at Prissy and saw her mutilated arms and didn't hide the horror on his face. She saw his look and told him that had all happened in the first couple of years after old man Willoughby died but hadn't happened anymore since. Ken took out the gold they had promised Chaplin and handed it to him. He took it and said it was generous. He told them they were welcome to use his landing at no further cost another time if they needed it. Ken said he wouldn't be coming back again until he heard that Willoughby was gone from this world. Chaplin said he didn't like to wish that on any man but came the closest to wishing it on him. He said that he was glad that Thomas would not have him to deal with when he took over the place, and Thomas looked up from his dolphin and turtle when he heard his name. Ashley went out and untied the boat from the end of the dock and brought it up to the bank, so Ken and Prissy wouldn't have to walk out on the rotten planks. Ashley got out, and he and Ken shook Chaplin's hand and thanked him. Thomas smiled at Ken and thanked him for the toys, and they got in the boat and left to go back to the sharpie.

Martin saw them coming and yelled for Henry who was down below with his accounting books. The skiff pulled alongside the sharpie, and the three climbed up, and Henry knew they had at least some success because they had Prissy with them. He smiled at Prissy and told her his name and pointed to Martin and told her his. He said she was a welcome sight and they intended to do everything they could to help her get a start in a new life and they had heard stories about her from Lucie.

Prissy couldn't think of anything to say, and that was unusual for her. In just two days her life as she had known it for the last fifty-five years had changed. Henry could see that she was overwhelmed. She asked who her massa was now, and Martin looked at Henry hoping he could explain it all to her. He tried, but it was difficult. He told her that Ken and Ashley had bought her just to get her away from Willoughby, but they didn't want to be massas, and she could be free. Martin said she could live on the island with Lucie and her family if she wanted, or she could live on their place near Savannah if she wanted. Henry saw that she still didn't understand and wished that Alice was here because she could explain things that were difficult, and this was difficult for Prissy. She had not been in possession of her own self her whole life and to understand that she owned herself now would take some time and much of Alice's clarity and kindness and she didn't understand how they were saying she was free, yet according to the sales contract, she was owned by Ken and Ashley. What she did understand and what she did feel was a sense of safety and goodness from her new owners, or whatever they were. Henry went below and handed out some tea and biscuits he had made earlier, and it was very awkward for Prissy being included and being served by these white men.

Martin changed the subject by saying that the wind had moved around and it looked like the beginning of the northeaster that Captain Jones had warned about. What Ashley and Ken had been doing for the last couple of days had been so unusual and crazy that, for the first time in years, they had not even thought about the weather. Martin's comment about the wind brought them back to what they were doing and what they were about to do and how they needed to go about it. Ken got up and walked to the bow and looked across the inlet and over Pritchard's Island toward the beach to try to gauge the wind. It wasn't blowing that hard where they were, but he knew that it would be blowing much harder on the beach side. He listened but couldn't hear the roar that came from a hard northeaster. Ashley walked up to him and asked what he thought. Ken said he wasn't sure and said they should explain things to Henry and see if he had any druthers. They went back to the cockpit and told Henry that the wind could increase by morning, and depending on how hard it was blowing, they could either go out in it or wait for four, five, or six days until it blew over, and then head back. Ken said they could go the inland route, but that might take three days or more. He said they had plenty of food for a week or more if they caught some fish and crabs, which would be easy. Ashley said they had returned to Tybee in northeasters before, but it could be rough. If they saw tomorrow that it was a bad one, they should wait it out or go the inland way. Henry said he didn't want to be delayed a week getting home, but he didn't care for an unsafe passage either and he would leave it up to them to decide. Ken said they would just have to wait and see in the morning.

Ashley went below and handed out some potatoes, string beans, onions, and carrots to Martin and asked if he could get them ready to cook, and Martin said he could. He asked Ashley for an extra knife, and when he got it he smiled at Prissy and handed it to her and sat the pot between them. She helped him clean and get them peeled and ready while Ashley rekindled the stove. Martin told Prissy about the island where Alice's family was while they worked. She listened, but Martin could sense how out of place she felt. He did the best he could to explain things, but he could tell that it would take some time for her to feel comfortable. He wondered whether it would be best to take her to the island with Alice's family or straight to the Milam place where Alice could talk with her and bring her around. He thought that Alice would be best, but she was about to have her baby and it might not be a good time for her to have someone new around that she would have to look after. He couldn't decide what would be best, and decided, like the northeaster, to think about it tomorrow. He handed the pan of vegetables to Ashley when they had them ready.

They had an early supper, and Martin noticed that Prissy had a distant look about her. He asked her if she would help him clean up the little galley area from supper and wash the tins. Ashley noticed how odd she looked when Martin asked her and how she didn't seem to know how to be. He realized that she was not accustomed to being asked, not ordered, to do something, especially by a white man or boy. He tried to explain to her that they didn't give orders, but he realized by her blank look that she didn't understand him. He smiled at her, and Martin waved his hand, and she went below with him. He talked to her about his home and his mother and father. She had heard of Savannah and she listened to what Martin was saying but she had that blank stare that told him that she didn't know what to think of things. He figured that it was all too much for her to understand all at once and hoped that she wasn't too uncomfortable and that she would feel better after some time. He thought of Maggie and Mary and how they would probably know better what to say to help her feel more comfortable.

After supper, Ken said he and Ashley would sleep on deck and let Prissy have their room, and Martin took Prissy below and showed her where to sleep. She had that look of disbelief and Martin told her that everything was okay and that things were better for her now. He still didn't think he was saying what she needed to hear and wished he could say something to help her feel better. He remembered that she could read and went and asked Ken if they had any books. Ken said that he had a few and told Martin where they were. Martin brought a half dozen to her. He saw her face light up. She opened one and immediately looked all around. He asked her what was wrong, and she said that she always had to hide when she had a book to read. Since Colonel Willoughby had died, if young Willoughby caught her or even heard of her with a book, he would whip her out in front of everybody. She showed Martin her forearms where she had shielded herself from the whip, and she said her back was worse than her arms. Martin was so nauseous that he was about to throw up and was barely able to endure the next couple of minutes. She saw the tears stream down his cheeks and didn't like that he was crying. He noticed that for the first time her wide-eyed look of bewilderment was gone as she realized that someone was having feelings for her. Martin filled the washbowl with fresh water for her to have in her cabin and told her to try and feel comfortable and not to worry. He saw that she was beginning to come around a little, and it made him feel better.

Next morning, Ashley and Ken were up early and joined by Prissy. They sat out on deck and had yaupon, and Ashley tried to help Prissy feel more comfortable in the new situation. She asked them if they had been to the island that Martin had talked about where Alice's family was, and they said they hadn't. She said she was lying in bed last night and thinking about a story that was told many years ago at the underground meetings they have on the island and they still talk about it sometimes. It was about hundreds of runaways being killed by white men dressed like Indians and the bodies piled up and burnt somewhere near Savannah. There was one little girl that survived and grew up to be real smart and could raise the spirit in people. She said she wondered if that could have been Lucie's little girl and how Lucie could have survived. Ken and Ashley looked at each other in surprise and told her that Alice was indeed that little girl and that Martin could best tell the whole story. Prissy was set back in amazement and wished she could tell some of the people back at the Willoughby place that had known Alice's family. Everyone had assumed that they all probably drowned trying to get off the island or that alligators or wild Indians ate them. Ken told her that she was gonna learn many things that were different from what she had learned on the Willoughby place and most were gonna be good and she had suffered enough. Prissy had been talked down to her whole life by white people. How Ashley and Ken were talking to her as an equal was a foreign experience that was going to take a good amount of time and talk before Prissy could get used to it.

Ashley went below to stir the grits and fix some eggs and bacon. When he was done, he handed out tins for Ken and Prissy. Again, it was awkward for Prissy to be served by a white man, especially one of the ones that had bought her. Ken urged her to relax and enjoy her food and she tried but was still uneasy about it. Martin and Henry came out, and Ashley handed out a mug of coffee and a mug of yaupon. They greeted Prissy, and she smiled slightly back at them. Martin mentioned that the wind had picked up some from yesterday, and Ken said it had. Ashley handed out two more tins of grits, eggs, and bacon and then came out with his own. They all ate, and then Martin motioned for Prissy to follow him below to clean up the galley.

Once they were done with breakfast, Ashley said he wanted to talk about their options on returning, considering the northeaster that was blowing. He said that he and Ken had discussed it first thing this morning and they thought that, even though it would be a little rough, they would like to go back the way they came. He said it was a medium size blow and they had handled them before going into Tybee Roads and it was good that high tide was early afternoon with good visibility. They could go in, with the centerboard up, and not have to worry about the shoals. It would definitely be a rough ride, and once they started, there could be no turning back. He told Henry that the final decision was up to him and there were the options of waiting it out or of going the inland route. Henry asked what Captain Ben would do, and Ashley and Ken looked at each other and chuckled. Ken said if Ben would have noticed the wind shift like it did yesterday, they would have been on their way to his friend's house here on Saint Helena for a week to wait it out. But, if there were something important waiting in Savannah, and it was not a real strong northeaster, like now, he wouldn't hesitate to go out in it, especially if they would be coming into the south channel at high tide, in the daylight, with good visibility, as they could today. Without hesitating, Henry said to go for it, and Ashley said they would. He said that the trip back would be much quicker than it had been coming and, since they wanted to go into Tybee a little before full tide, they would move to the mouth of the inlet, wait about an hour, then set out. Martin had been listening closely and was filled with excitement and a little bit of fear, but he trusted Ashley and Kens judgment. He said that, once they reached Tybee, they could go up into Lazaretto Creek and stay the night, or they could head straight up the south channel and, with the northeaster, blow a good ways toward home before dark, then they could anchor for the night and catch the tide in the morning and be back at the Milam place by noon tomorrow. Henry liked the idea of getting home to resume his many duties, but he also liked the idea of getting Prissy to the company of his mother, Ellie, and especially Alice, to help her adjust and feel comfortable. He told Ashley that his choice would be to head home only if they considered it safe.

The tide was coming into Trenchards Inlet, but with the northeaster, the only sail needed to power against the current was the jib, and before long they were at the front of the inlet. Martin looked out beyond the shelter of the land and marsh toward the ocean and saw solid white caps, and he could hear the sound of the wind and surf on the beach. They set one anchor, and Ashley and Ken began fastening everything down extra tight, including the skiff on deck. When Martin thought they had tied enough extra rope around everything, Ken would send him below to bring out more rope and tie down things more. When the time came to go, they were on the hook and into the wind, and they lowered the centerboard and hoisted the big jib. They brought the bow anchor in and the big sharpie whirled around and they went out toward the ocean with the northeaster on their beam. As they got farther out into Port Royal Sound, Ken let out some line on the jib, and Ashley steered more southward with the wind more on their stern quarter. The big jib was almost more than enough sail and pulled them faster than the ocean waves as they came to the north end of Hilton Head. Martin watched the shore go by quickly, and every wave was a thrill. Henry and Prissy didn't feel well and went below, but Martin was enjoying every minute of the rough ride. He looked at Ashley's face to see if there was any hint of concern, but Ashley smiled real big at him. Ken came and sat by Martin and aid that the most fun was yet to come, and Martin wondered what that would be. He looked around, and anything that was not tied tight was flapping, but most was tied good, and he understood why they had spent so much time doing it. The waves were huge but the sharpie road each one with grace. The big jib was pulling them, but Martin could feel the wind pushing the hull of the boat too, especially when the stern rose up on a wave. If the wind were to have its way, they would be blown up quickly onto the beach of Hilton Head, but the power of the jib sail and the angle of the rudder and the resistance of the big centerboard allowed Ashley to steer a bit eastward, and they crabbed ahead swiftly. Martin thought about how important a rudder was and how things could go bad if something broke or went wrong with it on a day like this.

Martin didn't have a clock to look at, but in what seemed not much more than two hours, they were within a couple of miles of the south end of Hilton Head. In a half hour, as they cleared the island, Ashley steered southwestward and let the jib blow over to the other side, and with the wind behind them, he steered directly at the west end of Tybee. Ken motioned for Martin to help, and they cranked the centerboard up. The wind seemed to get more violent as it swirled around Hilton Head and was mostly behind them. The big sharpie was sliding down every other wave, and the waves were breaking harder because they were sailing right across the shoals. Martin knew this was the more fun that Ken was talking about. He looked to read the expressions on Ken and Ashley's faces and he didn't see fear but saw a stern seriousness that he hadn't seen before. He looked to the south over at the north Tybee beach and remembered being there during a northeaster and looking out to where he was now, and thinking then what it would be like to be out in it and here he was out in it. Henry looked out from below, wondering if everything was okay, and Martin saw that he didn't look well. Henry looked at Martin, Ashley, and Ken and didn't see looks of panic that he might have imagined, and he turned back. Martin felt sorry for him but knew things would settle down soon, as the boat was moving quickly toward the entrance to the south channel but the rough ride was not over yet. Martin was not very worried but was fully aware that a broken mast or plank coming loose could bring disaster very quickly in water this rough. If they grounded out, the power and violence of the waves would smash the hull to pieces. He was glad of two things, one was that, with the centerboard up, the sharpie was shallow enough to go over the shoals, and the other thing was how thorough Captain Ben was in taking care of his boat.

They were now about a mile from the south channel, and Martin recognized the tree top pattern of Cockspur. He remembered Daniel saying that his father had been asking that a lighthouse be built on the eastern tip of Cockspur to mark the entrance to the south channel, and he now saw how helpful that would be to steer by. He shuttered to think of trying to get into the channel in weather like this, in darkness or fog, or in rain without a lighted beacon. He looked again over at the north beach and wondered if anyone had seen and recognized them coming in. There were no pilot crews on the beach because they knew there would be no ships that would risk coming in for a few days until the northeaster had quit. He couldn't see well enough to tell if the Captain was outside, but he thought he would be staying in. Maybe Charles or Daniel might have seen them from up on the lighthouse.

Ashley was steering straight for the middle of the south channel and when they were up in it a ways, Martin went to the cabin door and yelled to Henry that they had made it safely. Henry groaned a response, and Ken said he would be fine in a little while once they had gotten a ways up the river and into calmer water. He asked Martin if he still wanted to go on trips with them. Martin grinned and said more than before and made Ashley and Ken both laugh out loud. Ashley came about and into the wind long enough for them to untie all the lines they had bound around the booms to keep the big sails from flapping to pieces. He motioned for Martin to help hoist the big mainsail. Martin watched how Ken managed the sails and got them before the wind smoothly. He realized that he had a lot to learn but that he had some good teachers. With the big mainsail out on one side and the big jib out on the other, the sharpie was moving up the river rapidly, even as the tide had turned and started out against them. As the current increased and the wind was blocked more by the riverbanks, Martin saw the bank go by slower and slower until Ken said it was probably time to drop the hooks. He and Ashley talked for a few minutes and decided to set the anchors over a shallow area, safe from any ships with deep drafts.

Once the boat was secured, Martin sat with Ken and Ashley waiting for Henry and Prissy to feel better and come up. Prissy was first and looked a bit woozy and asked if there was any more rough water ahead, and Ken said there wasn't. Martin told her that they were not that far from his home and would be there about midday tomorrow. She said she had wondered if the sea would swallow them all up. Henry came out next and looked a little rough, but it made him feel better to know how close to home they were. He told Martin that he didn't care if he never went on a boat again and didn't understand why he liked it so much. Martin said he had felt as bad as Henry was feeling now, while he was in the little school in Savannah for that short time. Henry said they were full-blooded brothers but had their differences and that he loved every minute being in the school. It was getting dark, and Ken ran a lantern up the mast. He said he didn't think it would be necessary but that Captain Ben always wanted it done. Ashley said he would start supper. Henry said he would be skipping supper, and Prissy looked like he could be speaking for her too. Martin told Ken he was right about the extra fun. Ken said the northeasters blow so hard because they have the whole Atlantic from England to fetch up, and when they hit the end of Hilton Head, they swirl around and get violent, and he was terrified the first time he had gone through it. He added that today's blow was just a medium northeaster and they could be a lot worse. Ashley asked Henry if he had any regrets about agreeing for them to go out in the blow today. Henry was able to crack a smile and said now he didn't, but hours earlier while they were being tossed about in the worst of it, he did.

The next morning Ashley didn't start breakfast, so that everyone who wanted could sleep a little longer. There was no hurry because they had to wait before the tide would start in. After the sun was fully up, he went into the little galley, and his noise woke Henry, Martin, and Prissy. He had hot food ready when they ventured out. Henry and Prissy looked better, and Martin was fine. He had been a little extra tired, and it was rare for him not to be up early. A ship had drifted by while the tide was still going out, but it had not come near the sharpie because with its deep draft it had to stay in the deepest part of the channel. Six pulling boats were tied to it to keep it in the channel and away from the edge of the river. The sharpie was barely above the bottom of the river in the shallow area where they had set the anchors. Had they anchored in the deep water, it would have been a problem for the ship to pass. Captain Ben had taught his men well.

When the tide turned, they pulled the stern anchor. Once the sharpie turned and faced the wind, they set the sails, cranked the bow anchor and let it turn before the wind. They moved up the river swiftly with wind and current. Henry and Prissy felt better, but Prissy still had a look of uncertainty. The men were all feeling very happy and relieved over the success of the trip. Their good mood helped Prissy feel better even with her uncertainty. They were soon within a few miles of where the Wilmington River branched off of the Savannah River, with the Milam place not far away. There was still plenty of that wind from England in the sails, and Martin watched the river bank go by swiftly as they turned south into the Wilmington River. The wind was full on their beam, and the Milam bluff was in sight. As they got closer, they saw that everybody had come down to greet them. Martin said that Charles or Daniel must have seen them coming the day before and signaled the Milam's. The group on the bank was singing a chantey song, and it made Prissy feel better. Everybody was there except Walter and Martha. They saw the extra person aboard, and not knowing what she was about and they stared with quizzical looks. After the anchors were set and sails dropped, Ashley said he and Ken could come back later and secure everything else. They maneuvered the skiff over the side and all climbed down in it and were soon on the bank. It took a few minute for Martin and Henry and Prissy to adjust to the land and they felt unsteady to walk until they got their land legs back, and some of the group waiting wondered if something was wrong.

Everybody paid close attention to Prissy, wondering who she could be. Martin saw Alice, and she seemed to have gotten much bigger during the week he was gone. He held Prissy's hand to signal that she was special and walked her straight to Alice. He told her who she was and asked if she could, without difficulty in her condition, talk to her and assure her that everything was fine. He said hello to Johnny, Ellie, Jacob, Maggie, Izak, and little Thomas, who were standing together. He asked them to come to the house with them, and he and Henry would tell the story of the trip to them all together. Martin saw Alice say a sentence or two quietly to Prissy and saw her nod in agreement. He was glad that they had come straight home instead of stopping over at Tybee. Henry had been with Claudia and his kids, and they came over and hugged Martin. Martin said he thought that Jacob, Ellie, Johnny, and Alice should come to the house. Johnny had fetched Alice in the carriage, and Martin asked him to take her to the house in the carriage and the rest of them would walk to get their land legs back. Martin saw Alice talking more to Prissy, Ashley and Ken were about to go back out to the boat to sort and clean and get everything buckled down, but Martin asked them if it could wait until after they had gone up to the house a bit. They hesitated, but then he said that there would be meats, casseroles, pies, and cakes. Ken laughed because of how Martin had come to know how to get their attention.

At the house Walter and Martha were waiting on the porch and were extra happy to see both their sons return from what was an uncertain and hazardous quest. Martin had not known for a fact that there were pies and cakes when he had told that to Ashley, but he was more than right. When they had gotten the signal from the Dyers the day before that they had come in, Walter had suspected they would make it a ways up the river and catch the tide in the morning. He had bet Martha that they would be in by midday, and she had asked Claudia to help fix a special meal. They had kept it warm and ready and waiting to set out.

Henry introduced Prissy, who still had a look of disbelief and shyness and clung close to Alice. Prissy briefly said that she and Alice's mother and father had known each other as children and were always together until they had run away. Henry said they had much to tell, and it would take at least an hour and probably two, so maybe they should eat first. Martha agreed, and she and Claudia got up to bring out the food, and Ellie went in to help them. Martin told his father about the trip in the northeaster as the food was being set out. Walter beamed through it all, and Ken and Ashley were proud of their soon-to-be shipmate. The table was full of food, and Walter spoke of thankfulness for all their blessings before they ate. Martin caught Ashley's eye and smiled big at him and said he told him so. Ashley got that giddy way he always got when he was happy and didn't know what to say, and Martin and Ken laughed at him.

Before the meal was over, Henry told them about their visit with the Dyers, and how the Dyers were looking forward to Walter and Martha's visit, and how they had fixed up the guard house so nice with private bath facilities. He had thought of leaving that as a surprise, but he knew that his mother, even though she had not said so, was probably worried about where they would fit. Then he told the story of how they learned about Prissy before they had gotten there. He said that they should hear the whole story straight from Ashley and Ken because they were the ones that did all the work and were in all the action. So, for the next hour, Ashley and Ken took turns and told of the events that happened on Saint Helena, starting from when they first met Benjamin Chapman and his young nephew Thomas. Although Martin knew the story, he enjoyed hearing Ken and Ashley tell it again and saw how they were good storytellers and had everyone's complete attention, including his, Henry's, and Prissy's. After they had finished, there was much discussion including what might happen next with Prissy and Alice and her family.

Henry said he wasn't sure, but one thing he was sure of was that they were out of harm's way. He pulled the sales contract papers from his satchel and said that they were technically owned by Ashley and Ken and no longer owned by Willoughby. Ken said that they were free as far as he and Ashley were concerned. Alice asked to speak and said that she had asked Prissy if she would stay with her and Johnny and help her until she had the baby and for a week or so afterwards. And then, if Martin was willing, she could go and stay on the island with Alice's family for as long as she liked. Henry and Martin applauded that, and they saw that Prissy had a better look about her. The whole afternoon had passed, and Ken said they needed to go finish up on the boat and asked to be excused. Martha went up and hugged them both. And Walter told them that if they had been under his command in the royal navy, they would have gotten several medals and promotions, and he was proud to know them and they were family. Alice, without getting up, thanked them and Martin and Henry for what they had done to free her and her family, including Johnny and the new baby, from so many uncertainties. Martha told them to wait just a minute and for her to get them some cake and pie for later.

The next morning Ashley and Ken had plenty of time to go up to the Milam house to have a big breakfast, relax a bit, and bathe before leaving on the tide to go back to Savannah. Once back in Savannah, they went and found Ben right away because they knew he would like to know they were back. He said he had heard Captain Sandy's weather report about the northeaster and had thought they might be delayed, but they told him that they had decided to come on in with it. Ben asked if they had done what they had set out to do. Ken said they had done that and more, and Ben said he was glad to hear it. He said that he had a delivery waiting for Darien and, if there was no cargo for the return trip, he could haul some ice back to the Milam's whether they were in immediate need or not. Ashley told him that they had a lot of food left from the trip and he could join them for supper tonight if he liked. He said that would be fine and that they should probably get the cargo loaded first thing in the morning, leave for Lazaretto, spend the night, then leave for Darien the next morning. Ben said, if they were lucky, they might catch the tail end of the northeaster and get blown down to Darien if the two of them could stand a little rougher water, and they both nodded.

At the Milam place, Henry had a letter from John telling him the date they were leaving and that everything had gone well with Mable and her brother James. They would be moving with them to Savannah, and James might stay downstairs with Mable until the new barn was finished. He said that Lancy Jenkins had been very helpful and had arranged a huge wagon and horses that he and James would bring loaded with furniture. Julia and the kids would come ahead on the coach and might need to stay with them a night or two till he and James got there.

Another letter from Boston was from Thomas the engineer. He said that he had submitted the boat plans and had also spoken with some people that regularly sawed ice for ballast and for the area icehouses, and they already had standard sizes and weights. They said that it would be difficult to forecast what size the ice would be when it arrived, because of it melting some and the time it might take for different ships, but they would cut to their standards and make adjustments as became necessary. He also said he had visited some ice houses and thought their design with the thick cotton-insulated walls was superior to what he had found up there.

Jacob had told Henry just the day before that the foundation and floor were ready for the insulated panels to go up at the small icehouse. Henry had been very pleased that Jacob had decided on his own to insulate the ice house floor with four layers of cork slabs instead of cotton. The floor could leak as ice melted, and cotton would not hold up as well as cork. He thought to himself how resourceful Jacob was on the water as a boatman and on land as a builder and how lucky he was to have his help.

Henry thought about something else that Thomas had mentioned. He had heard about the man from Maine who had tried to market ice in Charleston but hadn't followed through. But some ice cutters said there had been other inquiries from people in the south since then. Thomas had spoken with a wagon maker and had given him the go-ahead to make two heavy-duty wagons of the height they needed. It would be costly to have them shipped but would simplify things in the long run because they could have them to copy when making their own. The wagons would be ready to ship in about a month, and the cork-insulated cover would need to be done after they arrived. Henry felt thankful that he had Jacob and Thomas to help him. Thomas said he would be there in a month, and he, Henry, and John could develop their first business plan.

Henry had been making his list of tasks, now up to 19. It was the longest task list he had ever made, and he sighed. Claudia walked in, saw the look on his face, and asked what was bothering him. He showed her the long list, and with no hesitation, she said he needed an overseer so he could not have the Milam place to worry about so much and do his ice business. She said he had been trying to do too much by himself, and now starting a new business, he needed help. Smart as he was, Henry sometimes lacked common sense, and he was lucky to have Claudia and Martin to offer advice. He admitted to Claudia that she was probably right and asked if she had any suggestions of who he could get to help. She said Jacob came to mind. Henry said that might work because Jacob was slowly learning to read from Maggie and got along good with everyone. He was already planning on having Jacob oversee the site work and construction of the new buildings. After the four or five months that would take, perhaps he could just continue and be the overseer of the whole Milam place.

Claudia told him she had just come to call him for lunch and left. Henry sat for a minute and thought about Abraham, the overseer at the Willoughby place, that Ken and Ashley had dealt with. They said he ran the whole place. As he got up to go for lunch, he thought how thankful he was to have people around to help him to think beyond his own self sometimes.

Martin went by Alice's house to check on Prissy and found the two of them sitting outside in the sunshine. He saw immediately how Prissy's face was so much more relaxed and could feel right away that just one day with Alice had helped her out of her nervousness. She smiled big at Martin and said she wanted to find Ashley and Ken to thank them some more. Martin said they were on a boat trip again but would probably be around again soon. She said that Alice had been telling her so many things about him and his family and her and her family. She also said that she would bring her some new books to read. She said she had been reading the same books over and over and some she had read twenty times. Young Willoughby had carried off most all the books, and she had only been left with a dozen, but it had been enough to teach a few others to read. Martin said that maybe there was a way to smuggle some new books in with Abraham's help. That possibility had never occurred to Prissy, and she was just about overcome by the idea. She declared to Alice that Martin was a Godsend, and Alice said she had known that for a long time. Martin was uncomfortable with the attention and said that Alice was the Godsend and Prissy was too and that without her help, they might still be in South Carolina trying to deal with Willoughby and she owed a lot to her own self. "Own self" was a strange concept to Prissy, and Alice was reminded of how Johnny was when they had their first intimate talks. She determined that in the next few weeks she would introduce Prissy to her "own self" just as she had learned to do with other people on the Milam place. Martin said he was just on the way to the boathouse and had wanted to check on Prissy and would continue on his way knowing she was fine. He left, and Alice told stories to Prissy of Martin from when he was little when she had him every day, and how his Geechee talk got so strong his own father couldn't understand him.

20
MILAM PLACE CHANGES

The Milam place had continued along every day and every week and every month smoothly, but now after the big important trip to South Carolina, there were some unusual things about to happen. Alice's baby, Walter and Martha's trip to Tybee, the Wilcox's moving to Savannah, Mary and Daniel's visit, and Martin going off with Ashley and Ken. The first thing to happen was Alice's baby, and it came with Ellie and Prissy at her side. Johnny was so upset while waiting for it to come out, that Jacob had to take him for a ride around the place in the carriage. Each time they circled the place, they would stop, Jacob would go in and check, and Ellie would say to go around again. After the fifth trip, they heard the baby's cry coming from in the house, and Jacob had to help Johnny off the carriage because he was so nervous, but he managed to get inside and see his new baby daughter, Jochebed, named after the mother of Moses and honoring Jacob.

The next big thing to happen was Walter and Martha going to the Tybee lighthouse as his doctor had suggested. There had been a plan for them to go on the supply boat, but Henry suggested a separate trip, and a day was set when the outgoing tide started about midmorning and there would be no hurry to rush off early, but they would still get to Lazaretto with plenty of daylight left. When they arrived, Daniel and Mary came to pick them up and brought them back to the compound. Walter had not been to the lighthouse since Alice was found after the massacre, and Martha had never been there, so it was quite the occasion. The Dyers always kept things clean and nice but had especially gone over everything to make it perfect for the Milam's. The new copper tub had been installed with a drain by the small ship stove, and the old guard house was perfectly detailed and bright and cozy, and Martha's fears of being in the Dyers' way were removed. It took them both a few days to get used to being someplace new. Daniel took over most of the lighthouse duties, so Walter and Charles could spend a lot of time talking about old times and new things. Like the new tower to be built at the point between the lighthouse and the ocean and the massive fort about to start on Cockspur Island that was supposed to be unconquerable because of its location on the river and surrounding marsh. Charles said he would prefer a small lighthouse to mark the entrance to the south channel over the two forts because of all the shipwrecks there. Charles reminded Walter that he and Daniel had watched Captain Ben's sharpie with Martin and Henry aboard come in with a northeaster blowing pretty hard but it was daylight with no rain or fog, and they were in a boat with a shallow draft, and Ben had taught Ashley and Ken well. He said it would only take a fifty-foot lighthouse there to save a lot of ships.

On their second day there, while the four of them were having tea on the porch, Walter, in length and detail, went through all that was discussed and determined during the big meeting that Charles and Margo missed. In conclusion, he said that he was satisfied with the outcome and that it was all in the hands of Henry now. Martha added that Walter had spent his life in the service of others and it was now his time to take care of himself and told them how thankful she was to them on the comfortable accommodations and Margo said she hoped they came regularly.

Margot asked Martha if she had heard how Mary and Martin were behaving toward each other lately and Martha said that all she heard Martin talk about was boats. Margo said that Mary was that way about her writing but she had seen the sparks fly between them when they were together. She mentioned how upset Mary was when Martin had left. Martha said they seemed so young but it was at about their age that she had gotten married. Margo said that in a few weeks Daniel and Mary would be visiting and there would be ample time for Mary and Martin to be together. The women exchanged a knowing smile that Charles and Walter could not see.

During those weeks, Mary got to know Martha better because Mary had asked her to tell her all about herself and Walter and the early days of the Milam place and Martha got to know Mary much better from the exchange in those conversations. Martha was continually at how seriously Mary took what she had to say and her diligence in documenting everything in her notes. Sometimes, it was Martha asking the questions and Mary telling her story. Martha asked Mary what had inspired her to do this and what she had learned so far. Mary said that seeing how Martin was so determined about what he wanted to do caused her to take her own self more seriously and to ask herself what she really wanted to do. Thanks to the Milam and Savannah library, and her isolation, she began reading extensively at an early age. One day during Martins long stay, it dawned on her that she was in the middle of a more exciting story than any of the books she had read and it became clear that she should record it all now and worry later about a publishable story. Most of what she was documenting, if became known, would cause a lot of very serious trouble for the Milams and the whole Milam place, her family, Alice and her family, and Ayana and her people. She admitted that gathering material for a book that couldn't be published was not a practical endeavor but she felt compelled to do it while the events were still somewhat fresh.

Martha asked Mary what she had learned so far in her work. Mary said that in the beginning, she simply recorded facts but realized that her favorite literature conveyed passion and emotion and it wasn't easy, but she began to not just focus on the facts but also the heart of the mater and the feelings and emotions involved. She said that saved historical facts would stay the same but she was not certain that boxed up feelings and passion and emotions would have the same impact ten years down the road or whenever it would be safe for all involved to publish the truth.

Mary told Martha about something that happened at the Lazaretto landing with Jacob and Johnny and the rest of the boatmen, the day before Martin and Henry went off to South Carolina. She said she had written it all down but it was more meaningful than just the facts.
She said the boatmen were all grieving prematurely about the certain death or worse that would happen to Henry and Martin as they went off to deal with the evil master that Alice and her family had run away from."They didn't say much aloud, but there was a gloom about them and at the same time a deep and rich love for your two sons. It was like the deep kind of love and respect that only happens after a loved one dies, and I was struck deeply by it, and their feelings came over me. And I knew I must try to learn to capture feelings like that in my notes somehow that could be reconstituted later without any loss of it all."

When Mary was not sitting with Martha, she was often with Walter, questioning and adding to her notes. Mary realized that there was a volume of work just in what all Walter had to say, and the same could be done with all the stories of Captain Jones, down on the beach. Mary occupied so much of Walter and Martha's time that she occasionally apologized but they insisted that they liked what she was doing and encouraged her.

Some days, Charles would take Walter in the wagon up a ways from the lighthouse and cross over to the beach where the dunes were not so big. The big dune in front of the lighthouse was too steep for Walter to walk down or climb up. They would ride back down the beach to see Captain Jones, and the three would sit and tell stories until Margo would have to send Daniel to tell them to come home. Mary would walk down with her notebook and write as fast as she could while they talked. For one reason or another, they would sometimes ask Mary to walk up the beach a little ways so they could tell a certain story that they didn't want her to hear and she hated that. And sometimes they would let her stay but wished they hadn't after the story was told.

After four days at Tybee both Martha and Walter were doing so well that Walter suggested they stay another week, and Martha agreed. While they were there, Mary's notes tripled, and when she wasn't listening and writing while Walter or Martha told her stories, she was in her room re-writing the notes and adding her own thoughts and feelings. Daniel was also very busy, doing his regular work plus what his father normally did. He did all the things to maintain the lighthouse. He hauled the oil up and kept the lamp full and trimmed the wick. He cleaned all the small pieces of mirror inside the parabolic reflector and cleaned the glass surrounding the top of the lighthouse. His hardest thing to do was the delicate task of removing the lamp's tall glass chimney and cleaning the soot from the in-side. He also sent and received messages with the Milam place every day, and occasionally with Ayana. He wrote out a report of the day and filed it in the box that contained all the daily reports going back many years. Daniel was doing almost everything.

While Martha and Walter were at Tybee, the Wilcox's moved from Darien to Savannah. Mable traveled with Julia and the kids on the coach, and James went with John on the big wagon that Lancy Jenkins sent. Julia and the kids and Mable went to the Milam place. A couple of days later John and James came to the townhouse, unloaded things, and sent the wagon back. Mable was happy and excited about leaving Darien, es-pecially now that their land was secured, but James was shy and insecure and a bit uneasy, being in a new and unfamiliar place. When John brought James to the Milam place the first time, Henry took James to Jacob's house and asked him to take James over to the boathouse to show him around and to meet Jehu, who had been staying there. Henry mentioned that James might be more comfortable there by the river with Jehu than in the townhouse in Savannah. Henry asked Jacob to talk to James and try to help him feel better about his new home and tell him about the new place that he and Jehu would be helping build. Henry told Jacob, there and then, that he was gonna be the new overseer of the whole Milam place after they had gotten the buildings done and Jehu and James were his two help-ers to get that done. He told Jacob that he wanted him to keep working on his reading and writing with Maggie. Jacob asked if he would go to the boathouse anymore. Henry said he would not be going there every day, but being the overseer of the whole Milam place meant that he was the boss man of all the work that went on, and the boathouse was part of it, and Johnny would take his place there. Henry asked him what he thought about being the overseer and Jacob said he would try and see if he could. Henry said good and told him not to worry about anything else until the new buildings were done, then he could worry about the other things, and he would keep looking after things until then. He asked Jacob to bring James by the house often so James could see Mable, while she was there the next few days, so he would know that she was okay.

When Jacob brought James to see Mable the next morning, Jehu was with them, and James was a little more at ease. Mable told Jacob that James could catch fish when nobody else could, and Jacob said that was good because a lot of people went fishin but not enough went catchin. Jacob told Henry that they were gonna start on the walls of the icehouse today and he had asked a couple of the strong boatmen to help. Johnny had said it would be fine because they could hear the bell from there if there was any kind of emergency. Henry said that sounded good and was pleased that Jacob had thought things through. He thought to himself how unusual it was that two free black men had a black slave for a boss, but he was more concerned about how it might go with the work crews he brought out from Savannah, with Jacob looking over things.

Martha and Walter were able to enjoy leisure that they hadn't expected and Charles and Margo were enjoying their company. Charles was plenty impressed with Daniel's good job, doing everything on his own. He told Walter that he could feel better now taking a few days off but would prefer to have another person there to help Daniel. Mary backed off some, so her mother and father could spend more time with Walter and Martha. She knew she would have more time to talk to them when she was in Savannah soon. She wanted to go over to Little Tybee and see Ayana and Alice's family before they went to Savannah, but she realized that Daniel was too busy now to take her. There would be a few days available after Martha and Walter left, and she asked Daniel if he might take her then. He said he would when the tide was right, so he could take her very early in the morning on the high tide and pick her up just before dark when the tide was high again. He said, if they did, he could signal Ayana that Mary was coming. Mary was so pleased with Daniel that she did something she rarely did and hugged him and gave him a kiss and said what a good brother he was. They asked Margo, who said she didn't like that she might be gone on one of the few days she had before being off to Savannah, but if she really wanted to, she would go along with it if her father did. Mary asked Charles that night at supper, and he said he didn't see any problem with her going.

Walter and Martha's visit had gone well with everybody, and after two weeks and a day, Henry sent a boat for them. The whole Dyer family saw them off at Lazaretto and watched the boat leave out of the creek and turn up into the south channel toward Savannah. It had been a big occasion for the Dyers to have company and they enjoyed the visit. Martha said they just had two extra people and now they were about to be without two extra people when Daniel and Mary were gone. Mary said she thought that they should ask Henry if he could send someone to help them while Daniel was gone because she had seen how busy Daniel had been for the last few weeks and the guards were not there to help anymore. Margo said she could help, but Mary said she had enough to do already. Daniel said he agreed with Mary, and they were all surprised because he usually didn't agree with anything she said. Charles said he would ask Henry if there might be someone that could help.

There was a big crowd at the boathouse to welcome Walter and Martha home. The chanty made them both tearful as they got close. Henry had the carriage waiting, but they said they had been sitting for so long they wanted to walk home. Henry took the carriage, and Martin walked along with them home and told what had been going on while they were away. He asked how they liked the fixed-up guard house, and Martha said she liked it a lot and they were planning to go back in about a month.

The supply boat had been to Tybee the day before, so it would be almost a week before the next boat came that would take Daniel and Mary to Savannah. Daniel told Mary that the next few day's tides were good for him to take her over to the Indian Islands. Mary said the day after tomorrow would be fine. Daniel said he would signal Ayana. Mary told her mother about it, and Margo said she was glad for her to go. She said that someone should know the story of Ayana's people and what she learned and wrote could come to be all there was of them one day. She said the story of Alice's family and friends needed telling too but less was known about Ayana and it was also important. Mary was glad her mother liked what she was doing. Margo told Mary that Charles had wanted to talk to her tonight about something, and Mary said she thought she knew what it was about.

After supper, Charles told Mary that he was happy with what she was doing, and proud of her for being so dedicated to what she believed in, but he was concerned that what she wrote in her notes could somehow get in the wrong hands and serious charges could be levied against them and the Milams and Ayana and her people. He went on to say that even though the ownership of Alice and her family was secured by their ownership of Ashley and Ken now, particularly Ayana and her group. They could be expelled to who knows where for supporting Alice's family in their illegal activities and transporting the runaways up the Ogeechee. Mary said she was aware of the risks and she and Daniel had planned to put her notes in a clay crocks and seal the lids with wax and bury them. Her father said that there was a risk but he believed in the importance of what she was doing and he urged her to take extreme caution and to bury a crock as soon as it was full of notes. Mary assured him that she would.

Daniel signaled Ayana the next day, and Ayana said she would be waiting happily to meet Mary early. Daniel had been keeping his little dugout that Martin had given him down on the beach by the Captain's shanty. He went down and shoved it into the water and sailed around the point and down Tybee beach and around the south end and into the Back River to the landing and left it pulled up above the high water line to be there for them the next morning. Margo packed Mary a lunch and a few treats for Ayana and Alice's family.

The next morning, before sunup, Martha had made breakfast for Daniel and Mary, and they left out and were shoving the little dugout into the Back River with the sun just beginning to peek over the horizon. There was hardly any wind, and they paddled across, just as the tide was full and had slacked, and entered the edge of the marsh grass. Daniel handed over one of the poles with the fork at the bottom and showed Mary how to push off the bottom of the marsh grass, so it wouldn't sink in the mud, and they started across the top of the marsh. Mary caught on quickly and they were soon near Long Island and could see Ayana and a few others waiting at the first landing. Daniel unloaded and told Ayana that he needed to go back right away while there was still enough water to cross over the marsh and told Mary that he would be back in about twelve hours.

Martin had told Mary about how Ayana's mother had learned that the diseases of the colonials were contagious to the Indians by the air they breathed and how Ayana would keep a distance from her and might even have a doeskin mask on. Mary had taken a silk scarf for herself to cover her nose and mouth. This morning Ayana had a doeskin mask on and so did the few people that were with her, and Mary had her silk scarf over her nose and mouth. Ayana motioned for Mary to follow her, and she went down a path along the edge of the island, and the people with her went down a different path. The wind this morning had picked up a little and was out of the south and they followed the path around to the south side of the island to a cleared spot with some log seats, and Mary could feel the breeze blowing from across the marsh and onto the little clearing. Mary was glad that Daniel had told her about how careful Ayana was and why. Once sat down, with the breeze moving from Ayana toward Mary, Ayana took off her doeskin mask and motioned for Mary to do the same and smiled beautifully, and it broke the smile out on Mary's face too. They were silent for a few minutes, and Ayana asked about Martin. Mary told her a little about him and what he and his brother Henry had done recently and explained a little about it all and what it meant for Alice's family and the others. Mary could see Ayana's face glow when she talked about Martin. Ayana told her how much she liked Martin. She said she liked her brother too, and how he had taught her to use the signaling mirror. Mary showed her the new notebook she had brought and told her that she had already completed three other notebooks and told her what they were about and all and that her story was no less important than anything else she had written about. She said she had heard some, from Martin, about her and her people but she wanted to hear it all straight from her if she didn't mind telling it. She said that she didn't want to presume that it would be okay with Ayana to tell her about her people and added that the notebook was to be buried on the island and why. Ayana agreed with that right away. She said she would like very much to tell the story of her people to Mary, and she would tell it all. She added that she had read many history books while she was staying in Savannah and explained that her people had a different way of recording history and that was by telling stories from one generation to the next. She said that the number of her tribe left had gone down in every generation since the colonials had first come to their land and now there was only eighteen of them left. She said that only a few were children and there was not enough of them to safely make more babies, so this might be the time we need to record our history in written words. Mary was in awe at the elegance and clarity that Ayana expressed. Ayana said it was a longer story than she had told Martin, and that she could tell that Martin had a hard time keeping his attention on her words, so she had made it short. Mary laughed and said she understood Martin well, and they both laughed. Then Ayana said something that shocked Mary. She asked when she and Martin were to marry. Mary showed her surprise and wonderment at Ayana's statement and asked her how she came to ask it. Ayana said that it showed in her face every time she said his name, and it was as sure as the wind and tide that they were to be together. Mary was a little befuddled, but she had known what Ayana was saying but had not heard it spoken. She saw an all-knowing smile on Ayana's face that she had never seen on anyone, including her own mother. Before she could answer, Ayana said that day when they were to be bound together would be a fine day and said she wished somehow she could be there. Mary could never have been prepared for this kind of sharing, but she felt completely comfortable and a warm friendship in just these first few minutes like they had known each other forever. Just then one of the little people who had been with Ayana earlier came with two cups and a pot of yaupon, and Mary saw that she had a doeskin mask on. She poured them each a cup, set the pot down, and left.

Mary told Ayana that she had planned to spend the day here with her and then spend tomorrow with Alice's family. She told her that she and Daniel were going to Savannah next week and would be gone for a few months or maybe more and would come back then to take more notes. Ayana said that was good because more time would be needed. Mary said she would come as many times as was needed. They sat and drank the tea for a bit, and then Ayana began to speak.

Her story started a hundred mothers ago, before the first Europeans showed up. She was very detailed in her telling and would speak a bit and wait for Mary to get it written and then speak some more. They went on like this for a few hours, Mary sipping tea while Ayana talked, and Ayana sipping tea while Mary wrote, until the pot was empty. The time flew by, and another one of Ayana's people, with a doeskin mask, came with some snacks. They ate, and Ayana suggested that they walk a little. They put their masks on and followed the path along the edge of the island a ways and Ayana pointed in one direction. She told Mary that through the woods there was where Alice's family was. She turned, and they walked back to the clearing, and someone had come and brought more tea. They sat again and carried on as they had in the morning, and the time went by quickly again. When most of the day had passed, Ayana said that was enough for today, and Mary said it surely was because they had covered about a two hundred years and filled more than half of her notebook. Ayana said that she expected the last fifty years of her people's lives would take much longer than what they covered today. Mary said she would have however long a time she needed to do it when she came back from Savannah, and this had been far more interesting than she could have imagined. They walked back to the landing and sat and waited for Daniel to come. With an hour of daylight left, they saw Daniel poling across the marsh. He set out the sack of sweets his mother had sent. Mary stepped in, and they turned and set out back across the marsh toward Tybee. Daniel set the sail, and the south wind and their poling got them across the marsh. Once in the river, the little dugout shot across the river to the landing. Mary had hardly noticed the river or Tybee or anything because she was thinking about many of the things that Ayana had told about. When the little boat bumped into the bank at the landing, she was startled back out of her mind, and she reminded herself of how Martin was often distant in his imagination and jumped when he came back to the present. Daniel asked her how it went, and she said better than she expected. Daniel stowed the rudder and sail and stuff, and he and Mary dragged the boat up above the high-water line.

He went and got the tackies out of the small dunes and hitched them to the wagon, and they headed back home.

After supper, Mary told some of the story to Daniel and her parents and how kind and elegant Ayana was. She added that it would take at least another few days to get the rest of the story from Ayana, and then there was Alice's family's story, but she didn't expect it to take as long. Daniel said she should go over and stay for a week. Mary said she might do that, when they were back from Savannah, and she looked at her mother and father to see their response.

High tide was an hour later the next day, so they didn't have to get up and leave as early as the day before. Daniel told his mother that it would probably be dark when they got home and told her not to worry. She said she would worry if she wanted to. Daniel said, even if it was dark when they left Long Island, all they had to do was head straight for the light-house, and they would hit right on the landing on the Tybee side. He said that when they got back from Savannah, Mary could stay over on the island for a few days if she wanted, or he could take her when the tides were right, like today. Margo said they could talk about that more when the time came. She said it just occurred to her that Alice would be wanting to take her baby over to see her parents soon, and probably before they were back. Daniel said it would be Martin taking her and he had heard something about Martin taking Prissy over to the island too but didn't know when that would be.

The wind was still out of the south the next morning, and Daniel and Mary paddled the boat over the river and across the marsh against the wind, but Daniel's trip back was easier with the wind behind him. He could have left the tackies hitched, but he knew how much they loved sea oats, and let them loose. After he was back and dragged the boat up the bank, he hitched them back and went home to help his father. That afternoon he included in the messages to the Milam place that his father could use some help while he and Mary were gone. He received a message back that Henry would send someone on the supply boat next week, and he told his parents that when he went down. Later in the day, after taking some food down to the Captain, it was time to go get Mary.

Mary had another full day of note taking. Alice's mother and father and her brother, his wife and kids, and the others were happy to see her and happy about the sacks of treats that Margo had sent. She explained what she had come there to do, what she had been doing, and what the crock pot was for, and she showed them the notebook that was already almost filled with the story from Ayana.

They had only heard that Henry and Martin were safely back from

South Carolina and wanted to hear about it all, so for the first hour she told the story of their trip to the place they had run away from all those years before. They were all deeply entranced and horrified hearing about their old Master Melvin and glad to hear of Ben Chaplin. But what sent them in a state of blissful weeping was hearing about Prissy and how the deal may not have happened without her help. And what put them all over the edge was that Prissy was at the Milam place with Alice and that Martin would probably be bringing her there soon, with Alice and the baby.

Mary explained how they were still owned by someone, but it did not have the usual meaning. It was a way so if they were ever discovered and hauled in, there would be proof of who owned them now. Otherwise, they could be sent back to Willoughby, or they would become property of the state and could be auctioned off and go back in slavery to anybody that paid for them. She explained about Ashley and Ken and how they had risked their lives in going to the Willoughby place to buy them, and how they came about finding Prissy and again how helpful she was in getting the deal done with Abraham and all. She explained again that Ashley and Ken had no desire to own someone but it was simply a way to preserve their security. It was quite a story, and they were in awe about it. Mary told them that they didn't have to live in the fear that they had been accustomed to, but they looked like they couldn't believe it and it would take some getting used to.

After Mary's talk and some tea, she explained to them what she wanted for her notes. She said there was no hurry because she was coming back as much as she needed to when she and Daniel got back from Savannah. She emphasized again that what she wrote would be buried on the island until the story could be told without fear. They all looked at her and asked who should tell the story first. She said she guessed that Lucie could start, and they could go from there but she wanted to hear from them all eventually.

Lucie began by saying that her earliest memory was when she was very little and playing every day with Prissy on the Willoughby place, but she didn't know who her mother and father were, and she stayed in several cabins on the place, sometimes with Prissy too, because she didn't have a mother or father either. She said she didn't remember many unpleasantries until after Colonel Willoughby died. She said that every day she and Prissy played all day in the dirt yard of the big house and splashed in the cold water that was piped over to the house from where the water shot up from the ground. Mary saw that Hester, (one of the people that ran away with Alice's parents) looked like she wanted to talk, so at a break in Lucie's story she asked Hester to speak some. She told of her sister that had died of fever and her mother and her grandmother who had been bought together by old man Willoughby when he had started the place. Hester talked for a bit, and then Alice's father talked for a while. Just like with Ayana, Mary would stop the person talking every few minutes to write down what they were saying. Then when they saw her stop writing, one or the other would talk some more. It was slow going, but they all enjoyed hearing one another's ways of telling things. Just like with Ayana, there was a lot of sipping yaupon, and they were all delighted with a little of the honey for their tea that Margo thought to send. By late afternoon, Mary had forty pages of notes, and she said she thought that it would take her another few days being there to get all their stories. She read the notes back to them, and they all laughed at hearing what they had said. Mary put her notes in the crock and melted the wax before setting the lid on. She told them all again why it needed to be kept a secret, and she asked Lucie to take it and give it to Ayana to bury and to remember where it was buried in case something ever happened to Ayana. They all went out to the point of the island and watched back toward Tybee for Daniel. It was late in the day, the tide was not yet at its highest and as the sun was dipping below the marsh to the west, Daniel came poling across to the island. Mary hugged them all and told them that she would be back in a few months, and Daniel said he would signal Ayana when he heard when Prissy was coming. Mary got in the boat and Daniel poled it out a ways, set the sail, and they headed out across the marsh and directly at the Tybee lighthouse. Daniel pointed at the landing and told Mary to look at the tackies waiting by the wagon. He said they like sea oats, but they don't like being out after dark. Mary said she didn't like it much here after dark because of the massacre.

They got home after dark, and Margo asked Mary how it went. Mary said good, but it was gonna take much more time than she thought, but she liked it. She told her mother how much they liked the treats and especially the honey for the yaupon tea. Margo said she should send things more often. Mary thanked Daniel again for taking her and picking her up both days. Charles asked if they all looked healthy, and Mary said they did. She said there were two runaways on the quarantine island, and Lucie said they shipped out three runaways last month. Margo said they had three more days here before leaving for Savannah and Mary said she was ready to go. Daniel said he didn't like going that much because he didn't like leaving his father with all the work. Charles said he would have some help and had put an extra bed for whoever Henry sent in the guard house. Margo said she thought Daniel would like it after he had been there a few days. She said he would be staying in Martin's room, and Mary was staying with Henry and Claudia in their end of the house.

Mary didn't say it but she was very pleased that she wasn't staying with her aunt as was first planned. Claudia had moved their kids in her and Henry's bedroom so that Mary could have the kids bedroom so she could have quiet and privacy to do her writing.

Daniel asked if there was anything particular that needed doing before he left, and Margo answered immediately that his room needed a good cleaning, and she wasn't going up there to do it. He didn't like hearing that but said he would do something with it. She told Mary that her room could use some help too, and Mary reluctantly said she would work on it. Charles said he should bring his boat off the beach and put it in the barn to let it dry out real good while he was gone and then oil it really good when he got back when it would be good and dry and soak up the oil. Daniel said that was a really good idea because it seemed a little heavy lately like it might be soaking up water. Charles said that ought to be done twice a year.

For the next few days, Daniel and Mary attended to things that needed doing. Daniel was uneasy about leaving and told his mother and father so, and Margo assured him that he would be fine, and if he didn't like being away, he could just come back on the next supply boat. Daniel said he didn't know if he would like to be around so many different people. His mother said that was because he lived way out there on Tybee and didn't see many people and was worried about how to act. She said Martin did fine when he left home alone to come there, but Daniel said that Martin loves Tybee and wanted to come. Margo said okay, then don't go, and Mary can go alone. Daniel said he didn't like that either and said he would go and come back if he wasn't comfortable being there. Mary wanted to go and was driven by her goal to finish a complete history with personal accounts of everybody involved with the Milam place from when Walter Milam first came from England to the present day. She had covered Walters's life up to and through the Revolutionary War and meeting Martha, while he was at Tybee, but that left a lot to be told all the way up to the present. She had just heard the same story from Alice's parents but wanted to hear it straight and thoroughly from Alice. Plus, there was John and his family, Captain Jones and the pilot crews, Henry, Jacob and Ellie and Maggie and more.

She thought to herself that she would need a lot of notebooks.

Besides Mary, only her mother knew the other reason Mary was so happy to be going to Savannah.

21.
MARY AND DANIEL AT THE MILAM PLACE

The day came for Mary and Daniel to leave, and Charles and Margo went on the wagon with them to the Lazaretto landing. They had packed what they thought they would need, knowing that if there was anything forgotten, it could be sent on the next supply boat. They watched the boat come out of the south channel and into Lazaretto creek and saw that there was an extra man to help Charles. When the boat got closer, they recognized it to be Izak, who had been there helping on the bridgework and was now a boatman in training. Mary said she had heard that Martin had taught him how to swim and had asked Henry and Jacob if he could train to be a boatman. She said that she had also heard that he had become very sweet on Jacob's daughter Maggie and that Maggie had taught him to read. Margo was surprised that Mary knew so much. The tide was at its lowest point, and everyone stepped out onto the two rails and walked up and cranked the boat up the rails. Johnny said hello to everybody and introduced Izak, and they all said they remembered Izak from when he had been there working on the bridge. Johnny said that Izak had reasons to not want to be away for a couple of months, but since he is the newest and youngest boatman, he was the one to go. Izak managed a smile and said he had liked being at Tybee before and would be a good helper, and he liked being a boatman, and he was ready to do whatever was needed of him. All the men helped, and shortly, the weekly supplies for the Dyers were unloaded from the boat and into the wagon, including two chunks of ice for their icebox. Margo handed Johnny a sack of big egg and bacon biscuits and he smiled big and thanked her. He told Izak that Mrs. Margo's cooking would help him a bit with his love sickness.

Most trips, the boatmen spent the night at Lazaretto and rowed back the next day, but when they arrived at Tybee before noon at dead low water, sometimes they would unload, and turn right around, same as the tide, and row back in the same day. Since Daniel and Mary were to go back with them, today was one of those days. They lowered the boat and after pausing for a few minutes for the Dyers to hug and say good bye to Daniel and Mary, they left in the slack of the tide and rowed out Lazaretto Creek and up the south channel as the tide began turning. After watching a minute or two, Charles said the ice was melting and they needed to get it in the icebox, and they left for home. When they got there, Izak commented that the last time he was there was with Jacob and a few others, and they were there to carry the big icebox up the stairs and onto the porch. Charles said he would go up and open the icebox door if he would bring up the first block of ice. He opened the door and set out the small chunk of ice that was left onto the porch floor. Izak put one new block at a time down in the copper pan, and Charles sat the small piece he had taken out on top of the fresh ice. Then they loaded some of the supplies into the icebox and some into the house, and Charles told Izak that the rest was to go elsewhere, and he would go and show him where they went and how to unhitch the horses and what care they needed. After they finished, Margo had egg-and-bacon biscuits for them, and Johnny was right, because they were so good that Izak forgot his blues for a few minutes about being away from Maggie. After lunch, Charles showed Izak the bed they had fixed for him in the old guard house and told him how the place and big bed had been fixed up for Walter and Martha to come and stay in and showed him about heating water for a bath and keeping water in the toilet tank so it could be flushed. Izak told Charles that Johnny told him it was part of his boatman training to keep everything clean and tidy and he was on duty the whole time he was there and should keep things shipshape and do all that he could to help. Charles told Izak to relax a little bit, and he would be back and take him up on the lighthouse and show him some of the daily tasks. Izak thanked him and said he hadn't ever been up in a lighthouse and would try not to be afraid. Charles told him that if he got too worried going up, they could go half way and he could go back down, and he could do the tasks today himself and they could try again tomorrow. Izak said no, he would do it, afraid or not, because it was his job. Charles was impressed with Izak's attitude and determination and said he would be back in an hour or so.

When Charles returned, Izak was waiting and ready. Charles motioned him to follow, and they went to the little oil house. He showed him the big tank inside and the four big tins of oil that had just been brought on the supply boat as part of their weekly delivery. He showed him the funnel and how to pour them into the big tank, and how to fill the smaller jugs from the big tank. He let him carry one and followed him into the lighthouse and up the stairs. Charles paused at each window on the way up for Izak to peer out, so he could gradually see how high they were. When at the top, Charles took a few minutes to catch his breath and noticed that Izak was barely winded. Charles motioned for Izak to follow him and showed how to top off the lantern tank and pointed out the wick and globe, the big parabolic reflector, and all the small pieces of mirror lining it. He said that over the next week, as different things needed doing, he would teach him how to do them. Izak had forgotten for a moment, while listening to Charles, how high they were. Charles said the next thing they did about this time every day was to go out on the balcony and signal the Milam place about daily ship arrivals and departures and Captain Sandy's weather and tide information which they get from the Captain down on the beach every day. Charles added that he was also signaling that Daniel and Mary were on the supply boat and headed there. Izak said he learned about Captain Jones when he was here before. Charles opened the door to the balcony and stepped out first and nodded for Izak to follow and told him to not look down but just pay attention to what he was doing. Charles went inside and brought out the signaling box, then turned and tilted it so that it was pointed between the sun and the Milam plantation. He opened and closed the wood shutter a few times and waited and told Izak to watch out to where he was pointing. In a few moments they saw multiple flashes, and Charles told Izak that those came from the Milam place. They were letting them know that they were there up on the top-floor balcony and were ready to receive the message. He looked at the paper he had brought and operated the shutter rapidly, sending the message on the paper. Izak was so fascinated that he forgot his fear of where he was. Then Charles stopped sending and watched and wrote down the messages that were sent back. He showed Izak the last message written on the paper, and Izak recognized the name Maggie. Charles told him that Mary, before she left, had asked him to send a message to Maggie that Izak arrived safely and that he missed her. Izak was overcome with a combination of emotions, and the one he expressed to Charles was gratitude, and Charles saw a few tears leak from his eyes. Charles told him to thank Mary next time he saw her because he would never have thought of doing this. Charles purposely did not say anything about signaling to Ayana because it was top secret, and he would do that alone. Signaling with Ayana was not an everyday thing, but she knew the times that Charles was up on the lighthouse and would flash him if anything was important, and he hadn't seen anything today. He thought he might not keep it a secret from Izak later. Next Charles set the monocular up in several places around the balcony and let Izak look out and told him what he was seeing. He was particularly interested in looking out toward Lazaretto and back toward Savannah and seeing the winding path of the Savannah River and the vast areas of marsh. Charles had done such a good job of keeping Izak's attention that he had forgotten his fears, and when he did look down, he wasn't that afraid.

Meanwhile, Daniel and Mary were enjoying the boat ride back to Savannah. The boatmen all knew them, and the three who were resting and waiting their turn to row cut up with them and told funny jokes about the three who were rowing and the jokes were directed at them when they rowed. They kept Daniel and Mary laughing most of the time. After a while, Mary took out her notebook and sat back with Johnny, at the helm, and asked him questions. He tried to answer, but the boatmen would make jokes about what he said. They said that Johnny didn't know about anything but boats, and that Alice had to teach him about everything, even about how babies were made. The boat almost came to a stop several times when the joking about Johnny caused the oarsmen to laugh so hard that they couldn't row. Mary saw that it would be impossible to get much from Johnny and just wrote about the boatmen in general without any questions. She would have more opportunities later.

Daniel and Mary were so entertained that the trip went by quickly for them, and they were soon turning into the Wilmington River with plenty of daylight left. Martin and Claudia, Prissy and Alice with her new baby girl were at the boathouse waiting for them as they pulled up to the boat ramp. They had made good time, and the tide still had another hour to come in. Daniel and Mary got out first and went straight to Alice to see her baby and they were overjoyed to see it, and Alice glowed with happiness. Next, Mary hugged Claudia and Martin. Martin felt pleasure as he smelled her sweet scent again and was also a little shy and awkward. He smiled big at Daniel, and they embraced and laughed at each other. Claudia hugged them and said they looked like grown people. Mary asked about her children, and she said they were with Walter and Martha, and her biggest kid, Henry, was busy as usual. Mary hugged Prissy and saw tears rolling down her cheeks. Johnny left the rest of the work of cleaning the boat to the others and came up and hugged Alice and smiled big and proud at his daughter. Martin asked Johnny to take Alice and the baby in the carriage, and that he, Mary, and Daniel would walk back because they needed to get their land legs back.

On the walk back to the house Martin told them that he knew how they hardly ever left Tybee and he wanted to help them do whatever they wanted while they were there. Mary said she wanted to meet with everybody and put their stories in her notes. She said she had filled up two whole notebooks from her talks with his mother and father while they were at Tybee, and she asked Martin who he thought she should talk to first. He said that was easy - she should talk to Alice because she knew more about the place than anybody else including him and his family. He said that a whole book could be about Alice. Martin said that Jehu's story was also one that she should hear, and Mary said she would. Martin said there was John and Julia, and Mable and her brother, and what happened to them and all. He said that John's mother and father would probably visit while she was there, and they would have plenty to tell. She said that Captain Jones was another that could be a book and the same for Walter. Martin said then there was Captain Ben and Ashley and Ken for her to get notes from, and their adventures could be a book. Mary told Martin that he had left out one of the most or maybe the most important character, and his brow wrinkled as he tried to think of who he may have overlooked. Then Mary put her finger in his chest and made Daniel laugh. Martin said he was only going on sixteen years old and didn't have much to say. Mary said he was wrong about himself, and by the time she had finished asking him all her questions, he would think differently. Martin then spouted off other important people for Mary to talk to and mentioned Jacob and Ellie and Willy. Mary said she came with a list of about twenty people in the order that she would talk to them, but maybe she ought to see how it goes and take things in the order they come.

At the house, Luisa and Mathew, Claudia and Henry's kids, came over to meet Daniel and Mary. Luisa said they had fixed up their room for Mary and seemed excited to show it to her. Claudia came out and said for them to go see Walter and Martha first. Mary and Daniel went on the porch and hugged them both. Martha said she had thought of more stories, and Walter said he had too. Mary said she planned on talking to everyone on the place before she went back and thought she would start with Alice. Martha said that she would be a good place to start. Luisa was pulling on Mary's hand to come see her room. Claudia said that Luisa had helped and was excited about it, so they went around to the end of the house. Mary was surprised when she went into the room. Luisa had watched her face to see her reaction, and she smiled big when she saw how much Mary liked things. They had taken out the two smaller beds and brought in one bed and put bright bed coverings on it. There was one big window, and by it they had put a small desk that had been Claudia's when she was little. Mary liked how the light flooded in over the desk and saw that they had put a small lantern so she could work at night. Mary hugged the two kids and Claudia and said it was perfect, and Louisa's face lit up with happiness when she saw how Mary was so pleased.

Martin took Daniel in to his room and showed him his bed and told him that he thought they might go for a horse ride to show him the whole place. Daniel liked that idea, and they went back out, and Martin told his mother where they were going. They walked to the barn, and Martin pointed out everything to Daniel and told what things were. Willy was at the horse barn, and Martin let Daniel meet Willy. He told him that Willy was good with horses and could sew and repair tack and keep a wagon in good shape better than anyone. Willy asked Daniel how his mother and father were and said he had met them when Captain Milam had taken him and others down to Tybee after all the runaway killings and had stayed with Walter until he went home with Alice. He said Daniel was a big little boy then. Daniel said he could barely remember all that but remembered that it was a dark time. Willy helped them get the horses ready, and Martin led the way. They rode out of the Milam place to where all the new buildings were to be built. Then they rode to where Jacob was building the icehouse and from there down to the boathouse. Martin took Daniel into the boathouse and showed him around and then outside and showed him the boat he got from the Captain. Daniel was stunned and impressed and said it looked like a different boat. Martin said he might be making a trip soon to take Prissy to stay with Alice's family, but it depended on how much longer Alice needed help, and Alice and the baby could be going too. He asked Daniel if he would like to go, and Daniel said he sure would, mainly because he didn't want to be left there while Martin was gone off. Martin said he expected to hear any day because Alice seemed to be doing well. Martin said they would be going the back way into Tybee, and Daniel said that might be interesting. They took the horses back to the barn. Daniel asked about the stacks of big cork slabs, and Martin explained how it was bark from trees and was what people made wine bottle stoppers out of but they were using it to make iceboxes with because it was very good at keeping out heat.

The next morning Martin and Daniel went early to have breakfast at Henry and Claudia's kitchen and let Walter and Martha sleep late. Mary was at the kitchen table with them. Henry had come in late from John's house in Savannah the day before and had not seen Mary or Daniel and said how much they had grown in only the short while since he had seen him. Henry said he was looking forward to sitting with Mary and telling what he could for her documentary, just as he had said he would while at Tybee. He asked her who she would talk to first. She said Alice. and Henry said that Alice knew more than anybody. Mary said that while she was here, she wanted to bring the story of the Milam's up to the present day. She said she expected to complete four or five more notebooks. Henry asked, what then? Mary said she wasn't sure but expected to go through the notes and write a book of some sort based on the notes, but that might be many years down the road. She said she figured getting all the information together would be better done now while it was fresh. Henry said he wished she could go to The College of Charleston, where he had gone, but they don't admit women. Mary surprised Henry when she replied that it was very much their loss for being so narrow-minded. Claudia almost choked when she heard Mary say that. Henry said that he knew that and wished that his old school would change their policies but doubted that it would be any time soon. Mary said she hadn't thought much lately about school but she should. Her note taking had consumed all her time, and she was satisfied doing it. Martin and Daniel had sat quiet listening. Claudia asked them what they had planned for the day, and Martin said he guessed that he would keep showing Daniel around and maybe today they would ride to the Savannah waterfront and then maybe to see John Wilcox and family and maybe even go by and see Jason at his shop. Henry said John wouldn't be home today because he was coming there to work with him in his office. Martin said he wanted to take Daniel out in his new boat too.

Mary asked if it would be too early to go see Alice, and Claudia said it would be fine because she got up early most days. Martin said he and Daniel would walk her over to see Alice. Once at Alice's, Martin and Daniel peeked in at the baby for a couple minutes and then went to the barn for horses and their trip to Savannah. Alice and Prissy welcomed Mary, and Alice said she heard what Mary was doing. She said she knew who would like to listen in and Mary was surprised and asked who? Alice said Maggie, Jacob and Ellie's daughter. Alice explained how Maggie was the first person on the place she had taught to read, besides Martin and how she was now helping others to read and how she had learned so much from the books in the Milam library just as Alice had and how she might be going to Philadelphia to the Quaker school. Mary said that would be just perfect and she would like to hear what she had to say about things too. Mary said this could be more than she expected with Alice, Prissy, and Maggie getting interviewed all together. Alice said that it might be the only room in South Carolina where there were three black women who could read, and Alice and Prissy smiled at each other. Alice said that if Prissy would watch the baby, she would go and see if Maggie could come and motioned for Mary to come along.

They went to the chicken house and found Maggie and her mother. Alice told them why they had come, and Ellie told Maggie that she would do her work and for her to go. Maggie was a bit shy but would rather do anything than take care of chickens, and asked her mother if she was sure. Ellie said most sure and if it took a couple days she should be there for that too. Alice hugged Ellie and thanked her for all the dishes of food she had sent over since her baby came, and Ellie said it was no bother.

On the way back, Alice told Maggie what Mary was doing, and Maggie said she was glad someone was doing it. Mary said she bet Maggie missed seeing Izak, and Maggie said she did and she didn't. She said she had been teaching him to read and he was at their house lately more than when he was away. She said that she cared for him greatly but had things to do on her own that he didn't care about. Mary asked what that was, and Maggie said mostly reading and writing poetry, and she had her work with her mother and the chickens, and now she was also trying to teach her father to read and things had gotten too busy. Alice recognized something she could do to help and said that Jacob could come and learn reading with Johnny because she had been teaching him. She said Johnny might be a little further along than Jacob but that was fine because Johnny could help Jacob and probably learn better himself from doing it. Maggie said maybe when Izak got back she would do that and thanked Alice for the offer. They went back into Alice's house. Prissy had made tea, and they sat and chatted and drank some tea, and Alice asked Mary if she was ready for her to start. Mary said she could start when she wanted, and Alice said that maybe Prissy should start because she was at the Willoughby place before she was even born and knew her mother and father and other background. Mary said that would be just fine. Maggie sat quietly and listened in amazement that this all was happening.

For the next hour Prissy told of her life at the Willoughby plantation from when she was just a few years old, playing with the other children, which included Alice's mother and father. She told of her fond memories of Colonel Willoughby reading stories and giving them all sweet treats and letting her come in the big house a lot and how she learned to read by sitting on his lap while he read to them. The same stories would be read over and over until she memorized some of them. He delighted in letting her tell them to the other children, and she just picked up reading a little more every week until she could read the stories from the book instead of from memory. She was able to get Colonel Willoughby to do nice things for the rest of the slave children, and things were good. The Colonel's son Melvin was a few years older than her and didn't like his father's kind treatment of the slave children and was jealous of all the attention he gave her. She said how they started getting tasks to do when they were about ten, and life was not as much fun anymore. They still had it better than most, but they seemed to grow up fast after they began having a lot of work to do. After that, the most fun they had was all riding in a wagon on most Sundays to the village market on the north end where there was a preacher for anybody that wanted to listen and people selling sweet treats and vegetables and squirrels and fish and shine. Prissy went on to tell about when the Colonel died and how bad things got when his son took over. How there was a lot of beatings and not enough food, and it was most often spoiled and bad and how he hired a new overseer who was mean and how Abraham was not the overseer anymore. And how things went from tolerable for all the slaves to terrible for them all. She told of the old, crippled slave who Melvin ordered to be beaten for not much of a reason and how they were made to watch and how awful they all felt when he was found dead the next morning after being tied to a post all night in the cold. She told of how the word got out that the overseer had told Willoughby to sell off most of his slaves and to get all new ones who didn't have bad habits, and how many slaves began talking about running away, and how Alice's family and a few more took off one night, never to be heard from again until when Ashley and Ken came. She told of the years that went by, and how Melvin almost lost the place to creditors, and how they had meetings among themselves, and how they manipulated Melvin when he was drunk and on laudanum. And how for the last ten years Abraham had practically run the place and they didn't have any more beatings but were still horrified when Melvin would sometimes rant and rave. Prissy told how Melvin was as evil to her as his father had been nice to her. She was beaten often. She showed them her arms, all scarred from her fending off the whip. And she pulled her dress down and showed them her back that was covered with deep scars from beatings. Everyone listening was horrified, and Prissy said she was sorry to share that. Mary told her that it was okay, and she wished that it hadn't happened. Prissy said thankfully it only happened the first year or two after Melvin took over. After Melvin came within a hair of losing it all after months of rum and laudanum, he began to let Abraham run things mostly, and things improved. Then, she said, out of the blue, her saviors Ken and Ashley came. And with Abraham helping they did their dealings and here she is. But it didn't seem like she would get here when she was on the boat coming back when she feared she would be swallowed up by the ocean. After an hour of tears and laughter, Prissy brought her story right up to the moment of them there at Alice's house and said that was all she knew of everything and looked at Mary. Mary said she needed some time to catch up on her note taking because she had only jotted down parts of the story and she wanted, while it was fresh in her mind, to fill in some parts left out. Alice said it was a good time to have something to eat and drink.

After refills of yaupon and a meal of beans and corn bread, Alice began her story on the Willoughby place as a child. She had fun everyday playing with the other kids in the dirt yard of the big house, and everyone was sad when the Colonel died. They couldn't play at the big house anymore, and she was made to start working in the fields every day. She knew something was going on when she saw and heard many of the slaves speaking in whispers to each other but didn't know that they were planning to run away. She had no idea of a larger world and many other things going on. When her mother and the rest of her family and a few others left in the middle of the night, she thought they had been hired out to help at another plantation. She peeked out of her blanket in the wagon and saw her father handing a bag to the ferry man, and then they all went on the ferry and crossed over the river as the sun was coming up and went deep in the nearby woods to wait for night. When night came, she told of her brother running ahead to look for slave patrols camped along the road. He would run back, and they would all go a mile or so, and he would run out ahead again to check, and they would hide in the woods again when the sun came up. She told of the people that helped along the way and how they would hide them and give them food to take with them and take them across rivers. Alice's story went into greater lengths and detail, and she paused every few minutes for Mary to catch up. They took a few breaks for Alice to feed and take care of her baby. It was getting late, and Alice said she had some work to do before Johnny came home, and they could meet again tomorrow about mid-morning if that was ok. She told Mary that she was glad she started with Prissy and her because she had gotten her strength back and could do without Prissy's help now. She said Prissy could go to see Alice's mother and father over at the Indian Islands as soon as Martin could take her, and she asked Mary to tell him that when she saw him later. She said she wanted to go soon to show her mother and father their granddaughter, but she would wait a while yet. Mary looked at how she had filled a whole notebook just in that one sitting. She had brought four notebooks that her father had ordered from Henry that were brought on the supply boat, and if she needed more, she reckoned she could ask Henry for more. She was very pleased with her first day and the stories she was able to understand. Tomorrow she might finish with Alice. It could take a third day there but she didn't care what it took.

Maggie said she would walk Mary home, and Mary thanked her. They hugged Alice and Prissy, and Maggie thanked Alice for coming to get her so she could hear all this. Alice said she was glad she was there and her story was important and she could tell it tomorrow. Maggie said she didn't think what she had to tell was very important because her life had not been as exciting as hers and Prissy's. Mary told her that it all was important, and that her learning how to read was something special, and it was even more special that she was teaching someone else to read, and she might be the first to go off to school and get manumitted. Mary's words and enthusiasm made Maggie feel good about herself, and she was thankful to meet her. Mary told her that she would let her read some of the notebooks she had done so far if she liked to sometime, and Maggie said she would like that. They heard Claudia's kids playing and yelling as they got near, and Claudia was out on the porch with Walter and Martha. When Martha saw who was with Mary, she asked her in and got up and hugged her. She asked Maggie if she wanted to eat supper with them. Maggie was shy about it but said she would but wanted to let her mother know. Martha said that Martin would probably be home soon, and he could run over and tell Ellie that you were eating here. She said it would be an hour or so before they ate. Mary said she wouldn't mind walking around the place some more. Maggie said she would just go and tell her mother while they were out walking, and Martha said that would be fine. Maggie asked Mary what she would like to see. Mary said everything, and Maggie said there wasn't enough daylight to see everything but they could walk over to where her father and two others were building an icehouse down a bit on the river, and Mary said that sounded good.

Mary and Maggie had only known each other for a few hours, but it seemed like they were good friends already. Mary told her about life at the lighthouse and her brother and mother and father, and about some of the exciting things that happened when Martin was there. Soon after Mary began telling about it all, she saw just a tiny bit of sadness in Maggie and realized that she was telling of all these things, and that Maggie probably had never gone off much or done many things. She didn't say anything but kept that in mind. When Maggie talked, it was mostly about things she had read. Mary wished there was something she could do to help Maggie. Maggie sensed Mary's empathy and didn't want her to feel uneasy and told her that Alice had told her about how Henry could manumit her, but she would have to leave the state and could go to a school in Philadelphia for freed and runaway slaves and could come back after a few years when she was finished if she wanted. She went on to say that she would like to go to school, but going through the court to get manumitted, and going way off to Philadelphia to do it was very worrisome, but she really wanted to go to school and see more of the world. She said that Alice said someone would have to escort her to Philadelphia, and she didn't want to be so much trouble. Mary said that Walter Milam had wanted to free all the people on the place, but there are a lot of complications and the southern states have laws to limit what free slaves can do. Walter and Henry would like nothing better than to legally free every person on the Milam plantation and would be glad to pay legal fees and escort her to another city and pay any costs there or for her to return. The important question is if this would be what she really wanted. Maggie liked Mary's clarity and was already thankful to know her. They got to Maggie's house, and Ellie was home and getting supper ready. Maggie said that Martha had asked her to eat supper there, and Ellie said that was fine with her but didn't Martha have a house full enough already? Mary said that Martha said she hadn't seen enough of Maggie and it seemed she really wanted her to come. Maggie said she was taking Mary to show her where all the new building was going on.

On the way, they ran into him on his way back to the boathouse with Jehu and James. He smiled real big at the two of them. Jehu and James didn't say much more than a nod. Mary said that Martin had told her about him and how they had met and all. Hearing Martin's name brightened Jehu's face, and he smiled at Mary. She looked at James and told him that she knew he was from Darien and was Mable's brother and that he could catch fish when nobody else could, and James smiled slightly. Maggie admired how Mary helped the two of them feel comfortable. Maggie told her father that she was just showing Mary around, and they were headed to see them at the new icehouse but maybe now they would walk to the barn and see the horses instead. She told him that she was eating supper at the Milam's and she had told her mother.

At the barn Maggie showed Mary the horses. Mary asked Maggie if she liked to ride, and Maggie said she was afraid of horses and had never tried. Mary said maybe while she was here, she could learn if she liked, and Maggie said maybe but it wouldn't be her favorite thing to do. Mary said it was fun, and Maggie said she needed some fun. Willy came with the carriage while they were there, and Maggie told him who Mary was, and he said he had seen her brother earlier. Maggie told Willy that Mary wanted to teach her how to ride, but horses scared her. Willy said to get the new man Jehu to accompany her. He said that man could talk to horses just like we are talking here. He can tell the horse to take care of you. Mary said she had heard the stories about Jehu, and they should do that. Even if they didn't ride, it would be fun to listen to Jehu talk to them. Maggie said she would be agreeable to doing that.

Mary and Maggie were about to go back home when Martin and Daniel came up to the barn from Savannah to put the horses away. Martin was noticeably excited to see them. He jumped off and asked Mary if she wanted to take a short ride while his horse was all saddled. She said the horse was soaked in sweat and had ridden enough for a day, but she did want to ride sometime and might teach Maggie to ride.
Martin said that was hard to believe because he had offered many times to teach her, but she had said no. Mary said that they had a secret way to make it easy for her. He asked what that could be, and Mary said it was a secret and smiled at Maggie.

Daniel had been quiet and listening to them. He knew who Maggie was but had not been introduced. Mary remembered that and told Maggie that the quiet one on the horse was her brother, and Maggie said she had heard about him from Martin. They smiled at each other. Mary said that Maggie was eating supper with them tonight, and Martin said if they waited a few minutes for them to take care of the horses, they would walk with them back to the house.

On the way to the house Mary told Martin that Alice said that she had her strength back and Prissy was ready to go visit with Alice's mother and father on the Indian Island whenever he could take her and Prissy was excited about seeing them. Martin said he and Daniel had talked about that today when he took Daniel down to the Savannah waterfront. He said they had stopped to see Ashley and Ken. Martin said he had previously told them that he would be making a trip to Tybee to take Prissy, and that Ashley said he wouldn't mind going, but Ken said he liked staying off the water on his days off. Today he had told Ashley that he thought that trip would be coming soon. He asked Daniel what he thought about going home for a few days, and Daniel said he wouldn't mind that. All of them had been over there except Maggie, so the rest of the way home Mary tried to describe how it was and about Ayana. Maggie said she would like to go herself one day.

It was like a holiday at the Milam home. John Wilcox and family were there plus Mary and Daniel and Maggie, and Ellie had brought Thomas over, and the house and yard were full. John and Julia were pleased to meet Mary and Daniel for the first time. They had heard much of them. Henry told John and Julia that Mary would be visiting them soon and said what she was doing and that she had heard a little about Mable and her brother and wanted to talk to them too. They congratulated her and said what a fine endeavor that was and asked when the book was coming. Mary said it might be years before much of what she wrote could be revealed, but she would have it ready when the time came. Henry said he had wondered about that. Mary said all her notes would be buried until the world was ready to hear about them. Julia was listening and intrigued by Mary's project. She asked what it would take for it to be safe for her work to be public? She said it must be frustrating to do all this work and then for it to be hidden away. Mary said she wasn't frustrated a bit but when she thought about doing this, she knew that it would be better to be done now rather than later, and she didn't mind that it would be hidden until slavery was ended. Henry said that could be a long way off. John said it was coming but might be twenty years or more. Mary said she hoped it wouldn't take that long. She added that documenting all these things now would be easier and more accurate than later, and she felt very good about what she was doing, and it had been very educating so far. Mary asked John when his mother and father were coming because she wanted to sit and hear their story. John said they would be here in a couple weeks, and his dad was a big talker and liked to tell stories and listen to stories and knew a lot of people through his hardware business. Martha had been watching and listening to the talk surrounding Mary and was impressed at how she handled herself and answered so clearly and was so certain and secure about herself and how her words commanded attention but were spoken with humility. Martin had been watching too and saw how she seemed so grown and smart and talked as an equal with people older than herself.

Food was brought out and supper served, and it was another fine meal at the Milam place. With just enough daylight to get back to Savannah, John and Julia and their kids left, and Martin and Mary and Daniel walked Maggie and Thomas home. Daniel thanked Ellie for all the good eggs and Jacob for all the supply-boat trips he had made to bring them all the things they needed. Mary said she would be seeing them soon to write their story of things on the Milam place. Ellie said she knew what Mary was doing and had already started thinking up things for her story, and Mary said she liked hearing that. Daniel picked up Thomas and held him high over his head and set him down. Thomas asked for more, and he did it again and again until Ellie told Thomas that it was enough. He wanted to play more, and Daniel said he promised he would do it more another day.

On the walk back to the house Mary asked Daniel what he thought about being away from home. Daniel said he worried about the extra work his father had to do, but other than that, he liked being somewhere else for a change. Mary said that their father had help, and he could quit worrying about that. Daniel said the other thing that he noticed was that he didn't hear the constant sound of the ocean waves breaking and the squawks of the sea gulls all the time. Mary said she missed that a little but not much. She said the most interesting thing here for her so far was talking to different people and hearing how they sound. She said she had gotten accustomed to only hearing Daniel and her mother and father.

The next day Martin took Daniel with him in his boat to Savannah. They left about mid-morning on the last two hours of the incoming tide, rowed out the Wilmington River against the tide, then rowed with the tide into Savannah. Martin wanted to see if Ashley had time and wanted to go along on the trip to take Prissy. He also wanted to see how he and Daniel could handle rowing his boat with just the two of them, and they did fine. The boat was light and with its sharp entry, cleaved the water cleanly with only a small wake. When they got there, Ashley and Ken were doing maintenance work on the sharpie and were glad to see them and take a break. Ken asked Daniel if he was enjoying the time off from the island, and Daniel said he was, but Martin was already taking him back to Tybee. Martin said they had come to see if Ashley had time and still wanted to take a trip to Tybee the back way. Ashley said he did, but it depended on when they were to be gone. He said they had a trip coming up in a few days and looked at Ken. Ken said they were just waiting on some hardware to arrive for them to haul to Darien, and it could be two days or a week. Ashley asked Martin when he would want to leave and Martin said day after tomorrow early, then spend two nights and come back. Ashley looked at Ken again, and Ken said go ahead, if the hardware gets here, it can wait a day or two until you get back. Martin told Ashley to come tomorrow night and stay with them, and they could leave early the next day, and all he needed to bring was a bedroll, and he would take care of the rest. Martin knew what Ken's answer would be but he asked if he wanted to go and he said he liked to stay put between trips. The tide had turned, and Martin said they should get back and shoved off from the side of the sharpie. Ashley said he would see them tomorrow. After Martin and Daniel were out a ways, Ken grinned and told Ashley that Martin might be their captain before long. Ashley laughed and said Martin would start being his captain day after tomorrow.

There was no wind to sail by, so on the way back Martin and Daniel practiced rowing together at precisely the same time and adjusting the speed of each pull on the oars, to where it seemed like they attained the most progress with the least effort. Martin said he understood why a chantey helped the boatmen at their task. After they turned off the Savannah River onto the Wilmington River, the last mile to the Milam plantation was against a strong tide, and it was a lot of work and almost an hour to go that last mile. They pulled onto the bank at the boathouse, and some boatmen came down and helped pull the boat up past the high-water line. Martin told Daniel they ought to go right away and tell Alice and Prissy about going to the Indian Islands.

They found them inside Alice's house. Alice had been telling more while Mary took notes. Prissy and Maggie were listening, and the baby was quiet as if it was listening too as its mother talked. Mary continued writing without looking up at Martin and Daniel. Martin said he came to say he could take Prissy day after tomorrow if that suited them, and Alice said she was fine with that. Prissy said that would work, just as long as she would have time to hear the rest of what Alice was saying about everything. Alice said it was slow story telling because it only went as fast as Mary could take notes, but she would probably be done after today and maybe a couple hours tomorrow. Mary was caught up and told Martin and Daniel that this was better than she had ever imagined and said they should have heard all that Alice had said today. Alice smiled at Mary and told Martin that she had never seen so much enthusiasm as Mary had about what she was doing, and it made her feel good and hopeful about things. Maggie heard what Alice said to Mary and thought to herself how glad she was that Mary had come because it inspired her to dream more of the things she wanted, and she knew now that she wanted an education more than anything. Alice had told her that there was a way for her to get an education, but it was so complicated she wasn't sure if it was worth all the difficulty. Mary inspired her to forget the complications and try for what she wanted.

Martin said he had things to do to get ready for the trip and said they would leave about daylight, day after tomorrow at the same time the regular supply boat was leaving but would be going to the Back River landing instead of the Lazaretto landing, and camp there overnight, and take Prissy over to the island the next morning. Prissy going to see her old friends was big news but the girls were so enthralled by Alice's story, they didn't react to the news like Martin expected. He and Daniel left, and Alice began talking again. Mary continued her notes, and Prissy and Maggie and Jochebed became entranced again.

Martin told Daniel that Henry had ordered a well point, pipe, and a hand pump, like they had used at the old guard house, for Ayana and her people on the island. If it had come in, they could take it over and install it while they were there. They went back to the house and found Henry. He told Martin that he would check when he went to Savannah tomorrow, and if it was there, he would bring it back. Martin asked Henry if he would include in the messages to Charles tomorrow that they were coming but would be spending the night at the Back River landing. Henry asked when they expected to arrive. Martin said at little after noon, and Henry said Charles would probably like to pick them up and bring them back to the lighthouse for supper. Daniel asked why they didn't just stay at the lighthouse instead of camping at the Back River, and his father could take them back the next day. Martin said he guessed that would be fine if it wasn't too much for his parents. Daniel said his mother and father would be disappointed if they didn't spend the night there. Martin said they would need to spend the next night on the island with Alice's family because with his newer and bigger boat he wouldn't be able to go directly across the marsh and would have to follow the creeks and the tide had to be at least half full.

Henry said he would be in Savannah tomorrow and that two guards would be here at the house at the regular time for signaling with the light-house, and Daniel can come and tell his father about what y'all are doing. Daniel said that he had always wanted to be on this end of the signaling for a change, and he would enjoy surprising his father. Henry asked Martin if he and Daniel would ride over to see Jacob at the new icehouse being built to see if he needs anything for him to pick up while he was in Savannah tomorrow. Martin said they would like to do that.

Martin and Daniel left the house and walked to where the icehouse was being built. Jacob was always glad to see Martin, and Martin was always glad to see Jacob and that went for Jehu too. James was still shy but managed a smile at Martin. They were lifting the pre-made panels up onto the floor and then tilting them up and setting them in place to form the outside walls. The panels were about three feet wide and about eight feet tall and almost two feet thick and were heavy, but once they were stood up, they were so thick that they could stand on their own and be slid into place. Jacob had skillfully set two panels at each corner and nailed them together forming a corner and were carefully plumbed and leveled. Then, with a string line from one corner to the next, set more panels to form a wall in between. There weren't many panels left to fully enclose the building and there was an opening in front where a large, insulated door was to go. Martin and Daniel helped them set the last few panels, and Jacob said he was glad to see them all in because they were heavy. Jacob took his measuring stick and checked the opening that was left for the door frame and went over and checked the door frame and smiled and said it was a good fit and said that Jason had done a good job on making all the panels the right size to fit the floor plan. He said they were ready to quit for the day, and Martin told him that Henry was going to Savannah tomorrow and wanted to know if he needed anything. Jacob smiled like he had a trick or something and puzzled Martin. He picked up a small scrape of board and took his charcoal marker and wrote the number "24" and then "nals" and grinned real big and said, "number twenty-four nails" Martin was shocked even though he had heard that Maggie had been teaching him to read and write. Martin put his hand out, and when Jacob extended his, Martin slapped it and he and Jacob laughed at each other. Daniel asked for the charcoal marker and squeezed an "I" between the "A" and "L."

Martin asked Jehu how he was doing, and Jehu just smiled big and nodded his head. He then asked James if he was okay, and he nodded like Jehu. Jacob said that James had been catching enough fish to feed the whole place every day, and the attention caused James to look down. Daniel liked fishing and asked James if he could go. He just nodded yes, and Jacob said he went every day after work and that Daniel could just come to the boathouse, and James usually was not far up or down the river bank from there every afternoon. Daniel said if Martin didn't have anything for him to do this afternoon he would be there. Daniel told James he didn't have a pole. James mumbled something in a strong Geechee talk that Daniel didn't understand. Jacob said he said he had everything.

Martin took the scrap board with Jacob's writing, and he and Daniel walked back home. Martin couldn't wait to show what Jacob had written and went straight to Henry's office and set the board down on Henry's desk and said this is what Jacob had written. Henry didn't know what to say and just said he wanted to show his father, and the three of them went out and around to the porch, and Henry showed Walter and Martha the board. They both looked puzzled until Henry said it was what Jacob had written for him to bring from Savannah. They were both thrilled, and Walter said he wished that every man, woman, and child old enough could learn to read and write. He said that he was very glad when he heard that Alice was teaching Johnny and Maggie was teaching Izak but most glad to hear that Jacob was learning too. Martin said that Jacob had learned faster and better to read than he had and in a few weeks could probably be a better than him at it. Henry said that Jacob was happy about being the overseer, and he wanted to do good. Martha said she agreed with Walter that it was especially pleasing to see that Jacob was becoming literate. She said he would be a fine example to everyone else and inspire them to learn.

Martin told them about his plans to take Prissy and that it was all set if they approved. Martha said she knew Martin couldn't go too long between boat trips. She laughed and said it worked out good for Prissy to help Alice and it would make her feel good to see her friends after not seeing them for so long. Martin said when they first took Prissy off Saint Helena, she was glad to go, but she didn't know how to act and had a distant look about her. Martha said he would have a distant look and more if he had been through what she had been through. Martin said Alice was just the medicine Prissy needed because she is happy now, and that distant look is gone. Henry said he intended to hang that board with Jacob's writing on his office wall.

Late in the day Martin and Daniel went down to the boathouse so Daniel could fish with James. They saw James on the bank. When he saw them, he put his pole down and picked up another pole he had and handed it to Daniel. It was the longest bamboo pole Daniel had ever seen. It had a line that was the same length as the pole and a hook and a split buckshot ball as a weight. Daniel had never used a pole to fish with. He always fished with a hand line. James took a live minnow out of his bucket and carefully put it on the hook and handed the whole rig to Daniel. Then James picked up his pole and skillfully held the end of line near the hook and pulled back on the line until the pole bent a little and flicked the minnow out about thirty feet into the river. Daniel tried to do what James had done and managed to get his minnow out a ways, and James nodded and smiled at him.

Martin had other things in mind and went inside the boathouse and got a rag and some whale oil and came back out and began wiping a thin coat on the inside of his boat so it would have time to dry before they left for Tybee. Johnny came out and watched him for a bit, and Martin told him they were going to take Prissy day after tomorrow to stay with Alice's family for a while. Johnny said he would miss Prissy because she was such a good help for Alice. He said she was glum acting at first, but now she was happy all the time. Martin said they would leave with the supply boat early with the tide but would be going the long way to the Back River landing. Johnny said it had been a while since they had to go that way. He said he hoped that it would be a good long while before they did it again because he thought that end of the island was spooky. Martin said he liked it there and liked it even better across the river at the Indian Islands. They heard some yelling, and it was Daniel dragging a big striped bass up on the bank, and Martin looked and saw James laughing out loud for the first time. He and Johnny walked down and looked at the big fish. James took the fish off and put another minnow on for Daniel and pointed for Daniel to flick it out. He got it a little further out this time. While Johnny and Martin were still there, James hooked another bass and dragged it up on the bank, and before he could get it off, Daniel was dragging another one in. When he got that one in, James put their poles up under the boathouse and began scaling and cleaning the three big fish and told Daniel that he had somebody to take them to.

When Martin and Daniel got back home, Mary was talking with Claudia and Martha on the porch. She was reading from her notes what Alice had talked about. Martha and Claudia had heard the story many times but were not bored hearing about it again, especially the part she was on when Martin and Daniel came in. It was about Alice and Johnny when they first got to know each other, and Martin fixing up the little dugout he found in the river. Mary was so excited about it and showed Martin how she had filled one whole notebook from just what Alice had talked about and she had a long list of others to talk to. Martin said he didn't expect that everyone would have as much to tell as Alice and said she had started in the right place. Mary said she had a lot of notes from Martha and Walter and expected to get a lot from Henry. Claudia reminded her of how talkative

Richard Wilcox was and how he liked to tell stories. Mary asked when Martin wanted to tell his part of the story, and Martin said he wanted to be last and his would be the shortest. Mary said she doubted that and went back to reading her notes to Martha and Claudia. Martin thought to himself how things were not how he thought they would be when Mary was there. He thought they would be around each other a lot, but she was totally into her work. He didn't mind that she was and didn't mind that she spent all her time doing it, but was simply surprised, and now he was going off to Tybee. He thought to himself that it was a waste of time to try and think how things would be because they were usually different anyhow. Martha told Martin and Daniel that they were eating mostly leftovers tonight, and it would all be set out on the table in Claudia's kitchen in a bit after they got cleaned up. Martin added that James had more to say today than he had heard him say before and told them about him showing Daniel how to fish and what they caught and how he had laughed out loud when Daniel caught a fish. Claudia said that Julia and Mable would be glad to hear that because they were worried that he was sad about leaving Darien. Martin said that Jehu was not only good with horses but was good for James too.

The next day Mary was off to Alice's again. Maggie and Prissy were there. Henry had left at daylight to go work with John on their business, and Daniel said he wouldn't mind helping Jacob build the icehouse and said that he liked building things. Martin said that was fine because he had a list from Henry of things to be done and he needed to get their supplies packed for the trip. Martin reminded Daniel about being back for the daily signaling from Tybee.

When Daniel showed up at the icehouse to work, Jacob was delighted. He knew that the other buildings couldn't start until this one was done, and Daniel was strong and was a good hand. Also, the whole ice thing interested him, and he was curious if this building would keep ice as long as the sawdust pile did. After the doorframe was set, they started on the ceiling joists. Daniel could not have picked a better day to show up because the ceiling joists were extra big, so they could span the building without any walls or posts so the big slabs of ice could slide around without anything in the way. Jacob measured the joists and marked them, and Daniel cut them to length with a big handsaw. Jehu and James moved what he cut off the sawhorses and set another one until they had them all cut. Then Jacob marked the top of the walls where they went, and they began setting the joists up on the walls and nailing off each one as they went. By lunch most of the joists were set. Daniel hadn't brought any food, but Jacob brought more than enough for them all. Daniel told Jacob that he needed to leave early because he had to help send messages to his father today. He said he would like to help some more when he got back from Tybee, and Jacob said he hoped they would have the roof on by then but there was always plenty of work.

Martin was at the house later when Daniel got there and told Daniel to follow him to Henry's office so he could show him how things worked every day with signaling the lighthouse and Savannah. He picked up a piece of paper from the corner of Henry's desk and showed Daniel what was written on it to be signaled. He said today Daniel would also be sending the message about them coming and asking his father to signal Ayana that they would be going over there day after tomorrow. Martin got the paper plus a clean sheet of paper and a pencil and told Daniel to follow him up and said he had sent the guards back because they were doing the messaging today. He said it wasn't near as high as the lighthouse but had a clear view to the east toward Tybee, and on the other side of the house, had a clear view to the west to a spot on the bluff of Savannah. He said they always started with Tybee first and brought out the signaling box just like the one used at Tybee. He also got the monocular. The distant profile of Tybee Island could be seen but not the lighthouse without the monocular. Daniel looked through it and said it felt good to see his home. Martin positioned the signal box just right and did the standard signal to let Charles know they were there and ready for his daily messages. They saw a few flashes back, and there was a pause, and Martin got the blank paper and pen and wrote the letters that were signaled in the flashes from Tybee about ship arrivals and departures and then Captain Sandy's weather and tide report. Then, he told Daniel to signal his father about them coming tomorrow and about signaling Ayana and the ship information. Martin was amazed at how fast Daniel operated the shutter, and when he was done, they waited a few moments for a signal to come back that the messages had been received. Next, they moved things over to the roof patio on the other side of the house toward Savannah. The bluff in Savannah was about three and a half miles away, and Daniel looked at it with the monocular. Martin handed the paper with the ship information and after a few signals to let them know they were there; Daniel sent the ship information and the weather report to Savannah. After the messaging with Savannah, they put up the instruments, and Martin said that was it. Daniel said he enjoyed doing that and knowing that his father was up on the lighthouse where he usually was every day. Martin said yes, and today it was his father and Izak. Martin said he wondered how Izak was doing and guessed he was doing fine or else Charles would have let them know. Also, Jacob had told Izak, before he left, that if for any reason he didn't want to continue on there, he could take the supply boat back.

As Martin and Daniel were going down, they heard a carriage outside. It was Henry, and he had Ashley with him. Martin also saw the wellpoint pipe sticking out the wagon and was glad to see it and Ashley. Henry said he happened to see Captain Ben in town, and Ben had mentioned that Ashley was hiring a carriage ride out to their place to go with Martin to Tybee, and Henry had said he could ride home with him. Martin told Henry that he would take the carriage with the pipe down to the boat. Mary came up from Alice's with Maggie as they were standing out in the yard about to go. She said that Maggie was with her to help rewrite what she had written hurriedly in her notebook the last few days. Martin said he hoped to see her at supper tonight because he would be gone to Tybee for three or four days. Mary said good, and to remember everything so he could tell her about it all later, and to please tell Ayana that she was coming back soon to finish her notes with her and Alice's family. Martin said he would. He thought again to himself how Mary was much less interested in him than when he had gone down to stay with them. He didn't understand. He asked Ashley if the bunkroom at the boathouse was okay with him, and Ashley said he hadn't forgotten how much he had liked it when he and Ken stayed there before. Martin said to come on, and they could get him settled in there and then come back here for supper. He, Ashley, and Daniel got in the carriage and went to the boathouse. Daniel took the well pipes, and Martin handed the pump to Ashley and grabbed the sack of fittings and the sledgehammer to drive the wellpoint into the ground with. Once there they set the things down by the boat to load in the morning. Martin said he had stacked the supplies for the trip in the boathouse, and they would load them in the morning. Ashley grabbed his bag from the carriage and followed Martin and Daniel into the boathouse and he set his things in the bunkroom where Jehu and James were staying temporarily. Johnny followed them and asked Ashley where Ken was. Ashley said he was on the hill where he liked to be between trips.

Claudia and Martha knew Ashley would be there for supper. After Ashley and Ken had done what they had done for Alice's family and Prissy, they would have a special place at the Milam place forever and they knew Ashley loved good food, especially desserts, and they fixed blackberry cobbler. It was also a special occasion because of the trip to Tybee with Prissy. Martin dropped Ashley off at the house and told him that he and Daniel would take care of the horses and wagon. The weather had turned off a little cool, and they were eating in the big dining room and had extra chairs pulled up, and Claudia had already started setting things out. Walter had lit a small fire in the wood stove in the living room. Mary came in, and Claudia asked where Maggie was. Mary said she was eating supper with Johnny and Alice and Prissy tonight and had left. She said that Maggie had shown her some poems she had written, and they were quite good. She said that Maggie was a fast writer, and she had been helping her. She said after making corrections on her notes, she then read it out loud and Maggie wrote it all again as she spoke it. She said Maggie wanted to help the rest of the time she was there, but she was concerned that it would be too much work left for her mother. Claudia said they could do something about that by getting Ellie some help, and she would speak to Henry about it. She said that everybody was proud of what Mary was doing, and she was particularly proud that Maggie was helping. Claudia said that she would help Ellie with her work herself if she needed to, so Maggie could do something she liked. Mary was quite impressed with Claudia's reaction and gained a bigger respect for her. She would remember to include this kindness of Claudia in her notes.

It was another big supper at the Milam house. Everybody liked the blackberry cobbler, especially Ashley. Martin vowed to himself that he would make some ice cream to go with the cobbler next time it was cooked. Walter was telling Ashley stories about Captain Ben from way back before Ken and Ashley were around. Ashley wished Ken were there to hear the things about their captain. Daniel told Henry about how Martin had showed him the boxes of record keeping they had on all the ships coming and going over the years. Henry removed the oldest box of records from the closet and read some of the notes and messages about ships and read some messages that his father had sent when they first started. Martin asked Mary if she wanted to go for a walk. She said she did, and they walked along the river toward the new icehouse. She told Martin how much she liked being there. She said they hadn't been together much because she was so busy doing her work. He said that was fine because he knew how important it was to her and said he was the same way about boats. She said that the most interesting thing so far was Maggie and how bright she was and how she was conflicted about staying there or being the first Milam slave to be manumitted and going way off to Philadelphia to school. Martin said he knew how smart Maggie was and that she was something like a sister because they were everyday playmates when he was little and taken care of by Alice, and he was at Jacob and Ellie's house more than he was at his own home. He said he hoped she went off to school because she would not ever be happy staying here. Mary said that Maggie was also confused a little about Izak, since they had gotten to be so close. Martin said he didn't know what to say about that, but Maggie didn't seem very upset when Izak had to go to Tybee.

Mary surprised Martin when she asked what about her and him. He didn't know what to say, and she spoke first to answer her own question. She said that they were locked together, and nothing could change that. Martin nodded in agreement. She said that he had some things he needed to do, and she had some things to do too. Martin admitted that he thought about her all the time while he was doing whatever he did, but he knew it would be better to wait a year or so before asking her to be married. Mary about fell over at the shock of hearing what Martin said. She hugged him tightly, and they kissed a long kiss. She told him that she had known this would happen from the first minute when he first came to Tybee. He said he didn't know it that fast. Mary said there were some big questions that time would have to answer like how things would work when he was off on trips and where would they live. Martin said that he surely didn't know those answers. She said she could still decide to go off to school but didn't know where or when, but it would be soon if she did. Something came out of her mouth without any forethought, and she heard herself say that maybe she would go to the school in Philadelphia with Maggie. It was a further surprise to hear Martin say that it might be a good idea. She said that she was worried that Maggie might not go alone, and if it came down to it, she would go with her. Martin said that he intended to have his captain's license in two years or less, and maybe she could learn what she wanted in two years, and then they could be married. Again, Mary was surprised at how candid Martin was. She said she liked that idea but her side of that was more complicated than his, and she would just continue in her work, and time would reveal some answers about their next couple years.

Back at the house, Martin and Mary went into the living room where the rest were. Martha and Claudia noticed the glow about Mary as she came in the room and her beautiful smile. Since she had come, she had been only about her work. She had been pleasant but serious all the time, and she was almost like a different person when she came in the room with Martin tonight. Martha remembered to herself what Margo had said about how they were when they were together. It was almost dark, and Ashley was getting up to leave as they came in. Martha told him he could come there for some breakfast, and he said that he had told Johnny that he would eat with the boatmen in the morning. He told them all thank you and goodbye and hoped to see them when he got back from Tybee. Martin walked Ashley outside and said he would see him early. Walter and Martha hugged Martin, and Martha reminded him to not forget the life float he had promised her to always have in his boat, and he said he would, and she gave him a hug and kiss. When she kissed him, she could smell an unusual and sweet smell on his neck, and she knew where it came from and smiled to herself.

In the morning Claudia had some breakfast for Martin and Daniel ready early, even before Henry had gotten up. They were leaving with their bags as Henry was coming into the kitchen. Henry told them good-bye, and Claudia hugged them both. She couldn't help it and told Martin how beautiful Mary looked last night when she came in with him, and he said he had noticed that himself. Daniel rolled his eyes and pulled Martin toward the door. The morning was cool, and Ashley and the boatmen had just finished up breakfast inside with the woodstove going. A big pot of fish and grits had been brought over from the outside kitchen, and the last little bit of it was put outside and being eaten by a dozen cats that lived around the boathouse. There was a big pot of yaupon and some fresh milk and plum preserves on the table. Jacob poured Daniel and Martin a mug of it. Ashley fit in perfectly with the group of boatmen, and they liked him. They had heard the story of him and Ken dealing with the terrible plan-tation master in South Carolina. They had all liked him before, but now after what he and Ken had done in South Carolina, they were looked on as real heroes. Johnny came in the carriage with Prissy, and Martin saw a somewhat troubled look on her face and asked her what was wrong. She said she had been thinking about her last boat ride when they came from Saint Helena, and Martin said they were not going in the ocean and would only be in rivers and always near the edge of land and showed her the life float and said she could have it near her all the time. Johnny told her that everything Martin was saying was true, and her deep brow furrows evened out some, and Daniel reminded her that she would be with her old friends soon.

22.
REUNION

A dozen or so people had come to see them and the supply boat off. News spread fast and thoroughly on the Milam place, and everybody knew Martin was taking Prissy to be with Alice's family and the others hiding out on the Indian Islands. Prissy had become one of the most talked-about people since she had come, and everybody loved her. They saw the roughness of the healed scars on both of her arms where she had tried to protect herself from all the beatings from Melvin Willoughby. Both boats were loaded, and after rowing out a short distance they ran a line and tied Martin's boat to the stern of the supply boat. Martin took the tiller and Daniel and Ashley were on the oars and Prissy was seated back by Martin with her feet on the life float. When they were tied together, only the supply boatmen rowed until Martin's boat trailed straight behind. Johnny motioned for them to row, and he began a chantey by singing a verse alone. Then everyone in the boat and the people on the bank sang the chorus. They all sang until the voices on the boats and the voices on the land separated but stayed in rhythm from the sight of the long oars dipping into the water.

The two boats together were like one very long narrow boat and required less effort to row than two separate boats. It could go faster without making a wake, and they slipped rapidly with the tide out the Wilmington River into the Savannah River and headed east as the sun was just coming up. There was nothing much doing on the tiller as Martin's boat followed perfectly along behind the lead boat. Martin spelled Daniel on the oars after a while, then Daniel spelled Ashley for a bit. The boatman hadn't even broken a sweat and looked as if they could row forever without getting tired. About halfway they stopped at a usual spot to let everyone stretch their legs and relieve themselves. Johnny warned them all to watch for rattlers.

In what seemed like the fastest trip ever, they were approaching Lazaretto Creek and landing before noon. When Martin had first thought about this trip, he thought he would go the roundabout way to Tybee. But when he told Jacob, he was told that with people on the oars that were not used to rowing a long way, he would be better off going with the supply boat to Lazaretto, then catching the tide from there and going around to the Back River landing. Martin was glad he had followed Jacob's advice. He thought they could leave from there in the morning, but he might decide to catch the last of the incoming tide late today and time it so as he got where Lazaretto met the Back River as the tide started out, and it would be an easy row from there to the landing at the Back River. He would wait and see how things went at the lighthouse and decide. Leaving from the Back River in the morning would make for an easier day than leaving from Lazaretto.

Izak was at the landing with the wagon, and the supply boat was winched up the ramp, and they left Martin's boat in the water. Martin shook Izak's hand and asked him how it was going. Izak said he didn't like it at first, but now he liked it, and he was learning new things every day. He said he missed Maggie but not as much as at first. He told Daniel that his father was a hard-working man, and he and his mother had been treating him very kindly. He said that he had never eaten so much good food. Martin told him that he needn't worry about Maggie because she was with Mary almost all the time, and they were busy reading and writing. Izak said that he had told Charles and Margo that Maggie had been teaching him to read, and Margo had given him several books that were easy to read and a pen and ink and paper, and he had been practicing every day reading and writing, but what had helped him most was learning the signal code and writing down the signal letters, with Charles telling him later what the words were. He said it was getting easier, and he would surprise Maggie when she saw how much he had learned.

Martin introduced Ashley and Prissy to Izak. Everyone helped, and in a minute or two the supplies were loaded onto the wagon. Last were the two chunks of ice for the icebox at the lighthouse. Izak gave a big sack of egg-and-bacon biscuits to Johnny, and he said they would be heading back home after eating and resting for a while. Martin said they still had a couple of hours before the tide shifted, and Johnny said they might have time for a nap. Martin helped Prissy up front with Izak, and he and Ashley and Daniel climbed in the back for the return trip. When they got there, Charles and Margo were very happy to see Daniel. He said he missed being there but was glad to be where he was. He said his only concern was the extra work for his father. Charles said that Izak was doing a very good job helping and was learning how to help more every day. Margo said he was really helping and for Daniel not to worry about that. She turned to Prissy and said they had heard so much about her and were glad she was here. She said she would be staying in Mary's room tonight, and they had made Ashley a bed on the floor in the old guard house with Izak, and

Martin could stay where he always did in Daniel's room. Daniel suggested that his parents go inside with Prissy, and they would put the ice and supplies away. Margo said she had a lunch for them when they finished.

After lunch Daniel told his father that he would take Izak up on the lighthouse and do the signaling. Charles said that would be fine. He mentioned that he could tell it was him sending the messages yesterday because of the speed. Martin told Daniel that he wanted to take the boat around to the Back River landing later if he would give him a ride to Lazaretto and then pick them up about two hours later at the Back River. Izak said he would do that so Daniel could be with his parents, and Margo thanked him for his thoughtfulness. Izak said he would fish while waiting for them. Late in the afternoon Izak rode Ashley and Martin to the boat and told them that he would go on down to the Back River and fish until they got there.

Ashley and Martin caught the tide perfectly. They caught the last of the incoming tide, and just before they got to the Back River, the tide slacked, and shortly after they turned east toward the landing, the tide had started out, and they were at the landing well before dark. Izak had about twenty pan-size whiting on a stringer in the water. When he saw them coming, he cleaned them on the edge of the river and put them in a box Charles had given him with a piece of ice in it. He helped Ashley and Martin drag the boat up above the high-water line, and they loaded up and headed home. Margo was expecting the fish and already had a vegetable stew cooking and added the fish when Izak got there. She and Daniel and Prissy had been talking, and she told Prissy that it was nice to hear from her all about her life and especially the last part since she was able to leave. Charles and Margo both complimented Ashley for what he and Ken had done.

Not long after supper Margo saw how tired Daniel and Martin looked and said they should get to bed early because they had another long day ahead of them tomorrow and would be leaving to go hours before sunup. Ashley said he was tired too. Prissy said she was probably tired but was so excited about seeing Alice's family that she didn't know if she would be able to sleep. Margo said she had some tea that would calm her and went in the kitchen to make some. Martin said that they should be able to be back by dark tomorrow and would leave as soon as the creek got high enough. He said they should get there about mid-morning and leave a little after mid-afternoon.

In what seemed like the middle of the night, Martin woke to the familiar tapping of Margo's broom stick on the floor below him. He got up quickly and jiggled Daniel's shoulder, but Daniel didn't stir. Then instead of jiggling, he poked his finger into Daniel's ribs and woke him enough that he could smell the coffee and biscuits that his mother had going and rolled out of his bed. Martin stayed until he stood and told him that he was going out to wake Ashley. Martin woke Ashley and Izak and told them that their coffee and egg-and-bacon biscuits were waiting for them. They went in, and Charles and Daniel and Prissy were drinking coffee at the table. Margo had plates set and a big platter of biscuits and asked Ashley if he preferred coffee or tea, and Ashley said coffee. Margo pointed to several sacks of things for them to take. One sack was for Ayana and her people and the other sack for Alice's family. Izak finished and went out to hitch the tackies and brought the wagon around. Everyone hugged, and they loaded up and left for the Back River. There was about half of a waning moon, and it lit the two sandy-white wagon ruts in the road but not much else. Martin said he was glad they had moved the boat the day before, so that it was an easier trip today. When they got to the other end of the island and over the small dunes, the tackies were acting restless, and Daniel told Izak they wanted to eat some sea oats, so they unhitched them, and they went straight into the small dunes and started eating. Izak said he would remember that.

Martin said that by the time they got across the river, the tide would still be high enough in the creek to go up it. He thanked Izak and said it would probably be late afternoon before they were back. Izak helped get the boat down to the water and saw them off before getting the tackies out of the dunes and returning to the lighthouse. As he left, he looked back at the boat halfway across the river and thought to himself that he would like to go over there one day. Martin stuck the mast in place so that Ayana would be able to see them coming, but the winds were not favorable to use the sail. When they were across the back river and into the creek, they had to use the oars like paddles because the creek was narrow in most places.

About noon as they came near the island, Martin saw Ayana standing alone at the first landing. He knew she was alone because she was being protective of any of her people catching any sickness from them, and he told the others that. She had a doeskin mask covering her nose and mouth, but Martin could see the kindness and gratitude in her eyes. He set out the bag of things that Margo had sent. He knew that she would, like he had seen her do before, wash those things in the creek and the sack they were in before sharing them with her people. After looking closely, Martin could see the rest of her group just inside the trees on the edge of the island. Martin told Ayana that he would be back after a while. He pushed the boat off the bank and continued into the smaller creek that went to the other landing and the water was so low by then that he and Daniel had to get out and drag the boat. Ayana had told of them coming and the whole group was waiting on the edge of the landing for them to get there. Alice's mother was first to recognize Prissy and screamed, and then the others started yelling. Martin thought to himself that if someone didn't know better, they might think something terrible was happening, but the yelling and screams were out of happiness. Once the boat was pulled up on the bank, Ashley and Martin and Daniel stood aside for all the happy commotion to settle down, and they followed the group up to their camp. Martin introduced Ashley, and Prissy told that he and his friend had rescued her from the Willoughby place, and they all praised Ashley like he was a disciple out of the Bible or something and made him all embarrassed and teary eyed. They all sat, and tea was served. Talk was loud and animated in a strong Gullah-Geechee dialect. Martin understood the words, but it really wasn't necessary to understand them to feel the excitement and love as the stories and talk went on and on at a high and rapid pitch.

Things calmed only a little over the next hour. Martin stood and said that he and Daniel were going to see Ayana for a bit, then would come back and visit and would be leaving later when the tide got high enough. He looked at Ashley and asked if he would be fine. Ashley laughed and said he had never been praised like this and he was beginning to like it. Martin had wondered why the bigger sack Margo had sent was so heavy, and now he saw that Alice's father had pulled out four bottles of plum wine from the sack and was trying to get the cork out of one. Daniel reached into his pocket for a corkscrew. He said his mother had shoved it into his pocket as he left, and he handed it over. Martin thought to himself that until recently all he had ever known about cork was that it worked for stopping up wine bottles.

Martin and Daniel tied on the masks that Ayana had handed them when they had stopped and followed the trail to the other camp. They didn't know it but eyes had been on them the whole time they had been on the island. The people of those eyes went ahead of them and told Ayana they were coming and she met them. She motioned them to follow her to the meeting place on the edge of the island where the wind was coming off the marsh, and she told them where to sit so the breeze was blowing from her to them. Then she took off her mask and told them they could take theirs off now. Daniel was familiar with this because he had been coming over to teach Ayana how to use the signaling mirror. Ayana smiled beautifully to them both and told Martin that he was growing into a man. She praised Daniel to Martin for bringing the signal mirror and teaching her how to use it and how good it made her feel to be able to signal with him or his father every few days or if there was an emergency. She told them that there were three runaways over on the quarantine island now and they were regularly helping about three or four runaways every month. She said that Alice's mother still talked about where they were from and what it was like and how they happened to come there. Most came from around Savannah and South Carolina. Some told her of how in the underground meetings, they talked about this being a place for runaways to come to get away. She said that this had always worried her because, if the story of them helping runaways got out, it would mean big trouble for them. She said they had seen more boats than ever coming near and this worried her too. Martin said that more and more people were coming to Savannah, and he didn't know how long these islands would be overlooked. He said that his family was concerned about that too and she could count on them for help if the need ever arose. He said they were as important to them as Alice and her family, and he saw the tears well up in Ayana's eyes.

Martin told Ayana the story about Prissy and her being from the same place that Alice's family had run away from. He told how Henry had given the money to Ashley and Ken to buy Alice, her family and friends, and Prissy. Ayana asked Daniel about Mary, and he told her that she said she was coming back there soon after they finished visiting at the Milam place. Ayana said that she and Mary shared the understanding of how important it was to preserve history. She said it was particularly important for her and her people now that there were so few left."Our stories have been passed down for a hundred generations, and these few of us could be the end of what is known of us." She said Mary was a blessing because she had been worrying about the story of her people ending, and then along came Mary, wanting to know all about it and write it down so their past could live on even if they didn't. For the first time, Martin saw a deep sadness in Ayana as she said a few more things. She said she and her people were tired of hiding and she was tired of Alice's family hiding and for people to have to run away just for being different. She said she understood why the Milam's and Dyers had to hide the way they treated people and did things. Ayana said that Mary shouldn't have to hide the true stories that she was writing about."What is wrong when people have to hide the truth?" Martin and Daniel were not the victims as Ayana and her people were, but her words gave them a glimpse of the wrongness of it all through her. Martin had not expected this sadness from Ayana, and he and Daniel were affected by it. It was hard for Martin to know what to say, but he wanted to say something to help Ayana feel better.

After a few minutes of silence, words came from thoughts he had never had and as he said them, he felt like he himself was also a listener to them. He told Ayana that in the troubled times, some good had come that was like a light in darkness. He said that her people had helped the runaways and even saved Alice's family and a few others from the massacre and sheltered them for all these years, and they were able to help hundreds of runaways to freedom. He said because Alice survived and was raised by his family, he was able to meet her and her people and now they had a little security by being able to signal with the Dyers. And Mary would soon have the story of her and her people preserved. And they have the Milam's and the Dyers to help if there are problems. He said that she and her people, Alice and her family and friends, all the people on the Milam place, and the Dyers were all like his family to him, and that he would do all he could do to protect and help any or all of them. He said she had helped others, and now others were standing by to help her. Daniel was a bit in awe at hearing Martin speak because he was talking like a wise grown-up and not the younger, sometimes slow-witted, friend he had known. He saw tears of gratitude on Ayana's face as she listened. Martin told Ayana that he wished she could visit his family but that he understood her concern about sickness. She said that she felt like she was knowing his family through his visits. He said he didn't know if Prissy would be staying or what her future was, but if she didn't want to stay, he or Daniel would be back to get her.

Martin stood and told Ayana that they should be going back to the other camp and visit a little then be on their way back to Tybee. He told her about the well point they had brought, and that Daniel had told Alice's father and brother how to hammer it into the ground, and they had left tools for them to do it with. He said that he should have brought two instead of one but would get another one for them, and Daniel would bring it when he brings Mary back in a few months. Ayana said it was about signal time, and Martin asked her to signal that they would be leaving in about an hour and be back to the lighthouse about dark or a little after.

When they got back to the other camp, there was still plenty of carrying on, and half the wine was gone and the spirits were high. There was a lot of laughter and tears as Prissy was doing most of the talking about the people and the many things that had happened at the Willoughby place since their big runaway. Prissy said that they all wanted Ashley to stay, but they knew he had things to do, and they had made him promise to come back and bring Ken. There was a big pot of fish stew cooking that smelled good, and Alice's mother gave them a big bowlful and some tea with some honey in it that Margo had sent. Martin said he didn't know he was hungry until he started eating and added that they should be going soon after they ate. When they finished a second helping of stew, Martin got up and said it was time to go. Prissy was the first to hug Martin and Daniel and Ashley, and then everyone else did, and they all expressed their thankfulness for them bringing Prissy and freeing them for good from Melvin Willoughby and all were crying tears of happy gratitude. Martin mentioned that he would send another well point with Daniel later and for them to put the one now on their end of the island.

They had to walk and pull the boat for the first hour until the tide had come in enough. In about two hours they came out into the Back River and rowed to the landing where Izak was waiting with the wagon and tackies. Martin told Izak that he might end up spending the night there at this landing when he was one of the boatmen sometime, because during a strong northeaster the supply boat would land there instead of at the Lazaretto landing. They pulled the boat up high on the bank and flipped it over because Daniel had said that Captain Jones had predicted rain starting tonight.

It was after dark when the wagon pulled into the lighthouse compound, and Charles and Margo were anxiously waiting for them. Margo had made a big casserole and fresh biscuits, and after they had gotten cleaned up, they came to the supper table and ate and talked about their trip. Margo said that she had been thinking about something Prissy had told her. She said Prissy came close to going with the runaway group all those years ago and said she probably would have died in the massacre if she had. Margo said she was just thinking of how nice it was that, after all these years, she was freed from the Willoughby place, and now with the group that she regrettably stayed behind from. Ashley said that Prissy said she didn't run away with them then because she had for so long, starting with old man Willoughby, tried to make life better for the other slaves that she thought she ought not to go, for fear of what might happen to them without her. He added that it was good as it happened because, without Prissy's help, he didn't think that they would have been able to deal with Willoughby. Margo said she sure was glad Mary was doing what she was doing because this all was quite a story, and it would be impossible for someone to make up something more interesting than what it was. Daniel said that Ayana sure liked what Mary was doing and told what she said about how her people knew their history only by it being told from one generation to the next and how there had gotten to be so few of them and Mary's written history of them may be all there was and it was important to her. He added that Ayana had said something that he had been thinking about since she said it. She said that the truth shouldn't have to be hidden. Margo told Daniel that Mary would like to hear that he had been thinking deeper than he usually did. Daniel said he probably wouldn't have said what he did if Mary had been there, and that made Martin laugh.

Margo went and brought out a blackberry pie and sat it on the table. She said it wasn't warm anymore because they were later than she had expected. Margo told Martin that it was the last of the blackberries that she had preserved that he had helped pick when he was there and said that the season for them would be there again soon, and that the white blackberry blooms were how she always saw another year had passed. Martin said he hoped he would be there again to pick some more. Ashley said he hoped he would be there again to eat some more soon, and Margo served him another piece. Charles asked if they were going back in the morning and said Captain Jones said there were a few rainy days ahead. Ashley said there was a load waiting for him and Ken to take to Darien, and he should get back soon. Martin said they had slickers and could stand the rain. Charles poured more tea and said he wouldn't want to be out in the rain, but if Ashley needed to be back, then they probably should go tomorrow. Daniel asked Izak how he liked helping a lightkeeper, and he said he liked it more than he would have guessed. He said that the first few days going up so high bothered him, but he really liked it now. He said the hardest job was cleaning glass and the mirrors in the reflector, and Daniel said he didn't like cleaning those things either. Izak said his favorite job was setting up the monocular and looking at what kind and where the ships were from. He had come to learn the flags of about a dozen countries, and he took a long time to write the short reports, but Charles let him take all the time he needed, but he was getting better and faster at it. Charles went and got one of the papers with the ship reports on it and showed them all. He showed the first one Izak had written and then the most recent one and said how much his printing had improved. Izak said he had Martin and Maggie to thank for his learning. Martin first encouraged him to learn when he had helped him check the list of materials that came when they were loading the barge for the work to be done there on Tybee. Then Maggie had been very patient at how slow he had been to learn to read. He said he now had Charles and Margo to thank. He said he actually seemed to learn better on his own with the books Margo gave him, because if he didn't have Maggie right there to tell him every word that he didn't know, he would have to try harder on his own. He said that he liked doing the ship reports and writing down the signal letters for the messages, and that doing something you like makes it easier. Charles and Margo smiled at Izak. It made them feel good to help him and that he was taking to it and that he showed some genuine gratitude. Charles told Martin that if they had had Izak's help sooner, he and Margo could have gone to the big meeting at the Milam place a while back. He said that Daniel was very good at everything that needed doing, but it was good to have two people, not just to share the work, but also in case there was an accident or something. He said that after a little more training, Izak would be able to be that second person to help Daniel so he and Martha could go off for a few days. Izak said he would do whatever Johnny or Jacob told him and would like to come back there. Martin asked him what about Maggie. He said that Jacob and Ellie liked him, but they were probably ready to be rid of him for a bit because he was at their place a lot, and that Maggie had some big plans. He said she had been talking about going up north to a school in Philadelphia for three years and getting manumitted while she was there. Henry would send someone to travel with her to Philadelphia and then send someone to bring her back afterwards, or whenever she wanted, and would pay for everything including the fee that the law required a freed slave to pay every year. Izak said that Alice had explained it all to Maggie, Jacob, Ellie, and him. Martin said that Mary said that Maggie had become her best friend and said how smart she was and had educated herself from the books from the Milam library after Alice had taught her to read and that she wanted to learn more than she was able to teach herself. He said it would make his father very happy to officially manumit someone from his place because it had been what he had wanted from the beginning. Izak said that he had even thought of asking Henry to manumit him but had to think about where he would go and what he would do, and nothing sounded as good as living where he was, and he liked learning to be a boatman. He said he was treated like a real person where he was, and he had heard how bad things were in other places. He said if he did get manumitted and was out on his own and didn't have a job and couldn't pay his fee every year, he could be taken by the state and declared unable to provide for himself and be auctioned back into slavery again and end up somewhere that was bad. Martin added that Henry would pay his fee if he couldn't for some reason. Izak went on to say that Alice was going to each person on the Milam place and explaining all this carefully so that they would understand that they had choices about things and explained what those choices were and to begin with, they could learn to read and write. Charles said that all these changes were good, but Henry sure had a big job ahead of him to deal with it all.

It had been raining all night and was still coming down when Daniel and Martin came down the next morning. At breakfast with everybody, Martin asked Ashley and Daniel what they wanted to do, and they said they would let him decide. Martin said maybe it would be best to wait until tomorrow instead of going up the river in the rain. He asked Ashley if he could wait one more day and Ashley said he didn't want to get back and be sick and maybe it would be best to wait. Martin said he had not been to see Captain Jones yet and could do that today. Izak said that when he had taken his food down the day before, he was moving mighty slow, and he told him that Martin was there. Margo said that was good because the Captain was always asking about Martin. Daniel said he had been getting quite frail and that Martin should take his food down and visit him in a bit. Ashley said he would like to go along if that was okay, and Martin said that would be even better. Daniel said he would like a long nap while listening to the rain as he had done many times and would like to help his father and Izak with lighthouse work. Charles said there wouldn't be any signaling today because of the rain, but there was plenty of work to do cleaning the inside of the glass and the mirrors in the reflector and cleaning soot from the lantern glass and refueling the lantern tank and trimming the wick. Daniel told his father to take the day off because he and Izak could do it all. He said he could teach Izak a few things about cleaning glass and reflector mirrors that would make his job easier. Izak said he would like that. Charles said there wasn't much to do for now and said he would make some more yaupon and they could sit on the porch and have some and watch the rain. Margo said she wanted to hear more from Ashley about their trip to Saint Helena to buy back Alice and her family and Prissy. She said she had heard many stories but that was her favorite and wanted to hear it first hand from Ashly. So, while sipping yaupon, they all listened to the long version of the trip from Ashley. Martin had not known before what a good storyteller Ashley was. He was slow and had many pauses and had them all very attentive, trying to guess what his next words would be, and Martin noticed for the first time how Ashley used his hands often to help describe what he was saying. There were parts that brought tears and parts that brought laughter, and Ashley was very modest and made little of his and Ken's doings in it all and tried to lay the credit on everyone else, and everyone liked it when Ashley would get a bit giddy trying to explain some parts. After the story Margo said she would go and fix some food for the Captain and in a few minutes returned with a sack and a covered dish with the last piece of blackberry pie. Daniel and Izak got up to do the lighthouse work, and Martin and Ashley got into their slickers and started out in the rain with the food for the Captain.

23.
TURTLE ISLAND TREASURE

Down on the beach, there were no pilot crews or any signs of anybody. Martin knew the Captain would be in his shanty and went and first knocked and then pushed the door open. The Captain was lying down, and Martin had to control his shock at how feeble and ashen the Captain looked. But when he woke and saw Martin, his face lit up, and some color came over him, and he smiled real big. Martin helped him sit up and out of the bed and into his chair. He gave him the jar of yaupon, and the Captain said that was just what he needed and took a big drink. Martin shuddered to himself, knowing that the Captain was not long to this world, and was glad that the rain had caused them to stay an extra day so he could see him again. In his shudder was the understanding that there would be a time soon that he would come to Tybee, and the Captain would not be there. The Tybee north point would not be right without the Captain. Martin left those thoughts quickly so the Captain wouldn't notice his sadness. He told the Captain who was with him, and he really liked that he was meeting Ashley. He knew that he was a mate on Captain Ben's sharpie and that Ken was the other mate. He asked him about Captain Ben, and Ashley told how he and Ken would be taking over because of the Captain's back problems and how Martin would become the new mate in a few months. This made Captain Jones so happy he could hardly contain himself, and he asked Martin to hand him his pipe. He said it would be a very good thing for Martin because he knew that Captain Ben would have taught Ashley and Ken well and a good thing for them because Martin was such a good lad and was a piece of one of the finest captains ever, referring to Walter. He asked how his father was doing and told how much he had enjoyed visiting with him and Charles when he was there recently. He said the only thing that made him happier than seeing his father was seeing Martin. Martin told the Captain about their trip over to the island to take Prissy and what Mary and Daniel had been up to at his house in Savannah. The Captain particularly liked hearing about Mary and said she was so special, and he missed seeing her and her brother but was glad they were off seeing the world a bit. He said that he liked Izak and was glad that Charles had some help while Daniel was gone and said how Izak was a bit sad at first but had gotten happier after a week or so. Martin told him about Maggie, and the Captain shook his head in an understanding manner.

The Captain said he was particularly happy that Martin had come down today because there was something secretive in nature that he had wanted to tell somebody before he left this world, and he had decided sometime back that he wanted to tell Martin. He said he had meant to tell only him but would tell it even though Ashley was here because he had a liking for him and had heard what he and Ken had done for the Milam's in South Carolina. He said he was concerned that if something happened to him before Martin came back, the secret would never be told.

The Captain sipped and looked distant for a minute or so before he began. He said that what he was about to tell was the real reason he had come to Tybee from piloting ships into Warsaw sound where he and his two mates lived on what Martin now calls Claw Island, overlooking War- saw Sound. We spent our days, the only pilot crew around, waiting for a ship to show up wanting to come into the "Back Door" to Savannah. It was all contraband. It was a risky job because many of the ship captains and crews were desperate and unpredictable, although some were nice and gentlemanly, but just outlaws."We were young and foolhardy and al- ways believed that lady luck was always on our side." The captain paused and said there was something he wanted to say before he told anymore and said that he had forgotten more than he could remember about much in his life, but what he was about to tell was etched in his brain as clearly as scrimshaw was on a powder horn.

The Captain paused again for a moment and looked at Martin and said, There we were one day, sitting just above the high water mark, be- side that same boat that you now have, looking and hoping for a ship, and up comes a half dozen Indians from their camp that was nearby. They camped closer to the little inlet that splits the point, and we stayed more toward the ocean side of the point where we would be closer to get out to a ship. Usually they stayed to themselves, but occasionally they would bring us some fish, crabs, or conch, but this day they were holding up a young man that looked half dead. They set him down in front of us and left. His skin was parched from the sun, and his lips swollen. We carried him up and over the dunes to our shanty, laid him on the shady side and made him as comfortable as we could. We gave him little drinks of water every half hour for the rest of the day, and by afternoon he was able to sit up. That night he was able to eat a little, and he began to come around a bit. His pitiful state began to change, as he became less dried out and was able to swallow some beans. He didn't appear to want to run away or have the strength to, and we made him a comfortable place to rest for the night.

He woke up the next morning looking a lot better and was able to talk a little and began telling us how he had gotten there. First he said he needed to get far away and asked if we could help him, and I said I would try but he first needed to tell me who he was running from and why. He said he had decided to go to sea and had gone down to the wharfs in Charleston a while back and gotten on the first ship that would take him and was excited and happy that it had been so easy when he had no experience other than messing about in small boats and being only sixteen. He thought he had found a way to go off and return with some money to help his destitute family. He was given a place to sleep and fed food and grog and everything seemed fine, and he was told that the ship would leave in a week or so. During the week, and in the night, wagons would come alongside, and things would be loaded onto them from the ship's hold and sometimes from them to the ship. He was told to stay in his bunk and not to help. He thought it odd that all the loading was done in the middle of the night but didn't know enough to know what to think of it. After a week in port, he said the ship left and sailed south for a few days. Once out he learned the true nature and purpose of the ship, and it wasn't good. The sailors would drink grog at night and talked about the places they had been and what the Captain bought and sold. He said the crew and captain were the worst kind of characters. He said the bosun took him down in the bowels of the ship every day and made him crawl into the deepest part of the bilge and shovel sludge. It was a mixture of human waste and accumulated filth of all kinds and had become so putrid that the sailors would puke sometimes when they went below to stow or retrieve the stolen goods. And what they puked just added to the stench. He said the bosun showed him two barrels and said he couldn't come out every day until they were filled with the sludge, and he would either be lashed or be unfed until they were filled. He said he did the work as quickly as he could and then waited a while before banging on the decking above to be let out so he could look into the boxes and see what was there. Most of it was fancy silver tableware. Mugs, dishes, tea sets, platters, and everything silver and boxes jumbled full of silver that were too heavy to pick up. He understood what the sailors had talked about how the Captain only liked the kind of goods that were heavy and the most valuable because they were also the best ballast there was, and he specialized in trading in it. He had also heard them talk about the gold that the Captain had always separated out and kept in his cabin locked away. They continued south, stopping at a few places without going ashore and were met by smaller boats that off-loaded boxes of the silver goods onto and sometimes from. He said he began to understand that these were not the kind of pirates that raided ships, but they were the smuggling kind that bought and sold what pirates and thieves had pillaged. After a month of going south, they began meeting ships offshore and loading on more and more goods into the hold. Then they headed back north, and he learned from the drunken sailors at night that they were to go near Tybee and wait for a ship to come and meet and sell their entire hold full of silver. He said they went in from the ocean, but no further than the mouth of the Savannah River, and moored out by an island across the water from the Tybee lighthouse.

Martin and Ashley looked at each other, knowing what island that had to be. The Captain saw their recognition and said, yes, it was Turtle Island. The young man went on to say that they were there for a couple weeks waiting before the other ship showed up, and he continued in his everyday routine of shoveling the filthy sludge waste from the bilge into the barrels, and they would hoist them up from above and dump them over. He said he even got on good with a couple of the sailors at bedtime and imagined that they were not evil but had simply fallen into the whole ordeal like he had. They gave him treats that they bought from the bosun and told him all about what was going on. One day the bosun told him that the Captain needed someone to row him ashore the next day, and he gladly said he would do that, thinking it would be a break from his nasty job below. That night he told the two sailors that liked him about what he was asked to do, and instead of being happy for him, their brows furrowed, and both had a sad look about them that he didn't understand. The next morning a pulling boat was let over, and four boxes that were very heavy for their size were lowered in. He and the Captain climbed down into the boat, and the Captain took the tiller, and he took to the oars. The Captain had timed it so they caught the last of the incoming tide and went around to the back of the island and followed a creek. And as the tide reached full in, they were able to get up close to the back of the island. He said the Captain had him carry two of the small boxes, and they were so heavy that he would have to stop often and get his strength back. There was a ridge of higher ground that ran the length of the island, and they followed that a ways and stopped, and the Captain told him to go back for the other two boxes. When he got back with the other boxes, the Captain gave him the shovel he had carried and pointed and told him to dig. He said when the hole was over waist deep and plenty wide, he was told to put the boxes in it and cover them up.

The young man said that after the hole was filled and smoothed over and leaves and pine straw strewn over, the tide had dropped too low for them to leave, and they had to wait for it to go out and come back to be able to leave. They sat down right there and ate some hard bread and smoked meat and water, and the Captain dosed off. He said when the Captain was hard asleep, he stood up and looked around. He said he walked over to the east side of the ridge and looked to the southeast and saw the lighthouse on the island across the water and it looked peculiar because in its background was a clump of trees slightly higher than the lighthouse and much higher than the other trees on the island.

Martin spoke up again and said that was the tall pines where they hid Mallie and was one of his favorite places on Tybee. Captain Jones smiled at Martin and continued. After the lad had seen the lighthouse aligned with the tall trees behind it, he understood why the Captain picked this spot, so he could later come and find it again. He was stretched out on the ground like he had been napping when the Captain awoke and said the tide would be high enough soon and they could start back, which they did. When the tide was half in, the Captain had him drag the boat in the shallow water out to where it was deeper, and they returned to the ship.

That night, his two befriended sailors came to him and told him why they were so troubled about him helping the Captain. They said that the Captain would not want anyone around who could find their way to his gold and that his time alive was limited. They told him that the Captain would probably let him live long enough for him to finish the work in the bilge, which was almost done. But they had seen the same kind of thing happen twice before, and both times the helper had mysteriously disappeared. They said they were fond of him and would help him get a pulling boat over that night, and he could get away, and that's what they did. He said that, as he was crossing the mouth of the river, the swift river current and an offshore wind swept him out to sea before he could cross over, and he was so exhausted from trying to row against it that he fainted into the bottom of the boat and woke up hours later to a blazing sun, a few miles out and a bit south of Tybee. He had slept past midday and then drank what little water he had and started rowing toward the nearest land, and it got dark before he got there, and he saw fire light and went for it, and that was the campfire of the Indians. He said he was afraid of who it might be but felt near death and had no other choice, but they were friendly and they gave him water, and the next day brought him here to us.

The Captain said he told him that he would help him get off the island and explained that he had met the leader of the Indians who stayed on the long island across the marsh but came over there regularly to meet colonials that would come out from Savannah and trade. He spoke good English, and over many years of trading had made friends in Savannah and accumulated a small amount of wealth. The Captain said that the next time he came, he would ask him if he would take the marooned lad to Savannah, and that's what he did. Since then, Captain Jones said he had wondered often if he had been able to make his way back home to Charleston and hoped he did.

Captain Jones said he didn't want to take this story to his grave but had never found anyone he wanted to tell it to until Martin came along. He went on to say that there was a side of Savannah that Martin did not know about, but Ashley probably did, and Martin asked him to tell him more about what he meant. He said, just like the ship the lad got on in Charleston, many of the ships coming into Savannah are up to no good. They may look like the rest of the ships but have devious intentions and you never know. He said that, for those reasons, he was glad that Martin had got on with someone like Captain Ben. Martin asked if he thought the gold might still be there on Turtle Island.

The Captain said he didn't know, but there was many a captain or sailor that intended to return for buried gold that didn't return for various reasons. Their lives are full of uncertainty, and the company they keep is seldom to be trusted, and very few of them live a long life. Once in port, some are apprehended and some are killed and some quit their lawless ways. Some don't and have early endings or die in jail. The Captain said he would bet that the boxes of gold were still there, but he didn't want to see Martin going after it anytime soon. He said that the only people that went to Turtle Island were up to no good. Most were slave smugglers now that it had become against the law to import slaves. Many are simply looking for a place to hide something because they are worried that their ship could be boarded and searched in port or worried that his ship will be pirated by one of the pirates he deals with. Martin was surprised and asked if he meant that stolen goods could be stolen again. The Captain said yes and again and again and smiled at Martin's innocence. Martin asked if there was something left out of the story and mentioned that the Captain had said it was the real reason that he had left the beach by Warsaw Sound and came to work off the north Tybee beach. The Captain said he had told the most important part by revealing where and how Martin might locate the spot where the gold might still be, which is what he wanted Martin to know. All he had to do was walk along the ridge of the island until, look-ing back at Tybee, the lighthouse was in line with the clump of tall pines, and he would be at the spot.

The Captain took another long pause then started again and said the other part of the story was quite sad and was the real reason he had come to Tybee, and he had been bothered about it ever since. He said he and his two mates, who heard the lad's story, came to Tybee with the intention of the three of them going and getting the gold. He said he had some guilt about being part of those intentions, but the lure of it was too much, and he didn't think taking something that had already been stolen was a bad thing. Once they got to Tybee, they became just another pilot crew that waited for ships to guide in and kept their plans to themselves. He said it was summer and everyone knew about all the big rattlesnakes on Turtle Island and how they weren't as bad in winter. So, he warned his mates that they should wait till cold weather and the three of them could go after the gold. But they were impatient and made a plan without telling or including him.

Well, before summer was over, they told me that they were taking a few days off and going across the river fishing with a fellow crewman that had his own boat, and I was agreeable to it and would enjoy the time off. Anyhow, they left and said they were going to a spot on Daufuskie called Bloody Point, which is straight across, there on the southern tip of Daufuskie, and said they may spend a few nights. They never came back, and after a while I figured they either capsized or something foul was going on but didn't find out about it for a month or two afterwards. I didn't have a crew for a while and let the other crews know I was in need and why.

One of the pilots finally came to me and told what had happened. He said the crewman with his own boat, who he knew from here on the beach, came to him and told the story of what happened before leaving the state, out of fear that he could be blamed in some way for what had gone on. He said the captains two crewmen offered to give him a small share of gold that they had buried, if he would take them over to Turtle Island and bring them back and he said he would although he wished now that he hadn't. On high tide he took them around the back side of the island, and into a small creek that went up near the back of the island. He waited while the two of them went off with shovels to look for the gold. About two hours after they left, one limped back, dragging his leg that was swollen up huge from a snake bite and said that before they got to the gold, his mate was in front and was bit two times by a huge rattler and died in less than thirty minutes. He left him but was bit himself on the way back. He asked him to tell how he could find the gold, but he died a few minutes later. He said he left the one crewman there in the marsh for the crabs and the one up on the ridge for the buzzards and had been haunted by the ordeal and sold his boat and was going off to live somewhere in South Carolina.

The Captain said that he was not very proud of that part of the story, and he didn't like to think about how his mates had deceived him and was yet truly sad that they had died and was glad he had told it all before he died and was glad he had told it to them, particularly Martin. They sat quietly and listened to the rain. All were transported by the story, including the Captain, and they sat still and quiet, until they came back to the present moment.

Martin broke the silence and told the Captain that he was sure glad, for whatever reason, that he had come here to Tybee, but said he didn't like that his mates deceived him and died horribly. The Captain said coming to Tybee probably saved his life, because of how desperate and vile the captains and crews and they often narrowly escaped with their lives. Here, he was fed by the best cook in Georgia and looked after by the nicest folks around, meaning Margo and her family. that but getting fed regularly by the Dyers and having them as friends had been good for him. Ashley told him what a legend he had become in Savannah and all around as "Captain Sandy" and his weather reports. Captain Jones laughed heartily, and it made Martin feel good to see him laugh. Martin said that by his weather reporting he had saved people a lot of time and probably even saved lives.

The rain slacked and Martin asked the Captain if there was anything he could do before they left, and he said he was fine. The captain said he needed to get up and move about to get the stiffness out. Martin watched closely to see how able he was to get up on his own, but he was careful to not let the Captain know he was watching and pretended to be looking out the one window but watched the Captain out the corner of his eye. He saw that he strained a good bit and once up he teetered the first few steps toward the door but got better as he stepped out onto the rain-soaked sand. This worried Martin, and he would remember to talk to Charles and Margo about it. Ashley told the Captain how glad he was to meet him and hear the story about Turtle Island. Martin said he thought that the Indian leader that spoke English who had taken the lad to Savannah must have been Ayana's father. The Captain said it was, but he hadn't thought to mention that. The Captain said he suspected that Martin would one day go over to Turtle Island and line up things like in the story and hoped he only went in very cold weather. The Captain said to remember that there were a lot of big rattlesnakes there, but more importantly, to remember that there was a kind of snake that was more dangerous and they were easy to recognize because they had two legs. Ashley chuckled at what he said and told the Captain that they would go sometime but not anytime soon and held his hand out and softly shook the old captain's hand. Martin hugged him and told him that he would be back soon and once he was working with Ashley and Ken, he would be able to stop by more often.

Walking up the dune to the lighthouse was easier because the sand was wet. At the top, out of habit of being with Daniel, Martin looked for the lighthouse shadow, but because of the clouds there was no shadow today. Ashley could tell from Martin's silence that something was on his mind and asked what it was. Martin said it pained him to know that before long he would be coming here and there would be no Captain Jones. Ashley answered right away and asked if he would forget him. Martin said never, and Ashley said, then for you, in a way, he won't ever be entirely gone. When they got to the house, Martin stopped at the bottom of the stairs and told Ashley they should sit and clean the sand off their shoes because the only time he had ever seen Margo upset was when he and Daniel and Mary had tracked sand into the house, and he never wanted to see that again. Today the wet sand was caked up on their shoes, and they took so long that Margo came out to see what they were doing and smiled at Martin when she saw them cleaning their shoes. Charles came out, and they sat on the porch. Martin told them his concern about the Captain and how it was getting hard for him to get up and down. Charles said he knew that was coming and didn't know what to do but was sure they would do something. He said when the pilot crew was down there, they helped, and often they would leave one crewman behind to help him when they returned to Savannah. Martin wanted to but didn't talk about the story that the Captain had told them. He didn't like keeping secrets and decided he would tell them, but at another time. Instead, he just said that the Captain was one of the best storytellers he had ever heard, and he had heard some good ones. Ashley said he was so mesmerized by his story telling that an hour or more could go by without him knowing it. Margo said that between the Captain and the pilots and their crew, we hear a lot of stories, and she guessed that it was one of the reasons that Mary had wanted to write like she did. She smiled at Martin and said they were still telling stories of all that happened when Martin had come last year. She said Mary always said that real characters and stories followed Martin everywhere he went. Ashley said he could see that and said that it didn't seem so, but he must be a real character, and it made them laugh.

Daniel and Izak came in from their work up on the lighthouse, and Charles got up and brought some yaupon out. Daniel said that after not having been doing the work on the lighthouse for a while, he really liked it a lot. Izak said the work cleaning everything was even fun when there was someone to do it with and said he learned a lot from Daniel today. Margo said it sure seemed like the right thing for them to do was to wait and go tomorrow, and they all agreed. She asked Daniel how much longer he would like to stay at Martin's house. Daniel said being home today made him want to come back soon, but he had just begun to like being at Martin's before they came here, so he just didn't know. Charles said he needed to take his time and enjoy himself because it could be a while before he went off again, unless he found something there that he wanted more and was the reason for them sending him off. Being a light keeper is not for everybody, and if you didn't like being one, it could be a miserable existence. Ashley said he liked going on the short trips they did. When he went on a trip, he liked going, and when they were headed back, he liked that too. He said too long on the boat or too long on the hill didn't agree with him. Martin said he liked how that sounded for him too. He thought to himself about how he would not like being gone from Mary and wondered if she would care if he was gone. She seemed to be more interested in her work than him lately. He decided that he wouldn't think about that anymore and asked Izak if there was anything he wanted him to tell Maggie when he got back. Izak said to tell her that he missed her, but that he was doing just fine and that he might even go to Philadelphia with her and get manumitted and find a lighthouse there that needed a helper. Charles told him that he thought that might be possible and if he ever needed a letter of recommendation, he would provide one. He told Izak that he had improved his writing since he had been there and had gotten better at helping him and he really appreciated his good work. Izak wasn't accustomed to receiving such praise and was speechless. Margo looked on and saw the gratitude in Izak's demeanor and thought about who and where his mother and father might be. Daniel said he was going for the nap he had promised himself and asked Martin if he would like to take one. Martin said he was not sleepy but would like to go up on the lighthouse later in the afternoon. He asked Ashley if he wanted to go with him, and he said sure.

Everybody took a nap except Martin, and he spent his time looking at a few charts that Charles had of the islands to the north and south of the lighthouse. He studied the one with Turtle Island, since he had just heard so much about it from Captain Jones. Then he began studying Daufuskie Island. It was much bigger than Turtle but not as big as Hilton Head. He noted that Turtle, Daufuskie, and Hilton Head Island, together, were still not as big as Saint Helena Island. He thought he might like to explore Daufuskie or Hilton Head sometime since he had already explored the islands south of Tybee. He began looking all around Daufuskie on the chart. He was particularly interested in what was called Bloody Point on the south end of the island. He had often looked across from Tybee at low tide and saw how close it looked. The point of Daufuskie was a cotton plantation, and on a clear day you could see the big house from Tybee. On a full moon, when the tides were at their highest and lowest, and at dead low, it looked like you could walk across from Tybee, but he knew the

Savannah River channel was there and how deep it was and how swift the current was. He remembered the recent trip back with Ashley and Ken on the sharpie and how tall and steep the waves were. With the tide very low, he could see how shallow the water would have been everywhere except in the river channel. Now, looking at the chart, he saw where they had come by Hilton Head and steered directly to the South Channel. Because it had been high tide and the centerboard was up, they had been able to pass over the bars. Next he looked on the chart at the Lazaretto landing and at the entrance into the South Channel and across it at a point of land that went out a ways from Cockspur Island. He remembered Daniel saying that his father had been asking for a small lighthouse to be built there to help guide ships into the South Channel. Next he studied the big rivers that went around the west side of Daufuskie. He vowed to himself that in the next few years he would get himself as familiar with the area around Daufuskie and Hilton Head and Turtle Island, as he was with the islands south of Tybee. He had heard stories about some people on Daufuskie that were still secretly loyal to England and how it had high ground and thick dirt that was excellent for growing things. Tybee didn't have much high ground, and what was there was sand. There were the big dunes that were in front of the lighthouse and wrapped around the north end of the island and one ridge of high ground behind the dunes on the west end of the island. He thought about how the tall dunes in front of the lighthouse got there and looked at the chart and saw that the northeasters blew directly onto the north end of Tybee, fetching up across the whole Atlantic ocean. He remembered being on the beach in a strong northeaster and the air was full of sand, and you had to cover your eyes because it blew so hard and would sting any exposed sand and he thought about the story of Captain Jones sitting out on the beach in a northeaster and getting half covered with sand. He had learned from his father that beach sand had washed down from the mountains for thousands of years and then the northeasters had blown and piled it up into the high dunes, and the lighthouse was built behind them to protect it from ocean surge during hurricanes. Martin continued to look over the charts and his imagination had him swooping over the rivers and creeks and marsh like a gull, and he was so involved that he was startled when Daniel came in and it took him a moment to gather his attention from his imaginary flight. Daniel said he didn't have the rainy nap he wanted but did have a nap and was ready to do his work. He told Martin to come on and they would stop and get Ashley and Izak at the old guard house. Daniel's noisy climb down from the loft had woken his mother and father from their nap, and they were coming in as Daniel and Martin were leaving.

Ashley and Izak were outside, and Daniel motioned for them to follow him, and they went to the little brick building where they kept the lamp oil. Daniel filled up all four of the jugs with oil and handed the others one and kept one for himself and said that them toting these up would save Izak some work in the days to come. Once up top, Daniel let Izak set up the monocular while he got the signaling box and set it up. He gave Izak the paper with Captain Sandy's weather report and some ship information with a note about Martin returning with the tide tomorrow. The sky had some clouds but Daniel waited on a clear spot. After Daniel had sent the message, he handed Izak the paper and charcoal pencil so he could write out the letters of the incoming message. He wanted Izak to get all the practice he could while he was there. Charles had let them know on the Milam side that Izak was there in training and to be a little slower on the signaling. Daniel watched the flashes and what Izak was writing until he was finished. Martin said according to Captain Jones, the rain would be there all day, but the skies were clear. Daniel said that the Captain's pelican was allowed a little wiggle room in his forecasts, but he still knew better than anyone else. Martin said he didn't notice any flashes coming from Ayana. Daniel said he always looked, but she didn't signal unless there was something unusual going on. Martin let Ashley look through the monocular, which was set up to look at the Lazaretto landing. After Ashley had looked a bit, Martin moved it a little so they could see Turtle Island and Daufuskie. He looked at the rivers and creeks and the sound between Daufuskie and Hilton Head that he had just been looking at on the charts less than a half hour before. Next he looked behind the lighthouse at the clump of tall pines where they had taken Mallie and tried as best he could to extend an imaginary line from the pines through the lighthouse to see roughly where that hit on Turtle Island. Daniel wondered what hc was doing and thinking, but Ashley knew. Martin said he was just studying some things that Captain Jones had talked about and left it at that. Daniel knew that Martin could be a little strange in his imagination so didn't think much of it. Martin saw that if he was close in his sighting, the spot where the gold was buried was about in the middle of the island, but he knew that it would be more accurate to look from Turtle Island back this way. Martin wanted to tell Daniel about it all and intended to later.

Daniel let Izak put things up and fill the lamp, not to be a boss or anything like that but simply to let him gain the experience. While he was doing that, Martin and Daniel walked Ashley all the way around the balcony and pointed out what they were seeing. Daniel told Ashley what Martin had learned from his father and told him about the sun not rising and instead of how they were either spinning toward or away from it. Izak had finished and heard it, and they all laughed about it. While they were all together, Daniel pointed out where they had watched the duel on the beach and said he still thought about it every time he looked that way or went down on the beach. Daniel told them that he and his father had watched them when they came in from Saint Helena and said how good the sharpie did in the rough water but that it was probably a rough ride. Martin said it was the most fun he had ever had in a boat and made Ashley smile. Izak asked them if they could smell something. They stopped and sniffed the air, and Ashley was first to say he could. Izak said Margo was making something special, and Martin said everything she made was special, and Izak said he thought the smell was a combination of biscuits and sweet potato casserole because she had made it once before and he liked it. He said that the cooking had been very good, and he thought that the ocean breezes had made him hungrier too.

When they got down, they saw that Izak had been right because Margo had a big, deep iron pot set out to cool with sweet potato casserole and had biscuits keeping warm in the oven. Martin said that was Henry's favorite and he liked it too. She told them to get cleaned up, and she dished out a serving of the casserole and put a cloth around it and got two biscuits out of the oven and told Daniel to run it down to the Captain and come right back for an early supper. He took it down and put it inside the shanty and helped the Captain up and saw that he got into his small table and handed him his spoon and asked if there was anything else he needed. The Captain said he had more than he could ever want and told Daniel to hug his mother's neck for him and told him that he would miss him while he was away. He said one more thing as he left and that was to tell Martin that he had decided it was okay to tell him and his family about what they had talked about today. Daniel didn't understand what he meant but said he would tell Martin that and left.

After supper, he told the Captain's long tale. When he finished, Charles said that he had heard a little something about a small part of that but only about three pilot crewmen going off to Turtle Island and only one coming back. He said snakes, pirates, and treasure were always talked about when Turtle Island was the subject, and that probably would not change for a long time. Mary said she would leave certain parts of this story out of her notes, and Margo said that was a good idea.

There was no need to hurry off from the lighthouse the next morning because the tide to go home on didn't start until about midday. After breakfast, Daniel had a few things to do for Charles, and Izak helped him. Ashley asked Martin to take him back up on the lighthouse to look at things with the monocular one more time before they left. Margo found a big basket she had saved and some sail cloth to layer in it and planned to put a chunk of ice in it from the icebox and send some leftovers for their trip back. About an hour before low tide Izak hitched up the tackies and brought the wagon around. Margo added the ice and leftovers to the basket and she and Charles hugged the three of them. Izak took them to the Back River landing where they had left the boat, and just before the tide had finished going out, they left. The tide went slack, and they rowed in still water for a bit before it turned and started flowing in. Martin had hoped for a little ocean breeze once the tide started in, and they got it and put the lug sail up. After an hour the southeasterly was brisk enough for them to lay the oars down. Daniel asked to take the tiller because he had not sailed Martin's new boat before. The water was flat, but the wind was brisk and mostly behind them, and they made very good time. In a bit Ashley broke out the packed leftovers. The helm was so easy to manage that Daniel was able to tie off the tiller in a straight stretch of the river and sail while eating his lunch. Martin liked what Margo had done adding ice to the basket, and he told Ashley that he was thinking about talking to Jason about making a small ice chest, made only with cork and no wood on the outside so it would be lighter and he could take it in and out as it was needed. Ashley said that probably would work by gluing the cork parts together with pine resin. Martin said it could be another product for the new ice business.

After eating Martin looked back and saw that Daniel was having fun. Daniel saw him looking and said this boat was bigger and felt like a ship compared to the little dugout. Martin said yes and his father had said that a boat twice as long as another boat could be ten times bigger, and Daniel nodded in agreement. The longer the tide came in, the stronger the wind got, and Daniel whooped a few times when the boat caught a big blast of wind and leaned way over. As the river zigged and zagged, they simply let the sail out or tightened it up, and in a couple of hours they were more than halfway back, and the wind was still picking up. Daniel yelled that he was ready for a break, and he steered into the lee of a marsh hammock, and Ashley told Martin he would like to take the helm a bit, and Martin nodded. Ashley was a much more experienced sailor and drove the boat harder than Daniel or Martin knew how to. He knew just what to do to get the most speed by continually adjusting the sails just right. It was almost a solid thrill for more than an hour, and they were within sight of the Wilmington River soon after that. Martin was amazed because he could tell from the height of the water in the marsh grass that they could only have been gone three or four hours and would be back to the Milam place in an hour, and that they had come the long back way from Tybee quicker than many trips take from Lazaretto. The boatmen saw their sail and were waiting for them on the bank. Ashley tightened up on the sail and gained some speed and slid the boat way up the soft mud of the riverbank. The boatmen and Martin and Daniel had never seen such a sailing feat as that. The boat was high and dry with the sails still up, and they were able to step out without stepping in water. Martin was astonished and looked at Ashley, and Ashley said Martin would be doing just like that soon and laughed. Johnny laughed at Ashley and told him that he was teaching Martin dangerous ways, and Ashley said that a fast and hard landing could save his life one day. Johnny told them that they would take care of the boat and that they could just get their things and go on up to the house. Martin hugged Johnny when he got out and asked if everything was okay, and Johnny said it was and that everyone had been telling the same old stories and waiting on him to get back to have some new stories to tell. Martin said he would be over soon to see the baby and tell Alice about the trip and how her family was doing and how they were probably still carrying on large about Prissy being there. Johnny smiled at Martin and said he knew Alice was waiting to hear about all that, and he knew that within an hour of Alice hearing, the whole place will be talking about it for a couple days, and if the story gets back to him, there will be "things in it that you did that you didn't know you did." They all laughed more, and Martin said he knew how that went. Ashley watched and listened as Martin and Johnny talked and noticed that Martin's dialect changed and he spoke faster and that he and Johnny were talking different than the normal conversations he had been hearing with Martin and the Dyers. He had heard how Alice practically raised Martin the first six years of his life and that he was with the workers and their families so much that he learned the Geechee way to talk and that his own family could hardly understand him.

Martin's family knew they were leaving from the Back River landing about midday on the tide and expected them at dark or shortly after because it was a longer trip than from the Lazaretto landing. The strong southeasterly had most to do with their quick trip, but Martin's new boat had a lot to do with it as well as Ashley's hard sailing. The new boat was light and had a sharp entry and was fast, just like Captain Jones had said when he gave it to Martin. John had come out for the day to work with Henry, and they heard the loud greetings on the porch and came out and joined in the welcoming with Walter, Martha, Claudia, Mary, Maggie, and the kids. Somehow Ellie had already gotten the word that Martin was back, and within minutes she and Thomas had come. She said she could rest again now that he was back and knew that Prissy was with Alice's family. Ashley and Daniel were a bit in awe at all the commotion and how much everyone was so happy to see them back. After a little while, when Johnny and Jacob finished work, they and Alice and the new baby came, and Martin, Daniel, and Ashley all told about the trip to take Prissy. It was an extra special time, and it extended into the next day as the news was spread to everyone else on the place. It was one of those days of less work and more fun to carry on.

24.
THE NEXT FEW YEARS

Walter had handed everything over to Henry, and he and Martha visited Tybee every six weeks for a week and sometimes two. This is what Walter's doctor wanted him to do, and it was doing him and Martha good. Charles and Margo liked it too, especially during the times that Daniel and Mary were at the Milam place. Martha didn't like leaving home at first. She didn't like being on a boat and being away from her grandkids, which included the newest one, Jochebed. But after a few visits, she began to enjoy the salt air and the leisure and the

company of Margo. On each visit they went down on the supply boat one week and came back on the supply boat the next week or the week after that. Walter particularly liked the cooler days because it was like what he had grown up in. While Daniel was away, Izak had learned quickly what to do and allowed Charles plenty of free time to spend hours talking to Walter down on the beach with Captain Jones, the pilots, and the crews.

Back at the Milam place, Henry was the busiest man in Georgia. He liked Thomas, the engineer from Boston because he liked the idea of engineering being applied to business growth, just like it was to bridges, roads, and machines. The steam-powered saw mill was up and running, and his work there was done. Henry and John wanted him to relocate to Savannah with his family and work full-time in getting the ice business going, and to engineer the expansion that they expected. Henry told Thomas that he would guarantee him at least a year's work in Savannah and they wanted another set-up in Charleston that they expected to be bigger and that would probably take two years and that his work and involvement would probably always be needed to make the everyday operations of both locations efficient and innovative. Thomas and his wife only had one son who was grown and in the navy, so they did move to Savannah, and he came on full-time, with an arrangement to share in the profits.

With Thomas' help all the buildings were finished, insulated wagons built, and people hired. The Savannah newspaper was covering the progress of things every week, and so many people were signing up for ice delivery that they could barely keep up with it all. Jason had twelve workers building iceboxes for homes and icehouse components for businesses and plantation operations. On a visit to see John and his family, Richard Wilcox was so impressed with things that he ordered a large icehouse to make ice delivery part of his hardware business in Beaufort. Thomas had made arrangements with timber freighters in Maine, coming to Savannah, to leave their ice ballast at the new icehouse. Up until the Milam Ice Company, they had never been paid for their ice ballast. Now ice became cargo and income, and Thomas made trips to Maine and met with the suppliers to establish standards of how the ice was sawed and the purity of the source. Thomas designed systems for moving the ice from the ships to the icehouse with ramps to slide it on and a boom system for lifting. John was keeping the financial accounts of everything and was watching carefully because a lot of money was being spent without much money being gained, but he remained confident. Halfway through the first year, almost one hundred iceboxes had been delivered and components for twenty icehouses were delivered and put together in South Carolina and Georgia. Insulated wagons were leaving early every morning loaded with ice for homes. A large icehouse was built for Richard Wilcox in Beaufort. When his hardware customers heard of his new product, they began to order iceboxes, and some wanted small icehouses like the one on the Milam place. John and Henry did not anticipate the impact of Richard Wilcox making ice part of his business. He began getting orders from all around and even some inquiries from Charleston. A company from up in Maine had introduced ice in Charleston a few years before but had not followed through with ways to store the ice in homes and icehouses on plantations and fisheries. Henry, John, and Thomas went to Charleston, and with the Albert's help, they registered to do business there and bought property for a second location for the ice business and began plans for setting it up.

The people in Savannah were excited about this new business that Walter Milam's son was building. Not a week went by that the Savannah newspaper didn't have an article about it because it was something new and interesting and was supposed to improve the quality of everyday life. And it was becoming a major contributor to the local economy. Ordinary people were able to find employment, and word spread fast of the fair treatment of workers. The Savannah paper sent people out to see Henry often to ask about the operation. Henry was always busy but took the time because he realized that it was free promotion, and requests for ice increased every week. So, in the next year, the ice business grew in Savannah and Beaufort and began in Charleston, quicker than Henry and John had expected. And money coming in began to catch up with money going out, as iceboxes and icehouses were sold and delivered and weekly and monthly ice was delivered to them. Every week a few more workers were hired, and soon there were several wagonloads of workers arriving every morning. Jason's shop was the busiest because orders were coming from all over for iceboxes and small icehouses, and the demand for ice continued to rise. Ships were getting paid for something they had discarded in the past. Orders for iceboxes and small icehouses were scheduled for a year out.

Henry had worried about getting enough workers but working-class whites had limited opportunity because of the lower cost of slave labor. Most barely survived on small pieces of land, growing what they could. Many made "shine" and were involved in smuggling on the river. Many people worried that, if the white working class mixed with free blacks and slaves, they could unite and be a powerful and difficult force to deal with. False news was often spread to stir up dislike between them, but many were happy to have the work and were surprised at the fair treatment they received from the Milam's. About a third of the workers were fresh immigrants, just off the boat and eager and appreciative of the work and fair treatment. Many of them brought advanced skills and enhanced the work force.

After six months Mary and Daniel were still at the Milam's. Mary continued her note taking, and Maggie became her best friend. Henry arranged for some help for Ellie so Maggie could be with Mary. To Mary and Alice's surprise, Maggie said that she and Izak had talked before he had gone off to Tybee, and that if Maggie was sent to the new school in Philadelphia and manumitted, he would want to do the same. This was a big surprise because Izak had just started learning to be a boatman and had told everyone how much he liked it. The conversations that Mary had with Maggie and Alice were the most enlightening that Mary had ever experienced. There was nothing that they could not talk about together. She came to understand, even more, how special Alice was and was in awe at the clarity of her words and understanding and how she shared that understanding in the most pleasant way. Alice reminded her of Ayana. They both had a luminous way that spoke to the commonality of the heart and not the differences of the mind. Mary understood that what she got from them both was something that couldn't be learned from books or in a school. It went from person to person, and she was grateful, and it made a big difference in her writing from then on. She took notes from everybody over the months that she was there. She spent a couple of days talking to Walter's lawyer friends Hulbert and Sidney. They told her stories about themselves and Walter way back when they were children together in England. Walters's families were light keepers like her family. They didn't live on an island but were somewhat isolated on a piece of rocky land jutting out into the ocean. They were also a bit isolated from most because of their devout Quaker beliefs and had spoken out publicly and fervently against their country's participation in the slave trade, unlike the more popular churches.

For Mary the most amazing and informative times were when she asked Alice about her talks with all the people of the Milam place. She had made it her mission to inform them about the world around them and more importantly to introduce them to themselves, just as she had done with Johnny. Since the big meeting, she revisited everyone to explain that the door was open for any that wanted out. This had always been the case, but now there was a way that they could be escorted to Philadelphia, man-umitted, educated if they wished, and supported financially and escorted back to Georgia if they wanted. And the yearly fee required by the state would be paid for them until they could pay it themselves from income they could receive from their work for the Milam's or at the Milam Ice Company. Mary gained an understanding of how it was impossible for a person that was free all their life to understand what it was like for a person that was brought into the world belonging to someone else and missing the fundamental understanding of their own self. Alice said it was difficult for the first people that were brought to the Milam place because they were born in slavery, but the younger ones, born there, had more of a sense of self, and she just talked to them mostly about how things were on the outside. She said she wasn't sure what would happen in the coming years. Most on the Milam place were older, and there were only a few younger people. The majority of the work on the place was still to support itself, but the work had gotten more efficient and easier and leisure time increased.

Talking with Alice caused Mary to think of how similar things were with Alice and the people of the Milam place and Ayana and her people on the Indian islands. Not counting the Milam's themselves, the number of the two groups was about the same. The Indians were isolated as they had been for hundreds of years, and their numbers had decreased. Now they were few and were backed up to the last of their islands, and there were no more islands to back up on. In a way the Milam place was also like an island, with the world changing around them threatening their isolation and way of life. The abolition movement against slavery had grown in the north, but in the south people had embraced slavery more, and it was an integral institution of society. The Indians had Ayana, and the Milam people had Alice, and the Milam's had committed themselves to also help Ayana and her people. Mary was glad to have visited Ayana before coming to Savannah because it helped her understand that change was coming for both groups. She didn't know what those changes were but was glad to be documenting and learning what she could, to better enable her to help if need be.

Things were not like Mary had imagined about leaving Tybee. She thought she would be following Martin everywhere, but she wasn't. They were not any less in love, but they both had urgency about what they were doing, in preparation for later times. It was like they were at college, but they weren't away somewhere.

Things changed for Martin too. He began his boating career with Ashley and Ken before Mary returned to Tybee. Ben had said his back was getting worse and it was time for him to quit. Martha was a little shocked but had reconciled it all months before, and Walter would have agreed a year earlier if it had come up. To say that Martin was pleased would be an understatement. He had been counting the weeks and thought he was still months out from starting. Then, out of the blue, Captain Ben said he would go on one more trip and be back in about a week and he would retire. From then on Captain Ben's sharpie became a familiar sight moored out by the Milam Ice Company. It was a time of much learning for Martin, in boating and seamanship and about life from Ashley and Ken. The trips to Darien with sawmill equipment were less, but the trips with ice to Lands' End on Saint Helena Island and to Richard Wilcox's icehouse in Beaufort were frequent as demand increased for ice and iceboxes. On most trips the sharpie would be loaded with eight tons of ice and two or three iceboxes lashed down on the deck. They would make one stop at Lands' End on Saint Helena, and twenty wagons from the different plantations would meet them for ice or an icebox. Then they would deliver the rest to Richard Wilcox in Beaufort. Richard was selling more than they could deliver, and Henry began sending a large, insulated wagons loaded full of ice to Beaufort every week, so the sharpie could deliver to the places that only a boat could get to.

There was less time for Martin to be at home between trips than he had expected, unless there was bad weather, and much of that time was spent waiting at the Lazaretto landing at Tybee. They began to get more customers south of Savannah and go out in the ocean or take the inland waterways south to some of the large islands on the Georgia coast and deliver ice. The inland route was a lot different kind of sailing than simply going out into the Atlantic and heading north or south. Martin liked it. It required more detailed knowledge of the rivers and islands and much more attention to tides and the shallow areas. The big centerboard would stay up but often they would bump the bottom and sometimes run aground. Then they would have to wait for the tide to come up to continue and sometimes carry and anchor and line out in the skiff and pull themselves off with the windless. Nights were spent at anchor, except during clear weather and a full moon with high tide. This was Martin's favorite time to sail. On a high tide with a full moon and ample wind in flat water it was perfect, especially with a tide and the wind behind them. Often, in a good blow, the wind could be heard pounding the surf on the ocean side of the barrier islands, but on the lee side of the islands the water was mostly flat but could be choppy. The tall sails caught the wind above the riverbanks and marsh, and the big boat went fast, and the riverbank seemed to go by as fast as a horse galloping. Early on, Martin began making notes to go along with his navigation charts of the inland waterways. They included sand and mud bar locations and something else that was important. The ebb and flow tidal direction of the rivers on the back sides of the barrier islands come from and go to the sounds nearest them. A vessel can be drifting with the incoming tide and come to a place where the current slows and then starts coming in from the opposite direction from the next sound. Martin noted these locations on his charts. Moving north and south on these inland waterways could be done without any sails, by simply lowering or raising an anchor, taking advantage of the tidal direction, which changed every six hours, and the wind became a bonus when it was favorable.

The new boat was ordered from Boston but there were questions to be answered about the purchase and operation of another boat. What Henry had to say surprised Ashley and Ken. He told them that the boat would be theirs but the Milam Ice Company would pay for it, and they could pay it back from a portion of each trip. As usual, Henry was a step ahead and planned it out beforehand. He asked them when Martin could be ready to captain the new boat, and Martin was more surprised than Ashley and Ken. Ken said that he was already a capable captain on the inland waterways but still had some learning to sail outside and coming and going in and out the sounds. Henry said that he wanted Martin ready as soon as possible, and since he was paid by Ashley and Ken, they would say when he was ready to take a boat on his own. He said that they would need to be in charge of getting the new boat brought back. Henry said he would always be there to help them with problems and grow their shipping business and that he and his family were forever in debt to them for what they had done for them concerning Alice and their family in South Carolina. He said that final decisions were entirely theirs to make about their business, but to get them going there were several things he had looked into on their behalf. Ken and Ashley were taken aback with all that Henry had been saying, and Henry went on to explain that the engineer, Thomas, and he and John had mapped out the ice business for the next couple years, and if they could rise to the occasion, they could share in the business and prosperity. He said there were several leads that he wanted to pass on. He said that they had come on some good quality workers with various skills in the construction of the buildings and wagons and iceboxes for Jason. They had learned their skills in their home countries. Carpenters, masons, and metal smiths were highly advanced in their trades. A number of the carpenters were also shipwrights and sailors. He said they would be needing some extra hands with the extra boat, and could make inquiries through John, who has been issuing the pay to the workers. They confide in him about available workers and their skills. Henry went on to say that Richard Wilcox over in Beaufort, who they knew well from all the deliveries to and from his icehouse, had told him about something that didn't concern Milam Ice but may be of profit to them. He said his only concern was that it might interfere with their work with the Milam's, but Henry said he trusted that they could expand and still be accommodating.

Richard has been shipping, over land, an ever-increasing amount of yaupon tea to cities up north. The transportation over land was very difficult and expensive from South Carolina to Philadelphia, but from there to New York and Boston it was easier because they have roads that are maintained and some that are even paved. He has a customer that will store and distribute the tea from Philadelphia throughout the cities further north, and he thinks that he will soon have enough business in it to warrant a boat load to Philadelphia, so it will be up to y'all to decide to pursue that if you like. Ken said that they made several trips to Norfolk on the Chesapeake Bay every year and Philadelphia was up the Delaware Bay, which was the next bay up from the Chesapeake. Ashley thanked Henry and said they would talk to him about that on the next delivery to Beaufort. Now, Henry said, the last thing will be a surprise. Ashley said they were well surprised already, and Ken nodded in agreement. He went on to say that, with their expansion into a second distribution point near Charleston in the coming year, if they were interested, there would be a need for a couple more boats and crews or one particular kind of boat and crew. They didn't understand the last part of Henry's statement. Much of the conversation had been concerning Ashley and Ken and not directly having to do with Martin, and he had not been very attentive, but he perked up when Henry said the words, "a particular boat." Henry said that Thomas had suggested that the next boat they get might should be a steam-powered riverboat. He said it would be able to travel the inland waterways regardless of tides and winds and could carry ten times what the sharpie could carry with the same shallow draft and make more deliveries with one big crew than ten sail-powered boats and crews. Ashley and Ken had been focused only on their trips and teaching Martin and on the new sharpie to be built in Boston, and all this vision and planning by Henry was way beyond their thoughts and imagination. Martin startled them by saying he would start right away to learn about steam power and asked where he could learn, and Henry said to ask Thomas who had been telling him about the possibility. Henry said that there were three fundamental things about the ice business: receiving, cold storage, and delivery. He wanted them to take charge of the delivery and considered his time working and planning with them very important, and if they were up for the task, there was a large opportunity for them, but they would have to grow their capacity far beyond what it was now. It was a bit too much information for Ashley and Ken to take in, and Henry said for them to mull it over. He said that he would ask Thomas to check on the new boat and ask that it be completed as soon as possible and to let them know about a completion date so they could make plans to pick it up and bring it back.

Henry said he almost forgot something, and Ken and Ashley braced themselves for another surprise. Henry saw their look and said it was only a small detail that they would need to follow up on if they were interested. He said that Richard Wilcox had made this suggestion when he was discussing the possibility of hauling a load of yaupon up north. He didn't want his ice deliveries delayed then and while they were gone to pick up the new boat whenever it was done. He suggested that a barge could be used to deliver his ice then drift over to Saint Helena afterwards and unload the rest to the plantation owners. Richard told him that there was a man that used to haul cotton from Saint Helena Island on a barge and he could drift to Savannah in as little as eight days. Anyhow, Henry said that the Milam barge was theirs for the asking. It was seldom used and unused boats or barges deteriorate more quickly.

While Martin had been listening to all Henry was telling Ashley and Ken, he admired Henry's ability to enrich others while accomplishing his own goals. He had seen it happen over and over. Henry told them to talk things over and let him know. He said that he was not a sailor or any kind of boater, but from what Thomas was saying about a steam-engine powered river boat and what it could do, and considering how their orders for ice and iceboxes and ice houses was growing every month, Milam Ice Company would back them up on ordering a small steamship as soon as possible. Henry thanked them and said he had somewhere to go and hoped to hear back from them soon.

Ashley, Ken, and Martin left Henry's office, and they were stunned, even more than when Captain Ben had told them he was retiring and letting them take over the business. All Martin could think about was a steamship. They walked down to the boathouse and sat to talk about all that Henry had told them. Ken said that ever since Ben had handed things over to them he felt like they had been continually moving with the tide and wind behind them wherever they went. Ashley said that was a good way to put it. Another way is that we are riding the wake of the Milam Ice Business. Martin said that they weren't on a free ride because of what Henry said about delivery of ice being one third of the business. This made both Ashley and Ken feel better because it showed the great value and importance of what they were doing. Ashley said it would seem foolish not to go with the wind and tide and wake while they had it because it might not always be there. If Ken agreed and Martin was willing to help, he was all in to give it a go. Ken said he was too with one exception and that was he didn't want Martin to work for them but rather to be a partner in it all. Martin said he didn't care how things worked, he just wanted to get the new steam engine river boat ordered. He said he would get with Thomas to find out where to learn about steam power. He said nobody enjoyed sailing more than him, but he knew engine-powered boats were the new thing. He had seen more and more ships coming into Savannah with full sail rigging but also a steam engine. He mentioned that it was the steamship Savannah that Mallie and his owner had come to Savannah for, and he remembered that Captain Ben and his father were interested enough to go see it while it was at the dock. Ken said he and Ashley had a lot to do and said the most important thing was to get some deck hands and then get the barge set up with an icehouse on it to keep Richard Wilcox and his customers supplied. Ashley said that they could actually start loading ice directly onto the barge from ships if it had an icehouse built on it. Ken said that would free up the sharpie for their other deliveries, but he was concerned about the month or so it would take them to catch a ship up to Boston and sail the new sharpie back. Martin said that if they could get an experienced three-man crew for the sharpie, they might ask Captain Ben to come back for a month or so while they were gone. He said he had come to learn that Ben's back had not hurt as much as he had let on, but it had been a plan between him and Walter to get him on board sooner. Both Ashley and Ken liked that idea a lot because they missed Ben and wanted him to know about all the progress and to share in the business and prosperity if he wanted to. So, they decided to tell Henry that the three of them agreed to do what it would take to meet all the delivery needs. They would set a date to go get the new sharpie, turn the barge into an ice barge with an icehouse and crew accommodations, ask Captain Ben to come back for at least a month while they went to pick up the new boat, hire and train more crew for Ben, and learn more about a steamboat.

In the meantime, Mary and Daniel had finally returned to Tybee. Mary wanted to, even more than before, spend time with Ayana, and she had Daniel take her over to the islands often. It took her more days with Ayana than she had planned, but it was some of the most interesting of all her notes. After filling two of her notebooks, she read it back to Ayana, and there were only a few things to change. Ayana was more than relieved about it, and she gave Mary a beadwork piece like she had given Martin and carefully explained to her why she liked what Mary had done for her and her people. They were both brought to tears as Ayana said that Mary's notes might be all that was left of thousands of her people that had thrived on the Georgia coastal islands from the Savannah River south to the Altamaha River. She said they might all die there, or join with the Ogeechee people, or make the long trip to the far end of Florida to mix with all the different people that had gone there for refuge. She told Mary how thankful she was for what she was doing.

It would take Mary a year to finish her notes and two large crock pots to hold the thirty notebooks she filled. She didn't know how long it would be until she could weave it all into one story that could be safely revealed, but she wasn't worried about how long it might be. It had been an intense lesson for her of all the history and in how to combine the facts and her feelings so that she would be able to come back later and complete it. Things would have to change in the South before her story
could be revealed, and she didn't know how many years that would take. She continued to record the things going on at the lighthouse and what was happening at the Milam place that Walter and Martha would tell her about on their visits. Also, what Martin had to say about their trips and their growing fleet of boats, and an occasional story from the Captain Jones or one of the pilot crews. With the big part of her writing project done, she had time on her hands and helped Margo and began a separate notebook of her mother's recipes and cooking skills. She also got to spend more time with Martin, sometimes an afternoon and night if he spent the night with them, and sometimes a few days if the weather was bad, when they would have to wait at Lazaretto to leave.

Daniel had not thought about things much, but nothing about his trip to Savannah had changed his mind about continuing on after his father and being a light keeper. He had spent a lot of time with Martin until he started going off with Ashley and Ken. He had worked some with Jacob and James and Jehu on construction and decided that for any reason he could not be a lightkeeper, he would learn the building trade. He also had fished with James a lot but it was difficult to understand his strong

Geechee dialect, but there was not a lot to say about fishing. For James his experience with Daniel had been particularly good because it helped him become less shy. With his fishing skills, he was able to teach Daniel and others because he was always being asked for fresh fish, and that was another opportunity for him to speak up. Julia, John, and Mable saw him less and were pleased that he had come out of his shell and opened up and bloomed somewhat. Before any of those things helped him, it was Jehu who had first helped him adjust to his new home.

Alice was as usual, along with being a new mother, always talking with everyone on the place. From early on she had become the matriarch of the whole place, including the Milam's to a large degree, and her role had gotten even more important since Walter had stepped aside. She hadn't appointed herself or even considered herself as such, but she had grown into the position by her clarity and understanding. She was at first Walter and Martha's daughter and sister to Henry and Martin and even mother to Martin, and something of a daughter to Jacob and Ellie. Walter had left the operation of the place to Henry, but the real leadership came from Alice, and Henry went to her often about all issues other than business. One problem that Henry had asked Alice about was Jacob still being a property of the Milam's and how he had been advised by Sidney and his partner to keep the Milam place separate from the new ice business. He had done that with the exception of Jacob. He thought the way to settle that would be to manumit Jacob there in Savannah and then pay him as a worker if he was willing. But as they had learned, Jacob would be required to leave the state for a year, and he wouldn't ask Jacob to do such a thing. He wanted to ask Alice what she would think of her, Johnny, and their baby, as well as Jacob and his family and Izak, all going together to Philadelphia to be legally manumitted. He said they could go and come back, with no one outside of the Milam place knowing about it; and from what he understood, Maggie would probably want to stay for school for a year or more. Alice said that would please Walter more than anything she could think of, but it was a tall order. Henry said he had been thinking about it for a while, and he knew that it was most important that they all be in agreement. He said that the greatest difficulty was not the manumitting process because the Quakers in Philadelphia had a tried and true system that was quick and legal. They would actually buy the whole group and manumit them there in Philadelphia in a matter of days; the manumitted folks would be free to go as they pleased with proof of their free status on a court document. He said the biggest problem that he foresaw would be getting them all there and back securely and safely. Overland travel could take five or six weeks and no inns would take people of color. That would mean that there would be a lot of camping, where they would be vulnerable to local militias, slavers, and outlaws. In addition to all the gear needed, they would also need a couple armed guards and addition food and supplies for them.

However, Henry said that there might be another possibility. He explained that he had recently told Ashley and Ken that Richard Wilcox was interested in them hauling a boatload of yaupon tea to Philadelphia. Ken had said they had made regular trips to Norfolk, Virginia, and Philadelphia was just a couple days sail further. It dawned on Henry that he could hire Ashley and Ken to transport a number of people there and back to be manumitted. He hadn't said anything about it to Ashley and Ken because he wanted to talk with her first. Alice smiled and Henry asked what her smile was about. Alice said she felt gratitude mixed with a little bit of humor. Gratitude for Ashley and Ken helping again, and amusement at how Ellie would react if she were asked to face certain death in an ocean-bound boat. Henry said gratitude and humor was a pleasing combination of feelings. Alice said again that if all that happened, it would please Walter the most because it had been his hope for so long. and if Jacob and his family went along with it, others might follow. For herself, Johnny, and the baby, the answer was yes. She said she could see that over time a few people a year could go if they wanted without hindering the operation of things. Henry thanked her and said he would wait to talk with Ashley and Ken until after she had spoken with Jacob and Ellie. She added that if it were up to Thomas, she would know the answer, because he had been begging Martin to take him out on a boat but Ellie had forbidden it. Martin was like an older brother or uncle to Thomas, and he always wanted to go with him. Also, she was certain that Maggie would want to go and that would probably include Izak.

Ashley, Ken, and Martin were not long in getting back with Henry to let him know that they were willing to rise to the task of providing the Milam Ice Company with all of their delivery needs. They said that there was one thing they wanted to change about his recommendations and that was about Martin's involvement. They wanted to make him a full partner instead of a hired captain, and Henry said that was their business. Martin said again that it didn't matter to him how things were set up, he just wanted a steam-powered riverboat and told Henry how he had already talked to Thomas a lot about it all. He said that Thomas had mentioned something more than Henry had talked about. He said that in the not-too-distant future steam locomotives and railways would take over as the most practical way to transport goods between the northern and southern states, but that the coastal islands would always need to be serviced by boat.

He also told of a man named John Stevens, a prolific inventor of steam locomotive engines for railways and steam engine riverboats and screw propellers for boats. He said he currently operated a steam-engine-driven ferryboat service from Hoboken, New Jersey, to New York City. Martin said that there were lots of accidents with steam engines but that Thomas said that most were caused by inexperience or trying to gain more speed by over-firing the boilers. He suggested that he, Ashley, and Ken take a trip to New Jersey to see John Stevens and his operation. Martin had told Thomas that they were making a trip to Boston to pick up the new sharpie and sail it back. Thomas had suggested that they stop by Hoboken on the way back, and he mentioned that there were several steamboat operations on the Hudson River between New York City and Albany. Martin's enthusiasm was almost overwhelming, and Henry saw that Martin was on a mission and that there would soon be changes and new beginnings.

Ken told Henry that they had spoken to Richard Wilcox about the things Henry had mentioned. He liked the idea of the barge because it would be more practical and his ice sales were increasing every month and he was concerned that he may not get enough ice to fill his orders. He also liked that there would be more room on the barge so he could send his hardware orders over with the ice.

Ken said that they had met with John about finding deck hands and he put the word out that they would need six experienced sailors and he already had some inquiries. Also, they had spoken to Captain Ben and he said he would be glad to come out of retirement for a while to run the sharpie for them to be able to go to Boston and sail the new boat back, then again, while they made the trip to deliver the yaupon to Philadelphia. Henry said that was all great and especially that Captain Ben would help out because there might be some additional freight on the trip to Philadelphia that might add a few days that he would know more about later. They assured Henry that with the new barge in continual operation and the new sharpie and additional crewmen, and Captain Ben helping out, all the deliveries could still be completed while they were gone. Henry added that Thomas had heard back from the boat builder and the new boat would be ready in just two more months. Ashley said that would give them time to get the barge outfitted and a crew set up. Henry added that it wasn't always practical, but while they were gone, he could make some of their regular deliveries over land by wagon if it was needed to help keep up. Martin said he would go ahead and make inquiries about visiting Mr. Stevens in New Jersey. Henry added that he would ask his father to inquire about a ship for them to travel to Boston to pick up the sharpie. Normally the idea of an outside passage on a ship to Boston would have been a huge deal to Martin, but he was consumed with the whole steamboat ordeal and couldn't think of much else.

Alice picked a good time and sat with Jacob, Ellie, and Maggie to talk about the manumission process and all it would take to do it, She explained the difficulties of doing it in Savannah for many reasons including having to then leave the state for a year. She explained how it would be possible in Philadelphia and that they could travel there on the boat with Ashley, Ken, and Martin. Ellie said what would be the use in getting manumitted if they were all swallowed up by the sea which she was sure would happen. Jacob, having had years of boating on the river, was worried about his whole family going outside in the ocean, but he said he trusted Ashley, Ken, and Martin and would do whatever it took. He said it wouldn't make any difference in how they lived but he knew that it was something that Walter had always wanted and he would go along with it all if Ellie would. Alice explained the hazards of them traveling over land, and Ellie said they would probably die either way and she reckoned that the ocean might be a better way to die than from slavers and their dogs. Alice added that it would be best not to talk about what was happening until they got back and, when the time came to go, they could say that they were going to Tybee for a few weeks. She said they were in fact going to Tybee on their way, so it was partly true. She said that it would be good to tell everyone about it all when they got back because she hoped that more on the place would want to go and be manumitted. Alice said that a person couldn't be manumitted without being physically present in the court before a judge. She told them that Walter, Henry, and herself wanted everyone on the place to be prepared for anything that could happen in the years ahead. The yearly agreement with the U. S. government that sustained their place was not likely to change, but it was best to be prepared for anything. Jacob said he knew about how things could change. Ellie looked at Maggie and asked her if she was sure about going and staying way off somewhere for school. Maggie said she was but didn't like that she caused so much work and trouble. Alice quickly told her that all this was not just for her. She just happened to be the first, but all the trouble and bother was for the safety, security, and betterment of everyone on the Milam place. Maggie asked if Thomas, who was outside, would be going, and before Alice could answer, Ellie said he certainly was. Alice said that Thomas would need to be manumitted too. Jacob added that Thomas would go anywhere his big brother Martin went, with no questions asked. He has already decided that he would be a waterman, not a basic Milam boatman, but a crewman with Martin and then a captain. Alice felt a swell of gratitude on hearing that Thomas had aspirations because it meant that things, at least there, were going as they should. Being born and raised with a sense of self allowed Thomas to have aspirations and goals. Maggie said she had one question about the rule of a slave having to leave the state for a year after being manumitted and the annual fee afterwards. Alice said that was a good question, then explained that Georgia and South Carolina had those laws but Philadelphia didn't, thanks to the Quakers.

Captain Ben showed up sooner than was expected, and Ashley and Ken were glad to see him. They told him some of the things that had happened since he had left, about all that Henry was doing, and about the steam engine powered river boat that they would probably have in a year or so. He said that, after he and Walter had visited the steamship "Savannah" some years ago when it was in town, he knew that it was something that would eventually take over shipping. He asked about Martin, and they said he was with Thomas, the engineer from Boston, looking at the steam engine in the new sawmill upstream from Savannah. Ken said all he could talk or think about was steam engines now and that Thomas had ordered him some books about steam power. He said Thomas was planning for them to go see some steamboat operations in New Jersey and New York when they made the trip to Boston to pick up the new sharpie. Ashley said he wouldn't be surprised if Martin found a way to have them a steam-engine riverboat in less than a year, and at the rate of the growing ice deliveries, they would need it. The Captain told them that he was staying up on the hill at the usual place and for them to let him know when they wanted him. Ashley said they had hired six new deck hands that were supposed to be experienced sailors and explained how they came about them through John. Three were to be permanently on the barge, and three were to go with him so he wouldn't have to lift or strain on anything. He went on to say that he and Ken were planning to take three of them on a short trip to Daricn to see how competent they were before leaving them with the Captain. The Captain said that all sounded good and he was going next to visit with Walter and Martha.

Ashley and Ken had their hands full. Martin wasn't around to help much because he was studying steam engines every day. They were glad of it because they could see that it was what they needed after the talk with Henry. Ken set to work on remodeling the barge with three of the new crewmen. They had been sailors and shipwrights and needed very little instruction, and Ken drew on a board what needed to be built and pointed to the stack of lumber. They were to build a flat deck to cover the whole barge and then an enclosure for living accommodations and an icehouse with ramp and a boom for loading and unloading. Jacob had come and measured for the icehouse and took the measurements for Jason to build the panels. Jason had an efficient production operation building icehouse components by now and plenty of skilled men to do the work. He even built long insulated panels that could be joined to form the roof. Within a week he delivered all the panels to the barge, and his men taught the new barge crew all about putting the panels together. Ken brought roofing tar and paper to cover the roof deck and paint for the whole exterior and supplies to finish the interior.

Leaving the barge crew with more than a week's work, Ken and Ashley set out for a trip south to deliver ice to a dozen locations on the water south of Savannah. It was also a training run for the three new crewmen, so Ken and Ashley could confidently have them crew for Captain Ben. Not being able to speak their European language was not a problem because sailing a boat worked about the same way in any country, and they were in fact experienced and more than willing to do the job properly. They even taught Ashley and Ken a few things.

They had dropped Martin off at Tybee with several books on steam driven boats and planned on stopping to pick him up on the way back. A pilot on the beach saw them coming back and sent a crewman up to tell the Dyers, and Daniel and Martin took the wagon down to the landing and waited as the sharpie entered Lazaretto creek. All five loaded into the sharpie skiff and made their way slowly over to the ramp and piled out. Daniel told Ken and Ashley that they were expected to stay with them tonight, and for the next fifteen minutes, the three of them tried to explain to the three European immigrants that Ken and Ashley were staying at the lighthouse and would be back to leave for Savannah in the morning. They left for the lighthouse, not sure of what the men had understood but hopeful they would be all right. Ken said they had everything they needed and he didn't expect they would go anywhere.

Ever since Ashley and Ken had gone to get Prissy and buy Alice's family on Saint Helena from their dreadful owner, they were treated like special family members by the Dyers and Milam's. They hadn't been there long before Mary had her notebook out and was asking them to tell her all about what had been going on with them and Martin and the Milam Ice Company. Ken asked her if Martin had told her that he was an equal share with them in their shipping business. She said he hadn't told her anything about that and all he talked about was steam river boats and all. Ashley said when he got his mind on something it was hard to steer him in a different direction. Charles was listening and said he had a daughter that was that way and made them laugh. They told Mary about the barge and Ben coming out of retirement to help them a few months and their two long big trips coming up to Boston and Philadelphia. She said Martin told her about the Boston trip but what was the Philadelphia trip about and Ashley told her they were delivering a load of yaupon. Mary heard that and asked who in the world would buy that much yaupon and they told her what all Richard Wilcox told about it. They asked Charles what was new, and he said the most exciting thing was some new talk of a small light-house to be built on Cockspur Island to mark the south channel entrance. He thought it couldn't be done soon enough, and talk was still going on about the huge fort on Cockspur and the small fort down between them and the ocean. Martha said that Captain Jones was getting quite feeble and one of the pilots said that the only thing keeping him alive was looking forward to Walter's regular visits. She said that, if a crew member is not available to stay with him when they all return to Savannah, they send word and Daniel goes down to stay with him for the night but most of the time a crewman is there.

Martha had prepared another special supper, and after some rum and yaupon everyone served themselves. Ashley said every meal there was like a holiday meal. After supper and a little conversation, it was time for bed, and Margo asked Daniel to take Ashley and Ken out to the little house where she and Charles had put two cots with blankets. When he came back, he went up to his loft area where Martin was looking at one of his steam engine books. He showed Daniel the mechanical drawings of a small steam engine and told him how it worked. Daniel was interested but not as much as Martin, and after listening to Martin talk about it for just a few minutes, he got drowsy and went to sleep with Martin still studying the book by candlelight.

The next morning Martin heard the knocking on the floor and got up and roused Daniel a little and went downstairs. Ashley and Ken were already with Charles and Margo, having hot drinks. When Margo saw Martin, she started cooking the eggs and knocked on the ceiling again to get Daniel up. She listened before knocking some more and heard the ceiling boards creak as Daniel stood up, then went back to her eggs and in just a few minutes had a dozen on a platter set on the table with a big pot of grits and lard and biscuits and plum preserves. Then she set the biggest cup she had, full of dark black coffee, on the table for a sleepy-headed Daniel to drink. Mary got up and came in and sat by Martin at the table. Daniel finished his coffee and told Mary that she should bring her notebook because the three new sharpie crew might have some interesting stories. He winked at Ashley while saying it. Mary knew how Daniel's voice tone changed when he was saying something untrue or a joke. She wondered what it could be this time, but she always took her notebook with her anyhow. Daniel finished up and went out to rig the wagon and brought it around to the house where Ashley, Ken, Martin, and Mary were waiting to go. Margo handed a basket of biscuits to Ken for the new crewmen and hugged the three of them, and Charles said for them to come back soon.

When they got to the landing, one of the crew was waiting with the skiff and a big smile and repeated the word "Da" over and over. Ken commented that they must have understood more than it appeared the afternoon before. Ashley said they figured that we probably would leave when the tide started in toward Savannah and they had watched it go out and guessed that Ken and Ashley would be back to go as the tide started in. Ken handed him the basket of biscuits and pulled back the cloth covering them. They were still warm and smelled good, and Ken pointed his finger at him and then out to the sharpie, and he understood the biscuits were for them and repeated the same word again, "Da." It reminded Martin of the word that the Indians spoke when he first met them and said "Da" back. Mary told Martin that she understood now what Daniel was joking about at breakfast, and Daniel smiled. Martin told Mary that he wished she was going with him. She said she did too, and he said she could go with him when he got the new steamboat. Mary asked when that would be, and he said maybe a year and maybe less. She said she would be ready when the time came and kissed Martin. They loaded up, and the new crewman rowed them out to the sharpie. The crewmen were happy and excited and repeated the same word "Da!" over and over. Martin, Ashley, and Ken all said it back, and Ashley and Martin gestured at the basket of biscuits. The one crewman opened it up and handed the other two a big biscuit with bacon, lard and plum preserves. They said that same word again and ate the biscuits and every few minutes said "Da," and Martin said it back.

When the snacks were finished, Martin gestured toward Savannah. The new crew went to work, and Ashley and Ken sat back to let them do everything and were pleased at how they smoothly got the anchors up and the sails set and the sharpie under way and were soon in the south channel headed home. There was barely enough wind out of the southeast to bother with the sails, but occasionally a gust would come and power them ahead of the speed of the current. Ashley and Ken went to take a nap, leaving Martin to watch over things, but there wasn't much to watch over with the gentle wind and current, and the new crewmen attending to everything with much enthusiasm. The sharpie drifted over close to the bank and a mud bar, and Martin didn't say anything and just waited to see if the they noticed and what they would do. One said something to the others and pointed out to the mud bar, and two of them jumped down into the pulling boat, attached a line to the sharpie bow, and pulled it back into the deeper part of the river. When they came back aboard, Martin said

"Da" and they laughed. Other than keeping the sharpie in the channel, the trip was uneventful. Ken and Ashley stayed asleep, and Martin was able to study his steam engine book. After about five hours, they were at the Wilmington River, and two of the new crew got in the pulling boat again and guided the sharpie into the river and over to the west bank. They half drifted and half sailed, down to and in front of the boathouse, on the last of the incoming tide. Ashley and Ken had gotten up, and Ken smiled and said that was the easiest trip back he had ever had. The new men set the anchors and stowed the sails like they had been doing it for years. Martin said that Ben was going to like them.

It was always nice to arrive back home after a trip on the water, no matter how short or routine. They had all gotten onto the skiff and slowly made their way to the bank. Martin motioned for the new men to follow him, and they walked up to the boathouse where several of the boathouse men were sitting outside. He told them that these were the new sharpie crew that would be working with Captain Ben. He said they spoke a foreign language and the only word of it he knew was "Da" and that seemed to mean a lot of good things. He told them that he was going to get the wagon and come back to take them home to Savannah. Martin gestured with his arm out then brought it back and pointed it down, hoping that they understood that he was going but would be back there. He said "Da" and they said "Da" back, and he left.

When Martin got back, Ashley, Ken, and the new crew were back out on the boat doing some cleaning and making things ready for the next trip. They saw him and came over in the skiff. After they had dragged the skiff high up on the bank, they all loaded up on the wagon. Ken asked if they could stop by the Milam Ice place to see how the work was coming on the barge, and Martin said he was thinking the same thing. When they got to where the new icehouse was, they saw the barge and couldn't believe how much work had been done. Jason must have put all his crews together to make the panels so fast because they were all set. And the outside cypress boards were on, and the roof was framed and decked and the whole outside was painted grey. The three men were up on the roof, mopping hot tar onto the last section of tarred paper that had been rolled down over the roof decking. When they saw the wagon and their friends, they slopped on the last bit of tar and came down the ladder and started a lot of excited jabbering in their language. All Martin could understand of it was a lot of "Das" said after about everything, but he was able to feel the excitement they had about what each other had been doing and seeing. Martin asked Ken to give him a list of the additional building materials and he would get them there in the morning. Ashley said he would go in the morning to get a wood cook stove, stove pipe, water barrel, and wash tub. Ken said he would come back with the same crew tomorrow and finish up in a couple days, and if they were lucky, a freighter might be in, and they could load twenty tons of ice from it directly into the barge icehouse. Martin said the new sharpie should be done soon after the first barge trip to Beaufort and hopefully his father was able to get them on a ship to Boston about then. Ashley said that he could make a couple more deliveries with the new crew in the next three weeks, while Ken was gone, before handing things over to Captain Ben.

A freighter did come in to the Milam Ice Company, and the barge was loaded with a little over twenty tons of ice. The barge went from floating high on the water to sinking low but still only drew slightly less than three feet. Ashley brought a wagonload of provisions and the equipment and a surprise that Jacob had suggested. It was a chicken coop and a dozen hens for fresh eggs.

There was no problem keeping their food from spoiling because Ken built temporary shelves inside the icehouse for their vegetables, meat, and dairy items. After they had everything, the day and tide came to leave. Jacob brought Thomas, and them and Martin and Ashley watched as two crewmen in the pulling boat slowly pulled the barge out into the Wilmington River current. Ken was up on the platform with the third man, and together they skulled the big tiller to help get the barge to the deepest water where the current moved faster. The chickens seemed to know something was going on because they made a fuss that made Thomas laugh. Jacob told him that the chickens didn't want to leave Georgia but they needn't worry because they would be back in a few weeks.

The first couple of days on the barge were very slow because they had to do a lot of pulling to get across the south and north channels of the Savannah river. And once into South Carolina, the creeks between there and the first big island, Daufuskie, were small and difficult to navigate. A few miles before Daufuskie, the creeks got wider and deeper and became rivers, and the current and drifting was faster. Ken brought along the chart that Martin had noted on where tide direction changed along the way, so they knew what to expect about where the current would shift. It was more work than Ken had expected. There was more to it than sitting all day, drifting with the tide. Two men were almost always needed in the pulling boat to keep the barge off the bank and positioned in the deepest part of the river where the current was faster. One man always needed to be on the long tiller to assist the pulling boat in guiding the barge. Most cycles were for six hours drifting at about two miles an hour and then anchoring for six hours when the current headed the other way. Then when it shifted direction again, they would lift the anchor and drift for six more hours. Sometimes at certain points along the way, the incoming or outgoing tide could change directions based on land and riverbed elevations, so the cycles of drift and anchor could be shorter or longer. If there was enough moon or starlight, they would drift at night. When anchored, there were several duties. One was to saw the big chunks of ice into manageable size pieces of about one hundred and fifty pounds each, and slide and secure them, ready to be unloaded at Beaufort. Another duty was to bail out the bilge every two hours. With the added weight of the ice, the barge sunk two feet lower down in the water and the water pressure was greater and water leaked in between the planks faster. There was some leisure time, however, for fishing, playing cards, or sleeping while anchored and waiting for the tide to change. Although the new crew was from a country in Europe that Ken had never heard of, and only spoke a few words of English, there was never a problem understanding the work because they were familiar with boats and had a willing attitude. Overall, Ken was bored but glad to be setting things up to accomplish their goals and knowing that Ashley and Martin were busy doing different things to accomplish those same goals.

The hardest part of the trip was pulling the barge across the Broad River. It was a mile and a half wide. In order to get straight across, Ken started on the last half of the incoming tide and, with both pulling boats, got to the middle of the river by high tide, having drifted two miles upriver, then while crossing the other half of the river on the first half of the outgoing tide, drifted back the two miles and he ended up directly across from where he started from. It took eight days to reach Beaufort and a day to unload all the ice except what was needed to go to Lands' End. They took an extra day for the crew to spend a little time on the hill, and Ken was invited to Richard Wilcox's home for the night and given a tour of Beaufort. The city was set up on a beautiful bluff of live oaks overlooking the river. Richard knew everybody and their businesses, even some of their domestic goings-on.

The next day they were set to leave on the outgoing tide at about noon. While they were waiting, Richard sent the biggest bateau Ken had ever seen, loaded with hardware items that were supposed to be delivered with the ice. He came along on the boat and told Ken he had been so taken up with all the ice that he had almost forgotten all these other things. If they had gotten away before he remembered, he would have made a lot of good customers upset because they would be waiting to pick them up at Lands' End with the ice. He said he would be sending a message over to Saint Helena via the mail boat today to let the people of the island know that they would be there in a couple of days and to plan on being at the landing to pick up their ice and hardware. Lastly, he handed Ken a basket of a pie and desserts from Helen.

They left Beaufort and after drifting on one outgoing tide and some pulling, they anchored for the night. On the second day, with a westerly breeze behind them, they caught two outgoing tide cycles and set the anchors and watched the full moon rise behind Saint Helena Island. Ken wrote in the logbook that they were twelve days into their trip and noted that if they would have had a simple lugsail, and drifted all night they could have saved a half day. He thought about how quickly they could have gotten there in a steam-powered riverboat. He figured it could have gotten to Beaufort in ten hours, then another two hours or so to Lands' End after spending a day in Beaufort, then another ten hours to get back to Savannah. He was glad to have Martin so enthusiastically finding out about all that. He thought to himself that he and Ashley would have been content to operate the sharpie until they got old and quit like Captain Ben but was glad that things had gone the way they had. One of the crewmen came out with a bottle. He said "slivovitz" and poured everyone a glass of the clear spirits and toasted to Ken and said "Da!" Ken had never tasted it, but it was clear and had a faint taste of plums and was strong. They had a supper of fresh fried fish, grits, and biscuits and went to bed.

The next morning, they were up early and having some fresh eggs from the chickens and leftover grits as the sun was coming over the treetops of Saint Helena Island from the ocean side, and they could see wagons coming to the landing to pick up their ice and supplies. There came two skiffs out to the barge and told Ken they were there to help pull the barge in to the landing. Ken was surprised but glad to have the help and figured that Richard Wilcox had something to do with that. He threw them lines, the crew winched the anchor up, and in a half hour they were bumping up against a log bulkhead with secured lines from each corner of the barge to log pilings. The loading ramp attached to the front of the barge was lowered, and one by one the wagons were backed up and six hundred to a thousand pounds of ice was slid out of the barge onto each wagon. Ken had each customer sign his name on a list so Richard would know how much each customer got to be added to their bill at his hardware store. This went on until twenty wagons were loaded and covered and each left quickly to get the ice back to their small icehouses that they had gotten from the Milam Ice Company. The hardware was last to be distributed, and Ken recognized a wagon waiting with a man and small boy. He walked across the ramp and over to the wagon, and they recognized him before he got there. It was Benjamin Chapman and little Thomas Chapman. They had come to pick up some hardware that Richard had sent. Ben Chapman got down, and Thomas jumped off and reached a hand in each pocket and held up the two things that Ken had carved and given him. A dolphin was in one hand and a turtle in the other. Ben Chapman laughed and told Ken that he took them with him everywhere. They chatted for a minute, and Ken asked if he had seen Willoughby lately and he said thankfully not. Ken said he was worried that for some reason he might be at the landing. Ben Chapman said that Willoughby's father, Colonel Willoughby, had built a shed for keeping things cold by piping his very cold artesian water and drenching a row of cypress wood louvers inside it. It wasn't as cold as one of their iceboxes but plenty cold enough to keep produce and meats fresh for a while. He had seen it once before the old man died and his son had taken over. He then said he hoped he and Ashley made out profitably on their slave purchases from Willoughby, and Ken assured him that it was a very worthwhile endeavor but not the kind he would want to do over again, and Ben Chapman shook his head in understanding. They shook hands, and Ken lifted Thomas back up on the wagon, and they left with their hardware.

Almost half of the ice had been unloaded at Richard's icehouse in Beaufort and the rest was unloaded at Lands' End leaving only couple hundred pounds of ice shards in the barge icehouse scattered around on the floor. They pushed them up into a pile in one corner so it would keep their things cool for the trip back. Ken made notes in his log and put the two pages with all the signatures in a sealed package and put it in the mail drop box at the landing to go to Richard Wilcox on the mailboat. Now, with the barge empty of over twenty tons that they left Savannah with, the barge was floating high and drawing less than a foot of water, so they were able, even with the tide having dropped some, to be pulled away from the landing. They would have to sit at anchor for a few hours though for the tide to finish going out and start back in to go their way. Ken wished he could tell the crew that they would get paid the same for the trip whether they got back early or late, but it didn't seem to matter to them, and they were simply motivated to get back as soon as possible.

The trip back took nine days. Even though the barge was not loaded down, there was a southeasterly blowing, and the wind against them slowed things up. Ken was happy because they had figured it would take about three weeks. The crew would have a week off before the trip would start again. He wasn't sure that he didn't need to accompany the crew one more time before letting them go alone. They were over-skilled for the task but didn't speak the language, and it might be better to go along with them one more time and teach them a few more words in English. He was successful in teaching them a little on the trip, and one of them picked it up fast. He had written down a list of English words and combined them into a few dozen simple sentences and given it to the one that caught on the fastest. He went down the list with him, saying each word and then the sentences. He didn't know how to ask them to study it, but the one crewman surprised him and said, "English now." Ken understood that to say he needed to speak English and would study the list. Overall, it had been a good first trip, and Ken noted in his log that they could have easily carried another four or five tons of ice.

When they returned, Ashley was on a delivery with the sharpie and the other three new crewmen. Ken sent his three crewmen home on one of the three wagons taking workers back to Savannah from the ice company at the end of the day. He decided that he would just stay on the barge until Ashley returned. It was moored out by the big icehouse where it could stay until the next trip to Beaufort. The accommodations were more than adequate, and unlike the sharpie, the barge had a large deck to move around on and a lot of standup room and a pile of sand on the deck for an outside cooking fire and was a comfortable place to live.

The morning after the barge got back, Ken was surprised to see Henry and Martin up on the riverbank. He quickly rowed over to them in the skiff, and both were curious about how the trip went. Ken told about the first and last couple days being the slowest, navigating the small creeks just into South Carolina, and about the trip across the Broad River. Martin remembered that river from their trip to Saint Helena, and he had been in it a few times since he had gone to work on the sharpie. Ken said it took a total of twenty-two days and he thought he should make one more trip with the new crew before he sent them on their own. He added that they were able to take over twenty tons of ice and delivered it all except a few hundred pounds and added that they could have taken five more tons and still only draw three feet. Henry said that it was a long trip but still more efficient than sending that much by land on their big wagons over all the low swampy land between Savannah and Beaufort and the sharpie would have had to make two trips to deliver only sixteen tons. Henry said getting that much ice to Beaufort and Saint Helena made the barge trip very practical plus the extra hardware items from Richard Wilcox added some profit. He said that there would be a greater volume of hardware when the plantation owners began to rely on the regular monthly deliveries and Richard had orders for five more small icehouses on Saint Helena. Henry said it also freed up the sharpie for all the other deliveries he would have for them which would mean more income for their shipping business if they managed it efficiently. Ken said he was thinking that a steam-powered boat could make it to Beaufort in a day. Then it could have unloaded the next morning, made it over to Lands' End, unloaded there, left early the next morning, and been back to Savannah before dark. Martin added that also, from what he had been reading, a seventy-foot river boat could do all that with sixty tons of ice and pull a barge loaded with another twenty tons. Then after offloading the ice in Beaufort and Lands' End, it could leave the barge anchored and continue on up the inland waterway and deliver the rest of its load at other sea-island landings. All that with stand-up accommodations for a crew of eight plus and engineer's quarters and a suite for the Captain and a wife if he had one. Neither Henry nor Ken picked up on what Martin was thinking when he said a suite for a captain and a wife, but it was something that Martin had been contemplating. On the return trip, the boat could pick up the barge to go back to the Milam Ice Company, load up again and make deliveries to the sea islands to the south of Savannah all the way to Jacksonville in northern Florida. Martin concluded that ten days a month would be going and coming north and ten days would be going and coming south. All the sea islands to the north and south of them would get their monthly ice supply and hardware and all delivered regularly. The other ten days of the month could be spent at home for maintenance and time off for crew and captain. Henry and Ken were stunned that Martin had such clarity and understanding of how such a big task could be done. Henry said that at the rate of the increase in business, without something like Martin was talking about, they would have to start turning away customers. Martin added something else that was amazing, especially to Henry, because it would have some implications on the not-too-distant future of the Milam Ice business, and it was something he had never had the vision of. Martin said that, from reading about steam engine power in the publications that Thomas gave him, in about ten years, steam locomotives on railways built from up north to Georgia were going to have a big impact on shipping by water. But, he said, sea island shipping would still be a growing business because rails could not go over to the sea islands. Henry had been surprised before about the riverboat information, but now he was taken aback. His young brother had seen into future trends that he had not thought of, and he was almost speechless. Martin said that he had Thomas to thank for all the books he had gotten from Boston and New York and given him to study. He said Thomas had an engineering publication about steam engines and their various uses that came out twice a year and that Thomas allowed him to go to his office and read the current and back issues and that he had been there most of the last two weeks. He went on to say that the publication from six months earlier was all about Mr. Robert Fulton, the man who built the first commercial steamboat more than twenty years before. It went from New York City to Albany, New York, on the Hudson River and back at an average speed of five miles per hour. He died about fifteen years earlier, but now because of his inventions, there were several freight and passenger companies there with boat speeds almost ten miles an hour. Martin went on to say that the latest publication had just come last week, and it was about steam locomotives and all the places that railways would be built in the next ten years, connecting the northern and southern states. It said that freight costs over land would be less and more reliable, and much faster, and that the current shipping by sea could not keep up with the amount of agricultural products being produced in the south for the northern manufacturers and general population. Also, the coal that was dug in the north and all the manufactured goods could be hauled south to sell. He said a freight train, hauling what it would take fifty ships to carry, would be able to make the trip either way from New York to Georgia in three days and the loading and unloading on freight cars was ten times easier and faster than in and out of a ship's hold.

Martin said that is why he had been at Thomas' office every day for the last two weeks and how he had learned these things that he was saying. He said he was an awfully slow reader but spent a lot of time at it. Henry was in awe of Martin's knowledge and thought to himself that he, John, and Thomas had some important things to talk about having to do with the future of their business. He left Martin with Ken to go right away to see John and Thomas to discuss what Martin had talked about. Before he left, Martin told Henry that since Thomas would probably be with him and John today, he wouldn't go to his office today and that he was probably tired of having him anyhow, after having been in his way so much lately. Henry shook his head in amazement at his young brother and left. After Henry had gone, Martin told Ken that he had asked his father about any connections he might have to help them find a fast ship to Boston. He said that a ship hauling cotton would be lighter and faster than a timber freighter and all they had to do was let him know a couple weeks before they wanted to leave, and he would arrange it. Ken said it would be about four weeks before he was back from the next barge trip. Martin told Ken that they would be expecting him for supper. Ken said he would like that because the barge food was okay but nothing like the food at the Milam house.

Martin had ridden with Henry and walked back home. On the way he thought more about what he had told Henry and Ken about the spacious accommodations possible on a riverboat and what Mary might think of that idea. The idea appealed to him because he hadn't been able to imagine anywhere else for them to live or how they could be together with him being a river steamboat captain. He could see that it was going to take a lot of his time, and Mary had made it clear that she intended to be a writer and she could do that anywhere. Then he thought about the next few months of all there was to do. He would ordinarily be very excited about a trip to Boston by ship but there were so many other things happening that he simply thought of it as the fastest way to get Ashley, Ken, and him to pick up the new sharpie and sail it back. From Boston, with the new boat, they would stop at Hoboken, New Jersey, to see the river steamboats of Colonel Stephens' operation, then return home. After that there was the trip to Philadelphia to deliver a load of yaupon and the more important mission of transporting and manumitting the people from the Milam plantation. He knew that the Philadelphia trip was the most important thing he had to do, not for the yaupon, but for Jacob and his family and for his father to have something done that he had set out to do a long time ago. He had been taken up and obsessed with the whole steam engine and riverboat business lately but that was to satisfy the desires of his mind. The other thing with Jacob and manumission was about something deeper inside him and was to satisfy his heart.

This was the first time he had the clarity of those two parts of himself. And behind it all was Mary. He didn't know what to think about her but knew that the time was coming when they would be together. All these things were clear and certain in his mind, but how they would all play out was a curious mystery. But so had been the rest of his life up until now. The details of the coming months were not clear, but he had a curiosity about how it would unfold and an inner confidence about it all and an inner feeling of gratitude for everything. His introspection was interrupted by a shriek of joy from little Thomas, who saw Martin walking by his yard. Martin's attention came back to the moment and he was a bit jolted, and then Thomas almost knocked him over as he leapt into him. Thomas seemed to have almost doubled in size because Martin had been so busy the last year and gone much of the time and hadn't seen him as often. He was a big little boy now. Thomas said that his mother told him that he was gonna take the whole family for a boat ride to Tybee soon and he wanted to know when. Martin said she was right and it would be soon enough. Knowing when was not as important to Thomas as hearing Martin confirm what his mother had told him was true, and he could hardly control his happiness and ran in circles around Martin and did his little jig dance. Thomas asked if he would teach him to run the boat, and Martin said he had always planned to teach him and the trip to Tybee would only be the beginning of his lessons. Alice and Maggie had been in the house, and when they heard Thomas's screams, they came out to check on him and were glad to see Martin. Again, Martin was surprised to see how big the baby girl Jochebed had gotten. She squirmed in Alice's arms to be let down on the grass. She couldn't walk yet but could stand, holding onto her mother's leg. She let go and crawled to Thomas, who got down and let her crawl on him. Maggie said she had hardly seen Martin for months, and he said he knew but the trips with Ashley and Ken took up more of his time than he had expected, partly because they spent a lot of time at Tybee, waiting for favorable wind and weather, and he had been studying at Mr. Thomas' office in Savannah. He reminded Maggie that their trip to Philadelphia was coming up soon, and she said she thought about it all the time and so did her mother, but for different reasons. Her mother was worried about the boat ride, and she was worried about being in a school. She said she was afraid she would be slower and less educated than everyone else. Martin told her she didn't have to worry about that. He told her that she was gifted with intelligence and a desire to learn and would surprise the people in Philadelphia. Alice said that Maggie thought that everybody up north was highly educated and smarter than her and everybody down south. Martin said that, while trying to go to school, he had thought that everybody down here was smarter than him and he had learned that in many ways they were, but he had some talents of his own. Alice told him that he was up to some big travels in the next few months with his Boston and Philadelphia trips and local trips with Ashley and Ken delivering things. Maggie asked what he had been studying. Martin said steam engines for boats and told them about it and described the boat he wanted the Milam Ice Company to have in a year and how he planned to be the Captain. Also about the nice stand-up living accommodations it had, including a suite for a captain and a wife,   a private cabin for an engineer, and ample accommodations for a crew. Unlike Henry and Ken, who didn't get the connection when he said this, Alice and Maggie immediately looked at each other and smiled knowingly. Martin talked also about going to New Jersey and New York to learn more about steam riverboats. He stood up and said he should be going and he knew Thomas would want to go with him and asked if it was okay. Maggie said he could. Before Martin had taken three steps outside, Thomas, as usual, asked if he could go with him. Martin said his sister said he could, and Thomas did his happy jig around Martin again.

When Henry got to John's house in Savannah, he was glad to see that Thomas was still there. They had been discussing the estimated cost to open a Milam Ice Company in Charleston. They were really glad that Henry came unannounced to add his ideas and hear theirs. Henry said he just had an amazing conversation with Martin, and Thomas said he had been having one with him almost every day for the last few weeks. He said Martin was obsessed about steam engines on riverboats and what a big difference one could make for the Milam Ice Company. Yes, Henry said, that was half of what they talked about that morning. Thomas looked at Henry and pointed to the open steam locomotive publication on John's desk and told Henry that he had just brought it to show John. It was the recent issue and was the one that Martin had been studying at his office about steam locomotives and all the railroads coming in the next few years, and how much more practical than ships they would be to transport freight. Henry admitted that when he first heard the information from Martin, he worried that it would disrupt their business, but then he understood that it could greatly increase their business and profits. Thomas said he thought the same thing at first but then realized that train cars were perfect for building rectangular ice boxes onto and that two train cars could carry as much ice as a ship and could be in Georgia three days after the ice was sawn from a lake in Maine. There would be less loss from melting, it would be much easier to unload, and at locations that did not need to be on the water. He said it would quadruple the areas they could service. He added that the sea islands and many coastal towns would still need to be serviced by water, from North Carolina to northern Florida, especially since they were beginning to sell ice and ice boxes and ice house panels to the fishing industry. Henry said all that was why he had come to town to talk. John told Thomas that he probably hadn't been around long enough to know how insightful Martin could be in his simple way at unexpected times. Thomas said he had been seeing for the last few weeks how Martin had a guileless clarity about things where he himself often overthought and over-complicated what he was presented with. Henry said Thomas was spot on in his assessment of Martin.

Thomas said the railroads and locomotives were coming and they would have a huge impact on the economy in the north and south and a particularly big impact on our ice business, but that was ten years away. He said his biggest concern was the next few years and being able to dependably deliver what we sell. Henry said that they were not doing the selling because the ice was selling itself more every month. People saw their neighbors' iceboxes and heard how they could keep their food fresh for weeks and had to have one themselves. Fishing boats were able to stay out longer with ice in their holds, keeping the fish fresh and increasing their profits. Most every plantation ordered icehouse panels for their own icehouse and regularly got a thousand pounds a month and some got two thousand pounds a month. Restaurants and hotels were waking up to how they could keep their food fresh and frozen desserts and drinks had become all the rage.

Henry described what Ashley, Ken, and Martin were doing with the barge taking care of Beaufort. He talked about the new sharpie coming and the new crews. He explained Martin's plan of the steam-powered riverboat with a barge servicing the places north from Savannah ten days a month, returning to Savannah to reload, servicing south to Florida, returning in ten days to Savannah, using the other ten days of the month for boat and barge maintenance, then repeating the circuit. He said that each run with boat and barge loaded could deliver a two hundred tons of ice a month. Thomas said that seemed like a lot but ice was heavy and pointed at Johns desk and said a piece of ice that size was almost three thousand pounds. Thomas said they had probably heard that they had planned on observing a steamboat and barge operation and meeting with the inventor and steamboat designer in New Jersey while on their trip to Boston. John said he had not heard that and looked at the other two and laughed and said they had a young and unusual leader and were fortunate to have him. John asked Thomas how long it would take to get a steam-powered river boat in operation. He said he wasn't sure but if Martin had his way, it would be soon, maybe within a year. He then asked how long it would take to get their ice operation going in Charleston, and Thomas said if they started immediately, about a year or a little more. John said he had no idea what a steam-powered riverboat would cost but it sounded like what they would need and he knew that Ashley, Ken, and Martin didn't have that kind of money, but the bank did. He asked if they were that committed. Henry said they were all in and that he would talk to the three of them together soon to see if they could get going on the boat project. Thomas said he would put together a list of questions for Martin to ask about the riverboat operation in New York and about the design details from the man in New Jersey, but he bet Martin already had a long list. They all agreed to begin the set-up in Charleston right away. Henry would take Thomas there and introduce him to Albert because the professor knew so many business people there and could help them get a start.

Martin and big little boy Thomas walked straight to the boathouse. The sharpie had come in on the tide and moonlight late the night before. The new crew was fishing off the boat, and Ashley and Ben were sitting outside the boathouse with Johnny, having tea and cold biscuits. They were happy to see Martin and Thomas. Johnny wrestled with Thomas a bit and told him that he couldn't lift him over his head anymore because he had gotten so big. Martin asked how their trip was, and Ashley said all he and Ben did was drink tea and smoke because the new crew did everything including the cooking this time. He said he felt useless. Ben told Martin that they had seen a steamship coming in the river the day before, and Martin said he would go look for it tomorrow. Just then, Henry came and said he had stopped by the house. Claudia had heard that the sharpie was in, and she wanted Ashley, Ben, and Ken to come to supper if they were planning on staying the night. Plus, he had some business to talk to them about after supper. Ben said they would like that, and Ashley nodded in agreement. Martin said he would go get the wagon to take Captain Ben and Ashley to the barge and tell Ken about supper and Thomas went along. He had wanted to show Ben all the work they had done on the barge to carry ice and when he got back, he would take the sharpie crewmen over to the ice company to catch the afternoon wagon home. Henry told Ben and Ashley he would see them later.

When the wagon got to the Milam Ice Company ice house, the barge was sitting up on the river bank, where the tide had gone out and left it. Ken was so busy sawing and hammering, he didn't see them arrive, until Thomas jumped out and ran up the ramp and startled him. He smiled big, after not seeing Ashley and the Captain for almost a month and welcomed them aboard. The Captain was impressed and Martin proudly told him that it was the second boat in their fleet and brought a smile to the Captain's face. Ken grinned and said she as fast as the tide and before the next trip she would be slightly faster than that on occasion. He pointed to a long skinny pine pole on the bank and that was going to be an unstayed mast with a lug sail. It might only save them a half day in the three week round trip, but if the winds were favorable, maybe more. He motioned for the Captain to follow and opened the door to the crew accommodations. He said it had stand-up room even for Ashley. He pointed to the cook stove, to the big sink with a drain, to the water supply pipe coming from a tank on the roof, and to a cork-insulated and metal-lined icebox with a drain that Jason had just installed. He added that they had been keeping their meat and dairy in the icehouse, but the less often they had to open the door the colder it stayed so that's why they added an icebox to the galley. He pointed to the four bunks where he and the three crewmen could sleep and to three rough openings in the walls that he was in the middle of making operable windows for. Then he led them out and to the bow, which was the loading deck with a boom and lift ramp. He opened two big, insulated doors and showed the open area inside to store ice and said the walls were almost two feet thick, packed with cotton. He said the floor was insulated with eight inches of cork. He explained how they were able to off-load ice directly from a ship on the last trip, and he hoped to do that again before the next trip, or they would take ice from the icehouse on the hill. The

Captain said he was proud of them for growing their business. Ashley said it was because the Milam Ice Company was growing and they had agreed to try to keep up with their delivery needs and they were always helping them get bigger and better. He added that he thought what Henry wanted to talk to them about tonight after supper was those kinds of things. Ben said that in every conversation he had with Henry, he always mentioned what Ashley and Ken had done to free up Alice, her family, and friends and how it relieved him of the worst stress he had ever felt, and he would always do what he could to help them in any way. Ken said it really wasn't that big of a deal, but Martin said it was a huge deal and he felt the same as Henry about it. Martin called little Thomas, who had been in the pulling boat with a fishing pole, and said it was time to go. Ben said he was looking forward to getting cleaned up and supper. They loaded up, and Martin dropped them all off at the house and went down to get the new crewmen to take them to catch the work wagon home. When they loaded themselves up on the wagon and started talking to each other, he didn't understand much of what they were saying, but he sensed that they were happy about their new work.

Before Martin got back to the house, he could hear Walter and Ben talking loudly because they both didn't hear very well. When Claudia saw Martin, she asked him and Henry to help set out the food. Soon there was yaupon and rum, several meaningful toasts, and a big meal, and pies and pastries for dessert. After the meal, Henry said he had some business to discuss with Ashley, Ken, and Martin, and he would do it there because he wanted his father and Ben to hear it. Because his father was not privy to all that had been going on, he caught him up on the news about the growing ice business, the barge, steam engines in boats, locomotives and railways coming, the new Milam Ice business they hoped to set up in Charleston in a year or so. He told him that Thomas and Martin had been researching a steam-engine-powered riverboat that could pull a bigger barge and enable them to fill the growing demand for ice from locations between Jacksonville, Florida, to Wilmington, North Carolina. Even though this wasn't new information for Ken, Ashley, Martin, or Ben, the broad picture that Henry was painting made things clearer to them. Henry went on to say that the delivery side of the business was separate and was owned by Ken, Ashley, and Martin, but he and John wanted to help them rise to the growing delivery demands. From his research Thomas was sure that a steam-engine riverboat of about eighty feet with a wide beam, pulling a barge, could do the work required. He also researched the cost, and it was a very large sum of money. However, he and John have made the calculations, and the delivery fees should easily cover the costs and net a substantial profit. Henry paused for a few moments and said he was going to discuss some things that even Ken and Ashley and Martin were not yet informed about.

First, he said, if the three of them were willing, the Milam Ice Company would vouch for them at the bank in Savannah to have such a boat built. Second, he would ask that Captain Ben un-retire and captain the new boat for a year to help insure the large investment. From Thomas' research they figured that they would need an onboard steam engineer to operate the engine, along with a six-man crew on the boat, and maybe two crewmen on the barge. Henry said that this was his announcement and proposal but that it was certainly up to Ben, Ashley, Ken, and Martin to consider. Martin said quickly that he was all in if the rest were. He said he never believed the stuff about Captain Ben's back anyway, and that made the whole group laugh. Ashley and Ken were more in a state of mild shock at the possibility that sailing a boat might not be necessary much longer. Ben saw their state of mind and said he had seen this coming, but he didn't expect it to start with him and said he would like to be a part of this new shift in shipping to end his career on. Ken asked what would become of the sharpies, and Martin said with their insulated holds and Milam ice, they could easily be sold to commercial fishermen, but until we have the steam boat built, both sharpies will need to haul ice. Ken chuckled and said he didn't know how he would manage because the big sharpie had been his home for so long, and he was already attached to the new sharpie that he hadn't even yet seen. Ashley said he felt somewhat like Ken did but he liked to learn new things, but he wouldn't want to do it if it didn't feel right with Ken. Ken said if it were not for Henry and his partners and Captain Ben, he would not entertain such big changes, but he liked working with them all, and he was willing to go for it. Henry poured them a dram and proposed a toast to the new venture. After they drank, Henry said he would leave everything in their hands except that he and John would make the arrangements at the bank. He said Thomas was available and suggested that they begin working with him to learn more, and that they would be able to help gather information about steam-engine-powered riverboats and barges on their trip up north. He said that he wanted to tell them something that Thomas had told him that he had almost forgot to mention. He said his son was getting out of the navy in a few months and might be interested in working with them.

Walter insisted that they all stay the night at the Milam house. Ben agreed, but Ashley said they had to leave on another delivery of ice the next day and he was intent on drifting the sharpie on the tide in about an hour down to the ice house, so it could be loaded first thing in the morning, and he would just stay on it there. He said the new crew was coming early in the morning to load the ice and leave out on the tide soon after. He told the Captain that he and the new crew could easily handle the delivery and he was welcome to stay on the hill this trip. Ben said he was fine with that. Ashley asked Martin and Ken if they wanted to drift in the sharpie with him so they could talk about the things Henry had brought up, and Ken said it was an excellent idea. As they got up to leave, Ashley told Henry that he was sure he was speaking for Ken too, and thanked Henry and John for their generosity. He didn't know what to say except that they were filled with gratitude. Ken said he felt the same way. Henry answered quickly that their ice business couldn't grow without dependable delivery service and, friendship aside, they presented the best possibility. Secondly, he told them that he would be forever indebted to them for what they had done for his family and all. Ken said he needn't feel that indebted, and now might be the time to mention something that he and Ashley had talked about in light of the upcoming trip to Philadelphia to take Jacob, his family, and Izak to be manumitted. He said that he and Ashley felt awkward being the owners of Alice, her family, and friends and wanted to propose that the next manumitting trip be with that group including Prissy to officially set them free. Ashley piped in that it would make them both feel better. Henry said that was gracious of them and Captain Ben said he was proud of them but not surprised, having sailed with them for so long.

The sun was setting when the sharpie anchors were lifted, and the boat started drifting very slowly towards the icehouse. The tide was high and just starting out and they were far enough from the bank that there was no need for the pulling boat, so the three of them relaxed in the cockpit to discuss what Henry had talked about. Martin said what was most in his mind was their idea about taking Alice's family and Prissy and the others to Philadelphia to be manumitted. He said he had never seen his whole family so moved. Ashley said who could have imagined all this that has come upon them. Ken repeated that it was like riding a big wave ever since Ben had lied about his back and sold them the sharpie and asked Martin to join them.

In the first hour when a very high tide starts out, it moves very slowly especially along the edge of the river, so it took an hour for the sharpie to drift the quarter mile down to the Milam ice house, where the barge had been moored since it had gotten back from its first trip. The slow drift with the rising moon from the east was a perfect setting for the three men to review all the new things on their horizon and to meld their ambitions into a unified goal. Ashley would keep up the deliveries in the sharpie with the new crew. Martin would continue his research about steam-powered riverboats and make preparations for their passage and stay in Boston and New York. Ken would make another trip with the barge and new crew to prepare them to make the next trip on their own. Martin said it was a bit odd that they were talking about a new steamboat when they hadn't even picked up the new sharpie. Ashley said he had thought of that too but it could be a year or more before the new steamboat could be ready and since they had committed to keeping up with the deliveries, even if they used the new sharpie for a year it was worth getting. Ken said he thought there would soon be enough growing demand for ice on Hilton Head, Daufuskie, Warsaw, and Ossabaw to keep one sharpie and crew busy full-time and it could deliver other items as well. Ashley said they would have to wait and see, so the three of them decided that for the near future the two sharpies and the barge were what they would have for ice deliveries. Ashley added that he guessed they would wait to hear from Henry or John that they had been to the bank concerning the financing of the new steamboat, and Ken and Martin agreed. The moon was up and casting a beautiful light over the area, which added to the meaningful and memorable day for the three of them. Ashley rowed Martin to the riverbank for him to walk home.

There had been plenty of important things brought up in the last hours for Martin to think about on his walk home in the moonlight. But his mind up and flew to Tybee. He lingered on the essence of Mary and tried to remember her sweet scent. He couldn't remember it, but he could recall his feeling when he smelled it. He was in something of a trance, absorbed in his feelings and seeing her in his mind's eye. Not until he saw his house did his imagination fly back from Tybee and Mary. He had to pause a few moments and look around at familiar things to become grounded again before going in the house quietly and up to his room to bed.

The next morning the sharpie crew showed up early. They seemed particularly anxious to get aboard. When Ashley rowed over to pick them up, each one said, "Good morning, Captain Ashley," very proudly. Ken was on the bank and was amused and pleased because he realized that the sentences and words he had written out and had sent home with his crew had been shared and practiced with the sharpie crew. They continued saying English words and phrases while loading the four holds on the sharpie full of ice and were soon under way with the tide and a little wind in the sails.

Ken continued his work on the barge and was glad to see a ship drifting toward the icehouse and sent word for his crew to report in the morning. He quit the carpentry work, to be finished later while drifting, and set about gathering provisions for the trip from the Milam plantation. When the crew came very early the next morning, they were all repeating the English sentences and words that he had written and given them to take home and practice. Ken was appreciative amused. They had learned the words and phrases but didn't understand what some of them meant, and it reminded him of a parrot that a man in Savannah had. The crewmen were proud of what they had learned, and it made them feel more American. It would become a source of humor and learning on this second trip as Ken wrote out more words and some real progress was made in understanding what the words they had learned meant. Very little of their new vocabulary was necessary for loading the big blocks of ice from the ship onto the barge. They were very familiar with the mechanics of lifting and lowering with a boom and block and tackle but the clinching tongs that were used to secure a hold onto the ice blocks were new to them. Being experienced sailors, they had loaded, unloaded, and secured a lot of cargo, but ice was something new. It had some unique characteristics that made it easy in some ways and difficult in others. It was easy to slide a four hundred block around. The ice tongs made it easy to grapple onto the ice, but if there was a fissure in the block, it could break, and the heavy pieces could severely injure someone or crash through a deck or hull. Things had gotten easier since the ice sizes had become standardized, unlike before when it had been simply discarded ballast and different sizes. Thomas had gone to Maine and met with the people sawing the ice from the lakes. He had established size and quality standards and prices that enabled the cutters to deliver a consistent product of clear and clean ice with a profit incentive. Once the ice was set on the barge deck, one man could easily slide a huge block across a level surface. But this slipperiness also made it important to stack and secure the blocks side by side from one wall of the barge's icehouse to the other and to fill any gaps with wood blocking. This prevented it from shifting if the tide went out and left them tilted on a sand bar, or if they were ever in some big waves. A five-hundred-pound block of ice was slippery, and if one got going, it could knock out a wall or injure a person.

By noon the barge was loaded with five thousand more pounds than on the first trip. Ken measured the remaining freeboard and calculated they were drawing right at three feet of water. They winched up the anchor and began the slow drift to Beaufort as the tide started out. In the first few days out, Ken was able to explain that he would not be along on the next trip and they would be on their own. He assigned the crewman that had learned the most English to be in charge, but he insisted that they all look at the chart often and the islands they were going by. This was not new to any of them, since they had navigated rivers and coastlines in their own country, but what was new to them was the large rise and fall in the tides and mud bars. Navigating was very much about using the big rudder and pulling boats to keep the barge in the deepest part of the river for the most drift speed and so they wouldn't ground out before the end of the tide cycle. The chart had the major sand and mud bars marked, and Martin had added where the tidal shifts were. When conditions were fair, they tried out the new sail rig. It made only a slight difference in the speed of the heavy barge but could add a few miles to a day's progress if the winds were favorable.

Ken had asked Martin to send a message by coach to Richard in Beaufort about when they left and when to look for their arrival. They avoided any groundings and were able to use the sail with a favorable wind, so they made the trip in a half day less than the first trip. Boat arrivals at the riverfront were always quickly noted, so Richard soon sent two extra pulling boats to get them up to his icehouse to unload more than half the ice. Ken had become very satisfied with the new crew and was confident that they could complete the next trip on their own. He was still uncertain about their ability to communicate smoothly enough with the twenty wagons or more that would be waiting to pick up ice and hardware at Lands' End and to account for the quantity for each. Ken told Richard that he wouldn't be on the next trip, and he expressed his concern about the new crew interacting at Lands' End and asked Richard if he could supply a man to accompany them. Richard thought it was a good idea and that his man could go and return to Beaufort on the mail boat. He said he knew just the fellow and suggested he go along on this trip while Ken was still aboard to get familiarized with things. Ken thought that was an even better plan. The next day the ice was unloaded, and Richards's hardware cargo and the new man were all taken on, and they started drifting with the last of the outgoing tide toward Saint Helena Island.

Back at the Milam place, after Ken had left, Martin began planning the trip to New York. He told his father about when the needed to leave so he could check on ships leaving with a captain that he approved of. A few days later he gave Martin a short list with his recommendations. Martin asked Thomas to help him arrange accommodations and a meeting with the sharpie builder in Boston and with Colonel Robert Stevens in New Jersey. Being from the area, Thomas was happy and proud to help and said he would take care of it all. He also helped Martin prepare a letter of introduction to Mr. Stevens and stated Martin's intentions and expectation to pay for his consulting services. He described the cargo weight of the boat they would need and what the freight was and that it be able to tow a barge. Thomas also expressed a need for a chief engineer and an assistant engineer if necessary. Martin was very impressed with the letter's clarity. Martin said that they could stay on the new sharpie in New York City but Thomas said the weather would be cold and it would be best to stay at an inn so they could be comfortable and at their best.

The weeks went by, and the whole Milam place was abuzz with the upcoming long ocean voyage, and there were the usual doubts that Ashley, Ken, or Martin would ever return. Martin was busy studying all that Thomas could find on steam riverboats. He was obsessed with it all and became familiar with all the current knowledge available. He squeezed in one trip to see Mary, riding on the supply boat to Tybee, spending the night at the lighthouse and returning on the boat the next day. When he saw Mary, all the boat and ice things he was so consumed with vanished. Nothing in either of their circumstances lessened the commitment and growing love between them. Martin didn't mention what he had in mind about them on the new river boat. He wanted to wait and have the boat to show her.

25.

NEW ENGLAND

Ken was back in twenty-one days, and Ashley came in a day later. Martin began making daily trips to the Savannah riverfront to speak with the ship captains his father had recommended. Letters had come back to Thomas confirming their accommodations and appointments up north, so the three of them made themselves ready to leave on short notice on the first ship out based on his father's referrals. The ship and approval did come with short notice, and their departure tide was in the middle of the night. Henry got up to drive them to the Savannah riverfront. They boarded a fairly new freighter a few hours before daylight as the full moon set in the west. It was exactly one month after the memorable meeting when Henry had proposed to them his ideas about the new steamboat and Captain Ben helping.

The ship Captain came with high recommendations and was a close friend of a close friend of Walter's. Twelve pulling boats inched the big ship out into the middle of the river, and it began its long trip slowly by the power of the outgoing tide. Martin watched from the bow and remembered fondly his first trips in the little dugout sailing canoe from his house to the Savannah ship docks. All the same familiar smells wafted up to him. He was startled back into himself when Ken said that they were invited right away to eat an early breakfast with Captain Lawrence Missroon from Georgetown, South Carolina. Once they were seated at the table, the Captain was witty and entertaining with them. He said he knew of Martin's father but had not met him and asked a lot of questions about their trip up north. Martin explained a little about the ice business and their plans to learn about steam-powered riverboats and their hope of having one soon to deliver ice along the inland waterways from North Florida to North Carolina. When the Captain heard the word 'steam-engine boat,' his face lit up. He got up and got two books about steam engines to show Martin and said he too was fascinated with the subject. Then Martin rattled on about steam engines in boats almost nonstop. Ashley and Ken ate, and Martin and the Captain's food set and got cold. The Captain was astounded at young Martin's knowledge about a subject that he was interested in. The server saw what was happening and brought two more plates of hot breakfast for the two talkers. Ken and Ashley smiled to each other and excused themselves to go out on deck, leaving the two of them still talking. A good two hours later Martin came hunting Ashley and Ken and was a little disappointed that he had missed seeing the Wilmington River as they passed. For the nine days of the trip, Martin spent much of the time with the Captain in his cabin, telling him the things he had learned about steam engines on boats and ships from the books and publications that Thomas had provided him with. He, Ashley, and Ken were the Captain's dinner guests every night. They could not have possibly found and paid for better accommodations on any ship, because of the common interest of Martin and the Captain.

The trip was mostly uneventful, even during a three-day gale with huge seas. The big freighter liked the heavy winds. Other than adjusting to the angle of the ship, the ride was still somewhat smooth and stable, and when the wind slacked off, the five or six knots of speed seemed painfully slow. They were soon heading west, out of the ocean current, toward Boston. Martin watched as two pilots and crews raced out to guide the ship in. As usual, the first one there got the job, and it took another day to get safely into the port of Boston. Martin remembered what Thomas had said about how many ships and boats of all sizes there were in Boston harbor but he was still stunned at the biggest cluster of watercraft he had ever seen. Sixteen pulling boats brought them up to the dock, and the pace of things was much faster than in Savannah. The harbor and riverfront were much bigger but much more crowded because of so many vessels.

The Captain was looking out over the bow watching over the docking of his ship, and he saw the look of awe on Ashley, Ken, and Martin's faces and smiled at them. He said it was a smooth trip into the harbor this time but it could be, and often was, a hair-raising experience when the winds whipped up off the ocean. He added that it was a lot of different approach to the city than what they were accustomed to in Savannah. Getting in was quicker here but fraught with its own types of hazards, and there was no leaving at all when the wind was onshore. He asked where they were staying and sent a man ahead to arrange a carriage for them. He said that he wished he had time to make the trip to New York with them to learn about steam power in boats, but said he hoped to see them on his next trip into Savannah. Martin said he must come to his home and meet his family, and the Captain said he looked forward to that. He had made arrangements for their baggage to be taken off to the waiting carriage. He shook their hands and wished them good fortune in the freight business and told Ashley and Ken that Martin was fortunate to have them for partners and they were fortunate to have him as well.

When they set foot on land, there was not as much awkwardness as they would first feel when they got off the much smaller sharpie. They looked up, waved at the Captain, and took another look at the big freighter before loading onto the carriage. The driver had been given the address and paid in advance by their new captain friend, yet another case of a first class treatment they could have never imagined. When they got to the inn, Ashley showed the driver where they were to pick up the new sharpie and asked if he could be back in the morning to take them. He said he would be there and that he knew when breakfast was served at the inn and he would be there shortly after. He said they must be from Georgia or South Carolina because he could tell from the way they talked that they weren't from around there. Ken said he was right on both guesses. The driver said they would soon see that people talked a lot faster than they were accustomed to and to not be offended by people's abruptness and think it rude. It was just how they were. They were hard on the outside, but most were soft on the inside. They said they were going to New York after they picked up their boat in a day or two. The driver said that New York people were not just abrupt but point blank. They nodded but didn't know what that was about and wouldn't understand until they got to New York. Two porters came out and said they assumed they were staying at the inn. They said they were, and they picked up their baggage and led them inside. When the innkeeper heard their names, he welcomed them and said he was glad to meet Thomas' friends. He said he had them one small and one large room and that Thomas had asked that Martin get the small room that had the best view of the river. The three men continued to be amazed and thankful for the treatment that had been continually bestowed on them. They were led to their rooms, shown the bathing accommodations, and told when supper was served. They marveled at the building, and Ashley said it was probably older than most of the buildings in Savannah. He smiled and said he wished he could have witnessed, right where they had left the ship, only about fifty years ago, the event when colonials had dumped a shipload of tea into the river to protest the high import taxes the British had levied. Martin said his father was still a Brit when that happened and how much has changed since then. Ken said he was amazed at how much had changed in the last few months and laughed. He said just a couple weeks ago he had been slow drifting, swatting gnats and mosquitos with three men from a foreign country, struggling to speak each other's language. He said two of the men had learned a lot of English when they returned for the second trip, but the third man had learned very little, although he was the best sailor of the three. Ken said that no matter what you said to him, he would always give the same reply, "Thank you, my friend," one of the sentences Ken had written for them to learn. He said his reply worked every time he said it to Richard, the people in Beaufort, and the people at Lands' End. In any language, it was clearly the most important phrase to know for an immigrant. Martin thought to himself of the half foreign language of Gullah that some of his closest friends and his adopted family of Jacob's spoke, and how outsiders couldn't understand them, and how they used that to their advantage when it was useful.

After they had gotten cleaned up and come back downstairs, the inn-keeper personally saw them to their table for supper, and the waiter was very kind and told them what food was available for the meal. Ken saw a bowl of a dark reddish-brown casserole in a big earthenware bowl, served to a nearby table and asked what it was. The waiter said they were Boston baked beans and were on the menu every day. He explained that they were cooked, then baked with molasses at a very high temperature in a pork gravy, that formed a dark crust-like covering. The customer with the beans heard them and said that they were good. He asked where they were from, and when Ashley told him, he welcomed them to Boston. He said the beans were a local tradition and everybody had their own special way of cooking them, but they were all baked after being cooked and all had some amount of molasses in them that made them dark. Supper and the company was good, and they wondered where the abruptness that the carriage driver spoke about was. Then two men came in late to supper and had a harsh conversation with the innkeeper. It alarmed the three of them so much that they thought there would be a fist fight at any moment from the level of shouting. Then they heard the tones soften, and the innkeeper said he would have his man ready them a hot bath since they were running late and told them the desserts they could look forward to after their main dishes.

After supper, they took a stroll down to the riverfront and were all stunned again at how many boats and ships of all sizes crowded the wide port. They saw at least fifty sharpies from twenty feet to sixty feet and a lot of smaller boats that were pointy on both ends. There were at least a hundred ships, and a few dozen with stacks from steam engine boilers. Martin regretted he hadn't visited the one that came into Savannah recently but was very content knowing that he would be up close to a steam riverboat soon. The same east wind that had blown them in from the Atlantic was cold and damp, and they didn't stay out long before going back to the inn. Their rooms were three floors up and were quite cozy from the heat rising up from the lower areas. Once in his bed, Martin looked out the window at the sky like he had looked out the porthole by his bunk on the big freighter. He didn't see the movement of the sky or feel his body rock like it had for the last ten days. He thought of Henry's and his first sharpie trip with Ben, Ashley, and Ken to Darien, when they anchored for the night at the mouth of the big Altamaha River, near the two big timber freighters. He began to review the big things that had happened since then but was asleep before he got far.

Next morning, they got up early and unpacked their big overcoats. They were a bit early for breakfast and walked outside. Martin had seen the snow on his windowsill, and they saw that several inches of snow covered everything and looked magical, especially covering the decks and rigging of all the ships. Martin wished he could somehow show this to everybody back home. Ashley said he liked all the boats there but not the cold, and Ken agreed. It was more baked beans with potatoes and eggs, but no grits for breakfast and strong tea but no coffee. The beans felt like the perfect food for the cold weather. They had beans at home, but these were different with a deeper flavor, and they all had extra portions. Just as they had finished, the porter came in and told them that their carriage was waiting. They had their things with them and went outside and loaded up on the carriage. The driver knew the location, and after a fifteen-minute ride, they were at a large boat yard. There were at least thirty boats of all sizes, from twenty feet to sixty feet at different stages of construction, and at least a hundred workers. Old sails were lying all around the ground, in a pile of snow, that had been covering the boats during the night to keep the snow off. Ken asked where the office was, and they were directed to a small building with windows all around for observing the boat yard. They walked in and saw four men, each at a desk with a slanted top for drafting boat plans and high shelves above the windows with hundreds of rolled up boat plans. A gentleman at the desk nearest the door asked if he could help them, and Ken said they were here to pick up a boat. On hearing Ken's slow talk, the man exclaimed that they must be Thomas' friends from Georgia, and Ken said yes. The other three men looked up from their desks, interested to see what Georgia people were like. Introductions were made, and a man named Robert said they were expecting them and said their boat was ready and in the water. He excused himself for a minute, opened the door, called a worker over and told him to take a few men and pull the sailcloth from the new green sharpie at the dock and sweep any snow off. Robert told them that a man from the Milam Ice Company had sent a bank note, and the boat was paid for and ready to go. Ken said they would like to look at it today but would not be ready to leave until they had provisions for the trip back. He retrieved one of the rolled-up plans and opened them up. He showed them the drawings and the list of things they had requested plus another list of things they had added themselves.He added that they were able to locate cork slabs and went ahead and installed two layers in the four holds, on the hold hatch covers, and in the big ice chest in the galley. He said it was the first cork that the yard had ever used. He said their instructions were to use the most durable materials available to build the boat, and they had used New England white oak to frame it for strength and resistance to rot, and Georgia Long Leaf heart pine for the bottom planks that were full length without any butts. It resists worms and rot, and the extra weight of it down low will improve the stability. And they had used eastern white cedar for the upper planking and decks and the cabin. He said that the boat had more beam for its length than any sharpie they had ever built, but to hold the amount of weight they had asked for and keep the draft shallow like they wanted, she had to be wide. He said with the centerboards up and twenty thousand pounds in her holds, she would still only draw three feet. He said there was something special about her that the yardmen had told him. They were quite interested in the cork and had experimented with it by lashing one hundred pounds of ballast lead to a slab of cork, and it had floated. Robert said that they believed that, even loaded with ice and filled with water, she would not sink because they had used over a hundred and fifty slabs of cork in her holds and ice chest.

Robert grabbed his coat and motioned for them to follow, and they walked down to dock where the men were finishing up sweeping the fresh powdery snow off the boat. The new sharpie was beautiful. Ashley said it was gonna be hard to ever part with her, and Ken and Martin agreed. Every part was beautifully fitted and finished, not like on a fancy king's launch, but simple and sturdy and made to last. They looked below, and like the outside, form followed function, and the boat builders had included everything they had asked for and made it all fit with room to move about easily. Ashley had to tilt his head forward only a bit, but there was headroom for an average height man. Robert showed them the lowest section of the bilge, and there was some water, but he said the boat had only been in the water for a few days and there would be less water in a week after more swelling happened. Martin said it all looked good and it was soon to get a good test on the trip south. Robert said the boat was fitted out with any and all the equipment needed for their trip and all they would need were provisions, and Ashley asked if those were available close by. Robert said there was everything they could ever want and more. He said they could pick it out or there were companies that would pick it out and load it on at any date you want. He reminded them of how many boats were there and all the businesses around that specialized in every want and need for boats of all sizes and purposes. Ashley said he would like to pick out their provisions himself and asked for a list of suppliers, and Robert said he would give him one. Robert asked when they were leaving, and Ken said as soon as they could get their provisions and had favorable winds. Robert said that Thomas had told them that they were experienced, but he wanted to send two of his men with them for a day to show them a few things about the boat that would serve them well. They agreed and said they would be back in the morning and would do that first thing.

They walked out of the boat yard, and there were no carriages in sight. They began following the ballast stone cobbled streets close to the water and looking at all the boats as they went. Ken pointed out a particularly perky little boat at a dock with a wide beam about half of its length. There was an old man bailing out water, and Ken suggested they have a look. The man saw them approaching, saw their interest, climbed out, and said in a strong local dialect, thinking they were shopping for boats, no, she was not for sale. Ken said they had just bought a boat but couldn't help noticing his boat and just wanted to have a look. He smiled and recognized their unusual accents and asked them where they were from. They told him Georgia and South Carolina and said they were there to pick up a new boat at the boatyard just up the way. He said his boat was one of the first boats ever built at that same yard, many years ago. Ken asked what kind of boat it was, and he said it was a "cat" boat. Ken said he had never seen anything like it down in their part of the country. The man said there were many around here and most were used for the same thing as his and he pointed to some wood slat baskets on the dock and said he fished for "lobstas." He saw their puzzled looks and jumped back down in the bilge. He crawled around and said "Gotcha!" and came out with the most unusual looking crab they had ever seen. Martin said they called them crabs, but the man corrected him and said these were not crabs at all but the biggest bugs in the sea and called "lobstas." He said he had fished for them, and his father had, and his grandfather had even while in prison. Martin smiled to himself because there was something strongly familiar at this point in the conversation and he recognized it was how one of the pilots or crewmen or Captain Jones on the Tybee beach would lead into an entertaining tale. Ashley and Ken didn't notice that, and Martin didn't say anything but was no less interested to hear the story. As the man expected, Ashley said, "prison?." The man said yes and began his story that his grandfather didn't belong in prison to begin with but was put there simply because he was a poor immigrant. He said that at the time poor immigrants had been eating them for years but everyone else considered them sea bugs and too nasty to eat. In a game of chance with one of the prison guards, his grandfather had won a bet. He didn't like the prison food, so he told the guard that to settle his debt, he could fetch him a lobsta from his friends who lived in the old, rotted ship hull where they had picked him up. The guard had taken a liking to the old man and had often wished that he weren't in prison. He said he would get one and boil it and bring it to him. He did, but he brought a dozen instead. The man paused a moment and looked the three of them to see if he had their complete attention and Martin smiled to himself again because it was just like his own father and Captain Jones did when spinning a tale. He said he ate his lobsta and passed the others through the bars to the other prisoners, and they liked them much better than the prison food. From that day on it became a way that the guards could get inmates to behave or to clean up their cells, by telling them that they would bring them boiled lobstas. Soon, they became everyday food because they were so plentiful. Well, the man said, after another pause and look, soon a few guards tried some and then the warden did and before long everybody in Boston was eating lobstas, even the rich folks. All because of his grandfather, and he smiled proudly. Martin was sure that there was some truth in his story but wondered how much. Ken and Ashley didn't doubt much of the story, and Ashley asked about the boat and how she sailed. The man said she sailed better than the sailor and was very safe and forgiving. He lifted up a small hatch in the cockpit floor and pointed to a thick piece of glass about six inches square, inlaid in the bottom planking. He said it was his father's invention, but he had not been properly recognized for its valuable purpose. He saw again the unknowing look on their faces and asked Ashley to slide over one of the wooden-slat basket traps. He tied a short line to it, put a small smooth river rock inside to weigh it down, and shoved it over. He pulled it back up to within about five feet below the water surface and at the side of the boat near the glass. He told them to look through the glass and tell him what they saw. They said the trap with the rock inside. He asked if there were any lobstas or bait in it, and they said no. Then he explained that being able to see if you had caught anything or if there was bait remaining before pulling the heavy trap all the way up and over the side would save a man a lot of work. They were impressed with the work-saving idea, and he said again that his father didn't get his due. The old man asked them what kind of boat they were picking up, and they told him it was a fifty-five foot sharpie. He shook his head and said most all the boats that outfit builds now are sharpies, but they still turn out a few cats. He asked when they were heading out, and Ken said maybe in a couple days. He said this time of year he was tied at the dock more than he was out pulling traps and for them to stop by again. He said his name was Davie Franklin, and they told him theirs and said goodbye and continued their walk back.

When they got to the inn, they had a message from Captain Lawrence Missroon, asking them if they would join him for dinner and they didn't need to send an answer because he was going with or without them and the inn was on his way, and he would stop by about 6:00. Ashley said that sounded good to him because he always liked to rely on local knowledge, and the others agreed. Martin said he was a slow writer, but he wanted to sit and write a letter home to try to describe the waterfront and tell about their journey thus far. Ken said he would like to take a nap and then walk around some more until time to get cleaned up for supper, and Ashley said that sounded good to him too.

The Captain arrived on time. The three men were waiting out front and climbed into the carriage and were welcome company. The Captain said he would like to tell and show them some Boston history with a ride around town before dinner. He directed the driver where to go. He talked about the natives who had first inhabited the high ground where the town now sits. Two groups of Puritans displaced them and settled the area, the first coming in 1630, and the second about a half century later. The province was called The Massachusetts Bay Colony after the Massachusetts Indians. To Martin the story sounded similar to his father's story of Savannah and Tomochichi and the Yamacraw. The Captain talked about the years of British rule, the many tax Acts that the colonials rebelled against, the Tea Party, the Boston Massacre and the war that followed, the Battle of Bunker Hill, and other significant events. They stopped at Warren Tavern, named for Dr. Joseph Warren, who was killed at the Bunker Hill battle. They went inside, and the Captain was greeted by name, having been there often on his layovers. They were seated and treated like special guests. The Captain ordered them all some rum and asked the waiter to bring some samples of their different lobster dishes to start. The Captain toasted to their success in steam-engine boats and they began sampling the lobster preparations which were all good. With another round of rum, the Captain toasted their continued friendship. Next the waiter brought four big bowls of potatoes with various seafood bits in them. The seafood was cut up so small that they could not recognize what it was, but it was very good. Next, he brought out Boston baked beans and said that their cook had a secret ingredient in his beans that no one else used. Bread too was served in small earthenware cups. It had been baked in the cups and had risen and puffed up high above the cups and browned over perfectly, crusty on the outside, and soft on the inside. They were pretty full, but next came four small little meat pies, unlike anything Ashley, Ken, or Martin had ever had. And for dessert were bowls of cherry cobbler. They had to pause with some hot tea to let their food settle to have room for the cobbler.

Martin said that they had heard about the beginnings of people eating lobster. The Captain said that it had been prison food originally. Ashley, Ken, and Martin smiled at each other, and Martin told about the lobster fisherman they had met and his story. The Captain said he didn't know about the particulars but that the prison part was true. The proprietor had been listening and said they were talking about old Captain Davie and that he was privileged to know him as were a lot of other people on the docks. He was at least a third-generation fisherman, and he told a lot of tales, some more true than others, but the business about his grandfather was mostly true. Martin thought to himself that he wished old man Davie and Captain Jones could meet. After cherry cobbler and more tea and conversation, the Captain suggested that they go because he was having a particularly early start in the morning.

When the carriage got back to the inn, the Captain told them that he wished them a swift but safe journey home. He told them that he would be busy every day for the next few days, preparing to leave and probably wouldn't see them again until he was in Savannah sometime. He said he was sure they had what they needed for sailing into New York City but that he had something for them. He gave them a rolled-up chart of Long Island and the different approaches into the city. He said he had one of his officers add the latest new details from the most recent chart, so that this was probably better than what they had. He said with favorable wind and with the shallow draft of their vessel, they could just follow the coast south to Long Island. At that point, they could either go into Long Island Sound or stay east of the island to the Hudson River entrance at the south end. Once there, if they did not have a favorable wind, they could catch the incoming tide and drift to Hoboken, similar to how they could drift to Savannah from the Savannah River entrance. He unrolled the chart and put his finger on the mouth of the Hudson River at the bottom of Long Island to show what he meant. He added that, as they went home, they should stay far east of Cape Hatteras because a sudden northeaster could blow them up on the hill. Ken told him that they had made it by the Cape many times on their trips to Norfolk and that it was always the furthest they ever went out into the Atlantic for that reason. He shook Martin's hand and said he expected to hear all about their steam-engine riverboat plans on his next trip to Savannah. They all said goodbye, and the Captain went on his way back to his ship.

After breakfast the next morning, the three of them set out with the same carriage and driver. They explained that they were there to pick up a boat and sail it back to Georgia and needed food supplies for the trip and showed him the list of stores they had gotten from the boat builder. He replied that they were about to go to the most interesting market they had ever witnessed and said it was only a ten-minute ride and it would be one stop shopping for them. He said they were going to the world-famous Quincy Market.

Once there, they were astounded at its size. Ashley asked the coachman to wait, and they ventured in. The interior was vast and chock full of food from all parts of the world. As they walked through the fish section, Martin pointed out the crushed ice spread over everything and said there must be an ice business around somewhere. Ashley went to a long section of shelves with nothing but dried fish of all kinds. There was more dried cod fish than any other kind. Ashley said he had tried them once and they were good so he loaded a dozen packs on the wooden cart that Ken had gotten at the entrance. Again, Martin said he wished he could show the people back home what this was like. Ashley had a list, but for the first hour, all they did was wander and marvel at the quantity and variety of foods, many of which they had never seen. They all smelled something familiar. It was a coffee smell coming from an area with shelves and shelves of tea of all kinds. There was a man turning a crank on a grinding machine with a hopper full of coffee beans into a large tin container. They let him finish, and Ashley said he would like two pounds. The man put a small tin on a hanging scale and added the ground coffee until it balanced and then put a lid on it and marked a price with a narrow piece of colored wax.

Martin asked where the yaupon tea was, and the man said that he didn't know what that was. Martin said it grew wild in Georgia, and the man said to wait a minute. He went behind the shelving and came back with a printed booklet with "British East India Company" written on the first page. The man said that at first he did not recall hearing of yaupon, but he then remembered something in the annual tea publication that his tea supplier produced. He said this was last year's publication and thumbed back to a section. He came closer and read aloud, while looking down his nose and through some half-circle spectacles."It says here that yaupon is the most worthless quality of tea that has ever been boiled in water. It is most commonly gathered and drank by savages and slaves and the many poor and illiterate people of the southern states of America. The best of it tastes like heated water that was used to wash dishes." He asked Martin if he was sure of the name of the tea that he asked about. Martin said he was certain and figured that, for some reason, the publication was seeking to falsely discredit a wonderful beverage that he and his family had drank for years and still do enjoy. Martin said all this in such a guileless way that the man was not affronted and said he guessed that he should like to try some before he could actually know of its value. Martin handed the man the tin of coffee they had just gotten and asked him to write his name on it. He said he would personally send him a tin of yaupon when he returned home. The man smiled and wrote "Basel." He said to send it to Quincy Market with his name on it and he would get it because he had been there from the day the market had opened and was well-known there. They thanked Basel and finished their shopping.

Back out front, the driver was still there, and most of the morning had passed. Ken said that they thought he probably would have gone because they were so long, but the driver said he suspected they would have been even longer. He said he guessed that they wanted to go to the boatyard, and Ashley said they did. Once at the boat, Ken paid the coachman in excess of his fare, and they thanked him for his service. He asked if they would like him to come back later to take them back, and Ashley said they wanted to walk and see the sights, but he could come after breakfast in the morning.

Once there shopping was stowed, they all three took a closer look over the boat. Someone saw them and went to the office to tell Robert and he walked down to see them. They said that they hadn't found a thing that they would have had done differently. Ken said that he hated that they would not to be using the boat very long. Robert asked why not, and Ken explained briefly about their business, how it was growing and chang-ing, and how they would be switching to a large steam-engine powered boat that would travel the inland waterways and make deliveries from the Carolinas to northern Florida. They were surprised that Robert was not surprised. He said that he could see the change coming and had gone to the maritime exhibition some years ago and seen the steam riverboats of Robert Fulton and Colonel Robert Stevens. He said that Fulton had died but that he and Stevens had partnered up before his death and had made many advances. He said Stevens' latest innovation was his favorite and it was the new propeller-driven boats with double-ended hulls that could be driven easier without the huge and cumbersome paddle wheels. Martin was surprised and excited at the new information and told Robert that they were leaving day after tomorrow and headed straight to Hoboken to meet Robert Stevens. He explained that two things happened after they had al-ready ordered the new boat. The Milam Ice company had grown quickly and was opening a new operation in Charleston. They had learned from their engineer Thomas about steam engines in boats. Martin said that they would need this boat for a year or so anyway and were pleased to have bought it. Robert said he knew steam power in boats was coming but he expected his sharpie boat building to continue growing because of how practical and efficient the design was, especially in shoal waters locally and even more so in Georgia and the Carolinas, which was where half their orders were coming from. He said he had buyers if they ever wanted to sell. Martin said he would stay in touch and might want to sell it in a year or so. Robert asked what size steamboat they were planning on, and Martin said they would not be sure until they found out more from Mr. Stevens, but probably about eighty feet with a lot of beam. Robert said there were plenty of good builders in the Carolinas and Georgia but that he had an advantage of having built more boats and he would be glad to bid on their new steamboat. He said that Fulton had liked getting engines from England, but the last he heard Stevens had gotten an engine from Philadelphia. Martin said all the discussion was making him eager to get on to New Jersey and wished they could leave tomorrow. Ken said he thought they should spend tomorrow getting to know this new boat. Robert said he could arrange a tow out into the harbor. He would send his two men that were not only master ship carpenters but also excellent sailors. They knew sharpies better than anyone and could show them all the ropes. Ashley said that sounded good. He said that, even though he had been sailing a sharpie for years, what he didn't know about sailing was probably more than what he did know. They agreed that they would take up Robert's offer of the two men and a tow. Robert said that he had heard that the northwester currently blowing would be getting stronger during the next few days. It would be cold and rough but clear. With their new boat's wide beam, there was little chance of capsizing, but he suggested that it would be better for them to get some rough weather experience with his men on board rather than later without them. They all agreed.

On the way back, Ashley had a few gifts for Davie, the catboat man, who they all liked, so they were glad to see him at his boat. He was glad to see them too and gleefully happy that they had brought him a gift. He opened it and discovered a two-pound tin of Quincy's best and most expensive tea, a tin of honey, a pound of butter, two large loaves of bread, and a pack of fine Virginia tobacco. Tears welled up in the old man's eyes, and he told them they had no right buying him all that. He said he would enjoy the "backer," but he wanted the rest for his wife and grandchildren. They would be surprised for him to bring something home besides lobsta. They told him that they were leaving for New York day after tomorrow then back to Georgia a few days after that. He wished them favorable winds the whole way home. He said the strong northwester was here for a few days and it would blow them out of the harbor and around Nantucket if they were going that way. Martin asked him what way he would advise.

He told them that it was calm there because that big hill that Boston was set on blocked the wind. But five miles out in the harbor there would be whitewater and every mile further out it would be rougher. He said if it were him, he would wait to see how things were when leaving. If it was blowing hard and the visibility was good, he would stay close when rounding the cape, and keep on staying close and pass on the inside of the islands and stay three or four miles out from land all the way to Long Island. They might make it more than halfway down to Long Island by the end of the first day, or further since their new boat would be empty and light. He added that, if the northwester kept up, they could be at the tidewater of the Hudson a few hours before sundown on the second day. Martin told him that the cook at the inn knew the story about his grandfather and lobsters, and Davie said he told them so. He said he was getting ready to fish in the morning, and with any luck he would be visiting Quincy's himself to sell his catch. He added that lobstas were hard to catch this time of year but they brought higher prices. The three of them shook his hand and told him they could be back again sometime. He said he hoped they did come back and thanked them again for the gifts.

Back at the inn, they relaxed a bit. Martin wrote a letter to Mary and tried his best to describe what they had seen and done. He wasn't satisfied with his writing and thought it sounded like a six-year-old, but he wrote on. He went downstairs to ask about a local post office. The innkeeper said they were on the mail route and Martin could leave his mail there, and he would see that it was picked up. Martin gave him the two letters, one for his family, and the other for Mary. The innkeeper asked how their stay was so far, and Martin said the rooms and accommodations were very good and that they were enjoying the town and were planning, if winds were favorable, to leave day after tomorrow, but they wouldn't know for sure until that morning.

Supper that night was the usual baked beans, lobster stew with potatoes, and cherry pie for dessert again. The cook came out of the kitchen and asked how they liked the food. They said the beans were just the thing for the cold weather which they admitted not being accustomed to. Martin told him about how much everybody at his home liked deviled crabs. The cook asked what was in them, but Martin didn't know what besides crab meat. Ashley told him some of the other ingredients. The cook said he might try something like that with lobsters tomorrow just for them.

The next morning was a bit colder, and after breakfast they went to their rooms and layered on clothes and their big coats. Then they went back downstairs and boarded the waiting carriage for the trip to the boatyard. At the boatyard, there were two pulling boats with lines attached and four oarsmen waiting in a lumber shed to go to work. Robert saw the three of them from the office and came out with a dark bundle and greeted them. He said that he didn't think they would be equipped for the weather there. It was a cold day and would be much colder out on the water. He had bought them each wool sweaters and caps like all the fishermen wore. He showed them the fabric. The sweaters were deliberately made much larger and purposely shrunk until the knitting was very tight. It is the only clothing that can get wet and still keep you warm. He said he had gotten two medium-sized ones and one large. The hats can be wet and stretched a bit to fit if necessary. He told them that with these under their over coats they would be comfortable. The two men going with them arrived, and he introduced them. They had the same type sweaters with slicker overcoats and looked plenty salty enough. Robert said he asked the men to take them out ten miles where the wind had room to fetch up strong so they could be in a good blow. One of the men said they could go out to the northeast for ten miles with the wind on one beam and come back with the wind on the other beam. He said they probably could have done without the pulling boats to get out today but would need them to come in. The other man said he was curious to see how this sharpie with an extra-wide beam and extra centerboard would do. The oarsmen had turned the sharpie headed out, and Ashley, Ken, Martin, and the two boatyard men went aboard and told the oarsmen to hold up a bit. They spent a while going over things about the new boat then set the jib sail. They then got the two mainsails set on the mast hoops and secured to the big booms and gave the signal to the oarsmen to start out. The sharpie slipped away from the dock, and in only a few hundred yards, the lines to the pulling boats went slack as the sharpie with only a jib caught up and passed them. They threw off the lines and immediately set the big sails. The top of the sails caught a gust of the wind up high, and in flat water the new boat swiftly headed toward open water. The farther out they got, the more the wind increased. By three miles out, there were whitecaps slapping against the windward side of the boat. And at about ten miles out, big waves were crashing against their beam and salty froth and water blowing up and over the boat. Ashley, Ken, and Martin were following instructions from the yardmen and observing how the boat was handling the rough weather. Martin thought about the time he had come into the Savannah River, returning from Saint Helena in a northeaster. This was rougher, but the waves were not as steep because the water was deeper and there was no current standing up the waves. The yardmen skillfully managed to direct the boat to go with the wind on the stern for a way to show how she behaved. A big wave would rise up and look like it would break over the cockpit, but the stern of the boat would lift up, and the wave would pass under. With the big sails reefed and way out on different sides, and the jib dropped, the sharpie behaved and handled the rough water, with the stern rising above every wave. Next the yardmen brought the sharpie around and the sails in and somewhat into the wind, and the new boat did surprisingly well, considering the extra wide beam. When they ordered the boat, they had asked for tandem centerboards to offset the extra beam for going better into the wind, and it was working as planned. One of the yardmen said the two centerboards were a good idea. After sailing at all possible directions to the wind for a while, and the yardmen yelling instructions to Ashley, Ken, and Martin, it was time to head in. They did with the wind on the other beam, and the seas calmed gradually as they became sheltered by the high ground that Boston was built on. The pulling boats were about a mile out from the dock waiting to help them back in. Ashley, Ken, and Martin were wet but their "worsted wool" sweaters were keeping them warm. The yardmen had slickers over their sweaters and strange-looking slicker material hats that they said keep the rain and spray from going down their necks. Robert had said before they left that he should have gotten them "nor'easter" hats to wear like the yardmen had.

Robert had been watching and was waiting when they returned and asked how she did. Ken said the boat did better than good but they had taken a beating and a drenching. Robert motioned for them to follow him up to the office and inside where they had a coal stove. He had them strip off down to their skivvies and warm up and dry out. The steam rose up off the wet clothes that Robert hung on the backs of chairs pulled close to the stove. Ashley asked where the yardmen were, and Robert said he had told them to take the rest of the day off. Ashley said he and Ken had sailed a lot but those two were the best sailors they had ever been around, and he wanted to thank them. Robert said they were from a long line of boat builders and fishermen and started sailing soon after they could walk, and boats and sailing were no nonsense to them whatsoever. Ken said they really put the new boat through every possible angle of the wind and wave. Ashley said they could have gone hull speed with only the jib. Robert said this outing would help them better understand how the boat behaves in a good blow. He asked if they were still leaving in the morning, and Martin said he thought they would if the wind remained favorable and began putting his clothes back on. They were still damp but warm. Ashley said he wanted to go back on the boat and stow everything back that had been tossed around in the rough water. Robert said he got there early and hoped to see them off in the morning. He asked if there was anything that they still needed, and Ashley said he thought they had everything. Robert said they should be in New Jersey in a few days and there were even more chandleries there than in Boston. He added that for provisions they should visit Fulton Market in Brooklyn. They thanked him again for the sweaters and hats, and Martin said he intended to get the supply boatmen at the Milam plantation all a sweater like them.

They walked back to the inn and noticed that Davie and the catboat were gone. Martin said he hoped he was all right out in the rough weather, and Ken said it would take a bigger blow than today to swamp that wise old man and his boat. Martin looked uncertain and said he hoped so.

There wasn't much to do to get ready for leaving. Ken stopped to see the innkeeper on the way to supper and said that it looked like they could leave in the morning and asked about the bill. The innkeeper said that it had ben prepaid by the Milam Ice Company. Ken said that they had enjoyed the rooms and food and especially the Boston style beans. The innkeeper said he appreciated that and they all enjoyed having them. The cook was waiting for them to come to supper. He brought out a platter with six lobster shells full of a mix of lobster meat and the things that Ashley had told him were in deviled crabs like Margo and Ellie had made."Deviled Lobsta," he said, beaming with pride, and said he had made extra for him and his kitchen help to try, and they thought it was extra good and planned to make it a regular dish. When it cooled, they ate it and found it to be different from deviled crab but very good. Again, they had Boston beans, and the cook gave them a crock full of beans to take with them since he had heard they were leaving.

There was a dusting of snow in the morning as Martin looked out his window before light. He looked for any hint of red as the sunlight was just beginning to show over the horizon but there was none. He doubled up the clothes that he had hung to dry during the night and pulled on the tight knit wool sweater Robert had gotten him. He had a feeling of gratitude about Robert's thoughtfulness and about everything so far on their trip, and he looked forward to New York. They went down for breakfast earlier than usual and were surprised to see their carriage driver having tea in the dining room. He said he had guessed that they might be wanting to leave a little earlier today. After breakfast and farewells from the inn people, they left for the boatyard. On the way, all three were anxiously waiting to see if the little catboat was there. It was, and they all breathed a sigh of relief. Robert had been watching out for them and came down to cast off their lines. He said he hadn't set up the pulling boats because he didn't think they would need them. They thanked him, and he said he hoped to hear from them concerning their next boat. Martin said he might, and Robert added that he would appreciate hearing that they had made it home safely too. Just like the day before, the mainsail and foresail was made ready to go up, and the jib was hoisted, and the new sharpie glided silently away from the dock. The three looked at each other and smiled, and Ken said, "Here we come, Long Island."

While things were still calm, Ashley pulled out the chart Captain Lawrence had given them. He pointed to the hook of land that was called the Cape and then to the two islands called Marthas Vineyard and Nantucket, on the other side of the big hook of land. Captain Davie had said they could sail between them. He pointed to the vast shoals indicated on the chart around them. He pointed to the shipping channel and said, if it was the Georgia or South Carolina coast, he would be more comfortable in shoal waters. But it was not, so they might be better off following the shipping channel. He got a nod of agreement from Ken and Martin, and when they were well clear of the cape, they came about. With the strong northwester mostly on their stern quarter, and the new sharpie empty and light, they practically flew south, surfing every few waves with surprisingly very little spray blowing over them. It was the fastest sailing any of them had ever done, and by afternoon they sighted Long Island. They saw on the chart the Montauk lighthouse on the tip of Long Island and continued down the coast until almost dark. They looked at the chart from Captain Missroon and saw that there was enough depth to anchor out about three quarters of a mile offshore where the land would block most of the wind and dropped the anchors as the sky darkened and lashed the sails tight. Once inside, Ashley looked at the chart again and said he believed they had sailed further in a day than he had ever gone.

It was time to try out the new galley. The coal stove was a thing of beauty in craftmanship and heated up and Ashley soon had biscuits baking, eggs frying, Boston beans warming, and the cabin got cozy warm. Ken said New England was nice but that he preferred the warmer weather of the South. After a hearty supper, all three were dog tired from the rough and windy ride and were soon to put themselves to bed. Martin lay in his bunk, and his imagination raced down the coastline. In two seconds, he was flying over the Indian Islands and landed on Tybee, and in his mind's eye he saw Mary in her small room at her small desk with a pen in hand. The candlelight shown over her face as she looked up from her writing, searching for the clarity of the next sentence. He hovered close, trying to smell the light scent of her essence. In a moment, he saw her face change slightly as it came to her what to write next, and she bent with her usual determination over her notebook and continued.

The next thing Martin knew, some pots were clanging, and he smelled bacon and leftover biscuits warming and coffee brewing. He paused for just a moment, remembering his last thoughts of Mary before sleep had come, and he smiled within himself. The cabin was already warmed by the stove, but when Martin went outside in the dark to look around, he was shocked at how cold it was. He couldn't understand how people operated in such cold weather and told Ken and Ashley he was glad they were heading south, and they agreed.

After a hearty breakfast Ken laid out the chart by candlelight and put a penny on where they were and a penny on where they were going. He opened the hatchway and looked out over the water surface toward where the sun would be coming up in an hour or so. He said the wind was still coming from the northwest but might have calmed a little, at least for now, but could pick up later. Ashley looked at the tide chart and said the Hudson River tide started in about noon. The land would block most of the wind, but with the tide and a little wind, they should be able to get up the entrance of the Hudson River a ways. It was a cold morning, but the sky was clear. The sun was not up yet, but there was enough light, so they set the sails with the bow anchor down. When it was lifted, the sharpie eased around toward the southeast and picked up speed as it moved away from land and the wind soon swooped down and filled the sails. It was the easiest kind of sailing with wind coming offshore onto their stern quarter without any worry of being blown in too close. The chart showed that the water was not that deep, but they were sailing just fine without the boards down and wouldn't need them until steering west at the bottom of Long Island, where they arrived about eight hours later. Then they dropped the boards and reached as close as possible into the wind and toward the Hudson River entrance. As they came closer, the wind slackened because the land blocked it, but the incoming tide grew stronger.

The tidal current was like the Savannah River but not as strong. The higher riverbanks were different but what was most unlike coming into Tybee were the hundreds of buildings and wharfs and hundreds of boats and ships of all sizes, especially as they drifted by where the East River forked off to the north. Martin again wished there was a way to show the people back home the spectacle of it all. As they moved slowly along, the three of them were struck by all that was built up on both sides of the river unlike the endless stretches of marsh coming into the Savannah River. Very little wind was blowing over or against them, so they let down and secured them and were glad to be just drifting slowly so they could better see everything. Martin was looking ahead and let out a shout when he saw his first fully steam-powered boat crossing the river. They were nearing Hoboken and soon saw the sign saying "Stevens Ferry." He asked who wanted to go with him in the pulling boat and Ken said he would.

They attached a line and began inching the sharpie over to the side of the river where another steamboat was secured bow-first to a dock with a wide ramp in place. Wagons loaded with freight were crossing over the ramp and onto the ferry. It was routine work for the wagon teams, but the carriage horses were skittish to cross the loading ramp. The loading dock floated up and down with the tide and was made of steel. It was bigger than anything in Savannah and was secured by huge steel pilings. A man on the dock saw their intentions to come in and sent another pulling boat out to help them in. They were soon secured on the inside of the dock and out of the way of all the loading commotion. The man asked them, in no uncertain terms, if they had business coming there. That reminded them of what they had heard in Boston about people there being "point blank." Ashley said they had appointed business with Colonel Stevens, and the man's tone softened. He pointed to a building up on the hill and said he was up on the top floor where the row of windows were.

Martin wanted to stay and watch the ferry depart, but Ashley said it was getting late in the day and they should go before the office closed. Martin said he was right and that he could look later. They followed the long dock up to the huge shop building that had a railed slipway that went from the river up and into it for hauling boats. The shop building was vaulted about forty feet inside and was a couple acres big. There were a hundred or more men building all sorts of metal panels and parts for a boat about eighty feet long that was hauled up inside. Its hull was complete, and the decks were being installed with steel panels being lifted by an overhead crane and set in place. It reminded Martin of the sawmill operation they had visited in Darien except that most everything there was wood and here it was steel. There was an outside stairway that went up to two landings before reaching a wooden building on top of the shop building with the row of windows they had seen from the river. They continued their trek up the stairs to the top and knocked at the door. A man opened the door and asked them in. They were surprised at how quiet it was, with the door closed, from all the noise below. Ken said who they were and that they had come to see John Stevens. Mr. Stevens was at a big, cluttered desk by the windows that had a panoramic view of the docks and river out front. He heard his name and got up. He walked over to them and held his hand out and said he was Colonel John Stevens and asked what he could do for them. Ashley introduced them, and Stevens exclaimed that they were who the Boston engineer had written to him about and that he had been looking forward to their visit. He said they must have come in the smart looking sharpie he had seen arrive, and Ashley said they did. He motioned them over to his desk and asked the man who had answered the door to get a few chairs for them. He shuffled through his clutter and pulled out the letter from Thomas. He said he had read over it and asked them to tell him more about what the inland waterways were like in their part of the country. Ken went over things with him, and he said that, based on the cargo weights and other information he had been given, and the tidal range and swift currents, he thought they would need a boat about seventy to eighty feet in length. He said designing a vessel was a series of compromises. A long narrow boat would be capable of greater speed against their strong currents but would be difficult to navigate in smaller rivers with the current especially. A shorter and wider boat would be easier to navigate the small rivers but would be at almost a standstill in a strong current. Ken added that the inland waterways in the South have many sand and mud bars and that depth of draft was a major concern. Stevens said he was aware of that. Then he started talking about steam engines. Ashley and Ken knew very little of what he was talking about, but Martin understood most everything he was saying. Martin also asked about the new screw propeller operations, and Stevens was impressed with all that the young Martin knew.

He went on to talk about the advantages of propellers over paddle wheels. But he said the propeller system would require just a little more draft because it would need the keel to be lower than the props so the vessel could ground without damaging the shafts and props. He added that the propeller system was much better for hauling a barge like the engineer had mentioned that they would tow. He went on to explain how each prop could be controlled separately, so steerage in combination with a rudder was much better than with a side wheeler, because one prop could be run in reverse and the other in forward.

Robert said abruptly that it was getting late and they would need to catch the last ferry out and they had tomorrow to continue conversations. Stevens asked where they were staying, and Martin handed him the notes that Thomas had given him with the location of the rooms he had reserved. Stevens said it was close to the ferry landing on the other side and their boat would be fine overnight where it was. He said he would come over to their side in the morning and accompany them to look at the river freight and passenger company that he and Robert Fulton started. They were surprised that Stevens would take his day to show them around, but pleased that he would, and they expressed their thanks to him. Mr. Stevens jotted a note on a piece of paper and told them to give it to the dock master and said he knew where their inn was and would come there first thing in the morning. He added that he would think some more about their boat and barge setup and would have some more to say about it tomorrow. He said he had a few things to do before the day was out and said they needed to go now to catch the ferry and walked them to the door.

The ferry was just arriving back at the dock, and the long ramp was let down, and wagons and carriages were lined up to leave. They watched and waited for a half hour for the boat to empty. Then twenty men, each with a flat blade on edge with a wood mop type handle, began pushing the fresh horse manure over the sides into the river and in less than ten minutes they had it cleared, and the line of wagons waiting began to load up. Martin gave the note to the dock master, allowing the sharpie to stay at the dock. They took their bags from the sharpie and boarded the big ferry. Martin noticed how wide the ferry was and thought about how it never went against or with the river current but always across it. It looked as if it was about half as wide as it was long, and other than a pilothouse and a flat roof over the engine and boiler, it was all open deck for wagons and carriages with no accommodations for walk-on passengers. The three of them walked around the engine and marveled at the machinations of it. Martin pointed out the parts and what the engineer and his helpers were busy doing. About halfway across the river, they saw the other ferry headed back to the dock for the night, and Martin asked one of the deckhands when the first boat departed in the morning. He said it started loading at 4:30 and departed at 5:00 and that the boat they were on now left at the same time, but from the other side of the river, and in the fourteen-hour day, each would make six round trips. He said they operated six days a week and that Sunday was maintenance day. Being accustomed to their own transporting of ice and hardware and how long it took, the three of them were astounded at how much freight the two boats handled in one day.

It was getting dark when they walked off the ferry on the other side. They had made arrangements with a driver with an empty carriage on the way over, and they loaded up after he had come across the ramp. In fifteen minutes, they were at their inn, and again it had a view of the river with wharfs and ships and boats in both directions. Two porters met the carriage, took their bags, and led them inside. They were told about supper and shown their room, which was one big area with three single beds and a copper tub in the corner and a small water closet.

One of the porters opened a water valve to the tub and said he would be right back with a bucket of hot water. Once he had brought it he said he would be back again in twenty minutes, and then again in twenty minutes, for each of their baths. When they were all bathed, they went down and were the last to eat supper in the dining room. The food was unusual to them but good. Ken commented that he had liked everything they had been having but that he missed a few things like biscuits, cornbread, grits, and yaupon. Martin said he missed all the pies, cakes, and pastries that his mother, Claudia, and Ellie always made, and Ashley agreed. They were all tired and went back up and were in bed soon.

The street along the river, just outside their inn, was busy and noisy with cargo wagons early the next morning. The noise of the wagon wheels and horses' hoofs on the river stone woke them up well before sun-up, but they were well rested, having gone to bed early. Breakfast was stewed potatoes with shreds of beef and yeast bread with cheese curd. It wasn't something they had never had for breakfast but was hearty and suited to the cold weather. No sooner had they gone up after breakfast to get their overcoats, that a porter came and said there was a carriage waiting outside for them. They went down. Colonel Stevens was there, and they got in. He told them that he was a busy man with a lot of different things to do but that his favorite thing was to design a new steam-engine powered boat but that he didn't like much to be confined to his office all the time. He said he had designed several locomotives and actually had built the first one ever in the country some time ago, but he had become more interested in boats since then. He said he went to bed thinking about what kind of boat would be best for them and woke up with the perfect design to fulfill all they had said they wanted and some things that they needed but didn't know they wanted. They were surprised at his enthusiasm, especially so early, and Martin asked what he had in mind. Stevens said he wanted to show them a boat or two before he told them, so they would better understand and appreciate his design ideas, and that sounded like an agreeable plan.

In about twenty minutes they were just inside the East River that they remembered passing the day before. The carriage stopped at a long dock with two steam-powered boats at it, both about a hundred feet long. Two dock attendants recognized Steven's usual carriage and rushed out to accommodate him. He was getting up in age and was spry but still appreciated the hand in getting off. He told the two that he was fine and didn't need any more help, and that he wanted to show his friends around, and they went back to their work. He said that he had come early because he wanted to show them before the boat was crowded with people who would start boarding in about half an hour. Freight was already being loaded, and the boat captain was watching over things. He saw Stevens and came over to greet him. Stevens introduced Ashley, Ken, and Martin and told him they were his friends from Georgia and they and he would be on the boat this morning to Fort Washington and get off there and come back on the southbound boat. The Captain said that would work because more often than not the two boats stopped there at about the same time. Stevens said all he needed was, if it were possible, for the engineer to show his friends the engine for a bit. The Captain said he would send him shortly after they were underway. Stevens walked them to the stern and showed them the big paddle wheel. He said he didn't have a paddle wheel in mind for them but just wanted to point out how big it was and how difficult and inefficient it would be with a barge in tow with the big backwash they would soon see once underway. He added that the stern wheel was more efficient for going straight ahead but difficult when changing directions. The side-wheelers were better at that by stopping one wheel and powering the other to turn, but with the wheels on each side, they were extra wide, and the wheels lacked the protection of the hull like the stern-wheeler and were damaged more often by snags. As they continued around the boat, passengers began coming on, and he said he should have come earlier. He showed them the engine area and said they would come back to that when the engineer joined them, and he took them to the bow area where the ramp was and the freight area nearby. Then they went up into the pilothouse and saw the Captain again as he was giving orders to get under way after the last passengers were on. Stevens asked the Captain if he could show his friends his cabin, and the Captain said he could show them anything on the boat since it was, after all, his boat. The pilothouse was elevated a few steps with half-windows on three sides and two narrow windows in the back on each side of a narrow door so the Captain could look astern. Out the narrow door and down a couple of steps were the Captain's quarters that were well-appointed with a bath and water closet, a small galley with a sitting area, and two bedrooms that were small but adequate. There was a door that led out to a narrow balcony with a ladder down to the second level, giving the Captain a second route of access and egress. He told them that this captain lived alone but that most had wives and some even a wife and a child or two that lived aboard. This particularly interested Martin for his own reasons. Ken laughed and said the Captain's cabin was a big step up from Captain Ben's sharpie accommodations. Stephens said he didn't climb ladders, so they went back to the pilothouse and then down stairs that were steep but not as steep as the ladder and could be gone down forward.

When they were back down on deck, the bow of the boat was being shoved out by ten men on one end of a long pole that lodged in a niche in the bow. When the bow was out a short ways and the stern not yet let loose, the outgoing current pushed against the bow and began turning the ship. The wheel was engaged and the stern lines cast off, and the boat eased out into the river and northward against the current. Stevens said they would be making about seven knots against the current but that the boat would do about nine knots in slack tide and about eleven knots with the current and they would be at Fort Washington in about an hour. He said they would then get off and board a side-wheeler to return and that he hoped there might be another boat with a barge being loaded at the dock when they got back. The engineer came up, and Stevens introduced him. He said that he was designing a boat for them to use in Georgia and the Carolinas and wanted them to see the engine operation. Martin was keen on this, and the engineer could see his interest above the rest. He led them to the boiler room and pointed to the coal bin and said the coal was the source of their power. Martin said they would probably be using wood, and the engineer said he had started with wood ten years earlier and with the right wood that was properly cured, he liked it better because it was cleaner than coal. He added that steam power was the best way to move a vessel but could be fraught with danger, and Ashley asked him to explain why. The engineer said the biggest danger was not the engine but the operators. He said many explosions happened because of a captain's desire to go faster than the machinery was designed to perform. He said steam was a very powerful process and could expand beyond control without careful operation and patience. He said that with many things you could make a stupid mistake and live to do better and not make it again, but that by making a mistake with a boiler generating steam you didn't get a second chance. Stevens interrupted and said this was the main reason he had wanted them to come on the boat and the most important information they could acquire about steam engines and everything else was secondary. He motioned for the engineer to continue. He went on to say that coal was dirtier to deal with but what was good about it was that it was consistent. He said it was difficult to get wood that had the same burning power all the time. He said some woods were hotter than others and that uncured or wet wood was difficult to get a hot fire. He said if they burned wood, the cleanest and hottest was red oak or hickory, and they needed to have a stockpile that had been curing properly under cover for a year minimum. He said problems happened to many boats that would need fuel and stop and gather wood along the river. They would gather uncured wood of different kinds, load too much in because it was slow to catch or would burn too cool, and because they had a schedule to make. Then it would dry out all at once in the firebox and produce more heat than could be controlled. The steam would expand too quickly, and she would blow. He apologized for dwelling on the frightful things but he felt obliged to his boss to tell the truth to his friends or to anybody about to enter into this business. Stevens nodded his approval to the engineer, who began pointing out the different parts of the engine and what they did. He said he hoped his boss would agree but that he believed the English engines were still the best, and Stevens said he was generally correct except for the latest engines being made by a company in Philadelphia. Martin said they were making a delivery to Philadelphia soon and he would like to see that company. The engineer was with them for a while longer, and then Stevens continued the tour of the boat. When they had about finished, several short whistles sounded. Stevens said they were at Fort Washington and looked at his pocket watch and said, "one hour and twenty minutes."

The other boat was not at the dock but could be seen a ways up river. Stevens said they would be there quickly because they were moving with the current. Ashley, Ken, and Martin were astounded at how fast the second boat approached and went past them a short distance and turned to come up to the dock against the tide. Stevens was right about how easily the side wheeler maneuvered, quickly turning to come back to the dock. And he was also right about it being very wide, and it was a bit awkward laying close to the dock with the big side wheel holding it off a ways. There was a flurry of passengers and cargo again with the first boat leaving. Then they boarded the second boat and were soon away and moving quickly downstream. Martin looked at the riverbank, as he always had, to gauge speed, and it was passing rapidly.

On the trip back, they toured the boat again. Other than the side wheels, the two boats were almost exactly alike. The engineer had similar things to say but added a few things about the side wheeler.

When Martin asked him how he learned to be an engineer he smiled and said he had gone to the Stevens school of steam power. Stevens smiled too and went on to say that it was a four year school, starting as a deck hand, then a waterman, then a stoker, and then an engineer's assistant, and finally an engineer. He added that the engineer on the boat they were on started on a locomotive before switching to a riverboat, but he still had to do some time as a deckhand. Martin said they would need an engineer, and Stevens said that Thomas had mentioned that in his letter. He said that was a while off, and he would be looking for a good one who didn't mind moving down south. Stevens added that it was of great importance that the Captain and the engineer get along. He added that it was good for the engineer to have private quarters for extended trips like they would have. His quarters didn't need to be as nice as the Captain's but needed to be nicer than the crew quarters. The two whistles sounded again. Stevens looked at his watch and said, "just a minute more than one hour." They docked, and sure enough there was a boat at the dock with a barge attached, and after docking, they went straight to look at it. Stevens said the engine was the same as the two other boats, but they could see that it only had a pilothouse raised up one level with minimum accommodations for the Captain, engineer, and crew above, a galley and rest area below for the crew, and the largest area for freight. He pointed to the barge and said that it was twice as long as the one they had specified. He said that he would talk about that later in the office. It was about noon, and Stevens said they were expected for lunch with the Captain on the side-wheeler. They went back aboard and up to the Captain's quarters just as covered plates were being carried from the galley. Ashley, Ken, and Martin were impressed that the food quality was so good. Stevens said his boats were known for their quality meals and, other than the Captain and engineer, it could be said that the cook was the most important man aboard. After the meal, they headed back to catch the ferry back across the river.

Back in the office, Stevens pulled out a roll of paper and weighed the ends down on his desk. He told them he had stayed late after he had talked to them yesterday and sketched his ideas and thought more about it last night. He added that it's hard to account for but he was just as excited now as he was early on in his career designing boats. He pointed to a rolled-up chart and said it was of the coast of the Carolinas and Georgia. He had looked at it before contemplating what would serve them best, and he thought of a design he had built a few years back. He said they could see that this sketch showed a double-ended vessel not as narrow as the boat he had built before. Theirs needed the beam to carry the specified cargo weight without having a deep draft, but not too wide so it could maneuver with ease and buck their stronger tidal currents. Then he showed them a detail of the stern. Just above the keel on each side was a very large pro-peller. This was the new and best system, and he had been developing it for years, and it had improved each time he had it built. It was a propeller that was mostly submerged, but with the top foot or so above the water surface. He said there was a French word for it that he couldn't remember but it meant "splash prop."

Stevens went on to say that the boats he had taken them on had flat bottoms and were very wide and only drew two and a half feet. And he thought their boat should not have a perfectly flat bottom. He said that it should have a slightly rounded bottom, so that it could handle the rougher water of the many sounds they would cross. He said they could see that he had only drawn a bare hull and went on to say that the rest would be easy by simply applying the needed accommodations to match the crew and engine areas and the large, insulated ice-storage space they needed. He said there were two more things he would recommend. The first was to use a combination of wood and steel for the construction. There was no better wood to plank a boat than their own southern Long Leaf Pine but for the ribs and other framing, he would propose using steel. The second recommendation was to use an American-made steam engine by the outfit in Philadelphia he had mentioned earlier. He thought their engine was now as good as the English and French engines, and additional parts for maintenance and repairs would be more readily available. Stevens said that he could only give a rough estimate of cost until they were a little further along with the plans. He expected the propeller-driven system would cost more than the paddle wheels but the long-term cost would be less because paddle wheels had to be replaced every few years. He suggested one more thing, and that was about increasing the length of their barge, and it was a project that they had done often. He said the extra length would make very little difference in how hard it would be to pull and add a good bit to the cargo capacity, and that was something they could do locally.

About the boat, he said what he liked to contract for was only the hull design and construction and the engineering and installation of the engine. He said that he had worked before with the Boston Boat Works that had built their sharpie, and they could finish it out at their place while in the water. He said there would need to be some coordination between his company and theirs in the upper design so that the completed boat floated on the intended waterline, but he had worked with them on a dozen projects, and all went smoothly. Ashley, Ken, and Martin looked at each other and all seemed satisfied with what Stevens had to say. Martin asked how long the building would take to finish from when the plans were complete. Stevens said about four months for his side and maybe a little quicker for the Boston Boat Works.

He said that at this point, if they were in agreement, he would have one of his draftsmen refine his rough plans and make a list of recommendations for the build out and send it up to the Boston Boat Works to give an estimated cost. By that time, he would have a cost for the engine and be able to give a price for his company's part of the work. He added that he would be sending a payment request for the initial design and consulting. Ashley, Ken, and Martin looked at each other again and were in agreement, and Ken said they would look forward to receiving the plans, estimates, and his payment request. He added that, if they didn't have any more questions, he had a few things to do before the end of the day. They stood and thanked Colonel Stevens. He handed them a note for passage on the ferry and asked when they planned to leave for Georgia. Ashley said they hadn't known how long they would need with their business there, but now that it was done, they would need a day to add some provisions and could leave on the early outgoing tide day after tomorrow. Stevens said he had written in the note for them to have free passage on the ferry for as many times as they would need it and first class treatment. He glanced at his pocket watch and said there was one departing in about fifteen minutes.

Ashley, Ken, and Martin were silent walking out to the ferry. They were full of more information than they could think about from all that Stevens had told and shown them. The last of the wagons and carriages were boarding. The last carriage horse was rearing up and was hesitant to cross over the ramp, and Martin remembered the two bridges going from Lazaretto landing to Tybee, and the tacky horses being skittish and hesitant to walk over the widely spaced decking boards. This had been a big and busy adventure, and he was ready to go home.

Once they were on the ferry and crossing the river, Ken said that all that had come upon them since Captain Ben had handed over the business to them was like different waves they would ride. Ashley said that was so, and this one they were riding was the biggest so far. Martin said there was another one coming up that might be the biggest wave yet, and it would be to Philadelphia in just a month or so. They were back at the inn just before dark and asked if the carriage driver could pick them up in the morning, and he said he would. They let the porter know that they would need three baths pulled again, and he said he would see to it. They were all tired, and after a bath and supper, they lingered only a little while before an early bedtime. While waiting his turn to bathe and another hour before bed, Martin managed to write a letter to Henry, telling about their day and what they had done and the graciousness and knowledge of Colonel Stevens.

Next morning, after another hearty breakfast, Martin dropped his letter to Henry off with the innkeeper and they ventured out and found their carriage driver waiting. Ashley asked if he knew where Fulton Market was, and he laughed and looked at them and asked in that "point blank" way, "How long do you think I have been in this country?" He said everybody knew where Fulton was. Ashley laughed and asked back what was he waiting for. A smile broke over the driver's face and said fifteen minutes and moved out onto the roadway already crowded with hundreds of wagons and carriages of all sizes and shapes.

Fulton was even bigger than the Quincy Market they had been to in Boston. They still had a lot of what they had gotten at Quincy, but the place was huge, and they wanted to see it all. The driver told them that he could wait or come back in two hours, and Ken said to come back. Ken grabbed a small wooden wagon, and they got a few things but mostly gawked at all there was to see. There were different areas for different ethnic groups. They were surprised to see that the Oriental section was the largest, and Martin said that he had read in the locomotive publications at Thomas' office that thousands of Oriental people had come to America to work on all the new railways being built in the northeast. Two hours went by quickly, and their shopping wagon was full. They paid up and went back out front and found their carriage amongst many others. They loaded up and asked to go to the ferry dock. It wasn't yet midday, and they planned to take the rest of the day to ready the boat for an early departure with the tide in the morning. When the ferry landed on the other side, they looked up high at the row of windows, and they imagined Stevens looking at his pocket watch to check if the ferry was on time and looking down at them. Martin waved, hoping Stevens would see him.

Once on board, Ken checked the bilge for water. There was some but less this time, and he said she was swelling up tight. Ashley stowed the new provisions, and they ate some of the snacks they had picked up at Fulton. Then Ashley pulled out three charts that covered their trip back. He said he really didn't need to see anything from the Chesapeake down but wanted to study things from where they were to Virginia. He pointed out that there were only a few places to tuck in from the ocean until they got to Atlantic City. He pointed to an inlet about twenty-five miles north of Atlantic City and said they could go in there if necessary but only in daylight with decent weather, or they could continue and go in at Atlantic City. Martin said he wouldn't mind sailing at night and not stopping for a break until the Chesapeake. Ashley said a lot would depend on the weather and wind direction but there wasn't a lighthouse until the Cape Henlopen Beacon in Delaware. Then he thought about something and got the chart that Captain Missroon had given them and opened it up. It covered the coast a little ways down New Jersey, and he remembered the Captain saying his officers had updated it using the latest charts. Ashley looked at it and put his finger on a spot and said, "Yep, there is a new light penned in called Barnegat that has just recently been completed, and it has a lamp and mirrored reflector like Tybee, and it says here that with good visibility, it can be seen from seventeen miles out at night." He ran his finger down the coastline from there and stopped at the Cape Henlopen Beacon in the Delaware Bay, and said that was the next one, and then followed the coast with his finger to Norfolk, and said the Old Point lighthouse was next, and they were all familiar with that one. He said they could see what happened with wind and weather, but he wasn't up for taking undue risk at night, and they agreed on that. They felt good having seen and understood where they were going. The ferry whistle sounded, and they sat out in the cockpit and watched and waited for all the commotion of horses and wagons to load into the ferry before boarding themselves.

When they got to the inn, Ken told the inn keeper that they were planning on leaving in the morning and asked if there was anything that they needed to attend to. The inn keeper said that they had been paid up by the Milam Ice Company and wished them a safe return trip.

At 4:30 the next morning, there was already activity in the streets. They paused to look out from their room window at the spectacle of all the wagon and carriage lanterns moving about in the darkness. Again, Martin said he wished that there was a way to show these sights to the people back home, and Ken said they would just have to do their best to tell about it. They boarded the carriage and became one of the hundreds of faint lights slowly moving about in a frosty and foggy darkness. Once at the landing, they waited in the carriage until all the wagons and carriages had loaded before going aboard. The boarding attendant told them that they were expected in the Captain's quarters for a breakfast and told them that he would escort them as soon as they were underway. In a few minutes he was leading them up to the second deck and into the Captain's heated cabin where a table was set with covered dishes and a tea pot with a quilted cover to keep it warm. The attendant told them that the Captain couldn't join them because he had to stay in the pilot house during a crossing, but he thought they had everything they needed, and they could use the facilities here if they were needed. He pointed forward to the doorway and said they were welcome to go up into the pilothouse when they finished if they liked. They looked at each other in amazement, and Ashley said this might be their best meal for a while. Just as they finished up, they heard the whistle blow twice and left to go watch the approach from the pilothouse. The Captain welcomed them briefly while keeping his attention ahead as the long dock loomed out of the fog and the big ferry moved slowly up between two tall steel pilings and the heavy boarding ramp was lowered and lines secured and the parade of animals and wagons and carriages filed out over the ramp. From up above in the pilothouse, they looked down on the backs of the horses and wagons, some empty to go pick up goods, and some full to deliver goods. While they were peering out at the spectacle, the Captain properly introduced himself and said he had heard about what they had come to do and the boat that the Colonel was working on for them. His warm words made them feel like they had been around longer than they had. He asked them how they liked the big city and the Hudson River, and Martin said the city was nice, but he liked the river best. The Captain said he had enjoyed seeing their fresh new sharpie at the dock and that he had spent quite a few years on one about that length but not that wide. He said their builder in Boston was a good one and about one out of every three sharpies that you see came from them, and some were fifty years old and still going. He added that there would always be sails, but things were changing, especially there on the Hudson. Steam engines were getting smaller but more powerful and safer and more reliable, and the Stevens Works was turning them out nonstop. He saw their readiness and said the tide was almost full and soon be slack and that he knew they were needed to go. He bid them farewell and shook their hands. They left out and down to the main deck and out. Martin looked at the river and said a slack tide is a beautiful thing wherever it is. The dock master saw them and sent an attendant to help them get underway, and another surprise was that there were two pulling boats waiting with lines attached to get them out into the river. All they had to do was step aboard, and their lines were handed to them. The pulling boats easily, in the slack tide, expertly eased them away from the dock and out into the middle of the river, pointed eastward, and left them to wait for the tide to turn.

There were things to get the boat ready to sail, but there would be plenty of time drifting for the next few hours to do that, so they relaxed for the sacred ritual that they had done many times on the rivers in their home waters. There was a magical moment that could be felt in a calm and still river at slack tide. After the ocean surge had swelled and filled the riverbanks for thirty miles or so inland, somewhat like a giant liquid breath of air filling a body, there was a calm for about a half hour, and if you were keenly attentive, you could feel the surge turn and slowly start to breathe back out. They sat quietly and felt the flow change, and the new boat began, ever so slowly, moving with the water that began returning to the ocean.

When the fog lifted, they marveled at the hundreds of docks and buildings on the river. As they drifted closer toward the ocean, the riverbanks became more in their natural state. It was still calm, and there was no discernable wind direction yet, even when they were in clear view of the ocean and the current had slowed as it emptied out of the mouth of the river into deeper water. It was the only time they had been becalmed since they left Savannah. Martin said there was no logical reason for it but that he had somehow expected to be blasting southward in a favorable wind today but now realized that it was not to be.

Ashley said every sailor sailed in his mind as well as in the ocean and that both places had their tempests and their calms. He said that the wind always blew again after a calm just as it always slowed after a hard blow and although it could prevail from one direction, it eventually blew from every direction. Martin said that Captain Jones always said that the weather was something that men talked about often but could do nothing about. Ken said, "True that."

After hours of sitting idle, Ashley noticed that they were actually drifting very slowly backward and said that they should drop a hook. Ken said that was a good idea and they could get acquainted with the new windlass. He and Martin set about on the bow and let the anchor down. Ken reckoned the depth at about fifty feet and let out another hundred feet of line that just stayed bunched up in the water without much movement of the boat. Ashley said he thought it was perfect weather for a long nap. Ken said he agreed, but Martin said he would stay up and maybe fish a little because he didn't feel sleepy. Then he said he had forgotten that they weren't on the other sharpie with everything they needed. Ashley said he would look below because Robert had said that they had outfitted the boat with everything they could possibly need. After a few minutes he exclaimed that Robert was right and handed Martin a small wooden box with a hand line and hook and weight and handed him a pack of the dried fish they had gotten at Quincy market for bait. Martin rigged it all up and dropped it over the side. He became bored after only a few minutes, got a bit drowsy, and decided that he would nap like the others.

A few hours went by and Martin felt a little boat motion. He jumped up and went out to see the anchor line stretched out and the sharpie pointed southeast. He sighed because that was the exact direction they needed to go. He heard Ken say from below that he knew the wind direction from the look on Martin's face and said that they would make better progress becalmed than in a southeaster. Ashley came out and said Ken was right but that it offered the opportunity to practice with the new boat and see how close to the wind she would do. Ken stuck his head out and said it was cold and ducked back down and put some coal in the stove. He put on a pot of water for tea and found his worsted-wool sweater that Robert had supplied and went out with the others. Ashley said he would cook after they had set the sails on their own for the first time. They all went about it and, with the anchor still down and the boat pointed up, dropped both center boards. They hoisted the clean and crisp new sails, brought up the hook, and fell off to the east. Ken, at the tiller, played with their direction, easing into the wind, looking at the compass to see how close to the wind he could come. Then he came about to the west and did it again and again. After watching a while, Ashley went below and handed out heavy warm mugs of tea from Quincy Market. The smell of onions and potatoes was soon wafting out from below. Ken said he appreciated the ample supply of coal from Robert but much preferred the smell of oak or hickory wood to the smell of coal coming back over them from the chimney pipe. He said that it just occurred to him that the smell of the air over Boston and New York had been the many coal-burning fireplaces and stoves. Ashley came out and took the tiller to get the feel of it and he had Martin did some adjusting of the sails to see how things worked. After a half hour he offered the tiller to Martin, went below, and handed out some tins of soup. They had been sailing for about two hours, and Martin looked at the coastline and saw that they had only gone a few miles south, but it felt good to be moving. There was still plenty of daylight left, and Ashley asked what they thought they should do. He said they could tack back and forth in close until dark and set both hooks for the night. Or they could head out far to the east as close into the wind as possible for six or so hours, then come about and head westward as close as possible into the wind for about the same amount of time and look for the new Barnegat light about twenty five miles south. Ken said twelve hours might get them close enough to see the light that was supposed to be visible from seventeen miles. So, they set out east, keeping the sharpie as close into the wind as possible, and watching the compass for any change of wind direction. The wind increased some as they got further out, Ken tied off the tiller, and they were impressed with how, with the two centerboards down and all sails up, the wide sharpie held a steady course unattended. The sun set back over the distant shore, and Martin was reminded of what his father had taught him about the earth spinning away from the sun. They continued on until Ashley announced it was time to come about and that he hoped that they would see the new light in about seven or eight hours. Ken went below and made a big pot full of double strength tea. They were all warm and snug, thanks again to Robert for the worsted wool sweaters and toboggans.

They constantly peered toward the southwest for the Barnegat light, or the sound of surf. After five hours they really started looking hard for anything. After another half hour, Ken said he thought the swells were getting a bit steeper, and he started dropping a lead line, which showed that the bottom was getting closer. Martin screamed and said he saw the Barnegat light. They came about right away and headed east again for a few miles until the light almost disappeared. Then they headed westward again until it shown brighter. They continued that and took compass readings until they were sure of their position. They continued the tacking back and forth until the sun's light started over the ocean horizon. They were relieved and felt good to have made some progress. It had been more than a day and many miles of sailing, but they were still not far south, having only gained a little more than fifteen miles toward home. They had leftover soup and fresh biscuits for breakfast and took turns napping to catch up on their rest and at the end of the day they were even with the Barnegat Lighthouse.

Finally, they could no longer see the light from the lighthouse behind them that had been a reference since the night before. It was no longer visible and reckoned to be about fifteen miles south of it. Earlier in the night the moonlight reflected off the beach of the long barrier islands that stretched almost the full length of the Jersey coast. A couple of times the faint sound of the breakers could be heard to warn them to head back off-shore.

The wind began shifting to the east and with it on their beam, the shoreline began to pass more quickly and halfway into the third night the Henlopen light could be seen. Ashley said the coastline there turned more southward and their current wind would be presented to them even more favorably. If it continued its movement and came directly from the east, they would be able to go in a half-day farther than they had been in three days. He said that they could put in somewhere and rest or they could keep sailing through the night. Ken said he knew what Martin would want and said that he was a bit weary but was getting better at sleeping more often for shorter times, so while the winds were getting more favorable, he voted to go. Ashley said he was for going and it would be best that always two of them to be up while one napped. He added that the next lighthouse after the Henlopen one was a good ways off but it was the Old Point light that they were familiar with.

Sunup came at the beginning of their fourth day from New York, and they began the long stretch to Norfolk where they would finally be in familiar waters. The sharpie was moving along swiftly, due south, with a stiff east wind on its beam, staying parallel with the coast about five miles out, not far from Maryland. The wide beam of the new sharpie, with the two centerboards down, was stiff and heeled very little, and they were making the best progress so far and decided that they might take a land break once they reached the north side of the Chesapeake. It would be good to walk around a bit and rest up for the trip out and around Cape Hatteras and Diamond Shoals. Ashley looked over the chart again and said they were about one hundred sixty miles away but making good time and should, if the wind stayed the same, make it to Smith Island by the afternoon of the next day. They stayed on the same reach all day without any sail adjustments or having to cross the wind and took turns napping. The waxing moon was up before sundown and rose quickly out of the land.

Martin was on the tiller as the first sunlight shown out of the east and the mainland looked about ten miles away. Ken said he was looking forward to walking around on land and perhaps doing some fishing, but maybe they should sail on and try to pass the Cape ahead of what could be a northeaster coming on. Ashley said he was thinking the same thing, but he was tired too. Martin said he wished he could ask Captain Jones about tomorrow's weather. Ken tied the tiller off and went below and brought the chart out and laid it on the cockpit floor so the wind wouldn't blow it. He put his finger on Smith Island where they had planned to stop, and then he moved his finger along the coastline and around Cape Hatteras and stopped at an island called Ocracoke. He asked Ashley if he remembered them stopping there years ago on their first trip to Norfolk. Ashley said yeah but they had been heading north and Captain Ben had decided to hole up there, so they did and anchored in a creek, where there were several coastal trading sharpies bigger than theirs at some half rotted docks. Ken said the inlet was shallow but wide. Ashley said he remembered then being the first time he had heard of Cape Hatteras being called the "Grave Yard of the Atlantic."

Because of the easy and fast progress, the decision was made to go on past Smith Island and sail all night and head far out southeastward and around the Cape during the light of the next day. As the day passed, the wind began to move more toward northeast and the seas became steep and big over the Diamond Shoals. It was the biggest test for the new boat so far and it was wet as some of the biggest white capped waves broke against the stern and sent cold Atlantic spray over the cockpit. It wasn't till they were twenty miles out that the waves were less steep and they knew they were in deeper water and past the shoals and steered southwest back toward land and the stern lifted up over the waves without spray.

Ashley yelled, "Tybee Bight!" and Ken knew what he was excited about, but from the look on Martin's face, he could tell that he didn't. He told Martin that Captain Ben always shouted that when they were there, because it is the beginning of the Tybee Bight. He told Martin that from Cape Hatteras the coast ran southwest to Tybee, and from there it ran southeast to Miami, and Tybee was the westernmost spot on the east coast, and it looked like a big bite had been taken out of the coastline, and that's why it was called the "Tybee Bight."

Filled with excitement of passing by the "Graveyard of the Atlantic" and having the most favorable wind possible, and in a new boat, and headed for home with so many possibilities made this moment a particularly special one for the three of them. Martin's face muscles ached from smiling so big, and again he wished he could show the people back home what they were doing and seeing and experiencing. He didn't know how to do that, but he could at least tell it all to Mary and have her write it in her notes.

With the northeaster still blowing hard, the idea of making landfall at Ocracoke was out of the question. Rest would have to continue in two hour rotations and by the next morning the sharpie had passed by two hundred miles of the coast in about forty hours. They could be at Wilmington around noon the next day where they had gone in many times delivering freight. Martin went below for his rest time and Ken let him stay an extra hour before taking his turn, then Ashley did the same to Ken. As he always did, Martin watched the shore go by and thought about them getting closer and closer to the Tybee lighthouse and Mary. And he hoped that things worked for them to stop over for a night at the Lazaretto landing. He figured that with each ocean swell that passed under them, they were a hundred feet closer to Tybee. And he tried to calculate in his head how many swells to the mile, so he could know how many swells he would have to go over to get to Tybee. He gave up on that and just thought of the times he was there and stuff they did. He was interrupted when Ashley got up from the tiller and gestured for him to take over. He did but was soon thinking about Mary again. He didn't tire of thinking of her, but he tired of thinking of her and her not being there. He forced his mind to think about something else, but it wasn't easy. He thought about the riverboats Stevens had shown them and then about the Captain's quarters, and that made him think of Mary again. He thought about the big steam engines, and an idea popped into his head. It was what Henry had said about Thomas' son getting out of the navy and maybe needing a job. A while back when Martin had first started going to Thomas' office to learn about steam power, Thomas had mentioned that his son was somewhere on a navy steamship, but he didn't say anything then about him getting out. He thought about what Stevens had said about the best education for a steam engineer was the Stevens school of engineering, and he wondered if Thomas' son would be interested. Ashley interrupted his thoughts and handed out some beans and a hunk of hard cheese and biscuits and honey with some hot tea.

A couple more days and miles and miles of shore went by and they got better at resting in shifts on and off and the northeaster stayed steady. They headed farther offshore for the night sailing and checked the compass often. Martin skipped one sleeping shift and when the next one came he felt like he could stay up all night, but about midnight Ken told him he should get some sleep so that he would be rested in case they stopped over at Tybee. He laughed in a good-natured way. Martin grinned and said he was probably right and went below. He stayed for a few hours and came back out and grinned at Ken again. Martin asked if one of them wanted a break, and Ashley said he wanted one to fix some tea because he wanted to stay awake until sun-up because they would be getting close to Charleston by morning and there would probably be a lot of ships anchored waiting for the northeaster to finish so they could go in. Some of them anchor lights out and some didn't and he didn't want to get their new sharpie hung up under a yard arm or bowsprit or worse. This thought got Martin wide awake and his mind off Mary, and all three drank tea and peered into the dark. The first of the sun's rays lit the sky in the east, and Martin said he saw a light off the starboard beam. Ashley said that it had to be the Georgetown light, but he was surprised that they hadn't seen it earlier. Ken said the northeaster was kicking up a mist and they were twelve miles out. Ashley said he thought they would have been there sooner, but that maybe the wind had calmed a bit and the second reef slowed them some and they still had a few hours yet to get to Charleston. Ken said he liked Charleston but was ready to get home, and Ashley said stopping wasn't on his mind either. They looked at Martin, and he couldn't help grinning back at them and they knew what or rather who was on his mind.

An hour later it was light, and they began seeing a few ships on the horizon. Ken said the northeaster was slowing more and in about another hour and a half, they were seeing all the tall church steeples in Charleston and a few ships anchored a little closer in, probably waiting on a pilot. Charleston and Darien were probably the towns they had made the most deliveries to, and they were very familiar with both harbor entrances. Ashley was at the helm and had steered closer in so they could have a look as they went by, and Ken named the buildings, and they saw the two lighthouses, one on each side of Charleston. Martin said he hoped they would be delivering ice this far by next year, and Ken said he wouldn't be surprised if they were. As they passed the city, Ashley headed farther out. In another hour with the wind slowing a bit, he said he thought they could soon do without the reefs in the mainsail and set the foresail and move a little faster and be at Tybee by midnight or so. Martin said that high tide would be about an hour after midnight, and Ashley said that if they didn't get there soon enough to catch the last of the incoming tide, they would have to anchor out and go in the morning, but he would rather spend the night in Lazaretto creek if possible. He got up and told Martin to take the tiller and he and Ken would take the reefs out. The wind was slowing and moving around a little more eastward. Martin had thought he liked the wind on the beam best in this new boat, until they had come around Cape Hatteras and headed southwest with the northeaster directly behind them because they had sailed in strong winds in comfort for almost three hundred miles in two days. But now, with the wind on their beam, he liked how, with the wide beam and two centerboards down, she stiffened up without heeling over and moved along at a good clip without much effort on the tiller. Ashley came out with strong tea for them, and Martin tied off the tiller while they enjoyed the warming temperatures and sipped tea and watched the shoreline go by.

Martin said he had been thinking about the Philadelphia trip and where ten people would fit comfortably on the new boat. He said that he thought it would be a tight squeeze but Jacob, Ellie, Maggie, and Thomas could stay in the one room with the two bunks with Maggie and Thomas on the floor. Alice, Johnny, and the baby could be in the other room. The three of them and Izak could fit on the galley floor or, if it wasn't raining, there was plenty of room in the cockpit. Then he had another idea. He said the holds were about eight-feet wide by twelve-feet long and about six feet deep. He thought they could perhaps lay some tea boxes down in the bottom and lay some boards on top for a temporary deck with bedding on top of that. He said that the hatch cover on the hold could be propped up about a foot above the deck, giving about five feet of height to the inside and allowing some air in. He said they would have to bend over to move around, but it would be better than them bunching up on the galley floor. He said he thought Thomas could be with them, which would give more room for Jacob, Ellie, and Maggie. Ashley said that sounded fine and he guessed that the hatch could be let down in rain or a good blow. They didn't know yet how much tea that Richard wanted to send, but there would probably be room enough. Ken said they weren't back from one trip yet and Martin was already planning the next one. Martin said that he was the brother of Henry, who thought of all things practical, and he guessed some of Henry had rubbed off on him. Ashley said he guessed that it was also good that some of Martin had rubbed off on Henry and laughed.

The day passed without any sail adjustments as they continued beam to the wind, following the coast at a good clip. About an hour after sunset, they were passing Port Royal sound where the Broad River dumps out, and they could see the Tybee lighthouse fifteen miles ahead and a few hours or so away. Ashley went below to look at his watch by the glow of the stove and said they were ahead of what he had said by an hour and maybe they could be anchored in Lazaretto before midnight. Martin had never been so glad to watch the Tybee lighthouse get bigger and brighter as they got closer. Ken was on the tiller, and when they were straight out from the lighthouse, he steered directly west and said it was time to hoist the centerboards to go over the shoals outside and the mud bars closer in without worry of grounding. With the wind and tide , the big new sharpie slipped into Tybee Roads. The moon was getting closer to full and was straight up and moonlight shown off the lighthouse and the big dune in front of it and the little silver driftwood shanty of Captain Jones on the north beach of Tybee. All three sailors were spellbound at the beauty of it and very thankful to see it. At the same time, the weariness and fatigue that had been pushed back and ignored during the long back began to ache in their muscles and bones. They were completely spent, but in a good way and there was just a little more effort needed to get the sharpie a bit further to Lazaretto Creek, their favorite landing. Anchors were set and sails struck and the minimum tasks done and the rest left for the next day after the first snug harbor in eight days.

26.
Back to Georgia

They slept late in the morning. The sun was up, and the cockpit was already dried out from the dew when the three of them sat with coffee. Ken said if they had been more ambitious, they could have gotten up earlier and caught the beginning of the incoming tide to Savannah instead of sleeping until mid-morning. So now they would need to wait and leave late in the afternoon or wait until the morning. He eyed Martin who had already planned on what he would say to Ken and Ashley if they suggested leaving in the afternoon. He was careful to say it like he had just thought of it, and he casually mentioned that Margo would probably insist that they come for supper where she would probably have several kinds of casseroles, cake, and pie. Ken and Ashley smiled because they knew why Martin was saying that, but both agreed that it would most certainly be a mistake to disappoint Mrs. Margo by declining her offer. Martin smiled mostly to himself that the two of them saw through his talk, which was not entirely untrue. He said if he had some help with the skiff, he would go in and walk up to the lighthouse and Daniel would come get them in the wagon. Ashley said that sounded good but to wait until afternoon because he and Ken had some tidying up to do and some work to get things back in order, and they might like to have a nap. Martin said he would gladly stay and help out, and they said no and for him to go, so Margo would have plenty of time to make those pies and cakes.

Martin walked through the open gates to the lighthouse compound and saw Daniel and his father at the brick oil storage house filling the cans to go up top. They were so intent on filling the cans without spilling any oil that they didn't notice him. He waited until they had finished filling the can they were on, so he wouldn't startle them and cause a spill. Then he shouted, and it did startle them, and Daniel ran over and shook Martin's hand and gave him a bear hug, and Charles came and did the same.

Daniel said he was glad to see him, especially for Mary's sake because she had been moping around ever since he was gone and nothing he could do or say would cheer her up. They were interrupted by a scream, and it was Mary running out and hugging Martin. Charles laughed, and Daniel cringed a bit then laughed too. Margo heard Mary scream and came to see what was going on. She told them to come there because she had some things going on the stove that she couldn't leave. So they went into the house, and Margo said she had never been so glad to see someone and she knew that his family would be especially glad to see him too and hugged him. She moved her pots off the stove and put on some water for tea. Daniel asked him if they were in the same northeaster that they had just been in, and Martin said they were, and they had come by the "Devils Graveyard" in it, and Daniel said to tell them right away about it. Margo told Daniel to give Martin a bit to relax and have some tea first. Mary agreed with her mother and said she would have her pen and notebook whenever he wanted to tell them all about the trip. Martin said it would take a long time to tell all, and he would leave some for Ashley and Ken to tell. He asked how the Captain was and Daniel said he was very frail and he was worried about him and they could go down in a bit because he had been asking about him every day. Margo said she would assume that Ashley and Ken would be there for supper, and Martin said they certainly would and he had told them Daniel would come in the afternoon to get them. Charles said there had been a lot going on here and some new things happening at his home. Martin didn't think anything much about what Charles had said because there was always something going on at his home, and he asked Charles what had been going on with them. Charles said that some government engineers had come in a big sloop and anchored at Lazaretto to look at where to locate what they called a "Martello Tower" down at the bottom of the dune there and they walked around and around a spot at the point. They also wanted to go over to Cockspur to see about the big fort to go there and asked him to help. Charles said he had hired a crew and boat from out on the beach to take them to Cockspur, and on the way back he had them stop at the little spit of land coming out from the east end of Cockspur and told them how important and useful a small lighthouse would be there for navigating into the south channel. They said that the lighthouse was planned to be built but the forts would probably get going first and Charles said he told them that the lighthouse should be ahead of the others.

They left after three days, and it sounded like it would be a number of years before anything would start up, but the big fort on Cockspur would probably be first. He said another thing was that a ship had sunk while anchored out in the northeaster and as of yesterday you could still see the tip of the topmast above the water. Martin said they might have come near that last night coming in. Charles said a boat would be coming out from Savannah soon with a steel buoy, painted white, to mark the wreck. He said that the ship captain and crew had made it safely over to the Tybee beach and the Captain stayed in the old guard house, and the crew stayed with the pilot crews on the beach. He said he had signaled the Milam place and they sent both supply boats down the next day to bring the Captain and his crew to Savannah. Martin said there sure was a lot going on, and Charles said there was one more thing and told Daniel to tell it.

Daniel said they got a signal from Ayana asking him to come over, so he went right away. She told him about a boat trying to come up to their island. It got up to the first landing, and she had her people come out and stand with her. The people in the boat seemed to become frightened and abandoned what looked like an intent to come look at the island and left without saying anything. Ayana said it wasn't drunks or fishermen. It was three men with two slaves rowing the boat, and she said the men were well-dressed and looked important. Martin said that didn't sound good, and Daniel said that he had never seen Ayana so upset. She said she thought they wanted the island and were intending to look it over but were frightened by the sight of them. She is afraid they may come back with more people and guns. Martin said that sure didn't sound good, but he wasn't surprised because the population of Savannah was growing, and land investors were everywhere looking to make a profit. Daniel said he thought the islands belonged to the Indians. Martin laughed and said it did belong to them until a white man wanted it, and neither Indians nor slaves counted when it came to the law and a courtroom. Charles said, "true that." And Martin said he would ask Henry to ask if Sidney and Hulbert could find out if there were any land speculation rumors going on concerning the Indian Islands. Daniel said that was all that had happened there. Mary said it was the most that had happened there since Martin had come and stayed a while back. Margo came with tea and a big egg biscuit. Martin said he would tell some about the trip after a biscuit and said they had eaten pretty good while in Boston and New York but not near as good as the eating was here or at his home and they had eaten mostly beans the last eight days and he really looked forward to her casseroles and all.

After strong yaupon and the biscuit, Martin tried his best to describe all the wonders he had seen in the big cities they had visited, what they had set out to do, and what they had gotten done. Martin had not forgotten how he wished he could show them what he had seen of all the unusual people and places and things. He recalled how he had wanted to look at the art galleries for a painting of the waterfront or city view to better be able to show things, but they didn't take the time to shop for art. As best he could, he tried to paint a picture for the Dyers with his words as he reviewed the scenes in his mind's eye. It wasn't an entirely new way for him to tell a story but he just took more effort to make it more vivid. Whenever he paused a half moment, he saw their full attention and keen anticipation for his next words. He felt like he had learned more about story telling from Captain Davie with the "cat" boat. Mary was not only listening but jotting down important words or phrases to help her reconstruct later in the night. In an imperceptible instant while he was talking, Martin visualized the future with Mary, in their private quarters on a riverboat, with a pile of her old notes, putting together a book about everything that had happened since his father had come to Savannah. Martin tapered off his talking and said he wanted to leave some for Ashley and Ken to tell. He asked Daniel and Mary if they would go with him to see Captain Jones, and they said it was a good idea because it would do the Captain good to see Martin. Martin noticed a bit of melancholy about Margo and Charles and asked if everything was okay; Margo put on a more pleasant face and said they were fine. He and Daniel and Mary left to go down on the beach.

There were no pilots and crews on the beach because they were out with ships that had been waiting for the northeaster to blow over. There was no sign of the Captain either. They found him still in his bed in the shanty, and it was past noon. They walked in and were at first horrified because he was lying on his back asleep and he had a light grey ghostly pallor. His mouth was open like his last breath had gone out, and they thought he might be dead. Mary touched his shoulder, and they were relieved that he came to life and opened his eyes and looked at them, but he looked like he was not yet back from some place distant. After a few moments some color came back, and recognition showed in his eyes. When he saw Martin, a slight smile showed his more familiar way. He made an effort to sit up, and Daniel helped him and propped him up with a pillow. He said he had hoped to see Martin today but thought it would be a few days after the northeaster. Martin said they had ridden that northeaster for the last four hundred miles and it was terribly rough but they were thankful for it.

The captain surprised them and said he was hungry. Mary opened the basket and handed him half of an egg biscuit and filled his cup with warm yaupon. He ate a couple bites of the biscuit and a big swallow of tea and asked Mary to wrap up the rest for later. He said he had only wanted to eat a little because he wanted to tell them the dream he had been having, and his mother had always told him that it wasn't good to tell a dream before breakfast or something bad of it might come about. He said he didn't particularly believe that, but it was a habit put on him when he was too young to prevent it. He paused a moment and gazed out the one window in his shanty to recollect his dream. He said it was a dream of a war, and there were hundreds of cannons on the edge of the land from there almost to Lazaretto. They were shooting across the marsh and over the top of a small house, and he didn't understand why they were firing on the marsh, and why a house was built out in the marsh. Anyhow he said he had told it after breakfast and he didn't understand it, but that was the way of dreams.

Martin told the Captain briefly about their trip and coming around Cape Hatteras, and as the story went on, it got his blood flowing and the Captain perked up. He told the Captain that they would be picking up Ashley and Ken to spend the night at the lighthouse and the three of them would be leaving for Savannah in the morning. The Captain said Martin's mother and father had not come last week as usual, and he had looked forward to seeing them. Daniel said something that surprised them. He told Martin and Mary to go pick up Ashley and Ken, and that he wanted to stay and help the Captain get cleaned up and attended to and get him outside a bit. An unusual look of love and admiration came over Mary directed at her brother for his kindness. She placed a kiss on his cheek and then did the same to the Captain. Martin too was touched by Daniel's concern for the Captain and thanked him. Daniel told them that he would be up later, but if no pilot crew came back, he would be staying with the Captain for the night and that he kept a bedroll there for the occasion. Mary said someone would be down with supper if he wasn't back.

Mary and Martin were silent walking back up the dune. Mary said she couldn't stop thinking about the Captain's dream and said it made her think about what the engineering group had come this past week to see about. She said maybe the little house was actually a little lighthouse, and maybe the cannons were shooting at the big new fort. Martin was surprised that he had not made that connection, and he asked Mary why on earth cannons would be firing from Tybee on the new fort? Mary said dreams usually were odd and had more questions than answers and sometimes the answers came, and sometimes they didn't. Martin said he had plenty of odd times but not a lot of answers, and that made Mary laugh. He told her that he had thought about staying an extra day and riding back home with the supply boat and he was surprised and didn't understand why she said he should go home to see his family. Anyhow, they stopped and cleaned the sand from their shoes before going in and told her parents about the Captain and Daniel staying there. Margo said the time had come that the Captain needed more help, and Charles nodded his head in agreement. Martin went to hitch the horses and wagon, came back for Mary, and they set out for Lazaretto. Martin thought Mary to be unusually quiet. He said that he had noticed a smidgeon of melancholy about her mother and father and asked if all was well and Mary said there were just a lot of things happening lately. Martin was sufficiently convinced that things were okay, and the conversation turned to the upcoming trip to Philadelphia. Mary said she knew that was coming up, and she and Maggie had been exchanging letters every week by sending them on the supply boat. Maggie had told her that she was worried about going to a new place and being away from the Milam place and her family for the first time and if she would be smart enough for the school. She said she was worried about her father because he was older than her mother, and something could happen to him while she was gone for a year or more. Martin said Jacob would probably outlive them, and he knew Maggie was smarter than she thought she was. He cautioned about sending letters with confidential information. Mary said she knew that, but they were handing them directly to Johnny to carry and burning them after they had read them.

Ashley and Ken were sitting on the porch of the boatmen's shanty when Martin and Mary arrived. Mary hugged them both and told them she appreciated them keeping Martin safe on the trip and how he had told them some things about what they did but left a lot for them to tell, and she and her family hoped to hear it all after supper. Ken said he and Ashley both would agree to anything if it meant a supper from Margo's kitchen. She said there probably wouldn't be any "Boston baked beans" that Martin had told them about, but plenty of sweet potato casserole, green beans, fried chicken, cornbread, blackberry pie, and some sort of cake. Ashley asked what they were waiting for, and Mary spoke to the tackies, and they started back down the oyster shell road over the marsh to Tybee.

Ashley and Ken were like family to the Dyers and were always welcomed, and Lazaretto had become their most frequent layover coming or going on their trips. They became a source of news from Savannah and the nearby coastal communities. Lightkeepers were the independent type but always liked news from the outside. They were especially looking forward to hearing from them tonight more of what Martin had said. Margo had made a basket of food for Daniel and Captain Jones, and she asked Mary to take it down and come right back. The supper Margo fixed was like many in the past that had always seemed like the best supper ever. Margo not only was a careful cook and knew a lot of recipes but also was pleasant and that pleasant disposition somehow fused into what she cooked. Her big egg biscuits had become legendary in Savannah, not only because they were large and extremely good, and one could sustain a working man all day but what had made them a legend was the boatmen telling the people on the Milam place, and the pilots and crewmen telling the people in Savannah.

After supper Ashley and Ken tried as best they knew how to express their gratitude to Margo and her family for their generous treatment. Mary said that was enough about all that and she was ready to hear about their trip. It was a little cool out, so they stayed inside. After tea was poured, Ken started and said he didn't know what Martin had told or not but he would tell his favorite things. He talked a lot about the riverboats and the steam engines and how he had learned that transportation was changing fast. He carried on about how many more people there were up north and how they went about things in a hurry and even talked fast. But he added that he learned that, although they were a bit gruff and a bit direct in their way of talking, they were softer on the inside. Other than that, they were pretty much like everybody else in the world. He said that people down south tend to talk slower and sweeten their words more and say not so much what they feel and think, but what might preserve sensibilities. Ashley told a long story of all the things for sale at Fulton Market in New York and Quincy Market in Boston. To a family of lightkeepers on an isolated island, this all seemed otherworldly. He told of the Hudson River and how it had tides like the Savannah River, and about the snow and how many hundreds of wagons bunched up all over especially in the mornings and afternoons and about the huge task it was in keeping all the manure cleared from the streets.

Ashley said he regretted Daniel not being there, but they weren't long between visits and would see him again soon enough, and how it was big of him to be taking care of the old captain. Ashley described how well built the new sharpie was and how they didn't want to but might sell it in a year. He described the riverboat that Mr. Stevens had proposed for them and how much it would be able to carry including the barge which he had suggested be made bigger, and how far they could make deliveries both north and south. Besides what the new boat could carry and do, he added a bit about the accommodations for the Captain and his wife and family if he had one, and a section for the crew, and even a private room for the engineer. Ken told Ashley to talk about Captain Davie in Boston and lobsters and the little window in the hull. Ashley said he would, but they should be going soon. Margo said for him to hush up because they were staying here tonight and Charles had made them two bunks out in the guard house from the leftover wood from the temporary shanties that had been built at Lazaretto landing. She added that Martin had his place up with Daniel, even though Daniel will be down on the beach with the captain tonight.

There was no arguing with Margo, so Ken said he nor Ashley told about the trip up north in the big freighter but they would leave that for Martin, but he wanted Ashley to tell about the salty old Captain Davie.

Ashley talked slowly and used his hands as if he were molding the words from his mouth and tried his best to convey the unique character of the old man and repeated his tales about his father and grandfather and all and spun the story out for half an hour or more. He said he wished that he could adequately describe the look of his joyful gratitude on his face when they brought him the gifts and how his eyes welled up with tears and all. He finished up about Captain Davy by saying what the owner of the inn said to them. He said that of all the characters that were in the Boston harbor, they picked the most colorful one to just happen to meet up with and that most of his stories had a good bit of truth to them. Ashley looked at Ken and told him that he should tell Margo about the new dish on the Boston Inn's menu and Ken nodded.

Ken began by telling about the inn they stayed in and described all the ships in the harbor in full view and tried to describe the beauty of the fresh snow on the ships and yardarms and all. Then he told about how every-body ate the Boston Baked beans and how the cook said they made them and also how the cook at the famous restaurant that Captain Lawrence Missroon, the captain of the freighter that took them to Boston, told him how he made his baked beans. Anyhow, Ken spun things out for fifteen minutes or so before getting to his intended topic.

Then he told about Captain Davie's grandfather being in jail and all and what he did to cause "lobstas" to go from only being eaten by poor im-migrants to being eaten by everybody. Then, finally how the cook at the inn learning from Ashley and Ken about Margo's deviled crabs and what was in them and how he made "deviled lobstas" and all and how he was making it an item on their menu.

Margo noticed that Martin looked tired and asked him if he was okay and he said he was and Ken said he had skipped many of his two hour rest times and was wore out still from the trip, but Martin insisted that he was fine and there was much more to tell about their journey but Margo said there would be plenty of time for more stories later. She asked Charles to take Ashley and Ken out to the guard house and gave Charles a special look that no one else but Mary noticed.

Charles lit a lantern and nodded for them to come on and took them out and showed them the bunks he had built and the thick comforters, stuffed with cotton Margo had made for sleeping on. Charles said he hoped they could sleep alright in a bunk that didn't rock and roll and made them laugh. Charles had gone out earlier and fired up the little ship stove and filled two buckets of water on it to heat up for their baths.

Ken said a fresh water bath was gonna be nice for a change after the salt water baths they had been having on the boat.

Charles asked them to sit for a minute because he wanted to tell them something and they both noticed right away the serious tone in his voice. He said that he and Margo had decided to tell them something that had been going on at the Milam place that they didn't want Martin to hear about until he got home. It was that his father had taken seriously ill with his heart and had been laid up, with the doctor coming every day, and it had the whole place worried and stirred up. He said he had signaled today that they were there and coming on the tide tomorrow and they thought it best to let Martin find out when he got there. It was surprising news for Ashley and Ken. Ken said it was best that they let Martin find out tomorrow because he would have been a wreck by the time he got home. Ashley said that, in light of that news, he regretted all that carrying own and storytelling and all about their trip. Charles said that was okay, and had they not, it would have been unusual and they preferred that things be normal for Martin's sake.

After breakfast the next morning Daniel brought the wagon around and after extra warm farewells, he and Mary took Martin and Ashley and Ken to Lazaretto to catch the tide home. On the way, Martin mentioned that they were all unusually quiet. Mary said everybody was too full of breakfast to talk. Martin said he wasn't and told Mary some more things about their trip and talked about plans for the Philadelphia trip and where everyone could sleep and all on the new sharpie. Mary was thinking how upset Martin would be when he found out about his father and what would happen if he died. Her eyes welled up and spilled over several times, and she looked away out over the marsh so Martin wouldn't notice.

The tackies had made so many trips to Lazaretto that they knew the way without a word or tug on the reins. Martin commented again on how quiet Mary was, and she said some days were like that and not to worry and asked him to think of more that he hadn't told about their trip. He talked about all the different kinds of tea that they sold at Quincy's in Boston and about the man in charge of that department and what he had said about yaupon. Out of storytelling habit, he looked at Mary to see if he had her attention and instead he sensed she was somewhat distant, and it reminded him, for some reason, the feeling he had when they left the lighthouse to come to the landing. Charles and Margo had hugged him but it was somehow different than the normal farewell. His wondering thoughts were interrupted by the horses coming to a stop at the landing.

On the trip up the river, Ashley and Ken seemed unusually quiet, and Martin did most of the talking. He commented on how much more natural the area here was than in New York and Boston. Ken said he hoped it stayed that way. Martin laughed and said the area around here was a much better place for pirates and outlaws and runaways to hide. Ken said for alligators and big snakes and wild hogs too. Ashley said there were plenty of snakes up north and they were the worst of all kinds. That surprised Martin because he hadn't heard snakes mentioned at all while they were up north. He asked what kind of snakes Ashley was talking about and Ashley said the kind with two legs. Ken laughed, and Martin took a moment to catch on to what he said and replied that there were some of those locally too.

The sailing was easy, and after Ashley made tea, they opened the basket of biscuits and ate, and all agreed that it was good not to go for long without having Margo's biscuits. Martin said it was odd that people didn't make biscuits up north. Ken said he agreed, but he had liked the yeast bread that they had. Ashley said he wondered where their ice barge was now. Ken said it should be drifting back to Savannah about now, and he hoped that everything had gone okay with the new crew and he had been thinking about their other sharpie with Captain Ben and the new crew with it. He chuckled and said it was funny to think of Ben and the Europeans trying to talk to each other. Ashley said they were very experienced sailors, and not much would need to be said. Martin told them both that if they wanted to nap, it was easy sailing, and he could handle things. They thought that to be a good idea, and Martin was to himself for the next couple of hours. Most of the time his mind was on his time with Mary the day before and how good it felt to hold and kiss and feel her tenderness and smell her special sweetness. Of all the things there was for him to do in the next year or so, what he would do concerning Mary was the most unclear, but of all those things, it was the most certain.

Within a few miles of the Wilmington River, Martin's two captains came out on deck. Ken said the napping on the river was much better than the napping had been in the Atlantic. Ashley agreed and saw where they were and said he needed some tea and went back below to make some. When he handed out the tea, he said they had left only three and a half hours earlier, and that was good time. Martin said the sailing was too, as he steered toward the west bank of the Wilmington River within sight of home. When they got to the boathouse, they struck the sails and set the hooks. Martin commented that the only person waiting for them was Henry in a carriage and that was odd because usually there were more, but maybe everybody was busy. There were a few boatmen out front of the boathouse, and it was unusual that they stayed put and did not come down to haul up the skiff as usual. Ashley and Ken understood why but didn't say anything. Henry waved to Martin to come over, and Ken said go on and they would take care of things.

Martin walked up to Henry and saw immediately that something was amiss from the more than usual seriousness of Henry. He told him to get in and said something had happened to their father. Martin was shocked and asked what? Henry said that a couple days after they had left, their father was sitting out on the porch and called their mother and said he felt a tightness in his chest. She called for Henry, and he sent for the doctor. By that time Walter couldn't sit up, and they couldn't lift him, but managed to get him to the floor with a pillow under his head until some help came and they were able to get him to his bed. The doctor came right away and told them that his heart had failed him and there was not much that he could do. He said at that point, only rest, water, and his will to live could keep him alive. Henry said that their father had rested, and he had a strong will to live and was a little better but still gravely ill. It dawned on Martin the reason for the peculiar behavior of the Dyers, Ashley, and Ken. He murmured that they knew, and Henry said they did, but they all thought it better to let him find out when he got home. Martin said he didn't want to hear anymore and wanted to go see his father, so Henry shook the reins and headed the carriage home. Martha and Claudia were waiting, and Martin rushed past to go to his father's room. He was propped up in the bed and had dozed off but woke when Martin came in. His face brightened a little, and he extended his hand on the bed for Martin to hold. He asked Martin what took him so long and how was the new boat. It took Martin a moment to answer because he was overcome with the sight and condition of his father, but he managed to say that there had been much to do and the new boat was a good one. Walter said Henry had read him the letter that had come yesterday from him. He said he also knew that he was going off again with Alice and her family soon, and he didn't want his condition to delay his going. He barely cracked a smile and said that was not a request but an order. He added that he intended to live at least as long as it took him to get back from Philadelphia for him to know that what he had wanted for his people had at least begun. He said he wanted his order obeyed even if he died tomorrow, and if Martin would swear to it, he would consider it done. It was difficult to speak, but Martin managed to say that he did swear to do it. Upon hearing that, Walter drifted back to sleep.

Martin was still holding his father's hand when Henry came in and put his hand on Martin's shoulder and motioned for him to come. They went out on the porch with Martha and Claudia. Martha said the whole place had been outside all day and she had asked them to go home until after Martin had come and talked to his father. Claudia stared at Martin in a slight awe, and she remembered how he had seemed to change and mature so much when he had gone with Henry a few years ago to Darien.

She saw another change in maturity in him over the last few months, and especially now that he was back from this trip. Henry said their father might look bad now, but he had improved since he first was struck down. The doctor had been there in the morning and said that. since he made it this many days, he would probably make it for a while yet. Henry said that he had managed to stay awake a little longer each day and yesterday and today he was looking forward to Martin coming home. Martin said he had given him an order to leave for Philadelphia as soon as possible, no matter what his condition was, and he made him swear to do it soon, even if he died tomorrow, and he fully intended on doing so. Martha said the doctor said to not keep him in conversation for too long, so that he could sleep more. She said Ellie had been bringing her egg-white soup every day, but he didn't start drinking any of it until yesterday, and the doctor said that was a good sign. She added that they had only told a few people in Savannah because they didn't want a lot of visitors. Henry said he told Sidney and Hulbert and John and Thomas, and of course the Dyers knew what had been going on. He told Martin that he was glad he was back because their father had asked about him every day, and the letter yesterday relieved him a bit. Claudia said she would send her daughter to tell Alice and Ellie that they could now come over because she knew they were both nervous wrecks and would want to see Martin. In a little while Ellie and her family came, and Alice and Johnny with little Jochebed came. Ellie brought egg-white soup for Walter and two pans of sweet potato casserole for the others, and she said she had sent Thomas with a pan of it to Ashley and Ken. She said that she had been so uneasy and nervous that she didn't know what to do with herself, so she cooked. She then went over and hugged Martin and said that seeing him lifted her spirits and that everybody on the place already knew he was back and it did the same thing to them too. Jacob and Johnny said amen to that.

Henry had been sitting quietly. He got up, and when Martin looked his way, he nodded slightly. Martin got up and followed him to his office. Henry sat a minute and looked at his brother and saw a man for the first time ever. He said he didn't know what needed saying, but that he had known of their father's health problems before anyone else except Martha. He had tried to prepare himself for what was happening, but it had done little good and that he had never been so glad to see Martin return. He told Martin that he probably didn't know or understand how important he had been to the whole place, beginning way back when he was little and was with Alice at Jacob and Ellie's house more than he was at their own home. He said that he had been so taken up with his own life at school and with running things afterwards that he had hardly spent any time with him and said that he first saw how important he was to the place when he had gone to school and gotten so sick and how upset everyone was about him. Henry went on to say that, when their father fell ill, what everybody asked and worried about was how would Martin be when he got back. Martin said he didn't know what to think about all that, but he didn't feel any more important than anyone else and right now his feelings were all bunched up, and he didn't know what to make of anything. But what he had to do for now was simple and that was to fulfill the vow he had made to their father to get the people to Philadelphia and back as soon as possible. Henry said that was the first thing their father talked about, when he could first speak a few days ago. He told Martin that he didn't have to worry about ice deliveries because he, John, Thomas, and Captain Ben had devised ways things could work out with the one boat and barge and more wagon deliveries to fulfill their commitments and all Martin needed to do was to get the boat and preparations together for the trip. He said he had talked to Sidney and Hulbert, and they had begun to make the arrangements with the Quaker group back when the Philadelphia trip was first decided on. Names, ages, and legal details have been sent to the Quakers for the manumission process, and a large donation had been sent to cover everyone's legal expenses and accommodations plus tuition costs for Maggie's school. Martin was not surprised at all Henry had done so quickly because he had come to know what a master planner he was and saw to the details so completely.

Henry then said something that surprised Martin. He told him that Charles had sent a long, coded message about what had happened with the visitors that Ayana was so worried about. He had already talked to Sidney and Hulbert about it for them to look into it. Henry said he knew Martin would be worried about it. Martin said that he was and he knew their father would like that they were doing what they could. Another thing, Henry said, was that Alice had talked to Jacob and Ellie and told them that she expected they would be leaving soon. She assured them of how everything was being planned there for them, so they needn't be worried. Even Ellie now was being big about it all because she understood it was Walters's wishes. Henry said he had sent a letter on the stage to Richard in Beaufort, telling him about their father and that the tea delivery to Philadelphia trip would probably be happening sooner so he had asked if he could get the load of tea he had in his warehouse put on the barge to be brought back here so they would not have to stop there on the way to get it, saving a few days. Again, Martin was impressed at Henry's thoroughness.

Walter remained gravely ill but somehow was able to talk a little, mostly with Martha, and some with Alice and Ellie, who brought fresh soup every day, and with the doctor who came every morning. Jacob, Henry, and Martin came every afternoon but only stayed a few minutes because it was difficult for Walter to stay awake.

Martin, Ashley, and Ken met with Thomas to discuss the new riverboat plans, and John got them a business plan to present to the bank for financing and set up the meeting with the banker. It was the kind of thing that would normally have made Martin nervous, but in light of what was going on with his father, it became just another task that needed to be done before leaving. Just before they walked into the bank, Martin remembered the time before, when Henry had sent him with a bank note, to pick up the gold they used to pay Willoughby for Alice and her family and friends that had runaway. He remembered how Mr. Peters, the bank president, doubted his identification, and how Mr. Johnson had happened in at the very time and spoken so loudly about who Martin was that everybody stopped and looked at him. When they entered the bank this time, he asked to see Mr. Peters, and they were directed to his office upstairs. Mr. Peters had been expecting them because John had set it up, and he remembered how he had somewhat disrespected Martin before, and he was particularly gracious in receiving them. He was very impressed after Martin had gone over their plans for the new steam powered riverboat and that Captain Ben was to operate it. John had sent their business records and expected revenues and the Milam Ice Company's commitment to use them as their shipping company. Mr. Peters said the bank had a good customer named Captain Lawrence Missroon who he had become friends with. He was obsessed with steam power and said it was the future in shipping on land and water. He would be pleasantly surprised when he learned that his bank would be financing a riverboat powered by a steam engine. Martin, Ken, and Ashley looked at each other and smiled because Peters' good customer was the Captain who had them as guests every night in his cabin on the trip to Boston and who had taken them to dinner once they were in Boston. The other reason for their smile was that he was pretty much saying his bank was financing their boat. Before they could say anything, Mr. Peters said he remembered Mr. Johnson's words about Martin becoming the best captain around in a few years. Martin said that Captain Ben, Ashley, and Ken were the best captains there were, and they would always know more than him. Mr. Peters switched back to business and said that there would be a large down payment for their loan and a performance bond required. He said that, when he got more information from the Milam engineer about the total costs, he would let them know what their down payment and monthly payments would be. He added that their financial history was not enough to make such a large loan, but Henry Milam and John Wilcox were co-signing the loan agreement with them.

When they walked out of the bank, they were a little overwhelmed at the generosity of the Milam ice Company. Ashley and Ken both commented on that, and Martin reminded them it wasn't because he was a Milam but was because they couldn't sell ice if it couldn't be delivered. Ashley said how surprised Captain Missroon would be when he next talked to Mr. Peters, learning about his bank financing a steamboat and it being for them. Martin was going about business, but the cloud of dread hung over him about his father's condition.

They went from the bank to Thomas' office to discuss boat plans. Thomas was glad to see them and expressed his sympathy for Walter. Martin thanked him and said staying busy was helping him cope with it all and they had a lot to discuss. First that they had a tentative approval from the bank, and they would require further information on costs. Thomas said he had already received a package from Colonel Stevens with revised plans. It had come yesterday, but he hadn't looked it over yet. He opened the package and read the letter in it. The colonel said how much he enjoyed the meeting them and especially appreciated the youthful enthusiasm of Martin about steam-powered boats, which had been his passion for some time. He said he had his designers start the day they left on the hull plan with the surface-penetrating screw propeller drive system he had spoken of and using the latest engine and boiler from the Philadelphia outfit. He said this new model was smaller but just as powerful as the English and French engines, and he was able to keep the length of the vessel at eighty feet. It was a bit beamy at eighteen feet but would still be able to buck a tidal current and make six miles per hour loaded and a little less with a barge in tow. They should be able to travel three or four miles per hour with the barge and a full load against an average tidal flow. He added that he could adjust the length and beam and weight capacity and get more speed if they desired, but every adjustment was a tradeoff and what he was proposing in these drawings was what, after hearing about their needs, he considered the most practical. He also said that the bare hull was the quickest part of the construction and that they could turn out a bare hull with a steel frame and wood hull and deck planking in six weeks and have the engine and boiler installed in another month or two, but it would take another three months for the Boston Boat Works to finish up the build out. Thomas paused and said he was surprised that things could happen so quickly. He read that the colonel said he had gotten so enthusiastic talking to them about the surface-drive propellers that he had decided to build the bare hull with the engine on speculation to these plans, but he would let it be for them if they wanted it. He said an estimated cost for the bare hull, engine, and running gears was included, and with their approval, he would send another copy of the plans to Boston. Thomas unrolled the plans and weighed the corners, and they studied them silently for a few minutes. The area for the engine and boiler and wood fuel storage was shaded in and took up almost a third of the deck area. That left the other two thirds of the area for ice storage and loading deck with a boom that would be used to lower and raise the loading ramp and to lift ice slabs. Ashley said that he was confident that Robert and his designers, with all their experience, would know better how to do the build-out, and it might be best for them to make a plan for them to review. Martin and Ken nodded in agreement. Martin said that if Ashley and Ken agreed, he would like Thomas to handle and plan things with Colonel Stevens and Robert at the Boston Boat Works, and that he was satisfied with the hull and engine plan and trusted that Colonel Stevens had much greater experience than them and had their best interest in mind. Thomas said that he worked for John and Henry, and they had already told him to accommodate them because they had proceeded with the plans to open another facility in Charleston and they wanted them to have the new boat and barge going as soon as possible. Ken said that was generous of them, and Thomas said they had business reasons for what they do. Also, he said Henry had told him that y'all would probably want to leave for Philadelphia as soon as possible and wouldn't have time to deal with all this. Martin said Henry was right, but they had dealt with the bank and would still need to get them the final cost estimates. Thomas said that, with their approval, he would get a letter out right away to Stevens to say that they want the hull and engine he has specified in the drawings and will send a deposit, once the bank has what they need to issue the first of the progress payments necessary. Thomas said he thought that would satisfy Stevens for now, since he said he was building the boat for them on speculation anyway. Thomas said there was one more thing and that was about his son getting out of the navy soon. They all nodded. He said that, at his recommendation, when his son had first joined the navy, his son had asked for service on the Demologos or what was renamed the Fulton, after Colonel Stevens' deceased former partner. He said it was the first ever steam-powered gunboat of the U. S. Navy. He didn't think his son could have learned enough to be an engineer, but he probably had learned a lot about steam power. He said that all his son had told him was that he was assigned to the boat and that it was still a classified project so he was not able to elaborate on what he was doing. Martin said that Stevens had told them he had a training setup for aspiring steam engineers particularly for boats. Thomas said his son would be home in about a month, and they could talk to him. He added that they could go make their plans for their important trip and not to worry about the new boat because he would see to it all from there. They thanked him and left.

Ken said that the ice barge could be back, so they stopped at the Milam Ice Company. There was no ice barge. But there was another barge there with a pile-driving rig and dock-building crew, driving pilings for a dock. It was a surprise to Martin because Henry had not mentioned anything about it, but they all agreed that it was a good idea. Ken said the river here was beginning to look like things in New York. They left and went straight down to the boathouse to see if Ben may have gotten in. He had and was at the table in front of the boathouse talking to Johnny and yelled to them. Ben said he and Johnny were admiring the beautiful sight of the two sharpies anchored out there together. He said he had just said to Johnny that he hoped to see them because he wanted to get the new sharpie crew a ride down to the Milam Ice Company in time for them to catch the wagon into town so they could spend tonight at home. He looked at his pocket watch and yelled at the crewmen to come on in. They saw the wagon and knew what it probably meant and wasted no time in getting to shore. They were a happy crew. They smiled big at Ashley and Ken and began to say all the English phrases that Ken had written for them to learn. The one sailor who had caught on the quickest was able to say a few things to Ken that were not just memorized phrases. It was broken sentences but intelligible. He thanked Ken for writing out the English words. He said that Captain Ben had added some and repeated a phrase he had written, "Time to eat." That even made Martin laugh a little, and they were all impressed that he had not only understood the words but understood the humor of it. The new crew looked at Captain Ben closely every few minutes, and it was easy to see that he had gained their respect and friendship. The crewman next said, "Time to go," and the Captain told them to be there early the next day.

Captain Ben turned serious and told Martin how concerned he was for his father and he had stopped here hoping to hear some good news. Martin said he would talk a little every day and it would lift his spirits to see him. Ben said he had only expected to stop by and ask Johnny about Walter. He was going to spend the night on the boat, drift up to the icehouse before daylight with his crew, load up with ice, and leave out the next day for more deliveries to Hilton Head and Ossabaw islands. Then he would be back, load up again, and go to Sapelo, Saint Simons, and Brunswick. He said he had been busy with them gone, but it had been easy on him because the new crew did everything even the cooking. He said he would have them ready to go on their own soon because they had a lot of experience in their homeland and were studying the charts and learning quickly. Ben said he would like to see Walter but only if he could stand the company. Martin said he could ride with them up to the house when Ken got back. Johnny said that Alice said he generally had some strength until late afternoon and then was too tired and went to sleep for the night. Ben put his hand on Martin's shoulder and told him what a great man his father was. Martin's eyes welled up and spilled, and when they did, so did Johnny's, Ashley's, and Ben's. When they all got back to the house, Martha hugged Martin, and he could see the redness around her eyes from her salty tears. Ellie, Jacob, Alice, and her baby were out on the porch, and when Henry heard the wagon, he and Claudia came around from their end of the house. Everybody hugged Ashley, Ken, and Ben. Martin asked if his father was strong enough for Ben to visit. Martha said she thought so, and he might be a little better today because it was the first day he had finished the whole bowl of Ellie's soup.

Martin and Ben went in the room to Walter's bed. A faint smile came over Walter's face when he saw that it was Martin and Ben. He asked Ben if he had ever seen a sailboat come about on a sea of palmetto fronds. Ben didn't understand, but Martin remembered it like it was yesterday. Walter smiled and told Martin to tell Ben about it. Martin said it referred to his first boat. It was a small dugout that he found washed up on the riverbank. Johnny had helped him fix it up and Walter had a sail made for it. He was anxious to try it out, but Johnny was on a supply trip to Tybee so he spread some fresh green palmetto fronds and positioned his dugout on them. With the sail set, he was able to easily turn the boat at different angles of the wind and practice trimming the sail to get the feel of things. His father had walked up behind him, but he hadn't seen him until he heard him laugh. After telling his story, Martin noticed that his father looked better than he had the day before. He thought it was because he liked seeing Captain Ben, and he was glad that Ben had come in today. Walter told Martin that he wanted to speak to Ben alone and for him not to read much into it. Martin was a little surprised but pleased to do anything his father wanted. He told him that he would be back in to see him again soon. When Martin went out onto the porch, he told those waiting that he thought his father was better today than yesterday and Martha said she had thought that too. He told them that Walter had wanted to speak with Ben alone so he had left.

After a while Ben came out and told the others that Walter had some things to tell him that were of no great importance to anyone but him.

Martin was most curious about what those things were. Ken had returned and said he would almost bet that the ice barge had returned on the tide, and he suggested they ride in the carriage down and see, and Ben and Ashley said that sounded good. Once outside, Thomas ran up to Martin and asked him if he could go with him and Martin said he could but he had to first go inside and ask his mother. He did, and Martin helped him up into the driver's spot and handed him the reins. Thomas grinned wide, and his white teeth showed beautifully against his dark skin. Martin smiled and thought to himself it was like seeing a young Jacob. In a few minutes they were on the new Milam Ice Company land, and Thomas steered the horses toward the river where the big icehouse was and where they had been keeping the ice barge moored out between trips. The dock building crew had gone, but there sat the ice barge. Ken was most pleased because he had spent the most time with the new crewmen on the first two trips. He had worried since he left about how they would do on their own. They saw the wagon with Ken on it and began yelling "Captain Ken!" Ashley said their whole fleet was in now, and Martin became detached from his sadness a bit and grinned at Ashley's words. Ken yelled to bring two boats, but they didn't understand what he was saying. They all walked down by the edge of the river, and Ken motioned for them to come. Then they got it, and one sailor leapt in each boat and hurried to the riverbank. Ken was so glad to see them that he hugged them both, and they immediately began to recite the English sentences that he had written out for them. They all loaded up onto the two pulling boats and were rowed out to the barge. Ken was excited to show them what had been done, but once they were all aboard, the new crew began trying to tell Ken about their trip but with a lot of difficulty because they didn't know much English. Then one of them pulled out a folded-up paper from Richard Wilcox. The letter said that everything went fine, and his man had accompanied the barge from Beaufort to Lands' End on Saint Helena. He said the crewmen operated the barge expertly and that he would continue to send the same man over with them until he reported back that they could handle things on their own. He said the tea and shipping information was in the ice storage room and for them to make sure it was stored and maintained dry, and they didn't need to collect any money because his distributor in Philadelphia would take care of that. He said he really liked this new set up with the large ice delivery once a month and the delivery being taken directly over to Lands' End. He said he was getting more local customers every month and had orders for four home-size ice boxes to come on next month's barge. He had trained two carpenters there how to put them together instead of having them shipped all put together because they were so heavy. He added that he had also shipped more hardware and other items over to Lands' End this time because word had gotten out about doing that. He would send a bank note for that additional freight with his ice payment. The new crew watched Ken's reaction to the letter very intently, hoping that there were no complaints from Richard. They saw Ken's smile after he finished and celebrated a moment among themselves. Ken said, loud and clearly, "Da!" and the crew were all relieved and laughed. Ken led the tour of the new work done on the barge. They first went into the ice storage area and looked at the stacked up boxes of tea. Martin said as far as he knew, this was the first large shipment of yaupon ever in America. That reminded him that he had promised to send a one pound box of yaupon to the nice man at the tea department of Quincy Market in Boston. Ken said his name was on the box of tea they had gotten there, and he would see that it was done. Next Ken showed them the galley and the new stove and ice box that was made to fit by Jason. He showed them the new windows and the bunks, and they were all impressed; even little Thomas liked it all. Ashley looked at his pocket watch and said the crew had missed the worker wagons that took workers back to town. Ben said he wouldn't mind walking back to the sharpie if one of them wanted to take them in the wagon. Ken said if they all didn't mind walking, he would drive the crew home, and they all nodded in approval. Ken said, "time to go home" and was understood perfectly by the crew, and they grabbed their things to leave. Before Ken left with the crew, Martin suggested that they get together in the morning to plan out what they need to do for the trip. He said he would come down there if that suited them, and they said that was fine. Captain Ben said he hoped to be loaded and gone before they got there in the morning.

Ben and Ashley walked back to the sharpies, and Martin walked Thomas home and stopped in to visit. Maggie hugged Martin and said she had never thanked him for taking her to Philadelphia. Martin corrected her and said it was a lot more than him taking them on this trip and if there was someone to thank, it was his father and Henry. Ellie said Walter was why she was going. She said she didn't think she would feel any different after being manumitted but she knew that was his wish. And she knew it was his wish for the whole place to be manumitted and she hoped that her doing it would move the others want to do it too. Thomas said that if manumitting meant he could be a boat captain, then he was all for it. That made Martin laugh even with his worry about his father. Maggie told Martin that she knew Philadelphia was a big city but had often thought it might be possible for them to see Mallie. Martin was so taken up with thinking about what needed to be done that the thought of that had never occurred to him. He told Maggie that he had no idea how long the court process of manumission took but in Philadelphia he thought he might visit the outfit that was supposed to supply the steam engine for their new boat and there would be some time needed to get the tea to whoever it was going to. If there was enough time left after those things, he would ask around. Maggie said that would be a good idea but he should be careful about who and what he asked. Maggie said she wished she could know more about the school and what she could learn but she knew nothing about anything except that there was a school and Walter's lawyer friends had made the arrangements for her to be there, and she guessed she should be satisfied with that but wished she could know more. Martin smiled and said there would be plenty of choices for her, but he was more interested in what there would be for a free young and educated black woman to do when she was finished with her schooling. Maggie agreed but said she had thought about that but those thoughts didn't bother her like the unknown of what she might study. Martin saw the concerned look on Ellie's face. He knew she understood that there wouldn't be anything around there for Maggie to use her education and she might end up living in Philadelphia or someplace else far away. Martin told them about how he had planned for them to have one of the cabins on the boat, except for Thomas who could stay in a separate new cabin area with him, Ashley, and Ken, and Izak if he wanted to. Thomas said he wanted to be with Martin, so he could learn about being a captain. Martin reminded him that he was not a captain yet, and before you were a captain, you had to be a deckhand. Thomas said he just wanted to be like Martin, and Jacob and Martin exchanged a smile. Martin assured Thomas that he was about to get a lot of deckhand experience in a short time, and Thomas did his little jig that he did when he became overcome with excitement. Ellie asked Martin when they would be leaving. He said he, Ashley, and Ken would do some planning together in the morning, and he would let her know after that, but it would be sooner rather than later.

Martin next stopped at Alice and Johnny's house for a minute to let them know that it wouldn't be long before they set out, and he would know more about that the next day. He also told them they would get the other cabin, and Johnny was surprised about that. Martin said he, Ashley, Ken, and Thomas were getting the best accommodations and explained what they were doing to make one of the holds livable. Alice smiled to herself with affection for Martin, knowing he was saying that in a way to make Johnny feel better.

When Martin got back home, he first went around to Henry's end of the house. He and Claudia and the kids were all at the table, and he sat for a minute to tell Henry what he had been up to with Thomas and the banker. Henry had already gotten a message from Mr. Peters, who was obviously trying to make up for his lack of appropriateness with Martin the time he had gone for the gold. Henry reminded Martin that, even though Mr. Peters favored the Milams, it was business, and his bank was in the money business, and they charged for other people to use their money. Martin only vaguely understood that, in no way as clearly as Henry. He said he was in business because it involved boats and rivers and the ocean. Henry with a degree of sternness said that once all that bank money had paid for their new boat, he needed to be more in a business way about things. He said that Martin had been spared the cold realities of business that he had been educated in and been part of. Martin smiled and said that was why they needed each other. Henry could remind him of how to think sometimes in a business way, and he could sometimes help Henry think ways where business didn't fit. Henry shook his head in agreement because of the simpler way that Martin was able to understand things that his complicated mind couldn't cipher. Martin told them that he thought it might even be just a week before they left, but he would know more the next day. Claudia said she was always afraid of anyone talking about a boat trip because her life growing up on Wilmington Island was full of mishaps on the water, but she was glad to hear about this trip.

The next morning Ashley, Ken, and Martin met at the boathouse, had tea with Johnny, then went out to the new sharpie. Captain Ben and the new crew had left earlier in the old sharpie. Since Ashley and Ken were the co-captains, they had already made some plans about the trip and had decided that the three of them would be in charge of different aspects of preparing for the trip. Ken was to first see that the tea was loaded and secured on the sharpie and the barge provisioned for its next trip so all the new crew had to do was load ice and go. He then would assist Ashley, who would be in charge of provisioning the sharpie for the Philadelphia trip, which was the biggest task they had. It was a lot more involved than what had been needed when he, Ken, and Ben would set off for somewhere. Their trips were usually not more than a couple of days one way, and they would be in port for a day or two where they would often take meals ashore and could purchase additional provisions if needed. To clarify for Martin, Ken said that he and Ashley had begun, a few days before, thinking and talking about all the things that would be needed for eleven people including a baby, to have as comfortable a journey as possible. It could be as much as a two-week trip one way, and there was much to consider that they had not ever had to think about before. He added that it probably wouldn't take that long but it could if they were becalmed. There would be eleven aboard, and it was no small task to plan for. Ken said that he and Ashley thought that Martin could be in charge of raising temporarily the hatch over the one hold and making it weatherproof and livable for them and Thomas. Martin agreed and said he would get Jacob to help him and said he could start on that as soon as the tea was loaded. He added that this was a lot of work to do to get everybody to Philadelphia and back safely in a boat, but he considered it safer than overland travel through the Carolinas, Virginia, and Maryland. He said that Henry was told that every state had more militia patrols than ever that watched the roads, and there were slave catchers that would often haul away any person of color. There would be no inns that would accommodate such a group, and finding a secure place to camp every night would be difficult, and he had all he ever wanted to do with slave catchers. Ashley told Martin that he and Ken could do most everything to get ready and other than him getting the hold ready for them to sleep in, they wanted him to have time to spend with his father before leaving. Martin thanked them and said that doing this was what his father wanted most and told them about the vow his father had asked him to make.

Next they talked about when things could be ready to leave. Ken said he could be done with his part in a couple days and be ready to help Ashley. Ashley said, with Ken's help, he could be ready in four or five days. Martin said he thought, with Jacob and Johnny's help, he could be done in a couple days, So it was decided that they tentatively plan on leaving in a week. Martin said he would ask Daniel to begin asking Captain Jones about weather predictions a few days ahead of leaving. If there was a northeaster or north wind, there would be no use in leaving until there was a better forecast.

The next week was a busy one, and the whole Milam place was talking and anticipating the big trip. The secrecy they had hoped for was not possible so Alice went to everyone there, one on one, and explained what they were doing and why it was so important that news of it did not go beyond the Milam place. Johnny and Jacob caught on quickly to what was needed to make one of the holds livable, and they told Martin to spend the rest of the week with his father. Walter's condition improved somewhat, and Martin and Martha were together with him a lot. Alice and Ellie came every day, and Johnny and Jacob came the day before leaving to see him. They all expressed thankfulness to Walter, and every time, he reversed it and said he was the one needing to be thankful.

27.
PHILADELPHIA

The forecast from Captain Jones was for a northwest wind. Since the journey was somewhat northeast, this wind direction would be good to go, not just because of wind direction, but it usually meant cool and dry weather for a few days. The whole Milam place turned out for the departure, even Walter who was helped into the carriage to come and watch. Never had there been so many tears shed by the river and never had there been such a loud and beautiful chantey sung as the loaded new sharpie, full of their own, set sail and headed for Tybee. Their song could be heard from those on the boat and those on the land almost all the way to where they turned from the Wilmington River east onto the Savannah River toward Tybee. Once in the big river and headed east, all the sails were let way out, and Martin was satisfied to see the riverbank go by swiftly.

The timing of the tide and the wind behind them would put them at Tybee at early afternoon, and there was a surprise waiting for them, particularly for Alice. It was waiting at the shanty at the Lazaretto landing. No one knew about it except the Dyers, and it had been Daniel's idea, and Mary had said it was the best idea that Daniel had ever had. He had gotten the idea on a day that he had taken Mary over to sit with Ayana to continue writing about Ayana and her people's story. This particular time, instead of sailing back to Tybee and returning in the afternoon to pick Mary up, they had stayed on the other end of the island with the runaways. On his trips to teach Ayana how to use the signaling mirror and taking Mary over to see Ayana, he had gotten to know Alice's family better and told them about the Philadelphia trip. It occurred to him that her parents had not seen Jochebed, and neither had his parents. He decided that, if it could be arranged, he would ask Alice's mother and father if they would like to go over to Tybee and see Alice and the baby when they all stopped at Lazaretto for the night before leaving for Philadelphia. They were both overjoyed and unsettled about it because they had never left the island since they were brought over by the Indians after the massacre. When he first asked them, he hadn't asked his parents but was sure enough that they would go along with it. As they were leaving the island, late in the day at high tide, he told Mary about his idea, and she screamed so loud in approval, that a few of Ayana's people came out to the edge of the island because they thought something could be wrong. Mary and Daniel were only a hundred yards across the marsh, and Mary noticed that Ayana had come out with the rest. She knew they had heard her scream and stood up and instinctively waved both hands to let them know they were okay and put her pole down and reached for Daniel's hand and kissed it. Mary had never done anything like that to Daniel, but he understood her gesture. He told her that the thought of asking them had just come to him while having tea with them earlier, and he had some concern that he had done it without first asking his mother and father. Mary was still beaming about what Daniel had done and told him not to worry about that, and they would be proud of him. Daniel said he had already thought that he could ask Captain Jones to ask one of the pilots out on the beach to tow a small boat from Savannah for him to use to get them over the island in because his boat wouldn't be big enough. Mary said it would be fine for the Captain to know what was going on but no one else should.

So, a week later, when the sharpie pulled into Lazaretto Creek to spend the night, the whole Dyer family plus two special guests were there and there was a big pot of grits and crabmeat on the outside hearth of the shanty. After the sharpie was anchored, Daniel rowed out in the boat they had obtained from Savannah. He didn't say anything about Alice's mother and father being in the shanty. Martin thought it strange that Daniel would be in a different and bigger boat and noticed something different about Daniel. He was most always pleasant, but today he had a big grin across his face that didn't go away. Martin was surprised to see the whole Dyer family there but would be more surprised to see who was in the shanty. Ken told Martin to go on in with the group, and he and Ashley would be along after getting things in order. They put the sharpie skiff in, and slowly and carefully loaded the group into the two boats and rowed over to the landing. Johnny helped Alice and the baby up the ramp, and Jacob helped Ellie up. A few minutes later, cries and screams were let out, followed by a baby crying as little Jochebed was frightened by it all, and she wasn't the only one frightened. Ashley and Ken heard the commotion and thought someone must have slipped and fallen off the boat or something and were both straining to see what was going on. Martin saw them and yelled that all was well. Inside the shanty, Alice's mother and father were in tears looking at their granddaughter. The grin was still across Daniel's face, and everyone else had tears of joy.

When things settled down, Daniel rowed over to bring Ashley and Ken, and they were welcomed. Charles opened some plum wine and handed it out to everyone, and Margo laid out a big basket of biscuits and a big bowl of blackberry preserves and began filling bowls of crab grits for everyone. Mary hugged Martin and kissed him and told him how Daniel had thought of this and had brought Alice's parents over on the high tide that morning. She said he had asked Ayana to come, but she was afraid that she could bring some sickness back to her people, but she said she would come another time and see the Dyers only and wear her doeskin mask. The party continued until the sun had set, and Charles told Martin that they should be leaving because they likely would be getting up very early to leave in the morning, and he didn't like to leave the lighthouse unattended for long. Daniel told Alice that they had planned for her and Johnny and Jochebed to stay with her parents in the shanty and had made them some bedding. Alice hugged Daniel and told him that she would never forget what he had done, and he still had that grin. Maggie and Mary were together most of the time during the celebration. Mary gave Maggie a notebook and pen and asked her if she would keep a journal of the trip to go in her notes. Maggie said she would and send it back with Martin. Maggie again expressed her fears of being gone for a couple of years and of her worries of not being smart enough to be in school, and Mary convinced her again that she was more than smart enough and a couple years would go by quickly. Mary noticed that Izak had been listening and saw the tears well up in his eyes as he heard Maggie saying those things to her. Without thinking, Mary said that Izak should stay in Philadelphia too. The idea noticeably shocked both Izak and Maggie. Maggie said that Izak was in training to be a boatman, and Mary said that could wait if need be, and they would have plenty of time to think and talk about that on the trip up. Margo brought two small crocks of blackberry and plum preserves for them to take on the trip, and the Dyers said farewell and left in the dark to go back. Margo again told Daniel what a good thing he had done. All but Alice, Johnny, and Jochebed took the bigger boat out to the sharpie and were soon in bed.

Next morning a couple hours before daylight, Martin woke to the sound of Ashley and Ellie cooking and the smell of fresh biscuits, bacon, and coffee. Ashley told Martin that he had seen candlelight through the shanty window and he should row over and get Johnny and Alice and the baby so they could get underway while the wind and tide were in their favor. He nodded, and Ashley handed him a cup of yaupon. When Martin got over, Alice's mother was holding Jochebed, and she looked at Martin with a worried look. She said she had been so excited to see the baby that she had forgotten her fear of them all going off in the ocean so far away. She said she wished Alice would let Jochebed stay with them until they got back, but she guessed she should be with her mother. Martin said he would bring Alice and the baby over to their island before too long and said that both captains, Ashley and Ken, were ready to leave, and after hugs and tears he, Johnny, Alice, and the baby loaded onto the sharpie skiff and rowed back out. Ashley and Ken with Jacob's help had the sharpie into the wind with all sails up and one anchor still down. The stern anchor was lifted, and with the last two hours of the outgoing tide, the sharpie was able to clear the point of Lazaretto Creek and steer toward the open Atlantic, passing the lighthouse and Captain Jones' shanty and then heading northeast. It was a good wind to leave on because the northwester was blowing plenty hard off the land and the water was somewhat flat for a mile out. Ellie said she was afraid, but when she looked at how calm and peaceful the baby was, it made her feel better.

They were just passing the southern tip of Hilton Head when the sun started up over the ocean horizon. Ashley said that if the wind blew from this direction and speed every day and they did some sailing at night, they would be to the river leading into Philadelphia in seven days, but that wasn't likely to happen because the wind always changed. He said they could do alright with any wind except one out of the north or northeast. But a northeaster on the return, like they had just been in, would get them home quick but be a rough ride. The wind only stayed out of the northwest for another half day, and then moved around to the north. After a few days they were just a few miles past Charleston, but then the wind moved around to the east, and their progress tripled. The big wide sharpie barely heeled over and with its two centerboards down, and the wind on its beam made the coastline go by quickly. It was so pleasant that for the first time Ellie came out from inside and sat with Jacob.

Ken had taught Jacob and Johnny how to let a line out with a hook and a small shiny spoon-shaped piece of metal to fish for bluefish, and every once and a while they would haul one in. Izak would clean it over the side and cut it up and add it to a big pot of potato soup cooking on the stove inside. Everywhere on the boat that Martin went, young Thomas followed him asking questions. Martin liked answering them, and it reminded him of himself when he wanted to learn about boats. Except for the surprise when Alice and Johnny saw that Alice's mother and father were waiting for them at the Lazaretto Landing and there was so much loud screaming, little Jochebed had not cried a bit. She was happy but had to be watched carefully because she could crawl so quickly and could pull herself up on things and stand holding on. She was with Ellie more than she was with her mother. Alice saw how the child had helped Ellie to be not so afraid of the ocean, so she was always putting her in Ellie's arms. Once when she squirmed to get out of Ellie's lap to crawl around on the cockpit floor, Jacob tied a thin rope around and under her arms and around Ellie's waist, and they did this every time she came out of the cabin. Jochebed was a big entertainment for everyone. She smiled a lot and had a small streak of mischievousness about her. In just the few days they had been gone, she had begun to stand and hold onto the raised seat of the cockpit and walk around, with the rope tied to her. She liked to play with Thomas and would try to follow him as he followed Martin everywhere, but she could only go as far as the rope was long.

After four days out, the wind slacked off to almost nothing for a couple days. The surface of the ocean was calm, but the ocean swells continued. They only managed a few miles a day, and the smooth swells and sun caused everyone to nap a lot. Ashley spent hours with Thomas, teaching him how to tie many different knots because Thomas was the one most bored with the stillness. Maggie and Izak entertained each other, and Maggie wrote in the notebook from Mary what little there was of their journey so far and worked on a few poems. She thought about her heroine Phyllis Wheatley and her poem she read to Martin about sailing in a storm, and that is what she had expected the trip to be like. They were six days into the trip and still far away from the Delaware Bay which led to Philadelphia. Then after two days of stillness, the wind started out of the best possible direction, the southeast, and the coastline began going by more quickly than it had since they had left. It was an easy point of sail on the starboard stern quarter of the sharpie. It continued, and when they passed Cape Hatteras, the boat's speed increased even more as they headed more northerly with the wind mostly behind them. They cruised night and day for three days, and during the night after the third day, Ken spotted the only lighthouse marking the entrance to Delaware Bay. Cape Henlopen lighthouse could be seen from a good distance. Carefully studying their chart, they steered north of it almost ten miles and entered the middle of the bay as the sun was coming up with the southeast wind on their other stern quarter, and still cruising fast. Having plenty of room at the wide entrance, they pulled the centerboards up, not knowing where the shoals were, as they sailed westward. When it got full daylight, Ken, Martin, and Thomas stood at the bow, and they dropped the boards back down as the three of them looked across the water for any signs of shallow water. It was something that Thomas could catch onto quickly as Ken and Martin pointed out what they saw about the surface of the water and gave hand directions back to the helm. By midday the bay narrowed to a wide river, and they began to feel a current that was moving out, but the favorable southeaster was moving them ahead a little faster than the current. They passed several ships drifting out the river. Each one had a dozen pulling boats keeping them in the channel. Ken noted that the current in this river was strong but not as strong as the Savannah River. All but Maggie and Izak were outside in the cockpit. Ashley asked the group if they would like to continue up the river all night or find a spot out of ship traffic and anchor for the night. Jacob asked how much further it was to Philadelphia, and Ken said without wind they could almost drift there in one incoming tide. Jacob said if it were the Savannah River, he would continue all night, but he knew nothing of this river and he would probably choose to stop for the night. This was the answer that both Ashley and Ken were hoping for, and both said they liked what Jacob said and they began looking for an out-of-the-way spot to anchor for the night. Ashley steered the sharpie over to the side of the river while Ken dropped the lead line. They picked an area that was too shallow for a deep draft ship to drift up on them during the night.

The sky was red as the sun sunk low, and it was the first day since they left Tybee to be out of the ocean and stopping for the night. Ellie tied Jochebed's rope to Maggie and asked Jacob to put a line over and see what he could catch. He said he needed some bait, and Ashley said there was some dried fish they still had from their New York trip and got them for Jacob. Izak and Johnny joined him, and in a few minutes they were pulling in pan-size croaker fish. Ellie went below and put on a big pot of water and added onions and potatoes and started making biscuit dough. Jacob quit fishing and started cleaning fish over the side and told Johnny to stop fishing after they had three more fish. When all the fish were cleaned, he handed them down to Ellie for her stew. Ken went below and got the papers that Richard Wilcox had sent with the load of Yaupon they were delivering. There was a hand-drawn map of the Philadelphia waterfront and directions to the wharf and a name of the company and man they were making the delivery to. Ashley said he had been thinking while they were coming up the river about how best to go about things. He said perhaps, instead of taking a slip anywhere at a dock, they should anchor out and row in with the skiff, and once they found the place of delivery, they could go in and get unloaded and go back out and anchor. He said, although Philadelphia was a more tolerant place for runaways and free blacks, he had heard there were still a few slave catchers around, and he thought it could be safer for them to be anchored out. Martin said it might be a good idea for either Ashley or Ken to remain onboard all the time, and they both nodded in agreement. Their conversation had the full attention of Jacob and Johnny.

Next, Martin opened a satchel with two folders, one from Sidney and

Hulbert, and the other from Thomas (the engineer). He opened the one from Sidney and Hulbert, and it had a name and address of a law firm and the name of a contact person, with no other information. The folder from Thomas had some steam engine specifications and their new boat specifications and the name of the engine maker's company and address. Martin said the law firm would be the most important place to start, and Henry had said that they had all the information from having contacted the Quaker organization about the manumission process and the school arrangements for Maggie. He mentioned that Henry had said that all the details had been worked out about everything and all they had to do was show up. Martin said he guessed that he could go alone to the law office, or either Ashley or Ken could go with him. Ken said maybe after they make the delivery that could be decided. Next Ashley unrolled the chart that had the river and Philadelphia waterfront on it and took the hand-drawn map of the wharf they were going to and tried to cipher where the wharf was on the chart. He found what looked like where it might be and said if there was room for them, they could anchor out in front of that area. The smell of fresh baking biscuits wafted out of the cabin, and Ellie said it wouldn't be long until suppertime. The sun was going down in a red sky, and Ashley went below and handed out small cups of plum wine to have before suppertime. Shortly afterwards, Ellie handed out tin bowls of fish chowder and big biscuits with lard drippings and handed a bowl for herself to Jacob. She said she didn't know why, but she was not feeling steady on her feet. Jacob said she had adjusted herself to the ocean swells for the last ten days, and Ellie said she was still rocking and rolling. Jacob said she would be fine after a while and the plum wine might help. She said she was having that anyway because she wanted to celebrate their ocean crossing and made everyone laugh. While they were eating, Johnny said he was surprised how calm the water they had come across was and that they had gone through much rougher water in the Savannah River. Ashley said they had just been lucky, but chances were that they wouldn't complete the whole trip without some rough water. Ellie said she had begun to like the ocean the last few days. Jacob said he hoped she kept on liking it, but he agreed with Ashley that there might be some rough water ahead, but they were here and that was something big to be thankful about. Ken said that was a worthy toast and raised his cup of plum wine and said, "To Philadelphia and back," and all raised their cups and repeated it. Then Alice raised her cup and said, "to Walter Milam." Everyone raised their cups with even greater enthusiasm and repeated what Alice had said, and there was a silence as everyone felt both gratitude and hopefulness for Walter. Ken got up and hung a lantern on the mast, and Ellie went below and handed out more biscuits with blackberry preserves. Ken raised the lantern up the mast and told the group that they would probably hear a ship's horn more than once during the night and explained how shallow the water was where they were anchored, so they needn't worry because it would not be possible for a ship to drift up on them because it would run aground first.

They did hear three horns of ships coming in with the tide, and two more later, when the tide had turned as they drifted out. Just like always, Ashley was first in the galley early starting grits and coffee and tea. There was no hurry this morning because the tide wouldn't start in for two hours after daylight, and there wasn't enough wind to buck the outgoing current, so after breakfast there was an idle time. Ashley, Ken, and Martin had boat stuff to do, and Jacob and Johnny helped. Jacob had saved the fish heads from the day before and handed the bucket of them to Izak and suggested he and Thomas try to catch some crabs for supper. Ellie tied herself to Jochebed and helped her take her first-ever steps from one side of the cockpit to the other while Alice and Maggie gleefully watched. Ellie said her walking was the beginning of trouble, and she tightened the knot on her rope. Ellie would pick her up after she had gone back and forth a couple times and she bowed her back to be let down to totter some more and each time getting more confident, until she was able to stand without holding on and turn and go back. Ellie and Alice and Maggie's laughing and carrying on at Jochebed had everyone in light spirits, and it was soon time to get under way.

With the help of Johnny and Jacob, operating the sharpie was easier. Ken and Ashley were able to just say what and when, and Jacob, Johnny, and Martin with Thomas shadowing him, did all the work. Ken said it was like sailing with the new European sailors they had taken on except he could understand what was being said. He said he wondered where between their dock and Beaufort they were now. Ashley said he wondered similarly about Captain Ben and his crew. Martin commented that they had a fleet that was headed in three directions, and Ken said he could have never imagined how things with them had become. Martin said with an air of confidence, like an elder, that there was much more than that ahead of them, which made Ashley smile at their young partner. The southeast breeze was still blowing, but the river had narrowed, and the high, tree-lined riverbanks were now blocking the wind. They set all sails and drifted with an occasional gust of wind swooping down and filling the sails, and they would speed ahead for a quarter mile, then slow to drift speed again as the wind lifted up. Izak had caught almost a bushel of crabs and went below to cook them in a big pot of boiling water that Alice had put on once she had seen Izak start catching them. He was back in just a bit with them all red and steaming hot, and he, Johnny, and Jacob sat in the back of the boat and picked the meat out, saving the shells for Ellie to make deviled crabs later.

More than an hour before sunset they began to see the ship masts at the city waterfront. Martin noted that Philadelphia was not up on a hill like Boston and was farther away from the coast than Boston and New York, but it was a much more sheltered harbor than both of those cities. Ashley added that it was an older port than those cities too. They drifted with the last of the incoming tide slowly to the far end of the third large riverfront port city that Ashley, Ken, and Martin had been to in the last six weeks. Only the big jib sail was left up to pass through all the ships and boats of all sizes and shapes. When the jib was pulled down and the bow anchor dropped, the sharpie floated still, with the tide having reached full and for half an hour, there was no more tide coming in, and no tide going out. Them and the tide had come full in.

Martin commented that wherever they went, slack tide, be it at its lowest point or highest point, was his favorite time. Ken commented that he and Ashley had delivered many kinds of cargo, but he could have never dreamed or guessed that they would come to Philadelphia with a boatload of tea and people. As the sun was setting the whole group sat silent, in awe of the sunset colors in the sky and the feeling of relief and gratitude of having arrived. Alice was holding Jochebed with Johnny on one side and Martin on her other side. She squeezed Martin's hand and in a whisper that Martin could barely hear she said, "Thank you, Walter."

The tears that had been welling up in Martin flooded over his cheeks without a sob. The silence was finally interrupted by Ellie getting up and going below to bake the crab shells full of crab meat and dressing that she had prepared and left in the icebox, which only had a small chunk of ice left in it. It was dark, and Ken hung a lantern on the mast. Ashley handed out small cups of plum wine, and the whole group watched and laughed at Jochebed as she walked from one to the other of them sitting in the long sharpie cockpit. Ellie handed out bowls of hot grits with the last of the butter from the Milam cows and a platter of deviled crabs that she said was the best she had ever tasted. There was a lot of talk about the difference in the taste of northern crabs and southern crabs and which tasted best. These were so good that it was hard to say that anything else was better, and Johnny said something that was simple but true. He said that what was "now" was most always the best, and he picked up Jochebed and lifted her up and high and she laughed out loud and made everyone else laugh.

The next morning before the sun was up, after Ashley, Ken, and Martin talked over coffee and tea, it was decided that Ashley would row ashore with the shipping papers and set up the offloading of the tea. Ken, Martin, Johnny, and Izak would remove the floorboards and all evidence of their using the one hold for sleeping accommodations. They also decided that, while unloading, all but Johnny and Izak with Ken, Ashley, and Martin, stay out of sight below. It would not be unusual for there to be one or two black men as part of the crew. They would be thought of as slaves or free blacks and not raise any attention. But it might cause some unwanted attention if the whole group was seen. Ashley left and was back in an hour and said he had found the business and owner, and they had been expecting them, and three pulling boats followed him out to tow the sharpie in. Once at the dock, workers assisted them in unloading the tea, which went quickly, because it was light cargo, and the holds were soon empty. Once during unloading Jochebed had gas or something and cried a bit, and Ashley quickly said his wife was below with their baby and no one thought anything of it because captains often traveled with their family and there was no difference in a black or white baby's crying. After the unloading, the pulling boats towed the sharpie back out, and Martin directed them out to the far side of the cluster of ships and boats. It was just past noon, and Ken and Martin set out in the skiff to find the office of Sidney and Hulbert's associates.

They went to the wharf where the tea was unloaded and asked if they could leave the skiff there, then picked one of the many carriages for hire and showed the driver the address. He nodded and said it was not too far and set out over cobblestone streets like those in Savannah. They stopped at a brick two-story building with a small sign outside that said, "Norley and Norley - Counselors in Law." The driver asked if he should wait, and Martin said they could walk back. The door was locked, and Ken knocked. An elderly gentleman came and seemed a bit tired, but when Martin announced who they were, his overall look changed dramatically and he became animated and happy to see them and said his name was Joseph Norley and to call him Joe. He ushered them in and up the stairs to an office with one window and the rest of the walls with bookshelves packed with books. A somewhat younger man met them, and Joe introduced him, saying his name was Nathan and his only son. Nathan said he and his father had been expecting them and asked how their trip was. Ken said that, except for a few days of doldrums, the winds had been favorable. Martin presented a small gift to Joe and he was delighted and opened it. When he saw that it was dried leaves, Martin said it was "Yaupon tea." and it was the cargo that they had delivered early that morning and explained a little about it and said it was the first ever shipment of it, and if it caught on, he expected they would be bringing more in the future. Joe thanked them and told a little about how he had been lifelong friends with Sidney and Hulbert and Walter since they were very young in England and had come to America soon after Walter. He had relatives in Philadelphia and settled here, and Sidney and Hulbert went to Savannah to be near Walter. Martin said that he, Ken, and Ashley who had remained on the boat were business associates in a new shipping company. Joe said that Sidney and Hulbert had conveyed to them that Ashley and Ken were like family to the Milam's and were to be trusted completely in all matters. He went on to say that Nathan had done just about all the work in setting up and co-ordinating with the Quakers to accomplish the manumission process and he was proud of Nathans zeal for abolition, and thanks to the Quakers, the abolition movement was growing. He nodded to Nathan, and Nathan said he was grateful to his father and mother for giving him the correct under-standing about human rights and to the Quakers for all they had done.

He said everything was set up for them and he had been just waiting for them to arrive to set it all in motion, and he would go this afternoon and notify the Quakers that they had arrived. He said he would tell them a little about how things worked and looked at his father to see if he had anything to say about it first, and his father said he would enjoy hearing it all again himself.

Nathan took a long breath and said that the Quakers were attending to a small but important detail that had been left out by the founding fathers concerning our African and Indian brothers and sisters in that they were no less entitled to the inalienable rights enjoyed by everyone else. He said he didn't go to their church services but had great respect for what they did and how they had been able to stick to the fundamental truths of the Bible. They not only preached about it but did the practical work to free those who had been left out of the proclamations about freedom in this country. He said there were still a few Quakers that had slaves themselves, in the western part of the state, but that was rare. He said he didn't know how much they knew of things there, but the Quakers had created something of a free zone in the Philadelphia area, despite the slave-based economy in surrounding states including Virginia which had the largest slave popula-tion of any state and more than twice that even of South Carolina. Not too long ago slave catchers could come there looking for a particular runaway and grab any black person they wanted, and every day there were groups of blacks chained together making the trek back south. The slave catchers were working within the law that allowed them to come after runaways, and there was nothing in place to stop or regulate them for decades. But, starting in the lower courts, the Quakers worked and changed the laws to make the slave catchers appear in a full courtroom and submit documents to prove that they were taking who they had come for, and that cut down by three quarters the number of slave catchers around.

Nathan went on to say that Philadelphia was the first place to abolish slavery in 1780. It was a gradual process by which all slave children born after that were considered free. He said that the freedom laws had a head start there because the founder of the state, William Penn, was a Quaker and the city was fortunate to have leaders early on who opposed slavery. One was named Anthony Benezet, an educator who started the first school for blacks in the city, and one of its students was a black man named James Forten, who currently was a very wealthy man and the biggest supporter of the many opportunities for free blacks and runaway slaves.

"He works with the Quakers with lawyers and their agents to carry on the system of manumission and the operation of the Quaker school for Negros; both being what your trip here is about." Joe interrupted his son a moment and said that Nathan was being somewhat lengthy but was zealous about his beliefs. Nathan apologized if he was, and both Ken and Martin said they were not tiresome of his words and appreciated all he was saying. Nathan said he was only hitting the high spots, and it would take him days to tell all. He said he would just like to tell a couple more things about James Forten. He said he was a child soldier in the war, aboard a Patriot ship, hauling powder up to the ships cannons. His ship was captured by the British, and he was held prisoner. When the Brits learned that he was very bright and educated, they afforded him special privileges. After the war he did several jobs, and his last was a sailmaker, eventually buying the company he worked for. He was bright and there was a great demand for sails and he grew his company and became one of the richest people, black or white, in Philadelphia and had become a leader and the biggest contributor to the abolitionist movement and had spearheaded a petition to the U. S. Congress in 1801. He not only worked with and supported the Quakers but also started the first black church called the African Methodist Episcopal Church in efforts toward real equality. His influence and orations helped convince some of the founding fathers that they had grossly ignored the rights of Africans that should have been allowed no less freedoms than anyone else. He said that Benjamin Franklin was one of those founding fathers and now had become a leader in the movement.

Now, Nathan said, he had finished his speech making and was ready to get down to the details of their coming there and the plan that they had made on behalf of Sidney and Hulbert. He went on to say that he and his father's roles in things were limited to simply setting up things and handling the transfer of funds for the manumission process and that the Quaker organization would handle the rest, including the school plans for the one young lady that will be staying. Also, during the process, we will be here for you if there are any problems, which we don't expect. Again, thanks to James Forten, there are several law firms that have young agents that will represent each of the people up for manumission. They may not be lawyers themselves but advisors in court under the legal auspices of their lawyer bosses, who are paid by James Forten. He said that a couple of the agents were blacks, but although the state was ahead in many aspects of legal rights, it was still lacking in other areas including the possession of a law degree by a free black. He said that the system was an everyday all-day process, and they had made it quick and efficient. From the time the court date was set until the process was completed would only be a day or two at the most. Martin asked what they needed to do. Nathan said not much because they had the names of the people for manumission. He said that, even though he had just told of how Philadelphia was such a free zone, he would advise their people to stay mostly out of sight. He would send a messenger to see them before the end of the day, after he had informed the Quakers that they were here, telling when and where to meet to take the people to a secure location to wait for their courtroom appearance. He said the Quakers would arrange transportation during darkness from an agreed upon location and that might even be in his message later today.

Nathan said he would go ahead and leave them with his father and go and tell the Quakers that the process can begin. Then he said he had forgotten something. He needed a description of their boat and its location in the harbor and took out a map of the waterfront. Ken pointed out their location and said they were out a ways from the group of boats and said it was a new boat and was a new grey fifty-five foot sharpie. Nathan said he had asked, in the same situation, for a captain to tie a line to the stern of their skiff and let it be out backwards from their boat. He said to tell him a password that could be given to the messenger. Martin said "Yaupon" and wrote it down on a piece of paper and pointed to the box of tea he had given them.

Nathan left, and Joe asked Ken and Martin to sit a minute with him for tea and tell him about the Milam place that he had heard about from Sidney and Hulbert. There was a cook stove piped into the fireplace chimney, and it had a kettle of hot water on it. Martin suggested he try the yaupon. Joe said that was an excellent idea, and he handed Martin a teapot and spoon and asked him to show him the proper amount to use. Martin put in three heaping teaspoons full and said it took about five minutes to brew. Joe asked where the tea grew, and Martin said all over the South but especially along the northern Florida, Georgia, and South and North Carolina coasts. He said that on the Georgia coastal islands more than half of the short greenery that you saw in the woods was yaupon. He went on to say that it was getting popular, especially with the more common folks, because it was free, plentiful, and stimulating. Joe poured the tea and asked Martin to keep talking because he was interested. Martin told him about meeting the man over the tea department of the big store in Boston and how he showed them a bulletin from the big British trading company, saying how the tea was only for poor people and less-than-human Indians to drink. Joe said that sounded like something they would say. He said he wasn't accustomed to the taste but could already tell it was stimulating and he needed that. Martin said a little honey was good in it. Joe said he knew that Walter was sick, having just gotten a post from Sidney, and wished him better health. Martin explained how this had been his father's wish for all the people on the Milam place to be manumitted, even though few would want to leave. Joe looked at Ken and asked him what his thoughts were. Ken said that the Milam place was unlike any other place of its kind in the South. It was somewhat isolated, and Walter had special privileges, he reckoned, because of what he provided the city in security and prosperity, and he ran the place like it was his ship and the workers were his sailors. Martin added that his older brother, Henry, was worried that what they were doing near Savannah was not something that they could count on lasting, because there were people that didn't like that they treated the workers like servants instead of slaves. Joe said he had heard a little about the Milam Ice business from Sidney and Hulbert and asked them to tell him more about that. Ken told what he knew about it and about the boats they had and delivering ice. Martin told him about their new boat and the boat's engine coming from there in Philadelphia. Joe said it must be coming from Philadelphia Shipbuilding. Martin said it was and that he planned after this manumission process was completed, to visit and learn what he could about their engine. Joe said that company was the oldest and best around and he heard that they were building more engines than ships these days, but still had their shipyard next door to the metal works. Ken said that they should be getting on and stood and thanked Joe, and so did Martin. Joe thanked them for the tea and the interesting information about it and their other stories and said he admired what they were doing and he hoped for them to stop again before they left and let them know how it went and have some more tea and tell him more about Georgia.

It was about a twenty-minute walk back to where the skiff was. Just like the Boston, New York, and Savannah waterfronts, there were lots of businesses that sold what ships and boats needed, and the area was full of wagons hauling in and hauling out goods to and from ships. Martin said there was a smell in every port they had been to, and they were each different. Ken said he had noticed the smell but hadn't thought about it, but he reckoned it must be the particular mud and marsh for each place. Martin said that Savannah had the strongest smell, and Ken said there was more mud there than any place they had been. When they got to the skiff, Martin said he had wished in all the ports they had been to that he could have a picture of it to take home and show everybody. Ken told him that he needed to take landscape painting lessons, and he was surprised that Martin said he might do that. When they got back out to the sharpie, Ken tied a line to the stern of the skiff and let the tide take it out to the back. Johnny and Jacob saw him, and Ken saw their quizzical look. He explained why he did it and told them the word that the messenger would say to let them know he was real. Ellie brought out tea, and Ken and Martin told the rest about Joe and his son Nathan and how everything was taken care of and how organized the Quakers were and that they would only be a day or two and be done. They explained that they would have a lawyer's agent in a courtroom with a judge and that the agent would explain it all to them beforehand. Johnny and Ellie were the most worried about it. Ellie said she had never been in a courtroom with a judge, and Johnny said he hadn't either and were it not for Alice and Jochebed, he wouldn't go. Alice said it was their good fortune to be here and, even though none of them except Maggie would probably be doing anything different afterwards, she was glad to be doing what Walter had wanted for a long time. What Alice said shored up the resolve of Ellie and Johnny and the rest and eased their fears.

Just before dark, a lone man in a skiff came out, and all eyes were on him as he approached the sharpie. When he got near, he said the word, "Yaupon," and everyone let out the breath they were holding. It was a young man, and Ashley put a hand out to get him onboard. He saw their anxious looks and told them that a ship's boat would be out in the morning before daylight to pick them all up and for them to bring a change of clothes. He said they were told that there were to be eight of them going and asked if that was still so, and Alice said it was. He then said that they would be staying at sympathizers' homes tomorrow night. They would be split up into two groups of four and stay in different homes, and each group would have their own agent because the law limited to four people at a time that an agent could represent in the courtroom. The agent would tell them what to say and when to say it, and it was an easy but important procedure. He said there was a special message and that was a request that Martin Milam come because he was listed as having power of attorney and his signature would be required. He then asked who Maggie was, and everyone looked at her. The young man asked her if she was still planning on staying for the school, and she said she was. He said someone would talk to her about it tomorrow and answer any questions she might have. Ellie asked if Maggie would come back to the boat or stay once she was there, and he said she could stay on the boat if she liked. He asked if there was anything else. No one said anything, and he got up to go and said that the boatmen in the morning would use the same password and to leave the skiff tied backwards. Ken pulled his skiff alongside, and he left. Everyone was silent a bit until Alice smiled and said this is what we came for and eased the tension, especially for Ellie and Johnny.

Ashley said he would go tomorrow and pick up a few things they were short on and just to see what was available to add a few more things before they left. Ken said he guessed he would stay on the boat alone since everyone else would be gone. Martin said he thought that it was a good idea for someone to be here all the time. Ellie said they were having sweet potatoes and rice and beans for supper and it was almost ready, and Ashley went below to serve up some plum wine. After supper Jochebed was the entertainment again as she walked back and forth to everyone seated in the cockpit. Martin noticed how Maggie was quiet and sat close to Ellie with her head on her mother's shoulder. Martin told more about the abolitionist leaders that Nathan had told about earlier, and it was soon bedtime.

Ashley was up earlier than the rest as usual. He was joined in the galley by Ellie, and together they had a big breakfast with eggs and grits and salt pork and biscuits and blackberry preserves. Everyone was somewhat solemn and, just as they were told, the ship's boat came out with two boatmen and said the word "yaupon" again, and all nine of them loaded on and, in the dark, headed for the docks. A large coach was waiting, and they were off and soon at a brick two-story building similar to the one Martin had been to the day before, except it didn't have a sign outside. The place was simple and clean inside and had a wood stove in the middle of the main room with a fire to break the early morning chill. A lady in muslin clothing came in and smiled and asked if everyone wanted tea. All nodded their heads yes, and she left and came back with cups and poured tea from a pot that was on the wood heater. She said her name and said that this would be where they would wait until their time came up and that two agents would be there in about an hour to talk to them. She showed them the water closet and asked if they had any questions, and nobody but Maggie spoke up. She said she was staying for the school and asked if the lady knew anything about that. The lady said she did, and Maggie asked how it worked. The lady said that she would first talk with a school counselor and advisor to find out what her skill level was and what she was interested in and then be assigned to a class that suited her best. She said that she would be taken to the home that she would be staying in while she was in school. She saw the worried look about Maggie and told her that she would have some choices about what she wanted to study and even about who she stayed with if she was not comfortable. The way the lady talked and what she said made Maggie and her mother feel more comfortable. The lady went on to say to the whole group that they would all be free by the end of the day or tomorrow, and they all had a choice to stay in Philadelphia or go back to where they were from. Their agent would explain much more to them about what their rights were and what obligations they would have if they stayed there or went back to the state they had traveled from. She warned them that even though they would be classified as free blacks, in southern states, they would still be faced with difficulties, sometimes greater than being a slave. Most southern states had annual fees that had to be paid by free blacks, and if they weren't paid, they could become property of the state and be sold into slavery again. She said that because of numerous slave rebellions in the last fifteen years, things had become stricter for free blacks because owners were always concerned that it would cause their slaves to be unsettled and unsatisfied with their lot. She went on to paint a realistic picture of what could be expected for them with their new life status. She couldn't have known how things were where they had come from, but the information was still interesting for all to hear.

There came the sounds of horse hoofs clopping on river stone paving, and the lady went to the window quickly and peeked out and announced that the two agents had arrived, and they would have a lot more to say than she did and encouraged them to ask as many questions as they wanted. She looked at Maggie sitting by her mother and told her not to worry, because they had been doing this for a long time, and everyone was there to help her in any way that she would need it and if she liked learning, she would be very pleased and happy in their school. Maggie said she was worried that she wouldn't be as educated as the rest, and the lady smiled and told Maggie that she could tell that she was plenty bright, and it didn't matter at what level she was because she had never seen anyone that was not suited to their comfort level of learning.

The two agents were let in. One was a black man, and one was white, and when they walked in, Martin screamed and scared everyone in the room and Jochebed, who had been quiet, started crying. The black agent smiled and said "Martin!" and surprised everyone that he knew Martin. Martin said "Mallie!" and Maggie and Alice were the only two to catch on right away. Martin got up and hugged Mallie, and the lady and the other agent were somewhat shocked. Martin exclaimed to the group that this was Mallie, who they had helped escape the slave catchers on Tybee.

Martin laughed and called him "Le Mal "like he had signed the coded letter that he sent to the Dyers. He said that Charles Dyer was not thrilled about him doing that. Mallie told the lady and the other agent that he could explain the whole story in five minutes and then they could go ahead as planned. So, Mallie started with his lawyer boss that had mistreated him in Augusta and how he learned to read. Then, how during a trip to Savannah with his owner, he escaped during the night onto a ship loaded with cotton bales and was discovered while going down the Savannah River to head out into the Atlantic and how he was let out on Tybee Island at the edge of the Atlantic. He told about the work crew, staying on Tybee from the Milam plantation, and how he was so hungry and ate up with bugs that he walked into their camp thinking that he was giving himself up to be returned to his evil master, but instead they fed him and gave him a blanket to cover up from the bugs. Then he told how he met Martin and Daniel and Mary and how the slave hunters came and they were barely able to stay one step away from them. He told of the trickery that Martin played on the slave hunters to make them think he had left from one end of the island, when he had actually escaped from the other end. He stopped and asked if Martin could tell about where he went and Martin said he guessed it would be OK. Mallie told of the runaways and the Indians on an island way out in the marsh and how they helped him get with some other Indians that hid him on a big canoe and took him way up a river to some other people that hid him again and took him to North Carolina then to other places and finally got here to Philadelphia. Martin asked how he ended up doing this, and he said that the only good thing about his time with the cruel lawyer in Augusta was that he learned about the law. Then, when he got there, they asked him what he knew about and they took him to the office of Mr. James Forten, who was in every way the opposite of his owner in Augusta. Mallie said that Mr. Forten gave him more law books to study and put him to work. There was not a dry cheek in the room after hearing what Mallie said. The lady told Mallie that he should get on with preparing the people here for their court appearance later today or tomorrow. Mallie said he could tell from how many people were left from yesterday that it wasn't going to be this afternoon but would be tomorrow. Alice asked if they should go back to the boat or stay here until tomorrow. The lady said that it would be better to stay. Mallie told Martin that he didn't need to stay unless he wanted to, but he would need to come back tomorrow, then he thought better of it, and said he had the papers with him that Martin needed to sign, and he could sign them and not have to come back tomorrow. Martin said he would do that because he had other things to attend to, but he wanted to see Mallie again and asked him if he could come out to their boat later in the afternoon. Mallie said he could do that, and Martin told him where the boat was and about the backwards skiff and Mallie said he could hire a pulling boatman to take him out. He added that there were papers that Ashley and Ken needed to sign pertaining to their ownership of Alice, and he could bring them. Martin got up and hugged Mallie and all the people from the Milam plantation. All eyes were on young Martin as he left. Mallie and the other agent took turns explaining everything and helped everyone feel more at ease. When they finished, Mallie went off and came back in half an hour with the same large coach. and they loaded up to go to where they would be staying for the night.

Martin hired one of the many pulling boatmen that were waiting around for work, to take him back out to the sharpie and smiled to himself as he saw their skiff tied to the stern of the sharpie backwards. The boatman pulled alongside and was paid, and Martin climbed aboard. Ken and Ashley were glad to see him and asked about the others. Martin said they were fine and the manumission would be completed by the next day and told them about Mallie, to which Ken said it was a small world indeed. Martin said he had done all that was wanted of him, and he had thought about going to the Philadelphia Ship Company but wanted to wait for them to go together. Ashley said he had thought he would go ashore to pick up a few supplies, but he would just wait until later. He said he and Ken had made the hold back into sleeping arrangements again, and even Ashley could stand up in it now that the boxes of tea were gone. Martin told them about the things Mallie had said about how he got there and what he was doing, and that he was coming out to the boat in the afternoon for a visit to have them sign some papers about Alice. After a snack Ken and Ashley both went into their new sleeping arrangements in the hold for a nap.

Martin was too keyed up for a nap and sat in the cockpit, contemplating things. He felt somewhat like he had when he finally went over to the Indian islands to look for Alice's family after having vowed years before to do it. Now, it was a vow to his father to see this all done, but he knew his urgency wouldn't calm until he got back home and told his father of it being completed. He didn't expect it to happen, but after a few minutes, the warm sun made him drowsy. He went below and got a pillow and stretched out in the cockpit. Martin must have been more tired than he thought and slept for a couple hours and would have remained asleep, except for feeling a bump against the sharpie hull and hearing Mallie call his name. He felt like he had only just laid down but saw that the sun had moved over to the west and the sky was turning pinkish. Mallie climbed aboard and hugged Martin as Ashley and Ken came out to see what was happening.

Mallie grinned big at them and thanked them for bringing Martin and everybody to Philadelphia. Ashley went below to put some water on for tea and came back up to hear Mallie telling of all the places he had been taken to on his trip from the Indian Islands to Philadelphia. When he went below again to get the tea, he came back with Martin telling Mallie the rest of the story about what had happened with the slave hunters after he had gone across the Back River. It was one of Martin's favorite stories to tell of the slave hunters coming and the head man fuming over seeing where he thought a boat had picked up Mallie. His most favorite part of the story was telling how the blind Captain Jones had told them about seeing him leave the beach with two men in a boat headed for Turtle Island. Mallie laughed until he cried, and Ken, Ashley, and Martin laughed uncontrollably with him, even though they had heard the story a dozen times. After the laughter settled a bit, Mallie said there was something that had come up that he wanted to tell Martin about, and Martin was very interested in what that could be. He said that after Martin had left, Izak had asked if it would be possible for him to stay after things were finished in court, and Mallie had said he would be free then to choose anything about what he wanted to do.

This surprised Martin, but not completely because he had seen how Izak had looked worried sometimes when the subject came up about Maggie staying in Philadelphia for school. He told Mallie that they had talked about marriage but were waiting to see how things here were and how everyone would be surprised because Izak had been training to be a boatman. He was a good swimmer and had been doing everything being asked of him, even going to Tybee to help out at the lighthouse while Daniel and Mary had come to stay with them for a while. Martin asked Mallie what he thought about it and what Izak's prospects might be. Mallie said there would be no problem whatsoever if that is what he really wanted. He said with his skill on the water, there was plenty of need for a pulling boatman, and that Philadelphia even had a waterfront rescue operation that was part of the fire department and had a boat with a water pump for ship fires and for any other kind of water emergency. He said it wouldn't be a problem at all for Izak to fit in, and if he and Maggie were married, that wouldn't be a problem either. He said he had told them both all the same and said he would help them in any way he could and be glad doing so. Martin said he would probably do the same if he were Izak. Mallie said that Maggie had told him about his father's health, and he wished him to be better when they returned. Ashley told Mallie something that made him particularly happy and that was about their plans to bring Alice's family and friends, from over on the island, up to Philadelphia for manumission before too long. Mallie said that he thought of them often and how he had considered staying there with them but hadn't and how kind they all were to him. He asked about Ayana and her people. Martin said their future was uncertain because of how the Savannah population had doubled in the last few years and out-of-the-way places like the Indian Islands were getting colonials looking for opportunities. It didn't matter that the islands had been granted to the Indians because they had no more voice in a courtroom than a slave. Mallie shook his head and said that it might be a long time coming, but he said changes were coming for equal rights for all. He told of one of the founding fathers of America, Benjamin Franklin, taking an active role in the abolitionist movement and how he spoke about his regrets that all people, including black people and Indians, should not have been left out of the Declaration of Independence and the Constitution in the beginning. He said that he felt like he had escaped from one island to another, and that Philadelphia was like an island of equal rights for all people surrounded not by water but by slave-holding states. It was a situation where he saw that his island was getting bigger because the understanding about abolition was growing and spreading. Mallie said he had come to know about how the churches in Augusta were the biggest supporters of slavery in how they reasoned for it to be a good thing for the Africans according to the teachings of the Bible and how the consciences of the people were salved by this in the churches. But, he said, he had come to learn there about what a great force the Quaker church was and how they used the same Bible to show how that all men were equal in the eyes of God and deserved the same choices and rights as everyone else. He said they were on a mission to change things, and he had witnessed how they had organized and had, within the law, eliminated slavery in the area and had their sights on doing it in the whole country and they were getting support from higher-up people in the government, and even some of the original founding fathers were rethinking their views and having great influence in changing the laws. Mallie said it was a powerful experience when you helped them achieve their goals because you could feel a force of good and of doing something that was already happening and you were just an instrument in it being done. Martin said he had heard his brother Henry say something like that. Mallie asked more about Mary and Daniel. Martin told him about Mary's driven desire to write the history of her parents and the Milam operation and their origins and how she was hiding all her notetaking until a time when it could be openly shared, and her intent was to put it all together in a book. Martin said Mallie was already part of it, and that made Mallie laugh.

He said she could publish it there in Philadelphia now but there would always be a chance that it would get back to Georgia and make trouble for everyone there. Ashley asked Mallie if he could stay for supper and he or Ken could take him over in the skiff afterwards or at any time he wanted. Mallie said he would like that but he needed to get Ashley and Ken to sign the documents in regard to Alice and Jochebed first. After they had, Ken went below and handed out some plum wine, and Ashley went below and started some supper and, in a few minutes, the smell of baking biscuits wafted up from below and then the smell of potatoes and onions.

After supper and more spirited talk, Mallie said he should be going. Martin said he wanted to row him over, and they left in the skiff. Since it was dark, Martin asked if Mallie would be fine alone. He said this wasn't Augusta or Savannah and that he would be safe. Martin said he believed him but insisted that he wait and see that he was on a carriage to go home. They sat and talked some more, and Martin told Mallie about his plans to marry Mary and take her on the new steamboat they were having built. He told Mallie that he was the first person he had told that to. Mallie said he wished he could be there for the wedding. He added that who could have ever dreamed that they would see each other again. Mallie told Martin that a day hadn't gone by that he didn't think of him, Mary, Daniel, and the people over on the island and how thankful he was for them risking so much to save him. He said that he didn't want a long time to go by without seeing or hearing from them again. Martin reminded him of the risk in letter-writing. A carriage with a lantern came along the riverfront looking for a customer, and Mallie hailed it. He hugged Martin and left, and Martin rowed himself back out to the sharpie. Ashley and Ken were still up when Martin came back, and they sat and talked. Ken said things sure were different with only the three of them left on the boat, and Ashley said he missed little Jochebed already. Martin said that everyone but Maggie and Izak should be back tomorrow afternoon, and all they had to do before going back to Savannah, was to visit the ship and engine building company.

The sky was red the next morning, and they all three knew what that meant. Ken said a cold front was coming and probably would be pushing some wet weather over them soon. Martin said yes, but that usually meant a northwester and clear skies for a few days after that and that would blow them out of there and down the coast a ways. They all shook their heads in agreement. They sat together with coffee and cold biscuits and preserves, watched the colorful sky as the sun rose, and then Ashley and Ken made ready to go ashore. As they were leaving in the skiff, Martin told them not to buy any fresh fish or crabs because he would catch something while he waited on the boat, and for them to take the whole day and see the town and enjoy themselves some if they liked because there may not be another landing for a couple weeks.

Martin sat in the cockpit a while and watched the colorful sky fade as the sun rose higher. He thought of his father and hoped that his health had continued to improve. He thought of his mother and Henry and his family. Then he settled on thinking about Mary and pondered what she might say about his idea of her living with him on the new steamboat after they were married. Next, he thought about the things Henry had talked to him about how things could change after their father was gone. He didn't like thinking about his father not being there and maybe even the Milam place and their lighthouse support operation ceasing to exist if the annual contract was not continued. His father had been the solid rock that had anchored everything but he knew Henry was a rock like his father, and he knew Henry had been making plans to ensure the security of everyone if big changes came. He was confident in Henry's vision and planning skills and glad the place didn't depend on his skills in that area. He thought about Ayana and her people and knew changes were coming for them. He knew that Ayana was a wise and good leader, but he had uncertainty about what might happen to them. In his solitude he made a solemn vow to himself, like he had made to his father about fulfilling his wishes about the people of the Milam plantation, to help Ayana to preserve and protect her people. Martin sat in silence for a while longer, letting his wishes sink in deep within himself, before setting about getting some baited lines overboard. In a few hours, he had enough fish and crabs and cleaned them all and put them in the biggest pot they had with the last of the potatoes and started a stew cooking slowly that would feed everyone later. After more cold biscuits, he took a nap and woke and had a bowl of the stew that had been cooking.

About an hour before dark, the ship's boat that had taken the group over returned, and right behind it were Ashley and Ken in the skiff. Martin was surprised and glad that Maggie and Izak and even Mallie returned with the group. There was an air of happiness and relief, and the sharpie cockpit was full as the plum wine was passed from below and Alice spoke of what they all had gone through and where they stayed. She said she could never have imagined the concern of the people that they stayed with and how much fervor and empathy they showed to help them. They were on a mission of freedom, for not only them, but for every slave in America. She said the manumission in court was fast and most of the time they were educated about what were their rights and obligations they would have as a free black and warned about the ways they could be repossessed by the state and resold back into slavery under certain conditions. They were each given documents to prove their free status. Alice, with Jochebed in her arms and tears in her eyes, told Ashley and Ken again how thankful she was for how they had done such a heroic thing by going to Saint Helena Island and negotiated the sale of her and Jochebed and her family and the others, so that they were the official owners, just to protect them from ever being returned to South Carolina or repossessed by the state. She said she and Jochebed both could have been taken from Johnny. Ashley and Ken were both choked up from what Alice said, and Ken said the next yaupon delivery would have her family and the others to bring for their manumission.

After all the talk, Mallie said he had a surprise for everyone. Martin noticed Izak and Maggie smiling real big and figured that Mallie would let Izak announce that he was staying in Philadelphia. But what Mallie did was hold a paper up and read a law about how a boat captain could perform a legal marriage ceremony. He looked at Ashley and Ken and said he guessed they could perform it together. Then he looked at Izak and Maggie and said that there was to be a marriage there on the sharpie and asked them to stand up. He handed two sheets of paper to Ken and said that he and Ashley would both have to sign but only one had to read the vows to Maggie and Izak. Ellie and Jacob had learned about Izak staying but the marriage today there on the boat was a surprise. Ellie had not always approved of Izak, but she was overcome with emotion and got up and hugged them both. Jacob just sat and smiled, and everyone was filled with joy. Mallie said he wanted to do the marriage first off so they would have some time to all celebrate. He showed Ken, who had the papers in his hand, where to read from and asked Maggie and Izak to stand. Ken offered the paper to Ashley, and Ashley told Ken that he stuttered when he read aloud, so Ken stood and read the vows to each. When they had both agreed, Izak took a thin gold band that Mallie had given him earlier and placed it on Maggie's finger, and the boat rocked a bit as they all stood and some cried and some laughed. Alice passed Jochebed to Maggie and told her that she would have one soon and Maggie said yes but not real soon. Izak, with tears on his cheeks looked at Martin and said he hoped he hadn't disappointed him about staying and how he had liked training to be a Milam boatman. Martin said he couldn't be happier for him, and he had done all that had been expected of him and more. Izak said that he owed everything to him for teaching him how to swim and inspiring him to learn reading and taking him to meet Maggie. Mallie said he had already made inquiries about a job on the riverfront fireboat for Izak and that the same people who had been having Maggie stay with them had a carriage house with a small room above that they both could stay in. Mallie asked Martin when he thought they would leave. Martin said he thought they could do their business at the shipyard tomorrow and leave the next day with the northwester they thought would be blowing. The sun was getting down near the horizon, and the sky was getting colorful. Plum wine flowed, and the big pot of fish and crab stew was eaten, and much merriment was shared. When Mallie announced that it was time for him to go, Izak and Maggie stood to go with him, and another round of laughing and crying erupted. Martin brought the skiff alongside and rowed the newlyweds and Mallie in and waited until they were on a carriage before heading back.

Next morning, Ellie made a big pot of grits with the leftover fish and crab stew added to the pot. Johnny fashioned a rope harness around Jochebed because she had learned to climb from the cockpit floor up onto the seat and needed watching every minute. Martin, Ashley, and Ken took some time to go over the plans of the steamboat that Colonel Stevens had done to make them fresh in their mind. When they finished, they loaded onto the skiff and rowed to the wharf area where they had been leaving the skiff. When they were stepping out, a pulling boat was leaving with Maggie and Izak, going out to spend the last day on the sharpie before it left for South Carolina. Martin yelled at them, and they both smiled real big back at him.

The Philadelphia Ship Building Company was on the southern end of the city up a small river not even a quarter mile. They hailed a carriage. It wasn't far, but the shipyard was huge and spread out. They asked the driver to take them to the machine shop area. He set them off and pointed to a two-story building next to the small river a hundred yards from the biggest enclosed shop they had ever seen. The noises coming from inside the big shop were loud and unfamiliar to them. The loud banging and clanging of steel and iron was not something they ever heard in Savannah. They walked in, and there were a half dozen men at drawing desks. The man nearest the door asked if he could help them. Martin told them the name of the man, Mr. Watson, that Colonel Stevens had told him to ask for. The man said his office was upstairs and pointed to a door and told them to go through that and up the stairs. They did and entered a large office, and an older gentleman stood up from his desk and welcomed them in and asked if he could help. Martin said that Colonel Stevens was building a steamboat for them, and he had suggested they come here to look at the engine he was planning to use. Martin announced their names, and Mr. Watson instantly became very much alive and said the Colonel had said they were coming soon. He said he and the Colonel had decided to build the hull and set the engine here instead of at his shop, because of the difficulty in moving the big engine and boiler and running gear from here over to his place.

Mr. Watson got up and motioned for them to follow, and they went down the stairs and outside and headed over to the big shop. The noise got louder as they got closer, and Martin recognized the hull form as soon as they walked inside. It was built on two flat railway cars that were on the rails leading out to the river. Watson first led them around the framed hull then pointed to the engine parts and to the overhead crane on trolleys that would be used to set the heavy steel parts of the engine in place. He commented that he liked the combination of materials because the steel frame better supported the weight of the engine, and there was no better hull planking material than the Longleaf Pine from Georgia. He pointed to a huge stack of planking intended for their boat that had planks as long as fifty feet. Watson said if they had come next week, they would have seen the engine in place and the shafts, which they intended to do before the planking. There was a plan table set up with the framing plan and engine placement, and he showed them the heavy-duty steel framing that would support the engine and boiler. Martin briefly thought of his new friend, Captain Lawrence Missroon, and how he would like to see all this. The noise was somewhat deafening, and Watson had to yell for them to hear him. He asked if they were interested in seeing more, but they were ready to leave because the noise was disturbing. Watson led them back up to his office where they could speak without yelling. He said he didn't know how long the Boston outfit would need to do their work, but he expected to splash their hull in a couple months. But it would take another month of testing and modifications to have it ready to leave for Boston. Ashley said that even if it took four months in Boston, they would be ahead of the time they expected it to take. Watson said that Stevens had mentioned that they were in search of an engineer, and he would be looking out for one that wouldn't mind moving to Georgia. Martin, thinking of Thomas's son, said they might have one that would need some additional training. Watson said he could supply one temporarily if that was what they needed. Martin asked how long it took to train an engineer, and he said it depended on how much education and experience he had beforehand, and of course on the individual himself. He said a smart man with some experience could be ready in a couple years. Martin mentioned that they may be getting a navy man that had been on the first navy steamship. Watson said that his and Colonel Stevens outfit had built that boat in secrecy years before with an engine from France. He said they had made improvements on the engine going in their boat and it was lighter than the French and English engines but just as powerful. He added that they should send the navy man to Colonel Stevens because there was not a better place in the world for him to learn how to safely operate a steam engine. Ashley said he had heard stories about steam engines exploding and blowing up the boat and everyone onboard. Watson said it did happen, but it was mostly because of inexperience and impatience. He went on to say that the inexperience was easy to fix by teaching the engineer and crew how to properly operate the engine but patience was difficult to teach. He added that steam was very powerful and could expand beyond control, and the explosions were very powerful. If you add too much fuel to a firebox, you can't pull it out, and it converts the water in the boiler to expand to an uncontrollable level and can be a disaster. He said that and other reasons is why it is so important to have a capable engineer.

Watson said, the engineer should oversee everything, including wood quality and storage. And it's the Captain's job to have a good engineer around always. That's why the engineer gets his own private quarters like the Captain. Martin said he hoped this wouldn't be the last boat that they built for them and asked what else he thought they should know at this point. He said not much and to let him know if they would be needing an engineer on loan. Martin quickly said that he could say now that they would, because Thomas' son would not be trained in time for when the boat would be ready. Watson said he had just the man but would need to ask if he would be agreeable to go to Georgia for a year or so. Martin added that the bank was ready to make a payment whenever it was needed. He said that wouldn't be until the hull, with the engine and running gear installed, was launched and tested, and he would let them know. He said he would send for his personal carriage to take them back and walked downstairs with them and asked one of his people to see that his carriage and driver were summoned. Once in the carriage, Martin said he was already starting to think about the second steamboat that he was sure that they would soon need. Both Ashley and Ken shook their heads in disbelief and awe at Martin.

They were back sooner than they thought they would be and found the sharpie full of much merriment and gladness. It was all about Maggie and Izak, but Jochebed was causing most of the laughter. Maggie had been holding onto her, sometimes in her lap and sometimes by the rope harness Johnny had put on her. Ellie was both happy and sad about Maggie. She didn't like that she would be gone from home, but the visit with the people where she would be staying, and the fact that Izak would be with her, helped ease her mind. She worried that Thomas would be lonely but worried also about him leaving after seeing how much he liked boats and Martin. He said all the time that he wanted to be a captain like Martin. Jochebed was like her granddaughter, and she knew she would have plenty of time yet to enjoy her. Johnny and Jacob were pleasant and happy with everything, but they were both ready to be home with all the things they felt like they had to do. They were happy to hear Ashley say that they would start home in the morning.

Early in the afternoon, a skiff came with Mallie. He said he knew they would probably be leaving the next day, and he couldn't help but want to see them a while more. Ellie fed him and gave him some plum wine like they had been sipping all day. The tears flowed from his eyes as he proclaimed that his run in with all of them at Tybee was the greatest thing that had ever happened to him. He looked at Jacob and said he would have been back in Augusta with his awful master had not Jacob taken him in when he had surrendered to them at Lazaretto Landing. Then, how the Dyers had risked everything to help him stay one step ahead of the slave hunters and dogs. He looked at Martin and expressed his gratitude so sincerely that he had everyone shedding tears. There was laughter as Martin told again of the blind Captain Jones telling the fuming slave hunters that he had seen him leave the beach in a boat with two others headed for Turtle Island. Then the others told their favorite parts of that story. Jacob told the part about the boatload of slave hunters and their dogs coming to Lazaretto, and the swarm of gnats following and biting so bad that they couldn't row the boat, and all the arguing they were having. It was a good thing that they had anchored the sharpie a ways from the other boats because of all the loud laughing and carrying on that was happening.

At sunset Martin hailed a pulling boat nearby to take Izak, Maggie, and Mallie back in. Before they loaded up, Martin reminded them that he expected there to be more yaupon deliveries to Philadelphia before long. Ellie made them all laugh when she said she would think about being a deckhand on that boat and Martin had never seen Jacob laugh so hard at anything because he knew how Ellie had been so afraid of the ocean. Mallie told Ellie that he owed everything to them all and that he would keep special watch over Maggie and Izak, and that made Ellie feel good. Izak asked Johnny to tell the boatmen that he would miss them. Thomas cried and told Maggie that he wanted to be on that next yaupon boat too. Alice hugged Maggie and told her how proud she was of her and to keep writing her poems and the time had come for her to shine. Maggie picked up Jochebed and hugged her, and next she hugged Martin and said he was her brother from another mother and for him to watch over Thomas. The group going in climbed down in the boat and it pulled away.

The sharpie coasted away from the Philadelphia waterfront the next morning with the outgoing tide and a northwesterly breeze behind it with the last sprinkle of showers that had come during the night. All aboard were in a somewhat somber mood, except for Jochebed who was her happy self, going from one lap to the other. After about an hour, her joy and happiness won over their sadness, as the sun lifted up and cleared the clouds that were hung over the river and marshes. The blue of the sky began to show up, and the air began to dry out and was chilly. The sails were set wing on wing with the wind mostly behind them. By midafternoon, when the tide turned, they were in the Delaware Bay, and Ashley and Ken told everyone that their intent was to sail on through the night while the weather and wind were favorable. To themselves, they hoped that a west or southwest wind would be with them to get past Cape Hatteras, but they knew it was unlikely for a northwester to blow for two more days. If it did blow for a couple more days, with no cargo in the holds, they might, if they sailed night and day, cover the two hundred and fifty miles between them and the Cape.

There was a different mood going back than there had been coming up to Philadelphia, and not just because Maggie and Izak were not along. For Martin, it was one of contemplating the future, concerning his father mostly and then Mary. As he learned from Ken, sailing offshore without constantly watching two sides of a channel gave him time to think more than usual. He had seen the look on Henry's face when they were around their father. Henry, fifteen years older, was often something more like a parent than a brother, and Martin often took his lead. Henry had told him of his planning for things when their father was not around, and that was hard to think about. Martin thought about Mary, and there was no doubt about her becoming his wife but he wasn't sure when and if she would go with him on the boat and thought of where else they might live and came to the simple fact that it would be her choice. Then, the thing next most on his mind was Ayana and her people. He knew change was coming for them and helping them was almost more important than Mary. Helping them was another vow of his. There were other things that Martin thought about, but those were the three that were most on his mind. His father, Mary, and Ayana and her people.

The rest of the people on the boat were also somewhat thoughtful on the trip back home. Ashley and Ken were mostly intent on getting the boatload of people safely back home to Georgia. They also had plans to think about concerning the shipping business and they had also vowed to bring Alice's family and friends to Philadelphia to have them manumitted.

Alice's thoughts were with Walter. She contemplated life at the Milam place without him. She found solace in knowing that they had just accomplished what he had wanted and hoped that he would be alive when they got back so he could know it was done. She gazed at Martin and thought what a blessing he had been to unite her with her family and do what his father had wanted. Alice wasn't sure that her mother would want to go for manumission, or how long she would stay on the island and continue helping runaways. Her father would stay or go, depending on what her mother's wishes were. Alice was not sure about what her brother would want to do, having an Indian wife with their son and all. He would want to please his wife and her choices for their child. She was concerned about Prissy and the others too. Besides being a mother and wife, Alice was aware that she had become somewhat of a matriarch and many depended on her council, especially Henry.

Johnny was a man of simple thoughts and deep feelings. His thoughts and feelings on the trip home were not much different than usual. He really didn't know what had come over him after having met Alice, but he felt gratitude about it every day. Although he may have been regarded as nothing more than livestock when he was born and early life, he now had a sense of his own self and what he wanted and that was to take care of his family and be a useful part of the Milam place and he felt contentment every day.

Unlike the trip up to Philadelphia, Ellie was in high spirits on the way home. She had been worried about Maggie going to a strange place and being alone. Izak would not have been her pick, but she was glad Maggie had someone to be with. She was touched deeply by the Quakers' zeal and sincerity to help them and others. Before being sent to the Milam's, she had seen and felt the torment, separation, and ill treatment of her people. Much of this underlying despair now was displaced by hope and optimism that truth and light would prevail. Jacob was also affected by the kind treatment of the Quaker people and the betterment they wanted for Maggie and the rest of them. He was glad Maggie was getting an education because he had seen her boredom when helping her mother with chickens and eggs and her excitement when she spoke about the books she read. Jacob didn't feel any different being a legally free black but felt an even greater thankfulness especially toward Henry for working so hard to fulfill his father's wishes for them. Jacob was a man of tasks. Although he was getting up in years, he was looking forward to getting back to his overseer job of the Milam place and thought about the things he needed to do when he got home.

As night fell at the end of the first day out from Philadelphia, they were nearing the mouth of the Delaware Bay, and the Henlopen lighthouse was easy to spot. In the darkness, Ashley steered them southeasterly until they were about five miles out, then they followed a compass course south, checking the wind direction often by the compass to best guess their distance from shore and they made sure there was always two people awake at the helm and there was usually three. Ken was at the helm at when the Cape Henry lighthouse tower in Virginia was spotted. Ken happily reported that they had gone almost two hundred miles two days. However, the cool dry wind of the northwester was slowing, and it was many hours more before they were past the lighthouse and the Chesapeake Bay. The shore went by slowly all night without any lighthouse sighting, and by morning the wind was out of the south, in the opposite direction of home. They went windward as much as possible, and as the wind continued shifting around to the southeast, they actually lost ground in order to gain some distance from shore, with the Cape still seventy miles south. With no inlets to tuck into, Ashley and Ken decided, to go in and anchor out for the night at about three miles offshore and wait until there was a wind shift before attempting Cape Hatteras.

It took two days on anchor before the wind became favorable enough for them to safely go out and around the shoals of Cape Hatteras. Once past the Cape, the coastline slants back southwestward all the way to the Tybee bight. Now, with an east wind on their quarter it was like going downhill and the big new sharpie surfed down every other huge ocean swell and Martin saw the shoreline racing by and in two nights and a day of sailing, they were counting all the church steeples of Charleston, and twelve hours later, they were entering Tybee Roads. Martin thought about Mary up at the Tybee Lighthouse and saw the pilot crews out on the beach and Captain Jones by his shanty as that came in. He had sensed Ashley and Ken's urgency over the last few days to deliver their cargo of people safely. And he saw the relief on their faces as they came in from the Atlantic. They got to within three miles of home before the tide turned back toward Tybee. The east wind was still behind them, but it took three hours to go the last three miles against the current. The river was passing swiftly under them, but the riverbank was extremely slow in going by.

As soon as they came about into the Wilmington River and the Milam bluff was visible, Jacob started the chantey with a solo verse, and the rest chimed in the chorus. The Dyers had been watching out for their return every day for the last week and had seen them come in and signaled that they were on their way. The whole Milam place, except Martha and Walter, were out watching them come slowly up the river. When they heard the chantey enough, they joined in. There was not a dry cheek on the boat or the land as Ashley, with the centerboards up and with sails still set, plowed the boat up onto the soft mud bank and threw a line out. He said they could just let the tide go out from under her, and she could spend the night on the riverbank. Ken laughed and said she was tired and needed that.

Martin had not seen so much weeping, frolic, yelling, and carrying-on as the people in the boat climbed out and joined the people on the hill. He went straight to find Henry to ask about his father, and he saw the answer on his face before reaching him. Henry didn't have to say anything. He just hugged Martin and told him to go with him now to the house. Martin hadn't noticed, but Alice was right behind him and had seen Henry's expression and followed them to the carriage. She left Jochebed with Ellie, and the three went ahead. They went in the house together and straight to Walter's room where Martha was with him. He saw Martin and Alice, and a little color and brightness came over him. Martin's first words were to tell his father that they had done what they had set out to do and Walter managed a slight smile of understanding. He put his hand out to Alice and told her he loved her like his own and looked at them all and said to tell everyone that he loved them too. He reached for Martha's hand and squeezed it. His last breath came out and he was gone.

Walter was buried near the Milam plantation on a beautiful bluff that later became a famous cemetery called Bonaventure.

28.
TEN YEARS LATER

After Walter's death, and the deaths of most of his close friends and allies in Savannah, there came many changes to the Milam place. As Henry had expected, within four years of his father's death, the Milam place was investigated for crimes against the state, because of their treatment of the blacks that lived and worked there. However, by that time, all had made the trip to Philadelphia and had been manumitted. Some were too old to work and continued living there and were supported and The Milam's still had enough influential allies in Savannah, so their penalties were financial. Their ice business was renamed "The Southern Ice and Works Company" and employed those left on the place that could still work, along with many immigrants and poor whites that were sparsely employed because of the slave labor economy. Maggie stayed in Philadelphia and was teaching at the school she had attended, and Izak was a fireboat captain on the Philadelphia waterfront. They became close friends with Mallie, who continued assisting the growing number of slaves through the manumission process. Little Thomas grew up and was the first mate on the steamboat on which Martin was the Captain with his wife, Mary and she continued her journal and writing. The son of Thomas (the Boston engineer) had become the engineer, and he had his own small cabin on that boat. The Milam's lost the annual contract to supply and manage the Tybee lighthouse, although the Dyers were allowed to remain. Daniel Dyer had found a wife and had two children. He was now the light keeper, and Charles and Margo had built a small house on the Milam property. Everybody's favorite Tybee character, Captain Jones, (Captain "Sandy"), had passed shortly after Walter. His body was taken in a procession of pilot boats, along with the old Milam supply boats, Martin and Mary, Johnny, and Daniel and his father and mother accompanied his body, aboard his old pilot boat that Martin had restored, and he was laid to rest at Bonaventure with Walter. John and Julie Wilcox also built near the Milam's, with one daughter off at a girls' school in Virginia and one married and living in Charleston. Mable married and was living in the part of the old Milam home place where Henry had lived. Her brother James still worked with Jehu, and they lived in the apartment in the huge horse barn of the ice company. Martha was still living in the same place, in part of the big house, with her sister. Henry and his wife built a new house nearby and Henry, as always remained managing the large ice company. Their daughter was off at the same girls' school in Virginia as John's daughter, and his son was working at the ice company and still at home. Alice and Johnny had another son, JohnJohn and Johnny worked at the ice company. Alice became the matriarch and her and

The Southern Ice and Works Company grew much bigger and became one of the largest companies in Savannah, and one of the few that operated without slave labor. They opened another plant in Charleston that was bigger and handled more ice than the one in Savannah. Some ice continued to come on ships from up north, but most was coming by the new railways and steam locomotives in insulated train cars. More and bigger icehouses were built that kept ice longer. The market expanded inland, and Jason was still building many residential iceboxes and icehouse parts, and thirty ice wagons left every morning to deliver ice to Savannah residences. However, the only way to deliver to the coastal islands and towns was still by boat and demand continued to grow. Soon after Ashley, Ken, and Martin had their first steamboat built, they had another one built by the same companies in Philadelphia and Boston. They also had a bigger barge built with steel. Ashley and Ken co-captained the new boat, with the barge, from Beaufort, South Carolina, to Wilmington, North Carolina. After Martin worked under Captain Ben for a couple years, Ben retired to the north end of Saint Helena Island and Martin became the Captain and the boat became the home of the wedded Martin Milam and Mary Dyer. Their boat delivered to the islands and coastal towns from Savannah to Jacksonville Florida, returning to Savannah a few times a month to load more ice. Both boats also carried supplies and hardware to island plantations, as well as occasional passengers. Usually, Martin's boat docked at the ice company dock near the Milam place, and sometimes they stopped over at the Lazaretto landing and spent time with Daniel.

Stopping at Tybee to see Daniel was not the only or even the most important reason for using the Lazaretto Landing every month. It was still Martin's vow and mission to be of assistance to Ayana and her people and to Alice's family, Prissy, and the others who continued helping the few runaways every month. With the steamboat anchored at Lazaretto, Martin and Mary would take his little dugout or the bigger boat he was given by Captain Jones and go over to the Indian Islands for a day or two. Sometimes they would leave, as before, on an early morning high tide, from the Back River landing, pole over the marsh to Long Island to see Ayana and return on the high tide late in the day, and Daniel or his son would pick them up at the back River Landing. Mary continued taking her notes from both groups, and as before, visiting with Ayana on the breezy side of the island. There had been several rumors that the Indian Islands would become farm land, but the lack of good water and thick dirt halted investments. Like the good leader she was, Ayana had already planned for her people to join the people at the Indian settlement on the Ogeechee when the time came.

Alice's family and friends had been taken to Philadelphia, early on, and manumitted by Ken and Ashley. They continued to take a boatload of yaupon tea to Philadelphia a couple times a year and to have maintenance done on the steamboat engine at the place it was built. In doing so, they had carried the remaining people of the Milam place to be manumitted. Alice's mother and father continued to help one or two runaways every month to recover and to continue their flight, hidden in the long trading canoes of the Ogeechee people.

Martin and Mary never thought about settling down to a house on land. They both liked being able to stay at Tybee sometimes, near the Milam place sometimes, or at some of the coastal towns that they delivered ice to, and some of their favorite places along the inland waterways.

About eleven years after Martin's father died, he asked Mary if she ever thought about writing a book from all her notes. Mary said she didn't feel inclined to do it because it could still bring trouble to so many people, especially then, with such a big divide in the country over slavery. Mary thought about it and said that it would be good to string all the notes together roughly into a story while they were still somewhat fresh in their minds and said she was surprised that Martin was so interested. Martin said that she shouldn't be surprised because she knew how much he liked a good story. Mary said, yes, he was good at spinning a tale, and that she would never forget the conversation that they and Daniel had with their father after listening to Captain Jones on the beach telling tall tales. It was about telling an untruth in a story, and their father had said that well-to-do people all over the world went to elaborate playhouses to see and hear stories that had little or no truth to them. He said that there could be nothing wrong with people like Captain Jones and the pilots and crews on the beach telling tall tales for entertainment. Martin said that Captain Jones said that every story should have at least a small amount of truth to it because there was nothing that a man could imagine that was as amazing as the truth. Martin laughed and said that the Captain started most all his stories by saying with a solemn sincerity that what he was about to say was the whole truth with a twinkle in his eye. But, when he told a story that was really the whole truth, he would say that he wanted what he was about to say be known, and there was no twinkle, just an air of concern. Martin went on to say that it was like that in the story about how the Captain came to be on Tybee and the gold on Turtle Island. He said that it was something that the Captain wanted him to know about before he died. Mary could see Martin's eyes well up, and she said she missed the Captain too. Martin said that his crew, there on the steamboat, liked to hear some of Captain Jones' stories and sometimes he told one but he regretted that he could not tell his best story about the treasure on Turtle Island. He said he had made a vow to go to Turtle Island to see if the gold was still there. Mary said he might get snake bit and die like the Captain's mates did and Martin said he would go on a cold winter day when the snakes were in the ground. Mary reminded him of the wise thing that the Captain always said about the worst snakes on Turtle Island having two legs and could do harm in any weather. There was a long pause and Martin saw that Mary was deep in thought and he knew to ask her what she was thinking when he saw her like that. She said she knew Martin would go look for the gold because he always did what he had vowed to do. But, she said she knew of a greater buried treasure than the gold and Martin looked puzzled and asked what that could be. Mary said it was the contents written about in those thirty notebooks, still buried near the orange tree at the base of the Tybee Lighthouse.

After hearing what Mary said about real treasure, Martin made them some tea and they sat quietly, contemplating what they had been talking about. Martin said he would go dig up the crocs full of her notebooks soon and bring them to the boat. There were places down in the bilge that no one but the boat builder and him knew of. Mary said that would be good because she wanted them, together, to go through them all and refresh their memory while it was still somewhat new and she could string all her notes together in a rough account of all that had happened.

That they did, and for the next year, where ever they stopped for the night along the waterway, Mary would read a section of her notes and they would discuss and reconstitute the events till it became almost alive again. Then at Mary's insistence, Martin would slowly tell it in his own simple way and Mary would dress it up some and write it all down. They stopped the story at the point when Walter died, but Mary continued her journal of events and happenings and all for more than a dozen years afterwards.

Some of those events were the big fort on Cockspur being built, and the Martello Tower out in front of the lighthouse as well as the small lighthouse marking the South Channel. She wrote about what led up to Ayana and her people being displaced from the Indian Islands and joining the Ogeechee Indians. Another big happening was when Martin eventually did go looking for the gold on Turtle Island and the surprising and startling discovery he found. However, the biggest event and most precarious time for Henry and the Milams and friends was the increased animosity between the North and South over slavery. No time, since the time leading up to the Revolutionary War when Patriots were against Loyalists did the country become so divided.

What Mary wrote about in her journal was that the North became more determined in their cause of abolition and the south became more devout in their slave based economy. In Savannah, she told of friends becoming enemies and families splitting over their beliefs and a time when there became tension in the city and surrounding area instead of peace. She wrote about the many days and hours that her and Martin and Henry and Alice met and agonized over the critical choices that had to be made for the future of the Milams and those they felt a responsibility to look after.

She and Martin knew that they would eventually string the two periods of her journals together into one saga. They believed that there would come a time when the whole thing could be revealed without negative consequences but they sensed that there were some rough times ahead before that could happen.

ACKNOWLEDGEMENTS

Many people played a part in bringing this book of mine, a labor of love, to fruition.

First and foremost, I want to thank my wife Mavis for believing in me when I didn't believe in myself.

I am especially grateful for the "village" experience of Tybee Island in the 1950s through the early 1960s, when your friends' mothers and fathers were called aunts and uncles.

I thank my longtime friend and fellow writer Bo Bryan, the first author officially appointed by the city of Myrtle Beach, South Carolina, as its poet laureate.

I thank my dearly departed big-hearted friend Sidney Snelgrove, owner of Sloppy Joe's Bar in Key West and Tombee Plantation in Frogmore, South Carolina.

I celebrate the vision of Georgia governor Zell Miller for dedicating the island of Little Tybee a Heritage Preserve to prevent its development and construction of a causeway to it.

I thank my brother Joel Anderson for no particular reason except love. He understands.

I thank my publishing team, Tybee residents Lauren Clackum, Ben Goggins, and Will Strong for their patience with my mess.